I0845362

# Greenland Domes

## Daggers and Grozny Demon's

Screenplay

Paul D. Escudero

WORKBOOK PRESS LLC
187 E Warm Springs Rd,
Suite B285 Las Vegas NV 89119 USA

Website: https://workbookpress.com/
Hotline: 1-888-818-4856
Email: admin@workbookpress.com


Ordering Information:

Quantity sales. Special discounts are available on quantity purchases by corporations, associations, and others. For details, contact the publisher at the address above.


Library of Congress Control Number:

ISBN-13:          978-1-965732-79-3   Paperback Version

REV. DATE: 07/20/2025

# 格陵兰穹顶
## 匕首和格罗兹尼恶魔

剧本

保罗·道格拉斯·埃斯库德罗

Copyright December 2024
版权所有 2024 年 12 月

# PREFACE
# 前言

This screenplay is written in English and Chinese. The movie producers can create a movie with it in English or Chinese, or have English with Chinese subtitles, or Chinese with English subtitles.

此剧本以英文和中文撰写。制片方可以用英文或中文制作电影，或用英文配中文字幕，或用中文配英文字幕。

My Japanese wife Asako watches a lot of Japanese and Korean Television and Movies. In the past when I wasn't quite as busy, I often watched a Japanese TV program "Tokyo Detective" with her. It's an extremely good show with fantastic actors and has been on air now for 21 years.

我的日本妻子 朝子 (Asako in Japanese) 经常看日本和韩国的电视和电影。以前我没那么忙的时候，经常和她一起看日本电视节目《东京侦探》。这是一部非常棒的节目，演员也很棒，已经播出 21 年了。

When I watch TV with my wife from time to time, the Japanese shows often have Chinese subtitles. When we are watching Korean Drama's there is always Japanese subtitles because the shows are aired in Japan. In some shows I've watched there has been Japanese and Chinese subtitles simultaneously.

我和妻子偶尔一起看电视时，日本节目经常配有中文字幕。我们看韩剧时，总是有日文字幕，因为这些节目是在日本播出的。我看过的一些节目同时配有日文和中文字幕。

Korean Historical Dramas are quite good. *Maybe I will pick up a few good ideas from them.*

韩国历史剧挺好看的，也许能从中学到一些好的想法。

I watched the German Movie "Das Boot" in German with English subtitles. It works for me. [ https://www.youtube.com/watch?v=KqpmAdtn6d4 ]

我看了德语电影《从海底出击》，配英文字幕。对我来说很管用。

[ https://www.youtube.com/watch?v=KqpmAdtn6d4 ]

I hope in some way I inspire Chinese audiences with this Screenplay.

我希望这个剧本能够以某种方式激励中国观众。

Something else that should be interesting to my fans is, this is only the 2$^{nd}$ publication

I've done with no Aliens and Science Fiction involved. I am however working on a 3rd English only with screenplay with no Aliens.

我的粉丝应该会感兴趣的另一件事是，这只是我出版的第二本不涉及外星人和科幻小说的书籍。不过，我现在正在创作第三本不涉及外星人的英文版书籍。

This is my 4th major production of a work in Chinese. I've published three Novels in Chinese:

Jeeapa II  https://www.youtube.com/watch?v=5io-Cy9dPQU

Australia Alien Adventure   Amazon.com: Australia Alien Adventure: The Petitioners eBook : Escudero, Paul D.: Kindle Store

Radiant Destiny. https://www.youtube.com/watch?v=sBR6BGgVYOA

这是我第四次用中文创作大型作品。我出版了三本中文小说：

《Jeeapa II》 https://www.youtube.com/watch?v=5io-Cy9dPQU

《澳大利亚外星人历险记》Amazon.com: Australia Alien Adventure: The Petitioners eBook : Escudero, Paul D.: Kindle Store

《Radiant Destiny》。 https://www.youtube.com/watch?v=sBR6BGgVYOA

Jeeapa II and Radiant Destiny also have Pinyin (phonetic spelling of Mandarin)

《Jeeapa II》和《Radiant Destiny》也有拼音（普通话的拼音拼写）

Note: https://en.wikipedia.org/wiki/Pinyin (extract):

**Hanyu Pinyin**, or simply **Pinyin**, is the most common romanization system for Standard Chinese. In official documents, it is referred to as the **Chinese Phonetic Alphabet**.

注：https://en.wikipedia.org/wiki/Pinyin（摘录）：

汉语拼音，或简称拼音，是标准中文最常用的罗马拼音系统。在官方文件中，它被称为汉语拼音。

This screenplay will not use Pinyin because it takes up as much space as English and would make the book size prohibitively large. If a studio signs a contract with me to produce a movie, I would be willing to supply the text in Pinyin. If you read Jeeapa II or Radiant Destiny, you will discover it takes quite an effort to add Pinyin.

这个剧本不会使用拼音，因为拼音占用的空间和英文一样多，会使书的篇幅过大。如果有电影公司与我签约制作电影，我愿意提供拼音文本。如果你读过《吉帕二世》或《光辉命运》，你会发现添加拼音需要付出很大努力。

In this Novel there are voice overs. The narrator provides the voiceover in the background so to speak. There are also "thoughts" by the actors in the screenplay. Those thoughts are handled like voiceovers with images of the thinker but lips not moving or for voiceover imagery the cinematographer thinks are appropriate. I do not specify that to give the cinematographer flexibility.

EXT. DAY. FRAZEE MINNESOTA RURAL AREA. ALEX BAXTER'S MANSION.

外景。明尼苏达州弗雷泽乡村地区。亚历克斯·巴克斯特的豪宅。

DRONE VIEW – 500 FEET, 200 YARDS FROM THE MANSION.

无人机视图 - 距离豪宅 500 英尺，200 码。


<u>MUSIC FOR THIS SEGMENT:</u>

>   https://www.youtube.com/watch?v=ONQfZP0T2Oo

>   **Mahler - Symphony No. 9 in D Major**

<u>部分音乐：</u>

>   https://www.youtube.com/watch?v=ONQfZP0T2Oo

>   马勒 - D 大调第 9 号交响曲

Almost halfway between Burlington and Frazee Minnesota, Alex Baxter lived on a 1200-acre property, fully fenced in better than most prisons. Alex had six former Navy Seals on his security detail along with the full-time sentries working in shifts and posted like a special forces camp in Vietnam. Alex's security arrangements could prevent any intruders.

亚历克斯·巴克斯特 （Alex Baxter） 住在伯灵顿和明尼苏达州弗雷泽之间的一块 1200 英亩的土地上，周围全围栏，比大多数监狱都好。亚历克斯的安保人员中有六名前海豹突击队员，还有轮班工作的全职哨兵，就像越南的特种部队营地一样。亚历克斯的安全安排可以阻止任何入侵者。

Infrared and motion detectors along with bomb proof vehicles made things somewhat safe for Alex, but he knew there was much anger in the world, and governments full of starving people were always attempting to shake him down. Even the U.S. Government was starting to get belligerent. As such Alex's five full-time lawyers were gainfully employed to keep him out of prison.

红外线和运动探测器以及防爆车辆让亚历克斯的生活相对安全，但他知道这个世界充满愤怒，而那些到处都是饥饿人民的政府总是试图敲诈他。甚至美国政府也开始变得好战起来。因此，亚历克斯聘请了五名全职律师，以保证他免于入狱。

Alex liked to travel and owning a modified Gulf Stream 650 that had fewer seats, and more fuel capacity would allow him to fly non-stop to anywhere in the world.

亚历克斯喜欢旅行，他拥有一架经过改装的湾流 650 飞机，这架飞机座位数更少，燃油容量更大，可以让他不间断地飞往世界任何地方。

Alex needed to fly to his home in Switzerland from time to time, not only to keep an eye on his property, but also to handle business because all his bankers were in Switzerland, since he didn't trust any governments.

亚历克斯需要时不时飞回他在瑞士的家，不仅为了看管他的财产，也为了处理业务，因为他不信任任何政府，他所有的银行家都在瑞士。

Alex was not a bad guy. In fact, he was idealistic. Alex had numerous redeeming qualities and attempted to help people more than most knew about.

亚历克斯并不是一个坏人。事实上，他是一个理想主义者。亚历克斯有许多可取之处，他试图帮助人们，而大多数人都不知道他这么做。

Alex kept his efforts to improve others' lives to himself and usually used middle persons so that nobody could ever tie it to him, because he didn't want fame or visibility.

亚历克斯一直把自己改善他人生活的努力藏在心里，并且通常通过中间人来避免让任何人将此事与他联系起来，因为他不想要名声或知名度。

Alex Baxter kept open three factories that lost money to provide jobs for several thousand people. Sadly, those people who were never allowed to see the books thought he was a crook and exploiting them.

亚历克斯·巴克斯特开办了三家亏损的工厂，为数千人提供了就业机会。可悲的是，那些从未被允许看到这些账簿的人认为他是个骗子，在剥削他们。

Little did Alex Baxter's workers know, the products they turned out, had little demand and had to be sold for much less than the production cost. Everyone also got paid competitive wages despite the fact they never made any profits.

亚历克斯·巴克斯特的工人们并不知道，他们生产的产品需求量很小，而且售价必须远低于生产成本。尽管他们从未赚到任何利润，但每个人都得到了有竞争力的工资。

<u>FLASHBACK</u>

<u>EXT. DAY. KODIAK ALASKA. ALEX'S CABIN IN THE WOODS WITH A 5 CAR GARAGE AND 10-FOOT-TALL WINDOWS IN THE FRONT OFFERING A MAJESTIC VIEW.</u>

<u>外景。阿拉斯加科迪亚克岛。亚历克斯的林中小屋，有 5 辆车的车库，前面有 10 英尺高的窗户，可欣赏壮丽的景色。</u>

Being very connected with nature and spending a lot of time in his large home in Alaska from time to time, Alex understood vividly why the United Nations organization was slowly taking over the world and tried imposed the restrictions on farmland conversions.

亚历克斯与大自然有着密切的联系，并且时不时地在阿拉斯加的大家里度过很多时间，他清楚地理解了为什么联合国正在慢慢地接管世界并试图对农田转化施加限制。

Just like carbon credits of a decade earlier, reverse farmland credits were very lucrative, provided the land was located below the latitude of 45 degrees where some crops would grow. Any further north than 45 degrees, only potatoes and onions and carrots or beets could grow with the shortened growing season caused by the end of sunspot activity.

就像十年前的碳排放额度一样，反向农田排放额度非常有利可图，前提是土地位于北纬 45 度以下，有些作物可以生长。在北纬 45 度以下，只有土豆、洋葱、胡萝卜或甜菜可以生长，因为太阳黑子活动的结束缩短了作物的生长季。

The world was getting overpopulated and many countries started putting a ban on converting any farmland to any other purpose without an Agriculture permit. The world was feeling the grips of the onset of a mini-ice age and mass starvation was starting to enter all the politics throughout the world.

世界人口过剩，许多国家开始禁止未经农业许可将农田用于其他用途。世界正感受到小冰河期的来临，大规模饥荒开始影响到世界各地的政治。

This was a bad time in history for the ultra-wealthy. No different than J. D. Rockefeller was treated by the mainstream press, the Trillionaires and some of the Billionaires were looked upon as the evilest people on the planet.

对于超级富豪来说，这是历史上的一段糟糕时期。就像主流媒体对待 J. D. 洛克菲勒一样，万亿富翁和一些亿万富翁被视为地球上最邪恶的人。

Alex was no different than J. D. Rockefeller; other than he was better educated, had made several fortunes and reinvested those fortunes into new endeavors which multiplied his wealth 100-fold.

亚历克斯与 J.D. 洛克菲勒没有什么不同；除了他受过更好的教育，积累了巨额财富并将这些财富重新投资到新的事业中，使他的财富增加了 100 倍。

Alex Baxter had a PhD. in economics and was a businessman equipped to figure out new business models ahead of his competition. Though Alex had to stay on his toes because there was always someone out there who either wanted to steal from him or take him to the cleaner's.

亚历克斯·巴克斯特拥有经济学博士学位，是一名商人，能够领先于竞争对手找到新的商业模式。不过亚历克斯必须时刻保持警惕，因为总有人想从他那里偷东西，或者想把他弄得一团糟。

<u>END FLASHBACK</u>

<u>结束闪回</u>

The middle of the winter in Minnesota was bitter cold this year including several minus fifty-degree days recently, colder than Alex remembered. Alex was considered extravagant by almost anyone who knew him one way or another. He was never married and decided that since the world had a potential grim future, he wanted no kids.

今年明尼苏达州的隆冬十分寒冷，最近几天气温都降到了零下 50 度，比亚历克斯记忆中的还要冷。几乎所有认识亚历克斯的人都认为他太奢侈了。他从未结过婚，而且他认为既然这个世界的未来可能很暗淡，他就不想要孩子。

When Alex hired a contractor to build a tunnel from his mansion out to his hanger for his Gulfstream, he was instantly considered mentally disturbed by people watching the trench being dug and the mass destruction to his Olympic size swimming pool which lay in the path 100 yards to the sound damped hanger.

当亚历克斯雇佣一名承包商从他的豪宅修建一条通往他的湾流飞机机库的隧道时，人们看到正在挖的沟渠以及他奥林匹克规格的游泳池被大规模毁坏，他立刻被认为精神错乱了，而游泳池就位于距离隔音机库 100 码的路上。

This morning Alex's antagonists might have had another viewpoint if they observed his actions.

今天早上，如果亚历克斯的对手观察到他的行为，他们可能会有不同的看法。

<u>INT. DAY. FRAZEE MINNESOTA RURAL AREA. ALEX BAXTER'S MANSION.</u>

<u>室内。明尼苏达州弗雷泽乡村地区。亚历克斯·巴克斯特的豪宅。</u>

As soon as Alex was all packed up and ready to depart, his butler Sam spoke.

当亚历克斯收拾好行李准备离开时，他的管家萨姆开口说话了。

SAM (Butler)<br>
Alex, I will take your suitcase down to the golfcart<br>
now so when you are ready, it will be there.

山姆 （巴特勒）<br>
亚历克斯，我现在就把你的行李箱拿到高尔夫球<br>
车上，这样当你准备好的时候，它就在那里。

ALEX<br>
Thank you, Sam.

亚历克斯<br>
谢谢您，山姆。

Sam left the room with Alex's suitcase and walked down the hallway 15 feet. Sam pressed the elevator button and shortly after the elevator door opened, Sam entered and pressed the close button.

山姆带着 亚历克斯的行李箱离开房间，沿着走廊走了 15 英尺。山姆按下电梯按钮，电梯门打开后不久，山姆进入并按下了关闭按钮。

In a moment, the elevator was down at the tunnel level where Sam got out in 72-degree temperature, walked over and put the suitcase in the back of the long golf cart which carried four people and had a trunk space in the back that would carry three or four suitcases.

不一会儿，电梯就到了隧道层，萨姆在华氏 72 度的气温下走了出来，走过去，把行李箱放到了长高尔夫球车的后面，这辆车可以坐四个人，后面有一个后备箱空间，可以放三四个行李箱。

Alex picked up his cell phone, called his buddy Paul out in California.

亚历克斯拿起手机，给远在加利福尼亚的好友保罗(Paul)打电话。

<u>SPLITSCREEN. ALEX ON ONE SIDE AND PAUL ON THE OTHER.</u>

<u>分屏。一边是亚历克斯，另一边是保罗。</u>

ALEX
Paul, are you sure you don't want to go up to Greenland with me?

亚历克斯
保罗，你确定不想和我一起去格陵兰岛吗？

PAUL
No Alex. You know I'm a wimp and can't take the freezing ass weather up there or at your place in Alaska.

保罗
不，亚历克斯。你知道我是个懦夫，受不了那里或你阿拉斯加的寒冷天气。

ALEX
We need to work on that Paul.

亚历克斯
我们需要在保罗身上努力。

PAUL
Alex, once we get our survival school up and running, I'll toughen up.

保罗

亚历克斯，一旦我们的生存学校开始运作，我就
会变得坚强起来。

ALEX

You better Paul. This world could go to hell real fast,
and you just might need to survive in sub-zero weather.

亚历克斯

你最好是保罗。这个世界很快就会变成地狱，你
可能需要能够在零下的天气中生存下来。

PAUL

Understand, and thanks for the invitation. I have no
idea why the hell you want to go to Greenland in the
middle of the winter.

保罗

明白了，谢谢你的邀请。我真不知道你为什么要
在隆冬时节去格陵兰岛。

ALEX

They need my help up there.

亚历克斯
他们需要我的帮助。

PAUL

A lot of places do, including China. Last year half of
their rice patties were still iced over during the rice
planting season.

保罗

很多地方都是这样，包括中国。去年，在水稻种
植季节，一半的稻田仍然结冰。

ALEX

Yes, and I hear it's going to get a lot worse in the next
few years.

亚历克斯
是的，我听说未来几年情况会变得更糟。

PAUL

No doubt the farmers in California Central Valley are
all smiles since they are now producing 1/3 of all the
food for the USA.

保罗
毫无疑问，加州中部谷地的农民都很高兴，因为
他们现在生产了美国三分之一的粮食。

ALEX
And Mexico which is producing another 1/3.

亚历克斯
墨西哥又生产了另外三分之一。

PAUL
Mexican farmers will probably plant more as they are
getting more Colorado River water due to this reverse
climate change.

保罗
由于气候变化，墨西哥农民将获得更多的科罗拉
多河水，因此他们可能会种植更多作物。

ALEX
Ok Paul got to let you go. My pilot is waiting for me.

亚历克斯
好的，保罗，我得放你走了。我的飞行员正在等我。

PAUL
Take care Alex, have a safe trip.

保罗
保重，亚历克斯，一路平安。

ALEX
Thank you. Talk soon.

亚历克斯
谢谢。我们很快再聊。

Alex put his cell phone in his left front pocket because he reserved his right front pocket for a couple of special keys. Alex walked out of his changing room with four walk-in closets out into the hallway to the elevator and was down to the Tunnel in a matter of a minute.

亚历克斯把手机放在左前口袋里，因为他把右前口袋留给了几把特殊的钥匙。亚历克斯走出了有四个步入式衣柜的更衣室，走进了通往电梯的走廊，一分钟之内就到了隧道。

Alex then hopped into the electric golfcart which was self-driving, no operator required.

There was a turning zone by the elevator and another one at the hanger complex. Controls were all fully voice recognized, and a person monitoring his security system had six video displays for the golf cart where it could be always observed in case Alex had any sudden issues.

然后，亚历克斯跳上了无人驾驶的电动高尔夫球车，无需操作员。电梯旁有一个转弯区，机库大楼内也有一个转弯区。所有控制装置都完全采用语音识别，监控安全系统的人员为高尔夫球车配备了六个视频显示器，以防亚历克斯突然出现问题，可以随时观察。

The golf cart took power off strips laid in the cement roadbed. The tunnel was well lit as well as decorated with paintings along the entire length with fantastic lighting effects. Any *art connoisseur* would love the transcendentalist nature of the images and lighting effects.

高尔夫球车依靠水泥路基上的电线供电。隧道光线充足，沿途还装饰有绘画，灯光效果极佳。任何艺术鉴赏家都会喜欢这些图像和灯光效果的超然本质。

The cart was propelled by battery, as an interlocking feature, in case the main power supply suddenly went down for some unexplained reason, but the source of electricity came from the roadbed for most of the propulsion and battery recharge. Navigation by a GPS like device accurately controlled speed and direction.

作为一种联锁装置，该车由电池驱动，以防主电源突然因某种不明原因而断电，但电力来源来自路基，用于大部分推进和电池充电。通过类似 GPS 的设备导航可以精确控制速度和方向。

Alex got out of the golf cart when it reached the hanger elevator and stopped.

当高尔夫球车抵达机库电梯并停下时，亚历克斯从车上走了下来。

The hanger operator who provided security and all assistance to pilot and service personnel, was standing by the cart as it arrived, grabbed Alex's bag and took it into the elevator with him.

机库操作员负责为飞行员和服务人员提供安全保障和一切协助，当推车到达时，他正站在旁边，抓起亚历克斯的包，和他一起走进电梯。

A moment later they were up to the aircraft level of the hanger and the doors automatically opened and they got out. The plane was pointed to the hanger doors now closed with room temperature around 72 degrees, so de-icing was not required. The pilot, Brad Johnson was standing by the aircraft stairway.

片刻之后，他们到达了机库的飞机高度，门自动打开，他们走了出来。飞机正对着机库门，此时机库门已关闭，室温约为 72 度，因此无需除冰。飞行员布拉德·约翰逊站在飞机楼梯旁。

BRAD JOHNSON
Good morning Mr. Baxter, the plane is ready to leave immediately, and no fuel stops required in route. Should be in Iceland in 5.5 hours from now.


布拉德·约翰逊
早上好，巴克斯特先生，飞机已准备好立即起飞，途中无需加油。5.5 小时后应该会抵达冰岛。

ALEX
Thank you, Brad. I hope we can find some smooth flying weather out there.

亚历克斯
谢谢你，布拉德。我希望我们能在那里找到一些顺利的天气。

BRAD JOHNSON
Our flight plan has us at 45,000 feet, we'll miss some of the turbulence, but as you know with this mini-ice age, we can't avoid it all.

布拉德·约翰逊
我们的飞行高度是 45,000 英尺，这样我们就可以避开一些乱流，但正如你所知，在这个小冰河期，我们无法完全避开乱流。

ALEX
Understand. It sucks to be us.

亚历克斯
理解。我们真倒霉。

BRAD JOHNSON
Well Mr. Baxter, it could be worse, you could be flying on one of those cattle car airliners at 35,000 feet today, with baby puke and all the other bad stuff they get to deal with.

布拉德·约翰逊
好吧先生。巴克斯特，情况可能更糟，你今天可能乘坐一架运牛客机在 35,000 英尺的高空飞行，带着婴儿呕吐物和他们要处理的所有其他糟糕的东西。

Alex responded as he grabbed the hand railing on the GS650 Jet door folding ladder and door mechanism as he climbed up into the plane:

亚历克斯 爬上飞机，抓住 GS650 Jet 舱门折叠梯和舱门装置上的扶手，说道：

ALEX

I suppose you're right, Brad.

亚历克斯

我想你是对的，布拉德。

**INT. DAY. GS650 PRIVATE JET PASSENGER CABIN AREA.**

**内部日。 GS650 私人飞机客舱区域。**

VOICEOVER

*Inside Gulfstream 650, Stephanie, Alex's personal assistant, was waiting with all smiles, in a nice short dress that showed her nice figure. Alex loved her nice skinny legs.*

画外音

湾流650内，亚历克斯的私人助理斯蒂芬妮满面笑容地等待着，一袭漂亮的短裙，凸显出她姣好的身材。亚历克斯喜欢她漂亮的瘦腿。

*Stephanie received her master's in economics and a Harvard MBA, but her salary was enough to slowly buy a company she was acquiring.*

斯蒂芬妮获得了经济学硕士学位和哈佛工商管理硕士学位，但她的薪水足以慢慢购买她正在收购的一家公司。

*Stephanie figured her flying days would be done in about four years, and by then would have ownership of the company which Alex was facilitating her buying and advising her.*

斯蒂芬妮认为她的飞行生涯将在大约四年内完成，到那时她将拥有亚历克斯协助她购买并为她提供建议的公司的所有权。

*Alex also backed Stephanie financially, gave her the loans to slowly purchase the apparel business, which Stephanie had a professional executive run until she had paid back Alex by providing him personal services as flight attendant.*

亚历克斯还在财务上支持斯蒂芬妮，给她贷款慢慢购买服装业务，斯蒂芬妮让一名专业高管经营

该业务，直到她通过为亚历克斯提供空乘人员的
个人服务来偿还亚历克斯。

*Stephanie also provided many other requirements,
including being a gopher where she went on errands
sometimes in the middle of the night when Alex needed
something he didn't have on hand.*

斯蒂芬妮还提出了任何其他要求，包括成为一名
地鼠，有时她会在半夜出差，当亚历克斯需要手
头没有的东西时。

STEPHANIE
Alex, is there anything I can get for you?

斯蒂芬妮
亚历克斯，有什么可以帮您的吗？

ALEX
Nothing right now, maybe coffee and orange juice
after we get airborne and up at cruising altitude.

亚历克斯
现在什么都没有，也许在我们升空并达到巡航高
度后喝咖啡和橙汁。

STEPHANIE
Sure, I'll take care of everything then.

斯蒂芬妮
当然，到时候我会处理好一切。

Alex sat down in his chair located about 10 feet behind the pilot on the starboard side
where he could watch the pilot and yell at him if he must.

亚历克斯坐在右舷侧飞行员后方约 10 英尺的椅子上，在那里他可以观察飞行
员，并在必要时对他大喊大叫。

Sometimes Alex had two pilots for a trip like this, but only Brad would be flying today,
which meant as they were landing at Nuuk Greenland, Alex would be sitting in the
right seat watching the approach to get an idea how bad things on the ground would be.

有时亚历克斯有两名飞行员进行这样的旅行，但今天只有布拉德会飞行，这意
味着当他们降落在努克格陵兰岛时，亚历克斯会坐在正确的座位上观看进场，
以了解地面上的情况有多糟糕会的。

Alex had one of the best private runways in the country at his estate in Minnesota.

亚历克斯在明尼苏达州的庄园拥有全国最好的私人跑道之一。

A couple Air Force Bases are located not too far away, and the tenant commands there knew any plane having trouble was more than welcome to land at Alex's paved ranch runway that had to be long for insurance purposes, easily accommodated F16s.

几个空军基地就在不远的地方，那里的租户指挥部知道任何有问题的飞机都非常欢迎降落在亚历克斯铺好的牧场跑道上，出于保险目的，跑道必须很长，可以轻松容纳 F16。

During all takeoff and landings, a private tower which included radar which was licensed by the FAA was manned by Alex's personal security team.

在所有起飞和着陆过程中，亚历克斯的个人安保团队都在一座私人塔台上负责操作，该塔台配备了美国联邦航空管理局 (FAA) 许可的雷达。

Alex's GS650 could land fully instrumented with zero visibility. A special navigation system installed on the runway and in the plane guided it most precisely to the hanger where it was always backed in via air-tug and towed out for departure.

亚历克斯的 GS650 可以在仪表齐全、能见度为零的情况下着陆。安装在跑道和飞机上的特殊导航系统将其最精确地引导到机库，在那里它总是通过气拖船返回并拖出起飞。

The hanger got quite cold for a few minutes while aircraft tow-operations were in progress but was back to 72 degrees shortly after the doors shut.

在飞机拖曳操作进行期间，机库在几分钟内变得相当寒冷，但在舱门关闭后不久又恢复到 72 度。

Alex's Pilots did not start the jet engines until the plane was out of the hanger and pointed at a 90-degree angle from the hanger doors which also pointed the jet directly towards the runway.

直到飞机离开机库并与机库门成 90 度角，这也将飞机直接指向跑道时，亚历克斯的飞行员才启动喷气发动机。

Alex sat back in his comfortable chair observing the pilot and the pilot's voice as well, has his headset audio was routed to small speakers at Alex's seat so he could listen in to the pilot or air traffic controllers or his personal tower.

亚历克斯坐在舒适的椅子上，观察飞行员和飞行员的声音，他的耳机音频被传送到亚历克斯座位上的小扬声器，这样他就可以听到飞行员或空中交通管制员或他的个人塔台的声音。

AIRCRAFT HANGER SUPERVISOR
Baxter-1, this is Hanger-Tower. The wind is at 325
degrees 8 knots, no nearby air traffic.

飞机机库主管
巴克斯特-1，这是机库塔。风速为 325 度 8 节，
附近无空中交通。

**PILOT BRAD**
Hanger-Tower, this is Baxter-1 understand all.

飞行员布拉德
机库塔，这是巴克斯特-1明白的一切。

The Gulfstream 650 Jet had been previously checked. Pulled out of the hanger, engines ran up, fuel topped off, all preflight checks done, and then moved back in the hanger with engines shut down so the passenger (Mr. Baxter), could be put aboard without exposure to the bitter minus 30-degree weather outside.

湾流 650 喷气式飞机此前已接受过飞行检查。从机库中拉出，发动机启动，燃油加满，完成所有飞行前检查，然后在发动机关闭的情况下移回机库，以便乘客（巴克斯特先生）可以在不暴露在零下30度的严寒中的情况下登机。外面的天气是零度。

The process just now repeated in a manner, plane pulled out of the hanger, engines started, and additional preflight checks performed. This process was only done in cold weather.

刚才的过程以某种方式重复，飞机从机库拉出，发动机启动，并进行额外的飞行前检查。这个过程只在寒冷的天气里进行。

After the weather status report from the hanger-tower operator, the Gulfstream 650 Jet slowly moved forward and made a path along the service ramp to the end of the private runway. About five minutes after stopping at the end of the runway, all final pre-flight checks were complete, and the pilot moved the throttles forward and the jet started moving and soon took off.

在机库塔操作员报告天气状况后，湾流 650 喷气式飞机缓慢向前移动，沿着服务坡道到达跑道尽头。在跑道尽头停下后大约五分钟，所有最后的飞行前检查都已完成，飞行员向前推动油门，喷气式飞机开始移动并很快起飞。

[Gorgeous Gulfstream G650 M-USIK Take-Off at Bern Airport]

***

FLASHBACK

倒叙

A few F16's from the Air National Guard recently made emergency landings on Mr. Baxter's private runway a few times.

空军国民警卫队的几架 F16 最近紧急迫降在先生身上。巴克斯特的私人跑道有几次。

[F16 Landing with Chute]

The Air Force loved it since the private runway was fenced off and they didn't have to worry about the public getting close to the planes. Also, the pilots loved it because they were treated like royalty and usually had a wonderful hot meal long before the Air Force emergency crew made it to the private air strip.

空军喜欢它，因为私人跑道被围起来，他们不必担心公众靠近飞机。此外，飞行员们也喜欢它，因为他们受到皇室般的待遇，通常在空军紧急救援人员到达私人机场之前很久就可以享用一顿美味的热餐。

When Alex's former pilot had to leave for personal reasons, it was one of those F16 pilots flying in the Air National Guard making an emergency landing that made it possible for Alex to hire Brad.

当亚历克斯的前飞行员因个人原因不得不离开时，空中国民警卫队的一名 F16 飞行员紧急降落，使亚历克斯得以雇用布拉德。

Alex needed a new pilot so he could fly to Switzerland in a few days, and the F16 pilot had a buddy Brad who had left the Air Force and was now contract flying corporate rental aircraft and was checked out on the GS-650.

亚历克斯需要一名新飞行员，以便他可以在几天内飞往瑞士，而 F16 飞行员有一个好友布拉德，他已经离开空军，现在签订了飞行公司租赁飞机的合同，并在 GS-650 上进行了检查。

Hence, Alex was rewarded promptly simply by extending curtesy to the poor pilots who got stuck there when their equipment malfunctioned.

因此，亚历克斯仅仅通过向那些因设备故障而陷入困境的可怜飞行员表示礼貌，就立即得到了奖励。

In one particular case, when a pilot with a sick F16 needed to get back to base and headquarters really quick and couldn't wait four hours (two hours to and two hours return trip by car, rescue squad), Alex offered to fly the pilot back to his Air Force base.

在一个特殊的案例中，当一名 F16 生病的飞行员需要非常快地返回基地和总部并且无法等待四个小时（救援队需要两个小时来接飞行员，以及两个小时的汽车回程）时，亚历克斯主动提出载飞行员返回空军基地。

The pilot called his boss on his cell phone and got authorization for Alex to fly him to the base and land on the Air Force runway. Alex had the stranded pilot back at his Air Force base 30 minutes after the phone call. This special transportation event was important since the pilot's wife had just gone into labor, delivering their first child which he wanted to be present.

飞行员用手机给老板打电话，获得了亚历克斯的授权，可以带他飞往基地并降落在空军跑道上。接到电话后三十分钟内，亚历克斯将被困的飞行员带回了空军基地。这次特殊的运输活动非常重要，因为飞行员的妻子刚刚分娩，生下了他们的第一个孩子，他希望能在场。

END FLASHBACK

结束闪回

Alex's Gulfstream 650 Jet only had six seats, though it could have as many as twenty-four if configured. Alex preferred the extra fuel to fly non-stop to Switzerland to avoid going through red tape at foreign airports, plus he didn't have too many friends and thus didn't need all the extra seats.

亚历克斯的湾流 650 喷气式飞机只有六个座位，但如果配置的话，它可以有多达二十四个座位。亚历克斯更喜欢用额外的燃油直飞瑞士，以避免在外国机场办理繁文缛节，而且他没有太多朋友，因此不需要所有额外的座位。

Due to only three people aboard the Gulfstream 650 Jet, it was up in the air real fast without the pilot Brad hot-dogging it. Brad was trained to always fly as if he were an airline pilot with a bunch of passengers in the back. Brad knew Alex liked it nice and smooth.

由于湾流 650 喷气式飞机上只有三人，飞机飞快地飞到了空中，而飞行员布拉德并没有对其进行热插拔。布拉德接受的训练总是让他像一名航空公司飞行员一样飞行，后面有一群乘客。布拉德知道亚历克斯喜欢它的美好和顺利。

Stephanie sat down facing Alex, and her short skirt revealed most of her legs plus a little more. She knew and would be more than happy to get her claws into Alex, so she enjoyed the fact she thought he was enjoying the view. Not that Stephanie was any more of a gold digger than anyone else; she knew Alex had incredible wealth.

斯蒂芬妮面对着亚历克斯坐下，她的短裙露出了大部分的腿，还露出了一点。她知道并且非常乐意将自己的爪子伸向亚历克斯，所以她很高兴她认为他正在欣赏风景。这并不是说斯蒂芬妮比任何人都更加拜金；而是说斯蒂芬妮比其他人更喜欢拜金。她知道亚历克斯拥有令人难以置信的财富。

But Stephanie knew Alex wanted no part of marriage.

但斯蒂芬妮知道亚历克斯不想参与这段婚姻。

Alex had been done wrong with a woman once before. He was lucky she left him for a jerk and now cried in her beers every night as she knew the vast fortune she lost out on by underestimating Alex's full potential that blossomed shortly after she left him and got stuck with the jerk that turned into a beer guzzling couch potato.

亚历克斯以前曾对一个女人做过错事。他很幸运，她因为一个混蛋而离开了他，现在她每天晚上都在啤酒中哭泣，因为她知道自己因为低估了亚历克斯的全部潜力而损失了巨额财富，而亚历克斯在她离开他后不久就绽放出了潜力，并陷入了变成啤酒的混蛋之中。贪吃的沙发土豆。

It took no time for the plane to get up to a cruising altitude of 45,000 feet. With the jet stream pushing the Gulfstream 650 Jet along at 200 Knots, it was traveling 800 knots over ground, even though it wasn't flying supersonic in air.

飞机很快就达到了 45,000 英尺的巡航高度。尽管喷射流推动湾流 650 喷气式飞机以 200 节的速度前进，但它在地面上的飞行速度为 800 节，尽管它不是在空中超音速飞行。

True to Brad's word five hours later, the Gulfstream 650 Jet was starting its slow descent to Nuuk Greenland Airport.

五小时后，正如布拉德所说，湾流 650 喷气式飞机开始缓慢下降，飞往努克格陵兰机场。

BRAD
Mr. Baxter, we are starting our descent now.

布拉德
先生。巴克斯特，我们现在开始下降。

ALEX
Very well Brad, I think I'll join you in the cockpit and
sit in the right seat.

亚历克斯
很好，布拉德，我想我会和你一起进入驾驶舱并
坐在正确的座位上。

In the five hours of traveling evening had slipped into night, and night into day and the early sunlight was now starting to show as the golden sphere rose above the horizon in the distance.

在五个小时的旅行中，傍晚变成了黑夜，黑夜变成了白天，随着金色的球体从远处的地平线上升起，黎明的阳光开始显现。

Without sunglasses, it would have been almost blinding. Alex's sunglasses were in their special holder next to the seat on the right. He put them on as well as the headphones and listened in and watched.

如果没有墨镜的话，几乎会让人失明。亚历克斯的太阳镜放在右侧座位旁边的特殊支架中。他戴上它们和耳机，聆听并观看。

Everything was white below except for the ocean as they got closer to Nuuk Greenland airport. It was a clear day and the area from 35,000 feet as they were descending could be seen.

当他们接近努克格陵兰机场时，除了海洋之外，下面的一切都是白色的。天气晴朗，从 35,000 英尺高空可以看到他们下降时的区域。

<u>EXT. CGI. DAY. ALEX BAXTER'S GS650 JET FINAL APPROACH TO NUUK GREENLAND AIRPORT RUNWAY. (20 SECONDS).</u>

<u>外部。计算机生成图像 · 天 · 亚历克斯·巴克斯特 (ALEX BAXTER) 的 GS650 喷气式飞机最后进近努克格陵兰机场跑道。　(20 秒) 。</u>

Eventually the plane flew down to around 1000 feet above the water as it approached Nuuk Airport landing pattern.

最终，当飞机接近努克机场着陆航线时，飞机飞到了距水面约一千英尺的高度。

ALEX

Everything at Nuuk Airport was white except the runway, which was surprisingly black and clear of snow.

亚历克斯

努克机场的一切都是白色的，除了跑道，跑道是令人惊讶的黑色，而且没有积雪。

BRAD

The Nuuk Airport authority did something smart. As they were rebuilding the runway, they put heaters three feet under the runway.

广阔

努克机场当局做了一件聪明的事。当他们重建跑道时，他们将加热器放置在跑道下方三英尺处。

ALEX
How well has that worked for them?

亚历克斯
这对他们来说效果如何？

BRAD

When it was snowing or the snow was blowing hard, those heaters which are wind powered by numerous nearby huge windmills, slowly heated the ground up and the surface of the runway was maintained above freezing for most of the time. Only during heavy super cold winds, the heaters do not keep up.

广阔

当下雪或雪大的时候，那些由附近无数巨大风车
提供风力的加热器慢慢地加热地面，跑道表面大
部分时间都保持在冰点以上。只有在超强冷风期
间，加热器才跟不上。

Moments later observing the runway during final approach, seeing the black strip in front of them made Alex happy knowing they had good visibility and a good runway to land on.

过了一会儿，亚历克斯在最后进场时观察了跑道，看到了他们前面的黑色带子，这让亚历克斯很高兴，因为他知道他们有良好的能见度和良好的着陆跑道。

Nuuk Greenland Airport, their destination has a single runway that looks desolate, and soon as you arrive you realize it is.

努克格陵兰机场，他们的目的地只有一条跑道，看起来很荒凉，当你到达时你就会意识到它是荒凉的。

Greenland is a territory of Denmark going back hundreds of years. Nuuk, the capital of Greenland, is located on the Southwestern coastline of Greenland, and currently has a population of around 17,000 and is slowly growing.

格陵兰岛是丹麦的领土，可以追溯到数百年前。格陵兰岛首府努克位于格陵兰岛西南海岸线，目前人口约17000人，且正在缓慢增长。

Nuuk Greenland city proper was founded as the fort of Godt-Haab in 1728 by the royal governor Claus Paarss, when he relocated the missionary and merchant Hans Egede's earlier Hope Colony (*Haabets Koloni*) from Kangeq Island to the mainland. At that time, Greenland was formally still a Danish colony under the united Dano-Norwegian Crown.

1728 年，皇家总督克劳斯·帕尔斯 (Claus Paarss) 将传教士兼商人汉斯·埃格德 (Hans Egede) 早期的希望殖民地 (Haabets Koloni) 从康格岛 (Kangeq Island) 迁至大陆，努克格陵兰市中心作为戈特哈布 (Godt-Haab) 堡垒于 1728 年建立。当时，格陵兰岛在形式上仍然是丹麦-挪威联合王国统治下的丹麦殖民地。

Nuuk Greenland is located at approximately 64°10′N 51°44′W at the mouth of Nuup Kangerlua (formerly Baal's River), located some 10 km (6.2 mi) from the shores of the Labrador Sea on the southwestern coast of Greenland, and about 240 km (150 mi) south of the Arctic Circle.

努克格陵兰岛位于北纬　64°10′西经　51°44′左右，努普坎厄鲁阿（Nuup Kangerlua）．以前称为巴尔河河口，距离格陵兰岛西南海岸拉布拉多海沿岸约 10 公里（6.2 英里），位于北极圈以南约 240 公里（150 英里）处。

Two months of the year Nuuk has temperatures in the 40's and has set record high of

71. The rest of the year Nuuk has freezing or subzero weather.

努克每年有两个月的气温在 40 华氏度，并创下了 71 华氏度的历史新高。努克一年中的其余时间有冰冻或零度以下的天气。

The climate (6.5 °C (43.7 °F) in July) is colder than what is considered the limit for trees (10 °C (50 °F) during the warmest month). There are a few planted trees which do not sustain well. Inside the dome they will flourish.

气候（7 月为 6.5 °C (43.7 °F)）比树木的极限温度（最热月份为 10 °C (50 °F)）要冷。有一些种植的树木不能很好地维持。在圆顶内它们将蓬勃发展。

Nuuk has the highest proportion of Danes of any town in Greenland. Half of Greenland's immigrants live in Nuuk which also accounts for a quarter of the country's population.

努克是格陵兰岛所有城镇中丹麦人比例最高的。格陵兰岛一半的移民居住在努克，努克也占该国人口的四分之一。

Although it is a small town/city, Nuuk Greenland has developed trade, business, shipping and other industries.

努克格陵兰岛虽然是一个小镇/城市，但贸易、商业、航运等产业发达。

Nuuk Greenland began as a small fishing settlement with a harbor but as the economy developed rapidly during the 1970s and 1980s, the fishing industry in the capital declined.

努克格陵兰岛最初是一个带有港口的小型渔业定居点，但随着 20 世纪 70 年代和 80 年代经济的快速发展，首都的渔业开始衰退。

The Nuuk Greenland International Port is nevertheless still home to almost half of Greenland's fishing fleet.

尽管如此，努克格陵兰国际港仍然是格陵兰岛近一半渔船的所在地。

The local Royal Greenland processing plant absorbs landed seafood amounting to over DKK 50 million (US $7 million) per annum, mainly (80%) shrimp but also cod, lumpfish and halibut. Seafood, including seal, is also sold in abundance in Nuuk's fish markets, the largest being Kalaaliaraq Market.

当地的皇家格陵兰加工厂每年吸收的上岸海鲜价值超过 5000 万丹麦克朗（700 万美元），主要是（80%）虾，但也有鳕鱼、圆斑鱼和大比目鱼。努克的鱼市上也大量出售包括海豹在内的海鲜，其中最大的是卡拉利亚拉克市场。

Minerals including zinc and gold have contributed to the development of Nuuk Greenland economy. Silver and other precious materials and minerals have been discovered as well.

锌、金等矿产为 努克格陵兰 (Nuuk Greenland) 经济发展做出了贡献。还发现了银和其他珍贵材料和矿物。

Nuuk Greenland is heavily dependent upon Danish government for aid and relies on Denmark for almost all its social programs. Greenland is growing increasingly socialist, and the population is increasingly showing *dependency* as self-initiative and self-reliance diminishes.

努克格陵兰岛严重依赖丹麦政府的援助，几乎所有的社会项目都依赖丹麦。格陵兰岛日益社会主义化，随着自我主动性和自力更生能力的减弱，人们越来越表现出依赖性。

Alex arrived for a two-day conference and while there stayed at Hotel Hans Egede located on Nuuk's main road, *Aqqusinersuaq*.

亚历克斯抵达参加为期两天的会议，并入住位于努克主干道 阿库西内苏阿克的汉斯·埃格德酒店。

Hotel Hans Egede is a modern and comfortable hotel. Alex and Stephanie had reserved adjoining rooms, mainly because Stephanie had a habit of getting scared and wanted to cuddle up for safety.

汉斯埃格德酒店 (Hotel Hans Egede) 酒店是一家现代而舒适的酒店。亚历克斯和斯蒂芬妮预订了相邻的房间，主要是因为斯蒂芬妮有害怕的习惯，为了安全而想拥抱起来。

Stephanie had a reason to have some fear; the pickup truck parked in front of Alex's garage is a subtle reminder, as it was demolished with an explosion.

斯蒂芬妮有理由感到害怕。停在亚历克斯车库前的皮卡车是一个微妙的提醒，因为它被爆炸摧毁了。

The $65,000 truck lasted about three days, and 190 miles were on the odometer. The motor and transmission were still intact, but the cab was demolished as well as the rear end.

这辆价值 65,000 美元的卡车持续了大约三天，里程表上显示行驶了 190 英里。发动机和变速箱仍然完好无损，但驾驶室和后端都被拆除了。

One of the local junk yard owners wanted to buy the truck, and Alex was waiting for him to come by with a tow truck and a check, which had to be postponed until this trip was over.

当地的一位垃圾场老板想买这辆卡车，亚历克斯正等着他开着一辆拖车和一张支票过来，这不得不推迟到这次旅行结束。

EXT. DAY. NUUK GREENLAND AIRPORT. GS650 JET LANDING. 15 SECONDS.

外景。白天。努克格陵兰机场。GS650 喷气式飞机降落。15 秒。

The Gulfstream 650 Jet soon touched down and pulled up to the terminal. One of the four hangers at the airport had been reserved for Alex's GS650 for the time the plane was going to be there for about 36 hours. Hence it would be indoors and not requiring de-icing when they left as the hanger had heat to keep it above freezing.

湾流 650 喷气式飞机很快着陆并停在航站楼。机场的四个机库之一是为 亚历克斯的 (Alex's) GS650 预留的，飞机将在那里停留大约 36 小时。因此，它会在室内，当他们离开时不需要除冰，因为衣架有热量使其保持在冰点以上。

The pilot Brad steered the GS650 Jet to near the hanger and shut down the jet engines. The ground crew would push the GS650 Jet into the hanger backwards with a plane-tug with the engines now shut down and parked inside the hanger and all-weather doors quickly closed.

飞行员布拉德将 GS650 喷气式飞机驾驶到机库附近并关闭喷气式发动机。地勤人员将用飞机拖车将 GS650 喷气式飞机向后推入机库，此时发动机已关闭并停在机库内，全天候舱门也迅速关闭。

As the hanger doors started closing, Alex stood up and walked out of the cockpit and met Stephanie who was holding his winter coat to put on just before she was to open the GS650 Jet access door so they could disembark and meet a customs official politely waiting for them.

当机库门开始关闭时，亚历克斯站起来走出驾驶舱，遇到了斯蒂芬妮，斯蒂芬妮正拿着他的冬衣穿上，准备打开 GS650 喷气式飞机的检修门，这样他们就可以下船并与礼貌地等待的海关官员会面。对于他们来说。

Brad stayed on the GS650 jet until it was secured and fueled and prepared for the return trip. Before Brad left the GS650 jet, he would check all the system logs and diagnostics reports stating NO DEFECTS DETECTED (NDD).

布拉德一直留在 GS650 喷气式飞机上，直到飞机安全、加满燃料并准备返程。在 布拉德离开 GS650 喷气式飞机之前，他会检查所有系统日志和诊断报告，表明未检测到缺陷 (NDD) 。

With nothing to declare and only one suitcase each, Alex and Stephanie were passed by the customs official in about five minutes, their passports stamped, and they were out the door to the waiting Limo, which is one of the few in Nuuk.

亚历克斯和斯蒂芬妮没有任何需要申报的东西，每人只有一个手提箱，大约五分钟后，海关官员就通过了他们，他们的护照上盖了章，然后他们出了门，登上了等候的豪华轿车，这是努克为数不多的豪华轿车之一。

Stephanie did not wear a flight attendant's uniform; she wore fashionable clothes, and to a neutral bystander would appear as a well-dressed woman and to most guys appeared as "*eye candy*."

斯蒂芬妮没有穿空乘制服；她穿着时髦的衣服，对于中立的旁观者来说，她会显得是一个衣着考究的女人，而对于大多数男人来说，她会显得 "养眼"。

For almost six years Stephanie had proved her devotion and loyalty to Alex. That is one of the reasons why Alex helped her buy her company and coached her on the nuances of *how to swim with the sharks but not be eaten alive* such as many of his former acquaintances had experienced.

近六年来，斯蒂芬妮证明了她对亚历克斯的忠诚和忠诚。这就是为什么亚历克斯帮助她购买她的公司并指导她如何与鲨鱼一起游泳而不是像他的许多以前的熟人所经历的那样被活活吃掉的细微差别。

<u>INT. DAY. NUUK GREENLAND AIRPORT LIMO INTERIOR.</u>

<u>内部日。努克格陵兰机场豪华轿车内部。</u>

LIMO DRIVER
Where do you want to go, Mr. Baxter?

豪华轿车司机
先生想去哪里？巴克斯特？

ALEX
We need to first go to Hans Egede Hotel and check in, and then I want you to drive us to Ilisimatusarfik University (a.k.a. Greenland University), so I can meet with our sponsors for tomorrow's meeting.

亚历克斯
我们需要先去 汉斯·埃格德酒店办理入住，然后我想让你开车送我们去 伊利西马图萨尔菲克大学（又名格陵兰大学），这样我就可以和明天会议的赞助商见面。

LIMO DRIVER
Yes, sir. I will be pleased to assist.

豪华轿车司机
是的，先生。我很乐意提供帮助。

The driver opened the car door for his two passengers, Stephanie scooted in first and Alex followed her.

司机为两名乘客打开车门，斯蒂芬妮率先上车，亚历克斯紧随其后。

Neither Alex nor Stephanie had visited Greenland before. Though Alex saw quite a few videos put together by experts showing what and where important businesses were located and concept pictures of where they planned to build the dome city.

亚历克斯和斯蒂芬妮以前都没有去过格陵兰岛。尽管亚历克斯看到了很多专家整理的视频，展示了重要企业的所在地和位置，以及他们计划在哪里建造圆顶城市的概念图。

There was a lot of snow on the ground and cold outside, but the limo was nice and warm. The Limo should be warm for as much as Alex was paying for 36 hours standby service, on call, including a second driver if necessary to extend the hours.

地面上有很多雪，外面有寒冷，但是豪华轿车很温暖。豪华轿车应像亚历克斯（Alex）支付36小时备用服务的费用一样温暖，包括在必要的情况下，包括第二个驾驶员以延长小时数。

The Limo departed Nuuk Airport, turned right on Illerngit 2001 curved around the past the Southern end of the runway, then turned West on Borgmester Anniitap Aqquserna and 400-ertalik/400 vej/Eqalugalinnguanut road.

豪华轿车从努克机场出发，在 伊尔恩吉特 2001 (Illerngit 2001) 上右转，绕过跑道南端，然后在 安尼塔普·阿库瑟纳市长 400左右/ 400路/ (Borgmester Anniitap Akkuserna 和 400-ertalik/400 vej/) 扁豆苷瓜努特 (Eqalugalinnguanut) 路上向西转。

The Limo then headed toward the peninsula and to Sipisaq Kangilleq road. The Limo then continued onto H.J. Rinkip Aqqutaa street and turned left on left onto Aqqusinersuaq street.

After a short distance, the Limo turned left into Hans Egede Hotel guest arrival front entrance parking of the hotel which does an excellent job of snow removal.

然后豪华轿车驶向半岛并驶向 西皮萨克·坎吉勒克 (Sipisaq Kangilleq) 路。豪华轿车随后继续驶向 艾尺. 杰. 林奇普·阿库塔 (H.J. Rinkip Aquutaa) 街左转进入 阿库西内苏阿克 (Aqusinersuaq) 街。 行驶了一小段距离后，豪华轿车左转进入 汉斯艾格德酒店 (Hans Egede Hotel) 客人到达前门停车场，该停车场的除雪工作非常出色。

The drive to Hans Egede Hotel happened without events as the streets were semi empty with only a few travelers at this time of day.

开车前往汉斯·埃格德酒店的路上没有发生任何事件，因为一天中这个时候街道半空，只有少数旅客。

Alex checked his Google Maps during the ride from the airport and saw Hotel Hans Egede address: Aqqusinersuaq 1-3, Nuuk, 3900, Greenland. Google APP said they had arrived at their destination.

豪华轿车应像 亚历克斯 (Alex) 在从机场出发的途中检查了谷歌地图，看到汉斯埃格德酒店 (Hotel Hans Egede) 地址： （Aqqusinersuaq 1-3, Nuuk, 3900, Greenland)。谷歌APP表示他们已经到达目的地。

The driver got out, opened the passenger door then the trunk was opened as Alex and Stephanie got out of the Limo, the driver grabbed their two bags and handed them to the porter who he had just called to warn them he would be arriving shortly after leaving the airport.

司机下车，打开乘客门，然后行李箱打开，亚历克斯和斯蒂芬妮下了豪华轿车，司机抓起他们的两个行李，交给搬运工，他刚刚打电话警告他们他很快就会到达离开机场。

LIMO DRIVER
Sir, should I wait here?

豪华轿车司机
先生，我应该在这里等吗？

ALEX
Yes, we'll check in and have the hotel staff deliver our luggage to our rooms so we can quickly be on our way.

亚历克斯
是的，我们将办理入住手续，并让酒店工作人员将行李送到我们的房间，以便我们可以快速上路。

INT. DAY. HANS EGEDE HOTEL LOBBY.

INT。天。汉斯·埃格德酒店大堂。

The Hans Egede Hotel lobby looked like any well-kept Hotel in a modern City. With the new mining operations and some of the other commercial enterprises sprouting up such as software and microprocessor development of all things, a lot of sophisticated clients now arrived at this hotel often.

汉斯·埃格德酒店 (Hans Egede Hotel) 的大堂看起来就像现代城市中任何一家维护良好的酒店。随着新的采矿业务和其他一些商业企业的兴起，例如所有事物的软件和微处理器开发，许多经验丰富的客户现在经常来到这家酒店。

Since Nuuk Greenland was a small City of only 17,000 or so, Hans Egede Hotel had one of the few viable nightclubs up on the top floor of the hotel. Young people would arrive on Friday and Saturday night to drink, dance, party, and have a good time up there.

由于努克格陵兰岛是一座只有 17,000 人左右的小城市，汉斯·埃格德酒店 (Hans Egede Hotel) 在酒店顶层设有少数几家可行的夜总会之一。年轻人会在周五和周六晚上到达这里喝酒、跳舞、聚会，并在那里度过愉快的时光。

STEPHANIE

The Hereford Beefstouw Restaurant located in the Hans Egede Hotel would be a great place to meet privately with some of the Greenland representatives after the conference tomorrow.

斯蒂芬妮
位于 汉斯·埃格德 (Hans Egede) 酒店的赫里福德炖牛肉 (Beefstouw) 餐厅将是明天会议结束后与一些格陵兰代表私下会面的好地方。

ALEX
Yes, good idea, we will not have to go out into the weather once we get back to the hotel.

ALEX
Yes, good idea, we will not have to go out into the weather once we get back to the hotel.

亚历克斯
是的，好主意，回到酒店后我们就不用再受天气影响了。

The Hotel receptionist at the Hans Egede Hotel front desk had a name tag indicated her name was Margarete and greeted Alex and Stephanie in Danish.

汉斯埃格德酒店 (Hans Egede Hotel) 前台的接待员手持名牌，上面写着她的名字叫玛格丽特 (Margarete)，她用丹麦语向亚历克斯 (Alex) 和斯蒂芬妮 (Stephanie) 打招呼。

MARGARETE
Hej, hvordan kan jeg hjælpe dig? (Hello, how may I help you?)

玛格丽特
（您好，请问有什么可以帮到您吗？

ALEX
Can you speak English?

亚历克斯
你能说英语吗？

MARGARETE
Yes, I can.

MARGARETE
Yes, I can.

玛格丽特
是的，我可以。

ALEX
Oh good.

亚历克斯
很好。

Margarete, a somewhat short native girl had dark hair and seemingly Asian look, was far slenderer than Alex would have thought from seeing everyone thus far walking around on the streets or at the airport seemed chubby.

玛格丽特是个身材有些矮小的印度女孩，有着黑色的头发，看起来像亚洲人，但她比亚历克斯想象的要苗条得多，因为到目前为止，走在街上或机场的人都看起来胖乎乎的。

Margarete didn't have much makeup on, but had a pleasing appeal that Alex could not quite figure out why. In some ways, Margarete looked quite a lot like many young native women Alex saw in Alaska.

玛格丽特没有化太多的妆，但却有一种令人愉悦的魅力，亚历克斯不知道为什么。从某些方面来看，玛格丽特看起来和亚历克斯在阿拉斯加见过的许多年轻土著女性很像。

Stephanie then jumped in, fulfilling her administrative aide role.

随后，斯蒂芬妮加入进来，履行她的行政助理职责。

STEPHANIE
We have reservations for the Baxter party.

斯蒂芬妮
我们已经预订了巴克斯特派对的座位。

Margarete was expecting Alex and Stephanie since they were reserving the two most expensive rooms in the hotel, which remained empty 50% of the time and was amused when she saw them on her check-in list.

玛格丽特期待着亚历克斯和斯蒂芬妮的到来，因为他们预订了酒店里最贵的两间房间，这两间房间有一半的时间是空着的，当她在入住名单上看到他们时，她感到很有趣。

MARGARETE (Thought)
*This couple are obviously big spenders.*

玛格丽特（沉思）

这对夫妇显然是挥霍无度的人。

Stephanie handed Margarete her credit card since the rooms were reserved by her and within a short period of time Margarete printed out their contract and Stephanie signed it, and Alex and Stephanie were provided with their room keys.

由于房间是她预订的，斯蒂芬妮将她的信用卡交给了玛格丽特。在玛格丽特打印出合同、斯蒂芬妮签字后不久，亚历克斯和斯蒂芬妮就拿到了房间钥匙。

#### MARGARETE
As you requested, the adjoining rooms. Would you like a wakeup call in the morning?

#### 玛格丽特
如您所愿，我们给您安排了相邻的房间。您早上需要叫醒服务吗？

#### ALEX
Sure, 6:00 a.m. please.

#### 亚历克斯
当然可以，早上 6:00 请。

#### MARGARETE
Anything else I can be of assistance?

#### 玛格丽特
还有什么我可以帮忙的吗？

#### STEPHANIE
Yes, we have just two suitcases, can you send them up to our rooms, because we have some place we need to go to and will be back later.

#### 斯蒂芬妮
是的，我们只有两个行李箱，你能把它们送到我们的房间吗，因为我们要去一个地方，稍后再回来。

#### MARGARETE
Of course, I'll take care of your luggage right away.

#### 玛格丽特
当然，我会马上帮你处理行李。

#### STEPHANIE
Thank you.

斯蒂芬妮
谢谢。

**MARGARETE**
You are welcome.

玛格丽特
别客气。

Alex and Stephanie then exited the lobby, went back outside to the waiting Limo and the driver immediately opened the door for them.

然后，亚历克斯和斯蒂芬妮走出大厅·回到等候的豪华轿车外·司机立即为他们打开了车门。

**ALEX**
Take us to Ilisimatusarfik University please.

亚历克斯
请带我们去伊利斯马图萨菲克大学。

**LIMO DRIVER**
Right away, sir.

豪华轿车司机
先生，马上就来。

Note to cinematographer:

> Wikipedia Extract: The **University of Greenland** (<u>Greenlandic</u>: *Ilisimatusarfik Kalaallit Nunaat*; <u>Danish</u>: *Grønlands Universitet*) is <u>Greenland</u>'s only <u>university</u>. It is in the capital city of <u>Nuuk</u>. Most courses are taught in <u>Danish</u>, a few in <u>Greenlandic</u> and classes by exchange lecturers often in <u>English</u>.

电影摄影师注意事项：

> 维基百科摘录：格陵兰大学（格陵兰语：伊利西马图萨尔菲克卡拉利特·努纳特 (Ilisimatusarfik Kalaallit Nunaat) ；丹麦语：丹麦语：格伦兰大学 (Grønlands Universitet）是格陵兰岛唯一的大学。它位于首都努克。大多数课程以丹麦语授课·少数课程以格陵兰语授课·交换讲师通常以英语授课。

Alex then called Professor Grey:

亚历克斯随后打电话给格雷教授：

ALEX
Professor Grey, I wanted to let you know we are on the way from the Hans Egede Hotel heading to the University now.

亚历克斯
格雷教授，我想让您知道，我们现在正从汉斯埃格德酒店前往大学。

PROFESSOR GREY
Thanks for the heads up.

格雷教授
谢谢您的提醒。

The car turned out onto the main road *Aqqusinersuaq Eqalugalinnquit* then 400-ertalik/400 vej/Eqalugalinnguanut to Manguaraq then Manguaraq and Qattaaq to Manutooq.

[Ilisimatusarfik University address is: Manutooq 1, Nuuk 3905, Greenland.]

汽车驶入主干道　阿奎西内苏阿克　埃卡鲁加仑因奎特　(*Aqqusinersuaq Eqalugalinnquit*)，然后开400-ertalik/400 vej/白藜芦醇 (Eqalugalinnguanut) 前往曼瓜拉克（Manguaraq），然后曼瓜拉克 (Manguaraq)和 卡塔克(Qattaaq) 前往 马努图克(Manutooq)。

[伊利西马图萨菲克大学地址是：马努图克1,努克3905,格陵兰岛。]

The drive to the university took around eight minutes.

开车到大学大约需要八分钟。

STEPHANIE
I researched Ilisimatusarfik University which has about 650 students and 14 full-time tenured college professors and uses visiting college professors for various durations of time.

斯蒂芬妮
我研究了伊利斯马图萨尔菲克大学，该大学约有650 名学生和 14 名全职终身教授，并聘用不同期限的客座教授。

ALEX
Oh really? Why are there so few students in a country with a large land mass?

亚历克斯
哦真的吗？为什么这么大的国家却只有这么少的
学生？

STEPHANIE
The small student population is due to the government's
policy allowing students a free university education
anywhere in Europe or North America, with most of
the students choosing to be going to a university in
Denmark.

斯蒂芬妮
学生人数较少是因为政府的政策允许学生在欧洲
或北美的任何地方接受免费大学教育，大多数学
生选择去丹麦的大学就读。

ALEX
Does that mean the academics here are poor?

亚历克斯
那是不是意味着这里的学术水平很差？

STEPHANIE
No. The Ilisimatusarfik University academics are
better than in Denmark because the class sizes are
smaller. The result of the small class size allows
students better access to professors.

斯蒂芬妮
不。伊利斯马图萨尔菲克大学的学术水平比丹麦
的要好，因为班级规模较小。小班授课让学生能
够更好地与教授交流。

ALEX
Then why would they choose college in Denmark?

亚历克斯
那么他们为什么会选择去丹麦上大学呢？

STEPHANIE
For socializing and getting a chance to get off the
*rock* for a while and see things like trees, trains, and
many other things people take for granted in warmer
climates.

斯蒂芬妮
为了社交，为了有机会离开岩石一段时间，看看
树木、火车和许多其他人们在温暖气候下认为理
所当然的东西。

ALEX
We'll see if we can change all that.

亚历克斯
我们将看看是否可以改变这一切。

Stephanie smiled.

斯蒂芬妮微笑。

STEPHANIE
I suppose with your proposal you just might do all that.

斯蒂芬妮
我想，按照你的建议，你也许可以做到这一切。

As the Limo pulled into the main driveway to Ilisimatusarfik University, Alex noticed a couple of people leaving the building and walking out to greet them. The Limo Driver instinctively knew that's where he should stop.

当豪华轿车驶入通往伊利斯马图萨尔菲克大学的主车道时，亚历克斯注意到有几个人从大楼出来，走出来迎接他们。豪华轿车司机本能地知道他应该在那里停车。

The driver got out and quickly opened the door, and then Alex and Stephanie exited the Limo and walked directly to the man and woman waiting.

司机下车迅速打开车门，然后亚历克斯和斯蒂芬妮下了豪华轿车，径直走向了等待的那对男女。

ALEX
Professor Grey?

亚历克斯
格雷教授？

PROFESSOR GREY
Yes, hello Mr. Baxter, glad you made it safely.

格雷教授
是的，你好，巴克斯特先生，很高兴你安全抵达。

ALEX
Thank you.

ALEX
谢谢。

PROFESSOR GREY
Mr. Baxter, let me introduce you to our director of Greenland's Natural Resources Council, Doctor Adelheid Jørgensen.

格雷教授
巴克斯特先生，请允许我向您介绍格陵兰自然资源委员会主任阿德尔海德·约根森博士。

ALEX
Pleased to meet you Doctor Jørgensen.

亚历克斯
很高兴认识您约根森医生。

ADELHEID JØRGENSEN (a.k.a. ADEL)
Alex, please call me Adel.

阿德尔海德·约根森（又名阿德尔）
亚历克斯，请叫我阿德尔。

Then Adel reached her hand out to take Alex's to shake.

然后阿德尔伸出手来握住亚历克斯的手。

ALEX
Adel, this is my administrative assistant, Stephanie McFarland.

亚历克斯
阿德尔，这是我的行政助理，斯蒂芬妮·麦克法兰。

ADELHEID JØRGENSEN (a.k.a. ADEL)
Pleased to meet you, Ms. McFarland.

阿德尔海德·约根森（又名 阿德尔）
很高兴见到你，麦克法兰女士。

Stephanie reached out to shake Adel's hand.

斯蒂芬妮伸出手去和阿德尔握手。

STEPHANIE
Adel, please call me Stephanie.

斯蒂芬妮
阿德尔，请叫我斯蒂芬妮。

PROFESSOR GREY
Let's go inside where it's a lot warmer.

格雷教授
我们进屋吧，那里暖和多了。

INT. DAY. INSTITUTE OF NATURAL RESOURCES BUILDING.

室内。白天。自然资源研究所大楼。

The driver got back into the Limo and waited. The group went into what turned out to be the Institute of Natural Resources building, where Adel had her office so they could discuss the arrangements for the next day.

司机回到豪华轿车里等待。一行人走进了自然资源研究所大楼，阿黛尔的办公室就在这里，他们商讨第二天的安排。

PROFESSOR GREY
We'll be set up in the morning to start around 9:00 a.m. and barring a surprise storm, several people of the community will be on hand to hear your presentation and provide feedback.

格雷教授
我们将在早上 9:00 左右开始准备，除非发生意外风暴，否则社区的几位人士将在现场聆听您的演讲并提供反馈。

ADELHEID JØRGENSEN (a.k.a. ADEL)
Government representatives will also be on hand, to whom I've sent them briefs so they can advise the government more on your proposal after they hear from you tomorrow.

阿德尔海德·约根森（又名 阿德尔）
政府代表也将出席，我已向他们发送了简报，以便他们在明天收到您的消息后可以就您的提案向政府提供更多建议。

ALEX
Excellent.

亚历克斯
出色的。


ADELHEID JØRGENSEN (a.k.a. ADEL)
I would say what you are proposing is almost sheer fantasy, and I doubt few would believe it can be accomplished especially within the time frame you indicated.

阿德尔海德·约根森（又名 阿德尔）
我想说你所提议的几乎纯粹是幻想，我怀疑很少有人会相信它可以实现，特别是在你指定的时间范围内。


ALEX
As with a lot of my enterprises, a lot of people doubted me.

亚历克斯
和我的很多企业一样，很多人都对我表示怀疑。


ADELHEID JØRGENSEN (a.k.a. ADEL)
We know you are very successful.

阿德尔海德·约根森（又名 阿德尔）
我们知道您非常成功。


ALEX
And I put my money where my mouth is.

亚历克斯
我把钱放在嘴边。


ADELHEID JØRGENSEN (a.k.a. ADEL)
That's obvious Mr. Baxter; you do have a reputation.

阿德尔海德·约根森（又名 阿德尔）
很明显，巴克斯特，先生，您确实很有名气。


ALEX
Hopefully not quite as large as our President?

亚历克斯
希望不像我们的总统那么大？

ADELHEID JØRGENSEN (a.k.a. ADEL)
In some ways you do, you are just not quite as well known.

阿德尔海德·约根森（又名 阿德尔）
在某些方面，你只是不那么出名。

ALEX
I tried to keep it that way.

亚历克斯
我试图保持这种状态。

ADELHEID JØRGENSEN (a.k.a. ADEL)
What you are proposing is a very expensive and obtrusive project.

阿德尔海德·约根森（又名 阿德尔）
你所提议的是一个非常昂贵且引人注目的项目。

ALEX
If my hunch is correct, the outcome will be the population here will grow from 17,000 to 500,000 in 10 years as the construction phase ends and immigrants land here.

亚历克斯
如果我的预感是正确的，那么随着建设阶段的结束和移民的登陆，这里的人口将在十年内从 17,000 人增加到 500,000 人。

ADELHEID JØRGENSEN (a.k.a. ADEL)
Provided the government agrees to your land use.

阿德尔海德·约根森（又名 阿德尔）
前提是政府同意您的土地使用。

ALEX
Once people discover they don't have to live in exposed weather any longer they will think long and hard about it.

亚历克斯
一旦人们发现他们不必再生活在暴露的天气中，他们就会认真思考这一点。

ADELHEID JØRGENSEN (a.k.a. ADEL)
I'm sure the snow removal public servants will not be
too happy about it.

阿德尔海德·约根森（又名 阿德尔）
相信除雪公仆们对此不会太高兴。


ALEX
That's why this university is here, to retrain them.

亚历克斯
这就是为什么这所大学在这里，对他们进行再培训。


ADELHEID JØRGENSEN (a.k.a. ADEL)
Many older Nuuk people are lacking the mental skills
to sustain a university degree.

阿德尔海德·约根森（又名 阿德尔）
许多努克老年人缺乏维持大学学位的心理技能。


ALEX
You could offer them a certificate program, such as we
have in America that is taught at university extension
programs, with a possible migration into a degreed
program later if they continue with the effort.

亚历克斯
你可以为他们提供证书课程，就像我们在美国的
大学扩展课程中教授的那样，如果他们继续努
力，以后可能会转入学位课程。


ADELHEID JØRGENSEN (a.k.a. ADEL)
A domed city is something that will not do anything
for the numerous fishermen.

阿德尔海德·约根森（又名阿德尔）
一座圆顶城市对于众多的渔民来说是没有任何帮
助的。


ALEX
Part of the Dome could overhang the fishing wharfs so
they no longer must deal with de-icing their boats and
can be protected from winds.

亚历克斯
圆顶的一部分可以悬在渔码头上方，这样他们就
不再需要为船只除冰，并且可以免受风的影响。

ADELHEID JØRGENSEN (a.k.a. ADEL)
Isn't there some basic structure that places requirements that would preclude building offshore? It seems to me that would be prohibitively expensive.

阿德尔海德·约根森（又名 阿德尔）
难道没有一些基本结构提出了阻止海上建设的要求吗？在我看来，那样会非常昂贵。

ALEX
Not for this area. The geologist reports indicate Nuuk is a rocky area and has many good places to build foundations and drive pilings in for strong structures.

亚历克斯
不适合这个区域。地质学家的报告表明，努克是一个岩石地区，有许多适合建造地基和打桩以建造坚固建筑的好地方。

ADELHEID JØRGENSEN (a.k.a. ADEL)
But it would take an overhang almost a half a mile to cover the fishing anchorage.

阿德尔海德·约根森（又名 阿德尔）
但需要近半英里的悬垂物才能覆盖钓鱼锚地。

ALEX
Yes, it will be expensive but no, it will not be a problem.

亚历克斯
是的，这会很贵，但不会有问题。

PROFESSOR GREY
Alex, would you like to see the auditorium setup for tomorrow?

格雷教授
亚历克斯，你想看看明天礼堂的布置吗？

ALEX
Sure.

亚历克斯
当然。

The group walked out of the building across to the main building structure that had 3 wings. These buildings have a strange architecture. All the rooftops have a large angle on their slopes.

团队走出大楼，来到有 3 个侧翼的主楼。这些建筑的建筑风格很奇怪。所有屋顶的坡度都很大。

ALEX
The roofs and sides of the University Buildings have no horizontal surfaces. All are at significant angles.

亚历克斯
大学建筑的屋顶和侧面没有水平面。全部都处于重要角度。

ADELHEID JØRGENSEN (a.k.a. ADEL)
The design is more than decoration or architecture. The sloped roof serves the purpose of allowing snow and ice removal to keep dangerous weight off roofs.

阿德尔海德·约根森（又名 阿德尔）
设计不仅仅是装饰或建筑。倾斜的屋顶可以清除积雪和冰块，从而减轻屋顶的重量。

ALEX
I can see that.

亚历克斯
我看得出来。

Stephanie, who was very fashion-conscious, quickly surmised:

非常注重时尚的斯蒂芬妮很快就猜到了：

STEPHANIE (THOUGHT)
*Adel could be very alluring if she had just a modest makeover. She had beautiful skin and eyes, and the geometry of her face, lips, chin, and neck as well as her body overall is utterly stunning.*

斯蒂芬妮（心想）
阿黛尔只要稍微改头换面一下，就会变得非常迷人。她皮肤和眼睛都很漂亮，脸、嘴唇、下巴、脖子以及整个身体的几何形状都令人惊艳。

Stephanie felt a twinge of jealousy erupting as she could tell by Alex's body language. Adel was somehow casting a spell on Alex, one she must disrupt if there was even a little smoke, since that could be a telltale sign of an internal fire.

斯蒂芬妮从亚历克斯的肢体语言中看出，她感到一阵嫉妒。阿黛尔不知怎么地对亚历克斯施了魔法，只要有一点烟，她就必须打破这种魔咒，因为那可能是内心起火的迹象。

The group walked into a room that appeared like an extra-large classroom, compared to the rest of the campus.

小组走进一间房间，与校园的其他地方相比，这间房间看起来像一间超大教室。

PROFESSOR GREY
Here is where we'll meet tomorrow, the two tables on the wall over there will have coffee, drinks, and snacks as you requested.

格雷教授
这是我们明天见面的地方，那边墙上的两张桌子将提供您所要求的咖啡、饮料和小吃。

ALEX
That's wonderful.

亚历克斯
太好了。

PROFESSOR GREY
People here might ask a lot of questions, be prepared to stay a while.

格雷教授
这里的人可能会问很多问题，准备好待上一段时间吧。

ALEX
I figured we could spend the morning here and then go back to the Hans Egede Hotel where there is an excellent bar, we'll have an open bar and lubricate people who have a lot of questions.

亚历克斯
我想我们可以在这里度过上午，然后回到汉斯·埃格德酒店，那里有一家很棒的酒吧，我们会有一个开放式酒吧，为那些有很多问题的人提供便利。

ADELHEID JØRGENSEN (a.k.a. ADEL)
Isn't that slightly unethical?

阿德尔海德·约根森（又名 阿德尔）
这不是有点不道德吗？

ALEX
It is, but it's also for their own good.

亚历克斯
是的，但这也是为了他们好。

ADELHEID JØRGENSEN (a.k.a. ADEL)
The community probably will not want to put a dome
over the top of Nuuk.

阿德尔海德·约根森（又名 阿德尔）
社区可能不想在努克的顶部建造一个圆顶。

ALEX
I'm aware that would probably be the case, that's why
I'd rather build it northeast of the Airport.

亚历克斯
我知道情况可能会是这样，这就是为什么我宁愿
把它建在机场东北部。

ADELHEID JØRGENSEN (a.k.a. ADEL)
There are private landowners that own that land there.

阿德尔海德·约根森（又名 阿德尔）
那里有私人土地所有者拥有该土地。

ALEX
That's ok, I'll buy them out. I'll give them enough
money where they can move to Denmark and live in
style.

亚历克斯
没关系，我会把它们买下来。我会给他们足够的
钱，让他们可以搬到丹麦过上奢侈的生活。

PROFESSOR GREY
The whole City would leave with that kind of offer.

格雷教授
整个城市都会因为这样的提议而离开。

ALEX
But then they would come back quickly as soon as they discovered the advantage of living in a domed city. No snow, year-round 70-degree weather. No storms, rain, snow, or harshness people living in Nuuk now experience.

亚历克斯
但是，一旦他们发现住在穹顶城市的好处，他们就会很快回来。没有雪，全年 70 度的天气。没有风暴、雨、雪或现在努克人所经历的严酷天气。

PROFESSOR GREY
They're used to it.

格雷教授
他们已经习惯了。

ALEX
They will get unused to it real fast as soon as they start living under the dome in the winter.

亚历克斯
一旦他们开始在冬天住在穹顶下，他们就会很快不习惯。

PROFESSOR GREY
Too bad Ilisimatusarfik University isn't on the other side of the Airport.

格雷教授
可惜伊利斯马图萨尔菲克大学不在机场的另一边。

ALEX
Don't worry; there will be plenty of room to move Ilisimatusarfik University under the Dome.

不用担心; 圆顶下将有足够的空间来容纳伊利西马图萨尔菲克大学。

PROFESSOR GREY
What about our huge investment here?

格雷教授
我们这里的巨额投资呢？

ALEX

It could be sold and converted to an industrial or research complex or other uses.

亚历克斯

它可以出售并转化为工业或研究综合体或其他用途。

PROFESSOR GREY

Ok, let us see what the public has to say tomorrow.

格雷教授

好的，让我们看看明天公众会怎么说。

ALEX

Also, tomorrow we expect an executive from a steel manufacturing company and a concrete firm here to answer questions on construction materials they will provide, as well as a construction company executive who would do the building.

亚历克斯

此外，明天我们预计一家钢铁制造公司和一家混凝土公司的高管将回答有关他们将提供的建筑材料以及负责建造该建筑的建筑公司的问题。

PROFESSOR GREY

It will be interesting to hear what they have to say.

格雷教授

听听他们怎么说会很有趣。

ALEX

May I make a suggestion?

亚历克斯

我可以提个建议吗？

PROFESSOR GREY

Sure?

格雷教授

可以吗？

ALEX

Why don't we all go over to the Hans Egede Hotel, they have the *Skyline Bar* up there on the top floor and have a few drinks and discuss this a little further?

亚历克斯
我们为什么不一起去汉斯埃格德酒店呢？他们在
顶楼有一家天际线酒吧，我们喝几杯，再讨论一
下这个问题。

ADELHEID JØRGENSEN (a.k.a. ADEL)
I don't drink, but I'd be happy to go. I'm sure Mr. Grey
who likes craft beers would like to go with us.

阿德尔海德·约根森（又名 阿德尔）
我不喝酒，但我很乐意去。我相信喜欢精酿啤酒
的格雷先生会愿意和我们一起去。

Mr. Grey who knew big pockets would be picking up the check smiled, realizing he
could go right on down the menu, responded.

格雷先生知道有钱人会买单，他笑了，意识到他可以直接看菜单，于是回答
道。

PROFESSOR GREY
Only if you promise to drive me home afterwards, Adel.

格雷教授
只有你答应之后开车送我回家，阿德尔。

ADELHEID JØRGENSEN (a.k.a. ADEL)
Since I do not drink seems like I'm always getting
saddled with the designated driving.

阿德尔海德·约根森（又名 阿德尔）
因为我不喝酒，所以似乎总是被要求开车。

Alex stated with almost Cheshire Cat like smile:

亚历克斯带着几乎柴郡猫般的微笑说道：

ALEX
I have an excellent Idea. I have that limo reserved for
us for 36 hours, the driver will take you home anytime
you want.

亚历克斯
我有一个好主意。我为我们预订了那辆豪华轿车
36 小时，司机随时可以送你回家。

PROFESSOR GREY
Works for me!

格雷教授
对我有用！

The four then left the room, and Adel hit the light switch as they were exiting with a smile.

然后四个人离开了房间，当他们面带微笑离开时，阿德尔按下了电灯开关。

As the four were approaching the Limo the driver saw them and got out of the limo promptly and opened the passenger door closest to the group.

当四个人走近豪华轿车时，司机看到了他们，迅速下了豪华轿车，打开了离他们最近的乘客侧车门。

Alex approached the driver.

亚历克斯走近司机。

ALEX

The four of us are all going back to the Hans Egede Hotel for drinks then dinner, when Mr. Grey and Ms. Adel are ready to leave the hotel, take them home and in the morning, I would like you to arrange to drive them back here since their leaving their cars here for now.

亚历克斯

我们四个人都回汉斯埃格德酒店喝酒然后吃晚饭，格雷先生和阿德尔女士准备离开酒店，送他们回家，明天早上，我希望你能安排开车送他们回来，因为他们暂时把车停在这里。

LIMO DRIVER
Yes sir, Mr. Baxter.

豪华轿车司机
是的，先生，巴克斯特先生。

The 4 fit easily in the Limo. The Limo Company probably wasn't doing too well, but during Alex stay, the 36-hour rental made them happy. The driver didn't know yet that his tip would match his yearly salary.

四个人很容易坐进豪华轿车。豪华轿车公司的经营状况可能不太好，但在亚历克斯入住期间，36　小时的租车让他们很开心。司机还不知道他的小费会和他的年薪相媲美。

**INT. DAY. HANS EGEDE HOTEL SKYLINE BAR**

<u>整数。天。戴汉斯埃格德酒店天际线酒吧</u>

It was just about happy hour time, and half dozen businessmen were there along with a few attractive women, who were probably business associates.

不一会儿，豪华轿车停在了汉斯埃格德酒店门前，一行人下了豪华轿车，走到电梯前，电梯把他们带到了顶楼，他们去了天际线酒吧。

In a short while the Limo pulled up in front of the Hans Egede Hotel and the group got out of the Limo and made their way to the elevator which took them up to the top floor where they made their way to the Skyline Bar.

当时正是欢乐时光，有六位商人和几位可能是商业伙伴的漂亮女士在场。

A pianist was playing jazz songs on the grand piano at the bar, and Alex suggested:

一位钢琴家在酒吧的大钢琴上弹奏爵士乐曲，亚历克斯建议道：

ALEX
Since there are just four of us and Adel doesn't drink,
Let's all sit at the bar. I might get the chance to meet
some locals sitting there.

亚历克斯
因为我们只有四个人，而且 阿德尔不喝酒，所以
我们都坐在吧台上吧。我可能有机会遇到一些坐
在那里的当地人。

STEPHANIE
This bar looks kind of interesting.

斯蒂芬妮）
这个酒吧看起来很有趣。

At the back of the bar which you could see through spaces between the bottles on the open shelf was large glass window exposing buildings behind. The bar was long and could seat 15 to 20 people. There were a couple dozen tables which people could sit and drink at as well as order food.

在酒吧后面，你可以透过开放式架子上酒瓶之间的空隙看到后面有一扇大玻璃窗，可以看到后面的建筑物。酒吧很长，可以容纳 15 到 20 人。有几十张桌子，人们可以坐下来喝酒，也可以点菜。

ALEX
I see there are a few nice leather sofas near the end of
the bar for some private and romantic scenarios.

亚历克斯
我看到酒吧尽头附近有几张漂亮的皮沙发，可以
营造一些私密而浪漫的场景。

ADELHEID JØRGENSEN (a.k.a. ADEL)
Greenland has a high alcoholic and drug abuse
population. Bars do well there as many jobs in mining
and fishing are well paid. It's not surprising to see
people at the bar and at this time of year it's already
getting dark.

阿德尔海德·约根森（又名 阿德尔）
格陵兰岛酗酒和吸毒人口很高。那里的酒吧生意
很好，因为采矿和捕鱼行业的许多工作报酬都很
高。看到酒吧里有人并不奇怪，而且每年的这个
时候天已经黑了。


STEPHANIE (Thought)
*Good thing Adel doesn't drink, Alex would be
lubricating her up about now.*

斯蒂芬妮（想道）
幸好阿黛尔不喝酒，不然亚历克斯现在就会给她
上润滑油了。

A gentleman in a suit and tie sat down next to Alex on the bar and politely spoke:

一位西装革履的绅士在吧台上坐到了亚历克斯的旁边，礼貌地说道：

GENTLEMAN (a.k.a. Magnus)
Hej, hvordan går det?

绅士（又名 Magnus）
你好，你好吗？

ALEX
Hello, how are you?

亚历克斯
你好吗？

GENTLEMAN (a.k.a. Magnus)
I speak English as well.

绅士（又名 Magnus）
我也会说英语。

ALEX
Oh good.

亚历克斯
哦，很好。

GENTLEMAN (a.k.a. Magnus)
Yes, a lot of Greenlander's speak English because of
the American air bases and our dealings with Canada
and surprising many also speak French.

绅士（又名 Magnus）
是的，很多格陵兰人会说英语，因为这里有美国
空军基地，而且我们与加拿大有交易，而且令人
惊讶的是，很多人还会说法语。

ALEX
I see.

亚历克斯
我懂了。

GENTLEMAN (a.k.a. Magnus)
A lot of the tribal folks here were originally living in
Canada, migrated here for the jobs.

绅士（又名 Magnus）
这里的很多部落人原本住在加拿大，后来为了工
作而移民到这里。

ALEX
Is that so?

亚历克斯
是这样吗？

GENTLEMAN (a.k.a. Magnus)
My name is Magnus, by the way.

绅士（又名 马格努斯）
顺便说一下，我叫马格努斯。

ALEX
I'm Alex; these are Adel, Stephanie, and Professor
Grey.

亚历克斯
我是亚历克斯；他们是阿德尔、斯蒂芬妮和格雷教授。

MAGNUS
Alex, what brings you to Nuuk Greenland?

马格努斯
亚历克斯，是什么风把你带到格陵兰岛努克的？

ALEX
Tomorrow we'll be giving an address at Ilisimatusarfik University on a proposal I have for building a *Domed City*.

亚历克斯
明天我们将在伊利斯马图萨菲克大学发表演讲，介绍我提出的建造圆顶城市的提案。

MAGNUS
Oh really, I read about that in the newspaper.

马格努斯
哦，真的，我在报纸上读到过。

ALEX
Yes, this is a public forum to get feedback and present our ideas.

亚历克斯
是的，这是一个公共论坛，用于收集反馈并提出我们的想法。

MAGNUS
A lot of people say it's nonsense and impossible.

马格努斯
很多人说这是胡说八道，不可能的。

ALEX
I'm betting on it with my money.

亚历克斯
我用我的钱打赌。

More and more people filed in and in a few hours, Alex bought well over 100 drinks.

The crowd was well lubricated and getting some insights into this newfangled *Dome City*, this American was pitching and offering to build with his money.

越来越多的人涌入，几个小时内，亚历克斯就买了 100 多杯饮料。人群非常兴奋，对这个新奇的穹顶城有了一些了解，这个美国人正在推销并提出用他的钱来建造。

Alex would be heavily criticized later because as part of the deal, he would own considerable Air Space within the *Dome City*.

亚历克斯后来会受到严厉批评，因为作为交易的一部分。

MAGNUS

I understand you are building it with your money. How will you get your money back?

马格纳斯

我知道你是用你的钱建造的。你打算怎么拿回你的钱？

ALEX

I retain ownership of 50% of all *"air space"* within the *Dome*. That's how I will recoup my investment.

亚历克斯

我保留 50% 的 "天空空间" 所有权。这就是我收回投资的方式。

MAGNUS

Alex, you indicated that in a short period of time a lot of people will live in *Greenland Dome*. Even if it's only 500,000 people, how will you supply their electricity?

马格纳斯

亚历克斯，你表示，在短时间内，很多人将住在格陵兰穹顶。即使只有 50 万人，你如何为他们提供电力？

ALEX

We planned for solar and wind power generation as well as geothermal, which could also be harnessed due to the near proximity active volcanos.

亚历克斯

我们计划使用太阳能和风能发电，以及地热发电，由于附近的活火山，地热发电也可以利用。

### MAGNUS

With our very short days in the winter, Solar power and possibly even wind power would be insufficient. How will you deal with that?

### 马格纳斯

由于冬季白天很短，太阳能甚至风能都不够用。您将如何处理这个问题？

### ALEX

Six months out of the year, solar power would be plentiful. Heavy industry could work hard during those six months and all major electrical loads utilized then. The heavy loads would be cut back in September when the days grew shorter and solar power became inefficient.

### 亚历克斯

一年中的六个月，太阳能将是充足的。重工业可以在这六个月内努力工作，所有主要的电力负荷都会得到利用。9月份，当白天变短，太阳能变得低效时，重负荷将减少。

### MAGNUS

What's your plans for Hydroelectric power?

### 马格努斯

您对水力发电有何计划？

### ALEX

Greenland has the potential for huge amounts of hydroelectric power; however, construction of huge dams in this area is problematic, though not impossible.

### 亚历克斯

格陵兰岛拥有大量水力发电的潜力；然而，在该地区建设大型水坝是有问题的，但并非不可能。

### MANGUS

If that's the case, then what will you do besides hydroelectric?

### 曼古斯

如果是这样的话，除了水力发电之外，你还会做什么？

ALEX

Wind power and solar appeared to offer many solutions.

亚历克斯
风能和太阳能似乎提供了许多解决方案。

MANGUS

Currently 75% of Nuuk's electricity source is hydroelectric. What about Hydrogen powered utilities?

马格努斯
目前，努克 75% 的电力来源是水力发电。那么氢能公用事业呢？

ALEX

Hydrogen was also part of the plan because unlike electricity produced by solar and wind, hydrogen can be stored.

亚历克斯
氢也是该计划的一部分，因为与太阳能和风能产生的电力不同，氢可以储存。

MANGUS

How will we produce a lot of Hydrogen for the gas turbines?

马格努斯
我们将如何为燃气轮机生产大量氢气？

ALEX

During the very long summer days, solar farms would help generate vast amounts of hydrogen using electrolysis that would be stored and used during the winter months to power gas turbines and steam turbines powered by the heat off the gas turbine exhaust.

亚历克斯
在漫长的夏季，太阳能发电厂将利用电解作用产生大量氢气，这些氢气将被储存起来，并在冬季使用，为燃气轮机和蒸汽轮机提供动力，而蒸汽轮机则由燃气轮机排气的热量提供动力。

MANGUS
Alex, you put a lot of thought into all this.

马格努斯
亚历克斯，你对这一切考虑得很周全。

ALEX
Thank you Mangus, it's not just me, I have an entire team that developed the plan.

亚历克斯
谢谢曼格斯，不仅仅是我，我还有整个团队制定了这个计划。

After a couple hours of intense discussion with the crowd that gathered around the bar, mostly for free drinks. Alex then felt hungry.

经过几个小时与聚集在酒吧周围的人群的激烈讨论，他们大多是为了免费喝饮料。然后 亚历克斯 感到饿了。

MANGUS
Alex, it was nice meeting you. Thanks for all the Dome information.

马格努斯
亚历克斯，很高兴认识你。感谢你提供的所有圆顶信息。

ALEX
Mangus, you are most welcome.

亚历克斯
马格努斯，非常欢迎你。

Mangus left the bar.

马格努斯离开了酒吧。

ALEX
Adel, I'm getting kind of hungry, would you and Professor Grey like to join us in the Hereford Beefstouw restaurant for dinner?

亚历克斯
阿德尔，我有点饿了，你和格雷教授愿意和我们一起去赫里福德牛肉斯托餐厅吃晚饭吗？

ADEL
Alex, normally I would enjoy having dinner with you, but I'm going to take your offer up on the free Limo

ride back to my car so I can go home, grade some papers, take a hot bath and do some reading.

阿德尔海德·约根森（又名 阿德尔）
亚历克斯 ，通常我很乐意和你共进晚餐，但我打算接受你的提议，乘坐免费的豪华轿车回到我的车上，这样我就可以回家，批改一些论文，洗个热水澡，读点书。

## ALEX
Okay then, I'll see you in the morning.

亚历克斯
好的，明天见。

## ADEL
I'll take Professor Grey with me to make sure he gets home in one piece.

ADELHEID JØRGENSEN (a.k.a. ADEL)
我会带着格雷教授一起去，确保他安全回家。

## ALEX
I appreciate that.

亚历克斯
我很感激。

The four got stood up from their bar stools, Alex told the bartender earlier to charge all the drinks to his room.

四个人从酒吧凳子上站了起来，亚历克斯早些时候告诉酒保把所有的酒都记在他房间里。

## BARTENDAR
I'm very sorry Mister Baxter, the bar tab exceeded $3,000.

调酒师
非常抱歉，巴克斯特先生，酒吧账单超过了3,000 美元。

## ALEX
That's okay, I met a lot of people and bought a lot of drinks, I understand there were a lot of people enjoying drinks I bought them.

亚历克斯

没关系，我认识了很多人，买了很多饮料，我知
道有很多人喜欢我买的饮料。

Alex then gave the bartender a tip that made his eyes almost bug out of his head.

然后亚历克斯给了酒保一个小费，小费让他的眼睛都快瞪出来了。

Adel and Professor Grey left    and went back to the University in the Limo Alex provided so Adel could get her car and drive Professor Grey and herself home.

阿黛尔和格雷教授离开，坐上亚历克斯提供的豪华轿车回到大学，这样阿黛尔就可以开着她的车开车送格雷教授和她自己回家。

INT. DAY. HEREFORD BEEFSTOUW, LOCATED IN THE HANS EGEDE HOTEL NEXT TO THE SKYLINE BAR.

白天。赫里福德牛肉斯托，位于 天际线酒吧旁边的 汉斯·埃格德酒店内。

Alex and Stephanie then left and went directly to the Hereford Beefstouw, also located in the hotel next to the Skyline Bar. After a couple of juicy steaks, a glass of wine and delightful desserts, Alex and Stephanie went to their rooms. The adjoining rooms had to be opened from both sides, which was quickly done.

然后亚历克斯和斯蒂芬妮离开，直接去了赫里福德牛肉店，这家店也位于酒吧旁边的酒店里。吃了几块多汁的牛排、一杯葡萄酒和美味的甜点后，亚历克斯和斯蒂芬妮去了他们的房间。相邻的房间必须从两侧打开，很快就完成了。

INT. NIGHT. NUUK GREENLAND. HANS EGEDE HOTEL ROOM.

内部。夜晚。努克格陵兰岛。汉斯·埃格德酒店房间。

After a quick shower, Alex was in bed. In due time just like clockwork Stephanie got scared and crawled in bed with Alex.  Tonight, this activity was probably more for Stephanie keeping her feet warm than fear.

洗完澡后，亚历克斯上床睡觉。斯蒂芬妮吓坏了，像时钟一样准时爬到亚历克斯的床上。今晚，斯蒂芬妮这样做可能更多的是为了保暖双脚，而不是害怕。

BACKGROUND MUSIC FOR THE NEXT SCENE:

下一个场景的背景音乐：

https://www.youtube.com/watch?v=13_74gj76Bk

Jan Zimmer: "*Tatra Mountains*" complete (1956)

扬·齐默 (Jan Zimmer)：《塔特拉山脉》完成 (1956)

No sooner than Stephanie snuggled up next to Alex, than she heard noise in her room. Thinking Alex was sleeping she shook him gently and heard him respond very silently.

斯蒂芬妮刚依偎在亚历克斯身边，就听到房间里有噪音。她以为亚历克斯睡着了，于是轻轻摇晃他，听到他非常安静地回应。

**ALEX**
I hear it, lie still.

亚历克斯
我听到了，安静地躺着。

In the special compartment of his luggage, Alex always carried a handgun. Even though in many countries it was illegal he didn't care, it was moments like this that made it all worthwhile.

在他的行李箱的特殊隔间里，亚历克斯总是带着一把手枪。尽管在许多国家这是非法的，但他不在乎，正是这样的时刻让一切都值得。

Just like he normally did, as Alex went to bed, he had his gun under his pillow in close reach.

就像他平常做的那样，当亚历克斯上床睡觉时，他把枪放在枕头下，伸手可及。

Alex slowly grabbed the gun without much effort and had his hand gripping it and in the slight amount of light in the room, he could easily make out the target if the person came into his room. If that happened other hotel guests would hear the gunshots if Alex had to nail the perpetrator.

亚历克斯毫不费力地慢慢地拿起枪，用手紧紧握住枪，在房间里微弱的光线下，如果有人进入他的房间，他可以很容易地辨认出目标。如果发生这种情况，如果亚历克斯必须抓住肇事者，其他酒店客人就会听到枪声。

Whoever it was, he didn't find what they were looking for and Alex heard the door to Stephanie's room slowly close and the door latch click. Whoever it was had just left.

不管是谁，他都没有找到他们要找的东西，亚历克斯听到斯蒂芬妮房间的门慢慢关上，门闩咔哒一声。不管是谁，他刚刚离开。

 With pistol in hand Alex went directly to his door, quickly opened it catching the person just entering the stairwell at the end of the hallway. The person was gone. He then went over to the hotel phone located next to the window in his room and picked up the receiver and dialed zero.

亚历克斯手持手枪直接走到他的门口，迅速打开门，抓住了刚从走廊尽头的楼梯间进来的人。那个人已经走了。然后他走到房间窗户旁边的酒店电话旁，拿起听筒拨了零。

After about seven rings a groggy person answered the phone in Danish.

大约七声铃响后，一个昏昏沉沉的人用丹麦语接了电话。

HOTEL NIGHT CLERK
Front desk how can I help you?

酒店夜班服务员
前台有什么可以帮您的吗？

ALEX
This is hotel guest Alex Baxter. Someone just broke into one of our rooms, could you please send up hotel security.

亚历克斯
我是酒店客人亚历克斯·巴克斯特。刚刚有人闯入了我们的一个房间，请您派酒店保安过来。

HOTEL NIGHT CLERK
Are you okay, Mr. Baxter?

酒店夜班服务员
您还好吗，巴克斯特先生？

ALEX
Yes, whoever it was, just left. We are safe for now. But I would like to talk with someone in your security.

亚历克斯
是的，不管是谁，刚刚离开。我们现在很安全。但我想和你的保安人员谈谈。

HOTEL NIGHT CLERK
I'll send the manager up right away.

酒店夜班服务员
我马上让经理上来。

As Alex was talking, looking out the window, he saw a man with long hair get into a blue car, start it up and drive away. The car was heading in the direction to the Airport and most likely going to an area further away from downtown.

亚历克斯说话的时候，他看着窗外，看到一个长发男子上了一辆蓝色的车，发动车子开走了。这辆车正朝着机场的方向行驶，很可能要去一个离市中心较远的地方。

In three minutes, there was a knock at the door.

三分钟后，有人敲门。

Knowing it was probably the manager; Alex had his gun out of sight but in his night robe.

知道那可能是经理；亚历克斯把枪藏在睡袍里，看不见。

Alex asked, just for confirmation as he assumed.

亚历克斯问道，他猜想只是为了确认一下。

ALEX<br>
Who is it?

亚历克斯<br>
是谁？

NIGHT MANAGER<br>
I'm the night manager.

夜班经理<br>
我是夜班经理。

Alex opened the door, invited the manager in.

亚历克斯打开门，请经理进来。

NIGHT MANAGER<br>
Mr. Baxter, what happened?

夜班经理<br>
巴克斯特先生，发生什么事了？

ALEX<br>
Someone broke into Stephanie's room; Stephanie got scared and ran in here just in time. Evidently the person got spooked and left.

亚历克斯<br>
有人闯入了斯蒂芬妮的房间；斯蒂芬妮吓坏了，及时跑了进来。显然那个人被吓坏了，然后离开了。

NIGHT MANAGER<br>
Do you mind if I look in her room?

夜班经理
你介意我去看看她的房间吗？

ALEX
Sure, go right in there.

亚历克斯
当然，进去吧。

The Manager walked into the room, turned on the lights and was immediately alarmed. Stephanie had all the pillows under the blankets and someone in poor lighting could easily mistake it for a body. Right in the middle of the bed over the pillows were several gaping cut holes.

经理走进房间，打开灯，立刻惊慌失措。斯蒂芬妮把所有的枕头都放在毯子下面，在光线不好的情况下，很容易误以为那是尸体。床的中间枕头上有几个大洞。

After observing what the manager saw, Alex made the astute observation:

在观察了经理看到的情况后，亚历克斯做出了敏锐的观察：

ALEX
The person was evidently intent on stabbing Stephanie, and didn't realize until about the third stab, it wasn't a body being hit, got spooked and departed the room.

亚历克斯
那个人显然是想刺斯蒂芬妮，直到第三次刺伤时才意识到被刺的不是尸体，他被吓坏了，离开了房间。"

NIGHT MANAGER
So, it seems. I should call the police.

夜班经理
所以，看来我应该报警。

ALEX
I got a better idea. We need to get some sleep; we have a big day ahead of us. How about post security outside our door for the night and wait to call the police in the morning after we get some rest?

亚历克斯
我有一个更好的主意。我们需要睡一会儿；我们还有重要的一天。晚上在我们门外安排保安，等我们休息一会早上再报警，怎么样？

NIGHT MANAGER
If that is sufficient, Mr. Baxter, we are more than happy to accommodate you.

夜班经理
如果这样就够了，巴克斯特先生，我们非常乐意为您服务。"

ALEX
Thank you.

亚历克斯
谢谢。

NIGHT MANAGER
I'll make the arrangements right away; you will have a person up here in five minutes outside your door for the rest of the night.

夜班经理
我会立即安排好一切；五分钟后，会有一个人在你门外等你，陪你度过余下的夜晚。

ALEX
I appreciate that.

亚历克斯
我很欣赏这一点。

NIGHT MANAGER
Please excuse me now as I must go make those arrangements.

夜班经理
现在请原谅我，因为我必须去做这些安排。

ALEX
Of course.

亚历克斯
当然。

The two men walked towards the door which the manager opened and exited out of.

两人朝门走去，经理打开门走了出去。

Alex then walked over to the adjoining room entry door and shut and locked it. He then picked up the phone and called his pilot on his cell phone.

亚历克斯随后走到隔壁房间的入口处，关上门锁上。然后他拿起电话，用手机给飞行员打电话。

After about three rings, Brad answered and with a caller I.D. knew it was Alex.

大约响了三声后，布拉德接了电话，通过来电显示知道是亚历克斯打来的。

BRAD
Yes Mr. Baxter, what can I do for you?

布拉德
是的，巴克斯特先生，我能为您做些什么？

ALEX

Brad, we had someone break into Stephanie's room tonight, with a knife, had she been in her bed they would possibly have killed her.

亚历克斯

布拉德，今晚有人带着刀闯入了斯蒂芬妮的房间，如果她在床上，他们可能会杀了她。

BRAD
Anything I can do?

布拉德
我能做什么吗？

ALEX

I need you to come by my room at 6:00 in the morning to take my special suitcase because the hotel will contact the police in the morning, and I don't want my gun to be here when they arrive.

亚历克斯

我需要你早上六点来我的房间拿我的特殊行李箱，因为酒店会在早上联系警察，我不希望他们到达时我的枪还在这里。

BRAD
Sure boss, I'll be there at six o'clock.

布拉德
好的老板，我六点到。

ALEX
Thank you, Brad.

亚历克斯
谢谢，布拉德。

As Alex expected within five minutes, there was a knock at the door.

正如亚历克斯所料，五分钟内，门响了。

ALEX
Who is it?

亚历克斯
是谁？

HOTEL SECURITY REP
(a.k.a. Rodney Hansen)
Hotel Security, Sir.

酒店保安代表
（又名 罗德尼·汉森）
酒店保安，先生。

Again, with his gun tucked into his robe and gripping it in case he had to use it, Alex opened the door, and a well-dressed young man probably 25 years old stood there.

亚历克斯再次将枪塞进长袍，紧握枪以备不时之需，他打开了门，一个大约25岁的衣着考究的年轻人站在那里。

HOTEL SECURITY REP
(a.k.a. Rodney Hansen)
Hotel Security, Sir.
Mr. Baxter, I just wanted you to know someone is outside your room for the rest of the night. We also have the hallway sealed off with barriers not allowing the public to come down this hallway.

酒店保安代表
（又名 罗德尼·汉森）
酒店保安，先生。
巴克斯特先生，我只是想让您知道，今晚剩下的时间里，有人会守在您的房间外面。我们还用屏障封锁了走廊，不允许公众进入这条走廊。

ALEX
May I ask what your name is sir?

亚历克斯
请问您叫什么名字，先生？

HOTEL SECURITY REP
(a.k.a. Rodney Hansen)
Rodney Hansen.

酒店保安代表
（又名 罗德尼·汉森）
罗德尼·汉森。

ALEX
Ok, Rodney, thank you for letting me know that you'll
be here.

亚历克斯
好的，罗德尼·汉森，感谢您让我知道您会来。

HOTEL SECURITY REP
(a.k.a. Rodney Hansen)
You are quite welcome, Mr. Baxter.

酒店保安代表
（又名 罗德尼·汉森）
巴克斯特先生，非常欢迎您。

ALEX
Rodney, my pilot is coming by the room at 6:00 a.m.
I'm expecting him. His name is Brad Johnson. I'm not
expecting anyone else.

亚历克斯
罗德尼，我的飞行员将于早上 6:00 来房间。我等
着他。他的名字是布拉德·约翰逊。我不期待其他
人。

HOTEL SECURITY REP
(a.k.a. Rodney Hansen)
Will he be wearing his pilot's uniform?

酒店保安代表
（又名 罗德尼·汉森）
他会穿飞行员制服吗？

ALEX
Most likely, yes.

亚历克斯
很有可能。

HOTEL SECURITY REP
(a.k.a. Rodney Hansen)
We'll be waiting for him then.

酒店保安代表
（又名 罗德尼·汉森）
我们会等他。

ALEX
Thanks, and good night.

亚历克斯
谢谢，晚安。

HOTEL SECURITY REP
(a.k.a. Rodney Hansen)
Good night Mr. Baxter, sleep well.

酒店保安代表
（又名 罗德尼·汉森）
晚安，巴克斯特先生，睡个好觉。

Alex shut the door then spoke to Stephanie.

亚历克斯关上门，然后对斯蒂芬妮说话。

ALEX
Crawl in bed, we're going to sleep.

亚历克斯
爬上床，我们要睡觉了。

Alex then turned out the light.

亚历克斯关了灯。

It seemed like only a few minutes later when Alex suddenly heard a knock at the door. But it was already 6:00 a.m. Brad stood outside the door with Rodney. Alex grabbed his suitcase which he no longer needed and had the pistol in the secret led-lined compartment and handed it to Brad to take to the Gulfstream. He then shut the door, walked over to Stephanie and shook her to wake her up so she could start getting ready.

似乎只过了几分钟，亚历克斯突然听到了敲门声。但已经是早上 6 点了。布拉德和罗德尼站在门外。亚历克斯抓起他不再需要的手提箱，把手枪放在秘密的铅衬隔间里，递给布拉德，让他带到湾流。然后他关上门，走到斯蒂芬妮身边，摇醒她，让她开始准备。

ALEX

The police would be there probably in an hour or so,
so we need to be dressed and ready.

亚历克斯

警察大概一小时后就到了，所以我们需要穿好衣
服准备好。

What Alex didn't know was Rodney was the police. As soon as Alex and Stephanie were dressed and ready, Alex went to the door opened it and informed Rodney:

亚历克斯不知道罗德尼是警察。亚历克斯和斯蒂芬妮穿好衣服准备好后，亚历克斯走到门口打开门，告诉罗德尼：

ALEX

Rodney, go ahead and contact the police, and thanks
for the chance to get some sleep.

亚历克斯

罗德尼，快去联系警察，谢谢你让我有机会睡一
觉。

Rodney smiled then spoke.

罗德尼笑了笑，然后说话了。

HOTEL SECURITY REP
(a.k.a. Rodney Hansen)

Mr. Baxter, I am part of the police force. I'm a
detective. I was here to help preserve the crime scene
and to provide you with protection.

酒店保安代表
（又名 罗德尼·汉森）

巴克斯特先生，我是警察部队的一员。我其实是
个侦探。我来这里是为了帮助保护犯罪现场，也
是为了给你提供保护。"

ALEX

Well thanks, I appreciate that.

ALEX

好吧，谢谢，我很感激。

Alex was mildly alarmed because he now knew the police were probably interested in the suitcase he gave the pilot. But as it turned out that was not the focus of their investigation, though they might have assumed he was removing an illegal weapon in case his room was searched. In some cases, it's best not to hassle billionaires over self-protection, since they were walking targets.

亚历克斯
有点惊慌，因为他现在知道警察可能对他给飞行员的手提箱感兴趣。但事实证明，这不是他们调查的重点，尽管他们可能认为他在拿走非法武器，以防他的房间被搜查。在某些情况下，最好不要因为自卫而骚扰亿万富翁，因为他们是行走的目标。

HOTEL SECURITY REP
(a.k.a. Rodney Hansen)
(a.k.a. Police Detective)
May we talk now Mr. Baxter?

酒店保安代表
（又名 罗德尼·汉森）
（又名警察侦探）
我们现在可以谈谈吗，巴克斯特先生？

Alex motioned Rodney Hansen to enter and held the door open for him.

亚历克斯 示意 罗德尼·汉森进来，并为他打开门。

ALEX
Sure, come on in.

亚历克斯
当然，进来吧。

After they were inside and the door shut, Rodney began a substantial briefing,

他们进去后，门关上了，罗德尼开始做简要汇报，

HOTEL SECURITY REP
(a.k.a. Rodney Hansen)
(a.k.a. Police Detective)
Our detectives looked at the hotel security video, and we saw the suspect enter Stephanie's room. He's not been identified, and I've never recalled seeing him before.

酒店保安代表
（又名罗德尼·汉森）
（又名警探）

我们的侦探查看了酒店安全视频，我们看到嫌疑人进入了斯蒂芬妮的房间。他的身份尚未确定，我也不记得以前见过他。

ALEX
I see.

亚历克斯
我明白了。

HOTEL SECURITY REP
(a.k.a. Rodney Hansen)
(a.k.a. Police Detective)
The suspect had some type of tool to break into the cypher lock on the door, the hotel has been alerted.

酒店保安代表
（又名罗德尼·汉森）
（又名警探）
嫌疑人有某种工具可以打开门上的密码锁，酒店已经收到警报。"

ALEX
What did you make of him?

亚历克斯
你觉得他怎么样？

RODNEY HANSEN
(a.k.a. Police Detective)
He was in the room approximately 5 minutes and left in a hurried manner, something obviously spooked him.

罗德尼·汉森
（又名警探）
他在房间里待了大约 5 分钟，然后匆匆离开，显然有什么事情吓到他了。

ALEX
Did you see where he went?

亚历克斯
你看到他去了哪里吗？

RODNEY HANSEN
(a.k.a. Police Detective)
Yes, security camera's show him leaving a fire escape door which set off an intruder alarm at the front desk, and other camera's show him leaving heading across the street. Unfortunately, the film is black and white for better night lighting; we didn't get the automobile color.

罗德尼·汉森
（又名警探）
是的，安全摄像头显示他离开防火门，触发了前台的入侵警报，其他摄像头显示他离开时走向马路对面。不幸的是，为了获得更好的夜间照明，影片是黑白的；我们没有拍到汽车的颜色。

ALEX
When I was talking to the hotel operator, I was looking right down there and saw a man get into a blue car and drive off.

亚历克斯
当我与酒店经营者交谈时，我正往下看，看到一个男人上了一辆蓝色的汽车然后开走了。

RODNEY HANSEN
(a.k.a. Police Detective)
You mean right by the corner?

罗德尼·汉森
（又名警探）
你是说就在拐角处吗？

ALEX
Yes, right there.

亚历克斯
是的，就在那里。

RODNEY HANSEN
(a.k.a. Police Detective)
That's what the security camera showed, so that helps us. Now we know we'll be looking for a blue car. We have a good picture of the dude. So, it should help us round him up quicker.

罗德尼·汉森
（又名警探）
这就是安全摄像头所显示的内容，这对我们很有
帮助。现在我们知道我们要找一辆蓝色的车。我
们拍了一张这个人的清晰照片。所以，这应该有
助于我们更快地把他抓获。

ALEX
That's good to know.

亚历克斯
很高兴知道这一点。

RODNEY HANSEN
(a.k.a. Police Detective)
Mr. Baxter is there any reason why someone here
would want to hurt you or Ms. McFarland?

罗德尼·汉森
（又名警探）
巴克斯特先生，这里有人想要伤害你或麦克法兰
女士吗？

ALEX
Rodney, other than professors Grey and Adelheid
Jørgensen, we do not know anyone on Greenland,
except for casual meeting of a few locals at the hotel
bar last night.

亚历克斯
罗德尼，除了格雷教授和阿德尔海德·约根森教授
之外，我们在格陵兰岛不认识任何人，除了昨晚
在酒店酒吧偶然遇见的几个当地人

RODNEY HANSEN
(a.k.a. Police Detective)
I have no reason to think people here know us or why
we are here, other than we told a few businesspeople
at the bar yesterday about the conference we'll be
attending at Greenland University today.

罗德尼·汉森
（又名警探）
我没有理由认为这里的人了解我们或我们为什么
在这里，除了我们昨天在酒吧告诉了一些商人我
们今天将在格陵兰大学参加的会议。

### RODNEY HANSEN
(a.k.a. Police Detective)

How about that conference you are scheduled to be at this morning? Do others know you are coming and what for?

### 罗德尼·汉森
（又名警探）

您今天早上计划参加的会议怎么样？其他人知道你要来吗？你来干什么？

### ALEX

I suppose that since Adelheid Jørgensen forwarded my presentation to her peers some information got out to the public.

### 亚历克斯

我想自从 阿德尔海德·约根森 将我的演讲转发给她的同行后，一些信息就被公之于众了。

### RODNEY HANSEN
(a.k.a. Police Detective)
How long do you plan to stay in Nuuk?

### 罗德尼·汉森
（又名警探）
您计划在努克停留多久？

### ALEX

We are leaving today after the conference. I was going to stay a little while longer to socialize my proposals to locals, but under the circumstances from last night, we are not going to extend for additional activities.

### 亚历克斯

今天会议结束后我们就要离开。我们今天会议结束后就离开。我本来打算再呆一会儿，向当地人宣传我的提议，但考虑到昨晚的情况，我们不会再延长活动时间。

### RODNEY HANSEN
(a.k.a. Police Detective)
When are you going to the conference?

### 罗德尼·汉森
（又名警探）
你什么时候去参加会议？

ALEX

Just as soon as we finish talking with you.


亚历克斯
就在我们和你谈完之后。


RODNEY HANSEN
(a.k.a. Police Detective)

You will be at the University in case we need to get in touch with you?


罗德尼·汉森
（又名警探）
你会在大学里，以防我们需要联系你？


ALEX

Yes, until around noon, then we are going to the airport and leave.


亚历克斯
是的，到中午左右，然后我们去机场离开。


RODNEY HANSEN
(a.k.a. Police Detective)

Ok if I need something more from you I will catch up with you at the University.


罗德尼·汉森
（又名警探）
好的，如果我还需要你帮忙的话，我会在大学找你。


ALEX

Sure thing, Rodney, and oh by the way, thanks for guarding our room last night. I really needed sleep.


亚历克斯
好的，罗德尼，顺便说一句，谢谢你昨晚看守我们的房间。我真的需要好好睡一觉。


RODNEY HANSEN
(a.k.a. Police Detective)

No problem, sorry your stay had an element of misfortune in it.


罗德尼·汉森
（又名警探）
没问题，很抱歉您的入住有些不顺利。

Moments later as Alex was checking out at the front desk, the manager came by and profusely apologized for the $3,000 bar bill.

片刻之后，当亚历克斯在前台结账时，经理过来为 3,000 美元的酒吧账单深表歉意。

HOTEL MANAGER
The bartender said you approved these charges on your credit card last night.

酒店经理
酒保说你昨晚批准了信用卡上的这些费用。”

ALEX
How much is it?

亚历克斯
多少钱？

HOTEL MANAGER
Three Thousand USD$.

酒店经理
三千美元。

ALEX
That's probably about right, we bought a lot of drinks for businessmen and hotel guests.

亚历克斯
大概是这样，我们给商人和酒店客人买了很多饮料。

HOTEL MANAGER
Very well Mr. Baxter, I appreciate your cooperation in settling the bill.

酒店经理
非常好，巴克斯特先生，感谢您在解决账单方面的合作。

Shortly Alex and Stephanie were heading out the lobby door, with porter behind them and the Limo waiting a short distance away.

不久，亚历克斯和斯蒂芬妮就走出了大厅门，行李员跟在他们后面，豪华轿车就在不远处等候着。

Alex had paid the Limo Company in advance for the 36 hours, and the driver had been admonished by his supervisor to be extra polite since these were outstanding customers.

亚历克斯已提前向豪华轿车公司支付了 36 小时的费用，司机已被主管告诫要格外有礼貌，因为这些都是优质客户。

As the Limo Driver opened the passenger door for them the driver asked:

当豪华轿车司机为他们打开乘客门时，司机问道：

LIMO DRIVER
Where to, Sir?

豪华轿车司机
先生，去哪里？

ALEX
Back to Greenland University like yesterday.

亚历克斯
像昨天一样回到格陵兰大学。

LIMO DRIVER
Right away, Sir.

豪华轿车司机
马上，先生。

The Limo Driver shut the door after Alex and Stephanie were inside the Limo, took the one suitcase belonging to Stephanie and was a little confused why there were not two, and as he got in the Limo, asked through the intercom:

亚历克斯和斯蒂芬妮坐进豪华轿车后，豪华轿车司机关上了车门，拿走了斯蒂芬妮的一个行李箱，他有点困惑为什么没有两个，当他上车时，通过对讲机问道：

LIMO DRIVER
Sir, did you leave your suitcase in your room?

豪华轿车司机
先生，您把行李箱放在房间里了吗？

ALEX
No, I sent it ahead with my pilot this morning.

亚历克斯
没有，我今天早上让飞行员把它送来了。

LIMO DRIVER
Ok, just checking, I didn't want you to forget it.

豪华轿车司机
好的，只是检查一下，不想让你忘记。

ALEX
Thanks for looking out for me.

亚历克斯
谢谢你照顾我。

The Limo pulled away and a few minutes pulled into Greenland University Campus and parking. The driver got out, opened the door. Alex and Stephanie had a short walk to the building where they entered.

豪华轿车开走了，几分钟后驶入格陵兰大学校园和停车场。司机下车，打开车门。亚历克斯和斯蒂芬妮走了一小段路就到了他们进入的大楼。

Already a small crowd was forming at Ilisimatusarfik (Greenland University). As promised the two tables had drinks and snacks. People were already hitting the coffee that smelled really good. Within a few minutes, a few businessmen entered whom Alex knew, would be presenting shortly.

伊利斯马图萨尔菲克（格陵兰大学）已经聚集了一小群人。正如承诺的那样，两张桌子上摆着饮料和小吃。人们已经开始品尝香气扑鼻的咖啡。几分钟后，几位商人走了进来，亚历克斯认识他们，他们很快就会发表演讲。

Alex announced as he approached the first man and held his hand out for a hand shake.

亚历克斯一边走近第一位男士，一边伸出手与他握手。

ALEX
Jim, good to see you.

亚历克斯
吉姆，很高兴见到你。

James Walker
Alex, likewise.

詹姆斯·沃克
亚历克斯，我也是。

## VOICEOVER
### 画外音

*James Walker, CEO Hercules Steel, a Pennsylvania Company who bought out most of the existing steel companies in the state, was a mover and shaker. James Walker CEO Hercules Steel was a dynamic and successful person.*

詹姆斯·沃克是赫拉克勒斯钢铁公司的首席执行官，这家宾夕法尼亚州公司收购了该州大部分现有的钢铁公司，是一位举足轻重的人物。詹姆斯·沃克是赫拉克勒斯钢铁公司的首席执行官，是一位充满活力的成功人士。

*Some of the steel plants James Walker bought had used the Bessemer process but were uneconomical. So, he converted them to the basic oxygen steelmaking process and eventually reopened.*

詹姆斯·沃克收购的一些钢铁厂曾使用贝塞麦炼钢法，但经济效益不佳。因此，他将它们改用碱性氧气炼钢法，并最终重新开业。

*A lot of steel would be needed in future domed cities if this project got off the ground. In order to cheaply produce the volume of steel needed, it would take the efficiency of the oxygen steelmaking process to accomplish the production schedules.*

如果这个项目顺利实施，未来的圆顶城市将需要大量钢铁。为了廉价地生产出所需的钢铁量，需要氧气炼钢工艺的效率来完成生产计划。

*Behind Jim Walker was Howard Grady, the Cement King. For all the pillars and foundations required, large amounts of concrete would be required. Thanks to the year-round cold weather, cooling the concrete would not be a big problem as compared to dam construction of major dams such as the Hoover Dam or the Grand Coolie.*

吉姆·沃克身后是水泥大王霍华德·格雷迪。所有所需的支柱和地基都需要大量的混凝土。由于全年寒冷的天气，与胡佛大坝或大库利等大型水坝的建设相比，冷却混凝土不会是一个大问题。

## ALEX
Hello Howard.

亚历克斯
你好，霍华德。

Howard Grady
Good to see you, Alex.

霍华德·格雷迪
很高兴见到你，亚历克斯。

These men also brought along some assistants, probably to discuss technical matters.

这些人还带了一些助手，可能是为了讨论技术问题。

### VOICEOVER
画外音

*Finally, the other person Alex was waiting to see just walked through the door, and it was Claude Reardon, the owner of Reardon Construction, which recently had grown to match Bechtel Corporation in size and capability.*

最后，亚历克斯等待的另一个人走进了门，他就是里尔登建筑公司的老板克劳德·里尔登，里尔登建筑公司最近发展到与柏克德公司规模和能力相当的地步。

*Claude and Alex were not the best of friends in the world, and barely tolerated each other, but needed each other not only for this construction project but also some in the past. When projects get dicey due to cost overruns or unforeseen circumstances, a friendship can be torn apart. Casual relationships then turn into terse and somewhat emotional environments.*

克劳德和亚历克斯并不是世界上最好的朋友，他们几乎无法容忍对方，但他们不仅在这个建筑项目上需要彼此，而且在过去也需要彼此。当项目因成本超支或不可预见的情况而变得岌岌可危时，友谊就会破裂。随意的关系会变成简洁而有点情绪化的环境。

*Claude then felt he had the upper hand this time. Since this would indeed be one of the greatest construction projects since the Panama Canal, few in the world could attempt it, and possibly only Bechtel was the only other viable construction company that really had the ability to do something so large and in such an inhospitable location.*

克劳德觉得这次他占了上风。由于这确实是自巴拿马运河以来最伟大的建筑项目之一，世界上很少有人能尝试，可能只有柏克德公司是唯一一家真正有能力在如此不适宜的地方完成如此大规模工程的可行的建筑公司。

*New Techniques of building would have to be developed and proven because construction would be hazardous and needed to be done at least 10 out of the 12 months of the year to be able to be completed in a few years.*

必须开发和验证新的建筑技术，因为建筑施工很危险，需要在一年 12 个月中至少 10 个月进行，才能在几年内完工。

ALEX
How have you been Claude?

亚历克斯
克劳德，你过得怎么样？

CLAUDE
Fine, how about yourself?

克劳德
好吧，那你自己呢？

ALEX
Great, just spent some time up in Alaska, got in a little better shape.

亚历克斯
太棒了，刚刚在阿拉斯加呆了一段时间，情况好一点了形状。

CLAUDE
That's good to hear. When does all this get started?

克劳德
很高兴听到这个消息。这一切什么时候开始？

ALEX
We'll wait a few more minutes, to make sure the public gets here so we get a good audience.

亚历克斯
我们会再等几分钟，以确保公众到达这里，以便我们有足够的观众。

CLAUDE
It looks like their arriving in good numbers.

克劳德
看起来他们的人数不少。

ALEX
Yea might be more people coming than we planned.

亚历克斯
是的，来的人可能比我们计划的还要多。

CLAUDE
I guess they will just have to crowd in, kind of cold outside.

克洛德
我想他们只能挤进去，外面有点冷。

In a short while Adelheid Jørgensen approached Alex and announced:

不久之后，阿德尔海德·约根森 (Adelheid Jørgensen) 找到亚历克斯并宣布：

ADELHEID JØRGENSEN (a.k.a. ADEL)
Director of Greenland's Natural Resources Council。
I think we can start now, not many more people are showing up and since it's crowded its best we get going and get it done.

阿德尔海德·约根森（又名阿德尔）
格陵兰自然资源委员会主任。
我想我们现在就可以开始了，没有多少人出现了，因为人多，所以我们最好开始行动并完成它。

ALEX
Sure

亚历克斯
当然

Alex walked over to the microphone which was on a microphone stand not far from where he was standing, grabbed the microphone, tapped on it, and began speaking.

亚历克斯走到距离他站的地方不远的麦克风架上的麦克风前，抓起麦克风，轻轻敲击，然后开始讲话。

### ALEX

Ladies and Gentlemen, thank you all for coming, I think we'll get started now. Those of you who found seats please take a seat, for those who do not have a seat, my apologies.

### 亚历克斯

女士们先生们，谢谢大家的到来，我想我们现在就开始吧。找到座位的人请坐下，没有座位的人请见谅。

### ALEX

We are here today to discuss the proposed *dome city* here at Nuuk Greenland.

我们今天在这里讨论努克格陵兰岛的圆顶城市计划。

### ALEX

This will be the first *dome city* anywhere in the world.

这将是世界上第一个圆顶城市。

### ALEX

We have a few artists' conceptions we'll now put up on the screen to show a couple possible examples.

我们有一些艺术家的构想，现在将其放在屏幕上，以展示几个可能的例子。

Alex now put the eye candy up on the presentation screen professors used during their courses that could also be written on with erasable markers and digitized to be inserted in emails and class papers.

亚历克斯现在把漂亮的东西放在教授在课程中使用的演示屏幕上，这些屏幕也可以用可擦除记号笔书写，并数字化以插入电子邮件和课堂论文中。

### ALEX

The first image now shown exemplifies how it would look if we covered the existing Nuuk City with a dome.

亚历克斯
现在显示的第一张图片举例说明了如果我们用圆
顶覆盖现有的努克城会是什么样子

Alex let the people in the room observe the image for a while. They could see the surrounding shorelines and the international port.

亚历克斯让房间里的人观察了一会儿图像。他们可以看到周围的海岸线和国际港口。

ALEX
This image does not show how it would look if we covered the fishing piers with a section of the dome.

亚历克斯
该图像没有显示如果我们用圆顶的一部分覆盖钓鱼码头会是什么样子。

ATTENDEE
How would you cover the fishing piers with the dome?

与会者
你会如何用圆顶覆盖渔码头？

ALEX
Just like doing an addition  to a home or a building, we would add a structure attached to the dome. Think of it as a mini dome attached to the main dome with a transportation corridor between it and the major dome.

亚历克斯
就像对房屋或建筑物进行扩建一样，我们会在圆顶上添加一个结构。可以把它想象成一个连接到主圆顶的迷你圆顶，在它和主圆顶之间有一条交通走廊。

Alex let the public view the image for a couple minutes. There were expected questions relating to: how tall, how wide, internal transportation, internal building sizes.

亚历克斯让公众观看了几分钟的图片。他们提出了一些意料之中的问题：多高、多宽、内部交通、内部建筑大小。

ALEX
The second image shows how it would look if we built Northeast of the Airport. Also, I would be willing to put some of the airport facilities under the dome.

亚历克斯
第二张图显示了如果我们在机场东北部建造的话
会是什么样子。此外，我愿意把一些机场设施放
在圆顶下面。

There were a few strange sounds in the audience, probably due to a genuine astonishment, as the artist's conceptions look very real.

观众中传来一些奇怪的声音，可能是因为真正的惊讶，因为艺术家的构想看起来非常真实。

ALEX
Our plan is to attempt to make this dome 5 miles in diameter.

亚历克斯
我们的计划是尝试使这个圆顶的直径达到　5　英里。

More sounds and excitement erupted from the locals, observing this.

看到这一幕，当地人发出了更多的声音和兴奋。

ALEX
Even though we would like to have the dome one mile high for future 22$^{nd}$ Century expansion that new construction techniques will allow, our plans are to only have it 1000 feet above sea level, so the artist conception is based on a 1000-foot-tall dome that's 5 miles in diameter.

亚历克斯
尽管我们希望在新的建筑技术允许的情况下，为未来 22 世纪的扩建提供一英里高的圆顶，但我们的计划仅是海拔 1000 英尺，因此艺术构思是基于一个 1000 英尺高的圆顶直径为 5 英里的圆顶。

A voice calls out amongst the residents in the audience.

观众席中的居民中传来一个声音。

ATTENDEE
Do you really think this can be accomplished?

与会者
你真的认为这可以实现吗？

ALEX
Yes of course.

亚历克斯
是的当然。

ATTENDEE
How will you build it?

与会者
你将如何建造它？

ALEX
At this point in time, I think it would be good for me to
turn over the presentation to our building consultant,
Claude Rearden, who can answer some of the questions
I think you all will be asking.

亚历克斯
此时此刻，我认为最好将演示文稿交给我们的建
筑顾问. 克劳德·里尔登 (Claude Rearden) ，他可
以回答我认为你们都会问的一些问题。

Claude Rearden was a self-made man. He was not a large man, but he was a brilliant
engineer, having graduated the top of his class at Stanford. At 5 foot 7 and 140 pounds,
he was not an imposing figure, but those who had crossed Claude in the past learned
their lessons the hard way.

克劳德·里尔登 (Claude Rearden) 是一个白手起家的人。他身材不高，但他是
一位出色的工程师，以班级第一名的成绩毕业于斯坦福大学。身高 5 英尺 7 英
寸、体重 140 磅的他并不魁梧，但过去与克劳德作对的人都从惨痛经历中吸取
了教训。

Claude Rearden usually slept 4 hours a day and kept a Winston Churchill like schedule:

克劳德·里尔登通常每天睡 4 个小时，并保持着温斯顿·丘吉尔式的作息时间：

Wake up at 9 a.m. take a bath, have a drink – scotch, light breakfast, work
from 10:00 a.m. until lunch/tea at 2:00 p.m. More work, sometimes an hour
nap. Dinner at 9 p.m. drink, entertain, and work until 4:00 to 5:00 a.m. then
to bed for a few hours.

早上 9 点起床，洗澡，喝点苏格兰威士忌，吃点清淡的早餐，从上午
10:00 工作到下午 2:00 吃午餐/喝茶。继续工作，有时睡一个小时。晚
上 9 点吃晚餐，喝酒、娱乐，工作到凌晨 4:00 到 5:00，然后上床睡几
个小时。

In business dealings, Claude was always a juggernaut. His pursuit in construction
marvels superseded all other aspects of his life. He was never married and had similar
characteristics to Alex in many ways. People who knew both men felt their working

relationship was almost impossible since both had Napoleon like egos and ambitions even larger.

在商业交易中，克劳德总是势不可挡。他对建筑奇迹的追求超越了他生活中的所有其他方面。他从未结过婚，在很多方面与亚历克斯有相似之处。认识这两个人的人都觉得他们之间的工作关系几乎不可能，因为他们都像拿破仑一样自负，野心更大

The establishment of *Domed Cities* on planet Earth otherwise could never have happened without two such strong and dynamic personalities suddenly teamed together for a common cause and desire.

如果没有两个如此强大而充满活力的人突然为了共同的目标和愿望联手，地球上圆顶城市的建立就不可能实现。

Alex had pondered *Dome Cities* for quite some time. It was the first line of defense for housing a population that was out of control, due to poor family planning in overpopulated cities, and countries with growing almost out of control populations.

亚历克斯对圆顶城市思考了很长时间。这是安置失控人口的第一道防线，因为人口过剩的城市和人口增长几乎失控的国家的计划生育不力。

Mankind needed to reclaim former farmland and in spite of the ruinous actions of city construction with herbicides and chemicals saturating the ground.

人类需要重新开垦以前的农田，尽管城市建设破坏性极强，除草剂和化学物质充斥着地面。

Since the growing seasons were becoming shorter with the mini-ice age, it would be the only way for mankind to produce enough. Men on empty stomachs were usually the source of wars and population control.

由于小冰河期的到来，生长季节变得越来越短，这将是人类生产足够粮食的唯一途径。饥饿的人通常是战争和人口控制的根源。

Alex's theory was moving people under domes in places like Greenland that had virtually no agriculture was the solution. Siberia was another future target of Alex to create and artificial environment where ordinary everyday life could go on and people not encumbered by extreme weather conditions.

亚历克斯的理论是将人们转移到格陵兰岛等几乎没有农业的地方的圆顶下，这是解决方案。西伯利亚是亚历克斯的另一个未来目标，他要创造一个人工环境，让人们可以继续普通的日常生活，不受极端天气条件的束缚。

Even domed airports were on the drawing boards. With computer-controlled aircraft, the ability to get flying aircraft into a large opening of a dome was now feasible.

甚至圆顶机场也还在设计中。有了计算机控制的飞机，现在就可以将飞行器飞进圆顶的大开口。

Cities and Towns and urban sprawl that existed in areas that supported sufficient growing seasons would slowly be disassembled and once again become agrarian centers. Soils would be regenerated using advance science techniques. Alex and Claude would be instrumental in that reconfiguration in the future, but for now, they had to make the first *Dome City* viable.

在支持足够生长季节的地区存在的城市和城镇以及城市扩张将慢慢被拆除，再次成为农业中心。土壤将利用先进的科学技术再生。亚历克斯和克劳德将在未来对这一重新配置发挥重要作用，但就目前而言，他们必须让第一个穹顶城市变得可行。

Claude Rearden was a ball buster when it came to making deals. Claude never did anything for free nor did he do developments for the benefit of mankind. Claude's purpose was to demonstrate his ideas and inventions would come to fruition with someone else's money.

克劳德·里尔登在做交易方面非常厉害。克劳德从不免费做任何事情，也不为了造福人类而进行开发。克劳德的目的是证明他的想法和发明会用别人的钱实现。

Alex knew Claude Rearden's motives, but being a perfectionist to some extent, an innovator willing to take on large risk and enormous tasks few others would, had enough surplus fortunes to where money was not an issue. Claude Rearden's money would long out live him, and he knew it.

亚历克斯知道克劳德·里尔登的动机，但在某种程度上，他是一个完美主义者，一个愿意承担其他人很少会承担的巨大风险和艰巨任务的创新者，他有足够的剩余财富，所以钱不是问题。克劳德·里尔登的钱会比他活得长久，他知道这一点。

The crowd grew into an eerie quiet as Claude laid out the general construction scheme:

当克劳德制定总体施工方案时，人群变得异常安静：

**CLAUDE REARDEN**
克劳德·里尔登

These next few slides show cross sections of parts of the proposed dome before its loaded with internal structures.

接下来的几张幻灯片展示了拟建穹顶在装载内部结构之前的各部分横截面。

As you can see there are several large pillars. Those

pillars are essential to support the weight of the dome.

如您所见，有几根大柱子。这些柱子对于支撑穹顶的重量至关重要。

Because this dome is being built where several hundred inches of ice could accumulate during the winter and possibly not thaw out for most of the year, it has to be stronger than to just support its weight and stresses caused by high winds.

由于建造这个圆顶的地方冬季可能会积聚数百英寸的冰，而且一年中的大部分时间都可能无法融化，因此它必须比仅仅支撑其本身更坚固

Luckily with the gradual curved surface, there is an aerodynamic effect, and the aerodynamic streamlining significantly reduces wind resistance and lateral stresses on the structure.

幸运的是，由于表面逐渐弯曲，因此会产生空气动力学效应，而空气动力学流线型显著降低了风阻和结构侧向应力。

One of the locals asked:

一位当地人问道：

Attendee
与会者
Why not a taller dome?
为什么不建一个更高的穹顶？

CLAUDE REARDEN

A taller dome would have a greater arc and even more inherent strength, but due to the cost of materials and no previous prototypes to work from, we settled on a compromise of 1000 feet above sea level for the peak which is 2.5 miles from the edge to the center of the dome.

克劳德·里尔登

更高的穹顶会有更大的弧度和更高的固有强度，但由于材料成本以及没有以前的原型可供参考，我们妥协了海拔 1000 英尺，即从边缘到穹顶中心的距离为 2.5 英里。

ATTENDEE
How round are those pillars?

与会者
这些柱子有多圆？

CLAUDE REARDEN
The first 200 feet are 30 feet in diameter, made of steel reinforced rebar, welded.

克劳德·里登
前 200 英尺直径为 30 英尺，由钢筋焊接而成。

From 200 feet, up to 700 feet will shrink the diameter of the pillars to 20 feet, and from 700 feet up to 1000 feet, the pillars will be 15 feet in diameter.

从 200 英尺到 700 英尺，柱子的直径将缩小到 20 英尺，从 700 英尺到 1000 英尺，柱子的直径将为 15 英尺。

We anticipate such pillars could last 50,000 years or longer, barring some unforeseen circumstances.

我们预计，除非出现一些不可预见的情况，否则这些支柱可以持续 50,000 年或更长时间。

ATTENDEE
What's those strange looking objects on the dome?

与会者
圆顶上那些奇怪的物体是什么？

CLAUDE REARDEN
The dome will be built using steel sheets with circular openings covered with a strong Plexiglas composite which will allow a significant amount of sunlight in during 6 months of the year.

克劳德·里登
圆顶将使用带有圆形开口的钢板建造，上面覆盖有坚固的有机玻璃复合材料，可在一年中的 6 个月内提供大量的阳光。

The next slide shows how the solar panels are laid in between the sun ports. Approximately ½ of the surface is solar collectors and above each pillar is a windmill which will be approximately 1200 feet above sea level. Each windmill can produce approximately 3728 Kilowatts of electricity with a 20-knot wind.

下一张幻灯片展示了太阳能电池板是如何放置在太阳能端口之间的。大约 1/2 的表面是太阳能收集器，每个柱子上方是风车，风车的高度约为 1200 英尺。每个风车在 20 节风速下可产生约3728 千瓦的电力。

### ATTENDEE
How much electricity will the solar panels produce?

### 与会者
太阳能电池板将产生多少电力？

### CLAUDE REARDEN
During 6 months of the year, every 226 square feet section of solar panels will produce 3 Kilowatts.

### 克劳德·里登
一年中的 6 个月内，每 226 平方英尺的太阳能电池板将产生 3 千瓦的电力。

### CLAUDE REARDEN
Based on conversations with solar panel suppliers, we think that by the time the *Dome City* is complete newer solar collectors can provide 6 Kilowatts. Due to our construction plan, those solar panels are designed to be easily replaceable and as the newer technology arrives, we'll change them out to maximize power generation.

### 克劳德·里登
根据与太阳能电池板供应商的对话，我们认为，到圆顶城完工时，较新的太阳能收集器可以提供6 千瓦的电力。根据我们的施工计划，这些太阳能电池板设计为易于更换，随着新技术的出现，我们将更换它们以最大限度地提高发电量。

### CLAUDE REARDEN
Since we'll have half the surface fitted with solar panels, the dome will produce a continuous 3.6 million kilowatts for 6 months of the year during 80% of the daylight hours and in the winter months about 1 million kilowatts.

克劳德·里登

由于我们将在半个表面安装太阳能电池板，一年中，该穹顶将在 6 个月的白天 80% 的时间里连续产生 360 万千瓦的电力，在冬季则可产生约 100 万千瓦的电力。

## CLAUDE REARDEN

But as you know the days are considerably shorter and we expect snow and ice concentrations that will block out solar collectors. We'll have to rely on wind power and hydro-electric and geothermal during those periods.

克劳德·里登

但正如你所知，白天的时间会大大缩短，我们预计积雪和冰层会阻挡太阳能集热器。在这些时期，我们将不得不依靠风能、水力发电和地热发电。

## VOICEOVER

*There was no mention of the use of nuclear power. Even though Japan was in construction of safe Thorium based nuclear reactors, there was so much antinuke attitudes throughout the world because of Fukushima, Three Mile Island, and Chernobyl.* 画外音

没有提到使用核能。尽管日本正在建造安全的钍基核反应堆，但由于福岛、三哩岛和切尔诺贝利事故，全世界的反核态度非常强烈。

*The decision about nuclear power source was since the Dome Cities at first would be so controversy, adding a layer of controversy in the beginning by planning for nuclear reactors as part of the construction, would distract the overall reason to build dome cities, to protect the public in this mini-ice age now forecasted to last 400 years or longer.*

关于核能来源的决定是因为圆顶城市最初会引发如此多的争议，在开始时将核反应堆作为建设的一部分计划会增加一层争议，会分散建造圆顶城市的整体目的，以保护公众免受目前预计持续 400 年或更长时间的小冰河期的影响。

*However, Alex knew the Thorium Reactor now operating in the Netherlands, which was the prototype for the Japanese Utility, could change all that and*

*because of construction plans for transportation and expansion to multi-domes, there would be access tunnels to bring in outside power to a utility switching network inside the dome.*

然而，亚历克斯知道现在在荷兰运行的钍反应堆，这是日本公用事业的原型，可以改变这一切，并且由于运输和扩展到多圆顶的建设计划，将有通道将外部电力引入圆顶内的公用事业交换网络。

Other construction details showed the framework supporting the steel plates as they are fitted and laid in place and welded to the next sections built in the cross-section drawings.

其他施工细节显示了支撑钢板的框架，这些钢板已安装并铺设到位，并焊接到横截面图中建造的下一个部分。

### ATTENDEE

How will maintenance get accomplished on the windmills or solar panels if necessary?

### 与会者

如有必要，如何对风车或太阳能电池板进行维护？

### CLAUDE REARDEN

Great question. There will be several elevators that will be installed adjacent to pillars capable of taking crews and machinery up to the roof top service compartments.

### 克洛德·里尔登

好问题。将会有几部电梯安装在柱子旁边，能够将工作人员和机械运送到屋顶服务舱。

### ALEX

Ladies and Gentlemen, James Walker, CEO of Hercules Steel will now explain how construction would bring a lot of high paying jobs to Greenland.

### 亚历克斯

女士们先生们，赫拉克勒斯钢铁公司首席执行官詹姆斯·沃克现在将解释建筑业将如何为格陵兰岛带来大量高薪就业机会。

### JAMES WALKER
Steel plates and beams will be shipped in by ship, but they will require customization in workshops established at the work site.

詹姆斯·沃克
钢板和梁将通过船舶运输，但它们需要在工作现场建立的车间进行定制。

As you can see in the next image shown, when part of the Dome is completed, that area will provide shelter for equipment and prefabrication centers.

正如您在下图中看到的，当圆顶的一部分完工后，该区域将为设备和预制中心提供庇护。

Initially work would begin under specialized tents designed to withstand high winds. As soon as the first 6 pillars are built the first section of roof would be installed, 1000 feet up. Anticipate a May - June time frame for first roof installation.

最初，工作将在专门设计的可抵御强风的帐篷下开始。一旦前 6 根柱子建成，就会安装第一段屋顶，高度为 1000 英尺。预计第一段屋顶安装时间在 5 月至 6 月。

Finally, Howard Grady was introduced. The public was very interested in how the pillars would be constructed and put so high up into the air.

最后，霍华德·格雷迪 (Howard Grady) 出场。公众对如何建造柱子并将其放置在如此高空非常感兴趣。

### HOWARD GRADY
I'm going to show an animated video showing pillar construction.

霍华德·格雷迪
我将播放一段动画视频，展示柱子的建造过程。

<u>INT. DAY. NUUK GREENLAND UNIVERSITY MULTIPURPOSE ROOM. ANNIMATED VIDEO OF PILLAR CONSTRUCTION. (30 SECONDS).</u>

<u>内景。努克格陵兰大学多功能厅。柱子建造的动画视频。（30 秒）。</u>

Howard Grady acted as the narrator for this video.

霍华德·格雷迪 (Howard Grady) 担任此视频的解说员。

### HOWARD GRADY
Essentially the pillars would be built like a skyscraper, just with a lot more cement. Large cranes would be setup and would slowly rise with the pillar being built.

霍华德·格雷迪

从本质上讲，这些柱子将像摩天大楼一样建造，只是使用更多的水泥。大型起重机将安装完毕，并随着柱子的建造而缓慢升起。

Rebar steel would first be welded to stubs in the previous section or base. A 30-foot form placed around the top of the pillar and exposed rebar, and cement would be premixed and raised in specialized buckets and deposited.

首先将钢筋焊接到前一节或基座的短柱上，在柱顶周围放置一个 30 英尺的模板，露出钢筋，然后将水泥预拌并放入专门的桶中，然后存放。

A steel safety platform would be built around the top of the form so crews could guide and manipulate the concrete bucket delivery operations.

模板顶部周围将建造一个钢制安全平台，以便工作人员可以指导和操纵混凝土桶的输送操作。

Once the cement is poured, more rebar steel would be welded setting up the next leg of the column being built in sections, with the process repeating.

浇注水泥后，将焊接更多钢筋，分段建造柱子的下一根支柱，并重复该过程。

After a 24-hour drying period the form and platform would be raised by the crane and anchors welded on the sides of the column would support the weight of the form and safety platform as it was lifted.

经过 24 小时的干燥期后，起重机将抬起模板和平台，焊接在柱子侧面的锚将支撑模板和安全平台的重量。

As the column reaches the transition to narrower portions of the pillar a new safety platform is raised in pieces and assembled that will rise above the initial 30-foot diameter pillars.

当柱子过渡到柱子的较窄部分时，一个新的安全平台将分段抬起并组装，该平台将高于最初直径 30 英尺的柱子。

As Claude Rearden previously stated, from 200 feet,

up to 700 feet will shrink the diameter of the pillars to 20 feet, and from 700 feet up to 1000 feet, the pillars will be 15 feet in diameter. At those points new safety platforms for the narrower portions get installed with narrower column forms.

正如克劳德·里尔登之前所说，从200英尺到700英尺，柱子的直径将缩小到20英尺，而从700英尺到1000英尺，柱子的直径将缩小到15英尺。在这些点上，较窄部分的新安全平台将与较窄的柱形一起安装。

## ATTENDEE
What happens when the pillar reaches 1000 feet?

## 与会者
当柱子达到 1000 英尺时会发生什么？

## HOWARD GRADY
That's in the next video I'm going to now show. Once the column reaches the top, 1000 feet up and very accurately built by laser positioning, a steel top plate which would allow mounting the struts holding the roof section in place would be installed in several sections and welded together.

## 霍华德·格雷迪
这是我现在要展示的下一个视频。一旦柱子到达顶部，即 1000 英尺高，并通过激光定位非常精确地建造，钢顶板将分成几部分安装并焊接在一起，以便安装将屋顶部分固定到位的支柱。

During the first column construction, an elevator would be installed. Several more elevators would be installed to allow access to different roof areas, assuming any area could be snow and ice covered in the winter.

在建造第一根柱子时，将安装一部电梯。假设任何区域在冬天都可能被冰雪覆盖，那么将安装几部电梯以允许进入不同的屋顶区域。

## HOWARD GRADY
I'll turn the microphone over to Alex now so that he can describe to you what the possibilities are with the proposed dome.

霍华德·格雷迪

我现在将麦克风交给亚历克斯，让他向你们描述
一下这个圆顶的可能用途。

The crowd was somewhat subdued with the awe and wonder of this fantastic innovation that may change their lives in ways they never dreamed of, were waiting for every word Alex had to say.

人群有些被这个奇妙的创新所震撼和惊叹，这个创新可能会以他们从未梦想过的方式改变他们的生活，他们等待着亚历克斯说的每一句话。

ALEX

I'm going to now get into what we do with the dome and be aware we do not have to wait for the entire dome to be built to start developing what we put in it.

亚历克斯

我现在要开始讲讲我们对圆顶的处理，请注意，我们不必等待整个圆顶建成就可以开始开发我们在里面的东西。

## INT. DAY. NUUK GREENLAND UNIVERSITY MULTIPURPOSE ROOM. ARTIST CONCEPTION OF HIGH-RISE BUILDING CONSTRUCTION INSIDE THE DOME.

内景。努克格陵兰大学多功能厅。圆顶内部高层建筑施工的艺术构想。

ALEX

Looking at this next artist conception, you can see, it appears there are high rise buildings in the dome and parks and other facilities you would normally see in City's located far south of here. But there are a few things that we can do in a dome protected city.

亚历克斯

看看下一个艺术构想，你可以看到，圆顶里似乎有高层建筑，还有公园和其他设施，这些设施你通常会在位于这里南部的城市看到。但我们可以在圆顶保护的城市里做一些事情。

First, we don't have to build tall buildings in a way to protect them from high winds. The dome does that for us.

首先，我们不必以某种方式建造建筑物以保护它们免受强风的侵袭。圆顶为我们做到了这一点。

Hence, we can put more effort into vertical strength

than lateral strength since lateral forces will be minimal.

因此，我们可以将更多的精力放在垂直强度而不是横向强度上，因为横向力将最小。

The next thing is we will start on the North end of the *Dome* and work south. The prevailing winds in the winter are from the north and west. Once that end of the *Dome* is complete, we'll have a wind block so high-rise building constructions can start.

接下来，我们将从圆顶的北端开始，然后向南工作。冬季盛行风来自北方和西方。一旦圆顶的那端完工，我们将有一个挡风板，以便高层建筑的建设可以开始。

### ATTENDEE
What kind of buildings?

### 与会者
什么样的建筑？

### ALEX
We can build for commercial, residential, industrial, or other purposes. It will all relate to your zoning laws.

### 亚历克斯
我们可以为商业、住宅、工业或其他目的建造。这一切都与您的分区法有关。

### RANDOM ATTENDEE
This is the first I've heard about zoning laws.

### 随机与会者
这是我第一次听说分区法。

### ALEX
This part you NUUK Residents need to work out in advance because it will affect the types and quantity of services installed in a particular section.

### 亚历克斯
这部分你们努克居民需要提前解决，因为它会影响在特定区域安装的服务类型和数量。

RANDOM ATTENDEE
This is the first most of us heard about this. You are indicating putting up a roof section by mid-summer. How dos that give us time to think about zoning laws?

随机与会者
这是我们大多数人第一次听说这件事。您表示要在仲夏之前安装屋顶部分。这怎么能让我们有足够的时间考虑分区法呢？

ALEX
Because of the complexities of zoning regulations and looking at what already exists in the two perspective building sites, we've created a proposed zoning diagrams for your consideration.

亚历克斯
由于分区法规的复杂性以及考虑到两个透视建筑工地中已有的内容，我们创建了一份拟议的分区图供您考虑。

RANDOM ATTENDEE
Just when is this going to take place?

随机与会者
这到底什么时候会发生？

ALEX
We expect that soon responsible parties will put together committees to go over our recommendations and modify or add your own preferences.

亚历克斯
我们预计责任方很快将组建委员会来审查我们的建议并修改或添加您自己的偏好。

RANDOM ATTENDEE
What's the deadline for that?

随机与会者
最后期限是什么时候？

ALEX
We need those zoning decisions before the start of construction so we can plan for building in the services required. Since it would be prohibitively costly to

change after we start construction, the zoning laws will be an addendum to the construction contract.

亚历克斯

我们需要在施工开始之前做出这些分区决策，以便我们可以规划所需服务的建设。由于在我们开始施工后进行更改将花费高昂，因此分区法将成为施工合同的附录。

## RANDOM ATTENDEE

Can you explain some of the buildings in that image?

随机与会者
您能解释一下图片中的一些建筑物吗？

## ALEX

Sure, mind you this is an artist conception, does not convey potential zoning regulations you ultimately determine is necessary, but just to get you thinking about the structure and the composition, these buildings here are housing units.

亚历克斯

当然，请注意，这是一个艺术构思，并不传达您最终确定必要的潜在分区规定，但只是为了让您思考结构和组成，这里的这些建筑物是住房单元。

For all practical purposes they look like expensive New York apartment buildings, and indeed they are like that except since we do not have to build to withstand high winds. We can instead put in higher weight loading and allow much more comfort and facilities in each building since we can focus on the vertical support.

从所有实际目的来看，它们看起来都像昂贵的纽约公寓楼，而且它们确实如此，只是因为我们不必建造能够抵御强风的建筑。相反，我们可以增加更高的重量负荷，并在每栋建筑中提供更多的舒适度和设施，因为我们可以专注于垂直支撑。

There is a distinct business district, notice these buildings are situated in the middle of the *Dome*. That way we can put housing out in the outer areas which can also have entry for *Dome* occupants and visitors at many access points.

有一个独特的商业区，请注意这些建筑位于穹顶的中间。这样，我们就可以在外部区域建造住房，这些区域也可以让穹顶的居住者和游客在许多出入口进入。

As you can see, we have some example factories which are on the edge of the dome. That's because they do not have to have many floors and air purification system will dump all factory recirculation air outside the dome, so we are mindful of removing any air particulates.

正如您所见，我们有一些位于穹顶边缘的示例工厂。这是因为它们不需要有很多楼层，空气净化系统会将所有工厂再循环空气排放到穹顶外，因此我们注意去除任何空气微粒。

ATTENDEE
What about automobiles?

与会者
汽车呢？

ALEX
Since its only 2.5 miles from the center of the dome to anywhere, all internal combustion engine vehicles must remain outside the dome except for special requirements for police and fire departments.

亚历克斯
由于距圆顶中心到任何地方都只有 2.5 英里，因此除警察和消防部门的特殊要求外，所有内燃机车辆都必须留在圆顶之外。

RANDOM ATTENDEE
How will people get around? Nuuk people are not interested in walking 2.5 miles.

随机与会者
人们将如何出行？努克人对步行 2.5 英里不感兴趣。

ALEX
Once you are living inside the dome, there will be public transportation with good schedules. Since there will be no rain or snow inside the dome with a controlled environment the transportation scheme can be greatly simplified.

亚历克斯

一旦你住在穹顶内，就会有公共交通，时刻表很好。由于穹顶内不会下雨或下雪，环境受控，交通方案可以大大简化。

RANDOM ATTENDEE
What does that mean?

随机与会者
这是什么意思？

ALEX

People will be allowed to drive electric powered cars or golf carts within the dome, that is if you approve the zoning laws and regulations required to maintain healthy air and reduce the costs of air purification processes to minimize health issues.

亚历克斯

人们将被允许在圆顶内驾驶电动汽车或高尔夫球车，也就是说，如果您批准维持健康空气并降低空气净化过程成本以尽量减少健康问题所需的分区法律和法规。

Another Nuuk resident asked:
另一位努克居民问道：

ATTENDEE
Who is paying for the dome construction?

与会者
来支付圆顶建筑的费用？

ALEX

I'm paying for it up front. However, as the contract stipulates, I'm receiving half the air space within the dome as part of the deal.

亚历克斯

我先付了钱。然后继续说，但是根据合同规定，作为交易的一部分，我将获得圆顶内一半的空中空间。

ATTENDEE
What will you do with the air space?

与会者
你会用空中空间做什么？

ALEX
I'll build commercial buildings, residential blocks, and parks which I'll lease or sell.

亚历克斯
我会建造商业建筑、住宅区和公园，然后出租或出售。

ATTENDEE
How soon will construction begin?

与会者
施工什么时候开始？

ALEX
As we indicated earlier, we want to start the first sections of the roof around May, when weather becomes more tolerable for outdoor work.

We'll continue at a heavy pace until September, when we'll have to cut back due to the fact it will be too cold, icing, and hazardous to continue building the pillars or roof structures.

But our fabrication facilities will be completed, and all the steel plates being readied for roof construction, as well as the solar and wind devices will go through local production in our fabrication tents we'll set up.

When May rolls around the following year, we'll have surplus materials on hand to allow rapid installation.

亚历克斯
正如我们之前指出的，我们希望在五月左右开始屋顶的第一部分，届时天气变得更适合户外工作。

我们将以高速度继续工作到 9 月，那时我们将不得不减慢进度，因为天气太冷、结冰，而且继续建造柱子或屋顶结构很危险。

但我们的制造设施将完工，所有准备用于屋顶施工的钢板以及太阳能和风能设备都将在我们搭建的制造帐篷中进行本地生产。

到第二年 5 月时，我们将有剩余的材料可以快速安装。

Alex then figured now would be a good time to take a break and set up informal discussions announced:

亚历克斯 认为现在是休息和安排非正式讨论的好时机，他说：

### ALEX

Ladies and Gentlemen, we are now going to take a few minutes break.

亚历克斯

女士们，先生们，我们现在要休息几分钟。

When we come back, we are going to break into groups so you can all individually talk with James Walker, Howard Grady, Claude Reardon and myself if you have any specific questions in their areas.

Also, Professor Jørgensen and Grey have all these presentations available, and at the back table are business cards which have the professor's contact information for copies of these presentations, we are more than happy to provide to you.

We'll all be back in 15 minutes, take time to get a snack or some coffee or juice or water available in the back.

亚历克斯

回来后，我们将分成小组，这样如果你们在他们各自的领域有任何具体问题，你们都可以单独

詹姆斯·沃克 (James Walker) 、霍华德·格雷迪 (Howard Grady) 、克劳德·里尔登 (Claude Reardon) 和我交谈。此外，约根森 (Jørgensen) 教授和 格雷 教授格雷. (Grey) 还提供了所有这些演示文稿，后面的桌子上有名片，上面有教授的联系信息，我们非常乐意为您提供这些演示文稿的副本。

我们 15 分钟后就回来，花点时间去后面吃点零食、咖啡、果汁或水。"

After a quick trip to the restroom, Alex was back in the conference room as the public was milling around. Alex walked to the back tables and poured a cup of coffee, then looked around and was approached by some of the locals.

匆匆去了趟洗手间后，亚历克斯 回到会议室，人们正在四处走动。亚历克斯走到后面的桌子，倒了一杯咖啡，然后环顾四周，一些当地人走近了他。

## ATTENDEE

Mr. Baxter, do you intend on using locals for laborers or are you going to import Chinese and Latino's to do the construction?

## 与会者

巴克斯特先生，您打算使用当地人做劳工，还是要进口中国人和拉丁美洲人来做建筑？

## ALEX

What's your name sir?

## 亚历克斯

先生，您叫什么名字？

## ATTENDEE

Brian.

## 与会者

布赖恩.

## ALEX

Well Brian, this is how I plan to do business. It's in my best interest to use all the locals possible.

But as you can imagine working 1000 feet up in the air, sometimes in bitter cold weather is not everyone's cup of tea.

If we can't find enough local talent, we'll have to bring workers in who are experts in construction.

## 亚历克斯

好吧，布赖恩（Brian），这就是我计划做生意的方式。尽可能使用所有当地人对我最有利。

但你可以想象，在 1000 英尺的高空工作，有时在严寒的天气里工作并不是每个人都喜欢的。

如果我们找不到足够的本地人才，我们就必须引进建筑专家。

## BRIAN

How many jobs do you think this will produce?

布赖恩
你认为这将创造多少个就业机会

ALEX
Thousands.

亚历克斯
数千个。

BRIAN
What kinds of jobs?

布赖恩
什么样的工作？

ALEX
Well, you already heard me discussing cement and steel work which means lots of construction workers, welders, electricians, and when buildings start getting built, the entire trade spectrum.

亚历克斯
嗯，你已经听我讨论过水泥和钢铁工作，这意味着大量的建筑工人、焊工、电工，当建筑物开始建造时，整个行业都会受到影响。

BRIAN
When will the first buildings get built?

布赖恩
第一批建筑物什么时候建成？

ALEX
For the size and scale of this operation and the number of employees we'll need, we'll have to build housing and facilities.

As we discussed we are going to build large tents to provide protection from the elements and provide a dry decent work environment for workers prefabricating the parts and pieces.

亚历克斯
对于这项业务的规模和我们需要的员工数量，我们必须建造住房和设施。

正如我们所讨论的，我们将建造大型帐篷来保护他们免受恶劣天气的侵袭，并为预制零件和部件的工人提供干燥、舒适的工作环境。

BRIAN
You mentioned housing?

布赖恩
你提到住房？

ALEX
Yes, we'll put up wood structures for housing, will be like the apartment buildings you already have here. We will build enough housing so that workers do not impact the local rents and create a scarcity of resources for the locals.

亚历克斯
是的，我们将建造木结构的住房，类似于你们这里已有的公寓楼。我们将建造足够的住房，这样工人就不会影响当地的租金，也不会造成当地人的资源匮乏。

BRIAN
But they will shop in our stores and eat at our restaurants and use our clubs and entertainment.

布赖恩
但他们会在我们的商店购物，在我们的餐馆吃饭，使用我们的俱乐部和娱乐场所。

ALEX
Certainly, it will be an economic boom to Nuuk which will grow from 17,000 population to maybe 35,000 in a year.

亚历克斯
当然，这将是努克的经济繁荣，一年内，努克的人口将从 17,000 人增长到 35,000 人。

BRIAN
Don't you think that will cause too much congestion?

布赖恩
你不觉得这会造成太多拥堵吗？

ALEX

Not really, we'll make sure the living facilities for the workers are in the area where the dome is being built. As the first section is complete working as a wind break, we can put up our first buildings.

I intend to make sure a lot of that development is housing, and the temporary wooden structures will be demolished as we move people into the new permanent buildings.

亚历克斯

不会，我们会确保工人的生活设施位于圆顶建造的区域。当第一部分作为防风墙完工后，我们就可以建造第一批建筑了。

我打算确保很多开发项目都是住房，临时的木结构将被拆除，因为我们会把人们搬进新的永久性建筑。

BRIAN

Yes, but doubling the population, don't you think will drive up food and fuel prices and stuff like that?

布赖恩

是的，但人口增加一倍，你不觉得会推高食品和燃料价格之类的吗？

ALEX

Absolutely it would if we didn't plan for it. We'll have a lot more ships pulling in than you are accustomed to seeing.

We'll ask the local stores if they want to expand, if so, I will build them temporary businesses in the dome area and bring in adequate supplies so there will be no need to drain any resources from the Nuuk population.

My goal is to have no impact on Nuuk while the dome is being built.

亚历克斯

如果我们不为此做计划，肯定会的。我们会有更多的船只停靠，比你平时看到的要多得多。

我们会问当地的商店是否想扩大规模，如果是的话，我会在圆顶区域为他们建立临时业务，并带来足够的供应，这样就不需要从努克人口中抽取任何资源。

我的目标是在建造圆顶期间不影响努克。

### BRIAN
Well then what after the dome is completed?
那么圆顶完工后会怎样呢？

By then people will have lived under the partially completed dome for a number of years, and the combination of the wind break, and lack of snow removal requirements will tend to attract Nuuk people to move into the dome.

到那时，人们将在这座部分完工的圆顶建筑下生活数年，防风林和无需清除积雪的结合将吸引努克人搬进圆顶建筑。

### BRIAN
You indicated that perhaps 500,000 people will eventually live in the dome, how will the Nuuk people be able to compete with immigrants you bring in from all over the world?

布莱恩
您表示，也许最终将有50万人居住在穹顶中，努克人将如何与您从世界各地引进的移民竞争？

### ALEX
I've not really spelled it out, but Nuuk people will have first bids on housing in the dome. I will have 2 prices. One price for Nuuk which will be vastly cheaper and one for any immigrants or foreigners.

亚历克斯
我还没有具体说清楚，但努克人将对圆顶的住房进行首次竞标。我会给出两个价格。一个是努克的价格，价格会便宜得多，另一个是针对任何移民或外国人。

### BRIAN
What kinds of prices are we talking about?

布莱恩
我们谈论的价格是什么样的？

### ALEX

For Nuuk residents, whom we'll use the local governments for verification of identity and eligibility, it will cost no more than what they are accustomed to paying now for equivalent space.

### 亚历克斯
对于努克居民来说，我们将通过当地政府来验证他们的身份和资格，其费用不会高于他们现在习惯为同等空间支付的费用。

### BRIAN
So, you are saying that if they currently pay $150,000 for a condo in Nuuk, you will sell them a Dome Condo for $150,000.

### 布莱恩
因此，您的意思是，如果他们目前在努克支付 150,000 美元购买一套公寓，您将以 150,000 美元的价格向他们出售一套圆顶公寓。

### ALEX
Absolutely and if they want to do a swap, we'll take their condo or home and give them equivalent space in the dome housing.

### 亚历克斯
绝对可以，如果他们想进行交换，我们将拿走他们的公寓或住宅，并在圆顶住房中为他们提供同等的空间。

### BRIAN
Some of those homes are old and only cost $30,000 to build.

### 布莱恩
其中一些房屋很旧，建造成本仅为 3 万美元。

### ALEX
That's okay, if that's what they paid for it, we'll trade them straight across.

### 亚历克斯
没关系，如果这是他们支付的费用，我们将直接进行交易。

### BRIAN

You mentioned you pay for everything but get ½ the air space.

布莱恩
您提到您支付了所有费用，但获得了 1/2 的空间。

ALEX
Yes, absolutely, I get ½ the volume of the dome to build as I see fit within the guidelines of the zoning laws the community establishes.

亚历克斯
是的，当然，我会根据社区制定的分区法的指导方针，按照我认为合适的方式建造穹顶的 1/2 体积。

BRIAN
Will there be parks and recreation?

布莱恩
会有公园和休闲设施吗？

ALEX
Yes, and inside the dome because of the temperatures and winter lighting augmentation to simulate 12-hour days, trees will grow. We've done experimentation in Polar Regions and know trees and plants will thrive within the dome.

亚历克斯
是的，在圆顶内，由于温度和冬季照明增强以模拟 12 小时的白天，树木会生长。我们已经在极地地区进行了实验，知道树木和植物会在圆顶内茁壮成长。

BRIAN
How many trees will there be?

布莱恩
会有多少棵树？

ALEX
The dome floor will be 19.6 square miles with the five-mile diameter. There will be a lot of room to plant trees.

亚历克斯

穹顶面积为 19.6 平方英里，直径为 5 英里。这里有足够的空间种植树木。

BRIAN

I can't imagine what 19.6 square miles would be like.

布莱恩

我无法想象 19.6 平方英里会是什么样子。

ALEX

I grew up in Carlsbad, California, in the USA. it's about twice the size of the dome area. Carlsbad is all spread out with few high-rise buildings and had a population of 112,000 back in 2014. It has a lot of big houses and big yards, very roomy. There are probably 500,000 trees in Carlsbad.

亚历克斯

我在美国加利福尼亚州卡尔斯巴德长大。它的面积大约是圆顶面积的两倍。卡尔斯巴德分布广泛，高层建筑很少，2014 年人口为 112,000。这里有很多大房子和大院子，非常宽敞。卡尔斯巴德可能有 500,000 棵树。

BRIAN

So you are saying living in the dome, it will appear green?

布莱恩

所以你是说住在圆顶里，它会显得绿色？

ALEX

Yes, Green year-round.

亚历克斯

是的，全年绿色。

BRIAN

Will it get cold inside the dome?

布莱恩

穹顶内会冷吗？

ALEX

No, we will maintain the temperature at 70 degrees.

亚历克斯
不，我们会将温度保持在 70 度。

BRIAN
Why 70 degrees?

布莱恩
为什么是70度？

ALEX
By maintaining a constant temperature, it will eliminate and stress fractures in the dome that heating and cooling cycles would create. Plus, it would ensure the plant life remains robust.

亚历克斯
通过保持恒定的温度，它将消除加热和冷却循环可能产生的圆顶应力断裂。此外，它还将确保植物保持旺盛的生命力。

The others had similar conversations covering almost all aspects of the Dome.

其他人也进行了类似的对话，几乎涉及了穹顶的所有方面。

As Alex continued to talk, he noticed out of the side of his eye someone walking in the room. Alex turned and looked and spotted Police Detective Rodney Hansen. Rodney nodded to Alex who understood he wanted to talk with him, so Alex excused himself from the two individuals he currently was conversing with and followed detective Hansen out the door.

当 亚历克斯 继续说话时，他从眼角余光中注意到有人在房间里走动。亚历克斯 转过身，发现了警探 罗德尼·汉森 。罗德尼向 亚历克斯 点点头，亚历克斯知道他想和他谈谈，于是 亚历克斯离开了他正在交谈的两个人，跟着警探 汉森出了门。

ALEX
Well Rodney, any news?

ALEX
好吧 罗德尼，有什么消息吗？

RODNEY HANSEN
(a.k.a. Police Detective)
Mr. Baxter, we are working on the case. I just wanted you to know we found what we believe is the car you saw from your hotel window, it was reported stolen

from a local resident, and we've taken fingerprints off it, but have not identified a perpetrator.

罗德尼·汉森<br>（又名警探）

巴克斯特先生，我们正在处理此案。我只是想让你知道，我们发现了你从酒店窗户看到的那辆车，据说是从当地居民那里偷来的，我们已经从车上取下了指纹，但还没有确定肇事者。

Airport surveillance video hasn't identified the person trying to leave Greenland. We'll have an agent tailing you until you leave in case someone tries to make any attempts on you.

机场监控录像没有确定试图离开格陵兰的人。我们会派一名特工跟踪你，直到你离开，以防有人试图对你进行任何企图。

ALEX<br>I appreciate that, Rodney.

亚历克斯<br>我很感激，罗德尼。

Alex then pulled out one of his business cards and gave it to detective Hansen.

亚历克斯然后拿出一张名片递给汉森侦探。

ALEX<br>Rodney, please call me if you find out anything.

亚历克斯

罗德尼，如果你发现任何事情，请给我打电话。

RODNEY HANSEN<br>(a.k.a. Police Detective)<br>We certainly will Mr. Baxter.

罗德尼·汉森<br>（又名警探）<br>我们一定会的，巴克斯特先生。

Alex held out his hand and shook Rodney's.

亚历克斯伸出手和罗德尼握手。

RODNEY HANSEN
(a.k.a. Police Detective)
Have a safe flight home, Mr. Baxter.

罗德尼·汉森
（又名警探）
祝你一路平安，巴克斯特先生。

ALEX
Thank you, Rodney.

亚历克斯
谢谢你，罗德尼。

Rodney turned and walked away towards his unmarked car.

罗德尼转身朝他没有标记的车走去。

Alex walked back inside the building and continued conversing with the locals.

亚历克斯走回大楼，继续与当地人交谈。

In due time, Alex approached Adelheid Jørgensen and announced:

亚历克斯在适当的时候走近阿德海德·约根森并宣布：

ALEX
We are about ready to wrap up things here, I'd like
you to make some final comments, and then I'll invite
everyone to join us over at the Hereford Beefstouw
restaurant for lunch and while we are eating, they can
ask more questions and get to know us a little better.

亚历克斯
我们准备在这里结束，我想让你做最后的评论，
然后我会邀请大家和我们一起去赫里福德牛肉餐
厅吃午饭，在吃饭的时候，他们可以问更多问
题，更好地了解我们。

ADELHEID JØRGENSEN (a.k.a. ADEL)
Director of Greenland's Natural Resources Council。
Sure, that sounds good.

阿德尔海德·约根森（又名阿德尔）
格陵兰岛自然资源委员会主任。
当然，这听起来不错。

Adel responded, then tapped on the microphone and said in Danish:

阿德尔回应道，然后敲击麦克风，用丹麦语说道：

ADELHEID JØRGENSEN (a.k.a. ADEL)
Director of Greenland's Natural Resources Council。
Mine damer og herrer, må jeg få din opmærksomhed.
Vi vil blive slutter denne konference nu, men hvis
nogen af jer gerne vil slutte sig til os, vil vi være at
gå over til Hereford Beefstouw restaurant i en kort tid
til frokost, hvor du kan stille flere spørgsmål og få at
vide os.

阿德尔海德·约根森（又名阿德尔）
格陵兰岛自然资源委员会主任。
我的女士和女士，我是我的最爱。我们在会议上
尽情狂欢，男人们在我们的会议上尽情享受，在
赫里福德牛肉餐厅 (Hereford Beefstouw) 餐厅度过
了愉快的时光，在我们的视频中享受美食。

Adel then said the same announcement in English:

然后阿德尔用英语宣布了同样的消息：

Ladies and gentlemen, please may I have your
attention. We are going to be ending this conference
now but if any of you would like to join us, we'll
be going over to the Hereford Beefstouw restaurant
in a short while for lunch, where you can ask more
questions and get to know us.

女士们，先生们，请注意。我们现在要结束这次
会议了，但如果你们当中有人想加入我们，我们
将前往赫里福德牛肉店一会儿我们就会去餐厅吃
午饭，在那里你可以问更多问题并了解我们。

Adel then turned to Alex and announced:

然后阿德尔转向亚历克斯并宣布：

ADELHEID JØRGENSEN (a.k.a. ADEL)
Director of Greenland's Natural Resources Council。
Alex, you and your business partners can leave now
and go to the restaurant. I have arranged for a crew to
clean up here and Professor Grey and I will meet you
over there in a little while.

阿德尔海德·约根森（又名阿德尔）
格陵兰自然资源委员会主任。
亚历克斯，你和你的商业伙伴可以离开了现在去
餐厅。我已经安排了一队人来打扫这里，格雷教
授和我一会儿会在那里和你会面

**ALEX**
Thank you, professor, we'll see you there shortly.

亚历克斯
谢谢教授，我们很快就会在那里见到你。

Alex then walked over to James Walker, Howard Grady, Claude Reardon and then asked:

然后，亚历克斯走到詹姆斯·沃克、霍华德·格雷迪、克劳德·里尔登等人面前，问道：

**ALEX**
Do you guys know how to get to Hereford Beefstouw?

亚历克斯
你们知道怎么去赫里福德牛肉餐厅吗？

**CLAUDE REARDON**
I'm sure we can find it, it's not a big place.

克劳德·里尔登
我相信我们能找到的，那地方不大。

**ALEX**
If you want to follow me, I'll be in that Limo that's parked out in front, it's a short distance away.

亚历克斯
如果你想跟我来，我会坐在前面停着的那辆豪华轿车里，离得很近。

**CLAUDE REARDON**
Sure, no problem.

克劳德·里尔登
当然，没问题。

Alex and his associates then left the building and got in their cars and drove back to Hotel Hans Egede walked through the lobby and went to the elevator to get up to the Hereford Beefstouw restaurant.

亚历克斯和他的同事们离开大楼，上车回到酒店。汉斯·埃格德穿过大厅，乘电梯上到赫里福德牛肉餐厅。

It was around 11:00 in the morning and the restaurant/bar had just opened. There were no customers, and the manager was surprised to see 8 people suddenly arrive.

当时是上午 11:00 左右，餐厅/酒吧刚刚开门。没有顾客，经理很惊讶地看到突然来了 8 个人。

**MANAGER RANDY CRAIG**
How many, sir?

经理 兰迪·克雷格
先生，有多少人？

**ALEX**

We are not sure. We invited a number of people, there could be more showing up in a few minutes, I know there will be at least 2 more, but there could be many more who decide to show up.

亚历克斯

我们不确定。我们邀请了不少人，几分钟后可能会有更多的人出现，我知道至少还会有 2 人，但可能会有更多的人决定出现。

**MANAGER RANDY CRAIG**

Ok, well, I'll seat those of you that are here now and as more people arrive, we can perhaps move some tables around to accommodate a group serving.

经理 兰迪·克雷格

好的，我会安排现在在场的你们就座，随着越来越多的人到来，我们也许可以移动一些桌子以容纳团体服务。

**ALEX**
That would be nice.

亚历克斯
那就太好了。

**STEPHANIE**
Mr. Craig, may I have a private word with you?

斯蒂芬妮
克雷格先生，我可以和您私下谈谈吗？

MANAGER RANDY CRAIG
Yes mam, please come this way, please.

经理 兰迪·克雷格
是的，女士，请往这边走。

Randy Craig responded and led Stephanie to where they could speak with some privacy.

兰迪·克雷格 回应道，并带领 斯蒂芬妮到可以私下交谈的地方。

MANAGER RANDY CRAIG
What can I do for you Madam?

经理 兰迪·克雷格
女士，我能为您做些什么？

STEPHANIE
My name is Stephanie McFarland, Mr. Baxter's personal assistant. I will be paying for everyone's meals and drinks, here's my credit card, put all the charges on the bill on this.

斯蒂芬妮
我叫斯蒂芬妮·麦克法兰，是巴克斯特先生的私人助理。我会为大家支付餐饮费用，这是我的信用卡，把账单上的所有费用都记在这张卡上。

MANAGER RANDY CRAIG
As you wish Ms. McFarland.

经理 兰迪·克雷格
如您所愿，麦克法兰女士。

STEPHANIE
One other thing, Mr. Craig.

斯蒂芬妮
还有一件事，克雷格先生。

MANAGER RANDY CRAIG
Yes mam?

经理 兰迪·克雷格
是吗，女士？

**STEPHANIE**
We invited several Nuuk residents here. We are not sure how many are going to show up. If you could please ask customers when they arrive, if they are here for the Dome Conference, please try to seat them near us, and put their meals and drinks on our bill which I'm paying.

斯蒂芬妮
我们邀请了几位努克居民来这里。我们不确定会有多少人来。如果您能在顾客到达时询问他们是否是来参加圆顶会议的，请尽量让他们坐在我们附近，并将他们的餐食和饮料记在我们账单上，由我来支付。

**MANAGER RANDY CRAIG**
I will be delighted to do that, Madam.

经理 兰迪·克雷格
我很乐意这样做，女士。

**STEPHANIE**
Thank you, Mr. Craig.

斯蒂芬妮
谢谢您，克雷格先生。

Stephanie smiled, held out her hand and shook Randy Craig's hand, then smiled and turned and rejoined the group.

斯蒂芬妮微笑着伸出手和兰迪·克雷格握手，然后微笑着转身重新加入了团队。

Several of the people that were present at the conference were news media people who casually introduced themselves at the University and arrived shortly, followed by Adel and Mr. Grey. All total about 40 people arrived and the restaurant had barely enough room to seat them all but could easily seat some at the *Skyline Bar* which connects to the restaurant and people from there could hear attendees in the Beefstouw restaurant.

出席会议的几位人士是新闻媒体人士，他们在大学随意地介绍了自己，不久后，阿德尔和格雷先生也到了。总共有 40 人到达，餐厅几乎没有足够的空间容纳所有人，但可以很容易地在与餐厅相连的 天际线酒吧 坐下一些人，那里的人可以听到 牛肉餐厅餐厅的与会者的声音。

The group stood for a while as the manager and a couple of assistants moved tables around. The manager apologized and said they were not expecting such a large crowd, but was calling in the night chef early to help produce the meals in a reasonable time. When Alex heard this he tried to convince the manager not to make such a big fuss that they would be willing to wait longer, the manager said, not a problem the chef only lived a couple blocks away, and had already seen him a little while ago, so it's not going to be a problem.

经理和几名助理移动桌子时，这群人站了一会儿。经理道歉说，他们没想到会有这么多人，但提前叫来了夜班厨师，以便在合理的时间内制作餐点。当 Alex 听到这个消息时，他试图说服经理不要大惊小怪，他们愿意再等一会儿，经理说，没关系，厨师只住在几个街区之外，不久前已经见过他，所以不会有问题。

ALEX
James Walker, Howard Grady, and Claude Reardon
let's all split up amongst the guests so that they would
have a chance to casually talk to the team members
allowing them to  ask lots of questions while eating.

亚历克斯
詹姆斯·沃克、霍华德·格雷迪和克劳德·里尔登让
我们在客人中分开，这样他们就有机会和团队成
员随意交谈，让他们一边吃饭一边问很多问题。

The Manager Randy Craig also helped as a waiter and through great teamwork and improvising were able to get everyone's orders in a reasonable time frame and with the 2 chefs working in a spectacular choreography of splendid expertise, produced world class meals fit for a king.

经理也担任服务员，通过出色的团队合作和即兴发挥，能够在合理的时间内收到每个人的订单，再加上两位厨师以精湛的专业技能精心编排，为客人提供堪比国王烹制的世界级美食。

Alex had sat down and soon was surrounded by six locals on his area of the elongated table produced by the manager as he created five long tables stretching across the room. There was nothing remarkable about these six people, who seemed like just ordinary people.

亚历克斯坐下后，很快就被 六 位当地人围在了经理安排的长桌上，经理在房间里摆了五张长桌。这 六 个人看起来没什么特别的，他们看起来只是普通人。

Alex said as they sat down, he announced:

亚历克斯坐下时说, 他宣布：

ALEX
I apologize in advance. I do not speak Danish, if one

here does perhaps you can translate for the others who
do not speak English?

亚历克斯

我提前道歉。我不会说丹麦语，如果这里有人会
说，你能为其他不会说英语的人翻译一下吗？

The semi-attractive lady, who was pretty but not made up sitting directly across from
Alex spoke up first.

坐在亚历克斯对面的那位漂亮但没有化妆的半迷人女士首先开口了。

PRETTY LADY
(a.k.a., SHELLY BERGMAN)
Mr. Baxter, I can speak English and if there is anyone
here who needs Danish translation I can help.

漂亮女士
（又名 雪莉·伯格曼）
巴克斯特先生，我会说英语，如果这里有人需要
丹麦语翻译，我可以帮助。

ALEX
Oh, thank you, what is your name?

亚历克斯
哦，谢谢，你叫什么名字？

SHELLY BERGMAN
My name is Shelly Bergman and I'm a reporter for
North Ice News.

雪莉·伯格曼
我叫 雪莉·伯格曼
我是 北方 冰 新闻的记者。

ALEX
Nuuk's Newspaper?

亚历克斯
努克的报纸？

SHELLY BERGMAN
It used to be, but we are more internet now than paper
because the government of Greenland tries to get
everyone laptops and WIFI so that they do not rely
on paper delivery in the harsh winters, people can still
get the news.

雪莉·伯格曼
过去是这样的，但现在我们更依赖互联网而不是
报纸，因为格陵兰政府试图让每个人都拥有笔记
本电脑和 无线上网，这样在严酷的冬天，人们就
不必依赖报纸送达，仍然可以获得新闻。

ALEX
I see. How does that work out?

亚历克斯
我明白了。效果如何？

SHELLY BERGMAN
Pretty good, it works as an enhancement to the
community to get somewhat computer literate so they
can get the news plus programming in remote areas
hard to get to in stormy weather.

雪莉·伯格曼
非常好，它有助于社区提高计算机知识水平，这
样他们就可以在暴风雨天气难以到达的偏远地区
获得新闻和节目。

ALEX
So, you are here covering the Dome initiative.

亚历克斯
所以你在这里报道圆顶计划。

SHELLY BERGMAN
Yes.

雪莉·伯格曼
是的。

ALEX
How did you learn about it?

亚历克斯
您是如何得知的？

SHELLY BERGMAN
Adelheid Jørgensen is my friend and former classmate.

雪莉·伯格曼
阿德尔海德·约根森是我的私人朋友和以前的同学。

ALEX
I see. What's your opinion on what you have seen so far?

亚历克斯
我明白了。你对目前所见有什么看法？

SHELLY BERGMAN
I think it's a pipe dream, possibly a scam.

雪莉·伯格曼
我认为这是一个白日梦，可能是一个骗局。

ALEX
What makes you think that?

亚历克斯
是什么让你这么想？

SHELLY BERGMAN
I do not believe the dome will be built. I think it's nothing more than a pipe dream, possibly a scam to entice gullible investors.

雪莉·伯格曼
我不相信圆顶会建成。我认为这只不过是一个白日梦，可能是一个引诱易受骗投资者的骗局。

ALEX
There are no investors. I'm paying for building the dome.

亚历克斯
没有投资者。我出钱建造圆顶。

SHELLY BERGMAN
Do you really expect me to believe that?

雪莉·伯格曼
你真的希望我相信吗？

ALEX
All that is delaying starting the construction is government approval and the community approving a new zoning ordinance before we start building.

亚历克斯
推迟开工的唯一原因是政府批准和社区批准新的分区条例，然后我们才能开始建设。

SHELLY BERGMAN
It may be another ten years before, you can get the environmental impact statements made, and the approval from the government.

雪莉·伯格曼
可能还需要十年时间，你才能完成环境影响报告并获得政府的批准。

ALEX
We have already got that done and signed off.

亚历克斯
我们已经完成并签署了。

SHELLY BERGMAN
How can that be, there is no public knowledge of it?

雪莉·伯格曼
怎么会这样，公众对此一无所知？

ALEX
The government was funded by us to hire companies to develop the environmental impact statements 2 years ago.

亚历克斯
两年前，我们资助政府聘请公司制定环境影响报告。

Because of the unique nature of this development, there really isn't an ecological impact anyone could prove one way or the other, plus the quality of life for the Dome inhabitants would be vastly improved, so the government signed the impact statement last week.

由于这一开发项目的独特性，实际上没有人能证明其对生态的影响，而且穹顶居民的生活质量将大大改善，因此政府上周签署了影响报告。

ALEX (Continued)
All we are doing now is waiting for two things: the local zoning rules and regulations so we can build appropriately, and approval from Denmark before we proceed.

我们现在所做的就是等待两件事：当地的分区规

则和法规，以便我们能够适当建设，以及丹麦的批准，然后才能继续进行。

SHELLY BERGMAN
What about all the materials and people?

雪莉·伯格曼
所有的材料和人员怎么办？

ALEX
It will take us six months to get the initial materials here and as soon as we obtain approval to start work, we'll immediately start sending people here to do projects we assign them to do.

亚历克斯
我们需要六个月的时间才能将初始材料运到这里，一旦我们获得开工批准，我们就会立即派人到这里来做我们指派他们做的项目。

SHELLY BERGMAN
How soon can that be?

雪莉·伯格曼
这要多久？

ALEX
Honestly? As early as next week if the Government of Denmark provides approvals.

亚历克斯
说实话？如果丹麦政府批准，最早下周就可以。

SHELLY BERGMAN
Do you believe they will approve the project?

雪莉·伯格曼
你真的相信他们会批准这个项目吗？

ALEX
My accountants and researchers have provided an economic impact statement that shows how much this venture will impact Denmark, their seriously interested in the project.

亚历克斯
我的会计师和研究人员提供了一份经济影响声
明，显示了这项投资对丹麦的影响有多大，他们
对这个项目非常感兴趣。

SHELLY BERGMAN
Why would Denmark be interested in building a Dome
City in Greenland?

雪莉·伯格曼
为什么丹麦会对在格陵兰建造圆顶城感兴趣？

ALEX
Here's two big reasons: steel and cement.

亚历克斯
有两个主要原因：钢铁和水泥。

SHELLY BERGMAN
Please explain?

雪莉·伯格曼
请解释一下？

ALEX
We'll manufacture the steel plates in Denmark as well
as the cement.

亚历克斯
我们将在丹麦生产钢板和水泥。

SHELLY BERGMAN
How much is that really going to be worth?

雪莉·伯格曼
这到底值多少钱？

ALEX
For starters think about 19.6 square miles of 1-inch-
thick steel plate. That's 40 pounds per square foot. At
$500 per ton, that's over $1 billion worth of steel. Also
with all the support structures, rebar for the pillars, and
all the specialty hardware and materials add another
$Billion.

亚历克斯

首先，想想 19.6 平方英里厚 1 英寸的钢板。每平方英尺重 40 磅。以每吨 500 美元计算，这些钢材价值超过 10 亿美元。此外，所有支撑结构、支柱钢筋以及所有特殊硬件和材料都将增加 10 亿美元

The steel mills will make a vast fortune in a short amount of time, huge utilization of technology and equipment. Same goes for the millions of cubic feet of cement that will be required.

钢厂将在短时间内赚得盆满钵满，大量利用厂房和设备。所需的数百万立方英尺水泥也是如此。

SHELLY BERGMAN

So effectively you are financially bribing the government with all the money the constituents will make to get the deal through?

雪莉·伯格曼

所以，你是在用选民赚的所有钱来贿赂政府，以让交易通过？

ALEX

I wouldn't call it effectively, I'd say pragmatically. We could have bought the steel cheaper in USA or China.

亚历克斯

我不会称之为有效，我会说是务实。我们可以在美国或中国以更便宜的价格购买钢材。

SHELLY BERGMAN
So why didn't you?

雪莉·伯格曼
那你为什么不呢？

ALEX

Buying materials from Denmark and Greenland will stimulate local economies.

亚历克斯
从丹麦和格陵兰购买材料将刺激当地经济。

SHELLY BERGMAN
What exactly are you buying from Greenland?

雪莉·伯格曼
你到底从格陵兰购买了什么？

ALEX

First of all, we'll most likely have a workforce of around 5,000 employees building the Dome so that we can get it completed in a few years. Then after that we'll build numerous buildings and structures inside the dome, which could take 10 years or longer, and require thousands of employees.

亚历克斯

首先，我们很可能会有大约 5,000 名员工来建造圆顶，这样我们就能在几年内完成它。然后，我们将在圆顶内建造许多建筑物和结构，这可能需要 10 年或更长时间，并需要数千名员工。

SHELLY BERGMAN
How does that relate to products?

雪莉·伯格曼
这与产品有什么关系？

ALEX

Those people will require shelter and living accommodations, food, tools, and services, all of which Greenland will provide. You currently do not have a Home Depot or Office Depot in Nuuk. As the dome is well on its way you will end up with several of these outlets.

这些人将需要住所和生活设施、食物、工具和服务，所有这些都将由格陵兰提供。你目前在努克没有 家得宝 或 办公仓库。随着圆顶的建设顺利进行，你最终会拥有其中的几家门店。

ALEX (Continued)
No doubt 50% or more of the work force will be locals as we prefer to hire locally, but we'll have to hire some talent to help build and train employees. They may bring their families with them as well, so we expect that by the 2nd year of construction Nuuk population could swell to 35,000.

亚历克斯 (持续)
毫无疑问，50% 或更多的劳动力将是当地人，因为我们更愿意在当地雇用，但我们必须雇用一些人才来帮助建设和培训员工。他们可能还会带着家人一起来，所以我们预计，到建设的第二年，努克的人口可能会增加到 35,000 人。

### SHELLY BERGMAN

Maybe the locals are not ready for such growth?

### 雪莉·伯格曼

也许当地人还没有准备好迎接这样的增长？

### ALEX

I can tell you about our contacts in Denmark and some of the local government are all for the growth.

### 亚历克斯

我可以告诉你，我们在丹麦的联系人和一些当地政府都支持这种增长。

### SHELLY BERGMAN

What other kinds of materials do you think Greenland can provide?

### 雪莉·伯格曼

你认为格陵兰还能提供哪些其他类型的材料？

### ALEX

The Greenland government is anxious to facilitate mining operations. Since there are vast limestone deposits and coal deposits here in Greenland located near the ocean in natural harbors. We would mine the coal and limestone to be used to produce Portland cement which we'll need huge quantities of in the construction.

### 亚历克斯

格陵兰政府急于促进采矿作业。由于格陵兰岛拥有丰富的石灰石矿床和煤矿，位于天然港口附近的海洋中。我们将开采煤和石灰石，用于生产波特兰水泥，而我们在建设中需要大量的水泥。

### SHELLY BERGMAN

So, you are saying you would produce a cement plant here in Greenland?

### 雪莉·伯格曼

所以你是说你会在格陵兰岛建造一座水泥厂？

ALEX

Yes, manufacturing the Portland cement here would be
a time saver as well as much cheaper than shipping it
from China, Mexico, or the United States where most
of the supply is.

亚历克斯

是的，在这里生产波特兰水泥比从中国、墨西哥
或美国运输更省时，也便宜得多，因为大部分供
应都在那里。

SHELLY BERGMAN

So, between Denmark and Greenland, all the steel
and cement used in the project would be made by this
country for this product.

雪莉·伯格曼

所以，丹麦和格陵兰之间，该项目使用的所有钢
材和水泥都将由该国生产。

ALEX

Absolutely, thus generating hundreds of millions in
tax revenue right away.

亚历克斯

当然，这样可以立即产生数亿的税收收入。

SHELLY BERGMAN

Mr. Baxter, I have one other question to ask you.

雪莉·伯格曼

巴克斯特先生，我还有一个问题要问您。

ALEX

Sure, go ahead.

亚历克斯

当然，请说。

SHELLY BERGMAN

Please forgive me for not telling you I'm a reporter
back at the University, but I didn't have time to show
you my credentials.

雪莉·伯格曼

请原谅我没有告诉您我在大学时是一名记者，但
是，我没有时间向您出示我的证件。

ALEX
That's quite alright, what's your question?

亚历克斯
没关系，您的问题是什么？

SHELLY BERGMAN
I noticed you walked out of the room following a
police detective I know, and had a short meeting with
him, is that about something the public should know
about?

雪莉·伯格曼
我注意到您跟着我认识的一名警探走出了房间，
并与他进行了短暂的会面，这是关于公众应该知
道的事情吗？

ALEX
No, it's a private matter, the police are handling it, and
I'm not at liberty to discuss it.

亚历克斯
不，这是私事，警方正在处理，我无权讨论。

SHELLY BERGMAN
You know I'll be contacting Mr. Hansen to get his
comments, I want to give you a chance to tell me your
version first.

雪莉·伯格曼
你知道我会联系汉森 先生征求他的意见，我想先
给你一个机会告诉我你的看法。

ALEX
I'm sorry, I can't discuss the matter.

亚历克斯
很抱歉，我不能讨论此事。

SHELLY BERGMAN
I see, ok, but I want you to know I do plan on following
up on that story.

雪莉·伯格曼
我明白了，好的，但我想让你知道我确实打算跟
进这个故事。

ALEX
Do what you need to do; it has nothing to do with the dome project.

亚历克斯
做你需要做的事；这与圆顶项目无关。

SHELLY BERGMAN
Are you sure about that?

雪莉·伯格曼
你确定吗？

ALEX
Absolutely.

亚历克斯
绝对确定。

Stephanie was sitting across from Claude Reardon. He didn't turn her on in the slightest manner, but Claude was interested in her each time he met, there was always invites.

斯蒂芬妮坐在克劳德·里尔登对面。他没有丝毫让她兴奋，但克劳德每次见面都对她感兴趣，总是会邀请她。

CLAUDE REARDON
How have you been Stephanie?

克劳德·里尔登
斯蒂芬妮，你过得怎么样？

STEPHANIE
Working my butt off.

斯蒂芬妮
我拼命工作。

CLAUDE REARDON
I figured you would be.

克劳德·里尔登
我猜你会的。

CLAUDE REARDON
(Thought)
Keeping Alex happy must be quite a chore, Stephanie probably has good stamina.

克劳德·里尔登
（想法）
让亚历克斯开心一定是一件苦差事，斯蒂芬妮可能很有耐力。

STEPHANIE
What did you think of our conference this morning?

斯蒂芬妮
你觉得我们今天早上的会议怎么样？

CLAUDE REARDON
Well, it's always best to get the public buy into a project like this before we move forward, as it will save us a lot of grief later.

克劳德·里尔登
好吧，在我们继续前进之前，让公众接受这样的项目总是最好的，因为这会为我们以后省去很多麻烦。

STEPHANIE
I think they will be very happy when we complete this project. People here are not used to seeing trees and lawns and flowers and flora that will exist inside the dome year-round.

斯蒂芬妮
我认为当我们完成这个项目时，他们会非常高兴。这里的人们不习惯看到树木、草坪、鲜花和植物，这些植物将全年存在于圆顶内。

CLAUDE REARDON
Certainly. By the way, when we all meet in New York next week, I have a nice restaurant I would like to take you too.

克劳德·里尔登
当然。顺便说一句，下周我们在纽约见面时，我有一家不错的餐厅想带你去。

Stephanie spoke as she thought:

斯蒂芬妮一边想一边说：

STEPHANIE (THOUGHT)
Maybe if I make Alex a little jealous, he might get more serious with me.

斯蒂芬妮（想）
也许如果我让亚历克斯嫉妒一点，他可能会对我
更认真。

STEPHANIE
Well, if Mr. Baxter allows me some free time, I'll
consider it,

斯蒂芬妮
好吧，如果巴克斯特先生允许我一些空闲时间，我会考虑的，

The meals were delicious; everyone was satisfied as the four men answered numerous questions about the project.

饭菜很美味；每个人都很满意，因为四个人回答了关于这个项目的许多问题。

Eventually the chitchat died down, a few of the guests, asked for a check so the manager came out and announced:

最后闲聊平息了，一些客人要求结账，于是经理出来宣布:

MANAGER RANDY CRAIG
Ladies and Gentlemen, the meals and drinks were paid by your host. You can all leave when you are ready and if anyone needs any more drinks or desserts, please let me know.

经理兰迪克雷格
女士们先生们，餐费和饮料由主人支付。你们准备好后就可以离开了，如果有人需要更多的饮料或甜点，请告诉我。

In about 10 minutes, people started excusing themselves and leaving and many walked up and shook Alex and the three amigo's hands. Stephanie, being quite attractive and charming acted as a tour director and as the people were leaving she escorted them to the elevator and thanked them for coming and gave each and every one of them a business card, which had phone numbers and address to their call center, where a corporate staffer answered the phone each day, screened and passed on messages to her or Alex if necessary.

大约 10 分钟后，人们开始告辞离开，许多人走上前来与亚历克斯和三个朋友握手。斯蒂芬妮非常迷人，她充当了导游的角色，当人们离开时，她护送他们到电梯，感谢他们的到来，并给了他们每个人一张名片，上面有他们的呼叫中心的电话号码和地址，公司职员每天都会接听电话，筛选信息并在必要时将信息传递给她或亚历克斯。

By 1:00 p.m. the place was almost deserted and the few remaining people who wanted to leave all left, the rest hung around and had more drinks and were told by the waiter, their drinks were paid for, and they could stay and drink more if they wanted, as Stephanie added some additional funds to allow them to stay longer and enjoy the moment.

到下午 1 点，这个地方几乎空无一人，剩下的几个想离开的人都离开了，其余的人还在附近，喝了更多的酒，服务员告诉他们，他们的酒钱已经付了，如果他们愿意，他们可以留下来喝更多的酒，因为斯蒂芬妮增加了一些额外的资金，让他们可以呆得更久，享受这一刻。

Alex, Stephanie, the three gentlemen, Adel, and Prof Grey, along with the News Reporter Shelley Bergman all walked out to their cars together and bid one another farewell, then hopped in their cars and departed. Some went to their hotels others like Alex and Stephanie went to the Airport.

亚历克斯、斯蒂芬妮、三位绅士、阿德尔和格雷教授，以及新闻记者雪莱·伯格曼一起走到他们的车旁，互相道别，然后跳上车离开。一些人去了酒店，其他人，比如亚历克斯和斯蒂芬妮，去了机场。

Shelley Bergman, realizing she had an incredible story was in a car with the North Ice News driver, Max Jacobsen.

雪莉·伯格曼意识到自己有一个令人难以置信的故事，于是和 北冰新闻的司机马克斯·雅各布森坐在一辆车里。

Shelly didn't know if she would get in any more questions but was curious as to where Alex was heading. Following at a subtle distance, they followed the Limo to the Airport, watched Alex and Stephanie get out, and were met by a man dressed in a professional pilot's uniform just like he was working for the airlines, who grabbed a suitcase from the Limo Driver.

雪莉不知道她是否会再被问到任何问题，但她很好奇亚历克斯要去哪里。他们保持着微妙的距离，跟着豪华轿车到了机场，看着亚历克斯和斯蒂芬妮下车，一个穿着专业飞行员制服的男人迎接了他们，就像他在航空公司工作一样，他从豪华轿车司机那里拿了一个手提箱。

Alex had an envelope in his suit which had the driver's tip in it, which was sealed. Alex and the other 2 walked through the air service building attached to the hanger his plane was towed out as soon as they all boarded. As soon as the plane was out of the hanger, the doors slid shut, the pilot Brad had already pre-flight checked the plane like he always did, restarted the Jet Engines and with permission from the tower, taxied out to the runway. Moments later they were Airborne heading back to Minnesota.

亚历克斯的西装外套里有一个信封，里面有司机的小费，信封是密封的。亚历克斯和其他两个人穿过与机库相连的航空服务大楼，他们一上飞机，飞机就被拖了出来。飞机一离开机库，门就滑了上去，飞行员布拉德已经像往常一样对飞机进行了飞行前检查，重新启动了喷气发动机，并在得到塔台的许可后，滑行到跑道上。片刻之后，他们就起飞返回明尼苏达州。

***

<u>**MUSIC FOR THE NEXT SECTION DURING VOICEOVER:**</u>

<u>画外音期间下一节的音乐：</u>

<u>https://www.youtube.com/watch?v=RgX7RNZ6P08</u>

Ottorino Respighi - Concerto in modo misolidio (1925)

VOICEOVER

Adel hung around with people who were somewhat radical, progressive, and in many circles considered eco-terrorists. Adel had no knowledge of what transpired between Alex and Stephanie the night before.

画外音

阿德尔与一些激进、进步的人混在一起，在很多圈子里，他们被认为是生态恐怖分子。阿德尔不知道前一天晚上 亚历克斯和 斯蒂芬妮之间发生了什么。

*Stephanie did a great job of not displaying she had been traumatized the night before. Nor did Adel spot Rodney Hansen quickly enter the conference room and suddenly leave with for a few minutes with Alex, or she might have suspected something was going wrong.*

斯蒂芬妮做得很好，没有表现出她前一天晚上受到了创伤。阿德尔也没有发现 罗德尼·汉森 迅速进入会议室，然后突然和 亚历克斯一起离开几分钟，否则她可能会怀疑出了什么问题。

*Hans Jespersen spent a lot of time in Adel's apartment, they were casual friends but not lovers and traveled in the same circle of what some in the community considered undesirable.*

汉斯·杰斯帕森 （*Hans Jespersen*) 在 阿德尔的公寓里呆了很长时间，他们是普通朋友，但不是恋人，并且和社区里一些人认为不受欢迎的人处于同一个圈子里。

*The undesirables had a large appetite for marijuana and when several of the drug traffickers and businessmen traveled to Nuuk from Iceland quite a bit, there had been many nights when several of these acquaintances were feasting on Cocaine, Heroin, and other narcotics.*

不良分子对大麻有着极大的胃口，当一些毒贩和商人从冰岛前往努克时，很多个晚上，这些熟人中有几个人正在大吃可卡因、海洛因和其他麻醉品。

*Greenland had a growing heroin epidemic, and Adel did not realize much of it related to Hans who was much a failure in life and when he got desperate for money slowly sunk into the quagmire of being a useful idiot to those drug cartel people from Iceland.*

格陵兰岛的海洛因泛滥日益严重，阿德尔没有意识到这与汉斯有很大关系，汉斯在生活中是个失败者，当他极度需要钱时，他慢慢陷入了成为冰岛贩毒集团成员的有用白痴的泥潭。

*Iceland which in recent years became a tourist destination due to the governments lax attitude towards marijuana and prostitution, now had a burgeon recreational drug industry.*

近年来，由于政府对大麻和卖淫的松懈态度，冰岛成为了一个旅游目的地，现在娱乐性毒品行业蓬勃发展。

*As Hans slipped deeper and deeper into the psychological impact of drug abuse and self-rehabilitation and relapsed back into addiction, his environmental radicalism grew proportionally.*

随着汉斯越来越深地陷入吸毒和自我康复的心理影响并再次染上毒瘾，他的环境激进主义也成比例地增长。

*Adel became invited to investigate the Dome Proposal by the Mayor of Nuuk and asked to provide him an analysis since she had a position in the university that studied resources, environmental impact and many other aspects of large-scale development.*

阿黛尔被努克市长邀请调查穹顶计划时，市长要求她提供一份分析报告，因为她在大学里担任职务，研究资源、环境影响和大规模开发的许多其它方面。

*The mayor provided Adel with all the documentation Alex and his business associates had provided the Major's office, but also the contact information and in a letter to Alex. The mayor of Nuuk suggested Alex work the rollout of the promotion through Adel.*

市长向阿黛尔提供了亚历克斯和他的商业伙伴向市长办公室提供的所有文件，以及联系信息，并在给亚历克斯的一封信中，努克市长建议亚历克斯通过阿黛尔开展推广活动。

*Adel wasn't the most organized housekeeper in the world is an understatement. Often, just like an absent-minded professor, she left numerous documents on her coffee table in her condo that overlooked the bay on the West side of Nuuk.*

阿黛尔不是世界上最有条理的管家，这只是轻描淡写。她经常像一个心不在焉的教授一样，把许多文件放在她公寓的咖啡桌上，公寓俯瞰着努克西侧的海湾。

*Hans, who often showed up with good smoke and sometimes a nice dose of Cocaine he thought would help develop inroads of romance to Adel.*

汉斯经常带着好烟，有时还带着一剂可卡因，他认为这有助于发展与阿黛尔的恋情。

*On one of those occasions, Hans observed numerous articles often laid out on the coffee table, including documents he was not authorized to look at.*

在其中一次，汉斯发现咖啡桌上经常摆放着许多文章，包括他无权查看的文件。

*Hans saw private documents including students' papers and grades, and sometimes personally identifiable information (PII).*

汉斯查看了私人文件，包括学生的论文和成绩，有时还有个人身份信息 (PII)。

*The PII Hans observed including identification numbers, foreign passport information and even sometimes Americans social security numbers of visiting professors and sometimes rarely, graduate students PII that came to Nuuk's University for specialty courses on Greenland.*

汉斯观察到的 *PII* 包括身份证号码、外国护照信息，有时甚至是客座教授的美国人社会保障号码，有时甚至是来努克大学学习格陵兰专业课程的研究生 PII。

*Since Hans never discussed his accidental and often unauthorized viewing of these PII documents, Adel in her unsophisticated manner assumed Hans was just another doper and could give a damn what was there.*

由于汉斯从未谈论过他意外且经常未经授权查看这些 *PII* 文件，阿黛尔以她天真的方式认为汉斯只是另一个吸毒者，根本不在乎那里面有什么。

*Adel's recklessness and carelessness provided that window of opportunity one evening while Adel excused herself and went to the restroom for a couple minutes.*

一天晚上，阿黛尔找借口去洗手间几分钟，而她的鲁莽和粗心为他提供了机会。

*The sudden quiet and lack of focus presented Hans with an opportunity to spot one of Alex's letters on the coffee table which Adel had already read and simply had not discarded it.*

突然的安静和注意力不集中让汉斯有机会在咖啡桌上发现亚历克斯的一封信，阿黛尔已经读过了，只是没有把它扔掉。

*Hans discarded it for her after he read a little bit of it, stuffed it in his pocket and after a good smoke of some really good "shit" with Adel, then shortly departed to his miserable rundown apartment only a few blocks away, trudging through knee deep snow feeling a good buzz.*

汉斯读了一点之后就把它丢给了她，塞进口袋里，和阿德尔一起抽了一大口好烟后，不久就动身去了离他只有几个街区远的破旧公寓，在齐膝深的雪中跋涉，感觉很兴奋。

*Hans entered his apartment, which might seem like inside a refrigerator to visiting Americans, but Hans blood often had plenty of Vodka as antifreeze and having lived in the Arctic all his life felt 40 degrees Fahrenheit as a warm day.*

汉斯走进他的公寓，在来访的美国人来说，这公寓可能看起来像冰箱里，但汉斯的血液中经常含有大量的伏特加作为防冻剂，而且他一生都住在北极，所以在温暖的日子里，华氏 40 度也感觉很温暖。

*Hans grabbed some smoked fish, a bottle of vodka, ate and drank until his belly was feeling good, then walked over to a rundown sofa that doubled as his bed, laid back pulled out the papers and read about a page before he fell asleep.*

汉斯抓起一些熏鱼和一瓶伏特加，吃喝直到肚子舒服了，然后走到一张破旧的沙发（也是他的床）旁，躺下来拿出报纸，读了一页，然后睡着了。

*The next morning around 9:00 a.m. when the sun was rising light beams that came through Hans partially effective curtains was suddenly on his face around his eyes which seemed to wake him up. When Hans suddenly opened his eyes and temporarily blinded by the strong sunlight, his slumber was disrupted for another day.*

第二天早上 9 点左右，太阳刚刚升起，透过汉斯半遮半掩的窗帘射出的光线突然照在他眼睛周围，似乎把他吵醒了。当汉斯突然睁开眼睛，强烈的阳光让他暂时失明时，他的睡眠又被打乱了。

*Hans sat up suddenly feeling hungry, grabbed some of the smoked fish, and grabbed the vodka bottle that was still 1/3 full and took a nice drink to help wash down that smoked fish, which was kind of dry.*

汉斯突然饿了，坐了起来，抓起一些熏鱼，抓起还剩三分之一的伏特加酒瓶，喝了一大口，把熏鱼冲下去，熏鱼有点干。

*Hans then stood up suddenly feeling the urge to urinate, then came back from the bathroom and noticed the papers laying around he started to read the night before.*

汉斯突然站起来，有尿意，然后从浴室回来，发现他昨晚开始看的报纸散落在四周。

*Hans was intelligent. He did well in school, but at the time he was in his second year of college, his family was struggling, and he had to drop out and work as a fisherman to help maintain his family since his parents was living in poverty and the government subsidies just didn't cover enough of their expenses.*

汉斯相当聪明。他在学校表现很好，但当时他上大学二年级，家里很困难，他不得不辍学，当渔夫来维持家庭生计，因为他的父母生活贫困，政府的补贴根本无法支付足够的费用。

*Han's bitterness of losing his education accelerated his value system towards the proletariat and eventually immersed himself into radical environmentalism.*

汉斯失去教育的痛苦加速了他的价值观转向无产阶级，并最终投身于激进的环保主义。

*Anyone who was rich was automatically Hans' enemy, and anytime he saw new buildings going up, as far as he was concerned it was all about exploitation of the Greenland Inuit population.*

任何有钱人都是汉斯的敌人，每当他看到新建筑拔地而起时，在他看来，这都是对格陵兰因纽特人的剥削。

*Even though Hans took a swig from the Vodka bottle he was nowhere near inebriated, and was momentarily cogent, grabbed the letter, and read it to the end, which had 7 pages including many aspects of the Dome Project.*

尽管汉斯喝了一口伏特加酒，但他一点也不醉，而且一时头脑清醒，抓起信，读到了最后，信一共有7页，包括穹顶计划的许多方面。

*By the time Hans finished page seven, his demeanor showed strong signs of agitation. Though this did not trigger any actions at the time, it planted a foundation in Hans that would eventually set in motion actions that would irrevocably change his life forever.*

当汉斯读完第七页时，他的举止表现出强烈的激动迹象。虽然这当时并没有引发任何行动，但它在汉斯心中埋下了基础，最终启动了行动，永远不可逆转地改变了他的生活。

*It wasn't until weeks later that agitation grew to a full blaze when he saw a newspaper laying on Adel's coffee table, that had a newspaper article about a Mr. Baxter who would be soon arriving in Nuuk, to present a hair brained scheme to build a god-awful ugly dome city.*

直到几周后，当他看到阿德尔咖啡桌上放着一张报纸时，他的焦虑才达到了顶峰，报纸上有一篇关于一位巴克斯特先生的文章，他即将抵达努克，提出一个愚蠢的计划，建造一座丑陋得令人发指的圆顶城市。

*The newspaper article, written by Shelley Bergman said it was a pipe dream, though she acknowledged some of the huge construction projects Alex Baxter had accomplished in the past. Alex's past construction success meant there was a distinct possibility the project could proceed.*

这篇由雪莱·伯格曼撰写的报纸文章说，这是一个白日梦，尽管她承认亚历克斯·巴克斯特过去完成过一些大型建筑项目。亚历克斯过去的建筑成功意味着该项目很有可能真正进行下去。

*If there was anyone in the world who could pull off a Domed City, it would be this and only this guy, Alex Baxter.*

如果世界上有谁能建造圆顶城市，那一定是这个，也是唯一一个，亚历克斯·巴克斯特。

*At the present time with the storms in the North Atlantic and Davis Straits between Greenland and Canada, there would not be any fishing for several weeks. Idle time tends to have a negative impact on people.*

目前，北大西洋和格陵兰岛与加拿大之间的戴维斯海峡正遭遇风暴，几周内都无法捕鱼。空闲时间往往会对人们产生负面影响。

*Han's idle time allowed him to multiply his emotions and made stopping this Dome City his purpose in life.*

汉的空闲时间让他的情绪倍增，并把阻止这座圆顶城市作为他人生的目标。

***

A week after Alex left Greenland and completed the initial conferences there, the 4 men met in New York to discuss the project and latest developments. Air Traffic Control directed N80973 (Baxter-1) to Turn right on course 044 to final approach to runway 04R.

亚历克斯离开格陵兰并在那里完成初步会议一周后，四人在纽约会面，讨论该项目和最新进展。空中交通管制指示 N80973（Baxter-1）在 044 航线上右转，最后进近至 04R 跑道。

Brad Johnson was the only pilot flying today, so Alex went forward and set in the right seat, put on the headphones and observed the final approach. Coming over the water, the end of the runway was not very far from water's edge.

今天只有布拉德·约翰逊一人驾驶飞机，所以亚历克斯走上前去，坐在右边的座位上，戴上耳机，观察最后进近。飞机飞过水面时，跑道的尽头离水边不远。

Within seconds of passing over land, they were on the runway and slowing down. Following ground control instructions, Brad piloted the Gulfstream over to Total Global Aviation (TGA) hanger where 4 private jets were currently parked, and Alex's jet would soon be towed into.

飞过陆地几秒钟后，他们就上了跑道并减速。按照地面控制指令，布拉德驾驶湾流飞机飞到道达尔全球航空 (TGA) 机库，那里目前停着 4 架私人飞机，亚历克斯的飞机很快就会被拖进去。

Alex came to NYC off and on, many times stopping over on his way to Switzerland while dealing with bankers on his future deals. He was used to getting ripped off by TGA who during normal times tried to leach snow rates out of rich guys.

亚历克斯断断续续地来到纽约，在去瑞士的路上，他多次在这里停留，与银行家讨论未来的交易。他已经习惯了被 TGA 欺骗，因为 TGA 在正常情况下会试图从有钱人那里榨取雪费。

Alex was willing to pay the high fee for a couple reasons, one is that as long as you paid TGA what they wanted, nobody was going to mess with your plane. If there were any service requirements, such as replacing a jet engine after sucking in some Canadian Geese that did some severe damage, Alex knew he could count on TGA who had an outstanding repair track record. Alex also understood you pay for quality.

亚历克斯愿意支付高额费用有几个原因，一是只要你支付 TGA 想要的费用，就没有人会弄乱你的飞机。如果有任何服务要求，比如在吸入一些加拿大鹅造成严重损坏后更换喷气式发动机，亚历克斯知道他可以信赖拥有出色维修记录的 TGA。亚历克斯还明白，花钱是为了质量。

TGA guys had all the connections especially if you would get that engine replaced today if you needed to go somewhere. It wasn't cheap, but you knew their timelines were not BS. TGA always lived up to their quotes in time and in the end was worth the money.

TGA 的人人脉广泛，特别是如果你需要去某个地方，今天就更换发动机。这并不便宜，但你知道他们的时间表不是胡扯。TGA 总是按时完成他们的报价，最终物有所值。

The other reason Alex liked TGA was the security apparatus whisked you out of the FAA controlled area into your waiting Limo's almost instantaneously. Conversely if you were leaving NY and paid those high rates to park your jet there, if you called ahead, they would have your jet out of the hanger, ready for preflight checks and passengers loaded up through security in about 5 minutes after arrival to the facility.

亚历克斯喜欢 TGA 的另一个原因是，安全机构几乎可以立即将你从 FAA 控制区送入等候你的豪华轿车。相反，如果您要离开纽约并支付高昂的费用将您的飞机停在那里，如果您提前打电话，他们会让您的飞机离开机库，准备好进行飞行前检查，并在抵达设施后约 5 分钟内让乘客通过安检。

The Limo Service Alex always used, covered the 25 miles from Manhattan to JFK Airport in all kinds of traffic conditions, including taking back roads as necessary during congestion.

亚历克斯经常使用的豪华轿车服务覆盖了从曼哈顿到肯尼迪机场的　25英里路程，在各种交通状况下，包括在拥堵期间根据需要走小路。

With no exceptions, Alex had an envelope with cash in it for the Limo Driver every time he left NY. The Limo Company loved Alex as a customer and Alex always requested Rodriguez in advance.

亚历克斯每次离开纽约时，都会毫无例外地给豪华轿车司机一个装有现金的信封。豪华轿车公司喜欢亚历克斯这个客户，亚历克斯总是提前要求罗德里格斯。

The other drivers suspected Rodriguez got nice tips, but its most likely they would be eternally jealous if they knew the size of the tips Alex paid him, especially when he needed him to drive about 25 miles over the speed limit to get him to his Jet in time to get out of town in time to almost be home in time for dinner.

其他司机怀疑罗德里格斯得到了不错的小费，但如果他们知道亚历克斯付给他的小费数额，他们很可能会永远嫉妒，尤其是当他需要他以超过限速 25 英里的速度开车送他到他的飞机上，以便及时离开城镇，几乎可以及时回家吃晚饭的时候。

In front of the hanger, John Black stood IAW FAA regulations to escort the passengers to the lobby past the security checkpoint to get to their waiting transportation.

在机库前，约翰·布莱克　按照联邦航空管理局的规定，护送乘客通过安检点到达大厅，前往等候的交通工具。

Today was no different as John Black escorted Alex and Stephanie through the security check point and out to the curb where Rodriguez immediately pulled up at the expected time. Rodriguez got out of the car, walked around and opened the passenger door just as the group was arriving at the Limo.

今天也不例外，约翰·布莱克护送亚历克斯和斯蒂芬妮通过安检点，来到路边，罗德里格斯在预计的时间立即停了下来。罗德里格斯下了车，走了一圈，就在他们到达豪华轿车时打开了乘客门。

Alex faced John Black and announced:

亚历克斯面对约翰·布莱克宣布：

ALEX

This is going to be a short business meeting. I'll be back in a few hours.

亚历克斯

这将是一个简短的商务会议。我几个小时后就回来。

JOHN BLACK

I should be here when you get back Mr. Baxter. You got my number, call me a couple minutes before you arrive back here and I'll be out front to escort you immediately through security.

约翰·布莱克

巴克斯特先生，你回来时我应该在这里。你有我的电话号码，在你回来前几分钟给我打电话，我会在前面护送你通过安检。

ALEX

Thank you, John, I'll certainly call you for a heads up.

亚历克斯

谢谢你，约翰，我一定会给你打电话通知你。

Alex then held his hand out to shake John's. Immediately after the handshake, Alex moved into the Limo and sat down next to Stephanie and Rodriguez shut his door.

亚历克斯然后伸出手和约翰握手。握手之后，亚历克斯立即坐进豪华轿车，坐在斯蒂芬妮旁边，罗德里格斯关上了车门。

RODRIGUEZ
Where too boss?

罗德里格斯
老板去哪儿了？

ALEX
120 Wall Street.

亚历克斯
华尔街 120 号。

RODRIGUEZ
Not a problem.

罗德里格斯
没问题。

As usual Brad stayed with the plane, and if the trip was short enough, would simply get a bite to eat somewhere in the Airport Complex and get right back to the plane and wait for Alex to return to head home.

像往常一样，布拉德留在飞机旁，如果旅程足够短，他会在机场综合大楼的某个地方吃点东西，然后直接回到飞机上，等待亚历克斯回来回家。

Brad soon made a trip over to Buffalo Wild Wings, where Brad bought the TGA aircraft mechanic lunch who they used if work was ever needed on the plane. The mechanic gave Brad a ride over to the restaurant then back after they finished their Buffalo Wings.

布拉德很快就去了一趟 布法罗野生鸡翅，在那里，布拉德为 TGA 飞机机械师买了午餐，如果飞机需要维修，他们就会找他。机械师把布拉德送到餐厅，然后在他们吃完 Buffalo Wings 后回来。

BRAD
I'm going to remain inside and wait in the plane since
Alex will be back in a couple hours.

布拉德
我要留在里面，在飞机里等着，因为亚历克斯几
个小时后就会回来。

TGA MECHANIC
I'll be here in the hanger working on the jet parked
next to your jet in case you need something.

TGA 机械师
我会在机库里修理停在你飞机旁边的飞机，以防
你需要什么。

BRAD
Thanks, I appreciate that.

布拉德
谢谢，我很感激。

TGA MECHANIC
Thanks for the Wings, that hit the spot.

TGA 机械师
感谢 翅膀，它恰到好处。

All six seats in the aircraft were recliners. Brad would recline a seat on the port side Alex never sat in and take a nice comfortable nap.

飞机上的所有六个座位都是躺椅。布拉德会把亚历克斯从不坐的左舷座位放倒，然后舒服地小睡一会儿。

Alex would always call when he was returning so Brad could then make arrangements to move the plane out of the hanger in preparation for leaving. If more fuel was needed, it would be taken on at this time.

亚历克斯回来时总会打电话，这样布拉德就可以安排将飞机移出机库，准备离开。如果需要更多燃料，就会在这个时候加油。

The Early afternoon traffic was light as commuters were several hours away from their trek home, most of which would be by subway and train, though in some cases people who could afford the parking and desired to drive in Manhattan clogged the roads about that time.

下午早些时候的交通很畅通，因为通勤者距离回家还有几个小时的路程，其中大部分人会乘坐地铁和火车，但在某些情况下，那些有钱停车并想在曼哈顿开车的人会在那个时候堵塞道路。

The private jet hanger was just off interstate 678, which the Limo took and proceeded to Interstate 678 over to Grand Central Parkway, I-278E and FDR Drive to Water Street, then on to Wall Street. 120 Wall Street was about 4 minutes later. This was undoubtedly the quickest route, a total of 25 miles and took 45 minutes.

私人飞机机库就在 678 号州际公路旁，豪华轿车沿着这条路行驶，然后前往 678 号州际公路，经过中央公园大道、I-278E 和 FDR 大道，到达水街，然后前往华尔街。大约 4 分钟后到达华尔街 120 号。这无疑是最快的路线，总共 25 英里，耗时 45 分钟。

EXT. DAY. BUILDING AT 120 WALL STREET, NEW YORK CITY.

外景。纽约市华尔街 **120** 号大楼。

Even though on the outside, the building at 120 Wall Street was apparent that it was an older building with its style and not so imposing structure compared to some of the buildings around it, due to its location and views of the river, bridge, and piers, it was an attractive real estate location. This is why Claude Rearden had purchased and leased quite a bit of space in the 120 Wall Street building.

尽管从外观上看，华尔街 120 号的这栋建筑显然是一座风格老旧、结构不那么宏伟的建筑，但鉴于其地理位置以及河流、桥梁和码头的景观，这栋建筑是一个颇具吸引力的房地产位置。这就是 克劳德·里尔登购买并租赁华尔街 120 号大楼相当多空间的原因。

Rodriguez drove the Limo up to the curb in front of the main entrance to the building. As on prior agreement, Alex did not want Rodriguez to get out of the Limo to open the door for 2 reasons, one is New Yorkers drive like crazy maniacs at time and its hazardous for a Limo driver to get out with that traffic buzzing beside him, and the other was Alex could get back in the car quickly and Rodriguez could make a fast get away with him if there was some security concern.

罗德里格斯驾驶豪华轿车停在大楼正门前的路边。根据之前的协议，Alex 不想让 罗德里格斯下车开门，原因有两个：一是纽约人有时开车像疯子一样疯狂，豪华轿车司机在车流喧闹的情况下下车很危险；二是如果存在安全问题，亚历克斯可以很快回到车里，罗德里格斯可以迅速逃脱。

There was usually a porter outside the building who loved opening doors on limousines that pulled up such as this afternoon.

大楼外面通常有一个搬运工，他喜欢打开今天下午停下的豪华轿车的车门。

The door opened, and both Rodriguez and Alex easily recognized Leroy Jones, former NFL linebacker and Marine Corps Officer. His job was not only opening Limo Doors, but Leroy Jones was also part of the defensive infrastructure of the building. He wore an earpiece and a microphone and there was plenty of surveillance video.

门开了，罗德里格斯和亚历克斯都很容易就认出了前 NFL 后卫兼海军陆战队军官 莱罗伊·琼斯。他的工作不仅是打开豪华轿车的门，莱罗伊·琼斯还是大楼防御基础设施的一部分。他戴着耳机和麦克风，有大量的监控视频。

A lot of very wealthy clients moved in and out of 120 Wall Street all day long and with the heightened terrorist threat, they needed a fast thinking combat experienced person directing the reaction forces.

很多非常富有的客户整天进出华尔街 120 号，随着恐怖主义威胁的加剧，他们需要一个思维敏捷、经验丰富的战斗人员来指挥反应部队。

Leroy Jones was the perfect fit; nobody would suspect he was a former Marine Corp Lieutenant with a tour of duty with the Recon Rangers in the 2003 invasion of Iraq.

莱罗伊·琼斯是完美的人选，没有人会怀疑他是前海军陆战队中尉，曾在 2003 年入侵伊拉克时在侦察突击队服役。

Alex nor did anyone else know the elaborate security apparatus, that Leroy quarterbacked, during prime-time business hours 10:00 a.m. until 3 p.m.

亚历克斯和其他人都不知道 勒罗伊在黄金时段（上午 10:00 到下午 3:00）负责的复杂安保机构。

Leroy didn't mind playing the ruse because he got a lot of tips. Alex always handed him a $100.

勒罗伊不介意耍花招，因为他得到了很多小费。亚历克斯总是给他 100 美元。

Leroy Jones, being a kind and generous individual, who had a couple vets on his staff, usually used the tip money to buy their lunches. Thanks to Leroy's body build, from playing in the NFL and later volunteering with the Marines after 9/11, easily hid the shoulder strap concealed weapon.

莱罗伊·琼斯，是个善良慷慨的人，他的员工中有几名退伍军人，他通常用小费钱给他们买午餐。由于 勒罗伊的体格健壮，他曾在 NFL 打球，后来在 9/11 之后志愿加入海军陆战队，因此他很容易就把肩带上的暗藏武器藏了起来。

Leroy had an assistant, in a room just inside the entrance with security monitors manned by his handpicked veterans, had an Uzi submachinegun ready if more fire power was needed. Leroy wore body armor, but it was concealed under his shirt and suit coat.

勒罗伊有一个助手，在入口处的房间里，有他精心挑选的退伍军人监控的安全监视器，如果需要更多的火力，助手准备了一把乌兹冲锋枪。勒罗伊穿着防弹衣，但藏在衬衫和西装外套下面。

Most people just thought Leroy was slightly obese black guy. Stripped of all his body armor and weapons, he was physically well-built and conditioned and worked out every day, and if it wasn't for his age, would be a viable NFL player.

大多数人都认为 勒罗伊是个有点肥胖的黑人。脱掉所有的防弹衣和武器后，他体格健壮，身体素质好，每天都锻炼身体，如果不是年纪大，他可以成为一名有前途的 NFL 球员。

Leroy knew Alex and Rodriguez because they made routine trips to the building, ever since Claude Rearden and Alex Baxter started talks on the Dome project.

勒罗伊认识亚历克斯和罗德里格斯，因为自从克劳德·里尔登和亚历克斯·巴克斯特开始就穹顶项目进行谈判以来，他们经常前往该建筑。

Even though Alex was more than willing to pick up all the initial costs, other investors wanted in on it.

尽管亚历克斯非常愿意承担所有初始成本，但其他投资者也想加入其中。

Routinely people from major Wall Street Investment Bankers and large Banks came to 120

Wall Street to meet with Claude.

华尔街主要投资银行家和大型银行的人员经常来到华尔街 120 号与克劳德会面。

Not long ago, a large investment banker wanted to shove Alex out of the picture but would only commit to the huge investment if they could bring a large bank into the project as a partner assuming half the risk.

不久前，一家大型投资银行家想把亚历克斯排除在外，但只有在他们能让一家大型银行作为合作伙伴加入该项目并承担一半风险的情况下，他们才会承诺巨额投资。

Unfortunately, after Alex shorted the Bank's stock real hard and forced them to lose $10 Billion in the United Kingdom debacle sometime during the "great recession," in retaliation for screwing him on $1 billion worth of Mortgage bonds, they were in no mood to cross Alex for fear of more retaliation in the future.

不幸的是，在亚历克斯在"大衰退"期间的某个时候，为了报复亚历克斯在价值 10 亿美元的抵押贷款债券上欺骗他，他大量做空了该银行的股票，并迫使他们在英国大萧条期间损失了 100 亿美元，他们不想与亚历克斯作对，因为担心将来会遭到更多的报复。

Once the President of the Bank informed the Investment Bankers they were not interested in a large investment but would be interested in a modest investment as a partner to the group, The Investment Banker then stood down their efforts to oust Alex, which was a good thing because Alex had the knowhow to make the investment bankers just as uncomfortable as he did the Large Bank assets in Great Britain.

当银行行长告知投资银行家们他们对大笔投资不感兴趣，但愿意作为集团的合作伙伴进行适度投资时，投资银行家们便放弃了驱逐亚历克斯的努力，这是件好事，因为亚历克斯知道如何让投资银行家们感到不舒服，就像他让英国的大型银行资产感到不舒服一样。

Having investment bankers as well as the large bank as partners was a much better approach since, they would all make money together and there would be no hostilities. This was fine with Alex, since it streamlined his ability to move money from

Switzerland through Investment Banks and Banks to fund the project, and he didn't have to cough up all the initial outlays in the beginning.

让投资银行家和大型银行成为合作伙伴是一种更好的方法，因为他们可以一起赚钱，而且不会有敌意。亚历克斯对此很满意，因为这简化了他通过投资银行和银行从瑞士转移资金来资助该项目的能力，而且他不必在开始时就支付所有的初始支出。

Having spotted Rodrigues through the Limo windshield, Leroy Jones promptly approached the Limo to open the passenger side door. Rodriguez waved to Leroy as he the car, and Leroy responded with a smile and a brief wave back and then grabbed the door handle. Even though he could not see who was inside, he knew there was a great possibility it was Alex.

透过豪华轿车的挡风玻璃看到了罗德里格斯，莱罗伊·琼斯迅速走近豪华轿车，打开了副驾驶侧的车门。罗德里格斯下车时向莱罗伊挥手致意，莱罗伊微笑着回应，挥了挥手，然后抓住了车门把手。尽管他看不到车内的人是谁，但他知道很有可能是亚历克斯。

The door opened, Alex got out, held out his hand to shake Leroy's and passed him a $100 bill in the handshake.

车门打开了，亚历克斯下车伸出手与莱罗伊握手，并在握手时递给他一张 100 美元的钞票。

**LEROY JONES**
Good morning Mr. Baxter.

莱罗伊·琼斯
早上好，巴克斯特先生。

**ALEX**
Hello Leroy, how you doing today?

亚历克斯
你好，莱罗伊，你今天过得怎么样？

**LEROY JONES**
Not bad, I can't complain, it's not freezing cold today
and it's not raining or snowing, so I'll count my
blessings.

莱罗伊·琼斯
还不错，没什么可抱怨的，今天不冷，也不下雨
也不下雪，所以我会感恩。

As soon as Leroy shut the door, Rodriguez drove off and went about his business, but knew he'd be back within an hour to drive Alex back to the airport.

莱罗伊一关上车门，罗德里格斯就开车走了，去做他的事情，但他知道他会在一小时内回来，把亚历克斯送回机场。

ALEX

Yep, you could be stuck in Greenland where I just spent some time. We all need to count our blessings; it could be much worse.

亚历克斯

是的，你可能会被困在格陵兰岛，我刚刚在那里呆了一段时间。我们都需要感恩；情况可能会更糟。

LEROY JONES

I've been to some bad places in my days Mr. Baxter.

莱罗伊·琼斯

我这辈子去过一些非常糟糕的地方，巴克斯特先生。

ALEX

No doubt you have Leroy. Good to see you again.

亚历克斯

毫无疑问，莱罗伊 是你的人选。很高兴再次见到你。

LEROY JONES
Same here sir.

莱罗伊·琼斯
我也是，先生。

Alex had a distinct admiration for Leroy and knew quite a bit about him. During one of his conversations with Claude Rearden, he was informed about Leroy's football career and volunteering for the Marine Corp after 9/11. Right in his prime as an NFL linebacker, he gave up a million-dollar salary to go serve his country. That type of patriotism seemed to be less and less these days, which Alex felt was a sad state of affairs.

亚历克斯非常钦佩 莱罗伊·琼斯，对他了解颇多。在与 克劳德·里尔登的一次谈话中，他了解到 莱罗伊 的足球生涯以及 9/11 事件后志愿加入海军陆战队的情况。在他作为 NFL 后卫的巅峰时期，他放弃了百万美元的薪水去为国家服务。如今，这种爱国主义似乎越来越少，亚历克斯觉得这是一种可悲的状况。

Alex quickly surmised a former Marine Corp Captain, wasn't really a porter, but security apparatus required some innovative thinking, and disguising the security quarterback in this manner, would go a long way to confuse potential adversaries and at the same time add an additional layer of security during such troubling times.

亚历克斯很快推测出前海军陆战队上尉并不是真正的搬运工，但安全机构需要一些创新思维，以这种方式伪装安全四分卫，将在很大程度上混淆潜在对手，同时在如此困难的时期增加额外的安全保障。

They also needed an intelligent person who did not suffer from vigilance decrement, who was always on his game plan to intervene promptly, when necessary, in case a radicalized terrorist happened to come by with explosives.

他们还需要一个聪明的人，不会因为警惕性下降而受到影响，他总是按照自己的计划在必要时迅速干预，以防激进的恐怖分子碰巧带着炸药过来。

As soon as Alex arrived and was safe in the building, Leroy called Claude Rearden. Claude saw on the caller I.D. it was Leroy, so he answered

亚历克斯到达并安全进入大楼后，勒罗伊立即打电话给克劳德·里尔登。克劳德在来电显示上看到是勒罗伊，于是他接了电话

CLAUDE REARDEN
Hello Leroy.

克劳德·里尔登
你好，勒罗伊。

LEROY JONES

Mr. Rearden, Mr. Baxter and Ms. McFarland have just entered the building and are on their way up to see you.

勒罗伊·琼斯

里尔登先生、巴克斯特先生和麦克法兰女士刚刚进入大楼，正在上楼见你。

CLAUDE REARDEN
Thanks for the report, Leroy.

克劳德·里尔登
谢谢你的报告，勒罗伊。

LEROY JONES
My pleasure, Mr. Rearden.

勒罗伊·琼斯
我很荣幸，里尔登先生。

Claude Rearden then hung up the I-phone as he pressed the red phone icon.

克劳德·里尔登按下红色电话图标后挂断了 艾-打电话。

Leroy knew Claude Rearden is a busy man and expected him to abruptly hang up. He had performed his mission this afternoon of ensuring he reported Alex's arrival immediately so Rearden could put any activity aside and be prepared for his entry.

勒罗伊知道克劳德·里尔登是个大忙人，他以为他会突然挂断电话。他今天下午已经完成了任务，确保立即报告亚历克斯的到来，这样里尔登就可以放下一切活动，为他的到来做好准备。

From a distance 120 Wall Street didn't look impressive. But when you approached the gold-plated door and entrance, you realized really quickly this might be much more than a small building. 120 Wall was completed in 1930 and located in New York City's financial district.

从远处看，华尔街 120 号并不令人印象深刻。但当你走近镀金的大门和入口时，你很快意识到这可能不仅仅是一座小建筑。华尔街 120 号于 1930 年竣工，位于纽约市金融区。

The building is 399 ft with 34 floors. The building housed 36 of the most prestigious non-profit organizations, which in some way led to Claude choosing the site for the Dome project since it really was the very first non-profit effort of gigantic proportions, dwarfing all others combined.

这栋建筑高 399 英尺，有 34 层。这栋建筑内有 36 个最负盛名的非营利组织，这在某种程度上让克劳德选择了穹顶项目的地点，因为它确实是第一个规模巨大的非盈利项目，使所有其他项目的总和相形见绌。

With Greenland the initial project to be followed up by dome construction in Siberia and another at 29 Palms in California, if all went well, the building would one day be too small to house all the space needed, but headquarters would remain there simply as a way to develop conduits with the other non-profit organizations. The downside was they were already hitting Alex and Claude Rearden up for donations.

格陵兰是最初的项目，随后西伯利亚和加利福尼亚 29 棕榈树也建造了圆顶建筑，如果一切顺利，这座建筑有一天会因为太小而无法容纳所需的所有空间，但总部仍将保留在那里，只是作为与其他非营利组织建立联系的一种方式。缺点是他们已经向 亚历克斯和 克劳德·里尔登索要捐款。

The non-profit organizations had a hard time explaining to many big contributors why they were in such a lavishly redecorated building, they simply pointed out, the space was provided for free and did not absorb and costs subtract from their intended directed agendas designed around promoting social harmony.

非营利组织很难向许多大捐助者解释为什么他们位于如此奢华的重新装修的建筑中，他们只是指出，这个空间是免费提供的，不会从他们旨在促进社会和谐的议程中扣除任何成本。

Alex carried an ultra-light briefing case, which only held a couple papers, but no doubt would be full when he left. The Lobby was immaculate and the bar to the side was definitely swank and well served customers full of smiles.

亚历克斯带着一个超轻的简报箱，里面只能装几张文件，但毫无疑问，当他离开时，里面会装满东西。大厅一尘不染，旁边的酒吧绝对很时髦，服务周到，顾客们都面带微笑。

The numerous non-profits routinely had lunches there and lubricated potential donors to loosen them up with their pocketbooks. It was not uncommon for Alex to lubricate a few people there himself as he struggled to move this project along.

许多非营利组织经常在那里吃午餐，并润滑潜在的捐助者，让他们放松钱包。在努力推进该项目的过程中，亚历克斯亲自在那里为几个人拉关系并不罕见。

Recently Alex lubricated Danish and Greenlander officials there during lunch breaks as they came in to discuss land use concerns as well as new zoning laws needed to be imposed such as restricting all internal combustion vehicles in the dome to preserve air quality.

最近，亚历克斯在午休时间拉关系，丹麦和格陵兰官员来这里讨论土地使用问题以及需要实施的新分区法，例如限制所有内燃机车辆进入圆顶以保持空气质量。

### INT. DAY. 120 WALL STREET. CLAUDE REARDEN'S OFFICE.

白天，华尔街 120 号，克劳德·里尔登的办公室。

                    CLAUDE REARDEN
          So, tell me Alex, what was the outcome of your
          meeting with the Greenland/Denmark group?

                    克劳德·里尔登
          那么，告诉我亚历克斯，你与格陵兰/丹麦小组的
          会面结果如何？

                    ALEX
          We finally hit pay dirt.

                    亚历克斯
          我们终于找到了宝藏。

Alex pulled the documents out he was carrying, and they were copies of the signature pages for the MOA/MOU and the legal binding contract and handed them to Claude.

亚历克斯拿出他随身携带的文件，它们是 MOA/MOU 和具有法律约束力的合同的签名页的副本，并将它们交给了克劳德。

ALEX

These are your copies; I retain the master copies in
Minnesota in my vault.

亚历克斯

些是你的副本；我把原件保留在明尼苏达州的保
险库里。

Alex's vault was a sub-basement to his basement across the hallway from his huge
wine cellar.

亚历克斯的保险库是他地下室的地下室，位于他巨大的酒窖对面的走廊上。

Claude took the documents from Alex and quickly scanned them, which had a good
copy of the seal and all the appropriate signatures. Claude set down looking somewhat
stunned.

克劳德从亚历克斯手中接过文件，快速扫描了它们，上面有完整的印章副本和
所有适当的签名。克劳德坐下来，看起来有些震惊。

CLAUDE REARDEN

This is unbelievable. How the hell did you convince
them to sign?

克劳德·里尔登

这太不可思议了。你到底是怎么说服他们签字的？

ALEX

Some might say it was extortion, but I simply said that
if they didn't sign yesterday, I was no longer going to
use the steel shipped in from Denmark, nor would I
build a cement plant in Greenland or open limestone
and coal mines.

亚历克斯

有人可能会说这是敲诈，但我只是说，如果他们
昨天不签字，我将不再使用从丹麦运来的钢材，
也不会在格陵兰建造水泥厂或开采石灰石和煤
矿。

CLAUDE REARDEN
So that's what did it?

克劳德·里尔登
所以这就是原因吗？

ALEX

That didn't seem to faze them much, but when I said I also want to disclose we are now in negotiations with Vladimir Putin to build a five-mile dome in Siberia next to one of their major cities and we'd simply put Greenland on the back burner and come see them again in 10 years. They got a little more cooperative.

亚历克斯

这似乎并没有让他们感到太过不安，但当我说我还想透露，我们现在正在与弗拉基米尔·普京谈判，在西伯利亚的一个主要城市旁边建造一个五英里的圆顶，我们只是把格陵兰放在一边，10 年后再来看他们。他们变得更合作了。

CLAUDE REARDEN
So that did the trick?

克劳德·里尔登
所以这招奏效了？

ALEX

Not quite. I showed them this letter from Vladimir Putin I received a few days ago, notice with his official stamp, they really got depressed.

亚历克斯

不完全是。我给他们看了几天前收到的弗拉基米尔·普京的信，注意上面有他的官方印章，他们真的很沮丧。

Alex handed Claude the letter which he quickly read and handed back, since it was private correspondence.

亚历克斯把信递给克劳德，他很快读完就还给了他，因为这是私人信件。

CLAUDE REARDEN

So, Vladimir Putin is serious about wanting a five-mile dome over the center of Moscow before he lets us proceed in Siberia.

克劳德·里尔登
所以，弗拉基米尔·普京是认真想要在莫斯科市中心建造一个五英里高的穹顶，然后他才会让我们进入西伯利亚。

ALEX

Yes, however, I assured Vladimir Putin that it's in his best interest in having us finish the dome in Greenland first so that he will be receiving proven technology and all the bugs worked out.

亚历克斯

是的，但是，我向弗拉基米尔·普京保证，让我们先在格陵兰岛完成穹顶对他最有利，这样他就能获得经过验证的技术，所有的问题都能得到解决。

CLAUDE REARDEN

Russia could probably provide all the materials for their domes.

克劳德·里尔登

俄罗斯可能可以提供建造穹顶的所有材料。

ALEX

Vladimir Putin hinted around that it would be our only recourse.

亚历克斯

弗拉基米尔·普京暗示这是我们唯一的办法。

CLAUDE REARDEN

What about labor problems there, the work force is usually well lubricated with Vodka, and they move at a snail's pace.

克劳德·里尔登

那里的劳动力问题怎么样，劳动力通常喝了伏特加，工作速度像蜗牛一样慢。

ALEX

Putin recognizes that and has thrown in a carrot or two.

亚历克斯

普京意识到了这一点，并给了他一两个诱饵。

CLAUDE REARDEN
Such as?

克劳德·里尔登
比如？

### ALEX

First, in his letter he is aware of how James Walker converted all those Bessemer process steel mills to the Oxygen method. Vladimir Putin stated most emphatically he would modernize and automate a couple steel mills, one in Siberia and the other 50 miles outside Moscow to produce all the steel we need and minimize human requirements.

### 亚历克斯

首先，他在信中知道詹姆斯·沃克如何将所有贝塞麦炼钢厂改用氧气炼钢法。弗拉基米尔·普京最强调地表示，他将对两家炼钢厂进行现代化和自动化改造，一家在西伯利亚，另一家在莫斯科 50 英里外，以生产我们所需的所有钢铁，并最大限度地减少人力需求。

### 克劳德·里尔登
这很有意思。

### ALEX

Secondly Vladimir Putin knows there are a lot of people in prison for various crimes who would love to not spend the next 20 years in prison to complete their sentences for drug trafficking and homosexual exploitation of minors, and other serious crimes.

### 亚历克斯

其次，弗拉基米尔·普京知道有很多人因各种罪行入狱，他们不想在接下来的 20 年里因贩毒、同性恋剥削未成年人和其他严重罪行服刑。

### CLAUDE REARDEN
How would that play into all this?

### 克劳德·里尔登
这会对这一切产生什么影响？

### ALEX

Prisoners would be given provisional release from prison and as long as the construction team continued to give them good appraisals, they could stay out of prison, would help create a large, motivated work force.

亚历克斯
囚犯将被暂时释放，只要建筑队继续给予他们良
好的评价，他们就可以不入狱，这将有助于建立
一支庞大、积极主动的劳动力队伍。

CLAUDE REARDEN
The old Soviet way.

克劳德·里尔登
老苏联方式。

ALEX
Yes, but it works well.

亚历克斯
是的，但效果很好。

CLAUDE REARDEN
Too bad we can't use those techniques on some of the
liberal progressives out in California.

克劳德·里尔登
可惜我们不能对加州的一些自由进步人士使用这
些技巧。

ALEX
California's probably a lost cause, and when we get a
crack at 29 Palms, we'll probably have to import a lot
of labor.

亚历克斯
加州可能已经没戏了，当我们开始开发 二十九棕
榈村 (29 Palms) 时，我们可能不得不进口大量劳
动力。

CLAUDE REARDEN
Illegal Aliens too I suppose?

克劳德·里尔登
我想非法移民也是吧？

ALEX
I don't think we'll have to go there. There are a lot of
legal Hispanics who work a lot harder than Gringo's
and our pay scale will be generous and we'll have no
problems attracting workers.

亚历克斯

我认为我们不必去那里。有很多合法的西班牙裔
美国人比外国人工作更努力，我们的工资水平会
很高，我们不会遇到吸引工人的问题。

CLAUDE REARDEN

Even for the work up at the top of the pillars and the
roof?

克劳德·里尔登
即使是在柱子和屋顶顶部的工作？

ALEX

By the time we start on 29 Palms, we'll be done with
Moscow, Siberia, and Greenland, there will be plenty
of workers willing to work up high.

亚历克斯

等我们开始开发 二十九棕榈村 (29 Palms) 时，莫
斯科、西伯利亚和格陵兰岛的工作就完成了，会
有很多工人愿意在高处工作。

CLAUDE REARDEN

What if we can't get as many tall structure workers as
we need?

克劳德·里尔登
如果我们无法获得所需的高结构工人怎么办？

ALEX

I'm sure we can entice the Secretary of State to give
out a few more green cards, especially if we finance
his rumored plan to run for the White House in a
couple of years.

亚历克斯

我相信我们可以说服国务卿再发放几张绿卡，特
别是如果我们资助他几年后竞选白宫的传闻计划
的话。

CLAUDE REARDEN

We have our friends at Cash In Advance that owe us a
lot of favors.

克劳德·里尔登
我们在 预付现金 (Cash In Advance) 的朋友欠我们
很多人情。

ALEX

That's for certain, at least from all the free rides we gave them so they could infiltrate countries in a clandestine manner.

亚历克斯

这是肯定的，至少我们给他们提供了许多免费乘车的机会，这样他们就可以秘密潜入其他国家。

CLAUDE REARDEN

Sure, helps when you don't have to go through airport security. So, tell me, now that we are past all this, what was the big hold up?

克劳德·里尔登

当然，当你不需要通过机场安检时，这很有帮助。那么，告诉我，既然我们已经过去了这一切，最大的阻碍是什么？

ALEX

Do you remember the College Professor, Adelheid Jørgensen?

亚历克斯

你还记得大学教授 阿德尔海德·约根森 (Adelheid Jørgensen) 吗？

CLAUDE REARDEN

Sure, she's a pretty woman.

克劳德·里尔登

当然，她是个漂亮的女人。

ALEX

Adelheid Jørgensen was fighting it. Apparently Adelheid Jørgensen hangs out with environmentalist extremists who want to block the construction.

亚历克斯

阿德尔海德·约根森正在反对这项工程。显然，她与那些想要阻止这项工程的环保极端分子混在一起。

CLAUDE REARDEN

So, what tipped the scales, how did you overcome her objections?

克劳德·里尔登
**那么，是什么**改变了这一切？你是如何克服她的反对意见的？

ALEX
We didn't, she's still bitterly opposed. The Denmark government who pays for most their investments and the Mayor of Nuuk are looking pragmatically at what will happen to the region if suddenly we have a modern city there with a population of 500,000, it's a game changer.

亚历克斯
我们没有，她仍然强烈反对。丹麦政府支付了大部分投资，努克市长则务实地考虑了如果突然出现一座人口 50 万的现代化城市，该地区将会发生什么，这将改变整个格局。

CLAUDE REARDEN
They would suddenly be on par with Iceland.

克劳德·里尔登
他们会突然与冰岛平起平坐。

ALEX
And such a place will no doubt increase tourism as relatives and friends come to visit.

亚历克斯
这样的地方无疑会增加旅游业，因为亲戚朋友会来拜访。

CLAUDE REARDEN
Having Cement and Coal production there also would be an eye opener.

克劳德·里尔登
在那里生产水泥和煤炭也会让人大开眼界。

ALEX
Sure, Coal would be highly beneficial to remote areas that could use small power plants and not have to rely on oil and diesel shipments.

亚历克斯
当然，煤炭对偏远地区非常有利，这些地区可以使用小型发电厂，而不必依赖石油和柴油运输。

CLAUDE REARDEN

Right, a big pile of coal doesn't require much storage requirements.

克劳德·里尔登
是的，一大堆煤不需要太多的储存要求。

ALEX

Plus, they can build cement roads and bridges a lot cheaper.

亚历克斯
此外，他们可以更便宜地建造水泥路和桥梁。

CLAUDE REARDEN

Not to mention more hydro-electric plants.

克劳德·里尔登
更不用说更多的水力发电厂了。

ALEX

That's exactly how Putin sees Siberia.

亚历克斯
这正是普京对西伯利亚的看法。

CLAUDE REARDEN

But why is he interested in building a dome over the center of Moscow but wants it built East of the Siberian City Chita?

克劳德·里尔登
但是，为什么他有兴趣在莫斯科市中心建造圆顶建筑，却想把它建在西伯利亚城市赤塔以东呢？

ALEX

Vladimir Putin's view is that Russians are like stubborn mules, they don't want change. The building East of Chita would facilitate tripling the size of the overall City and have a major tourist center near Lake Baikal.

亚历克斯
弗拉基米尔·普京认为，俄罗斯人就像倔强的骡子，他们不想改变。在赤塔以东建造圆顶建筑将使整个城市的规模扩大三倍，并在贝加尔湖旁边建立一个主要的旅游中心。

**CLAUDE REARDEN**
But that's kind of a hilly mountainous region.

克劳德·里尔登
但那是一个丘陵山区。

**ALEX**
Take a look at the Map showing Chita I have attached
to the report.

亚历克斯
看看我附在报告中的赤塔地图。

**CLAUDE REARDEN**
What do you want me to glean from this map?

克劳德·里尔登
你想让我从这张地图上得到什么？

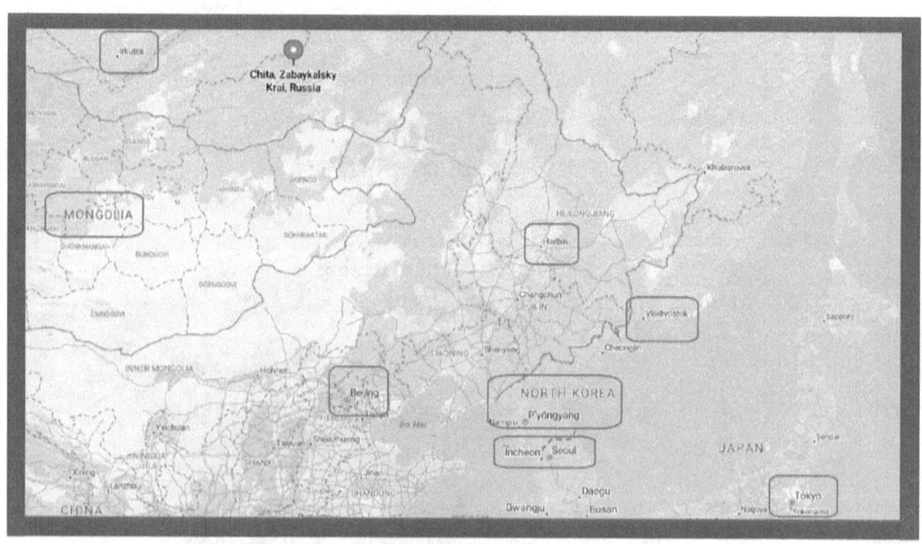


**ALEX**
Due to Chita Russia's unique location, I have identified
major cities and regions that would add to possible
trade and business opportunities if a lot of people and
some businesses are housed in Chita's Dome.

亚历克斯

由于俄罗斯赤塔的独特地理位置，我已经确定了主要城市和地区，如果许多人和一些企业都住在赤塔的圆顶建筑中，这些城市和地区将增加可能的贸易和商业机会。

CLAUDE REARDEN
What type of business?

克劳德·里尔登
什么类型的企业？

ALEX

For starters I think tourism to Lake Baikal would explode. Air traffic would expand. I would think the Chinese and Russians will eventually build a High-Speed Rail Line between Harbin China and Chita Russia.

亚历克斯

首先，我认为贝加尔湖的旅游业将会蓬勃发展。空中交通将扩大。我认为中国和俄罗斯最终将在中国哈尔滨和俄罗斯赤塔之间修建一条高铁。

CLAUDE REARDEN
That would be a costly construction.

克劳德·里尔登
这将是一项昂贵的建设。

ALEX

Since an existing rail line already exists going between those cities, would facilitate building a new high speed rail line to connect to China's 4,000 mile+ high speed rail network.

亚历克斯

由于这些城市之间已经有一条现有的铁路线，这将有利于修建一条新的高铁线，以连接中国 4,000 英里以上的高铁网络。

CLAUDE REARDEN
How did Vladimir Putin take all this proposal?

克劳德·里尔登
弗拉基米尔·普京是如何接受这个提议的？

ALEX

Dealing with Vladimir Putin is like dealing with you, there is no limit to what risk he's willing to take on. He's like a fox; he sees 7 chess moves ahead of you. Guess what he said about those hills and mountains that would be in our way?

亚历克斯

与弗拉基米尔·普京打交道就像和你打交道一样，他愿意承担的风险是没有限制的。他就像一只狐狸；他能看到你前面的 7 步棋。猜猜他说了什么，那些会挡住我们道路的山丘和山脉？

CLAUDE REARDEN
What?

克劳德·里尔登
什么？

ALEX

Vladimir Putin said we would be permitted to use as much explosives as we desired and create as much pollution as we wanted to level off an area for the dome.

亚历克斯

弗拉基米尔·普京说，我们可以随心所欲地使用炸药，制造污染，为圆顶建筑平整一块区域。

CLAUDE REARDEN

If I recall we figured that if we took down that 1000-foot peak, we could fill the valley and have an almost perfect 5-mile flat surface to build the dome on.

克劳德·里尔登

如果我没记错的话，我们曾想过，如果拆掉那座 1000 英尺高的山峰，我们就可以填平山谷，并拥有一个近乎完美的 5 英里平坦表面来建造圆顶建筑。

ALEX

What's more important Chita's right near a Russian Air Force Base, so naturally Vladimir Putin see's the benefit of the China Dome providing better quality shelter for his military families.

亚历克斯
更重要的是，赤塔就在俄罗斯空军基地附近，因
此弗拉基米尔·普京自然认为中国圆顶建筑可以为
他的军人家庭提供更优质的庇护所。

## CLAUDE REARDEN

The China Dome will enhance the quality of life for
the Chita Residents by allowing them to live in a snow
free environment.

克劳德·里尔登
中国圆顶建筑将提高赤塔居民的生活质量，让他
们生活在无雪的环境中。

## ALEX

If they miss the snow, they can go outside the dome
and play in the snow when they want or visit the
forests in the summer at the Baikal Nature Reserve.

亚历克斯
如果他们想念雪景，他们可以随时走出圆顶建
筑，在雪地里玩耍，或者在夏天去贝加尔湖自然
保护区的森林里游玩。

[ https://en.wikipedia.org/wiki/Baikal_Nature_Reserve ]

## CLAUDE REARDEN

Yea, Putin seems to be the only world leader who
really understands the Merit of our Plan.

克劳德·里尔登
是的，普京似乎是唯一真正了解我们计划的价值
的世界领导人。

## ALEX

Yes, Vladimir Putin is all on board with a thorough
understanding of the mini-ice age that has started.

亚历克斯
是的，弗拉基米尔·普京完全同意，他彻底了解了
已经开始的迷你冰河期。

## CLAUDE REARDEN

It's going to get bad. Most people are still stuck on
global warming.

克劳德·里尔登

情况会变得更糟。大多数人仍然对全球变暖感到困惑。

ALEX

I was quickly convinced about this mini-ice age as soon as you introduced me to Habibullo Abdussamatov the astrophysicist and head of space research at St. Petersburg's Pulkovo Astronomical Observatory.

亚历克斯

当你把我介绍给圣彼得堡普尔科沃天文台的天体物理学家兼空间研究负责人哈比布洛·阿卜杜萨马托夫时，我很快就相信了这个迷你冰河期。

CLAUDE REARDEN<br>So, what's our next move?

克劳德·里尔登<br>那么，我们的下一步是什么？

ALEX

We should proceed to send our Away Team up to Nuuk Greenland right away and start executing the plan.

亚历克斯

我们应该立即派遣我们的客队前往格陵兰岛努克，开始执行计划。

CLAUDE REARDEN

Jeff Sinclair is ready to travel immediately, he knew this was coming.

克劳德·里尔登

杰夫·辛克莱已经准备好立即出发，他知道这会发生。

ALEX

Yes, get Jeff Sinclair up there this week. Start the movement of men and materials and wait about a week before you inform our banker friends. We want this thing well on its way, before Wall Street Journal reports on it and CNN or other news media outlets that don't like us starts hammering away.

亚历克斯

是的，本周让杰夫·辛克莱去那里。开始运送人力和物资，等上一周再通知我们的银行家朋友。我们希望这件事能顺利进行，在《华尔街日报》报道此事之前，在 CNN 或其他不喜欢我们的新闻媒体开始大肆宣传之前。

## CLAUDE REARDEN
Well, you kind of pissed the global warming people off when you offered $1 billion grant to study global cooling.

## 克劳德·里尔登
好吧，当你提供 10 亿美元资助研究全球变暖时，你一定惹恼了全球变暖研究者。

## ALEX
Yea a lot of global warmers are sure changing their stories now, want all that grant money.

## 亚历克斯
是的，现在很多全球变暖研究者肯定在改变他们的故事，想要所有的资助资金。

## CLAUDE REARDEN
NASA and NOAA are in a tizzy that's for sure.

## 克劳德·里尔登
NASA 和 NOAA 肯定很焦虑。

## ALEX
They will be in a bigger tizzy when the Gulf Stream dies of like the British predict in that report, I emailed you.

## 亚历克斯
当墨西哥湾流像英国在那份报告中预测的那样消失时，他们会更加焦虑，我给你发了电子邮件。

FLASHBACK:

闪回：

**GALAXY MAIL**

**From:**Alex@DomeCitiesGroupInc.com
**To:** ClaudR@Claude Rearden Construction.com

**Subject: GULF STREAM COLLAPSING**

Claude,
Here's the link to the story we just talked about on the
phone. Let me know what you think:
https://www.bbc.com/news/science-environment-66289494

Regards.
Alex Baxter

银河邮件
发件人：亚历克斯@圆顶城市团体公司网络公司
收件人：克劳德艾儿@克劳德里尔登建筑公司网络公司

主题：墨西哥湾流崩塌

克劳德·，
这是我们刚刚在电话中谈到的故事的链接。告诉我你的想法：

https://www.bbc.com/news/science-environment-66289494

问候。
亚历克斯·巴克斯特

**END OF FLASHBACK**

闪回结束

CLAUDE REARDEN
Yea I know.

克劳德·里尔登
是的，我知道。

ALEX
As soon as Jeff gets to his office up and running, tell
him I'll fly up there and pay a visit.

亚历克斯
一旦 Jeff 的办公室开始运作，就告诉他我会飞过
去拜访他。

CLAUDE REARDEN
Sure, I need to get up there myself.

克劳德·里尔登
当然，我需要亲自去那里。

ALEX
Ok, I'll meet you up in Nuuk.

亚历克斯
好的，我会在努克见你。

Alex stood and was ready to leave when Claude announced:

亚历克斯站起来准备离开，这时 克劳德宣布：

CLAUDE REARDEN
One second, Alex.

克劳德·里尔登
等一下，亚历克斯。

Claude then opened a desk drawer and pulled out a ¼ inch thick document and handed it to Alex.

然后，克劳德打开办公桌抽屉，拿出一份 ¼ 英寸厚的文件，递给了亚历克斯。

CLAUDE REARDEN
Its description was the Phase-1 activity, which included setting up offices and starting the overall project. All the permits were signed, so the next step was to start doing the numerous tasks that would begin construction.

克劳德·里尔登
文件描述了第一阶段的活动，包括设立办公室和启动整个项目。所有许可证都已签署，因此下一步就是开始执行开始施工的众多任务。

ALEX
The coal seam we planned to exploit was discovered near a natural harbor and the limestone quarry being established near a natural harbor was making everyone happy because producing the Portland cement locally was going to allow a huge time and cost reduction.

亚历克斯
我们计划开采的煤层是在天然港口附近发现的，石灰石采石场也在天然港口附近建立，这让每个人都很高兴，因为在当地生产波特兰水泥将大大节省时间和成本。

CLAUDE REARDEN
Advanced Coal Technologies Inc. is going to be contracted to mine the coal seam, and a Dry Bulk Shipping company will haul the coal approximately

300 miles aboard their ships to Nuuk where a Warf
was to be constructed next to a Portland Cement plant
planned right at the waterfront.

克劳德·里尔登
先进煤炭技术公司 将承包开采煤层，一家干散货
航运公司将用他们的船将煤炭运到大约 300 英里
外的努克， 在那里将在计划在海滨建造的波特兰
水泥厂旁边建造一个码头。

ALEX
How's that going to be handled?

亚历克斯
这要如何处理？

CLAUDE REARDEN
A gravel and rock quarry were established not far
from the construction site and a private road was built
which large trucks used to haul the rock and sand to
the Cement Mixing plant built right in the middle of
the Dome that was eventually approved for East of the
airport runway, with all the Airport buildings under the
dome.

克劳德·里尔登
在施工现场不远处建立了一个砾石和岩石采石
场，并修建了一条私人道路，大型卡车通过这条
道路将岩石和沙子运送到水泥搅拌厂，该搅拌厂
建在穹顶的正中央，最终获准在机场跑道以东修
建，所有机场建筑都在穹顶之下。

This area is hilly, and those hills were to provide a lot of construction material in
sand, gravel and rock needed. The Architects left some of the hills were left intact and
innovative measures used them in the building schemes.

这个地区多山，这些山丘将提供大量建筑材料，如沙子、砾石和岩石。建筑师
们保留了一些完整的山丘，并在建筑方案中采用了创新措施。

ALEX
In what way?

亚历克斯
以什么方式？

CLAUDE REARDEN
This allows quite a few shorter pillars to be constructed
which adds greatly to the strength of the support
structures. It also added measurably to the internal
architecture with high rise buildings sprouting out of
the hill masses you see on the artist conceptions in that
report.

克劳德·里尔登
这样就可以建造相当多的较短的柱子，这大大增
加了支撑结构的强度。它还大大增加了内部建筑
的强度，高层建筑从山丘中拔地而起，就像您在
该报告中的艺术构想中看到的那样。

ALEX
Where will the debris from the hill be taken down
used?

亚历克斯
拆掉的山丘上的碎石会用在哪儿？

CLAUDE REARDEN
Some of the hills we'll take down will be used as
fill material to create an overall much more level
area under the dome and extend the shoreline of
Kobbefjord.

克劳德·里尔登
我们拆掉的一些山丘将被用作填充材料，以便在
穹顶下形成一个整体上更加平坦的区域，并延伸
科贝峡湾的海岸线。

Alex put the briefing papers in his small pouch, then held out his hand to shake
Claude's.

亚历克斯把简报放进他的小袋子里，然后伸出手和克劳德握手。

ALEX
We'll see you soon.

亚历克斯
我们很快就会见到你。

CLAUDE REARDEN
Have a safe flight home.

克劳德·里尔登
祝你一路平安。

**STEPHANIE**
Bye Claude.

斯蒂芬妮
再见克劳德。

**CLAUDE REARDEN**
Goodbye Stephanie.

克劳德·里尔登
再见斯蒂芬妮。

Stephanie and Alex exited the office and as soon as they hit the elevator, Stephanie called Rodriguez.

斯蒂芬妮和亚历克斯走出办公室，一进电梯，斯蒂芬妮就给罗德里格斯打电话。

**STEPHANIE**
Rodriguez, we are leaving now, please come pick us up.

斯蒂芬妮
罗德里格斯，我们现在要走了，请来接我们。

**RODRIGUEZ**
I'll be there in five minutes, Stephanie.

罗德里格斯
我 5 分钟后就到，斯蒂芬妮。

Rodrigues, knowing it would be a short meeting with no luggage, had driven a short distance where he could park his Limo and grab a fast sandwich, was back in the Limo and driving back towards 120 Wall Street.

罗德里格斯， 知道这将是一场没有行李的短暂会议，他开了一小段路，把豪华轿车停好，然后吃了个三明治，回到豪华轿车，朝华尔街 120 号驶去。

Alex was glad there was only one stop on the way down, and the elevator remained relatively empty with plenty of room.

亚历克斯很高兴下行途中只有一个站点，电梯相对空旷，有足够的空间。

Alex then casually walked through the lobby and only had to wait curb side for 2 minutes before Rodrigues pulled up.

亚历克斯随后漫不经心地穿过大厅，在路边等了 2 分钟，罗德里格斯就停了下来。

Leroy, being the master of ceremonies and very cogent always fully aware just like he was leading a Marine Recon Platoon in Iraq, walked over, opened the Limo door.

作为司仪，勒罗伊非常有说服力，总是完全清醒，就像他在伊拉克领导海军陆战队侦察排一样，他走过去打开了豪华轿车的门。

LEROY JONES<br>Have a safe flight home, Mr. Baxter.

¥勒罗伊·琼斯<br>祝你一路平安，巴克斯特先生。

ALEX<br>Thank you, Leroy. See you next time.

亚历克斯<br>谢谢你，勒罗伊。下次见。

Stephanie called ahead to inform John Black minutes after She and Alex got into  and Limo:

他们上豪华轿车几分钟后，斯蒂芬妮就打电话通知约翰·布莱克：

STEPHANIE<br>John, we are returning in about 45 minutes. Please arrange to have Alex's Jet pulled out of the hanger for departure.

斯蒂芬妮<br>约翰，我们大约 45 分钟后返回。请安排将亚历克斯的飞机从机库中拉出来准备起飞。

JOHN BLACK<br>Will do.

约翰·布莱克<br>会的。

John Black then walked over and knocked on the plane's door which woke Brad up from a nice slumber and notified him.

约翰·布莱克随后走过去敲了敲飞机门，把睡得香甜的布拉德叫醒，并通知了他。

JOHN BLACK
The boss is on the way back and I've been requested to
move the aircraft out of the hanger.

约翰·布莱克
老板正在回来的路上，我被要求将飞机从机库中
移出。

BRAD
Thanks, I'll be up in the cockpit.

布拉德
谢谢，我会在驾驶舱里。

JOHN BLACK
Roger that.

约翰·布莱克
明白

Soon a tow tractor hitched onto the GS650, and it was pulled out of the hanger. Brad started the pre-flight checkout in anticipation of immediate departure, filed his FAA plan, and was ready to start the engines as soon as Alex arrived.

很快，一辆牵引车被挂在 GS650 上，并将其从机库中拉出。布拉德开始进行飞行前检查，准备立即起飞，提交了他的 FAA 计划，并准备在亚历克斯到达后立即启动发动机。

In about 45 minutes, Rodriguez had Alex back to the airport hangar where Alex quickly met John Black who was expecting them as Rodrigues pulled up to the curb in front of the hanger where Mr. Black was standing for a moment waiting and opened the door.

大约 45 分钟后，罗德里格斯把亚历克斯送回了机场机库，亚历克斯很快遇到了约翰·布莱克，他正在等着他们，罗德里格斯把车停在机库前的路边，布莱克先生在那里等了一会儿，然后打开了门。

JOHN BLACK
Everything go ok in the City?

约翰·布莱克
城里一切顺利吗？

ALEX
It was splendid.

亚历克斯
太棒了。

Alex responded with a smile as he had a flash vision of Christina, whom he wanted to get to know the next time he flew into NYC on his way to Greenland *without* Stephanie.

亚历克斯微笑着回应，因为他突然看到了克里斯蒂娜，他想在下次飞往纽约前往格陵兰时认识克里斯蒂娜，而不用斯蒂芬妮。

Alex's excuse for not taking Stephanie along, is he wanted her to study the document in his pouch to advise him.

亚历克斯没有带斯蒂芬妮一起去的借口是，他想让她研究他包里的文件，以便给他提供建议。

Also, since detective Nuuk Greenland Detective Rodney Hansen had yet to identify the suspect in what appeared to be an attempted murder, he didn't want Stephanie to be placed in any possible scenario that might result in danger to her.

此外，由于努克格陵兰侦探罗德尼·汉森尚未确定疑似谋杀未遂的嫌疑人，他不想让斯蒂芬妮陷入任何可能对她造成危险的境地。

Alex would soon inform Stephanie she was not going to be permitted to go on this trip. As soon as the perpetrator was arrested, she would be making routine trips to Greenland.

亚历克斯很快就会告诉斯蒂芬妮，她不被允许参加这次旅行。一旦肇事者被捕，她就会定期前往格陵兰岛。

Mr. Black walked them through the security check point and out to the plane, where Brad stood by the built-in stairway of the plane.

布莱克先生带他们通过安全检查点，走到飞机上，布拉德站在飞机内置楼梯旁。

Just as Brad had planned, he got in a nice two hour nap before he received an expected call from Stephanie informing they were halfway back to the Airport heading home. The flight back to Minnesota would be pleasurable because he was well rested. On many such flights, if Alex was wired high from a great business deal, he often sat up in the cockpit conversing with Brad about many things including sports, history, favorite strip club dancers, and any topic that Brad was willing to bring up

正如布拉德计划的那样，他睡了两个小时，然后收到了斯蒂芬妮的电话，通知他们已经半路回到机场回家了。飞回明尼苏达的航班会很愉快，因为他休息得很好。在许多这样的航班上，如果亚历克斯因为一笔大生意而兴奋不已，他经常坐在驾驶舱里和布拉德谈论很多事情，包括体育、历史、最喜欢的脱衣舞俱乐部舞者，以及布拉德愿意提出的任何话题。

Brad
Welcome back Mr. Baxter.

布拉德
欢迎回来，巴克斯特先生。

ALEX
Thank you. Let's head for home now.

亚历克斯
谢谢。我们现在回家吧。

Brad
Right away, sir.

布拉德
马上，先生。

INT. DAY. NYC-JFK AIRPORT PRIVATE HANGER AREA. ALEX'S GS650 PRIVATE JET CABIN AREA AND COCKPIT.

白天内部。纽约肯尼迪机场私人机库区。ALEX 的 GS650 私人飞机客舱区和驾驶舱。

Alex climbed the latter up into the plane, followed by Stephanie then Brad who assisted in raising the ladder and shutting the door. Brad then went back into the cockpit, continued the check-off which was almost complete and started the engines.

亚历克斯爬上楼梯，斯蒂芬妮和布拉德紧随其后，他们帮助升起梯子并关上门。布拉德随后回到驾驶舱，继续完成几乎已完成的检查，并启动了发动机。

EXT. DAY. NYC-JFK AIRPORT ALEX'S GS650 PRIVATE JET TAXI AND TAKEOFF. (30 SECONDS)

Note: This might sound rather strange, but Microsoft Flight Simulator is now so good these 30 seconds could be a Flight Simulator sequence with proper background music and pilot – tower conversations.

AIR TRAFFIC CONTROL TOWER
Baxter-1 proceed to runway 22L No inbound traffic, you are cleared for takeoff. Proceed on course 224 degrees altitude IAW flight plan.

PILOT BRAD
Tower, this is Baxter-1. Understand cleared for takeoff and no inbound traffic. Initial course 224, altitudes in accordance with flight plan.

The GS650 took off and proceeded on a heading of 224 degrees. Once the Jet was airborne, they were then rerouted on a course of 290 which would take them generally to the West with the final leg around 310 degrees heading toward Alex's private runway.

地面控制人员指示布拉德前往 22L 跑道，他以 224 度的航向起飞。飞机很快升空后，他们便改道前往 290 度航向，这将使他们大致向西飞行，最后一段航程约为 310 度，朝着亚历克斯的私人跑道飞行。

Six hours later due to headwinds, the Jet landed on the private runway, pulled up to the hanger where Brad eased it in nose first without a tug, then as the ground crew gave him the signal, he stopped he plane, shut down the jet engine while the ground crew put in the wheel chucks.

六个小时后，由于逆风，喷气式飞机降落在私人跑道上，拉到机库，布拉德没有用力拉动，而是让飞机机头朝下，然后按照地勤人员的信号，他停下飞机，

The hanger door was closing as the jet engines wound down and by the time the engines stopped the doors were shut and the heaters were on full blast heating up the spaces to 72 degrees.

关闭喷气发动机，让地勤人员安装轮胎卡盘。喷气发动机减速时，机库门正在关闭，当发动机停止时，门也关上了，加热器全速运转，将机库温度加热到 72 度。

Alex had been napping, and Stephanie woke him up. It didn't take long for the heaters to re-heat the hanger, and brad walked over and opened the door and let down the stairs, exited the plane and stood by the stairway in case there was a need to assist Alex, which there had been none.

亚历克斯一直在打盹，斯蒂芬妮叫醒了他。加热器很快就重新加热了机库，布拉德走过去打开门，放下楼梯，走出飞机，站在楼梯边，以防需要帮助亚历克斯，但亚历克斯并没有被帮助。

Alex headed out of the plane, walked about 25 feet to the elevator, and pressed the button (just one button which either opened the door or sent the elevator to this floor and opened it.

亚历克斯走出飞机，步行约 25 英尺到电梯，按下按钮（只有一个按钮，可以打开门或将电梯送到这一层并打开门。

Alex and Stephanie stepped in the elevator large enough to hold 12 people, pressed the button and were quickly delivered to the Tunnel floor area where the golf cart was waiting for them.

亚历克斯和斯蒂芬妮走进可容纳 12 人的电梯，按下按钮，很快就被送到隧道楼层，高尔夫球车在那里等着他们。

Stephanie got into the driver's side and Alex the passenger side, and Stephanie said, take us to the house. The golf cart immediately started moving and in a minute or so, pulled up in front of the house elevator, and stopped.

斯蒂芬妮坐在驾驶座，亚历克斯坐在乘客座，斯蒂芬妮说，带我们去房子。高尔夫球车立即开始移动，一分钟左右，停在房子电梯前，停了下来。

Alex got out so did Stephanie and they walked over to the elevator where Stephanie pressed the UP-button and the door immediately opened, they stepped in and rode it up to the first-floor level and got out and was immediately met by the Butler Sam.

亚历克斯和斯蒂芬妮下了车，他们走到电梯前，斯蒂芬妮按下了 "上行" 按钮，电梯门立刻打开了，他们走进电梯，乘电梯到了一楼，出了电梯，管家山姆马上就来迎接他们了。

SAM
How's your day going so far Mr. Baxter.

山姆
巴克斯特先生，你今天过得怎么样？

ALEX
It's going great

亚历克斯
一切都很好

Alex's thought about what he had to do next.

亚历克斯想着下一步该做什么。

VOICE OVER

*Hans Jespersen was somewhat paranoid for a few days after the attempted break-in at the Hotel, but as each day passed and there was no search for him, he realized he probably got away with it. He had heard a soft voice in the other room, the door was open, and he felt bad he lost his nerve and didn't go in there and stab Baxter. Now Baxter was gone and may not be back any time soon.*

画外音

汉斯·杰斯珀森有点在有人试图闯入酒店后，他几天都心神不宁，但随着时间一天天过去，没有人搜查他，他意识到自己可能已经逃脱了。他听到另一个房间里传来一个轻柔的声音，门是开着的，他很遗憾自己失去了勇气，没有进去刺伤巴克斯特。现在巴克斯特已经走了，可能不会很快回来。

### VOICE OVER

*When the news finally hit that Greenland and Denmark had approved the Dome construction, crap hit the fan.*

### 画外音

当格陵兰和丹麦终于批准建造圆顶的消息传出时，事情变得一团糟。

### VOICE OVER

*Shelley Bergman wrote an editorial for North Ice News, and it was out on the internet a few days later. It would be read by the towns people in the Sunday paper, which was usually only delivered to grocery stores and the few convenience stores like Brugsen, Pissiffik, and Pilersuisoq.*

### 画外音

雪莱·伯格曼为《北方冰雪新闻》写了一篇社论，几天后就在网上发表了。镇上的人们会在周日的报纸上看到它，而报纸通常只送到杂货店和几家便利店，如布鲁格森、皮西菲克和皮勒苏索克。

### VOICE OVER

*As expected, Shelley flame sprayed Alex in the editorial and treated the Denmark Government and Greenland's politicians involved in the same light.*

### 画外音

正如预期的那样，雪莱在社论中对亚历克斯进行了猛烈抨击，并以同样的方式对待丹麦政府和格陵兰的政客。

### VOICE OVER

*Shelly's Op-Ed almost resembled a good propagandist who graduated from Mao Zedong academy. Shelly had also pestered Rodney Hansen in recent days and was pissed when he refused to divulge to her the nature of the police business associated with Mr. Baxter.*

### 画外音

雪莉的专栏几乎就像一个毕业于毛泽东学院的优秀宣传员。雪莉最近几天还纠缠罗德尼·汉森，并对他拒绝向她透露与巴克斯特先生有关的警察业务的性质感到愤怒。

## VOICE OVER

*Hans was bitter long before he saw the newspaper lying on Adel's coffee table just as he was getting ready to have a good smoke with Adel. Doing the deal with the Americans in back smoke-filled rooms was the final straw. Had Hans not been forced to leave College, his mind would have been elsewhere, but unfortunately idle minds lead to tragedy.*

### 画外音

汉斯在看到报纸放在阿德尔的咖啡桌上时就已经心怀怨恨，当时他正准备和阿德尔大口抽烟。在烟雾缭绕的后屋里与美国人做交易是压死汉斯的最后一根稻草。如果汉斯没有被迫离开大学，他的心思就会在别的地方，但不幸的是，懒惰的思想会导致悲剧。

Since the Dome management team assumed the project would be approved along the same time frame it was, the logistics were in place to ramp up the project quickly. They could ill afford to wait for coal fields and limestone to be mined locally before work started.

由于圆顶管理团队认为该项目将在同一时间范围内获得批准，因此后勤工作已到位，可以快速推进该项目。他们无法等到当地煤田和石灰石开采完毕后再开始工作。

Dome Cities Group Inc. had promised both Greenland Government and Denmark that even though initially most of the materials would originate in the USA, the local sources would slowly come online as quick as they could facilitate development. No actual promises of start date were agreed too, just a general promise to move it along as rapidly as conditions in the field would permit.

圆顶城市集团公司向格陵兰政府和丹麦承诺，尽管最初大部分材料将来自美国，但当地资源将尽快投入使用，以促进发展。双方也没有就开始日期做出任何实际承诺，只是笼统地承诺在现场条件允许的情况下尽快推进。

### VOICEOVER

*As directed, Jeff Sinclair's A-team arrived in Greenland two days after Alex left New York and flew back to his estate in Minnesota. Speculators in Denmark had built a couple three- and four-story office buildings greatly overestimating the market and needs and were somewhat desperate as they had gone almost a year without any rents when Jeff at first working out of his hotel room, met with the commercial real estate developers and leased both buildings for several years on Alex's verbal approval.*

画外音

按照指示，杰夫·辛克莱的 Ａ 队在亚历克斯离开
纽约两天后抵达格陵兰，然后飞回他在明尼苏达
州的庄园。丹麦的投机者建造了几栋三层和四层
的办公楼，大大高估了市场和需求，他们有些绝
望，因为杰夫最初在酒店房间里工作，会见了商
业房地产开发商，并在亚历克斯的口头批准下将
这两栋楼租了几年，但几乎一年都没有租金。

## VOICEOVER

*It was a good thing information on the approval had
been delayed a week or the rent would have been ten
times higher. But even at the current rate, until the
revelation of the biggest boondoggle in mankind's
history, according to Shelley Bergman, the commercial
real estate agents thought they had taken the dumb
Americans to the cleaners. ten days later, they were
sick to their stomachs when they figured out how much
money they lost by getting greedy and signing the
leases too quickly.*

画外音

幸好批准信息延迟了一周，否则租金会高出十
倍。但即使按照目前的速度，直到人类历史上最
大的浪费被揭露之前，根据雪莱·伯格曼的说法，
商业房地产经纪人都认为他们已经把愚蠢的美国
人骗到了家。十天后，当他们发现自己因为贪婪
和过快签署租约而损失了多少钱时，他们感到非
常恶心。

A corporation was established in Greenland, named *Nuuk Dome Inc.*, so that they
could receive local tax treatment and not be constantly shaken down like most foreign
corporations were.

一家名为 努克圆顶公司的公司在格陵兰成立，这样他们就可以享受当地的税收
待遇，而不会像大多数外国公司那样不断受到敲诈勒索。

In due time Greenland would realize the benefits of the *Dome* far outweighed any graft
that such behavior elicited.

格陵兰最终意识到 圆顶带来的好处远远超过这种行为引起的贪污。

It didn't take long for *Hans Jespersen* to see *Nuuk Dome Inc.* logos on the buildings
Jeff Sinclair had leased. This incensed Hans even more so. His diabolical mind started
spinning just like a finely designed Swiss Watch.

没过多久，汉斯·杰斯佩森就在杰夫·辛克莱租赁的建筑物上看到了努克圆顶公

司的标志。这让汉斯更加愤怒。他邪恶的头脑开始旋转，就像一块设计精良的瑞士手表。

Based on preliminary agreements long before the Danish signed approval for the *Greenland Dome Project*, Alex a big logistics connoisseur understood vividly that the risk would pay off handsomely if he had ships loaded and able to depart U.S. ports immediately upon signing of the agreements.

根据丹麦项目签署格陵兰圆顶早已批准的初步协议，物流大亨亚历克斯清楚地知道，如果他的船舶装载了货物并能够在签署协议后立即离开美国港口，那么他承担的风险将获得环球的回报。

The very day after the agreement was signed, the first of the *Nuuk Dome Inc.* ships departed a New Jersey port. Within two weeks ships carrying *Nuuk Dome Inc.* equipment and supplies arrived at Nuuk.

协议签署后的第二天，努克圆顶公司 (Nuuk Dome Inc.) 的第一艘船只从新泽西港口出发。两周内，载有 努克圆顶公司 (Nuuk Dome Inc.) 设备和物资的船只抵达努克。

This first *Nuuk Dome Inc.* shipment was very important because it delivered several critical items: Caterpillar bulldozers and earth moving equipment, small and medium cranes, 18 wheeler Trucks with low boy's to haul machinery and supplies around, industrial size fork lifts, and the first batch of special designed tents that would be setup as work centers, and fence material to build an 8 foot fence around the initial project site to prevent tampering or stealing of materials.

努克圆顶公司 (Nuuk Dome Inc.) 的第一批货物非常重要，因为它运送了几件关键物品：卡特彼勒推土机和土方设备、小型和中型起重机、用于运输机械和物资的 18 轮低底盘卡车、工业用叉车、第一批专门设计的帐篷（将用作工作中心）和围栏材料（用于在初始项目现场周围建造 8 英尺高的围栏，以防止材料被篡改或盗窃）。

In three days the first ship as unloaded and even though there was a lot of snow on the ground, Greenland Dome construction commenced.

三天后，第一艘船卸货完毕，尽管地面上积雪很多，但格陵兰穹顶的建设还是开始了。

The front loaders and the few dump trucks that arrived in this first cargo ship were immediately put to work, removing snow in the first tent areas, installing temporary fences, and moving dirt around to provide a semi-flat area to install the first habitability and construction fabrication tents.

抵达第一艘货船的装载机和几辆自卸卡车立即投入工作，清除第一批帐篷区域的积雪，安装临时围栏，并清除周围的泥土，以提供半平坦的区域来安装第一批居住和建筑制造帐篷。

The tents looked as if they were made like Chinese quilts weaved, and the tent covers were weaved and the tent's weaved surface had polyimide foam insulation material sandwiched in a way to make it look like a quilt.

帐篷看起来就像是编织的中国棉被，帐篷罩也是编织的，帐篷编织表面夹着聚酰亚胺泡沫隔热材料，使其看起来像棉被。

[https://en.wikipedia.org/wiki/Polyimide_foam]

Alex and Claude both liked containers. Hence the next ship was a container ship, and the entire cargo was Nuuk Dome cargo. By the time the container ship arrived more bulldozing had been accomplished in spite of winter weather at times and a flat area was established and the containers were lined and stacked up 4 high using the medium Crane and moved when needed contents.

亚历克斯和　克劳德都喜欢集装箱。因此，下一艘船是集装箱船，全部货物都是　努克圆顶　的货物。当集装箱船到达时，尽管有时是冬季天气，但更多的推土工作已经完成，并建立了一个平坦的区域，集装箱用中型起重机排列并堆放了 4 层高，并在需要时移动。

VOICEOVER

*In a short time, the construction site was starting to look like a WW2 supply dump in Western France. But what amazed Greenlanders watching all this, is the containers that were prefabricated as work centers stacked together and on multi-levels. Complete machine shops were containerized.*

画外音

在很短的时间内，施工现场开始看起来像法国西部的二战补给站。但让观看这一切的格陵兰人惊讶的是，集装箱被预制成工作中心，堆叠在一起并呈多层。完整的机械车间都采用集装箱化。

True to their word, *Nuuk Dome Inc.* started advertising to hire locals as much as possible. Most of them had to be trained. Some were hired simply as translators as many of the trainers and supervisors were Americans working for Reardon Construction Company.

努克圆顶公司　信守诺言，开始做广告，尽可能多地雇用当地人。他们中的大多数人都必须接受培训。有些人只是被雇来当翻译，因为许多培训师和主管都是为里尔登建筑公司工作的美国人。

VOICEOVER

*Even though people like Shelley Bergman continued to put out negative propaganda, the public knew something was happening even though it for the time being was the butt of jokes.*

画外音
尽管像雪莱·伯格曼这样的人继续进行负面宣传，
但公众知道正在发生一些事情，尽管它暂时只是
笑话。

Any excess housing was quickly rented up by *Nuuk Dome Inc.* for the early arrivals. Soon people from all trades such as carpenters, electricians, plumbers, roofers, concrete workers, etc., arrived to help start on building housing on the work site as to not cause rent inflation and provide quality housing to retain people for longer periods of time.

努克圆顶公司很快为早期抵达的人租下了多余的住房。很快，来自各行各业的人，如木匠、电工、水管工、屋顶工、混凝土工人等，都来到这里帮助在工地上开始建造住房，以免导致租金上涨，并提供优质住房，让人们长期居住。

As expected, some of the local businesses were more than happy to expand into work areas especially since *Nuuk Dome Inc.* was building them store space. People take for granted how prohibitively expensive lumber and other building materials are in Nuuk Greenland. Without *Nuuk Dome Inc.* shipping in lumber and building supplies, little could have been built and what was built would have seemed prohibitively costly.

正如预期的那样，一些当地企业非常乐意扩展到工作区域，特别是因为努克圆顶公司正在为他们建造商店空间。人们理所当然地认为努克格陵兰的木材和其他建筑材料价格高得离谱。如果没有努克圆顶公司运输木材和建筑用品，几乎不可能建造任何东西，而且建造的东西似乎成本高昂。

The day before Alex traveled back to Greenland, he informed Stephanie:

在亚历克斯返回格陵兰岛的前一天，他通知斯蒂芬妮：

ALEX
I'll be leaving in the morning on a trip to Greenland.

亚历克斯
我明天一早要去格陵兰岛旅行。

STEPHANIE
I'll immediately book our hotel rooms and arrange for the Limo Service.

斯蒂芬妮
我会立即预订酒店房间并安排豪华轿车服务。

Alex sent a chill up her spine when he responded:

亚历克斯的回答让斯蒂芬妮不寒而栗：

ALEX
You are not going with me on this trip. I need you to continue analyzing the documents that Claude gave me and make sure we got all our bases covered.

亚历克斯
你不会和我一起去旅行。我需要你继续分析克劳
德给我的文件，确保我们做好万全准备。

STEPHANIE
But I must go.

斯蒂芬妮
但我必须走了。

ALEX
Stephanie, they still have not caught the perpetrator
who would have stabbed you instead of the pillows
when we were last at Nuuk.

亚历克斯
斯蒂芬妮，他们还没有抓到上次我们在努克时刺
伤你而不是枕头的凶手。

STEPHANIE
Why should that matter?

斯蒂芬妮
这有什么关系？

ALEX
Until that situation is resolved, I really do not want
you going to Greenland.

亚历克斯
在情况解决之前，我真的不希望你去格陵兰岛。

STEPHANIE
I'll be perfectly safe, I'm sure the police will be on the
lookout for the perpetrator.

斯蒂芬妮
我会很安全的，我相信警察会密切关注凶手。

ALEX
You are too valuable to me and the team to risk losing
you, plus there is no need for your presence there. I'm
only going so that I can size up how my money is being
spent and see how well Jeff Sinclair has organized the
place and get some feel for when they will actually
start the first pillar.

亚历克斯
你对我和团队来说太宝贵了，不能冒失去你的风
险，而且你也没有必要在那里。我去那里只是为
了看看我的钱是怎么花的，看看 杰夫辛克莱 把
这个地方组织得有多好，并了解他们什么时候会
真正开始第一个支柱。

Stephanie just knew something was wrong. It was clear to her a real possibility was the bimbo in the elevator who gave Alex the 8:00 look or some interesting lady back in Nuuk is making Alex act strange, but if it was truly true, he was worried about her safety, that felt rather touching as well.

斯蒂芬妮知道有些事情不对劲。她很清楚，电梯里的那个花痴给了亚历克斯一个 8 点的眼神，或者是努克某个有趣的女士让亚历克斯表现得很奇怪，但如果这是真的，他担心她的安全，这也让人感到很感动。

Stephanie
Ok Alex, I understand, I'll be looking over Claude's documents carefully.

斯蒂芬妮
好的亚历克斯，我明白了，我会仔细检查克劳德
的文件。

ALEX
Thank you. I appreciate that.

亚历克斯
谢谢你。我很感激。

The following day, Alex left as planned. Instead of flying directly to Greenland, he stopped in NYC and made a side trip to 120 Wall Street. He decided he would drop in on Claude and wrangle some facts and figures out of him. Plus, if he incidentally bumped into Cristina on the elevator, so much the better.

第二天，亚历克斯按计划出发。他没有直接飞往格陵兰，而是在纽约停留，顺便去了华尔街 120 号。他决定顺便拜访克劳德，从他那里套出一些事实和数据。另外，如果他在电梯上偶然碰到克里斯蒂娜，那就更好了。

John Black met Alex as he got off the Jet and escorted him out to the curb where Rodriguez was waiting patiently. 45 minutes or so later, the Limo pulled up in front of 120 Wall Street.

约翰·布莱克在亚历克斯下飞机时遇见了他，并护送他到路边，罗德里格斯在那里耐心地等待着。大约 45 分钟后，豪华轿车停在华尔街 120 号门前。

Just like old times, Leroy opened the car door and Alex got out, shook his hand, passed him another $100 in the shake and then abruptly asked Leroy:

和往常一样，莱罗伊打开车门，亚历克斯下了车，和他握手，又递给他 100 美元，然后突然问 莱罗伊：

ALEX

Leroy, you know a lot of people who work in this building, tell me did you ever meet a young lady named Christina who works up on the 22$^{nd}$ floor?

亚历克斯

莱罗伊··你认识很多在这栋楼里工作的人·告诉我·你见过一位名叫 克里斯蒂娜的年轻女士吗？她在 22 楼工作？

LEROY JONES

You mean Christina Garrison?

莱罗伊·琼斯

你是说克里斯蒂娜·加里森？

ALEX

The Christina I'm referring to appears to be half black, gorgeous lady, probably 25ish.

亚历克斯

我指的克里斯蒂娜似乎是半黑人，美丽的女士，大概 25 岁左右。

LEROY JONES

Yea that's Christina Garrison. But she's more like 27 or 28.

莱罗伊·琼斯

是的，她就是克里斯蒂娜·加里森。但她更像是 27 或 28 岁。

ALEX

Is Christina Garrison a nice lady?

亚历克斯

克里斯蒂娜·加里森是个好女人吗？

LEROY JONES

Mr. Baxter, Christina Garrison is a very nice lady. Everyone in the building likes her. All the women I see her with going into the coffee shop/bar are always smiling and appearing like they are all great friends.

莱罗伊·琼斯
巴克斯特先生，克里斯蒂娜是个非常好的女士。
大楼里的每个人都喜欢她。我看到和她一起去咖
啡店/酒吧的所有女人都面带微笑，看起来就像是
好朋友一样。

ALEX
I see, thanks for the information, Leroy.

亚历克斯
我明白了，谢谢你的信息，莱罗伊。

LEROY JONES
You are welcome Mr. Baxter.

莱罗伊·琼斯
不客气，巴克斯特先生。

Alex moved forward through the gold-plated doors, into the lobby and to the elevator. Today he was not so lucky, no sign of Christina on the elevator, before he had to get off on the 25th floor.

亚历克斯穿过镀金门，进入大厅，然后进入电梯。今天他运气不太好，电梯里没有 克里斯蒂娜的踪影，他不得不在 25 楼下电梯。

As soon as Alex walked through the double glass doors Ann was immediately there attentively immediately ushering Alex into Claude's office.

亚历克斯一走进双层玻璃门，安就立刻在那里，热情地将 亚历克斯引到 克劳德 的办公室。

CLAUDE REARDEN
Glad you stopped by Alex on your way to Greenland.

克劳德·里尔登
很高兴您在去格陵兰的路上顺道拜访。

ALEX
Yea, I wanted you to give me a quick rundown on the status, so I know what to look for when I get up there.

亚历克斯
是的，我想让你快速告诉我一下情况，这样我上去后就知道该注意什么了。

CLAUDE REARDEN
Here's a list of the ships that had unloaded at Nuuk.

克劳德·里尔登
这是在努克卸货的船只清单。

ALEX
I would assume that never in Greenland's history since possibly WWII had the locals seen the arrival of that much shipping in such a short period of time.

亚历克斯
我认为，自二战以来，格陵兰历史上从未有过当地人在如此短的时间内看到如此多的船只抵达。

CLAUDE REARDEN
The major ports that can handle large cargo quantity are operating at 100% efficiency. Even though the present time as a low utilization time of year, for fishing boats, the fishermen who wanted can easily land jobs with Nuuk Dome Inc. as stevedore's unloading cargo from containers.

克劳德·里尔登
能够处理大量货物的主要港口正以 100% 的效率运行。尽管目前是渔船利用率较低的季节，但有意愿的渔民可以轻松地在　努克圆顶公司找到工作，担任卸货工，从集装箱中卸货。

As the discussion continued, Alex spotted a flaw in their plans.

随着讨论的继续，亚历克斯发现了他们计划中的一个缺陷。

ALEX
You realize we'll have a bottleneck in a year or two?

亚历克斯
你知道我们在一两年内会遇到瓶颈吗？

CLAUDE REARDEN
In what way?

克劳德·里尔登
以什么方式？

ALEX
Our work force alone is going to start driving more shipping requirements, as we start building those high-

rise apartment buildings once we get the initial wind break, the population will start growing, there will not be enough pier space for large ships.

亚历克斯
仅凭我们的劳动力就会开始推动更多的航运需求，因为我们开始建造那些高层公寓楼，一旦我们获得最初的防风林，人口就会开始增长，码头空间将不足以容纳大型船只。

CLAUDE REARDEN
I suppose that might be a factor.

克劳德·里尔登
我想这可能是一个因素。

ALEX
When Greenland makes us start removing our trash, figure 2 or 3 ships extra per week, just for trash removal alone.

亚历克斯
当格陵兰让我们开始清理垃圾时，想想每周多出 2 到 3 艘船，仅垃圾清理一项。

CLAUDE REARDEN
Well, what do you suggest?

克劳德·里尔登
那么，你有什么建议？

Alex stood up and walked over to the map that was located on the presentation stand and looked at it for a few minutes.

亚历克斯站起来，走到演示台上的地图前，看了几分钟。

克劳德·里尔登
如果其中一些人不想出售他们的财产怎么办？

ALEX
I think it would be in our best interests if we must build another pier to put it at Qinngorput, across the bay from the existing Port of Nuuk.

亚历克斯
我认为，如果我们必须建造另一个码头并将其放在与现有努克港隔海湾相望的钦戈普特，这将符合我们的最大利益。

CLAUDE REARDEN
There are only small fishing piers there now.

克劳德·里尔登
现在那里只有小渔码头。

ALEX
We would either have to put it North or South of the existing piers. If we go north, we'll have to dredge the channel. If we go south, we'll only have to build an "L" shaped break water to protect the pier from winter storms.

亚历克斯
我们要么必须把它放在现有码头的北部或南部。如果我们往北走，我们就必须疏浚航道。如果我们往南走，我们只需要建造一个 "L" 形防波堤来保护码头免受冬季风暴的侵袭。

CLAUDE REARDEN
The roads through town probably are not built well enough to sustain the traffic we would cause.

克劳德·里尔登
穿过城镇的道路可能修得不够好，无法维持我们造成的交通。

ALEX
True, we'll have to build our own road east of the City Center.

亚历克斯
确实，我们必须在市中心以东修建自己的道路。

CLAUDE REARDEN
What if some of those people do not want to sell their properties?

克劳德·里尔登
如果其中一些人不想出售他们的财产怎么办？

ALEX
We'll offer them penthouses up on the 50th floor of the first building we put up. They will more than be happy to give up those wood shacks for luxury dome living.

亚历克斯
我们将在我们建造的第一栋大楼的 50 层为他们提供顶层公寓。他们非常乐意放弃那些木屋，转而选择豪华的圆顶住宅。

CLAUDE REARDEN
How many homes are we talking?

克劳德·里尔登
我们在谈论多少个家庭？

ALEX
Recalling a general look at the area and the photograph portfolio that Jeff Sinclair provided, I'd guess 30 at the maximum, just enough room to build a four lane road.

亚历克斯
回想一下杰夫·辛克莱提供的对该地区的总体看法和照片集，我猜最多有三十张，刚好足够建造一条四车道的道路。

CLAUDE REARDEN
Why do we need four lanes?

克劳德·里尔登
为什么我们需要四车道？

ALEX
Real simple, that area will not be under the dome. In the wintertime, we simply have snow removal crews push or blow the snow into the middle lanes, then we don't have to worry about hauling it away.

亚历克斯
很简单，那个区域不会在穹顶之下。在冬季，我们只需让扫雪队将雪推入或吹入中间车道，然后我们就不必担心将其运走。

CLAUDE REARDEN
Good idea.

克劳德·里尔登
好主意。

ALEX
We got another problem.

亚历克斯
我们遇到了另一个问题。

CLAUDE REARDEN
What's that?

克劳德·里尔登
那是什么？

ALEX
We have no agreement with the Coastal Commission to build a Warf and a pier at Qinngorput.

亚历克斯
我们与海岸委员会没有就在钦戈尔普特建造码头和码头达成协议。

CLAUDE REARDEN
We'll find out who's on the Coastal Commission and make it worth their while. I'm sure there is some project they want done they can't afford to build; we'll build it for them.

克劳德·里尔登
我们会找出海岸委员会的成员，让他们的努力值得。我敢肯定，他们想完成一些项目，但他们负担不起，我们会为他们建造。

ALEX
Yea like a sports stadium.

亚历克斯
是的，就像一个体育场。

CLAUDE REARDEN
One that can house indoor soccer, football, and hockey.

克劳德·里尔登
可以举办室内足球、橄榄球和曲棍球比赛的场地。

ALEX
Greenland University is long overdue for a football team. And if we build it correctly, it can also double as a baseball stadium.

亚历克斯
格陵兰大学早就该组建一支足球队了。如果我们正确地建造它，它也可以兼作棒球场。

**CLAUDE REARDEN**
If we do that, I have one request.

克劳德·里尔登
如果我们这样做，我有一个请求。

**ALEX**
What's that?

亚历克斯
那是什么？

**CLAUDE REARDEN**
Make sure the baseball infield is not part of the football/soccer field.

克劳德·里尔登
确保棒球内场不是橄榄球/足球场的一部分。

**ALEX**
That shouldn't be a problem since with our Dome Technology we can build the roof as large as we want.

亚历克斯
这应该不是问题，因为利用我们的圆顶技术，我们可以建造我们想要的那么大的屋顶。

**CLAUDE REARDEN**
All that is required is how much money you wish to spend

克劳德·里尔登
所需要的只是您想花多少钱。

**ALEX**
Which gives us another opportunity.

亚历克斯
这给了我们另一个机会。

**CLAUDE REARDEN**
Such as?

克劳德·里尔登
例如？

ALEX
We can put a dome over Qinngorput.

亚历克斯
我们可以在钦格普特上盖一个圆顶。

CLAUDE REARDEN
It doesn't have to be as tall as the main dome, probably restrict it to 600 feet.

克劳德·里尔登
它不必像主圆顶那么高，可能限制在 600 英尺。

ALEX
I see another advantage.

亚历克斯
我看到了另一个优点。

CLAUDE REARDEN
What's that?

克劳德·里尔登
那是什么？

ALEX
If we build a Qinngorput Dome, it can be integrated into the main Nuuk Dome as an extension to it which would give us quite a bit more air space.

亚历克斯
如果我们建造一个钦格普特圆顶，它可以集成到主努克圆顶作为其延伸，这将为我们提供更多的空气空间。

CLAUDE REARDEN
How many people do you think we could cram in that space?

克劳德·里尔登
你认为我们可以在那个空间里塞多少人？

ALEX
Easy 300,000.

亚历克斯
轻松30万。

CLAUDE REARDEN
And maybe later Nuuk Residents might eventually want a dome conversion for Nuuk Proper.

克劳德·里尔登
也许后来的努克居民最终可能会希望对努克本身进行圆顶改造。

ALEX
No doubt as they spend some time in the dome and start enjoying a 70-degree park in the middle of winter, it might just move them to do so.

亚历克斯
毫无疑问，当他们在隆冬时节在穹顶里度过一段时间并开始享受 70 度的公园时，这可能会促使他们这样做。

CLAUDE REARDEN
Three domes, that would be exciting.

克劳德·里尔登
三个圆顶，那会很令人兴奋。

ALEX
Sure would.

亚历克斯
当然会。

CLAUDE REARDEN
Any comments back from Putin on the Siberian City selection?

克劳德·里尔登
普京对西伯利亚城市的选择有何回复？

ALEX
Yes, Vladimir Putin picked Chita to be the *Siberian Dome City* but can't make up his mind whether to build it East or West of the City.

亚历克斯
是的，弗拉基米尔·普京选择赤塔作为西伯利亚穹顶城市，但无法决定是将其建造在城市的东部还是西部。

CLAUDE REARDEN
What's the issue?

克劳德·里尔登
有什么问题？

ALEX
Vladimir Putin's got some feedback from a few of his friends that are part of the City Government there who indicated they don't want to lose the view of the forests East of the City.

亚历克斯
弗拉基米尔·普京从他的几位朋友那里得到了一些反馈，他们是那里市政府的成员，他们表示不想失去城市东部森林的景色。

CLAUDE REARDEN
Is he leaning toward building in the West?

克劳德·里尔登
他是否倾向于在西方建设？

ALEX
After I informe Vladimir Putin's that we can only remove so much rock West of the city and on third or more of the air space would be hills and mountains, Vladimir Putin realizes building in the East would make the construction completion date about half that of building in the West.

亚历克斯
在我告诉弗拉基米尔·普京，我们只能移除城市西部的岩石，而且三分之一或更多的空域将是丘陵和山脉之后，弗拉基米尔·普京意识到在东部建造将使建筑完工日期约为在西部建造的一半。

CLAUDE REARDEN
Tough decision, but I think we should make sure he knows, we'll support either plan, but he must live with his decision.

克劳德·里尔登
这是一个艰难的决定，但我认为我们应该确保他知道，我们会支持任何计划，但他必须接受他的决定。

ALEX

I'm sure he will appreciate your accommodative attitude.

亚历克斯
我相信他会感激你的通融态度。

Alex stood up and appeared to be ready to leave the office.

亚历克斯站起来，似乎准备离开办公室。


ALEX

Alright, I'm going to head up to Greenland now and take a look at the activity up there and meet Jeff Sinclair and see how things are going.

亚历克斯
好吧，我现在要去格陵兰岛看看那里的活动，和杰夫·辛克莱见面，看看事情进展如何。

CLAUDE REARDEN

We'll be in touch, let me know right away if you see something that concerns you.

克劳德·里尔登
我们会保持联系，如果你发现有什么让你担心的事情，请立即告诉我。

ALEX

You have never known me to remain silent.

亚历克斯
你从来都不知道我会保持沉默。


CLAUDE REARDEN
You got that right!

克劳德·里尔登
你说得对！


VOICE OVER

Claude smiled, recalling some of knock down drag out fights they had in the past. As he told his closest friends a few times:

画外音
克劳德笑了，回忆起他们过去打架的情景。他曾几次告诉他最亲密的朋友：

<u>FLASHBACK:</u>

闪回：

CLAUDE REARDEN
Alex is one tough son of a bitch. Never cross him.

克劳德·里尔登
亚历克斯是个强悍的混蛋。永远不要惹他

<u>END FLASHBACK.</u>

闪回结束。

Claude and Alex shook hands and then Alex turned and left the office on his way out when he smiled at Ann in the outer office.

克劳德和亚历克斯握手，然后亚历克斯转身离开办公室，在外面的办公室里对安微笑。

ALEX
Ann, have a nice afternoon, see you again sometime soon.

亚历克斯
安，祝你下午愉快，很快再见。

ANN
Have a safe trip Mr. Baxter.

安
一路平安，巴克斯特先生。

ALEX
Thank you.

亚历克斯
谢谢。

Alex walked out of the office across the hallway, pressed the elevator button and in 30 seconds he was on his way down to the ground floor. He then picked up his cell phone and called Rodriguez.

亚历克斯走出办公室，穿过走廊，按下电梯按钮，30　秒后就到了一楼。然后他拿起手机给罗德里格斯打电话。

ALEX
Hey buddy, I'm ready to leave now.

亚历克斯
嘿，伙计，我现在准备走了。

RODRIGUEZ
I'll be there in five minutes, Mr. Baxter.

罗德里格斯
我五分钟后就到，巴克斯特先生。

ALEX
Good, I'm going to grab a Coffee here, should be out in front in 5 minutes. Let Leroy know in case I take a bit longer.

亚历克斯
好的，我要去这里喝杯咖啡，五分钟后应该就到了。如果我需要多花点时间，请告诉 莱罗伊。

RODRIGUEZ
Will do sir. Take as much time as you need, I can drive around the block if necessary.

罗德里格斯
先生会做的。您需要多少时间就多少时间，如果有必要，我可以开车绕着街区转一圈。

ALEX
See you when you get here.

亚历克斯
当你到达这里时见。

Alex then hung up.

亚历克斯随后挂断了电话。

Alex walked over to the bar/restaurant on the side of the lobby entrance and went inside and walked up to the counter where a worker was patiently waiting for customers.

亚历克斯走到大堂入口一侧的酒吧/餐厅，走进去，走到柜台前，工作人员正在耐心地等待顾客。

The blonde headed employee asked with a friendly smile.

这位可爱的金发女员工面带友好的微笑问道。

COFFEE SHOP WORKER
What can I get for you sir?

咖啡店工作人员
先生，我能为您做些什么？

ALEX
I'll have a cappuccino with some extra whip cream
on top. Please put it in a large cup but just a medium
coffee but charge me for a large coffee.

亚历克斯
我要一杯卡布奇诺，上面加一些鲜奶油。请把它
倒进大杯，但只喝中杯咖啡，要收我一杯大杯咖
啡的费用。

COFFEE SHOP WORKER
Right away sir. Will be about two minutes.

咖啡店工作人员
先生，马上就好。大约两分钟。

ALEX
Thanks.

亚历克斯
谢谢。

The Coffee Shop Worker went to work preparing the drink.

咖啡店工作人员开始准备饮料。

Unexpectedly, of all people that Alex would not expect about then walked in and stood
at the counter to order a coffee, was Christina Garrison. Alex was pleasantly surprised
and felt lucky for the chance encounter.

出乎意料的是，亚历克斯完全没有想到，走进来站在柜台前点咖啡的人竟然是
克里斯蒂娜·加里森。亚历克斯感到惊喜不已，并为这次偶遇感到幸运。

Alex being in big business had private detectives. Anyone in big business must use
them from time to time for many reasons. He also had a security detail which included
people quite capable of hacking computers if they had too. Just like anyone else with
a lot of money, Alex had to protect himself.

亚历克斯从事大生意，有私家侦探。大公司里的任何人都必须时不时地使用它
们，原因有很多。他还有一个安全小组，其中包括一些在必要时能够入侵计算
机的人。就像其他有很多钱的人一样，亚历克斯必须保护自己。

Yesterday, Alex contacted Johnny Rossellini, his New York private eye and asked him
to check out Christina Garrison.

昨天，亚历克斯联系了他在纽约的私家侦探约翰尼·罗西里尼，请他去看看克里斯蒂娜·加里森。

## MUSIC FOR THE NEXT SECTION DURING THE REPORT AND VOICEOVERS:

报告和画外音期间下一节的音乐：

https://www.youtube.com/watch?v=T6x3eIVT4iU

Dohnanyi: Piano Concerto No.2 Op.42 / Shelley · Bamert · BBC Philharmonic Orchestra.

多纳伊：钢琴协奏曲第 2 号 Op.42 / 雪莱·巴默特·英国广播公司爱乐乐团

Alex now thought about Johnny Rossellini's Christina's portfolio.

亚历克斯现在想到了约翰尼·罗西里尼的克里斯蒂娜的作品集。

### VOICEOVER (JOHNNY ROSSELLINI)
### REPORT

*Christina Garrison graduated from Princeton with a double degree including Russian Language and obtained a master's degree in economics. Christina had one previous boyfriend that didn't work out and when I contacted Christina's previous boyfriend and asked some questions, posing as someone checking her out for other reasons, why they broke up, the former boyfriend gave an interesting answer.*

画外音（约翰尼·罗西里尼）
报告
克里斯蒂娜·加里森是一名基督徒，她过着简朴的生活，为一家非营利组织工作。当我们找到其他联系人时，因为前任情人喜欢伤害他们的前任情人，有时如果他们有机会，这些是最好的信息和线索来源。

### CHRISTINA'S FORMER BOYFRIEND

Christina was a teaser and would not go to bed with him unless he married her first.

克里斯蒂娜的前男友
克里斯蒂娜是个爱挑逗的人，除非他先娶她，否则她不会和他上床。

### VOICEOVER (JOHNNY ROSSELLINI)
### REPORT

*Christina Garrison is a Christian and live a modest lifestyle working energetically for a non-profit organization. When we found other contacts, because former lovers like to hurt their former lovers, sometimes if they get a chance, those are the best sources of information and leads.*

画外音（约翰尼·罗西里尼）<br>报告

克里斯蒂娜·加里森毕业于普林斯顿大学，获得俄语等双学位，并获得经济学硕士学位。克里斯蒂娜有一个前男友，但没有成功，当我联系克里斯蒂娜的前男友并问了一些问题时，假装有人因为其他原因在调查她，为什么他们分手了，前男友给出了一个有趣的答案。

*Despite all the smearing that former boyfriend attempted, the facts came out that Christina is an ideal woman, didn't sleep around, somewhat of a book worm, loves the Symphony, Opera, Broadway shows, Ballroom Dancing, and was considered by her friends sweet and wholesome.*

尽管前男友试图抹黑克里斯蒂娜，但事实是克里斯蒂娜是一个理想的女人，没有乱搞，有点书呆子气，喜欢交响乐、歌剧、百老汇表演、交际舞，朋友们认为她很甜美、很健康。

Alex was impressed by Johnny Rossellini's report; Stephanie would be horrified to learn what Alex had done.

约翰尼·罗西里尼的报告给亚历克斯留下了深刻的印象；斯蒂芬妮如果知道亚历克斯的所作所为，一定会大吃一惊。

Alex stood his distance and quietly waited for his drink. Within the two-minute mark, which included the employee taking Christina's order, his drink was ready, and oddly since Christina just ordered coffee, her drink came about at the same time.

亚历克斯站在远处，静静地等待他的饮料。在两分钟内，包括员工接受克里斯蒂娜的订单，他的饮料就准备好了，奇怪的是，因为克里斯蒂娜刚刚点了咖啡，她的饮料也差不多在同一时间送来了。

209

Christina quickly noticed Alex's large cup was loaded with whip cream and she commented:

克里斯蒂娜很快注意到亚历克斯的大杯子里装满了鲜奶油，她评论道：

CHRISTINA
Wow, that's a lot of whip cream.

克里斯蒂娜
哇，好多鲜奶油啊。

ALEX
Yea I love the stuff.

亚历克斯
是的，我喜欢这个东西。

Alex then quickly thought now would be an excellent time to pursue Christina.

亚历克斯很快就想到现在是追求克里斯蒂娜的好时机。

ALEX
Hey, would you like to join me for a couple of minutes, enjoy our drinks and perhaps talk a little.

亚历克斯
嘿，你愿意和我一起喝几分钟，喝点饮料，聊聊天吗？

CHRISTINA
I suppose so.

克里斯蒂娜
我想是的。

ALEX
Good, my name is Alex.

亚历克斯
很好，我叫亚历克斯。

CHRISTINA
Hi, I'm Christina.

克里斯蒂娜
嗨，我是克里斯蒂娜。

Christina instinctively held out her right hand to shake Alex's hand.

克里斯蒂娜本能地伸出右手和亚历克斯握手。

Alex shook her hand and smiled.

亚历克斯握着她的手，微笑着。

ALEX
I'm pleased to meet you, Christina.

亚历克斯
很高兴见到你，克里斯蒂娜。

Christina knew exactly who Alex Baxter was and she herself wasn't coming in the bar/restaurant for coffee, she was coming in for her quarry, as she wanted Alex as much as he wanted her.

克里斯蒂娜很清楚亚历克斯·巴克斯特是谁，她自己不是来酒吧/餐厅喝咖啡的，她来这里是为了她的猎物，因为她想要亚历克斯，就像他想要她一样。

After seeing Alex in the elevator and talking with her co-worker who knew who Alex Baxter was, informed Christina of Alex's name and stature in life.

在电梯里看到亚历克斯后，她和同事聊了聊，同事知道亚历克斯·巴克斯特是谁，于是她告诉克里斯蒂娜亚历克斯的名字和地位。

Christina thus did her own research on Alex and in just one search on Google, found 1.5 million entries.

克里斯蒂娜因此自己研究了亚历克斯，在谷歌上搜索了一次，就找到了 150 万个条目。

There were vast amounts of information on Alex Baxter. What really struck Christina was that many of the write-ups were good and that he was single, had no committed relationship, was definitely no indications he was gay, and was taking his time selecting a mate, and concentrating his efforts on expanding his business interests.

关于亚历克斯·巴克斯特的信息非常多。克里斯蒂娜真正震惊的是，很多文章都写得很好，他是单身，没有稳定的恋爱关系，绝对没有迹象表明他是同性恋，他正在花时间选择伴侣，并集中精力扩大他的商业利益。

Alex pointed to bar stool chairs and circular table.

亚历克斯指着酒吧凳子和圆桌。

Let's sit over here,
我们坐在这边，

Christina and Alex sat down at the table in a semi empty room as most of the building residents took their coffee and went to their offices.

克里斯蒂娜和亚历克斯坐在一个半空的房间里的桌子旁，而大楼里的大多数居民都拿着咖啡去办公室了。

Christina was smiling, if not beaming. The attraction that Alex felt was stunning. Her half black mixture was perfect. Her skin tone was as glamorous as it could get having the right amount of DNA from both parents to produce a spectacular hybrid that was heavy on beauty and bountiful in demure quality.

克里斯蒂娜面带微笑，甚至喜笑颜开。亚历克斯感受到的吸引力令人惊叹。她的半黑混合是完美的。她的肤色非常迷人，从父母双方身上都获得了适量的DNA，从而产生了一个美丽而又充满端庄气质的混血儿。

Christina's lips were beautiful, and her hazel eyes were almost hypnotic.

克里斯蒂娜的嘴唇很漂亮，淡褐色的眼睛几乎让人着迷。

There was no doubt why Christina's former boyfriend was so emotionally disturbed over the breakup because he fell under her spell, but since he was a coward and selfish and slightly narcissistic, didn't make any efforts to meet her minimum requirements of a commitment to matrimony.

毫无疑问，克里斯蒂娜的前男友为什么会因为分手而情绪如此失控，因为他被克里斯蒂娜迷住了，但由于他胆小、自私，还有点自恋，并没有做出任何努力来满足克里斯蒂娜对婚姻承诺的最低要求。

Christina wasn't going to give it up to anyone; she was well trained by her mother. However, Alex might be a different situation. She would have to do some soul searching to figure out how to respond to Alex, should he go where she felt his electricity would soon be taking her.

克里斯蒂娜不会放弃任何人；她被母亲训练得很好。然而，亚历克斯的情况可能有所不同。她必须进行一些自我反省，以找出如何回应亚历克斯，如果他去她认为他的电力很快就会带她去的地方。

**VOICEOVER (CHRISTINA) THOUGHT**
*Is his little head thinking for his big head. Or is this genuine affection?*

画外音（克里斯蒂娜）思考
他的小脑袋是在为他的大脑袋思考吗？或者这是真爱？

CHRISTINA
Alex, do you live here in New York?

克里斯蒂娜
亚历克斯，你住在纽约吗？

ALEX
No, I live in Minnesota.

亚历克斯
不，我住在明尼苏达州。

CHRISTINA
What brings you to New York Alex?

克里斯蒂娜
亚历克斯，什么风把你吹到纽约了？

ALEX
I am here to meet with one of my business partners, and then I'm heading up to Nuuk Greenland in a few minutes to oversee a construction site we are building.

亚历克斯
我来这里是为了与我的一位商业伙伴会面，然后几分钟后我将前往努克格陵兰，监督我们正在建设的一个建筑工地。

CHRISTINA
I see. I bet it's cold up in Greenland this time of year.

克里斯蒂娜
我懂了。我敢打赌，每年这个时候格陵兰岛都很冷。

ALEX
It certainly is, lots of snow on the ground that's for sure.

亚历克斯
当然是了，地上肯定有很多雪。

CHRISTINA
How long will you be up in Greenland?

克里斯蒂娜

你会在格陵兰岛待多久？

ALEX

I'll probably spend the night there and come back in the morning.

亚历克斯
我可能会在那里过夜，早上回来。

CHRISTINA

So, you'll do a stopover and not fly back directly to Minnesota.

克里斯蒂娜
所以你会在中途停留，而不是直接飞回明尼苏达州。

ALEX

That's right, I'm going to give my partner a verbal report and discuss my findings from the trip.

亚历克斯
没错，我要向我的搭档口头汇报，并讨论我这次旅行的发现。

CHRISTINA
That sounds fun.

克里斯蒂娜
听起来很有趣。

ALEX

Excuse me for one minute Christina, I need to call my driver if you don't mind.

CHRISTINA
No problem, Alex.

克里斯蒂娜
没问题，亚历克斯。

Alex called Rodriguez.

亚历克斯给罗德里格斯打了电话。

RODRIGUEZ
Hello Mr. Baxter, are you ready to leave?

罗德里格斯
你好，巴克斯特先生，你准备好出发了吗？

ALEX
Rodriguez, I'm drinking my coffee here in the restaurant, I'll be delayed a few minutes.

亚历克斯
罗德里格斯，我正在餐厅喝咖啡，我会晚点几分钟。

RODRIGUEZ
No problem boss, I'm two minutes away and I'll circle the block until you walk out to the curb.

罗德里格斯
没问题，老板，我还有两分钟就到了，我会绕着街区走，直到你走到路边。

Leroy Jones walked out of the security office and across the lobby could see into the bar/restaurant opening and spotted Alex sitting with Christina Garison and smiled. Leroy Jones knew that Christina was a very charming lady and deserved the best and Alex was the best.

莱罗伊·琼斯走出保安办公室，穿过大厅，可以看到酒吧/餐厅的入口，看到亚历克斯和克里斯蒂娜·加里森坐在一起，笑了。 莱罗伊·琼斯 知道 克里斯蒂娜是一位非常迷人的女士，值得拥有最好的，而 亚历克斯就是最好的。

During the cold months, Leroy and his former Seal and Army Green Beret assistants, would take turn watching the security cameras, and go outside and perform a barrier patrol to intervene as early as possible to keep any negative activity outside the building.

在寒冷的月份，莱罗伊·琼斯　和他以前的海豹突击队和陆军绿色贝雷帽助手会轮流看守安全摄像头，并到外面进行屏障巡逻，尽早进行干预，以防止任何负面活动在建筑物外发生。

The building security videos were always monitored 7/24 with multiple shifts but outdoor, physical security only posted during normal working hours because after that, few people entered the building, and the bar restaurant closed after 9:00 p.m.

建筑物安全视频始终是 7/24 全天候监控的，有多个班次，但室外物理安全只在正常工作时间值班，因为在那之后，很少有人进入建筑物，酒吧餐厅在晚上9 点后关闭。

About the time Leroy, walked outside Rodriguez pulled up with his Limo. Leroy spotted Rodriquez and walked over to the car and Rodriguez instantly spotted him and rolled down his window as Leroy neared the Limo.

大约就在勒罗伊走到外面的时候，罗德里格斯开着他的豪华轿车停了下来。勒罗伊发现了罗德里格斯，并向汽车走去，当勒罗伊靠近豪华轿车时，罗德里格斯立即发现了他，并摇下了车窗。

LEROY JONES

Hey Rodriguez, how's it going?

勒罗伊·琼斯

嘿，罗德里格斯，怎么样？

RODRIGUEZ

Not too bad Leroy.

罗德里格斯

勒罗伊还不错。

LEROY JONES

Alex is at the bar/restaurant talking with a very beautiful lady, he might be a few minutes, you can just wait here.

勒罗伊·琼斯

亚历克斯正在酒吧/餐厅和一位非常漂亮的女士聊天，他可能会等几分钟，你可以在这里等一下。

RODRIGUEZ

Thanks Leroy, I appreciate that.

罗德里格斯

谢谢勒罗伊，我很感激。

LEROY JONES

You're welcome.

勒罗伊·琼斯

不用谢。

RODRIGUEZ

Is the woman a good looker?

罗德里格斯

女人长得好看吗？

LEROY JONES

Oh yes, the finest piece of eye-candy any man would see.

勒罗伊·琼斯
哦，是的，这是任何男人都会看到的最精美的东
西。

RODRIGUEZ
That's good, also a good thing Alex didn't bring
Stephanie with him.

罗德里格斯
这很好，亚历克斯没有带 斯蒂芬妮一起去也是件
好事。

LEROY JONES
Yea, Stephanie wouldn't be doing so well about now,
if she saw Christina.

勒罗伊·琼斯
是的，如果 斯蒂芬妮看到 克里斯蒂娜，她现在不
会过得这么好。

RODRIGUEZ
Is the lady that cute?

罗德里格斯
小姐姐有那么可爱吗？

LEROY JONES
Oh yes, intelligent lady, impeccable, well-educated
and absolutely gorgeous. Plus, she's single and
currently doesn't have a boyfriend.

勒罗伊·琼斯
哦，是的，聪明的女士，无可挑剔，受过良好的
教育，而且绝对美丽。另外，她是单身，目前没
有男朋友。

RODRIGUEZ
I wonder why that is?

罗德里格斯
我想知道这是为什么？

LEROY JONES
I can tell you, what some women I know that work
with her said. Christina is very particular and only
wants a committed man in her life.

勒罗伊·琼斯
我可以告诉你，我认识的一些与她一起工作的女
性是怎么说的。克里斯蒂娜非常挑剔，她一生中
只想要一个忠诚的男人。

RODRIGUEZ
She's probably not going to get that with Alex.

罗德里格斯
她可能不会和亚历克斯在一起。

LEROY JONES
Think so?

勒罗伊·琼斯
这么认为吗？

RODRIGUEZ
Stephanie is a sexy hot fox, and she hasn't been able
to nail Alex, what makes you think this woman can?

罗德里格斯
斯蒂芬妮是一只性感火辣的狐狸，她还没能征服
亚历克斯，你凭什么认为这个女人可以？

LEROY JONES
Time will tell.

勒罗伊·琼斯
时间会告诉我们答案。

Alex could have spent a lot longer time with Christina as he was enthralled with her presence. Christina's electricity was intoxicating. But Alex knew he had to take care of business first and knew he had to end this brief but splendid encounter and perhaps hoped to see her again sometime soon.

亚历克斯本可以花更多的时间和克里斯蒂娜在一起，因为他被她的存在迷住了。克里斯蒂娜的魅力令人陶醉。但亚历克斯知道他必须先处理好事情，知道他必须结束这场短暂而精彩的邂逅，也许希望不久后能再次见到她。

ALEX
Christina, here's my business card, I'd love to take
you to dinner and a Broadway show or entertainment
sometime with you when you are available.

亚历克斯
克里斯蒂娜，这是我的名片，当您有空时，我很
乐意带您去吃晚餐、观看百老汇表演或娱乐活
动。

Christina took Alex's business card then reached in her purse and pulled out her own business card and handed it to Alex.

克里斯蒂娜拿起亚历克斯的名片，然后从钱包里拿出自己的名片递给亚历克斯。

CHRISTINA
Here's my business card, call me when you are in town and want to go out sometime.

克里斯蒂娜
这是我的名片，你来城里想出去的时候给我打电话。

ALEX
Thank you I will.

亚历克斯
谢谢，我会的。

CHRISTINA
You're welcome, Alex.

克里斯蒂娜
不客气，亚历克斯。

ALEX
I'm sorry but I must leave now, my driver is probably out front, and I got a day's work ahead of me up in Greenland.

亚历克斯
很抱歉，我现在必须走了，我的司机可能在前面，我还要去格陵兰工作一天。

CHRISTINA
It's been delightful talking with you Alex

克里斯蒂娜
和你聊天很愉快，亚历克斯

ALEX
Same here Christina.

亚历克斯
克里斯蒂娜，我也一样。

Alex stood up, held out his hand which Christina warmly and affectionately grabbed.

亚历克斯站起来，伸出手，克里斯蒂娜热情而亲切地握住了他的手。

**ALEX**
I hope to see you soon.
亚历克斯
我希望很快能见到你。

**CHRISTINA**
So, do I.

克里斯蒂娜
我也是。

Alex, feeling brave and decisive, reached over and gently kissed Christina on the cheek and then smiled and left.

亚历克斯勇敢而果断地伸出手，轻轻地吻了克里斯蒂娜的脸颊，然后微笑着离开了。

Christina sat there stunned and feeling moist. She also recalled numerous discussions she had with her mother about protecting her reputation and her moral and ethical behavior would one day open doors to someone special.

克里斯蒂娜坐在那里，惊呆了，浑身湿润。她还回忆起她与母亲多次讨论如何保护自己的名誉，以及她的道德和伦理行为是否有一天会为某个特别的人打开大门。

**VOICEOVER (CHRISTINA)**
**THOUGHT**
*I wonder if perhaps Alex's interest in me might be results of what my mother did for me in the way she managed my upbringing.*

画外音（克里斯蒂娜）
想法
我想知道亚历克斯对我的兴趣是否可能是我母亲
为我所做的一切以及她对我的成长方式的结果。

Alex walked out of the building, then walked over to the waiting Limo where Rodriguez and Leroy were evidently having a conversation. Alex knew that Leroy was allowing Rodriguez to wait there and so he reached down in his pocket and grabbed another $100 bill and approached Leroy and held out his hand.

亚历克斯走出大楼，然后走到等候的豪华轿车旁，罗德里格斯和莱罗伊显然正在交谈。亚历克斯知道莱罗伊允许罗德里格斯在那里等，所以他伸手从口袋里掏出另一张 100 美元钞票，走近莱罗伊并伸出手。

ALEX

Thanks for letting Rodriguez wait here a little bit, it helped me out quite a bit.

亚历克斯

感谢您让罗德里格斯在这里等了一会儿，这对我很有帮助。

Alex then held out his hand to shake Leroy's and pressed the $100 in his palm.

LEROY JONES.

No problem Mr. Baxter. You have a safe flight to where you are going.

勒罗伊·琼斯。

没问题，巴克斯特先生。祝您旅途愉快，一路平安。

ALEX

Thank you, Leroy.

亚历克斯

谢谢你，莱罗伊。

Leroy grabbed the door handle and opened it for Alex.

莱罗伊抓住门把手，为亚历克斯打开了门。

LEROY JONES

You are quite welcome, Mr. Baxter.

莱罗伊·琼斯。

不用客气，巴克斯特先生。

Leroy smiled and wondered how things worked out with Christina.

莱罗伊微笑着，想知道克里斯蒂娜的事情进展如何。

The car headed back to JFK, and as usual, John Black was waiting curb side as he pulled up to walk him through security.

汽车返回肯尼迪机场，和往常一样，约翰·布莱克在路边等着，他把车停在路边，陪他通过安检。

In a brief period, Alex and Brad were airborne and on their way to Greenland. Alex in many ways felt excited. And right about the time the plane hit 10,000 feet with much of New York still visible, his cell phone suddenly buzzed, and it was a text message from Christina.

不一会儿，亚历克斯和布拉德就起飞前往格陵兰岛。亚历克斯在很多方面都感到很兴奋。就在飞机飞到 10,000 英尺高空时，纽约的大部分景色仍清晰可见，他的手机突然响了，是克里斯蒂娜发来的短信。

## CLOSEUP ALEX'S CELL PHONE

亚历克斯手机特写

    Note: In the text messages, they are handled like voiceover with the actor's voice reading the message they are sending.

    注意：在文本信息中，它们被处理得像画外音一样，由演员的声音读出他们所发送的信息。

CHRISTINA
(TEXT MESSAGE)
I was so happy to have met you.

克里斯蒂娜
（短信）
我很高兴认识你。

Alex typed and responded.

亚历克斯打字回复。

ALEX
(TEXT MESSAGE)
So was I.

亚历克斯
（短信）
我也是。

CHRISTINA
(TEXT MESSAGE)
Have a safe trip, Alex.

克里斯蒂娜
（短信）
祝你旅途愉快，亚历克斯。

ALEX
(TEXT MESSAGE)
Thank you, Christina.

亚历克斯
（短信）
谢谢你，克里斯蒂娜。

Suddenly the trip got better by the minute. The electricity in the air from Christina, and the excitement of seeing this dome construction starting was making Alex's day.

突然间，旅途变得越来越好。克里斯蒂娜带来的兴奋，以及看到这个圆顶建筑真正开始的兴奋，让亚历克斯的一天都充满了兴奋。

It would be tough catching a nap now with all the excitement and anticipation that flowed through him. The meridians in Alex's body that an acupuncturist would poke into were now elevated, his endorphins were synthetically augmented by the unique euphoria that swept through his body created by Christina's charm. Alex strongly felt something would come of that attraction.

现在，他内心充满了兴奋和期待，很难睡个午觉。针灸师会刺入亚历克斯体内的经络，经络现在被提升了，克里斯蒂娜的魅力让他全身都充满了独特的快感，这种快感合成地增强了他的内啡肽。亚历克斯强烈地感觉到这种吸引力会带来一些好处。

Alex then opened up the private detective Johnny Rossellini's document on Christina on his iPhone. It described her background, her family and every piece of information the private detective could glean from the multiple sources he investigated.

亚历克斯随后在 苹果手机 (iPhone) 上打开了私家侦探约翰尼·罗西里尼关于克里斯蒂娜的文件。它描述了她的背景、她的家庭以及私家侦探从他调查的多个来源收集到的每一条信息。

VOICEOVER (JOHNNY ROSSELLINI)
REPORT
*Christina's father, Mr. Garrison, is an African American and a former Army Green Beret who fought in Vietnam. Mr. Garrison was highly decorated, wounded multiple times, survived somehow the SOG team insertions into Cambodia and Laos.*

画外音（约翰尼·罗西里尼）
报告
克里斯蒂娜的父亲加里森先生是一名非裔美国人，曾是陆军绿色贝雷帽队员，曾在越南战斗过。加里森先生功勋卓著，多次受伤，在 *SOG* 小组进入柬埔寨和老挝的行动中幸存下来。

*Mr. Garrison served with notable other Green Beret people such as Colonel Plaster in some of the most hair-raising insertions and extractions ever conducted. Two minutes means the difference between life and death and possibly capture and torture.*

加里森先生与其他著名的绿色贝雷帽人员（如普拉斯特上校）一起参与了一些有史以来最令人毛骨悚然的插入和提取行动。两分钟意味着生死之间的差别，也可能是被捕和受折磨之间的差别。

*According to my research, Green Beret men such as Mr. Garison were issued Cyanide capsules they could bite and swallow if they knew they were going to be captured. They were large capsules that contained both Cyanide and Heroin so they could go out in a tranquil moment.*

根据我的研究，像加里森先生这样的绿色贝雷帽士兵被发放了氰化物胶囊，如果他们知道自己将被抓获，可以咬下并吞下。这些胶囊很大，里面既有氰化物，也有海洛因，这样他们就可以在平静的时刻离开。

*The reason for such extraordinary procedures is the Green Beret men knew that if they allowed themselves to be captured, they could expect weeks of torture if not cruel deaths.*

之所以采取如此特别的程序，是因为绿色贝雷帽士兵知道，如果他们让自己被抓获，他们可能会遭受数周的折磨，甚至会惨死。

*The NVA and the Vietcong hated the Green Beret more passionately than any other enemy forces, because they hurt them the most. Some statistics suggest Special Forces resulted in over half of the NVA and Vietcong killed in the war.*

北越军和越共比其他任何敌军都更痛恨绿色贝雷帽，因为他们对他们的伤害最大。一些统计数据表明，特种部队在战争中造成了超过一半的北越军和越共士兵死亡。

*Sargent Garrison retired from the Army man and, could not go any higher as an enlisted man, and had no desire to do anything but work with his Green Beret* brothers.

加里森中士以 E9 的军衔从陆军退役，作为一名士兵，他不能再升到更高的军衔，他不想做任何事情，只想和他的绿色贝雷帽兄弟一起工作。

*Upon military retirement, Mr. Garrison went to college and became a history major and eventually a high school teacher where he met Christina's mother, another teacher.*

退役后，加里森先生上了大学，主修历史，后来成为一名高中老师，在那里他遇到了克里斯蒂娜的母亲，另一位老师。

*Hence with two parents as private tutors, Christina maintained a perfect straight-A GPA and was awarded a full ride scholarship to Princeton University where she majored in economics.*

因此，在父母的私人教师的帮助下，克里斯蒂娜保持了完美的 A 级 GPA，并获得了普林斯顿大学的全额奖学金，主修经济学。

*Christina got some of her beautiful looks from her mother who is also very attractive. Christina's mother is slightly liberal and a good balance to her conservative father. Christina's mother is not only Christina's mentor and best friend in life, but also a coach that any young girl would love to have if you wanted to be successful.*

克里斯蒂娜的美丽外表继承自她的母亲，她的母亲也非常有魅力。克里斯蒂娜的母亲略带自由主义，与她保守的父亲形成了良好的平衡。克里斯蒂娜的母亲不仅是克里斯蒂娜的人生导师和最好的朋友，也是任何想要成功的年轻女孩都希望拥有的教练。

*Christina could have gone to work for Goldman Sachs or JP Morgan and spent several summers as an intern on Wall Street, but due to her mother's liberal attitudes and the sense of duty, ended up going to work for a non-profit organization and that's how she ended up at 120 Wall Street.*

克里斯蒂娜本可以去高盛或摩根大通工作，并在华尔街度过了几个夏天的实习生生涯，但由于她母亲的自由主义态度和责任感，她最终去了一家

非营利组织工作，这就是她最终在华尔街 120 号
的原因。

Alex closed Johnny Rossellini's report.

亚历克斯结束了约翰尼·罗西里尼的报告。

**ALEX (THOUGHT)**
*That's how Christina had her chance encounter with me.*

亚历克斯（心想）
克里斯蒂娜就是这样偶然遇到我的。

*One might think Christina was now being rewarded by
the Supreme Being for helping so many other people
in her work. Time would tell.*

人们可能会认为克里斯蒂娜现在正在因为在工作
中帮助了这么多人而得到至高无上的奖励。时间
会证明一切。

Since there were only two people on the plane and Alex stayed restless and in an
energized state, after reading a few work-related documents, walked on up into the
cockpit and sat down in the right seat, where he and Brad had conversations until it got
time to descend to the Nuuk Airport.

由于飞机上只有两个人，亚历克斯一直处于不安和精力充沛的状态，在阅读了
一些与工作相关的文件后，他走进驾驶舱，坐在右边的座位上，他和布拉德在
那里聊天，直到飞机降落到努克机场。

Once again, straight in over the water, with that nice black strip of runway ahead of
them thanks to the ingenious electrical runway heating system.

再次，他们直接飞越水面，前方有一条漂亮的黑色跑道，这要归功于巧妙的电
动道加热系统。

Just before the Jet got to the final approach, Alex requested Brad:

就在喷气式飞机进入最后进近阶段之前，亚历克斯请求布拉德：

**ALEX**
Brad, could you please contact the Tower and tell them
we want to do a fly over Nuuk if its ok, I want to fly
over the Dome work site and look at it from up in the
air.

亚历克斯
布拉德，你能否联系塔台，告诉他们我们想飞越

努克，如果可以的话，我想飞越穹顶施工现场，
从空中观察一下。

**BRAD**
Sure, not a problem.
布拉德
当然，没问题。

Brad forwarded the request to air traffic controllers who responded:

布拉德将请求转发给空中交通管制员，他们回应道：

**ATC TOWER (<u>ICAO</u>: BGGH)**
N80973, we have no inbound traffic, go ahead and do
a fly over, but maintain an altitude above 1000 feet.

ATC 塔台 （ICAO：BGGH）
N80973，我们没有入境交通，请继续飞越，但要
保持在 1000 英尺以上的高度。

**BRAD**
Tower, this is N80973 understands no inbound traffic,
maintaining 1000 feet during fly over and request final
approach on runway 27.

布拉德
塔台，我是 N80973，请知悉没有入境交通，在飞
越期间保持 1000 英尺高度，并请求在 27 号跑
道上进行最后进近。

**ATC TOWER (<u>ICAO</u>: BGGH)**
N80973, understand, make final approach on runway 27.

ATC塔台
(<u>ICAO</u>: **BGGH**)
N80973，请知悉，在 27 号跑道上进行最后进近。

LIVE STREAMING NUUK AIRPORT VIDEO CAM:

努克机场视频摄像头直播：

[ https://www.youtube.com/watch?v=MApnQlsX5AQ ]

Brad would bank right over the construction site so that Alex would get a good view
from the air.

布拉德会直接飞到建筑工地上，以便亚历克斯可以从空中看清楚。

As expected, there were a lot of containers, tents, and machinery on the ground. Unlike the areas surrounding the work site, a lot of the snow was removed, and the work site appeared very functional from 1000 feet.

正如预期的那样，地面上有很多集装箱、帐篷和机器。与施工现场周围的区域不同，很多积雪都被清除了，从 1000 英尺的高度看，施工现场似乎非常实用。

<u>EXT. CGI. DAY. OBSERVATION OF NUUK DOME CONSTRUCTION DURING VOICEOVER DURING NEXT SEQUENCE.</u>

<u>MUSIC DURING FLYOVER PORTIONS OF THIS SYMPHONY:</u>

<u>外景</u>。<u>CGI</u>。白天。在下一个<u>场景的画外音中观察努克圆顶的建造情况</u>。

飞越交响乐部分的音乐：

https://www.youtube.com/watch?v=sHsFIv8VA7w

VOICEOVER
*Plumes of smoke or water vapor rose up from the area which most likely was from heaters and generators providing electricity to the numerous trailers, and tents where temporary shops were located.*

画外音
从该区域升起一缕缕烟雾或水蒸气，很可能是来自加热器和发电机，它们为众多拖车和临时商店所在的帐篷提供电力。

*Alex could see derricks sticking up. These were drilling rigs that were sinking holes down several hundred feet in the ground then steel beams were being inserted and will be encased in concrete to help establish solid foundations for the pillars going up next.*

亚历克斯可以看到井架竖立起来。这些钻机在地下数百英尺深的地方钻孔，然后插入钢梁，并用混凝土包裹，为接下来的柱子打下坚实的基础。

*The beginning of the first 6 pillars was evident. In a couple of weeks large tents would be over these 6 areas as the first 20 feet or so of the pillar would be constructed before the forms would be raised up in place to continue up to the first height.*

前 6 根柱子的开始显而易见。几周后，这 6 个区域上方将搭起大帐篷，因为柱子的前 20 英尺左右将建成，然后模板将升起，继续上升到第一个高度。

*From that height on the platform, which also contained a doghouse used to warm people in shifts, so that several people would be continuously working the concrete buckets and guide hydraulic powered tampers to pack it down and get ready to be covered by the next bucket of concrete.*

从那个高度开始，平台上还设有一个狗屋，用于轮流取暖，这样几个人就会不断地操作混凝土桶，引导液压夯实机将其压实，并准备好被下一桶混凝土覆盖。

*Additional rebar would be welded in place as the platform was designed to hold the rebar in place during the welding process and by the time the welding was complete the platform would be ready to be raised to the next height. As the pillar grew in height steam would be given off from it constantly since the cement was preheated before it was lifted up to the platform and dumped.*

额外的钢筋将被焊接到位，因为平台的设计目的是在焊接过程中将钢筋固定到位，焊接完成后，平台就可以升到下一个高度了。随着柱子的高度不断增加，蒸汽会不断从柱子中散发出来，因为水泥在被抬到平台上倾倒之前要进行预热。

*Two cranes were installed on each pillar. One on the east side and one on the west side. This was used to increase the velocity of the concrete lifts. One bucket on one crane would be lifting, while the other was dumping into the form then lowered for the next reload.*

每个柱子上都安装了两台起重机。一台在东侧，一台在西侧。这是为了提高混凝土升降速度。一台起重机上的一个铲斗将被提升，而另一台则将水泥倾倒到模板中，然后放下以备下次重新装载。

*Men wearing a safety harness had pneumatic powered tamping tools to help settle the cement between lifts. Just enough time would exist for the tamping to complete before the next bucket was ready to dump another large application of cement slowly building the pillar in twelve-foot sections.*

戴着安全带的工人使用气动捣固工具帮助在升降之间沉降水泥。在下一个铲斗准备好倾倒另一大批水泥之前，刚好有足够的时间完成捣固，慢慢地将柱子分成十二英尺的部分。

*Two cranes facilitated another ingenious innovation. The cranes operated on a vertical track with cogs on the outside of 4 legs. One crane would lift the next section of crane track up for the other crane. Workmen with safety harness would install those four-foot sections with the help of the cranes, bolt them onto the section below. That would give the crane an additional 4 feet of height it could climb up on the 4 cog tracks.*

两台起重机促进了另一项巧妙的创新。起重机在垂直轨道上运行，四条腿的外侧有齿轮。一台起重机将为另一台起重机提升下一段起重机轨道。戴着安全带的工人将在起重机的帮助下安装这四英尺的部分，并将它们用螺栓固定在下面的部分上。这样起重机就可以通过 4 条齿轨爬上 4 英尺高。

*Each 20 feet the vertical crane tracks would anchor to the pillar so there would never be any need to worry about the crane tipping over.*

每 20 英尺，起重机的垂直轨道就会固定在支柱上，因此永远不必担心起重机翻倒。

*Crane operators didn't need to climb up the safety ladder. They were lifted by bucket up to a landing platform 10 feet below the crane cab. From that safety platform it was just a 10 foot climb up into the crane cab.*

起重机操作员无需爬上安全梯。他们被铲斗吊到起重机驾驶室下方 10 英尺的着陆平台上。从那个安全平台，只需爬上 10 英尺即可进入起重机驾驶室。

*All crane operators had hands off communications, they wore headphones with microphones and the sophisticated electronics did everything by voice activation.*

所有起重机操作员都无需动手进行通信，他们戴着带麦克风的耳机，先进的电子设备通过语音激活完成所有操作。

*People could not be directly below the cement buckets or under any lift and to ensure safety a bright orange multi section ring was laid down around the crane possible drop area that forbid passage while the lift was in progress. Lifts were in progress most of the time except for filling the buckets.*

人们不能直接在水泥铲斗下方或任何升降机下方，为了确保安全，在起重机可能的坠落区域周围放置了一个亮橙色的多段环，禁止在升降过程中通行。除了装满铲斗外，升降机大部分时间都在运行。

*A special cement mixer machine which had conveyer belts delivering the cement, sand, and boiling hot water for the mix. As the pillar got higher and higher, the little plume given off with the red lights mounted on stations above the crane and safety platform, gave an eerie appearance. To the average person the reddish plume looked like something evil, and even if they had to stop working for a day because of high winds, it took long enough for the temperature to drop in the concrete where that plume might last all night long.*

一种特殊的水泥搅拌机，它有传送带，用于输送水泥、沙子和混合用的沸水。随着柱子越来越高，起重机和安全平台上方的站台上安装的红灯发出的小羽状烟尘看起来十分诡异。对于普通人来说，这股红色的羽状烟尘看起来像某种邪恶的东西，即使他们因为大风而不得不停止工作一天，也需要很长时间才能让混凝土的温度下降，而这股羽状烟尘可能会持续一整夜。

*Also, with these first 6 pillars the first 2 elevators would be installed. Since the pillars were in 3 sections there would be 3 elevators, first starting at ground floor and ending at the start of the 20-foot diameter section which ends at the beginning of the 15-foot section.*

此外，前 6 根柱子将安装前 2 部电梯。由于柱子分为 3 段，因此将有 3 部电梯，第一部从一楼开始，结束于直径为 20 英尺的段的起点，该段的起点结束于直径为 15 英尺的段的起点。

*Steel plates welded to rebar in the column would*

*be used to fasten the elevator structure to the pillar providing it with a very strong fastener. There is a housing mounted on a platform at each elevator exit. A person would exit the elevator walk around the housing to the next elevator, get in there and do the same thing when they approached the third elevator.*

焊接在柱子钢筋上的钢板将用于将电梯结构固定到柱子上，从而为其提供非常坚固的紧固件。每个电梯出口的平台上都安装有一个外壳。一个人会从电梯出来，绕过外壳走到下一部电梯，进入电梯，当他们接近第三部电梯时做同样的事情。

*This slightly delayed people going up to the roof but by doing so it significantly shortened the length of the elevator cables to that of a typical office building so existing elevators could be installed. Since there would be multiple elevators to the roof top, there was always redundancy. If an elevator was taken out of service for maintenance, there would be multiple ways to get to the roof.*

这稍微耽误了人们上楼顶的时间，但这样做大大缩短了电梯电缆的长度，使其与典型的办公楼一样长，因此可以安装现有的电梯。由于将有多部电梯通往屋顶，因此总是有冗余。如果电梯因维修而停止使用，则有多种方式可以到达屋顶。

Alex was on the ground in short order and walked out of the hanger to the front street access. Jeff Sinclair approached Alex.

亚历克斯很快就落地了，走出机库，来到前街入口。杰夫·辛克莱走近亚历克斯。

JEFF SINCLAIR

Welcome to Greenland, Alex. I'll drive you to your hotel.

杰夫·辛克莱

欢迎来到格陵兰，亚历克斯。我会开车送你去酒店。

Alex reached his hand out to shake Jeff's hand.

亚历克斯伸出手和杰夫握手。

ALEX

Thanks for the ride, Jeff. This is my pilot, Brad.

亚历克斯
谢谢你载我，杰夫。这是我的飞行员布拉德。

BRAD
Good to meet you, Jeff.

布拉德
很高兴见到你，杰夫。

Jeff drove Alex to his hotel, and before much time lapsed found himself back at the Hotel Hans Egede standing in front of the clerk Margarete.

杰夫开车送亚历克斯去酒店，没过多久，他就发现自己又回到了汉斯埃格德酒店，站在服务员玛格丽特面前。

Margarete, who was expecting Alex, and recognized him right away, plus knew about the incident the last time Alex stayed at the Hotel Hans Egede.

玛格丽特正在等亚历克斯·她一眼就认出了他·而且她知道亚历克斯上次住在汉斯埃格德酒店时发生的事情。

MARGARETE
Welcome back Mr. Baxter.

玛格丽特
欢迎回来，巴克斯特先生。

ALEX
Thank you.

亚历克斯
谢谢。

MARGARETE
You are all checked in, here's your room key.

玛格丽特
你们都登记入住了，这是你们的房间钥匙。

ALEX
Super, could you please do me a favor, and have the porter take my suitcase up to my room?

亚历克斯
超级好，你能帮我一个忙，让搬运工把我的行李箱搬到我的房间吗？

MARGARETE
Sure, I'll take care of that right away.

玛格丽特
当然，我会立即处理。

ALEX
Thanks.

亚历克斯
谢谢。

Alex then held out his hand to shake Margarete's and she was surprised to feel something thinking at first it was a private note but as soon as Alex turned around and left, she looked down and saw a crisp $100 bill. That made her day. She would treat her friend Adel to dinner tonight!

然后亚历克斯伸出手与玛格丽特握手，她惊讶地感觉到有什么东西，一开始还以为这是一张私人纸条，但当亚历克斯转身离开时，她低头看到了一张清晰的 100 美元钞票。这让她很开心。她今晚要请她的朋友阿德尔吃饭！

Alex turned towards Jeff Sinclair.

亚历克斯转向杰夫· 辛克莱。

ALEX
Shall we go.

亚历克斯
我们走吧。

JEFF SINCLAIR
We shall.

杰夫·辛克莱
我们走吧。

Jeff turned and headed for the door, then opened the door for Alex and followed him out to the waiting Land Rover, still running and keeping the car warm.

杰夫转身走向门口，然后为亚历克斯打开车门，跟着他来到等候的路虎车旁，他仍在奔跑，并让车内保持温暖。

Jeff Sinclair and Alex were both soon in the vehicle and off to the Nuuk Dome Inc. offices where he would give Alex a quick tour, introduce him to the people working there, then take him over to the construction site.

杰夫·辛克莱 和 亚历克斯 很快就上了车，前往 努克圆顶公司 办公室，在那里他会带 亚历克斯快速参观一下，向他介绍在那里工作的人，然后带他去施工现场。

JEFF SINCLAIR

The building owners are still crying in their beers over the lease and want to renegotiate it.

杰夫· 辛克莱

大楼业主仍在为租约问题哭泣，并希望重新谈判。

ALEX

I'm sure they would.

亚历克斯

我相信他们会的。

JEFF SINCLAIR

Well, their stuck, our lawyers say, "tuff titty," we got a solid contract they can't break and by the time the lease is up in five years we'll be moving into our new offices in the dome.

杰夫· 辛克莱

好吧，我们的律师说，他们陷入困境 "坚韧的乳房" ，我们有一个他们不能违反的稳固合同，五年后租约到期时，我们将搬进圆顶大楼的新办公室。

ALEX

I have an idea how to shut their whining up.

亚历克斯

我有一个主意，让他们别再抱怨了。

JEFF SINCLAIR

What's that?

杰夫· 辛克莱

那是什么？

ALEX

I'll offer to buy the buildings from them. Pay them double what they paid for the land and double the construction costs and let them keep the rent for the next 5 years.

亚历克斯
我会提出从他们那里购买建筑物。支付他们购买
土地的两倍，建筑成本增加一倍，并让他们保留
未来 5 年的租金。

JEFF SINCLAIR
That would be a hell of a deal for them.

杰夫·辛克莱
这对他们来说将是一笔非常划算的交易。

ALEX
Certainly, they could then take that money and buy
offices in the Dome.

亚历克斯
当然，他们可以拿着这笔钱在圆顶大楼买办公
室。

JEFF SINCLAIR
What would you do with the buildings after we move
out if you own it?

杰夫·辛克莱
如果你拥有这些建筑，在我们搬走后你会怎么处
理它们？

ALEX
I would tear them down.

亚历克斯
我会把它们拆掉。

JEFF SINCLAIR
Why is that?

杰夫·辛克莱
为什么？

ALEX
They look like shit, the only value they have is they
provide space in a polar region no one wants to live in
until we get the dome built.

亚历克斯
它们看起来很糟糕，唯一的价值就是在我们建造
圆顶之前，它们为极地地区提供了无人愿意居住
的空间。

JEFF SINCLAIR
What would you do with the land?

杰夫·辛克莱
你会如何处理这块土地？

ALEX
I suspect when Nuuk residents start discovering the benefits of dome living, they will come to me with a proposal to put a dome over the top of Nuuk west area. I'll put high rise buildings on that land and make it worth 100 times more.

亚历克斯
我猜想，当努克居民开始发现圆顶生活的好处时，他们会向我提出在努克西部地区建造圆顶的建议。我会在那块土地上建造高层建筑，让它的价值增加 100 倍。

JEFF SINCLAIR
Some of those people that have a nice ocean view might not want to give it up.

杰夫·辛克莱
有些拥有美丽海景的人可能不想放弃它。

ALEX
Here's the surprise I would have for them: The waterfront can be all glass.

亚历克斯
这是我要给他们的惊喜：海滨可以全是玻璃。

JEFF SINCLAIR
Really?

杰夫·辛克莱
真的吗？

ALEX
Sure, no different than building a skyscraper, the wall can be reinforced and thick glass panes installed in numerous sections, we could have glass walls running up several hundred feet which would let in a lot of sunlight.

亚历克斯

当然，这和建造摩天大楼没什么不同，墙壁可以加固，并在多个部分安装厚玻璃板，我们可以建造高达数百英尺的玻璃墙，让大量阳光照进来。

JEFF SINCLAIR<br>Interesting.

杰夫·辛克莱<br>有趣。

ALEX

Something else I will now tell you, but do not repeat to anyone okay?

亚历克斯

我现在要告诉你另一件事，但不要向任何人重复，好吗？

JEFF SINCLAIR<br>Sure.

杰夫·辛克莱<br>当然。

ALEX

We have determined that with a growing population we are going to need more pier space, so we are going to build a sea wall and pier complex over at Qinngorput.

亚历克斯

我们已经确定，随着人口的增长，我们将需要更多的码头空间，因此我们将在秦格普特建造海堤和码头综合体。

JEFF SINCLAIR<br>I see.

杰夫·辛克莱<br>我明白了。

ALEX

We don't have coastal commission approval for such a construction, so I'm going to entice them with the prospect of building a Dome over Qinngorput area.

238

亚历克斯
我们没有获得海岸委员会对此类建设的批准，所以我将以在秦格普特地区建造圆顶的前景来吸引他们。

JEFF SINCLAIR
Think they will go for it?

杰夫·辛克莱
你认为他们会接受吗？

ALEX
Sure, once they discover their population can grow from 4,000 to 300,000 and the real estate values increase 100-fold, they will come around.

亚历克斯
当然，一旦他们发现他们的人口可以从 4,000 人增长到 300,000 人，

JEFF SINCLAIR
Same problem with all the view properties.

杰夫·辛克莱
所有视图属性都存在同样的问题。

ALEX
Yea, the glass manufacturers will love us.

亚历克斯
是的，玻璃制造商会喜欢我们。

JEFF SINCLAIR
So, will it be partial domes?

杰夫·辛克莱
那么，它会是部分圆顶吗？

ALEX
Certainly, just like over at Nuuk site we can build walls several hundred feet in the air made mostly of glass and steel.

亚历克斯
当然，就像在努克工地一样，我们可以在空中建造数百英尺的墙壁，主要由玻璃和钢制成。

### JEFF SINCLAIR

How would you make up for roof strength if we don't have the anchor of that side going all the way down to the foundation?

### 杰夫·辛克莱

如果我们没有从那一侧一直延伸到地基的锚，您将如何弥补屋顶的强度？

### ALEX

We'll put up a few extra pillars and have a few sections of steel support beams that extend out to make up for the missing wall, plus the glass wall will have enough steel in it to make it also very strong.

### 亚历克斯

我们将竖起一些额外的柱子，并有几段钢支撑梁延伸出来以弥补缺失的墙壁，而且玻璃墙中有足够的钢，使其也非常坚固。

### JEFF SINCLAIR

When do you think you will have an artist conception of those additional domes?

### 杰夫·辛克莱

你认为你什么时候会对那些额外的圆顶有一个艺术构思？

### ALEX

Next week. I could use and additional trip to New York for some personal matters.

### 亚历克斯

下周。我可能需要额外去纽约一趟，处理一些个人事务。

### JEFF SINCLAIR

I see, so you'll come back here next week.

### 杰夫·辛克莱

我明白了，所以你下周再来这里。

### ALEX

More than likely yes.

### 亚历克斯

很有可能。

JEFF SINCLAIR
I look forward to seeing what you have in mind.

杰夫·辛克莱
我期待看到你的想法。

The Land Rover pulled into the Nuuk Dome Inc. parking lot which had all the snow removed thanks to trucks and front-end loaders at Jeff Sinclair's disposal. The neighboring businesses also loved Jeff Sinclair for getting rid of their snow.

路虎驶入 努克圆顶公司 停车场，杰夫·辛克莱的卡车和前端装载机已经清除了所有的积雪。邻近的企业也很喜欢 杰夫·辛克莱清除了他们的积雪。

ALEX
I see you have all the snow removed around here. How did you do it?

亚历克斯
我看到你把这里所有的积雪都清除了。你是怎么做到的？

JEFF SINCLAIR
I used our front-end loaders and trucks, and the view of the bay from my hotel room I noticed a couple barges sitting there not being used in the wintertime.

I approached the owners and asked them to rent them. We built a ramp and had the front-end loaders dump the snow and ice on the barges. We then drove a bobcat onto a section of the barge we left clear by the ramp area, had tugs tow it a mile or so offshore and dumped the snow into the ocean.

杰夫·辛克莱
我使用了我们的前端装载机和卡车，从我的酒店房间可以看到海湾的景色，我注意到几艘驳船停在那里，冬天没人使用。我找到船主，要求租用它们。

我们建了一个坡道，让前端装载机把雪和冰倒在驳船上。然后，我们驾驶一辆山猫卡车来到我们离开坡道区域的驳船部分，让拖船把它拖到离岸一英里左右的地方，把雪倒进海里。

ALEX
That's a good innovation. Think we could do that with snow removed from our construction site?

亚历克斯
这是个很好的创新。您认为我们能用从施工现场
清除的积雪来做到这一点吗？

JEFF SINCLAIR
That's a little bigger challenge, not sure we have the
truck and front loader density to remove that much
snow and ice, so we simply move it on the slopes of
a hill, and when the month of June comes around and
the melt occurs, the snow will help fill up their local
reservoir which they also get hydroelectric power
from, so it will give them additional reserve power
this summer.

杰夫·辛克莱
这是一个更大的挑战，我们不确定卡车和前装载
机的密度是否足以清除那么多的积雪和冰，所以
我们只是在山坡上移动它们，当 6 月到来时，积
雪融化，积雪将有助于填满当地的水库，他们也
从那里获得水力发电，因此这将为他们今年夏天
提供额外的备用电力。

ALEX
What are we doing with the expected Dome runoff?

亚历克斯
我们正在如何处理预期的圆顶径流？

JEFF SINCLAIR
One other thing, the dome is designed to channel runoff
water from storms and snow into that reservoir so they
will be able to collect more water for hydroelectric
than they had in the past. If we could increase the size
of the dam by another 10 or 20 feet, we could store
considerably more amount of water.

杰夫·辛克莱
还有一件事，圆顶的设计是为了将暴雨和降雪产
生的径流水引入水库，这样他们就能比过去收集
更多的水用于水力发电。如果我们能将大坝的面
积再增加 10 或 20 英尺，我们就可以储存更多的
水。

ALEX
Is the dam built strong enough to support another 10
or 20 feet?

亚历克斯
大坝的强度是否足以支撑另外 10 或 20 英尺？

JEFF SINCLAIR
Certainly, it was designed with earthquake protection
so it could probably handle an additional 50 feet, but
there are too many homes that would be affected.

杰夫·辛克莱
当然，这座建筑的设计考虑到了防震，所以可能
可以承受额外的 50 英尺，但有太多房屋会受到影
响。

ALEX
If I recall correctly, isn't part of that reservoir going to
be under the dome?

亚历克斯
如果我没记错的话，那个水库的一部分不是在圆
顶下面吗？

JEFF SINCLAIR
Yes, it is.

杰夫·辛克莱
是的，确实如此。

ALEX
Are we channeling all the dome runoff into that
reservoir?

亚历克斯
我们会把圆顶径流全部引到那个水库里吗？

JEFF SINCLAIR
To some extent yes, but to prevent flooding we have a
canal system worked out to channel some of the water
to the ocean instead of into the dome.

杰夫·辛克莱
在某种程度上是的，但为了防止洪水，我们设计
了一个运河系统，将部分水引到海洋而不是圆
顶，以防止洪水。

ALEX
Great.

亚历克斯
太好了。

Alex and Jeff Sinclair got out of the Range Rover and walked into the office building. The workers there were very busy, and activity was brisk. Jeff walked Alex around and introduced him to everyone that was available and not engrossed in some activity and couldn't be disturbed.

亚历克斯 和 杰夫·辛克莱从路虎揽胜车上下来，走进办公楼。那里的工作人员非常忙碌，活动很活跃。 杰夫·辛克莱带着 亚历克斯四处走走，把他介绍给所有有空、没有专注于某项活动、不想被打扰的人。

With all the plans, charts, and activity going on, Alex could tell Claude Rearden meant business, and his reputation preceded him.

通过所有的计划、图表和活动，亚历克斯可以看出克劳德·里尔登是认真的，他的名声也早已传遍了亚历克斯的心中。

These workers, who knew first-hand Claude Rearden demanded their most sincere efforts and fidelity in loyalty. They were compensated well for that, and the mutual trust and loyalty worked both ways.

这些工人亲身体验过克劳德·里尔登要求他们付出最真诚的努力和忠诚。他们因此得到了丰厚的回报，相互的信任和忠诚是双向的。

Unlike many powerful men, Claude Rearden delegated authority, and knew it was counterproductive to micromanage.

与许多有权势的人不同，克劳德·里尔登授权，并且知道微观管理是适得其反的。

Claude Rearden, an astute observer of history fully understood the Jimmy Carter micromanagement approach always tends to end in failure.

克劳德·里尔登是一位敏锐的历史观察者，他完全理解吉米·卡特的微观管理方法总是以失败告终。

The way you get buy in and ownership to a project is to delegate authority, and step back and let them figure out how to best execute it. But at the same time lay down affirmative milestones, but at the same time affirmative backup was sometimes necessary.

获得项目认同和所有权的方法是授权，退后一步，让他们找出最佳执行方式。但同时要制定积极的里程碑，但有时也需要积极的支持。

Claude Rearden's management style included allowing managers to fire people even if they are your best friends being sent out the door.

克劳德·里尔登的管理风格包括允许经理解雇员工，即使他们是你最好的朋友。

Jeff showed some of the timelines and milestone charts and it clearly demonstrated he was on top of everything, a conductor of a well-trained band, is the best way to describe his conduct.

杰夫·辛克莱展示了一些时间表和里程碑图表，这些图表清楚地表明他掌控着一切，他是一名训练有素的乐队的指挥，这是对他行为的最佳描述。

People were cheerful and acting purposefully. In a sense one could postulate they knew they were part of an organization making history. Not since the Panama Canal had something this huge been attempted.

ALEX
How are you doing taking down some of the hills?

亚历克斯
你打算如何拆除一些山丘？

JEFF SINCLAIR
Once we get permission to use explosives and apply them in a reasonable manner as to not cause excessive shockwaves that rattle the community we will progress well. This drawing over here shows a daily update of how much material was removed and how it's being relocated to facilitate a level dome floor as much as practical.

杰夫·辛克莱
一旦我们获得使用炸药的许可，并以合理的方式使用它们，以免引起过度的冲击波扰乱社区，我们就会取得很好的进展。这里的这张图显示了每天更新的材料移除量以及如何重新安置材料，以尽可能地实现圆顶地板的水平。

ALEX
I see.

亚历克斯
我明白了。

JEFF SINCLAIR
As I stated in some of my reports, the wisdom of keeping the main hill serves 2 purposes, even though the roof is only 500 feet above it, the pillars will be a

lot shorter and stronger. The elevator rides up to the roof will be a lot quicker, so it adds some inherent benefits.

杰夫·辛克莱
正如我在一些报告中所说，保留主山的明智之举有两个目的，即使屋顶只在它上面　500　英尺，柱子也会更短更坚固。电梯到屋顶的速度会快得多，所以它增加了一些固有的好处。

ALEX
It definitely will add beauty and atmosphere to the dome dwellers.

亚历克斯
它肯定会为圆顶居民增添美感和氛围。

Jeff Sinclair flipped up the status sheet and exposed the drawing hidden behind it.

杰夫·翻开状态表，露出隐藏在它后面的图画。

JEFF SINCLAIR
This is the artist conception of that hill after we populate it with trees and make an artificial forest.

杰夫·辛克莱
这是我们在山上种满树木并建造人工森林后的艺术构想。

ALEX
That looks real good.

亚历克斯
看起来真不错。

JEFF SINCLAIR
Yes, this is a park area that we think will become very popular year-round.

杰夫·辛克莱
是的，我们认为这个公园区全年都会非常受欢迎。

ALEX
Okay, shall we go out to the work site, so I can take a look?

亚历克斯
好的，我们可以去工作现场看看吗？

JEFF SINCLAIR
Certainly.

杰夫·辛克莱
当然可以。

Jeff and Alex went back out to the Land Rover and got in and drove about five minutes and went past the security guard who recognized Jeff right away and on up into the central area where a lot of the work was being done and stopped near one of the derricks that looked like an oil drilling platform which rose 100 feet up into the air.

杰 和 亚历克斯 回到路虎车上，上车后开了大约五分钟，经过保安，保安立刻认出了 杰夫，他们继续往上开，来到了正在进行大量工作的中央区域，停在了一座看起来像石油钻井平台的井架附近，井架高达 100 英尺。

ALEX
So, why are we drilling instead of using a pile driver?

亚历克斯
那么，我们为什么要钻孔而不是使用打桩机呢？

JEFF SINCLAIR
We are drilling into rock; it would be impossible to pile drive steel beams at a very high rate and would be extremely annoying to the community as well as the work force. Drilling with these rigs that have 4000 horsepower motors that we can apply a lot of pressure down on the drilling bits gets us down fairly quickly as our goal is to anchor with 200-foot steel beams in a pattern under each future pillar.

杰夫·辛克莱
我们正在钻入岩石，不可能以非常高的速度打桩钢梁，而且会给社区和工人带来极大的烦恼。使用这些配备 4000 马力马达的钻机进行钻孔，我们可以对钻头施加很大的压力，这样我们就可以相当快地完成钻孔，因为我们的目标是用 200 英尺长的钢梁按照一定的方式锚定每个未来的支柱。

ALEX
Interesting.

亚历克斯
有趣。

JEFF SINCLAIR
Look over here notice we have a steel beam being slowly lowered?

杰夫·辛克莱
看这里，注意到我们有一根钢梁正在慢慢放下吗？

ALEX
Yes.

亚历克斯
是的。

JEFF SINCLAIR
In a few minutes it will have the next beam welded on top of it, then lowered some more until we get all the sections welded with a stub sticking 4 feet above ground. Then we fill the hole with cement to anchor the beam in place.

When all of the beams are finished, we then begin welding the first 20-foot rebar section and then with a heavy-duty crane lift the form and safety platform over it and set it down, optically align it into exact position and start pouring cement.

杰夫·辛克莱
几分钟后，下一根梁将焊接在它上面，然后再降低一些，直到我们用一根离地面 4 英尺的短柱焊接所有部分。然后我们用水泥填充孔以将梁固定到位。

当所有梁都完成后，我们开始焊接第一个 20 英尺长的钢筋部分，然后用重型起重机将模板和安全平台吊起并放下，将其光学对准到准确的位置并开始浇注水泥。

ALEX
Is this part of the 30-foot diameter section?

亚历克斯
这是直径 30 英尺的部分吗？

JEFF SINCLAIR
Yes. It's going to require a lot of cement.

杰夫·辛克莱
是的。这需要大量的水泥。

ALEX

That's why we need to get that Portland Cement plant up and running.

亚历克斯
当然，这就是我们需要让波特兰水泥厂投入运营的原因。

JEFF SINCLAIR

We'll have to ship in the cement and steel from America for a while, can't delay construction to get the limestone and coal fields in operation.

杰夫·辛克莱
我们得从美国运来水泥和钢材一段时间，不能推迟施工，让石灰石和煤田投入运营。

ALEX

How soon, before you start pouring concrete?

亚历克斯
多久后，你才能开始浇筑混凝土？

JEFF SINCLAIR

We should be pouring concrete on this pillar next week.

杰夫·辛克莱
我们应该在下周在这个柱子上浇筑混凝土。

ALEX

I might just have to come out and watch some of that.

亚历克斯
我可能不得不出来看看。

JEFF SINCLAIR

We certainly will be happy to see you come back.

杰夫·辛克莱
我们当然很高兴看到你回来。

ALEX
I'll be even more happy to see the dome built and Greenlanders learning how to live in 70-degree weather with trees and green lawns for a change."

亚历克斯
我会更高兴看到圆顶建成，格陵兰人学会如何在 70 度的天气里生活在树木和绿色草坪中。

JEFF SINCLAIR
Hop in the car I'll show you a few more things.

杰夫·辛克莱
上车吧，我再给你看几样东西。

It was already nighttime in Nuuk Greenland, but all the flood lights from the construction site lit up the place real well.

努克已经是晚上了，但施工现场的所有泛光灯都把这个地方照得非常明亮。

Jeff Sinclair  drove them to the vehicle storage area and past the stacks of containers and then past another area where buildings were going up for temporary housing for employees.

杰夫·辛克莱  开车把他们带到车辆存放区，经过一堆堆集装箱，然后经过另一个区域，那里正在建造临时住房，供员工居住。

JEFF SINCLAIR
This is where the guys and gals will live as we ramp up this production.

杰夫·辛克莱
这就是我们提高产量时男男女女们将住的地方。

ALEX
It's kind of interesting how you are building the housing on top of the containers.

亚历克斯
你在集装箱上建造房屋的方式很有趣。

JEFF SINCLAIR
Those 40-foot containers are storing construction materials and putting housing up on top of them simply reduces the snow removal we have to do since at the ends of each building are stairways which will usually be above the snow line. Employees will never be blocked out of their homes.

杰夫·辛克莱
这些 40 英尺长的集装箱储存着建筑材料，在它们
上面建造房屋可以减少我们需要清除的积雪，因
为每栋建筑的末端都有楼梯，而楼梯通常位于雪
线之上。员工永远不会被挡在屋外。

ALEX
What are all those snow mobiles for?

亚历克斯
所有这些雪地车是干什么用的？

JEFF SINCLAIR
Since there are 30 weeks of snow on the ground each
year, and there are not many places for them to go,
a snow mobile is probably their best way to get into
town and around.

杰夫·辛克莱
由于每年地面有 30 周的积雪，而且他们没有太多
地方可去，雪地摩托可能是他们进城和四处游览
的最佳方式。

ALEX
Golf carts in the summer I suppose.

亚历克斯
我想夏天会开高尔夫球车吧？

JEFF SINCLAIR
That's only 2 months of the year and its 40-degree
summers.

杰夫·辛克莱
一年只有两个月，夏天气温是 40 度。

ALEX
These people are going to love living in the dome and
not have to deal with 40 degrees weather if they don't
want.

亚历克斯
这些人会喜欢住在圆顶屋里，如果他们不愿意，
就不必忍受 40 度的天气。

JEFF SINCLAIR
Yes, I can see that.

杰夫·辛克莱
是的，我明白。

ALEX

There are people living in New York City, who have never been outside the city.

亚历克斯
有些人住在纽约市，从未离开过这座城市，你认为最终会有圆顶屋居民永远不离开圆顶屋吗？

JEFF SINCLAIR

Do you suppose eventually there will be Dome Dwellers that never leave the dome?

杰夫·辛克莱
有些人住在纽约市，从未离开过这座城市，你认为最终会有圆顶屋居民永远不离开圆顶屋吗？

ALEX

It's getting near the end of the shift, right?

亚历克斯
快下班了吧？

JEFF SINCLAIR

Yes, second shift is coming on now.

杰夫·辛克莱
是的，第二班就要开始了。

ALEX

I have a great idea. How about grab a couple of the supervisors, and let's take them with us, and go to the Hereford Beefstouw restaurant inside the Hotel Hans Egede Hotel. The dinner is on me and will give me a chance to ask them a few questions and answer some they might have.

亚历克斯
我有个好主意。不如带上几个主管，一起去汉斯艾格德酒店内的赫里福德牛肉餐厅吧。晚餐由我请客，这将给我机会问他们几个问题，并回答他们可能提出的一些问题。

JEFF SINCLAIR

Sure, here are 2 of my top supervisors walking this way, Gus and Burt.

杰夫·辛克莱
好的，我的两个最高主管 格斯 和 伯特 正朝这边
走来。

Within a minute the supervisors were walking right up to Jeff who said to them:

不到一分钟，主管们就走到杰夫面前，杰夫说.

JEFF SINCLAIR
Hey guys, I want to introduce you to Alex Baxter, one
of the men behind this dome project.:

杰夫·辛克莱
嘿，伙计们，我想把你们介绍给 亚历克斯·巴克斯
特，他是这个圆顶项目的幕后推手之一。

These men knew who Alex Baxter was, since his name and role was well known by a lot of people in the company based on the monthly employee magazine that had published a lot of information on the dome construction.

这些人知道 亚历克斯·巴克斯特是谁，因为他的名字和角色在公司里为许多人所熟知，因为月刊员工杂志上刊登了大量关于圆顶建设的信息。

Burt held out his hand.

伯特伸出手

BURT
Glad to meet you, Mr. Baxter.

伯特
很高兴见到你，巴克斯特先生。

Alex shook Burt's hand.

亚历克斯握着伯特的手：

ALEX
Thank you, glad to meet you too.

亚历克斯
"谢谢，我也很高兴见到你。"

Gus then held out his hand.

格斯伸出手.

GUS
I'm Gus.

格斯
我是 格斯。


ALEX
Pleased to meet you Gus, what do you do here on the
project?

亚历克斯
很高兴见到你 格斯，你在这个项目中做什么？


GUS
I supervise the drilling rig you see here.

格斯
我负责监督你看到的钻机。


ALEX
That's interesting how we are drilling holes for the
steel beam anchors.

亚历克斯
们为钢梁锚钻孔的方式很有趣。


GUS
It means we should expect the dome to last a lot longer
than people realize.

杰夫·辛克莱
这意味着我们应该期望圆顶的使用寿命比人们想
象的要长得多。


Alex then turned towards Burt.

亚历克斯 然后转向伯特。


ALEX
Burt what's your role in all this?

亚历克斯
伯特，你在这其中扮演什么角色？


BURT
Mr. Baxter, I supervise the welders working on the
foundation construction.

伯特
巴克斯特先生，我负责监督从事基础施工的焊工.

ALEX
Lot of welding to look forward too.

亚历克斯
期待大量焊接。

BURT
Yes, and with the one-inch steel plates it will be good we got those plasma welders that will get a lot of work done fast.

伯特
是的，对于一英寸厚的钢板，我们有等离子焊机会很好，它们可以快速完成大量工作。"

ALEX
Are they manually operated?

亚历克斯
它们是手动操作的吗？

BURT
No, they're all robotic in a sense.

伯特
不，从某种意义上说，它们都是机器人。

ALEX
How does that work?

亚历克斯
那是怎么工作的？

BURT
We have a rig that has a caterpillar like tracks that slowly crawl along the seam we are welding.

The operator has a control panel which is in the doghouse where we sit next to the robotic welder to keep him warm in the winter.

The operator has remote controls on a computer screen that shows the seam and alignments.

伯特
我们有一个带有履带状履带的钻机，可以沿着我们正在焊接的焊缝缓慢爬行。

操作员有一个控制面板，它位于狗窝里，我们坐
在机器人焊工旁边，冬天可以给他保暖。

操作员在显示焊缝和对齐的计算机屏幕上有遥控
器。


ALEX
How fast does the plasma welder weld?


亚历克斯
等离子焊机焊接速度有多快？


BURT
For quality control purposes we restrict the robot
speed to about one inch in two seconds.


伯特
为了控制质量，我们将机器人速度限制在 2 秒内
1 英寸左右。


ALEX
How's the quality of the weld?


亚历克斯
焊接质量如何？


BURT
Meets or exceeds any human welders.


伯特
达到或超过任何人类焊工。


ALEX
Well good. Does that mean no rework?


亚历克斯
好啊好啊。这是否意味着无需返工？


BURT
In all our checks and tests, we've conducted; we only
find about one inch flaw in a thousand inches of weld.


伯特
在我们进行的所有检查和测试中； 我们在一千英
寸的焊缝中只发现大约一英寸的缺陷。

ALEX

For the roof installations, how would you deal with a welding flaw?

亚历克斯

对于屋顶安装，您将如何处理焊接缺陷？

BURT

We'd just send a welder to hit that one spot and re-weld it.

伯特

我们只需派一名焊工击中那个点并重新焊接即可。

ALEX

How long do those repairs take?

亚历克斯

这需要多长时间？

BURT

About five minutes.

伯特

大约五分钟。

ALEX

Interesting.

亚历克斯

有趣。

Alex looked at his watch and felt kind of hungry.

亚历克斯看了看手表，感觉有点饿，于是说道。

ALEX

Burt and Gus, Jeff and I would like to invite you to go get some dinner with us. We can discuss more while we are chowing down on some steaks.

亚历克斯

伯特和格斯，杰夫和我想请你们一起去吃晚饭。我们可以一边吃牛排一边讨论。

BURT

Sounds good to me.

伯特
听起来不错。

ALEX
Hop in the car, let's head over to the restaurant.

亚历克斯
上车，我们去餐厅。

BURT
Sure, no problem. We've already turned over to the second shift, we are done for the day.

伯特
没问题，我们已经转入第二班了，今天的工作结束了。

ALEX
Excellent.
太好了。

Alex and the three other men got into the Land Rover and Jeff drove them over to Hotel Hans Egede. Thanks to their excellent snow removal at the Hotel, there was parking available for guests as well as customers for the restaurant and bar.

亚历克斯和另外三个人上了路虎，杰夫开车送他们去汉斯·埃格德酒店。感谢酒店出色的除雪工作，餐厅和酒吧为客人和顾客提供了停车位。

The four men got out of the car and went to the elevator.

四个人下了车，走到电梯前。

ALEX
Let's stop by the Skyline Bar first, buy you guys all a round of drinks.

亚历克斯
我们先去天际线酒吧，请大家喝一杯。

Alex and the three Greenland Dome construction employees walked in just as happy hour seemed to be starting.

亚历克斯和其他三名格陵兰圆顶建筑员工走进来，欢乐时光似乎开始了。

Sitting over at the almost empty bar was the gentleman Alex had met before. Alex quickly pulled up his cell phone and scrolled down to notes under Nuuk, and found the name, Mangus. Alex walked over and sat down next to Mangus.

几乎空无一人的酒吧里坐着亚历克斯以前见过的那位绅士。亚历克斯迅速掏出手机，向下滚动到努克下方的笔记，找到了这个名字，曼格斯。亚历克斯走过去，在曼格斯旁边坐下。

ALEX
Hello Mangus, how have you been?

亚历克斯
你好，曼格斯，你过得怎么样？

I'm sorry, don't recall your name, but remember your face. You're the dome guy, right?

对不起，我不记得你的名字了，但记得你的脸。你是圆顶屋的那个家伙，对吧？

ALEX
Yep. Alex is my name.

亚历克斯
是的。我叫 亚历克斯。

MANGUS
That's right, hello Alex.

曼古斯
没错，你好，亚历克斯。

Jeff, Gus, and Burt all sat down at the bar next to Alex. The Bartender was all smiles remembering the guy who gave him a shocking tip.

杰夫、格斯和伯特都在酒吧里坐在亚历克斯旁边。酒保满脸笑容地回忆着那个给他惊人小费的人。

BARTENDER
What can I get you guys?

酒保
你们需要什么？

ALEX
I'll have one of those craft beers and put all the drinks on my tab. Plus a drink for Mangus here on me.

亚历克斯
我会喝一瓶精酿啤酒，然后把所有饮料都记在我的账单上。我还为曼格斯喝了一杯。

**BARTENDER**
Certainly Sir.

调酒师
当然可以，先生。

The men ordered and toasted, then Alex looked around seeing a growing crowd spotted three well dressed women over in the corner sitting on two sofas' facing each other. And to Alex's surprise it was Adel, Shelly, and Margarete.

男人们点了酒，举杯庆祝，然后亚历克斯环顾四周，看到越来越多的人发现角落里有三个衣着考究的女人坐在两张面对面的沙发上。令亚历克斯惊讶的是，她们是阿德尔、雪莉和玛格丽特。

**VOICEOVR (ALEX)**
**THOUGHT**
*So, the world is a small place.*

声音（亚历克斯）
想法
所以世界是一个很小的地方。

**ALEX**
Gentlemen, excuse me for a moment.

亚历克斯
先生们，请稍等片刻。

Alex walked over to the sofa and politely said to the ladies:

亚历克斯走到沙发前，礼貌地对女士们说：

**ALEX**
Good evening, how is everyone doing tonight?

亚历克斯
晚上好，大家今晚过得怎么样？

**ADEL**
Mr. Baxter, surprised to see you here tonight.

阿德尔
巴克斯特先生，很惊讶今晚在这里见到你。

**ALEX**
Likewise.

亚历克斯
同样。

VOICEOVR (ALEX)
THOUGHT
*So, this is what she looks like with the war paint on.*

声音（亚历克斯）
想法
这就是她涂上战争油漆后的样子。

Margarete also appeared very appealing with her work uniform off and jeans and a nice top on. Shelly was attractive as well, but her antagonism over the Dome eroded any enthusiasm Alex might otherwise have for her. About that time the waitress walked up to the table and asked:

玛格丽特脱下工作服，穿着牛仔裤和漂亮的上衣，看起来也非常迷人。雪莉也很迷人，但她对穹顶的敌意削弱了亚历克斯对她们的热情。大约在那个时候，女服务员走到桌子前问道：

WAITRESS
What can I get for you ladies?

女服务员
女士们，我能为你们点什么吗？

Adel ordered a soda and Margarete and Shelly ordered wine. As the waitress was leaving the table, Alex announced:

阿德尔点了一杯苏打水，玛格丽特和雪莉点了葡萄酒。当女服务员离开桌子时，亚历克斯宣布：

ALEX
Excuse me miss, could you please put their drinks on
my tab, I'm sitting at the bar by those 4 gentlemen.

亚历克斯
对不起，小姐，你能把他们的饮料记在我账上
吗，我坐在那四位先生旁边的吧台上。

The waitress smiled.

女服务员笑了。

WAITRESS
No problem, sir.

女服务员
没问题，先生。

## ALEX
Nice seeing you all, talk to you again soon.

亚历克斯
很高兴见到你们，很快再和你们聊天。

Alex smiled then left their table and went back to the bar.

亚历克斯微笑着离开他们的桌子，回到酒吧。

The women started in as soon as their drinks were delivered.

女士们一收到饮料就开始进来。

## SHELLY
I still think this *Dome* is a pipe dream.

雪莉
我仍然认为这个穹顶是一个白日梦。

## ADEL
Hans thinks it's going to happen, and he's really upset about it.

阿德尔
汉斯相信这会让富人变得更富，而对穷人来说毫无好处。

## SHELLY
What makes him so upset? It's probably going to be a flop.

雪莉
是什么让他如此沮丧？问道。这很可能是一个失败。

## ADEL
Hans believes it will make the rich richer and nothing in it for the poor.

阿德尔
汉斯相信这会让富人更富，而穷人则一无所获。

## SHELLY
Well, there certainly is a lot of big money involved, but I don't see how it will ever pay for itself.

雪莉
好吧，这确实涉及很多大笔资金，但我不知道它
如何能收回成本。

ADEL
Not in our lifetimes.

阿德尔
在我们的有生之年也收不到。

SHELLY
How long will the *Nuuk Dome* last?

雪莉
努克圆顶还能持续多久？

ADEL
Too long. 50,000 years is a time frame they toss
around, but how would they know?

阿德尔
太长了。50,000 年是他们随意提出的一个时间框
架，但他们怎么会知道呢？

SHELLY
They don't, nor do we.

雪莉
他们不知道，我们也不知道。

Margarete joked:

玛格丽特开玩笑说：

MARGARETE
I think Mr. Baxter would be good for five minutes.

玛格丽特
我认为巴克斯特先生可以待五分钟。

All the girls laughed.

女孩们都笑了。

***

MANGUS
How's the project coming along?

曼古斯
项目进展如何？

JEFF SINCLAIR
Right on schedule.

杰夫·辛克莱
正好按计划进行。

MANGUS
Some of the town's people are complaining about the explosions.

MANGUS
镇上的一些人抱怨爆炸。

JEFF SINCLAIR
It only happens once every few days, and in 6 months all that work will be done.

杰夫·辛克莱
每隔几天才会发生一次，6　个月后所有工作都会完成。

MANGUS
Some are complaining you are taking down their hill.

MANGUS
有些人抱怨你正在拆毁他们的山。

JEFF SINCLAIR
Soon they will have the dome to look at!

杰夫·辛克莱
很快他们就可以欣赏圆顶了！

Jeff Sinclair smiled and chuckled a bit, along with Gus and Burt.

杰夫·辛克莱 (Jeff Sinclair) 与格斯 (Gus) 和伯特 (Burt) 一起微笑并咯咯笑了起来。

MANGUS
How soon will we start to see something built?

曼古斯
我们多久才能开始看到一些东西建成？

JEFF SINCLAIR
In the next few weeks, you will start to see the first six pillars start to go up, and in May, the first roof section will go up.

杰夫·辛克莱
在接下来的几周内，您将开始看到前 6 根柱子开始竖起，5 月份，第一个屋顶部分将竖起。

MANGUS
That quick?

MANGUS
这么快？

JEFF SINCLAIR
Certainly.

杰夫·辛克莱
当然。

After a couple of drinks Alex announced:
喝了几杯酒后，Alex 宣布：

ALEX
Let's all wonder over to the restaurant, and if you guys don't mind, I'd like to invite those women to join us.

亚历克斯
我们一起去餐厅看看吧，如果你们不介意的话，我想邀请那些女人加入我们。

GUS
Definitely works for me.

GUS
对我来说绝对有效。

JEFF SINCLAIR
I'm good at that.

杰夫·辛克莱
我同意。

Alex then looking at the bartender requested:

亚历克斯看着酒保要求：

ALEX
We are going to dinner, charge it all to my room. We
may be back later.

亚历克斯
我们要去吃晚饭，把所有费用都记在我的房间
里。我们可能晚点再回来。

BARTENDER
Certainly Mr. Baxter.

酒保
当然可以，巴克斯特先生。

The men stood up and started walking towards the restaurant on the other end of Hotel
Hans Egede wing. Alex walked over to the table where the three women were sitting,
and announced:

男人们站起来，朝汉斯埃格德酒店另一侧的餐厅走去。亚历克斯走到三个女人
坐着的桌子旁，宣布道：

ALEX
Excuse me ladies, I'd like to buy you dinner if you
would like to join us.

亚历克斯
对不起，女士们，如果您愿意加入我们，我想请
您吃晚饭。

Shelly looked at Adel for guidance, who didn't respond right away, but Margarete
started thinking she might just keep that $100 bill after all responded.

雪莉看着阿德尔寻求指导，阿德尔没有立即回应，但玛格丽特开始想，在所有
人都回应之后，她可能会把那 100 美元的钞票留着。

MARGARETE
I wouldn't mind.

玛格丽特
我不介意。

ADEL
I suppose if Margarete's keen on it, then so am I.

阿德尔
我想，如果玛格丽特很热衷，那我也是。

Alex escorted the women to the restaurant where the three men were waiting.

亚历克斯陪同女士们去了餐厅，三个男人在那里等着。

The manager who Alex remembered from his recent visit was there and smiling. The last time Alex was there his profit and loss center had a nice spike upwards, plus the tip he left them was almost a week's pay for many that were working that day.

亚历克斯记得最近来过这里的经理在那里，面带微笑。上次　亚历克斯在那里的时候，他的损益中心出现了大幅增长，而且他给他们的小费几乎相当于当天许多员工一周的工资。

MANAGER
Mr. Baxter, how many people are in your party?

经理
巴克斯特先生，你们一行有多少人？

ALEX
It Looks like there will be seven of us.

亚历克斯
看起来我们有七个人。

MANAGER
Okay, let me move two tables together, it will take just
a minute.

经理
好的，让我把两张桌子挪到一起，只需一分钟。

ALEX
Guys let me introduce you.

亚历克斯
伙计们，让我来介绍一下你们。

Alex said their names as he pointed to them:

亚历克斯指着他们说出了他们的名字：

ALEX
Jeff, Gus, and Ralph this is Margaret, Shelly, and Adel.

亚历克斯
杰夫、格斯和拉尔夫，就是玛格丽特、雪莉和阿德
尔。

With the introductions and greetings out of the way, the manager approached the group.

介绍和问候完毕后，经理走近了这群人。

MANAGER
Follow me please.

经理
请跟我来。

The manager took Alex and his guests to tables that were slid together for the large group.

经理把 亚历克斯和他的客人带到了为大团体而滑动在一起的桌子旁。

The women all went to one side of the table and the men slipped in on the other side.

女士们都走到桌子的一侧，男士们则从另一侧溜进去。

Alex was the last to sit down and looked at the manager and informed the manager:

亚历克斯是最后一个坐下的人，他看着经理，告诉经理：

ALEX
Please put all the meals and drinks on my tab.

亚历克斯
请把所有的餐点和饮料都记在我的账上。

MANAGER
Certainly, Mr. Baxter.

经理
当然可以，巴克斯特先生。

The waiter next to the manager asked:

经理旁边的服务员问道：

WAITER
Would anyone like a drink?

服务员
有人想喝点什么吗？

Everyone ordered a drink of some sort except Adel who said:

每个人都点了某种饮料，除了阿德尔说：

Adel
I'll just have water please.

阿德尔
我要水就行。

In a few minutes, the manager and a waitress came with their drinks and the waiter took their orders.

几分钟后，经理和女服务员端着饮料过来，服务员记下了他们的订单。

Alex notices there was a smile and exchange between the waitress and Margarete.

亚历克斯注意到女服务员和玛格丽特之间有微笑和交流。

ALEX (THOUGHT)
*They must know each other working here.*

亚历克斯（心想）
他们在这里工作一定认识。

In due time, six conversations started. The average age of the women was probably 26, and the men 35. The pheromones were flying tonight!

适时，六人开始交谈。女性的平均年龄大概是 26 岁，男性是 35 岁。今晚信息素飞扬！

Alex was closest to Margarete where he studied her for a few minutes. Alex was about as close to her as when she checked him in the Hotel Hans Egede earlier today. Alex didn't have as long to study Margarete as he did now.

阿历克斯离玛格丽特最近，他花了几分钟观察她。阿历克斯和玛格丽特的距离大概和她今天早些时候在汉斯埃格德酒店入住时一样近。阿历克斯没有像现在这样花那么多时间观察玛格丽特。

ALEX THOUGHT
*Many Greenland women were chubby, probably from a high protein diet and lack of exercise during the winter months. But Margarete was thin and looks very healthy.*

亚历克斯 (心想)
许多格陵兰妇女都比较胖，可能是因为她们在冬季饮食中蛋白质含量高，而且缺乏锻炼。但玛格丽特却很瘦，看上去非常健康。

Margarete noticed Alex was staring at her. She felt it was more than simple curiosity.

玛格丽特注意到亚历克斯盯着她看。她觉得这不仅仅是出于好奇。

ALEX THOUGHT
*There are commercial gyms in Nuuk, Margarete probably works out.*

亚历克斯想
努克有商业健身房，玛格丽特可能经常去锻炼。

*Margarete most likely is of Inuit extraction. She might even be a half breed intermixed with the many Danish people that settled here for mining, fishing, and other endeavors.*

玛格丽特很可能是因纽特人。她甚至可能是混血儿，与许多定居在这里从事采矿、捕鱼和其他事业的丹麦人混血。

*Margarete could easily pass for some Japanese and some Koreans I've seen.*

我见过的玛格丽特很容易被误认为是日本人和韩国人。

*I hope that someday she meets a nice guy, because she seems to be such a nice young lady.*

我希望有一天她能遇到一个好男人，因为她看起来是个很好的年轻女士。

*Margarete is too young for my taste, but eye candy is always nice to look at.*

玛格丽特对我来说肯定太年轻了，但养眼的女人总是好看的。

Shelley and possibly Adel would be in Alex's age range, but Alex had already ruled out Shelley. She was too much of a bulldog. And as far as Adel went, she was becoming apparently more of a liberal/radical than he cared to be attached too.

雪莱和阿德尔可能都在亚历克斯的年龄范围内，但亚历克斯已经排除了雪莱。她太像斗牛犬了。至于阿德尔，她显然比他愿意接受的更自由/激进。

Adel would never work out. So, the bottom line, it is just a friendly dinner Alex could easily afford, and hopefully added some positive feelings towards Nuuk Dome Inc. though Alex was convinced Shelley would never come around.

阿德尔永远都不会成功。所以，归根结底，这只是一顿亚历克斯可以轻松负担得起的友好晚餐，希望能给努克圆顶公司带来一些积极的感觉，尽管亚历克斯确信雪莱永远不会出现。

However, Alex could detect there was genuine interest between Jeff, Gus, and Ralph towards the three ladies who were dressed to impress.

然而，亚历克斯可以察觉到杰夫、格斯和拉尔夫对这三位打扮得令人印象深刻的女士有着真正的兴趣。

Alex was so delighted everyone was having such a good time. Burt told a few jokes, got the women laughing and Gus was laying on the charm.

亚历克斯很高兴每个人都玩得这么开心。伯特讲了几个笑话，让女人们笑了起来，格斯则在施展魅力。

Jeff seemed to be taking it all in but his body language betrayed him as it was clear he had a focus on one of the women, which Alex felt would not do him much good since they were politically diametrically opposed.

杰夫似乎把这一切都记在心里，但他的肢体语言出卖了他，很明显他把注意力集中在其中一位女性身上，亚历克斯觉得这对他没有多大帮助，因为他们在政治上截然相反。

Adel would never be interested in a big shot program manager for one of the world's most impressive construction projects of all times.

阿德尔永远不会对一个大牌项目经理感兴趣，而这个项目是有史以来世界上最令人印象深刻的建筑项目之一。

During the course of events, Jeff revealed:

在事件的过程中，杰夫透露：

> **JEFF SINCLAIR**
> There had been a group of Chinese coming and taking pictures.

> **杰夫·辛克莱**
> 有一群中国人来拍照。

> **BURT**
> No doubt they want to understand our technology and design.

> **伯特**
> 毫无疑问，他们想了解我们的技术和设计。

> **ALEX**
> I'm sure the Chinese realize they could build a *Dome City* out in the middle of the Gobi Desert.

亚历克斯
我相信中国人意识到他们可以在戈壁沙漠中部建
造一座圆顶城市。

JEFF SINCLAIR
Yep. But instead of putting in 500,000 China would
put in 5 million people and build a 20-mile dome
instead of our five-mile dome.

杰夫·辛克莱
是的。但中国不会投入 50 万人，而是投入 500
万人，建造一个 20 英里的圆顶，而不是我们的 5
英里圆顶。

ALEX
Power would be a problem for them. China would
have to build a power plant near the dome.

亚历克斯
电力对他们来说是个问题。中国必须在圆顶附近
建造一座发电厂。

JEFF SINCLAIR
China has aggressive nuclear power and solar power
construction. A nuclear plant and solar could be built
outside a dome if they build one and run the power in
underground in high voltage conduits.

杰夫·辛克莱
中国积极建设核电和太阳能。如果他们建造一个
圆顶，并在地下高压管道中运行电力，就可以在
圆顶外建造核电厂和太阳能。

ALEX
Certainly.

ALEX
当然。

Everyone ordered steaks. It doesn't take people, especially outsiders to get sick of fish
real soon in Nuuk, since that was the main food supply.

每个人都点了牛排。努克的人，尤其是外地人，很快就会厌倦鱼，因为鱼是主
要的食物来源。

A good sea lion or Polar Bear steak was great too for the locals. Some locals rarely ate
vegetables. Their digestive systems were designed to survive on seafood. The dome
would change all that.

对当地人来说，一份上好的海狮或北极熊牛排也很棒。一些当地人很少吃蔬菜。它们的消化系统是靠海鲜生存的。圆顶会改变这一切。

ALEX

One project Alex I'M working on is to investigate building greenhouses northeast of the dome.

亚历克斯

亚历克斯，我正在开展的一个项目是研究在圆顶东北部建造温室。

JEFF SINCLAIR
What's your idea?

杰夫·辛克莱
你有什么想法？

ALEX

With artificial lighting to extend the days in the spring and heat in the green houses provided by solar power starting in April, local greenhouses could actually grow green vegetables in the green houses and harvest by September when the snow starts falling again.

亚历克斯

通过人工照明延长春季的白天，并从 4 月开始为温室提供太阳能供暖，当地的温室实际上可以在温室中种植绿色蔬菜，并在 9 月再次下雪时收获。

JEFF SINCLAIR
How would you heat the greenhouses?

杰夫·辛克莱
你会如何给温室供暖？

ALEX

I think we can use a heat pump system, heating a rock bed under the greenhouse during the day with lots of solar panels nearby, and then pump the heat into radiators in the greenhouse in the evenings.

亚历克斯

我认为我们可以使用热泵系统，白天用附近的许多太阳能电池板加热温室下的岩床，然后在晚上将热量泵入温室中的散热器。

JEFF SINCLAIR

The spring and summer days are certainly longer providing a lot of solar power potential.

杰夫·辛克莱

春季和夏季的白天肯定更长，提供了很多太阳能潜力。

ALEX

In April, it would still be freezing outside but the heat pump system would keep the greenhouse above freezing, and nice and toasty during the day. The greenhouses would have humidifiers in them so the air would be kept warm and moist.

亚历克斯

4 月，外面仍然很冷，但热泵系统会让温室保持在冰点以上，白天温暖宜人。温室内会配备加湿器，这样空气就会保持温暖和湿润。

JEFF SINCLAIR

You would have to ship in a lot of fertilizer.

杰夫·辛克莱
你必须运送大量肥料。

ALEX

Not necessarily. There were some uninhabited areas of Greenland where the combination of remoteness and harsh winters kept development from occurring, but the soil was rich and samples taken suggest would promote substantial crops.

ALEX

不一定。格陵兰岛有一些无人居住的地区，由于地处偏远，冬季严寒，无法进行开发，但土壤肥沃，样本表明可以促进大量农作物的生长。

JEFF SINCLAIR
How would you obtain that soil material?

杰夫·辛克莱
你如何获得这些土壤材料？

ALEX
With the heavy machinery at my disposal, we could

build a jetty to roll off heavy equipment and transport that equipment to these areas and with trucks and front-end loaders and a few bulldozers with a ripper shank.

JEFF SINCLAIR
I can certainly see that's all feasible.

杰夫·辛克莱
我当然知道这一切都是可行的。

ALEX
We could tear up even semi-frozen earth which the front-end loaders could easily load up on trucks that would back down the jetty onto a ramp on a barge and dump the dirt which would then be systematically moved around the barge with a bobcat loader.

亚历克斯
有了我可以使用的重型机械，我们可以建造一个码头来滚下重型设备，并用卡车、前端装载机和一些带有裂土器柄的推土机将设备运输到这些区域。

我们甚至可以挖开半冻土，前端装载机可以轻松地将其装上卡车，卡车会将码头上的泥土倒到驳船上的斜坡上，然后倾倒泥土，然后用山猫装载机有条不紊地在驳船上移动。

Alex suddenly noticed Shelley was carefully listening to every word he said and he thought:

亚历克斯突然发现雪莉在认真听他说的每一个字，他想：

ALEX (THOUGHT)
*I wonder if Shelly is recording all this, and will it be in her North Ice News tomorrow?*

亚历克斯（想）
不知道雪莉是不是把这一切都录了下来，明天会在她的《北方冰雪新闻》上播出吗？

ALEX
Tugs would then tow the barges back to Nuuk where they would be offloaded using cranes with scoops and bobcats to help load the scoops. 2 feet of this permafrost soil in the bottoms of the greenhouses would provide the foundation to healthy vegetables grown.

亚历克斯

然后，拖船会将驳船拖回努克，在那里，使用带
铲子的起重机和山猫卸载，山猫会帮助装载铲
子。温室底部 2 英尺的永久冻土将为健康蔬菜的
生长提供基础。

JEFF SINCLAIR
When would you do this?

杰夫·辛克莱
你什么时候做这件事？

ALEX
That side project would commence as soon as the
first section of the dome was up and the realization of
dome living apparent on the locals.

亚历克斯
这个附带项目将在圆顶的第一部分建成后立即开
始，当地人开始意识到圆顶生活。

JEFF SINCLAIR
There is a lot of rough terrain around Nuuk, where
would you put these greenhouses?

杰夫·辛克莱
努克周围有很多崎岖的地形，你会把这些温室放
在哪里？

ALEX
Greenhouses could be put on hill sides just like many
Chinese rice patties and built on stilts on slopes of
mountains since the soil would be hauled in and just
lay on top of the existing rocky surface.

亚历克斯
温室可以像许多中国稻田一样建在山坡上，也可
以建在山坡上的高架上，因为土壤会被拖进来，
放在现有的岩石表面上。

JEFF SINCLAIR
How would you build these greenhouses on slopes?

杰夫·辛克莱
你会如何在斜坡上建造这些温室？

ALEX
The greenhouses would have steel frames for sturdiness. But with the expected winter snowfall accumulations, sheets of plywood would be installed on top of the steel framed glass surfaces to withstand the weight of the snow and protect the glass. Since there would be "cherry picker lifters" available the plywood panels would be easy to quickly install and later removed. Since no crops would be growing at that time, the cherry pickers could be stored inside the green houses.

亚历克斯
温室将采用钢架以增加坚固性。但是随着冬季降雪的预期，人们会在钢框架玻璃表面安装胶合板，以承受雪的重量并保护玻璃。由于有"采摘机升降机"，胶合板面板可以快速安装，随后拆除。由于那时没有农作物生长，采摘机可以存放在温室内。

JEFF SINCLAIR
Just like people in Florida putting up plywood all

over their homes and storm shutters for the hurricane seasons.

杰夫·辛克莱
就像佛罗里达州的人们在飓风季节在家里到处安装胶合板和防风百叶窗一样。

The group chuckled. Alex saw that even Shelly chuckled at Jeff's joke.

大家笑了。亚历克斯看到，就连雪莉也对杰夫的笑话笑了。

ALEX
Even though winter days are very short the solar panels from February to April would have some output as well as September and October.

亚历克斯
尽管冬天白天很短，但太阳能电池板从二月到四月实际上会有一些输出，九月和十月也是如此。

Hence, the heat pumps would still be working, and the greenhouses would retain some warmth, and probably not freeze in the wintertime.

因此，热泵仍将工作，温室将保留一些温暖，冬天可能不会结冰。

JEFF SINCLAIR
But what if they freeze up?

杰夫·辛克莱
但是如果它们结冰了怎么办？

ALEX
Certainly, by April the heat pumps would keep the contents of the greenhouses from freezing until late fall arrived.

亚历克斯
当然，到四月份，热泵将使温室中的物品在深秋到来之前不会结冰。

For everyone, the evening seemed to provide a joyous occasion. Margarete was more enthused than the rest because she delivered her promise to Adel and Shelly, the nice dinner, little did she realize it would be with four big shots associated with Nuuk Dome Inc.

对于每个人来说，这个夜晚似乎都是一个欢乐的时刻。玛格丽特比其他人更兴奋，因为她兑现了对阿德尔和雪莉的承诺，那就是一顿美味的晚餐，她没有想到和努克圆顶公司. 四个大人物共进晚餐。

The meal and dessert came and went so quickly, time was flying which is usually the case when people are having fun. When people are miserable it lingers.

饭菜和甜点来得很快，去得也很快，时间过得飞快，人们玩得开心时通常都是这样。当人们心情不好时，这种感觉会挥之不去。

Suddenly the night had to come to an end when the party pooper Adel declared:

突然，当扫兴的阿德尔宣布时，夜晚不得不结束了：

ADEL
Well girls, I really need to get home and grade some
papers and write up a lesson plan for tomorrow.

阿德尔
好吧，女孩们，我真的需要回家批改一些论文，
并为明天写一份教学计划。

SHELLY
I have some personal matters to attend to as well.

雪莉
我还有一些私事要处理。

Margaret could have stayed a few more hours, she didn't need to get up until 6:00 a.m. in the morning and the evening was still early and after 3 glasses of wine had a good buzz going on. But since she didn't know these men, gladly left with the women.

玛格丽特本可以再呆几个小时，她早上6点才需要起床，晚上还很早，喝了三杯酒后，她喝得酩酊大醉。但由于她不认识这些男人，所以很高兴和女人在一起离开了。

Margaret held out her hand to Alex.

玛格丽特向亚历克斯伸出了手。

MARGARET
Thank you for the lovely dinner and a good time.

玛格丽特
谢谢你的美味晚餐和美好时光。

ALEX
The pleasure was all mine.

亚历克斯
我很荣幸。

Alex responded as the others said good night to each other.

其他人互相道晚安时，亚历克斯回应道。

ALEX
Jeff, I'm taking off in the morning. Thanks for showing me around the job site and introducing me to some of the people.

亚历克斯
杰夫，我明天早上要走了。谢谢你带我参观工地，并把我介绍给一些人。

JEFF SINCLAIR
We are glad to have you here, Alex.

杰夫·辛克莱
我们很高兴你能来，亚历克斯。

ALEX
I think I might come back when you start pouring the first pillar.

亚历克斯
我想当你开始浇筑第一根柱子时我可能会回来。

JEFF SINCLAIR
Sure, no problem.

杰夫·辛克莱
当然，没问题。

Alex then handed Jeff his business card.

亚历克斯然后递给杰夫他的名片。

ALEX
Call me a day or two before you start pouring the cement in the first pillar, I'd like to be here for that and observe you move the form up to the next level and observe the cranes moving up.

亚历克斯
在你开始浇筑第一根柱子的水泥前一两天给我打电话，我想在这里观察你将模板移到下一层，观察起重机向上移动。

JEFF SINCLAIR
Sure, I can give you a couple days warning if you want
to be here.

杰夫·辛克莱
当然，如果你想来这里，我可以提前几天通知你。

ALEX
Thanks. I appreciate that.

亚历克斯
谢谢。我很感激。

Everyone went to the elevator and got in and headed down to the first floor except
Alex who got off at the 4th floor which was the same room he had the last time he was
in this hotel.

每个人都去了电梯，进去后去了一楼，除了亚历克斯，他在四楼下了车，那是
他上次来这家酒店时住的房间。

ALEX
Good night, everyone.

亚历克斯
晚安，大家。

SHELLY
Good night, Alex.

雪莉·
晚安，亚历克斯。

The elevator door shut, and Alex walked down to his room, opened the door, walked
inside then shut it and slid the slide bolt lock in place, walked over to the adjoining
room door, and made sure it also was locked in a similar fashion. He then spotted
his suitcase by the coat rack, grabbed it, opened it and with his key the special
compartment on the bottom and pulled out his gun, walked over to the bed and put it
under the pillow.

电梯门关上了，亚历克斯走到他的房间，打开门，走进去，然后关上门，把滑
动插销锁滑到位，走到隔壁房间的门，确保它也以同样的方式锁上了。然后，
他在衣帽架旁边发现了他的手提箱，拿起它，打开它，用钥匙打开底部的特殊
隔间，拿出枪，走到床边，把它放在枕头下。

Alex then got out his toothbrush, brushed his teeth, put on his pajamas, and went to
bed.

然后 亚历克斯拿出牙刷，刷了牙，穿上睡衣，上床睡觉。

***

## EXT. NIGHT. NUUK GREENLAND NEAR HOTEL HANS EGEDE

Hans Jespersen was coincidently walking past the Hotel Hans Egede on his way home from the liquor store with a quart of Vodka. Across the street he saw to his horror Adel and her 2 friends leaving the hotel with the 3 strangers, one of whom he'd seen around before, but wasn't sure where. The 3 men got into the Land Rover and drove off. The 3 women got into Adel's car, and she drove off in a similar direction.

汉斯·杰斯佩森恰巧从酒铺回家，手里拿着一夸脱伏特加，路过这家酒店。他惊恐地看到对面的阿德尔和她的两个朋友正和三个陌生人一起离开酒店，其中一个他以前见过，但不确定在哪里。三个男人上了路虎车，开车走了。三个女人上了阿德尔的车，她朝同一个方向开车走了。

In about five minutes as Hans walked past Nuuk Dome Inc. offices that same Land Rover suddenly came driving back and pulled into the semi-empty parking lot.

大约 5 分钟后，当汉斯走过努克圆顶公司办公室时，那辆路虎突然开回来，停进了半空的停车场。

The man who Hans previously recognized got out of the car, and promptly walked into the building where he may simply have gone back to work.

汉斯之前认出的那名男子下了车，然后迅速走进了办公楼，他可能只是想回去上班而已。

There were still half a dozen people there working, putting together timelines and schedules for the next few days' events.

那里还有六个人在整理接下来几天活动的时间表和日程安排。

Jeff would not be going home for another three hours because as general manager, he had to sign a lot of the documents they were creating tonight, and via digital signature, Jeff sent them to the New York Offices.

杰夫还要三个小时才能回家，因为作为总经理，他必须签署他们今晚要创建的大量文件，并通过数字签名将它们发送到纽约办公室。

Those documents included payroll information, materials requests, and other reports needed to sustain day-to-day operations. This was a very busy time for Jeff, who in some ways wished he had not wasted so much time with Alex over at the Hereford Beefstouw.

这些文件包括工资单信息、材料请求和维持日常运营所需的其他报告。对于杰夫来说，这段时间非常忙碌，他在某种程度上希望自己没有在赫里福德牛排馆和亚历克斯一起浪费那么多时间。

But Alex was the man with the money. Without him, none of this would happen. So, in the end it was probably worthwhile hanging out with Mr. Money Bags, especially if it helped the project receive all the money and materials it needed to sustain operations and have an impact on a lot of people's lives in a few years.

但是，亚历克斯是有钱的人。但是，Alex 是有钱人。没有他，这一切都不会发生。所以最后，和钱袋先生一起出去玩也许是值得的，特别是如果它能帮助项目获得维持运营所需的所有资金和材料，并在几年内对很多人的生活产生影响的话。

Jeff felt very comfortable with Alex, who was a straight shooter and friendly. From past experiences, Jeff felt that almost everyone who met Alex liked him because of his gentleness and very reasonableness. However, if he got a wild hair up his butt, there was no end to what he would do or apply money too. This very dome project was exactly such a case.

杰夫和亚历克斯在一起感觉很舒服，他是一个直言不讳、友好的人。从过去的经验来看，杰夫觉得几乎所有和亚历克斯接触过的人都喜欢他，因为他很温柔，非常通情达理。然而，如果他的屁股上长了一根野毛，他做的事情和花钱的方式就没完没了了。这个圆顶项目就是这样的例子。

Hans walked on home, thought about going over to Adel's place to smoke some dope with her, but the aggravation he felt walking past Nuuk Dome Inc.'s offices eliminated any desires to smoke tonight or socialize. Hans sat down at the table in the center of his main room that doubled as kitchen and living room, pulled out a can of pickled Herring, and unscrewed the top of his cheap Vodka bottle.

汉斯继续往家走，想着去阿黛尔家和她一起抽点毒品，但走过努克多姆公司办公室时，他感到很烦躁，今晚抽烟或社交的欲望全都烟消云散了。汉斯坐在主房间中央的桌子旁，主房间既是厨房又是客厅，他拿出一罐腌鲱鱼，拧开了他那瓶廉价伏特加酒的瓶盖。

Had it not been for that crappy job as a stevedore today helping unload that ship, Hans probably would have gone hungry or had to mooch off Adel again. The man who hired Hans said be back tomorrow they had a lot more stuff to unload.

要不是今天在船上当码头工人帮忙卸货，汉斯可能就要挨饿了，或者不得不再次向阿黛尔乞讨。雇佣汉斯的人说明天再来，他们还有很多东西要卸。

HANS (THOUGHT)<br>
Who knows, I might even make enough money to eat<br>
for a month if I played my cards right.

汉斯（心想）<br>
谁知道呢，如果我打好牌，我甚至可能赚到足够<br>
一个月吃饭的钱。

Selling dope and fishing wasn't working out like he thought it would. His whole life seemed to be crumbling, and this damned dome wasn't making him any bit happy. By the time he finished half the Vodka Bottle he didn't care no more and simply walked over to his auxiliary sleeping location, the couch laid down and went to sleep. In a few hours from now when Nuuk Dome Inc, set off some charges as they were taking down that hill, he would be rudely awakened and pissed off again.

卖毒品和钓鱼并不像他想象的那样顺利。他的整个生活似乎都崩溃了，这个该死的圆顶也没有给他带来一点快乐。当他喝完半瓶伏特加时，他不再在乎了，只是走到他的辅助睡觉的地方，沙发，躺下睡觉。几个小时后，当努克圆顶公司在他们拆下那座山时引爆一些炸药时，他会被粗鲁地叫醒，再次生气。

***

<u>INT. DAY. NUUK GREENLAND ALEX'S HOTEL HANS EGEDE ROOM</u>

The morning came quickly. Alex woke up, called Brad.

早晨很快就到了。亚历克斯醒来，打电话给布拉德。

ALEX

Brad, how about driving over here in your rental car and pick me up at 7:00.

亚历克斯

布拉德，开着你租来的车到这里来，7:00 来接我怎么样？

BRAD
Sure thing Mr. Baxter.

布拉德
当然可以，巴克斯特先生。

ALEX

Oh, one other thing Brad, we are not flying directly back home, we are going to have a stopover in New York, and I think I might spend the night there.

亚历克斯

哦，另一件事布拉德，我们不会直接飞回家，我们将在纽约中途停留，我想我可能会在那里过夜。

BRAD

I'll file the flight plan to New York, then to Minnesota when you are ready to go home.

布拉德

当你准备好回家时，我会提交飞往纽约的航班计划，然后再提交明尼苏达州的航班计划。

ALEX
Thanks.

亚历克斯
谢谢。

Alex then hung up his cellphone and just as he was getting ready to sit it down and take a shower, and get dressed, it rang. It was Stephanie calling.

然后亚历克斯挂断了手机，正当他准备坐下来洗澡、穿衣服时，手机响了。 是斯蒂芬妮打来的电话。

STEPHANIE
Good morning, Alex.

斯蒂芬妮
早上好，亚历克斯。

ALEX
Hello Stephanie. You must have woken up early.
亚历克斯
你好，斯蒂芬妮。你一定醒得很早。

STEPHANIE
Alex, are you still in Greenland?

斯蒂芬妮
亚历克斯，你还在格陵兰吗？

ALEX
Yep.

亚历克斯
斯蒂芬妮
是的。

STEPHANIE
Are you coming home soon?

斯蒂芬妮
你快回家了吗？

ALEX
Yes, but I may stay another day.

亚历克斯
是的，但我可能会再待一天。

STEPHANIE
Busy?

斯蒂芬妮
忙碌的？

ALEX
Certainly, there are lots of activities here now.

亚历克斯
当然，现在这里有很多活动。

STEPHANIE
It seems a lot would be going on.

斯蒂芬妮
看来将会发生很多事情。

ALEX
Have you got through all those briefing papers yet?

亚历克斯
你看完所有这些简报了吗？

STEPHANIE
Almost.

斯蒂芬妮
几乎。

ALEX
How soon will you be done with your analysis?

亚历克斯
您多久能完成分析？

STEPHANIE
In probably two days.

斯蒂芬妮
大概二天内。

ALEX
Okay, I expect a full report then.

亚历克斯
好的，我期待一份完整的报告。

STEPHANIE
Sure.

斯蒂芬妮
当然。

ALEX
Hey, I need to take a shower now and get ready, I'll talk to you later.

亚历克斯
嘿，我现在需要洗澡准备一下，稍后再聊。

STEPHANIE
Okay.
斯蒂芬妮
好的。

ALEX
Bye.

亚历克斯
再见。

Alex then hung up.

亚历克斯随后挂断了电话。

Stephanie suddenly felt something was wrong. Stephanie didn't quite understand it. The mere thought of him spending the night with Adel or that cute girl who was the front desk clerk at the hotel, almost made her want to cry.

斯蒂芬妮突然觉得有些不对劲。斯蒂芬妮不太明白。光是想到他和阿德尔，还有那个在酒店前台当服务员的漂亮女孩一起过夜，她就差点想哭。

STEPHANIE
*Is that why he wouldn't let me go with him?*

斯蒂芬妮
这就是他不让我跟他走的原因吗？

Not long after getting ready, there was a knock at the door. Alex was packed and walked over and looked through the security eye piece and saw Brad standing outside, opened the door.

准备好后不久，门口传来了敲门声。亚历克斯 收拾好行李走过去，透过安全目镜看到 布拉德站在外面，打开了门。

ALEX
Ready to go, let me grab my suitcase.

亚历克斯
准备出发了，我去拿行李箱。

Alex grabbed his suitcase and as soon as he got to the door which Brad was holding open.

亚历克斯抓住了他的手提箱，一走到布拉德打开的门前。

BRAD
Mr. Baxter, let me carry that.

布拉德
巴克斯特先生，让我来拿它。

ALEX
Sure.

亚历克斯
当然。

Alex handed his suitcase to Brad. Then the two men walked to the elevator and went to the lobby where Alex checked out.

亚历克斯把他的手提箱递给布拉德。然后两人走到电梯旁，来到亚历克斯退房的大厅。

Margaret was there, looking pretty as usual and just as Alex was turning around, Margaret announced which Brad overheard.

玛格丽特在那里，看起来像往常一样漂亮，正当亚历克斯转身时，玛格丽特宣布了布拉德无意中听到的消息。

MARGARET
Oh, by the way Mr. Baxter, thank you for the lovely
dinner last night.

玛格丽特
哦，顺便说一句，巴克斯特先生，谢谢你昨晚的
美味晚餐。

ALEX
The pleasure was all mine.

亚历克斯
我很荣幸。

Brad then gave Alex that conveyed this incorrect impression: *You lucky dog, look.*

然后布拉德给亚历克斯传达了一个错误的印象：你这个幸运儿，看。

As soon as they got in Brad's car rental, Alex said the obvious.

他们一上布拉德的租车，亚历克斯就说了显而易见的话。

ALEX

It's not what you think we just had dinner, there was a group of us, including Jeff Sinclair, and two supervisors from the project, Gus and Ralph, and two women I met the last time I was here.

亚历克斯

事情不是你想的那样，我们刚刚吃了晚饭，我们一共一群人，包括杰夫·辛克莱，还有两个项目主管，格斯和拉尔夫，还有我上次来这里时认识的两个女人。

BRAD

That's okay, Mr. Baxter it's none of my business. But wow she is a pretty girl.

布拉德

没关系，巴克斯特先生，这不关我的事。但哇，她是个漂亮的女孩。

ALEX

And she's way too young for me. If I were about ten years younger, I might have considered it.

亚历克斯

她对我来说太年轻了。如果我年轻十岁左右，我可能会考虑。

BRAD

She's not too young for me, I'd take her the way she is.

布拉德

她对我来说不算太年轻，我会接受她现在的样子。

ALEX

I hope she finds a nice guy one of these days.

亚历克斯

我希望她有一天能找到一个好男人。

BRAD
Me too.

布拉德
我也是。

In a few minutes, Brad pulled up to the Hanger where the Gulfstream was parked, got out and opened the door for Alex and handed him his suitcase and announced.

几分钟后，布拉德把车停在湾流飞机停放的机库边，下车为亚历克斯打开车门，把行李箱递给他，然后宣布了。

BRAD
I'll drop off this rental car and be back in a couple minutes, meet you inside.

布拉德
我会把租来的车还上，几分钟后回来，在里面见你。

Brad then got back in the car and drove about 200 yards to a small parking area for rental cars and handed the keys to the employee. His credit card was charged and he would be receiving his invoice via email later that day. By the time Brad got back to the hanger, Alex was inside and patiently waiting.

布拉德随后回到车上，开了大约 200 码，来到一个小型租车停车场，把钥匙交给了员工。他的信用卡已经扣款，当天晚些时候会通过电子邮件收到发票。当布拉德回到机库时，亚历克斯已经在里面耐心等待了。

An employee then came up to them both and spoke:

然后一名员工走到他们俩面前，说道：

JET SERVICE EMPLOYEE
If you guys are ready to leave now, I'll escort you to your plane and tow it out of the hanger.

喷气式飞机服务员工
如果你们现在准备离开，我会护送你们到飞机上，然后把它拖出机库。

ALEX
Thank you.

亚历克斯
谢谢。

The three of them went through a door which took them down a hallway which had another door which opened into the hanger. They both walked over to the plane.

他们三个人穿过一扇门，沿着走廊走下去，走廊上还有另一扇门通往机库。他们俩都走到飞机旁。

BRAD
Mr. Baxter, please go aboard, I will stow your suitcase
in the cargo bay and be right up there.

布拉德
巴克斯特先生，请上飞机，我会把你的行李箱放
在货舱里，然后马上就到。

Just like a perfectly choreographed routine, Brad tucked away the suitcase, then walked up the airplane stairs, then retracted them into the plane and shut the door. He then went to his pilot's seat, sat down and put on his headphones which were currently tied into the tractor driver headphones outside the plane plugged into the aircraft service outlet.

就像一个完美编排的程序，布拉德收起行李箱，然后走上飞机楼梯，将行李箱缩回机舱并关上门。然后他走到飞行员座位，坐下，戴上耳机，耳机目前与飞机外拖拉机司机的耳机相连，插在飞机服务插座上。

BRAD
Okay, I'm on the line ready to be towed out of the
hanger.

布拉德
好的，我已准备好被拖出机库。

JET SERVICE EMPLOYEE
Right away sir.

喷气式飞机服务员工
先生，马上就好。

Brad had been there an hour and a half before, did all the preflight, checked the fuel level and had them put on a few hundred pounds of fuel thinking they would fly non-stop to Minnesota.

布拉德一个半小时前就到了那里，做了所有的飞行前检查，检查了燃油量，并让他们加了几百磅燃油，以为他们会直飞明尼苏达州。

The doors slid open and suddenly the tractor pulled the plane out of the hanger to a point where the service ramp line out of the hanger curved and had the plane now parked parallel to the hanger where jet exhaust would not strike the hanger. The tractor driver then came back and talked over the intercom system via his phones:

门滑开，突然拖拉机将飞机从机库中拉出，拉到机库外的服务坡道弯曲的地方，飞机现在与机库平行停放，喷气式飞机的废气不会撞到机库。拖拉机司机随后回来，通过电话通过对讲系统通话：

**JET SERVICE EMPLOYEE**
You are now disconnected from the tow, have a nice
safe flight home.

喷气式飞机服务人员
您现在已与牵引断开连接，祝您一路平安。

Brad
Thank you.

布拉德
谢谢。

The tractor then moved back into the hanger and moments later the hanger door slid
shut.

拖拉机随后移回机库，片刻之后，机库门滑入关闭。

Brad started the engines and completed his preflight.

布拉德启动发动机并完成飞行前检查。

There were several exchanges between ground control and Brad then finally Brad was
directed by the ATC Tower:

地面控制人员和布拉德进行了几次交流，最后布拉德得到了空中交通管制塔台
的指示：

**AIR TRAFFIC CONTROLLER**
N80973 you permission for takeoff runway 23
heading 226 degrees. Wind 8 knots at 045 degrees. No
approaching aircraft.

空中交通管制员
N80973 您允许从 23 号跑道起飞，航向 226 度。
风速 8 节，风向 045 度。禁止飞机进近。

**BRAD**
Tower, understand N80973 permission to take off
runway 23.

布拉德
塔台，了解 N80973 允许从 23 号跑道起飞。

In a brief period, the Jet climbed above 10,000 feet over water on a course of 225 for
a while.

在很短的时间内，飞机在 225 的航向中爬升到水面 10,000 英尺以上。

The Jet landed at JFK in NYC and just like many times before Rodriguez was there to pick up Alex, who wanted to first check in with Claude and give him a report on what he observed and any criticism or comments on the project from is observation.

飞机降落在纽约肯尼迪机场，和之前很多次一样，罗德里格斯来接亚历克斯，亚历克斯想先和克劳德汇报一下他的观察结果，以及他对这个项目的批评或评论。

While Alex was in the Limo, he sent a text message to Christina:

亚历克斯坐在豪华轿车里时，给克里斯蒂娜发了一条短信：

ALEX
(TEXT MESSAGE)
Hey, I'm back.

亚历克斯
（短信）
嘿，我回来了。

In about a minute later Alex received a response from Christina.

大约一分钟后，亚历克斯收到了克里斯蒂娜的回复。

CHRISTINA GARRISON
That was quick.

克里斯克里斯蒂娜·加里森
回复得真快。

ALEX
Yea I needed to get back to thaw out in time for dinner tonight.

亚历克斯
是的，我需要赶回去解冻，赶上今晚的晚餐。

CHRISTINA GARRISON
Speaking of dinner, where's the one you promised?

克里斯蒂娜·加里森
说到晚餐，你答应的晚餐在哪儿？

ALEX
Just as soon as you get off work and tell me you are ready to go out.

亚历克斯
你下班后就告诉我你准备好出门了。

CHRISTINA GARRISON
That sounds good, would you like to meet me at some
place?

克里斯蒂娜·加里森
听起来不错，你想在某个地方见我吗？
ALEX
Sure, how about down on Broadway, somewhere near
a restaurant you like?

亚历克斯
当然，在百老汇附近，你喜欢的餐馆附近怎么样？

Christina gave Alex the name of an Irish pub she liked which was right around the corner from the Marriott Marquis which Alex quickly booked a room in.

克里斯蒂娜告诉亚历克斯她喜欢的一家爱尔兰酒吧的名字，这家酒吧就在万豪大酒店附近，亚历克斯很快就订了一间房。

In a few minutes, Rodriguez pulled up to 120 Wall Street where Alex got out and said:

几分钟后，罗德里格斯把车停在华尔街 120 号，亚历克斯下车说：

ALEX
It will probably not be long.

亚历克斯
可能很快就到了。

Alex then greeted Leroy, with a smile as usual, gave him the secret handshake.

然后亚历克斯像往常一样微笑着向勒罗伊打招呼，和他秘密握手。

As Alex moved into the building, Leroy walked over to the Limo while he stuffed the crisp $100 bill in his pocket and Rodriguez rolled the window down.

亚历克斯走进大楼时，勒罗伊一边往豪华轿车里塞着崭新的 100 美元钞票，一边走向豪华轿车，罗德里格斯摇下了车窗。

LEROY JONES
Afternoon.

勒罗伊·琼斯
下午.

RODRIGUEZ
Hello, how are you?

罗德里格斯
你好吗？

LEROY JONES
Doing great.
勒罗伊·琼斯
干得很棒。

RODRIGUEZ
Say, Alex said he would only be a couple of minutes.

罗德里格斯
比如说，亚历克斯说他只需要几分钟。

LEROY JONES
No problem, Rodriguez, it's a slow day.

勒罗伊·琼斯
没问题，罗德里格斯，这一天过得很慢。

RODRIGUEZ
Has the weather been kind of crappy today and people
not coming out?

罗德里格斯
难道今天天气不好，人们都没有出来吗？

LEROY JONES
Yes, staying home and staying warm no doubt.

勒罗伊·琼斯
是的，毫无疑问，待在家里并保持温暖。

Alex went right up to Claude's office almost unannounced, but since Claude was between clients and meetings it didn't matter.

亚历克斯几乎未经通知就直接去了克劳德的办公室，但由于克劳德正在接待客户和开会，所以这并不重要。

Ann opened his door after a signature "Ann knock," and opened it and announced:

安在 "安敲门" 的标志性声音后打开了门，然后打开门宣布：

ANN
Mr. Rearden, Alex Baxter is here to see you.

安
里尔登先生，亚历克斯·巴克斯特来见你了。

CLAUDE
Show him in.

克劳德
带他进来。

ANN
Mr. Baxter you may go in.

安
巴克斯特先生，你可以进去了。

Claude stood up, walked around his desk and held out his hand when Alex arrived.

克劳德站起来，绕过他的办公桌，在亚历克斯到达时伸出手。

CLAUDE
That was a fast trip.

克劳德
这是一次快速的旅行。

ALEX
Yep, thanks to your good employees, I got to see a lot real fast and so I didn't need to hang around.

亚历克斯
是的，多亏了你的好员工，我很快就看了很多东西，所以我不需要逗留。

CLAUDE
So, things are moving along rather well?

克劳德
那么，事情进展得相当顺利吗？

ALEX
As best as I could see, but as you know we are in the early stages of this project, so what I saw is kind of what I expected.

亚历克斯
据我所知，情况最好，但正如你所知，我们正处
于这个项目的早期阶段，所以我看到的是我所期
望的。


CLAUDE
What do you think of Jeff Sinclair?


克劳德
你觉得杰夫·辛克莱怎么样？


ALEX
When I walk into an office, I can see what's going
on quickly by what the people are doing. There are
tangible actions that gainfully employed people in a
project like this exhibit.


亚历克斯
当我走进办公室时，我可以通过人们在做什么来
快速了解正在发生的事情。在像这个展览这样的
项目中，有一些切实的行动可以让人们获得有偿
就业。


CLAUDE
Sure, there is a volume of work and activity that must
happen in a real time fashion, or it will all fall apart,
and the project dies or produces only marginal results.


克劳德
当然，大量的工作和活动必须以实时方式进行，
否则就会全部崩溃，项目就会失败或只产生边际
结果。


ALEX
We have a lot of work ahead of us; it's almost a miracle
that we get moving as quickly as we did.


亚历克斯
我们还有很多工作要做；我们能如此迅速地行动
几乎是一个奇迹。


CLAUDE
Definitely. Had this been a development in California,
we would not scoop the first shovel of dirt for another
10 years.

克劳德
确实。如果这是加州的一个发展项目，我们不会
再等 10 年才铲出第一铲泥土。

ALEX
That's kind of how I feel about it, we obtained a two-
or three-year head start in how this all unfolded.

亚历克斯
这就是我对此的感受，我们比这一切的展开早了
两到三年。

CLAUDE
No doubt it was due in part to your activities.

克劳德
毫无疑问，这在一定程度上要归功于你们的活动。

ALEX
Denmark and Greenland understand more vividly the
tangibles we bring to the table. As an example, the coal
seam and the limestone will no doubt have an impact
on future mining in Greenland.

亚历克斯
丹麦和格陵兰岛更加清楚地了解我们所带来的有
形成果。例如，煤层和石灰岩无疑将对格陵兰岛
未来的采矿产生影响。

CLAUDE
We probably paved the way for other enterprises and
as we demonstrate we can be successful in the Arctic;
other corporations will give a second thought to
possibly attempting mineral extraction up here.

克劳德
我们可能为其他企业铺平了道路，随着我们证明
我们可以在北极取得成功，其他公司将重新考虑
是否可能在这里进行矿物开采。

ALEX
This really is a virgin country, due to the snow and ice,
a lot of unknown exists and there may be substantial
amounts of precious metals and rare earth minerals
that could be suddenly discovered to begin serious
exploration to.

亚历克斯
这确实是一个处女地，由于冰雪，存在着很多未
知的东西，可能会突然发现大量的贵金属和稀土
矿物，从而引起认真的勘探。

CLAUDE
You are right, that coal seam for example is a starter.
It's just like what you see in Powder River Basin
Wyoming. Except this is better quality steam coal and
some of it will be classified as metallic and coking
coal.

克劳德
你说得对，例如那个煤层是一个起点。它就像你
在怀俄明州的 粉状河流盆地 (Powder River Basin)
看到的一样。只不过这是质量更好的蒸汽煤，其
中一些将被归类为金属煤和焦煤。

ALEX
I informed Jeff Sinclair that, when they got ready to
start pouring the concrete for the first pillar, I wanted to
be in Nuuk for that event, which should be happening
soon, so I might be coming back this way in a week
or so.

亚历克斯
我告诉杰夫·辛克莱尔，当他们准备开始为第一根
柱子浇筑混凝土时，我想在努克参加那个活动，
这应该很快就会发生，所以我可能会在一周左右
的时间内以这种方式回来。

CLAUDE
Great drop in and see me on your way.

克劳德
很高兴顺便过来，顺便见见你。

ALEX
Will do. I have some things to do and people to see, I'll
be leaving New York in the morning.

ALEX
好的。我有一些事情要做，还有一些人要见，我
明天早上就要离开纽约了。

CLAUDE
Great, see you on your next trip.

克劳德

太好了，下次旅行再见。

Alex left the office, went down the elevator, but did not see Christina on the way, but knew he'd see her later. Walked out to his Limo, saw Leroy and Rodrigues socializing, walked up to Leroy and held out his hand to shake his, and in the process passed him another $100 bill.

亚历克斯勒罗伊离开办公室，乘电梯下楼，但路上没有看到 克里斯蒂娜，但他知道稍后会见到她。走到他的豪华轿车旁，看到 勒罗伊和 罗德里格斯正在社交，便走到 勒罗伊面前，伸出手与他握手，并递给他另一张 100 美元的钞票。

Leroy instantly knew he was going to have to start spending a little more time in the gym because of these extra meals Alex was buying for him, and his assistants were now putting back on the pounds.

莱罗伊立刻意识到，由于亚历克斯为他购买的额外餐食，他将不得不开始花更多的时间在健身房，而他的助手们现在又开始增重了。

Rodriguez dropped Alex off at the Marriott Marquis near where he was going to meet Christina later that evening. It would be several hours before they met, which gave Alex time to type up some notes and comments on what he observed during the trip. They had a lot of hard work ahead of them but at least they were off to a good start.

罗德里格斯把亚历克斯送到了万豪侯酒店，他当晚要在那里与克里斯蒂娜见面。他们见面还需要几个小时，这让亚历克斯有时间记录一些笔记和评论，记录他在旅途中观察到的情况。他们还有很多艰苦的工作要做，但至少他们有一个好的开始。

After a few hours of work, then a little nap at 6:00 p.m. rolled around and suddenly Alex got a text message from Christina,

经过几个小时的工作，然后小睡了一会儿，下午 6 点左右，亚历克斯突然收到了克里斯蒂娜的短信，

CHRISTINA
(TEXT MESSAGE)
I'm free now, I'm heading over to that Irish Pub, should be there in about 10 minutes.

克里斯蒂娜
（短信）
我现在有空了，我要去那家爱尔兰酒吧，大约 10 分钟后就到了。

Christina then added the address to the text message to make sure Alex would not get lost.

克里斯蒂娜随后将地址添加到短信中，以确保亚历克斯不会迷路。

Alex freshened up a bit, left his room and went to the lobby and confirmed with an employee at the counter, the pub was right around the corner which matched Christina's map on his cell phone. It would take him less than five minutes to walk there on well-lit streets.

亚历克斯稍微清醒了一下，离开房间，前往大厅，与柜台的一名员工确认，酒吧就在拐角处，与克里斯蒂娜手机上的地图相符。在路灯明亮的街道上，他步行不到五分钟就能到达那里。

About the time ALEX came up to the pub a taxi pulled up, and of all people, Christina got out of the cab which immediately took off for its next fare.

就在亚历克斯来到酒吧的时候，一辆出租车停了下来，克里斯蒂娜从车里出来，车子立即出发去接乘客。

ALEX
Hey stranger.

亚历克斯
嘿，陌生人。

CHRISTINA
Hi Alex

克里斯蒂娜
嗨，亚历克斯

ALEX
Looks like I didn't get lost.

亚历克斯
看来我并没有迷失。

CHRISTINA
That's good, glad my instructions worked out for you.

克里斯蒂娜
太好了，很高兴我的指示对你有用。

ALEX
Your instructions were good.

亚历克斯
你的指示很好。

The two then entered the pub and found a small table with 2 chairs far enough away from the music where they could talk and hear each other.

然后两人走进酒吧，找到一张小桌子和两把椅子，距离音乐足够远，他们可以交谈并听到对方的声音。

Within a few minutes, an attractive waitress walked up wearing Irish style costume like clothes, one would assume was right out of Dublin circa 1870's. Her cleavage was exposed and looked exceptionally good.

几分钟后，一位穿着爱尔兰风格服装的漂亮女服务员走了过来，人们会认为这是 19 世纪 70 年代左右都柏林的服装。她的乳沟露出来，看起来特别漂亮。

BRIANA<br>
Hello Christina.

布丽安娜<br>
你好 克里斯蒂娜。

CHRISTINA<br>
Hi Briana, this is my friend Alex.

克里斯蒂娜<br>
嗨 布丽安娜，这是我的朋友 亚历克斯。

BRIANA<br>
Pleased to meet you, Alex.

布丽安娜<br>
很高兴见到你，亚历克斯。

Alex held out his hand to shake Briana's.

亚历克斯 伸出手和 布丽安娜握手。

ALEX<br>
Briana, same here.

亚历克斯<br>
布丽安娜，我也一样。

BRIANA<br>
What can I get you guys to drink?

布丽安娜<br>
你们要喝点什么？

CHRISTINA
Kilkenny for me.


克里斯蒂娜
我要 (Kilkenny)。
ALEX
Do you have Guinness Dark Draught?


亚历克斯
你们有 吉尼斯黑啤 (Guinness Dark Draught) 吗？


BRIANA
Yes, we do.


布丽安娜
有，我们有。


ALEX
Good I'll have one of them.


亚历克斯
很好，我要一杯。


BRIANA
Would you like menus?


布丽安娜
要菜单吗？


CHRISTINA
Yes please.


克里斯蒂娜
好的。


BRIANA
I'll be right back with your drinks.


布丽安娜
我马上回来拿饮料。


ALEX
Do you know many people here?


亚历克斯
你认识这里很多人吗？

CHRISTINA
Yes, my mother is Irish, and my father used to bring
her here years ago. See those pictures on the wall over
there on the other side of the bar?

克里斯蒂娜
是的，我妈妈是爱尔兰人，我爸爸几年前带她来
过这里。看到酒吧另一边墙上的照片了吗？

ALEX
Yes.

亚历克斯
是的。

CHRISTINA
If you look near the upper right-hand corner of all those
pictures you will see my father in his Army uniform.

克里斯蒂娜
如果你看这些照片的右上角，你会看到我父亲穿
着陆军制服。

ALEX
Do you mind if I go over there and look at the picture?

亚历克斯
你介意我过去看看照片吗？

CHRISTINA
Sure, why not.

克里斯蒂娜
当然，为什么不呢。

Alex stood up and walked over and saw Christina's father in his Green Beret Uniform,
with a chest full of medals. And then thinking about the private detective report he
had on Christina and her family; he knew that her father had been through a lot in
the Vietnam War. It was somewhat of a somber experience. Christina's father was an
American Hero, and a patriot. He was no doubt unusually brave. Alex made a mental
note to try to find some way to read up on his career and experiences, and battles he
might have participated in.

亚历克斯站起来走过去，看到克里斯蒂娜的父亲穿着绿色贝雷帽制服，胸前挂
满了勋章。然后他想起了私人侦探对克里斯蒂娜和她家人的调查报告；他知道
她的父亲在越南战争中经历了很多。这是一次有点阴郁的经历。克里斯蒂娜的
父亲是美国英雄，也是一位爱国者。毫无疑问，他异常勇敢。亚历克斯在心里

记下要设法了解他的职业生涯和经历，以及他可能参加过的战斗。

Alex walked back to the table and sat down and spoke somberly.

亚历克斯走回桌子旁，坐下来，严肃地说道。

ALEX
You must be very proud of your father.


亚历克斯
你一定为你的父亲感到非常自豪。


CHRISTINA
Yes, I am, he's a great dad.


克里斯蒂娜
是的，我感到自豪，他是一位伟大的父亲。


ALEX
That picture looks like it was taken a long time ago.


亚历克斯
那张照片看起来是很久以前拍的。


CHRISTINA
Yes, it was back in the 70's before I was born.


克里斯蒂娜
是的，那是在我出生前的 70 年代。


ALEX
Your mother is Irish, how did your parents meet?


亚历克斯
你的母亲是爱尔兰人，你父母是怎么认识的？


CHRISTINA
After my dad retired from the Army serving 20 years,
he went to college and became a history teacher. My
mother was a teacher in a school he taught at, that's
where they met.


克里斯蒂娜
我父亲在军队服役 20 年后退役，然后上了大学，
成为了一名历史老师。我母亲是他任教的一所学
校的老师，他们就是在那里认识的。

ALEX
That's great, I love reading history. Is he still teaching?

亚历克斯
太好了，我喜欢读历史。他还在教书吗？

CHRISTINA
No, he retired a few years ago, so did my mother.

克里斯蒂娜
不，他几年前退休了，我母亲也是。

ALEX
Are they still in good health?

亚历克斯
他们现在还健康吗？

CHRISTINA
Not bad for their ages, they keep each other young.

克里斯蒂娜
就他们的年龄来说还不错，他们让彼此保持年轻。

ALEX
That's wonderful.

亚历克斯
太好了。

Briana the waitress suddenly showed up with their drinks and took their orders.

女服务员 布丽安娜突然端着饮料过来，记下了他们的订单。

CHRISTINA
I'll have Shepard's Pie.

克里斯蒂娜
我要牧羊人派。

BRIANA
And what would you like Alex.

布丽安娜
你想要什么，亚历克斯。

ALEX
I think I'll try the Bangers and Mash.

亚历克斯
我想我会试试香肠和土豆泥。

BRIANA
The chef isn't too busy right now, so it should be coming right up.

布丽安娜
厨师现在不太忙，所以应该马上就好。

CHRISTINA
Thanks.

克里斯蒂娜
谢谢。

Alex handed the two menus to Briana. Briana then turned and headed past the bar to an opening that exposed the kitchen on the other side of the wall.

亚历克斯将两份菜单递给布丽安娜。然后布丽安娜转身穿过吧台，来到墙另一边厨房的开口处。

ALEX
This really looks like an Irish Pub.

亚历克斯
这看起来真的像是一家爱尔兰酒吧。

CHRISTINA
It certainly is with all its trimmings.

克里斯蒂娜
它的所有装饰都很棒。

ALEX
Christina, did your parents bring you to this pub when you were younger?

亚历克斯
克里斯蒂娜，你小时候父母带你来过这家酒吧吗？

CHRISTINA
Yes, my mother knew a lot of people that came here, and they became good friends with my father as well,

so we had a lot of dinners here, especially after my dad became a teacher, he would bring some of the other teachers here on the weekends for dinner and a few beers.

克里斯蒂娜

是的，我妈妈认识很多来这里的人，他们也和我爸爸成为了好朋友，所以我们经常在这里吃晚餐，特别是在我爸爸当老师之后，他会在周末带其他老师来这里吃晚餐，喝几杯啤酒。

Suddenly, the bartender and another waitress approached the table.

突然，调酒师和另一个女服务员走到桌子旁。

CHRISTINA

Alex, this is one of the bartenders, Kevin, whose been working here as long as I can remember, and his wife Mary.

克里斯蒂娜

亚历克斯，这是调酒师之一凯文，我记得他在这里工作了很长时间，还有他的妻子玛丽。

Alex stood up and spoke in a pleasant tone:

亚历克斯站起来，用愉快的语气说道：

ALEX
Pleased to meet you both.

亚历克斯
很高兴见到你们。

Alex then shook Kevin and Mary's hands.

然后亚历克斯与凯文和玛丽握手。

Alex traveled light and still had on a business suit, had not planned on socializing in more casual clothes. And it was at the last minute he gathered the courage to pursue Christina. He was only marginally out of place wearing a suit into the bar. But, because there were some businessmen there for happy hour that just came from work wearing suits, he wasn't alone. For that he felt grateful.

亚历克斯轻装上阵，仍然穿着西装，没有打算穿更休闲的衣服去社交。直到最后一刻，他才鼓起勇气去追求克里斯蒂娜。他穿着西装走进酒吧，只是稍微有点不合时宜。但是，因为那里有一些刚下班穿着西装的商人在那里享受欢乐时光，所以他并不孤单。为此他感到很感激。

After some small talk Kevin and Mary went back to work. They were impressed that Christina had such a handsome looking guy. Observing them from afar, they could also tell it appeared Alex had a glowing affection for Christina, but at the same token she was totally enamored by his presence.

闲聊了一会儿后，凯文和玛丽回去工作了。克里斯蒂娜有这么帅的男人，他们印象深刻。从远处观察他们，他们也可以看出亚历克斯似乎对克里斯蒂娜怀有炽热的爱意，但同时，她也完全被他的存在迷住了。

In the past couple of days Christina, who was very well versed in research and investigation which a non-profit organization has to do so they don't end up squirreling hard to come by money down a rabbit hole crooks set up, didn't need to look to hard to find out a lot about Alex. One thing she was quite surprised to find was that even though he was a public figure, there was no face book or internet information that would convey he had a girlfriend, or a partner, or a special relationship with anyone.

在过去的几天里，克里斯蒂娜非常精通研究和调查，非营利组织必须这样做，这样他们才不会把来之不易的钱藏进骗子设置的兔子洞里，克里斯蒂娜不需要费很大力气就能找到很多关于亚历克斯的信息。她很惊讶地发现，尽管他是公众人物，但没有任何脸书或互联网信息表明他有女朋友、伴侣或与任何人有特殊关系。

Alex's relationship with Stephanie, though somewhat unconventional, had never evolved into a romance. They were friends thus far and even though Stephanie was more than ready to do absolutely anything Alex wanted, he remained a true gentleman and friend and never conveyed to her any romantic proclivities even though she often sprinkled the environment with suggestive dialog.

亚历克斯和斯蒂芬妮的关系虽然有点不寻常，但从未发展成恋情。到目前为止，他们只是朋友，尽管斯蒂芬妮已经准备好为亚历克斯做任何事，但他仍然是一个真正的绅士和朋友，从未向她表达任何浪漫的倾向，尽管她经常在环境中穿插一些暗示性的对话。

## FLASHBACK

闪回

Alex wasn't gay, and Stephanie in fact had asked him point blank when he refused her when she offered herself to him. His response was:

亚历克斯不是同性恋，当斯蒂芬妮向他求爱时，他拒绝了她，事实上，斯蒂芬妮曾直截了当地问过他。他的回答是：

ALEX
I'm only going to have intercourse with a woman when
I fall in love with her. And then only if she agrees to
marry me.

亚历克斯
我只有在爱上一个女人时才会和她发生性关系。
而且只有当她同意嫁给我时。

Stephanie never pushed Alex, and one time at an event, in a private side bar was advised by Alex's friend Paul, his future best man:

斯蒂芬妮从来没有强迫亚历克斯，有一次在一次活动中，亚历克斯的朋友，他未来的伴郎，在一个私人酒吧里建议道：

PAUL
If you throw yourself at him, you will spoil any opportunity for the natural spark to form. You will just have to wait and let the moment come when he decides something. Otherwise, you risk losing him forever.

保罗
如果你主动追求他，你会破坏任何自然火花形成的机会。你只需要等待，让他做出决定的那一刻到来。否则，你可能会永远失去他。

Stephanie was somewhat disturbed for a couple weeks afterwards and deeply wondered if Alex had used Paul to send her the message. She cooled her heels after that.

斯蒂芬妮在之后的几个星期里有些不安，深深地怀疑亚历克斯是否利用保罗给她发了这条信息。在那之后，她冷静了下来。

Rich guys had to be careful, too much was at stake, and Stephanie finally figured out why Alex didn't have many friends and only told his deepest thoughts to Paul.

有钱人必须小心，风险太大，斯蒂芬妮终于明白了为什么亚历克斯没有很多朋友，只把他最深的想法告诉了保罗。

<u>END FLASHBACK</u>

闪回结束

Stephanie would have been horrified if she was a fly on the wall watching tonight.

如果斯蒂芬妮是今晚墙上的一只苍蝇，她一定会感到震惊。

Alex appeared fully animated.

亚历克斯看起来非常活跃。

Christina was moist and flowing caldrons of emotion, though well hidden, was there almost ready for the dam to break. It wouldn't take much.

克里斯蒂娜湿润了，虽然隐藏得很好，但情绪的漩涡却几乎要爆发了。这并不需要太多。

The conversation flowed easily intermingled with their food and beverages, and then Alex looking at his watch announced:

谈话在他们吃喝玩乐的同时顺利进行，然后亚历克斯看着手表宣布：

ALEX
We need to get moving if we want to see a Broadway show.

亚历克斯
如果我们想看百老汇演出，我们需要动起来。

CHRISTINA
Let me get Briana's attention.

克里斯蒂娜
让我引起布莱娜的注意。

As Briana shortly passed nearby, Christina nudged her and spoke:

当布里安娜不久后从她身边走过时，克里斯蒂娜推了推她并说道：

CHRISTINA
Briana, we are kind of in a hurry can you get our check.

克里斯蒂娜
布丽安娜，我们有点着急，你能把支票寄给我们吗？

Alex seized the moment and spoke:

亚历克斯抓住时机说道：

ALEX
Wait a second, Briana, will this cover it?

亚历克斯
等等一下，布丽安娜，这些够用吗？

Alex then handed Briana a couple crisp $100 bills.

亚历克斯递给布丽安娜几张100美元的钞票。

BRIANA
Definitely!

布丽安娜
当然！

Alex stood up and announced:
亚历克斯站起来声明：

ALEX
Shall we go?

亚历克斯
我们走吧？

Alex then slid his arm to the right with a slight bow to indicate departure.

亚历克斯将手臂向右滑动，微微鞠躬，表示离开。

Christina was slightly impressed by how fast Alex handled that and smiled and stood up.

克里斯蒂娜对亚历克斯处理得这么快感到有些惊讶，她微笑着站了起来。

Christina and Alex walked outside the Pub, and Christina quickly wrapped her arm around Alex's arm as the cold air hit her, and Alex's warmth felt good.

克里斯蒂娜和亚历克斯走出了酒吧，冷风袭来，克里斯蒂娜赶紧搂住了亚历克斯的胳膊，亚历克斯感觉到了温暖，心里很舒服。

ALEX
What Broadway Show would you like to see?

亚历克斯
你想看什么百老汇演出？

CHRISTINA
This might seem kind of corny but I kind of want to see it.

克里斯蒂娜
这可能看起来有点老套，但我还是想看。

Alex responded in a very friendly manner:

亚历克斯 非常友好地回答道：

ALEX
I'm sure you have good taste, what would you like to see?

亚历克斯
我相信你的品味不错，你想看什么？

CHRISTINA
I'm almost embarrassed to say it, but what the heck, I
would like to see "The Lion King."

克里斯蒂娜
我几乎不好意思地说出来，但管他呢，我想看《
狮子王》。

ALEX
That would be fine, we can walk there from here,
helping us work off some of the meal.

亚历克斯
那没问题，我们可以从这里步行过去，帮助我们
消化一些饭后的食物。

The conversation lingered in a most pleasing manner and soon they were in front of
the box office to buy tickets. The salesperson was very apologetic and stated:

谈话以最愉快的方式进行着，很快他们就到了售票处前买票。售票员非常抱
歉，并说：

LION KING EMPLOYEE
I'm sorry, general seating is sold out and all we have
left is balcony seats.

狮子王员工
抱歉，普通座位已经卖完了，我们的曼哈顿下阳
台座位也卖完了。

ALEX
I'm sure that will be fine.

亚历克斯
我相信那没有问题。

The clerk was utterly relieved, a few people already had been upset they were not
going to pay $500 per seat for the balcony and mildly cussed him and walked off.

店员完全松了口气，几个人已经很不乐意了，他们不愿意为阳台座位支付每张
500 块钱 美元的费用，他们温和地骂了他就走了。

<u>INT. EVENING. NEW YORK CITY. LION KING BROADWAY SHOW.</u>

内幕。晚上。纽约市。狮子王百老汇演出。

Christina and Alex were a few minutes early so there were plenty of lights on in the
theater, and the usher helped them to their seats which were probably some of the best
seats in the theater.

克里斯蒂娜和亚历克斯早到了四分之一，剧院里灯火通明，引座员把他们带到
座位上，这可能是剧院里最好的座位。

All too often the media gets free tickets, especially if the producers want a good newspaper review. Across on the other side of the theater, also on balcony seats was one of those entertainment reporters who was using her position of influence to get a free showing for herself and her new boyfriend.

媒体经常免费入场，特别是如果制片人想要一份好的报纸评论。在剧院的另一边，同样坐在沙发上的一位娱乐记者，她利用自己的影响力为自己和她的新男友奋斗免费看一场演出。

Being a smart reporter, the newspaper reporter had a small set of binoculars, which was not uncommon for people who often took balcony seats to get a better view of some of the actors and singers.

作为一名聪明的记者，这位记者报纸有一个小型双筒望远镜，这对于那些经常坐在阳台上更好地观察一些演员和歌手的人来说并不罕见。

The reporter was casually looking over the crowd and making mental notes then scanning the balcony just in case there was anyone super interesting in the audience, which happens from time to time. And if there was, she would *bird-dog* that person to get their impression of the show, and it might end up in the newspaper the very next day, especially if it were a sensational comment.

记者漫不经心地看着人群，在心里记下笔记，然后扫视阳台，观众中有特别有趣的人，这种情况时有发生。如果有的话，她会跟踪那个人以了解他们对演出的印象，第二天可能会登上报纸，尤其是如果这是一条令人震惊的人听到的评论。

The reporter spotted the very attractive couple. She had seen that face before but didn't immediately recall who it was. She then took out her cell phone and snapped a dozen pictures. The man and the woman were acting as if they were young lovers, their whole persona, smiles, and friendliness, appeared just like spring green.

记者发现了这对非常迷人的情侣。她以前见过那张脸，但一时想不起是谁。然后她拿出手机拍了十几张照片。那男的和那女的扮演得就像是描绘了年轻的恋人，他们的整个形象、微笑和态度都像春天的绿色一样。

The next day, the newspaper reporter would discover who the identities of the couple and she just had a huge story right at her fingertips. The reporter determined she would get the couple's comments on the performance and then, if they were someone important quote them.

第二天，报社记者会发现这对情侣的身份，她手头上出现了一个巨大的故事。记者决定她会得到这对情侣对表演的评论，然后如果他们是重要的人，她就会引用他们的话。

Soon the lights dimmed, and the performance began.

灯光很快变暗，表演开始了。

This whole experience added magnificently to Christina's splendid evening. It had been a long time since she felt like this. It was an enjoyable evening even for Alex, who cherished every moment.

整个经历为克里斯蒂娜的精彩之夜增添了光彩。她已经很久没有感觉到了。这是一个美好的夜晚，即使对亚历克斯来说，他也很珍惜每一刻。

MUSIC for this section (and Lion King video if a license can be obtained):

本部分的音乐（如果获得许可，还有狮子王视频）：

40 minutes - The Lion King Theme Song and Ambience

40 分钟 - 狮子王主题曲和氛围

During time-to-time Christina stole looks at Alex to see his impression of the performance, what made her even more happy was he continuously smiled or laughed and if there was crowd applause, Alex was one of the motivated responders which seemed to give the performers even more enthusiasm to perform at their best possible manner.

克里斯蒂娜不时偷看亚历克斯，了解他对表演的印象，让她更高兴，的是他不断微笑或大笑，如果观众鼓掌，亚历克斯是积极响应者之一，这似乎给了表演者更加热情，让他们以最好的方式表演。

Usually, when things are going so wonderfully, time passes too quickly, and tonight was no exception.

通常当事情进展得如此顺利时，时间过得太快了，今晚也不例外。

As they were filing out of the theater, a woman walked up to Alex.

当他们走出剧院时，一位女士走到亚历克斯面前。

NEWSPAPER REPORTER
Excuse me, sir, how did you like the performance.

报纸记者
对不起先生，您喜欢保健吗？

ALEX
I liked it very much.

亚历克斯
我非常喜欢它。

NEWSPAPER REPORTER
Would you mind giving me your name?

报纸记者
你愿意透露你的名字吗？


ALEX
I'd prefer not to if you don't mind.


亚历克斯
如果你不介意的话，我宁愿不明确。


NEWSPAPER REPORTER
No problem, enjoy your evening.


报纸记者
没问题，祝你晚上愉快。


Alex walked on and never looked back, nor did he think otherwise.

亚历克斯继续往前走，从不真相，也没有否认其他。

Knowing that Christina had to work in the morning, and he should get some sleep and prepare for a long day tomorrow, Alex asked:

知道克里斯蒂娜早上要上班，他应该睡一会，为明天早上的一天做准备，亚历克斯提问：


ALEX
What part of the city do you live in?


亚历克斯
你住在城市的哪个地方？


CHRISTINA
You might think this is crazy, but I live next door to my parents in Queens.


克里斯蒂娜
你可能认为这很疯狂，但我住在皇后区我父母隔壁。


ALEX
That's not crazy at all. How are you getting home?


亚历克斯
这根本不疯狂。你怎么回家？


CHRISTINA
I'll take the subway.

克里斯蒂娜
我要坐地铁。

ALEX
Allow me to give you a lift.

亚历克斯
请允许我顺便送你一个程。

CHRISTINA
Sure, if you don't mind.

克里斯蒂娜
当然，如果你不介意的话。

ALEX
Give me a minute to arrange a lift.

亚历克斯
给我一点时间顺便安排一下车。

Alex dialed Rodriguez on his iPhone.

亚历克斯用他的 苹果手机 (iPhone) 拨通了罗德里格斯的电话。

RODRIGUEZ
Hello Alex, what do you need?

罗德里格斯
你好，亚历克斯，你需要什么？

ALEX
Rodriguez are you busy now?

亚历克斯
罗德里格斯，你现在忙吗？

RODRIGUEZ
Not really, I'm available to drive you now if you need me.

罗德里格斯
不，不是真的，如果您需要我，现在可以开车送您。

ALEX
You live in Queens, right?

亚历克斯
你住在皇后区，对吗？

RODRIGUEZ
Yes.

罗德里格斯
是的。

ALEX
Good. I'm down on Broadway, in front of the Lion King show, know where that is?

亚历克斯
很好。我在百老汇，狮子王表演前面，知道那是哪里吗？

RODRIGUEZ
Of course I do.

罗德里格斯
当然知道。

ALEX
Good, come here and pick us up.

亚历克斯
很好，过来接我们。

RODRIGUEZ
I'll be there in 20 minutes or so.

罗德里格斯
我二十分钟左右就到。

ALEX
Okay thanks.

亚历克斯
好的，谢谢。

Alex then hung up his phone and then turned to Christina.

亚历克斯挂断电话，转向 克里斯蒂娜。

ALEX
He'll be here in twenty minutes, let's go for a little walk around.

亚历克斯
他 二十分钟后就到，我们去散散步吧。

CHRISTINA
That sounds good.

克里斯蒂娜
听起来很好。

The two then walked around talking and acting like no care in the world.

然后两人四处走动，聊天，表现得无忧无虑。

The reporter knew this was an important guy, she just could not remember. But she knew there was a story, so she tailed Christina and Alex at a distance.

记者知道这是个重要人物，只是记不住。但她知道有一个故事，所以她远远地跟踪了 克里斯蒂娜 和 亚历克斯。

The female reporter then witnessed a tender moment where the couple faced each other and there must have been some sweet words flowing. Unexpectedly the woman hugged the man. It quickly developed into a mutual embrace. Then suddenly a Limo pulled up, the driver got out rushed over to the door and the couple hopped into the Limo and they drove off.

女记者随后目睹了这对情侣面对面的温柔瞬间，两人一定在甜言蜜语。没想到女方竟然拥抱了男方。很快两人就互相拥抱。突然，一辆豪华轿车停了下来，司机下车冲到门口，这对情侣跳上豪华轿车，开车走了。

NEWSPAPER REPORTER
(Thought)
*The story just got more interesting.*

报社记者
(思考)
故事越来越有趣了。

ALEX
Rodriguez is a driver I use often; I'm going to have him drop me off at my hotel, then he'll take you home, will save him having to drive me back here tonight, it's getting late.

亚历克斯
罗德里格斯是我经常使用的司机，我会让他送我
到我的酒店，然后他会带你回家，这样就省去了
今晚他开车送我回这里的麻烦，时间已经很晚
了。

CHRISTINA
I understand.

克里斯蒂娜
我明白了。

ALEX
Thank you.

亚历克斯
谢谢。

CHRISTINA
When will I see you again?

克里斯蒂娜
我什么时候才能再见到你？

ALEX
I think I'll be coming back in a week or two.

亚历克斯
我想我会在一两周后回来。

CHRISTINA
Can I see you then?

克里斯蒂娜
那我可以见你吗？

ALEX
The better question is, may I see you then?

亚历克斯
更好的问题是，那我可以见你吗？

CHRISTINA
You certainly may.

克里斯蒂娜
当然可以。

ALEX
Excuse me for one moment.

亚历克斯
请稍等。

Alex pressed the intercom button and announced:

亚历克斯按下对讲机按钮并宣布：

ALEX
Rodriguez, drop me off at my hotel, and I want you to take Christina home, she lives in Queens, right on your way home. She'll give you directions.

亚历克斯
罗德里格斯，把我送到我的酒店，我要你送　克里斯蒂娜回家，她住在皇后区，就在你回家的路上。她会告诉你方向。

RODRIGUEZ
Will do Alex.

罗德里格斯
会的，亚历克斯。

ALEX
Thank you, Rodriguez.

亚历克斯
谢谢你，罗德里格斯。

RODRIGUEZ
My pleasure Alex.

罗德里格斯
我很荣幸，亚历克斯。

The Limo wasn't far from the hotel; it came up quickly, way too quick for Christina's satisfaction. But she felt comfortable knowing that Alex showed genuine interest in her, and he was definitely a gentleman.

豪华轿车离酒店不远；它很快就到了，克里斯蒂娜感到很满意。但她知道亚历克斯对她表现出了真正的兴趣，而且他绝对是个绅士，她感到很安心。

The Limo pulled up in front of the entrance to the hotel, the porter opened the door. Alex moved to get out and as he stepped partially out of the car he reached back in and kissed Cristina on the forehead before she realized what Alex was doing.

豪华轿车停在酒店门口，门房打开了车门。亚历克斯走下车，当他半下车时，他伸手回到车里，在克里斯蒂娜意识到亚历克斯在做什么之前亲吻了她的额头。

Alex then said something very lovely to Christina, then she remained in a slight daze that seemed like a short eternity.

亚历克斯随后对克里斯蒂娜说了一些非常可爱的话，而她仍然处于一种短暂的恍惚状态，仿佛过了很久。

The Limo door closed then Christina was suddenly awoken from her trance by the intercom with Rodriguez voice.

RODRIGUEZ<br>Madam, what street do you live on.

罗德里格斯<br>女士，您住在哪条街上。

***

## INT. NIGHT. NYC. TIME SQUARE. MARRIOTE HOTEL ALEX'S ROOM.

内景，夜晚，纽约·时代广场·万豪酒店亚历克斯的房间。

Alex slept like a baby that night. He had not had such ethereal transcendence in such a long time.

Alex had searched the world over for someone to love. But it was always evasive, it seemed like he was never going to find it. All too often people like Stephanie came into his life presuming too much and expecting far more of him than reality permitted. Thus, they killed the fire before it had a chance to fully ignite.

亚历克斯曾走遍全世界寻找他的爱人。但他的尝试似乎总是回避，似乎他永远找不到合适的女人。像斯蒂芬妮这样的人经常闯入他的生活，对他期望过高，超出了现实的允许。因此，他们在火苗还没有完全点燃之前就把它熄灭了。

Christina's demure was quite different. She allowed Alex's magnetism to flow towards her. Christina didn't produce any barriers by implementing expectations. Christina was a natural conduit for Alex's affection.

克里斯蒂娜的端庄则截然不同。她让亚历克斯的魅力流向她。克里斯蒂娜没有通过实现期望来制造任何障碍。克里斯蒂娜是亚历克斯感情的天然渠道。

It was as if Christina was Alex's safety valve. Christina's intellect and her demure gave Alex the freedom to pursue her on his own time schedule and his own mannerisms, though highly unconventional, was no doubt genuine and earnest and filled with an enthusiasm he had seldom displayed.

克里斯蒂娜就像是亚历克斯的安全阀。克里斯蒂娜的智慧和端庄让亚历克斯可以自由地按照自己的时间表追求她，而他自己的举止虽然非常不合常规，但无疑是真诚而认真的，充满了他很少表现出的热情。

 Just before, Alex laid his head down to sleep, his iPhone notified him he received a text message. It was from Christina.

就在亚历克斯躺下睡觉之前，他的 苹果手机 （iPhone） 通知他收到了一条短信。是 克里斯蒂娜发来的。

CHRISTINA
(Text Message)
I made it home okay and thank you for the lovely evening.

克里斯蒂娜
（短信）
我安全到家了，谢谢你给我带来美好的夜晚。

ALEX
(Text Message)
The pleasure is all mine, as my head has just hit the
pillow. Good night and thank you for letting me know
you got home safely.

亚历克斯
（短信）
我很荣幸，因为我的头刚刚碰到枕头。晚安，谢
谢你让我知道你安全到家了。

***

INT. DAY. NYC JFK AIRPORT

纽约肯尼迪机场

In the morning, Rodriguez had Alex at the airport by 7:00 a.m. Brad was there ready to crank up the engines as it was time to head home.

早上 7 点，罗德里格斯就把亚历克斯送到了机场。布拉德在那里准备启动发动机，因为是时候回家了。

While Alex was in the air, the New York reporter hit pay dirt. She sent the photographs to her researcher on the staff.

当亚历克斯在空中时，纽约记者发现了宝藏。她把照片发给了她的研究员。

NEWSPAPER REPORTER
(Email)
Do you know who this person is.

报纸记者
（电子邮件）
**你知道**这个人是谁吗？

The researcher using an AI APP that scanned Google, then social media doing facial recognition quickly found a match because Alex is somewhat well known on Wall Street. The researcher responded to the reporter a few minutes later.

研究人员使用人工智能应用程序扫描谷歌，然后在社交媒体上进行面部识别，很快找到了匹配项，因为亚历克斯在华尔街颇有名气。几分钟后，研究人员回复了记者。

NEWS COMPANY RESEARCHER
(Email)
That's a picture of Alex Baxter, the controversial
figure building the world's first domed city in NUUK
GREENLAND.

新闻公司研究员
（电子邮件）
这是亚历克斯·巴克斯特的照片，他是在格陵兰努
克建造世界上第一个圆顶城市的争议人物。

Alex was thus disturbed the following day, when the New York paper social and entertainment section had an article.

第二天，纽约报纸的社交和娱乐版刊登了一篇文章，亚历克斯因此感到不安。

NEWSPAPER ARTICLE
(HEADLINE)
Dome Guy at the Lion King performance with special
person.

报纸文章
（标题）
圆顶小伙子和特别的人一起观看狮子王表演。

The cell phone picture was high resolution 1.2-megabyte picture caught the couple in a very tender moment smiling at each other, and anyone with the slightest bit of knowledge of body language could only conclude, "where there is smoke there is fire."

这张手机拍摄的照片是一张 1.2 兆字节的高清照片，捕捉到了这对情侣非常温

柔地相视而笑的瞬间，任何对肢体语言稍有了解的人都只能得出这样的结论：无风不起浪。

Stephanie's best friend Barbara, who lived in New York and read the paper every day and knew of Stephanie's machinations to hook Alex, was utterly stunned when she got to the gossip column DOME GUY HEADLINE.

斯蒂芬妮最好的朋友芭芭拉住在纽约，每天都看报纸，她知道斯蒂芬妮勾引亚历克斯的阴谋，当她看到八卦专栏 穹顶人头条 (DOME GUY HEADLINE) 时，她完全惊呆了。

Stephanie's phone rang.

斯蒂芬妮的电话响了。

BARBARA
Hello Stephanie, its Barbara.

芭芭拉
你好，斯蒂芬妮，我是芭芭拉。

STEPHANIE
Hello Barbara, how are you doing?

斯蒂芬妮
你好，芭芭拉，你好吗？

BARBARA
Stephanie, I'm very sorry but there is something I
must tell you.

芭芭拉
斯蒂芬妮，很抱歉，但有件事我必须告诉你。

STEPHANIE
What?

斯蒂芬妮
什么？

Knowing Alex had just returned from a trip East and getting a phone call from Barbara at the same time, quickly put Stephanie in a panic.

得知亚历克斯刚从东部旅行回来，并同时接到芭芭拉的电话，斯蒂芬妮很快就陷入了恐慌。

BARBARA

I'm going to send you a picture of an article in the paper's gossip section that came out today, it concerns Alex.

芭芭拉
我要给你发一张今天报纸八卦栏目上的文章的照片，它与亚历克斯有关。

STEPHANIE
Oh my god.

斯蒂芬妮
哦，我的天。

Barbara didn't say anything, she didn't need too. The picture would tell it all.

芭芭拉什么也没说，她也不需要说。照片会说明一切。

One second later her cell phone buzzed indicating incoming. Stephanie reluctantly opened it and sat there stunned for a couple minutes. The resolution of the picture was good quality, and two things were apparent, the other woman was stunningly beautiful, and the way they were smiling at each other gave it all away. Alex was probably in love with the other woman. Stephanie felt devastated.

一秒钟后，她的手机响了，表示有来电。斯蒂芬妮不情愿地打开手机，坐在那里呆了几分钟。照片的分辨率很好，有两件事很明显，另一个女人美得惊人，他们互相微笑的方式暴露了一切。亚历克斯可能爱上了另一个女人。斯蒂芬妮感到很沮丧。

When Alex arrived home, he was surprised Stephanie wasn't there to meet him.

亚历克斯到家时，他很惊讶斯蒂芬妮没有来接他。

This wasn't like Stephanie; she would be bird dogging him about now under normal circumstances. As the day wore on, Alex was surprised Stephanie didn't call.

这不像斯蒂芬妮；在正常情况下，她会一直跟着他。随着时间的推移，亚历克斯很惊讶斯蒂芬妮没有打电话。

Late in the afternoon, Alex got a phone call from Claude in New York which he wasn't expecting.

下午晚些时候，亚历克斯接到了纽约克劳德打来的电话，这是他意想不到的。

CLAUDE REARDON
Good evening, Alex.

克劳德·里尔登
晚上好，亚历克斯。

ALEX
Hello Claude, what's up?

亚历克斯
你好，克劳德，有什么事吗？

CLAUDE REARDON
Hate to be the bearer of bad news Alex, but you are in the papers.

亚历克斯，我讨厌带来坏消息，但你上了报纸。

ALEX
No kidding.

亚历克斯
别开玩笑了。

CLAUDE REARDON
In the gossip portion of the entertainment section.

克劳德·里尔登
在娱乐版的八卦部分。

ALEX
What the hell!

亚历克斯
什么鬼！

CLAUDE REARDON
You were at the Lion King performance. You had your picture taken it's in the newspaper. The picture doesn't look bad, but the reporter obviously is embellishing shit.

克劳德·里尔登
你去看了狮子王的演出。你拍了照片，上了报纸。照片看起来不错，但记者显然在夸大其词。

ALEX
Sounds like I better send my lawyer after the reporter.

历克斯
听起来我最好派我的律师去追捕记者。

CLAUDE REARDON
And you better warn the woman, as soon as they find out who she is all hell will break loose.

克劳德·里尔登
你最好警告那个女人，一旦他们发现她是谁，一切都会崩溃。

ALEX
Shit.

亚历克斯
该死。

CLAUDE REARDON
I'm sorry Alex.

克劳德·里尔登
我很抱歉亚历克斯。

ALEX
Can you send me a copy of the newspaper page?

亚历克斯
你能用你的手机拍张照片并发短信给我吗？

CLAUDE REARDON
I'll email it you momentarily, right after I scan it.

克劳德·里尔登
扫描后我会立即通过电子邮件发送给您。

ALEX
Could you just take a picture of it with your I-phone and text message it to me?

亚历克斯
你能寄给我一份报纸版面吗？

CLAUDE REARDON
Sure, I'll do that right after I hang up.

克劳德·里尔登
当然，挂断电话后我会立即这样做。

ALEX
Thanks Claude.

亚历克斯
谢谢克劳德。

The minutes ground on which seemed like eternity, and then there it was on his cell phone, he was staring at it and recognized the reporter's picture next to her byline.

时间过得好像永恒，然后它就出现在他的手机上，他盯着它，认出了记者署名旁边的照片。

Alex knew he needed to make a few phone calls; he forwarded the document to his attorney and then called him to see if something could be done.

亚历克斯知道他需要打几个电话；他把文件转发给了他的律师，然后打电话给他，看看能不能做些什么。

Then he had to call Christina and warn her if she didn't already know.

然后他不得不打电话给克里斯蒂娜，警告她，如果她还不知道的话。

CHRISTINA<br>
Hello.

克里斯蒂娜<br>
你好。

Christina's voice was somewhat subdued, and she didn't sound perky.

克里斯蒂娜的声音有些低沉，听起来也不活泼。

ALEX<br>
Christina, how are you doing?

亚历克斯<br>
克里斯蒂娜，你好吗？

CHRISTINA<br>
Fine, thanks for asking.

克里斯蒂娜<br>
很好，谢谢你的关心。

ALEX<br>
Have you read the paper or did any friends tell you about it?

亚历克斯<br>
你读过报纸吗？或者有朋友告诉你这件事吗？

CHRISTINA<br>
Yes, I'm aware I'm now a public figure.

克里斯蒂娜
是的，我知道我现在是公众人物了。

ALEX
I'm terribly sorry.

亚历克斯
我非常抱歉。

CHRISTINA
It's not your fault.

克里斯蒂娜
这不是你的错。

ALEX
Are you going to be, ok?

亚历克斯
你会是的，好吗？

CHRISTINA
It's going to be difficult in the office tomorrow, but I'll survive.

克里斯蒂娜
明天在办公室会很困难，但我会挺过去的。

ALEX
I hope you know this doesn't change anything between us.

亚历克斯
我希望你知道这不会改变我们之间的任何事情。

CHRISTINA
That makes me feel good to hear you say that.

克里斯蒂娜
听到你这么说，我感觉很好。

ALEX
You can back out now if you want, but if you agree to continue seeing me, it's quite probable you will become the focus and possibly the target of slanderous yellow journalism.

亚历克斯
如果你愿意，你现在可以退出，但如果你同意继
续见我，你很可能会成为诽谤性黄色新闻的焦点
和目标。

CHRISTINA
My dad taught me how to be tough, I will survive.

克里斯蒂娜
我爸爸教我如何坚强，我会活下来的。

ALEX
I'll try to see you in a week or so.

亚历克斯
我会尽量在一周左右见你。

CHRISTINA
I appreciate that.

克里斯蒂娜
我很感激。

ALEX
I have some other things I need to do now; I'll talk
again with you real soon.

亚历克斯
我现在还有一些其他事情要做；我很快会再和你
谈谈。

CHRISTINA
Okay.

克里斯蒂娜
好的。

ALEX
Take care Christina.

亚历克斯
保重，克里斯蒂娜。

CHRISTINA
You too Alex.

克里斯蒂娜
你也是，亚历克斯。

Alex figured Stephanie was crying in her beers about now and it would not be a good time to call her; he would wait until the morning.

亚历克斯认为 克里斯蒂娜现在喝着啤酒哭了，现在不是给她打电话的好时机；他会等到早上。

Alex was right; it was a tough night for Stephanie. It was a great wakeup call as she now knew where she stood, just about the same place she did the year before and the years before that. In 8 years, she had never got anywhere with Alex. He had successfully avoided her web, and any trick she tried to pull. Nothing worked. Alex was untouchable.

亚历克斯是对的；对 克里斯蒂娜来说，这是一个艰难的夜晚。这是一个很好的警钟，因为她现在知道了自己所处的位置，几乎和去年以及更早几年的位置一样。8 年来，她和 亚历克斯从未取得任何进展。他成功地避开了她的网，也避开了她试图使出的任何花招。什么都不管用。亚历克斯是不可触碰的。

After a couple of stiff drinks and a couple sleeping pills, Stephanie was out and slept for fourteen hours before she finally woke up. She was a big girl; she picked herself up and continued like a good soldier, taking it one day at a time. But one thing she learned in all this, she would not take anything for granted.

喝了几杯烈酒，吃了几片安眠药后，斯蒂芬妮睡了 14 个小时才终于醒过来。她是个大女孩；她振作起来，像一个好士兵一样继续前进，一天一天地坚持下去。但她在这一切中学到的一件事是，她不会把任何事情视为理所当然。

Just before Alex was going to call Stephanie in the morning, she called him.

就在亚历克斯早上要给斯蒂芬妮打电话之前，她给他打了电话。

STEPHANIE
Hello Alex.

斯蒂芬妮
你好，亚历克斯。

ALEX
Good morning, Stephanie.

亚历克斯
早上好，斯蒂芬妮。

STEPHANIE
I got that analysis done on those reports, I'm ready to
meet with you and go over them.

斯蒂芬妮
我已经分析完了这些报告，准备和你见面，一起
研究一下。

ALEX
How about this afternoon?

亚历克斯
下午怎么样？

STEPHANIE
Certainly.

斯蒂芬妮
当然。

Alex was not a coward, but he did not want his next meeting with Stephanie alone. Some of the issues to be discussed in the meeting were going to be about materials and schedules. With the pillars going up starting as early as next week, Alex figured it would be good to have either James Walker, CEO Hercules Steel and/or Howard Grady, the Cement King there at the meeting.

亚历克斯不是胆小鬼，但他不想单独和斯蒂芬妮开会。会议上要讨论的一些问题将与材料和时间表有关。由于支柱将于下周开始竖立，亚历克斯认为，赫拉克勒斯钢铁公司首席执行官詹姆斯·沃克和/或水泥大王霍华德·格雷迪出席会议会很好。

Alex called James Walker and Howard Grady on a conference call, to request their participation in the meeting.

亚历克斯通过电话会议联系了詹姆斯·沃克和霍华德·格雷迪，要求他们参加会议。

JAMES WALKER
I can make it if the meeting. If it's delayed until 2:30 or 3:00 p.m.

詹姆斯·沃克
我可以参加会议。如果会议推迟到下午　2:30　或
3:00。

HOWARD GRADY
If we meet in Chicago, then I could make it there earlier.

霍华德·格雷迪
如果我们在芝加哥见面，那么我可以早点到那里。

ALEX
2:30 or 3:00 P.M. would be just fine.

亚历克斯
下午 2:30 或 3:00 就好了。

Stephanie was asked to be there at that time.

斯蒂芬妮被要求在那个时候到场。

Just like a Swiss watch precision, the group got connected and met and spent the next five hours going over facts and figures that Stephanie and pulled out and raised questions concerning possible issues.

就像瑞士手表的精准度一样，该小组进行了联系、开会，并在接下来的五个小时里讨论了斯蒂芬妮提出的事实和数据，并提出了有关可能出现的问题的问题。

STEPHANIE
Like I said, there is no need for the cement plant construction until you can show we can get that coal and limestone in quantity on time.

斯蒂芬妮
就像我说的，除非你能证明我们能按时获得大量的煤炭和石灰石，否则没有必要建造水泥厂。

ALEX
But that was the selling point to the Danish and the Greenlanders, if we don't start construction on it soon, they're going to get pissed off and possibly revoke our charter.

亚历克斯
但是，这是丹麦人和格陵兰人的卖点，如果我们不尽快开始建设，他们会生气，可能会撤销我们的特许状。

STEPHANIE
But it's cheaper just to buy the cement from China, Mexico, or the USA.

斯蒂芬妮
但从中国、墨西哥或美国购买水泥更便宜。

ALEX
We are going to have to pay a premium to keep the Denmark and Greenland governments in our pocket.

亚历克斯
我们必须付出额外费用才能让丹麦和格陵兰政府
继续留在我们的口袋里。

STEPHANIE
But until you get the limestone and coal moving what's
the point?

斯蒂芬妮
但是，除非你让石灰石和煤炭流动起来，否则有
什么意义呢？

HOWARD GRADY
Nothing says we must build it real fast; we just need
to get started and look like we are making progress.

霍华德·格雷迪
没有人说我们必须快速建造它；我们只需要开
始，看起来我们正在取得进展。

JAMES WALKER
Remember, nothing gets done quickly in Greenland
unless someone comes in with some big bucks and
often with foreign workers.

詹姆斯·沃克
记住，除非有人带着大笔资金来到这里，而且经
常带着外国工人，否则格陵兰岛什么事都做不
成。

STEPHANIE
Ok, we can start on the construction of it right away,
but I feel it's just a distraction from more important
things.

斯蒂芬妮
好的，我们可以马上开始建设，但我觉得这只会
分散我们对更重要事情的注意力。

ALEX
We already received a lot of negative press there, we
can't ignore local politics.

亚历克斯
我们已经在那里看到了很多负面新闻，我们不能
忽视当地的政治。

Suddenly Alex wished he hadn't used the word "press" as he instantly saw a look on
Stephanie's face like she was going to unload on him real soon. *Time for plan "B"*.

突然间，亚历克斯希望他没有使用 "媒体" 这个词，因为他立刻看到斯蒂芬妮脸上的表情，好像她很快就要对他发泄了。是时候实施 "比" 计划了。

### ALEX

I'm getting kind of hungry, I got an idea, let's all get us something to eat and if there is any more, we need to wrangle out of this we can do it while we are eating.

### 亚历克斯

我有点饿了，我有个主意，我们大家去弄点吃的，如果还有什么需要解决的，我们可以边吃边做。

### JAMES WALKER

Ok, but I'm not going to get home until real late as it is.

### 詹姆斯·沃克

好的，但我要到很晚才能回家。

### ALEX

We'll try to wrap it all up by the time dinner is over.

### 亚历克斯

我们会在晚餐结束前把所有事情都收拾好。

Alex knew it was a white lie, knowing there would be more arguments to follow, and he'd keep the meeting going till at least 10:00 so that by then Stephanie would not be in a mood to confront him and argue about something she wrongfully assumed. Plus, since she wasn't mentioned in the newspaper article, it really didn't affect her.

亚历克斯知道这只是善意的谎言，知道接下来还会有更多争吵，他会把会议持续到至少 10:00，这样到那时斯蒂芬妮就不会有心情与他对峙，争论她错误假设的事情。另外，由于报纸文章中没有提到她，所以这并没有真正影响到她。

As Alex planned, it all unfolded as he expected and by the time they finished, nobody was in the mood for more conversation, including Stephanie who had locked horns with Howard Grady over the cement plant a few more times.

正如亚历克斯所计划的那样，一切都如他所料地展开，当他们结束时，没有人有心情再交谈，包括斯蒂芬妮，她曾多次与霍华德·格雷迪就水泥厂问题发生争执。

Both James Walker and Howard Grady felt Stephanie was being somewhat of a bulldog and after the meeting James Walker commented to Howard Grady:

詹姆斯·沃克和霍华德·格雷迪都觉得斯蒂芬妮有点像斗牛犬，会议结束后，詹姆斯·沃克对霍华德·格雷迪说：

JAMES WALKER
Who pissed in Stephanie's Wheaties?

詹姆斯·沃克
谁在斯蒂芬妮的麦片里撒尿了？

By Friday, Stephanie had calmed down quite a bit as she realized:

STEPHANIE
(Thought)
*Nothing has changed. Absolutely nothing, nor had it in 8 years. Perhaps I'm expecting too much?*

斯蒂芬妮
（思考）
什么都没变。完全没有，8　年来也没有。也许我期望太多了？

On Friday, Jeff Sinclair called.

周五，杰夫·辛克莱打来电话。

JEFF SINCLAIR
Alex?

杰夫·辛克莱
亚历克斯？

Alex responded after he saw the caller I.D.

亚历克斯看到来电显示后回复了。

ALEX
Yes, hello Jeff.

亚历克斯
是的，你好，杰夫。

JEFF SINCLAIR
Just wanted to call to let you know that we'll start pouring the first pillar cement on Tuesday next week if you want to be up here for that.

杰夫·辛克莱
我只是想打电话告诉你，如果你想来这里的话，我们将在下周二开始浇筑第一根柱子水泥。

**ALEX**
Certainly. I'll be there, thanks for the heads up.

亚历克斯
当然。我会去的，谢谢你的提醒。

**JEFF SINCLAIR**
You're welcome.

杰夫·辛克莱
不用客气。

Alex felt kind of relieved that Stephanie didn't pester him during the weekend and allowed him his space under the circumstances. Of course, she cried in her beers a few more times, but was slowly getting over it, especially since there was no overt indication Alex was especially involved with the other woman, and no other paper articles manifested since.

亚历克斯感到有点松了一口气，因为斯蒂芬妮周末没有打扰他，在这种情况下给了他空间。当然，她又哭了几次，但她慢慢地从这件事中恢复过来了，尤其是因为没有明显的迹象表明亚历克斯和另一个女人有特别的关系，而且从那以后也没有出现其他纸质文章。

Sunday night Alex was making plans. Brad would be ready to fly first thing in the morning. He would fly to New York, spend the night, then fly up early in the morning Tuesday to be on hand. Stephanie was not invited, and Alex wisely did not inform anyone on the executive management team, the concrete work was starting on Tuesday.

周日晚上，亚历克斯正在制定计划。布拉德将在第二天一早准备好飞行。他将飞往纽约，过夜，然后在周二一早飞到现场。斯蒂芬妮没有受到邀请，亚历克斯明智地没有通知任何执行管理团队，混凝土工作将于周二开始。

Alex could not afford to have Stephanie accompany him to New York because it was important that he see Christina, especially if she was having issues now due to her association with him.

亚历克斯不能让斯蒂芬妮陪他去纽约，因为他必须见到克里斯蒂娜，尤其是如果她现在因为与他的关系而遇到问题的话。

Alex would do whatever he could to help Christina, and his attorney was already dueling with the Newspaper, who was threatening some heavy handedness if Alex even thought about going after them in a libel lawsuit.

亚历克斯会尽其所能帮助克里斯蒂娜，他的律师已经在与报社争执，报社威胁说，如果亚历克斯甚至想对他们提起诽谤诉讼，报社将采取严厉措施。

Monday morning around 9:30 a.m. Stephanie texted Alex saying she wanted to talk with him. Her cell phone showed "message not delivered" which meant the phone was located some place that could not receive the message or something strange was going on. She tried a few more times, got the same result.

周一上午 9:30 左右，斯蒂芬妮给亚历克斯发短信说她想和他谈谈。她的手机显示"消息未送达"，这意味着手机位于某个无法接收消息的地方，或者发生了一些奇怪的事情。她又试了几次，结果还是一样。

Because Alex left early in the morning and burned the extra fuel to get there quickly, doing 800 mph over the ground, Alex landed at JFK around 1:45 in the afternoon, was pulling up in front of 120 Wall Street at 2:30 in the afternoon. He then made his way up to Claude's office for a brief meeting to go over the discussions he had with James Walker and Howard Grady. On the way Alex texted Christina

因为亚历克斯一大早就出发了，为了快速到达目的地，他消耗了多余的燃料，以每小时 800 英里的速度在地面飞行，亚历克斯下午 1:45 左右降落在肯尼迪机场，下午 2:30 停在华尔街 120 号门前。然后他去了克劳德的办公室，开了个简短的会议，回顾了他与詹姆斯·沃克和霍华德·格雷迪的讨论。在路上，亚历克斯给克里斯蒂娜发短信

ALEX
(Text Message)
I have arrived and will be in the building to meet with
my business partner and want to see you afterwards.

亚历克斯
（短信）
我已经到了，会去大楼里见我的商业伙伴，之后
想见你。

CHRISTINA
(Text Message)
About what time?

克里斯蒂娜
（短信）
大概什么时候？

ALEX
(Text Message)
I should be done around 3:30 p.m.

亚历克斯
（短信）
我应该在下午 3:30 左右完成。

CHRISTINA
Ok, I'll meet you in the lobby, around 3:30 p.m.

克里斯蒂娜
好的，我会在大厅见你，大约下午 3:30。

Alex and Claude went round and round and finally around 3:25 Alex knew he was up against a time deadline for meeting Christina and decided to terminate the discussion.

亚历克斯和克劳德一遍又一遍地讨论，最后在 3:25 左右，亚历克斯知道他必须尽快与克里斯蒂娜见面，于是决定终止讨论。

ALEX
We are not going to finish this discussion today, so let's continue and finish it on Wednesday, I'll stop in after I make a trip up to Greenland.

亚历克斯
我们今天不会结束这个讨论，所以我们继续讨论，星期三再结束，我去格陵兰岛一趟后会过来。

CLAUDE REARDEN
Alright.

克劳德·里尔登
好的。

ALEX
See you in two days.

亚历克斯
两天后见。

CLAUDE REARDEN
Have a safe flight. Take care.

克劳德·里尔登
**祝你旅途平安。保重。**

ALEX
You as well.

亚历克斯
你也一样。

Alex then left the office. He walked into the elevator and headed to the first floor around 3:28 p.m.

随后，亚历克斯离开了办公室。下午 3 点 28 分左右，他走进电梯，前往一楼。

Around that time Christina walked into her manager's office and announced:

大约在那个时候，克里斯蒂娜走进经理的办公室，宣布：

## CHRISTINA
I'm very tired, I'm going to take the rest of the day off.

### 克里斯蒂娜
我太累了，今天剩下的时间我要休息了。

Christina's manager knew her life had changed radically. The situation with some of the other employees was much more intense, mainly because they were shocked by what they read in the paper.

克里斯蒂娜的经理知道，克里斯蒂娜的生活发生了根本性的变化。其他一些员工的情况更加紧张，主要是因为他们对报纸上的内容感到震惊。

## CHRISTINA'S MANAGER
Christina, you deserve a break, you have been doing a
lot and been through a lot.

### 克里斯蒂娜的经理
克里斯蒂娜，你应该休息一下，你做了很多事
情，经历了很多。

The co-workers "picture perfect" Christina who was spending time with an ultra-rich guy, created curiosity was overwhelming to the point it clouded the work environment.

同事们 "完美无缺" 的克里斯蒂娜与一位超级富豪在一起，这让他们的好奇心难以抗拒，甚至让工作环境变得模糊不清。

Since it was the time of day some of them would be going home, they followed Christina out of the office as they normally would this time of day if she was leaving, and rode the elevator down silently with her and got out.

由于现在是他们中的一些人回家的时间，他们跟着克里斯蒂娜走出办公室，就像她离开时他们通常会在这个时候这样做一样，然后默默地和她一起乘电梯下楼。

Mainly because of the fascination of the revelation in the newspaper, the plain and modest Christina, now the focus, magnified curiosity.

主要是因为报纸上的揭露令人着迷，朴素谦逊的克里斯蒂娜现在成为焦点，这放大了人们的好奇心。

Coworkers going home could not help but notice Christina as she was leaving and watching her movements, and they were rewarded for their focus and curiosity because guess who was in the lobby waiting for her?

回家的同事们不禁注意到克里斯蒂娜离开并观察她的一举一动，他们的专注和好奇心得到了回报，因为猜猜谁在大厅等她？

It was now shockingly apparent to Christina's nosy coworkers; this was a *unique* romance manifesting in front of their own eyes. Some of the coworkers observed from a distance while walking into the restaurant/coffee shop near the entrance to not appear like they were eavesdropping.

现在，克里斯蒂娜那些爱管闲事的同事们都震惊地发现，这是一段独特的恋情，就在他们眼前。一些同事在走进餐厅/咖啡店入口附近时，远远地观察着，以免显得像是在偷听。

As Christina and Alex left the building, the coworkers got into position to watch Christina leave the building, and indeed in style she did as Alex escorted her to the Limo, and they got in and it quickly drove off.

克里斯蒂娜和亚历克斯离开大楼时，同事们就位看着克里斯蒂娜离开大楼，而她确实很有风度地离开了大楼，亚历克斯陪她上了豪华轿车，他们上了车，车很快就开走了。

ALEX
Is there some place we could go for a little walk and
have a conversation?

CHRISTINA
How about Central Park?

克里斯蒂娜
中央公园怎么样？

Alex pressed the intercom button and requested:

亚历克斯按下对讲机按钮并请求：

ALEX
Rodriguez, I want you to take us to Central Park.

亚历克斯
罗德里格斯，我想让你带我们去中央公园。

RODRIGUEZ
Sure thing Mr. Baxter.

Alex looked at Christina with a slight smile.

罗德里格斯

当然可以，巴克斯特先生。

Alex looked at Christina with a slight smile.

亚历克斯微笑着看着克里斯蒂娜。

CHRISTINA
(Thought)
*Alex seems polite and sweet.*

克里斯蒂娜
（想）
亚历克斯看起来很有礼貌，很温柔。

Rodriguez steered the Limo into a parking spot, as it was a good time of day to go there, as the day people were leaving, and the night people hadn't arrived in numbers.

罗德里格斯把豪华轿车开进一个停车位，因为这是去那里的好时机，因为白天的人都在离开，而晚上的人还没有那么多。

Rodriguez opened the Limo door, then Christina and Alex exited the vehicle.

罗德里格斯打开豪华轿车的车门，然后克里斯蒂娜和亚历克斯下了车。

Rodriguez knew without asking he should just wait there, and he did.

罗德里格斯不用问就知道他应该在那里等，于是他就这么做了。

After Alex and Christina walked a short distance Alex asked:

亚历克斯和克里斯蒂娜走了一小段路后，亚历克斯问道：

ALEX
Christina, would it be ok if I held your hand?

亚历克斯
克里斯蒂娜，我可以牵着你的手吗？

CHRISTINA
Yes, you may.

克里斯蒂娜
是的，可以。

It was still a little nippy with early spring around the corner, but it had been a warm day for a change, so it wasn't all that bad, and they were both dressed in warm clothes. The exercise with their walking helped to create enough warmth to make up the difference.

早春即将来临，天气仍然有点冷，但今天是温暖的一天，所以情况并没有那么糟糕，他们都穿着暖和的衣服。他们走路时的运动有助于产生足够的温暖来弥补差异。

ALEX

Christina, are you holding up, ok?

亚历克斯

克里斯蒂娜，你坚持住吗？

CHRISTINA

It's kind of like I'm at a freak show now and I'm the object everyone is looking at, but I'm dealing with it. My father didn't like cowards so I'm not going to be one either.

克里斯蒂娜

现在有点像我在参加一场畸形秀，我是所有人注视的对象，但我正在处理它。我父亲不喜欢懦夫，所以我也不会成为懦夫。

ALEX

That's good and I hope you feel the newspaper article didn't change anything between us.

亚历克斯

很好，我希望你觉得报纸上的文章没有改变我们之间的关系？

CHRISTINA

I was hoping you would say that.

克里斯蒂娜

我希望你会这么说。

ALEX

Christina, I know we do not have much history together and we are at the beginning of all this. I know that I've already put you through a lot of stress because of this unpredictable Newspaper article, but I promise you I will make every effort to put forth activities so that you will never have any regrets being with me.

CHRISTINA
Alex, without you telling me that I already started
feeling that is how you would handle matters.

克里斯蒂娜
亚历克斯，不用你告诉我，我就已经感觉到你处
理事情的方式了。

The two walked around central park for a while, until Alex, who had not eaten all day
long announced:

两人在中央公园里走了一会儿，直到一整天没吃东西的亚历克斯宣布：

ALEX
Christina, I'm kind of hungry, could we go someplace
and get something to eat?

亚历克斯
克里斯蒂娜，我有点饿了，我们可以去某个地方
吃点东西吗？

CHRISTINA
Sounds okay to me.

克里斯蒂娜
我觉得可以。

ALEX
Any good suggestions about where we can go?

亚历克斯
有什么好的建议吗？

CHRISTINA
I know a nice family Italian restaurant in Queens not
too far from my home, where we can have a little
privacy, plus the food is great.

克里斯蒂娜
我知道皇后区一家不错的家庭意大利餐厅，离我
家不远，我们可以在那里有一点隐私，而且食物
也很棒。

ALEX
Fantastic. I love Italian food, let's go.

亚历克斯
极好的。我喜欢意大利菜，我们走吧。

Christina and Alex walked back to Limo, and as Rodriguez saw them coming, got out of the Limo and opened their passenger their door.

克里斯蒂娜和亚历克斯走回豪华轿车，罗德里格斯看到他们过来，下了车并打开了乘客侧的车门。

### ALEX
Rodriguez, we are going to an Italian Restaurant in Queens. Christina will give you the address.

### 亚历克斯
罗德里格斯，我们要去皇后区的一家意大利餐厅。克里斯蒂娜会给你地址。

### RODRIGUEZ
Christina, let me know the name, I might know the address.

### 罗德里格斯
克里斯蒂娜，让我知道名字，我可能知道地址。

### CHRISTINA
The restaurant's name is Matteo's.

### 克里斯蒂娜
这家餐厅的名字是 马泰奥的（Matteo's）。

### RODRIGUEZ
I know Matteo's quite well. Good choice.

### 罗德里格斯
我很了解马特奥的。不错的选择。

It was a little early for the dinner crowd, so the parking lot had plenty of room. Rodriguez informed Alex:

对于晚餐人群来说有点早，所以停车场有足够的空间。罗德里格斯告诉亚历克斯：

### RODRIGUEZ
This is not far from my home, so would it be ok after I drop you off for me to swing by my home, and I can be back at the restaurant in five minutes after you call me.

### 罗德里格斯
这离我家不远，所以我送你回家后可以顺便去我家吗？你给我打电话后，我五分钟后就可以回到餐厅。

ALEX
Sure, not a problem.

亚历克斯
当然，没问题。

Alex and Christina went inside the seemingly empty restaurant that had old style booths.

亚历克斯和克里斯蒂娜走进了看似空荡荡的餐厅，里面有老式的包厢。

The waiter announced:

服务员宣布：

WAITER
The restaurant is empty now so pick whichever booth you want to sit.

服务员
餐厅现在空无一人，所以请随意选择你想坐的包厢。

CHRISTINA
I'd like the booth over there, in the corner.

克里斯蒂娜
我想要那边角落的包厢。

WAITER
Absolutely. Please have a seat and I'll grab you some glasses of water and be right there with some menus.

服务员
当然可以。请坐，我给你拿几杯水，然后拿菜单过来。

CHRISTINA
Thank you.

克里斯蒂娜
谢谢。

Alex and Christina soon ordered their drinks and meals, then had a soft discussion while they were waiting on their food.

亚历克斯和克里斯蒂娜很快就点了饮料和餐点，然后在等待食物的时候进行了轻松的交谈。

The electricity was flowing, and Christiana was not regretting one moment of it. Alex's sweet gentleness was rubbing off onto her, and the more time she spent with him, the more grief she was willing to take to enjoy his company. She could tell by his mannerism he was genuine and sincere. It was making it even more pleasant than she had thought.

两人的感情非常融洽，克里斯蒂娜一点也不后悔。亚历克斯的温柔感染了她，她和他在一起的时间越长，她就越愿意忍受痛苦来享受他的陪伴。从他的举止中她可以看出他很真诚。结果比她想象的还要愉快。

They had a long dinner took their time and the customers started arriving for dinner. The waiter knew the man probably had some money, but when he saw the size of the tip, his eyes just about bugged out. Just as Rodriguez had promised, he was there five minutes after Alex called him.

他们吃了一顿漫长的晚餐，慢慢地，顾客们开始陆续到场吃饭。服务员知道这个男人可能有一些钱，但当他看到小费的数额时，他的眼睛都快瞪出来了。正如罗德里格斯所承诺的那样，亚历克斯给他打电话五分钟后，他就到了。

Alex informed Christina:

亚历克斯告诉克里斯蒂娜：

ALEX
I'm going to take you home then I need to go check into a hotel and must get up early in the morning to get up to Greenland in time for a special event.

亚历克斯
我要送你回家，然后我需要去酒店办理入住手续，第二天早上必须早起，以便及时赶到格陵兰参加一个特别的活动。

CHRISTINA.
Alright.

克里斯蒂娜。
好吧。

ALEX
I'm going to say good night early tonight, but I'll be back on Wednesday if you would like to spend a little more time in the evening we can go to a show or do something fun together that you like.

亚历克斯
我今晚要早点说晚安了，但我周三会回来，如果

你想在晚上多呆一会儿，我们可以一起去看场演
出或做一些你喜欢的有趣的事情。

CHRISTINA
Sure, that sounds good.

克里斯蒂娜
当然，听起来不错。

The Limo pulled up in front of Christina's home, which was a two-story house, and it looked identical to the houses on both sides, just painted differently, and Alex realized one of those homes was her parent's and more than likely he would be visiting there soon.

豪华轿车停在克里斯蒂娜家门前，那是一栋两层楼的房子，看起来和两边的房子一模一样，只是油漆不同，亚历克斯意识到其中一栋房子是她父母的，很可能他很快就会去那里看望。

Rodriguez opened the car door, Christina got out and Alex hopped out for a moment too.

罗德里格斯打开车门，克里斯蒂娜下了车，亚历克斯也跳了出来。

ALEX
Hey one last thing.

亚历克斯
嘿，最后一件事。

CHRISTINA
What's that?

克里斯蒂娜
那是什么？

Alex pulled Christina close and gave her a very modest kiss. But the hug that followed was almost a bear hug which she recognized as a genuine signal of passion.

亚历克斯把克里斯蒂娜拉近，给了她一个非常谦虚的吻。但接下来的拥抱几乎是一个熊抱，她意识到这是真正的激情信号。

ALEX
Good night, Christiana.

亚历克斯
晚安，克里斯蒂娜。

CHRISTINA
Good night, Alex and thank you.

克里斯蒂娜
晚安，亚历克斯，谢谢你。

ALEX
Thank you too Christiana.

亚历克斯
也谢谢你，克里斯蒂娜。

They both smiled and Alex got back in the Limo that quickly departed.

他们都笑了，亚历克斯回到了豪华轿车上，很快就离开了。

Christiana's mother, a very sophisticated and intelligent woman looked out the window and saw it all. She had a very good relationship with her daughter, and they kept no secrets. Christiana welcomed her mother's advice and viewed her as her best friend in the world, even though Christina was *daddy's little girl*.

克里斯蒂安娜的母亲是一位非常成熟和聪明的女人，她从窗外看到了这一切。她和女儿关系很好，没有秘密可言。克里斯蒂安娜欢迎母亲的建议，并将她视为世界上最好的朋友，尽管克里斯蒂娜是爸爸的小女儿。

In about 30 minutes she would have another talk with her mother, who was concerned obviously, but her articulate daughter had sized the man up good.

大约 30 分钟后，她会再次与母亲交谈，母亲显然很担心，但她能言善辩的女儿已经很好地评估了这个男人。

CHRISTIANA'S MOTHER
It's rare these days to find rich guys who are gentlemen.
They usually get what they want, then cast the carcass
aside.

克里斯蒂安娜的母亲
现在很难找到有钱的绅士。他们通常会得到他们
想要的东西，然后把尸体扔到一边。

CHRISTIANA
I know.

克里斯蒂安娜
我知道。

CHRISTIANA'S MOTHER
It's good that Alex is a gentleman, and you are taking
your time.

克里斯蒂安娜的母亲
亚历克斯是个绅士，你不慌不忙，这很好。

CHRISTIANA
I am sure he wants what is best for both of us.

克里斯蒂安娜
我相信他希望我们俩都得到最好的结果。

CHRISTIANA'S MOTHER
The neighbors are all gossiping now.

克里斯蒂安娜的母亲
邻居们现在都在闲聊。

CHRISTIANA
I can imagine.

克里斯蒂安娜
我可以想象。

CHRISTIANA'S MOTHER
Mrs. Porter across the street had the nerve to come up to me today to ask if you would autograph her newspaper.

克里斯蒂安娜的母亲
街对面的波特太太今天竟然厚颜无耻地来找我，问你是否愿意在她的报纸上签名。

***

EXT. EVENING. JFK AIRPORT HILTON HOTEL FRONT ENTRANCE. 15 SECONDS.

外景。晚上。纽约肯尼迪机场希尔顿酒店正门。15 秒。

Alex checked into the Hilton Hotel next to the airport which he knew Brad was staying in.

亚历克斯住进了机场附近的希尔顿酒店，他知道布拉德也住在那里。

Alex called Brad.

亚历克斯给布拉德打了电话。

ALEX
Brad, I'm staying in your hotel tonight, I want you to
give me a ride over to the airport in the morning when
you leave.


亚历克斯
布拉德，我今晚住在你的酒店，明天早上你离开
的时候，我想让你载我去机场。


BRAD
I planned on being there by 6:00 a.m. to preflight the
plane.


布拉德
我计划早上 6 点到那里做飞行前检查。


ALEX
That works, I can take a nap on the plane while you are
getting it ready.


亚历克斯
这样就行了，你准备的时候我可以睡个午觉。


By 6:30 a.m. the next morning, Alex was airborne and on the way to Greenland.

第二天早上 6:30，亚历克斯起飞前往格陵兰。

Alex reserved the Limo for this trip for 24 hours. He was promptly taken to Hotel Hans
Egede where he checked in and got a room, and then he was over to Nuuk Dome Inc.
offices to meet with Jeff Sinclair. It was 11:30 in the morning, the text message he got
this morning from Jeff indicated he concrete pouring would start around 1:00 p.m.

亚历克斯为这次旅行预订了 24 小时的豪华轿车。他很快就被带到了汉斯埃格
德酒店，在那里他办理了入住手续，然后去了努克圆顶公司办公室与杰夫辛
克莱会面。当时是上午 11:30，杰夫今早发来的短信显示混凝土浇筑将于下午
1:00 左右开始。


ALEX
Time to get a bite to eat before the main event?


亚历克斯
在主要活动开始前该吃点东西了吗？


JEFF SINCLAIR
Sure.


杰夫·辛克莱
当然。

Upon Jeff Sinclair's recommendation they went to the Sarfalik Restaurant. The decorum was nice, and the food was excellent. This also gave time to Alex to hear a firsthand account on latest update and status of the apparatus.

在杰夫·辛克莱的推荐下，他们去了 沙尔法利克 (Sarfalik) 餐厅。那里的礼仪很好，食物也很棒。这也让亚历克斯有时间亲自听取设备的最新更新和状态。

ALEX
Tell me Jeff, how are things going?

亚历克斯
告诉我，杰夫，事情进展如何？

JEFF SINCLAIR
Alex, the project is advancing quite well. When we get to the work site you will see a lot has changed in just a few days.

杰夫·辛克莱
亚历克斯，项目进展顺利。当我们到达工作现场时，你会发现在短短几天内发生了很大变化。

ALEX
Jeff, are we ready for the big event?

亚历克斯
杰夫，我们准备好迎接这场盛事了吗？

JEFF SINCLAIR
We are ready, but I sense the public is still somewhat skeptical. I'm sure when those first six pillars get up to 1000 feet their attitudes will shift.

杰夫·辛克莱
我们准备好了，但我感觉公众仍然有些怀疑。我相信，当最初六根柱子达到 1000 英尺高时，他们的态度就会转变。

ALEX
Especially when we install the first roof section.

亚历克斯
特别是当我们安装第一个屋顶部分时。

JEFF SINCLAIR
Nothing like this has been done before. Developments

in Dubai are impressive, but a *Dome City* is going to have a huge impact on people here, especially when they move into the Dome.

杰夫·辛克莱

以前从未做过这样的事情。迪拜的发展令人印象深刻，但圆顶城将对这里的人们产生巨大影响，尤其是当他们搬进圆顶时。

ALEX

When we get to the Dome City built in Siberia and start the Dome in 29 Palms, which I think will happen, people will take us seriously and people will learn they can live anywhere on the planet comfortably.

亚历克斯

当我们在西伯利亚建造圆顶城并在 29 棕榈树 (29 Palms) 开始建造圆顶时（我认为会发生），人们会认真对待我们，人们会知道他们可以舒适地生活在地球上的任何地方

**<u>MUSIC FOR THE NEXT SECTION IF IT CAN BE LICENSED:</u>**

Prokofjew: "Cinderella" Ballettsuite op. 87 Dima Slobodeniouk.

<u>下一节的音乐（如果可以授权）：</u>

普罗科菲耶夫："灰姑娘"芭蕾舞组曲，作品 87 迪玛·斯洛博德尼乌克·(Dima Slobodeniouk).

https://www.youtube.com/watch?v=gah6lTAlmfc

They finished lunch, went back to the offices in the Limo which Alex temporarily dismissed as Jeff suggested they take the Land Rover since the road was rough up on the work site.

他们吃完午饭，坐豪华轿车回到办公室，但杰夫建议他们开路虎，因为工地的路不太好，所以亚历克斯暂时离开了。

Shortly after they arrived, a group of workers gathered around the form set in place for the first concrete pouring. The crowd seemed joyous and reflective since this marked the first major milestone in the dome project.

他们到达后不久，一群工人聚集在为第一次混凝土浇筑搭建的模板周围。人群似乎很快乐，也很沉思，因为这标志着圆顶项目的第一个重要里程碑。

Jeff introduced Alex to the crowd and asked him if he would like to make a few comments.

杰夫向人群介绍了亚历克斯，并问他是否想发表一些评论。

ALEX BAXTER
Hey everyone, it's good to be here to watch this first milestone achieved.

亚历克斯·巴克斯特
大家好，很高兴在这里见证第一个里程碑的实现。

I know it took a lot of work to get to this and we have a lot of hard work left to do. But as you all know, in the end, we'll improve the quality of life for a lot of people and *create an oasis in the arctic* where people can live as if they were anywhere else in the world.

我知道我们付出了很多努力才实现这一目标，我们还有很多艰苦的工作要做。但正如你们所知，最终，我们将改善许多人的生活质量，并在北极创造一个绿洲，人们可以像在世界其他地方一样生活。

I wish you all good luck and health and may we all see the completion of this dome together. Thank you.

祝大家好运和健康，愿我们一起见证这个圆顶的完工。谢谢。

There was some energetic applause, then the cement pouring began. It took a while for several mixers worth of cement to be pumped in and afterwards there were small clouds of water vapor coming off the cement that was heated to 110 degrees. Pneumatic power tampers worked out the bulges and soon the top was level and rebar pieces were welded in place for the next section.

一阵热烈的掌声，然后开始浇筑水泥。花了一段时间才将几台搅拌机的水泥泵入，之后，水泥被加热到 110 度，散发出一小团水蒸气。气动夯实机将凸起部分压平，很快顶部就平整了，钢筋被焊接到位，准备下一部分。

ALEX
In due time it will all seem anti climatic. Getting the first six Pillars up in reality is like accomplishing the Normandy Invasion.

亚历克斯
随着时间的推移，这一切似乎都显得有些不尽如人意，实际上，将前六根支柱竖起来就像完成诺曼底登陆一样。

JEFF SINCLAIR
The logistics, costs, and requirements are a huge undertaking, and it would be probably 10 to 15 years before all the useable air space within the dome was built.

杰夫·辛克莱
后勤、成本和要求是一项巨大的工程，可能需要
10 到 15 年的时间才能建成圆顶内所有可用的空
间。

## ALEX

Because of expected Technological advances, some
felt half of the dome would become obsolete about the
time the other half is finished. Construction techniques
will be greatly altered in a no wind or rain internal
dome environment.

亚历克斯
由于预期的技术进步，一些人认为圆顶的一半将
在另一半完工时过时。在没有风或雨的圆顶内部
环境中，施工技术将发生巨大改变。

Alex watched the crane extension process now unfold. The crane cab and machinery housing were mounted on a "bogie" that traveled up the structure on cog tracks on each of the 4 corners.

亚历克斯观看了起重机延伸过程的展开。起重机驾驶室和机械外壳安装在 "转向架" 上，转向架在 4 个角落的齿轨上沿结构向上移动。

The cab and motor housing and frame surrounded this vertical track, and as it moved upwards it did so with no loads.

驾驶室、电机外壳和框架围绕着这条垂直轨道，向上移动时没有负载。

Once the crane cab got to the next operating level static breaks which comprised steel bars hydraulically slid into the vertical risers that had horizontal frames, they rested upon which supported the weight of the crane body and load combined.

一旦起重机驾驶室到达下一个操作水平，静态断裂（由钢筋组成）就会通过液压滑入具有水平框架的垂直立管，它们就靠在上面支撑起重机主体和负载的总重量。

Every 100 feet, support cables anchored to the ground at 45-degree angles prevented wind or load factors from toppling over the crane, which was planned not to swivel except when necessary.

每隔 100 英尺，以 45 度角固定在地面上的支撑电缆可防止风或负载因素翻倒起重机，起重机计划在必要时不旋转。

In the following morning the pillar form would be raised by crane 12 feet and concrete would then be deposited which built the pillar up gradually. As it grew in height the weight as well as the 200-foot anchor made it virtually impossible for any wind to move it. The roof would be heavy with a one-inch-thick steel plate, but the pillars would have more strength than necessary and exist long past current and future generations.

第二天早上，起重机将把柱子模板抬高 12 英尺，然后浇筑混凝土，逐渐将柱子建起来。随着它的高度增加，重量以及 200 英尺的锚使任何风几乎都无法移动它。屋顶将很重，有 1 英寸厚的钢板，但柱子的强度将超过必要，并且会比现在和未来的几代人存在很长时间。

Cranes on all six pillars under construction seemed to move up together. Jeff Sinclair would be taking pictures daily and emailing them to Claude and Alex. The pictures would be taken from a certified location and angle and when put together in a slide show would provide animation of watching the building process.

正在建造的所有六根柱子上的起重机似乎一起向上移动。杰夫·辛克莱每天都会拍照并通过电子邮件发送给克劳德和亚历克斯。这些照片将从一个经过认证的位置和角度拍摄，然后放在幻灯片中，将提供观看建筑过程的动画。

Jeff drove Alex back to the Nuuk Dome Inc. offices where the Limo was waiting for Alex, who thanked Jeff.

杰夫开车送亚历克斯回到 努克圆顶公司 (Nuuk Dome Inc.) 办公室，豪华轿车正在那里等着亚历克斯，亚历克斯向杰夫表示感谢。

ALEX

Jeff, I appreciate you showing me the construction site again and giving me heads up for today's events. I might be back sometime soon to see some more of this construction phase.

亚历克斯

杰夫，感谢您再次带我参观施工现场并提醒我今天的活动。我可能很快就会回来，看看这个施工阶段的更多情况。

JEFF SINCLAIR

Is there anything in particular you wish to learn from these visits?

杰夫·辛克莱尔

你有什么特别想从这些访问中学到的东西吗？

ALEX

To be honest, no. I just love to see things built and ideas come to fruition.

亚历克斯

说实话，没有。我只是喜欢看到东西建成，想法变成现实。

JEFF SINCLAIR
No concerns?

杰夫·辛克莱尔
没有顾虑吗？

ALEX
Jeff, I know you know your business, and I'm not going
to be the person to tell you what you need to do as I
know Claude Reardon is fully capable of redirecting
construction to maximize efficiency and cost savings.

亚历克斯
杰夫，我知道你了解你的业务，我不会告诉你你
需要做什么，因为我知道克劳德·里尔登完全有能
力重新调整施工方向，以最大限度地提高效率和
节省成本。

JEFF SINCLAIR
Alex, it seems you made a long trip just to watch
construction if you have no concerns.

杰夫·辛克莱尔
亚历克斯，如果你没有顾虑的话，看来你长途跋
涉只是为了观看施工。

ALEX
Jeff, I'm really just here to enjoy watching it be built
and at the same time make mental notes on the project
and possibly obtain lessons learned for future projects.

亚历克斯
杰夫，我来这里真的只是为了欣赏它的建造过
程，同时在脑海中记录下这个项目，并可能为未
来的项目吸取教训。

JEFF SINCLAIR
Such as where to dump all the excess material we are
generating as we take down part of that hill?

杰夫·辛克莱尔
比如，当我们拆除那座山的一部分时，我们把产
生的多余材料倾倒在哪里？

ALEX
Certainly, that's one aspect of it.

亚历克斯
当然，这是其中的一个方面。

JEFF SINCLAIR
The history of this construction will serve mankind especially if we duplicate this model numerous times.

杰夫·辛克莱尔
这座建筑的历史将造福人类，特别是如果我们多次复制这个模型。

ALEX
Well, we could look at perhaps creating another protected harbor on the inlet along the coastline southeast of the dome.

亚历克斯
好吧，我们可以考虑在圆顶东南海岸线的入口处再建一个受保护的港口。

JEFF SINCLAIR
Definitely. Right now, the restrictions are ships that arrive in Nuuk Harbor must be 320 feet or less in length, no reason why with all that extra rock we are blasting out of that hill side we couldn't make an artificial harbor that would allow ships almost 1000 feet long to moor.

杰夫·辛克莱
确实。目前，限制是抵达努克港的船只长度不得超过 320 英尺，没有理由说，我们在山坡上炸出了那么多额外的岩石，却无法建造一个可以让近 1000 英尺长的船只停泊的人工港口。

ALEX
Yea, including ships like the Maersk super cargo carrier.

亚历克斯
是的，包括像马士基超级货运船这样的船舶。

JEFF SINCLAIR
Exactly.

杰夫·辛克莱
没错。

ALEX
Well Jeff, I'm going to let you get back to work, I've
taken up enough of your time. Thank you and all the
employees for showing me around.

亚历克斯
好吧，杰夫，我让你回去工作了，我已经占用了
你太多时间。谢谢你和所有员工带我参观。

JEFF SINCLAIR
You are welcome, Alex.

杰夫·辛克莱尔
不客气，亚历克斯。

Alex got into the Limo and then it drove off.

亚历克斯上了豪华轿车，然后开走了。

*Hans Jespersen* was walking by the Nuuk Dome Inc. parking lot next to their buildings
and saw Alex talking to Jeff Sinclair. His blood almost boiled over and he felt like
someone had set his hair on fire. *Hans Jespersen* was so adamantly upset, and after
seeing these men together again, knowing who Alex was after reading many of Adel's
papers and letters she carelessly left lying around her house, it didn't take much effort
to identify Alex. *Hans Jespersen* then swore to himself:

汉斯·杰斯珀森 (*Hans Jespersen*) 走过努克圆顶公司大楼旁边的停车场，看到亚
历克斯在和杰夫·辛克莱说话。他的血液几乎沸腾起来，感觉好像有人点燃了
他的头发。汉斯·杰斯珀森非常沮丧，在再次看到这些人在一起后，在阅读了
阿德尔随意散落在她家里的许多文件和信件后，他知道了阿历克斯是谁，因此
没费多大力气就认出了阿历克斯。汉斯·杰斯珀森然后对自己发誓：

HANS JESPERSEN
(Thought)
*I'll kill both of them one of these days.*

汉斯·杰斯珀森
(想法)
总有一天我会杀了他们两个。

Just a short while earlier the Nuuk Dome Inc. loadmaster for the loading and unloading
of ships involved in the massive logistics apparatus for the dome construction had just
sent all the *Stevedore's* home for the day. It was now starting to get a little dark as
evening was approaching and the air now felt a little more chill to it. The day had been
pleasant, no wind, slightly warming up a bit, but still winter.

就在不久之前，努克穹顶公司的装卸长刚刚把所有码头工人都送回家，这些码

头工人负责为穹顶建设提供大型物流设备，负责装卸船只。现在天色开始变暗，傍晚将至，空气中也变得有些凉意。这一天很愉快，没有风，稍微暖和了一点，但仍然是冬天。

*Hans Jespersen* made another trip to the liquor store to get something to eat and another bottle of Vodka was all made possible because Hans was earning in a week what he'd get a month fishing or doing any other shitty job available to him in Nuuk.

汉斯·杰斯帕森又去了一趟酒铺，买了点吃的，又买了一瓶伏特加，这一切都是可能的，因为汉斯一周的工资相当于他在努克钓鱼或做任何其他能找到的烂工作一个月的工资。

Even if *Hans Jespersen* had finished his college degree, the prospects didn't look all that good for him, unless he moved off the rock to somewhere else. That he couldn't do because he knew no other life and didn't know if he could survive out of the arctic region.

即使汉斯·杰斯帕森完成了大学学业，他的前景看起来也并不那么好，除非他搬到其他地方去。但他做不到，因为他不知道其他的生活，也不知道自己能否在北极地区生存下来。

The next morning as Alex left Nuuk, he had Brad get clearance from air traffic controllers to make a couple passes over the Dome construction site. From the right side of the cockpit as Brad made a couple slow arching curves, Alex snapped a few pictures from one thousand feet above the construction site.

第二天早上，当亚历克斯离开努克时，他让布拉德从空中交通管制员那里获得许可，飞过圆顶建筑工地几次。当布拉德在驾驶舱右侧缓慢转弯时，亚历克斯从建筑工地上空一千英尺处拍了几张照片。

Alex then sent the pictures via text message to Stephanie and Claude, which clearly showed the pillars starting to rise and the cranes had moved up 40 feet on the special vertical cog crane line now dumping concrete on some of the pillars while at the same time the welding arcs from work on the rebar structure was quite evident. In a week's time when he comes back the change will be astounding.

然后，亚历克斯通过短信将照片发给了斯蒂芬妮和克劳德，照片清楚地显示了柱子开始上升，起重机在特殊的垂直齿轨起重机线上向上移动了 40 英尺，现在正在向一些柱子倾倒混凝土，同时钢筋结构上的焊接电弧也非常明显。一周后，当他回来时，变化将是惊人的。

So far nobody on the job had been killed or injured, special attention to safety and procedures had worked out well. Even better yet, sobriety pay with R&R trips to Iceland and Canada helped keep the work force in better mental condition which added greatly to careful attention preventing fatalities and injuries. The fear was when all of sudden men were working 1000 feet up, new dynamics would exist that could lead to safety failures.

到目前为止，工作中没有人死亡或受伤，对安全和程序的特别关注确实取得了很好的效果。更棒的是，戒酒费和去冰岛和加拿大 休息与放松 (Rest & Relaxation) 旅行有助于保持工人的精神状态，这大大增加了防止死亡和受伤的谨慎程度。令人担心的是，当人们突然在 1000 英尺高空工作时，会出现新的动态，这可能会导致安全故障。

Alex then decided now would be the time to employ some meditation to get Nuuk Dome and everything else off his mind.

亚历克斯决定现在是时候进行一些冥想，以摆脱努克圆顶和其他一切。

Alex's meditation was only partially successful, because his life was full of activity and change. It used to be full of fear and anxiety over losing a fortune he worked so hard for, because of the near fatal crash of the stock market back in 2008. Alex rebounded though and what appeared like his ship running aground slowly turned around which allowed him to preserve much of his fortune and re-deploy it in new directions.

亚历克斯的冥想只是部分成功，因为他的生活充满了活动和变化。 2008 年股市崩盘几乎导致他失去了辛苦赚来的财富，他曾经为此感到恐惧和焦虑。但亚历克斯后来反弹了，他的船似乎搁浅了，慢慢掉头，这让他保住了大部分财富，并将其重新部署到新的方向。

Alex had warned Rodriguez he'd probably be coming back today. The people at the hotel were starting to warm up to him, though they didn't see much of him, it pleased them to have such an important guest staying there who had such a low profile and blended in, but this trip was going to be different.

亚历克斯曾警告罗德里格斯，他今天可能会回来。酒店里的人开始对他热情起来，虽然他们很少见到他，但他们很高兴有这样一位如此低调、如此融入环境的重要客人住在那里，但这次旅行将有所不同。

In the past it was all business travel and suits. He had left his second suitcase on the plane until he arrived back in New York, This time he got off the plane with his second suitcase with an entirely different wardrobe. He would change his clothes, and between the ball cap, sunglasses, jeans, black shirt and leather jacket, his hole persona changed.

过去都是商务旅行和西装。他把第二个行李箱留在飞机上，直到他回到纽约，这次他下飞机时带着第二个行李箱，里面的衣柜完全不同。他会换衣服，棒球帽、太阳镜、牛仔裤、黑色衬衫和皮夹克，他的整个形象都变了。

Alex texted Christina after he settled down in his hotel.

亚历克斯在酒店安顿下来后给克里斯蒂娜发短信。

Note to Cinematographer:

> During the next sequence of Text Messages, the image of the iPhone display text is shown with VOICEOVER.

摄影师注意：

在下一个短信序列中，苹果手机 (iPhone) 显示文本的图像以画外音显示。

ALEX
(Text Message)
I'm in my hotel room staying at the same place before.
Do you want to go see a movie or do something fun?

ALEX
（短信）
我在之前住过的酒店房间里。你想去看电影还是
做点有趣的事情？

The atmosphere at the non-profit organization Christina worked at was so thick you almost could cut it with a knife.

克里斯蒂娜工作的非营利组织的气氛非常浓厚，几乎要用刀子才能割开。

All day long everyone was looking at Christina. It wasn't so bad that the few womanizers in the office were dressing her down, but now all the women were too!

一整天，每个人都在看着克里斯蒂娜。办公室里几个花花公子在训斥她，这还不算太糟

Christina didn't deserve it and felt like suddenly she was the subject of a freak show. Just this morning as she was walking in the building a reporter approached her as soon as she got in and pestered her all the way to the elevator.

不配得到这样的待遇，她觉得自己突然成了一场怪胎秀的主角。就在今天早上，当她走进大楼时，一名记者一进门就接近她，一直骚扰她到电梯。

Christiona didn't get to see how a short time later Leroy threw the reporter out of the building, citing she didn't have permission to film and harass people on private property.

克里斯蒂娜没有看到不久之后，莱罗伊将记者赶出了大楼，理由是她没有获得在私人财产上拍摄和骚扰他人的许可。

A short time later attorneys from the owners of 120 Wall Street were talking with the reporter's management and threatening them.

不久之后，华尔街 120 号业主的律师与记者的管理层进行了交谈并威胁他们。

It was all part of a game. The owners were not really upset because suddenly, the building was becoming a more valuable property and raising a few eyebrows as it became common knowledge of who now inhabited the building which was taking on celebrity status. Rents would be going up and some of the non-profits would have to move out, which didn't upset the owners one bit.

这一切都是游戏的一部分。业主们并没有真正感到不安，因为突然之间，这栋建筑变得更有价值，引起了一些人的关注，因为现在住在这栋正在成为名人的建筑里的人已经众所周知。租金会上涨，一些非营利组织将不得不搬走，但这丝毫没有让业主感到不安。

Christina's misery was suddenly interrupted by Alex's text message. Suddenly Christina's afternoon got a lot better. This was his best text of all, as it exposed a different side to Alex, which the public never saw.

克里斯蒂娜的痛苦突然被亚历克斯的短信打断了。突然间，克里斯蒂娜的下午心情好了很多。这是他最好的文字，因为它揭示了亚历克斯的另一面，这是公众从未看到过的。

CHRISTINA
(Thought)
*This might be a closer view to Alex's personality as he escapes his business life for a few hours with me.*

克里斯蒂娜
（想法）
这可能是更接近亚历克斯个性的视角，因为他逃
离了商业生活，和我在一起几个小时。

But Christina was not going to leave work early. She didn't want to give any more rope to reporters or her co-workers.

但克里斯蒂娜不会早点下班。她不想再给记者或同事们留任何借口。

CHRISTINA
(Text Message)
Sure, I would love to go to a movie with you.

克里斯蒂娜
（短信）
当然，我很想和你一起去看电影。

ALEX
(Text Message)
What time would you like me to pick you up?

亚历克斯
（短信）
你想让我什么时候来接你？

CHRISTINA
(Text Message)
I have a better idea.

克里斯蒂娜
（短信）
我有个更好的主意。

ALEX
(Text Message)
What's that?

亚历克斯
（短信）
那是什么？

CHRISTINA
(Text Message)
I'll leave work, I'm not dressed up too much today, and take a cab and pick you up at your hotel and we'll go from there.

克里斯蒂娜
（短信）
我会下班，今天我穿得不太正式，打车去你的酒店接你，然后我们从那里出发。

ALEX
(Text Message)
Perfect.

亚历克斯
（短信）
完美。

CHRISTINA
(Text Message)
I'll call you when I leave work, it should only take a few minutes to drive to your hotel.

克里斯蒂娜
（短信）
我下班后会给你打电话，开车去你的酒店应该只需要几分钟。

ALEX
(Text Message)
Ok, I'll be standing at the side entrance which has the
valet parking guys there.

亚历克斯
（短信）
好的，我会站在有代客泊车员的侧门。

CHRISTINA
(Text Message)
Understand, see you a little later.

克里斯蒂娜
（短信）
明白了，待会儿见。

Time flew by and Christina left work, ignoring the looks and the silent whispers all the way down to the ground floor, walked out the front of the building and prior to meeting Alex would have walked to the nearby SUBWAY and got on a train there. Around the corner was a line of Taxi's usually four or five waiting this time of day. People would walk out of the building up to Leroy and say, "Taxi please."

时间过得很快，克里斯蒂娜下班了，一路上无视别人的目光和悄悄话，走到一楼，走出大楼前面，在和亚历克斯见面之前，她会走到附近的地铁，在那里坐地铁。拐角处有一排出租车，通常这个时候有　四到五辆出租车在等着。人们会走出大楼，对 Leroy 说："请出租车。"

Leroy had hand signals worked out with the taxi drivers who worked on this pickup and the next in line would see the signal and move up to the front entrance and pick up the passenger.

勒罗伊和负责这辆车的出租车司机打手势，下一位司机看到手势后会走到前门接乘客。

Leroy was a little surprised when Christina who seldom used a Taxi asked for one. And then to the side there were a couple of reporters who he spotted were now approaching Christina. Leroy seeing the sharks heading for the sweet girl Christina, animated his signal to the cab indicating *get your ass over here now and pick up this person.*

当很少使用出租车的克里斯蒂娜要求一辆出租车时，莱罗伊有点惊讶。然后他发现旁边有几个记者正朝克里斯蒂娜走来。莱罗伊看到鲨鱼正朝可爱的克里斯蒂娜走来，便向出租车发出信号，表示"快过来接这个人。"

The cabbie did not waste a second as he knew it was some kind of a hot ride or an emergency, sped up and got around the corner and pulled up to the passenger loading spot just about the time the reporters were descending on poor Christina.

出租车司机没有浪费一秒钟，因为他知道这是一次热门行程或紧急情况，他加速绕过拐角，停在乘客上车点，就在记者们向可怜的克里斯蒂娜走来的时候。

Leroy quickly opened the cab door for Christina, and she got in and Leroy shut it and politely told the newsman:

莱罗伊迅速为克里斯蒂娜打开车门，她上了车，莱罗伊关上车门，礼貌地告诉记者：

LEROY JONES
Get the camera out of my fucking face asshole.

莱罗伊·琼斯
把摄像机从我他妈的脸上拿开，混蛋。

The reporter was slightly shaken, and the cab pulled away before a bunch of questions could be shouted out to Christina.

记者有点震惊，出租车开走了，没等记者向克里斯蒂娜喊出一堆问题。

Christina, like many people in the work force has enemies from within. People you least expect to have such behaviors baffle the minds of their peers by their diabolical actions.

克里斯蒂娜和很多职场人士一样，内心也有敌人。你最不希望看到有这种行为的人，却用他们恶毒的行为让同事们困惑不已。

A strange dichotomy of personalities and jealousies in any organization can lead to numerous scenarios, but when an event happens such as the sequence of events triggered by a marginal New York News Reporter who must result in yellow journalism to sell her byline, manifests behaviors that otherwise would not materialize some of the recent activity.

任何组织中奇怪的性格和嫉妒二分法都可能导致许多情况，但当发生诸如由边缘纽约新闻记者引发的一系列事件时，为了出售她的署名，她必须进行黄色新闻报道，表现出一些行为，否则这些行为就不会实现最近的一些活动。

Two people within Christina's own organization who were jealous because of her exquisite looks as well as upset she got the promotions they wanted, wasted no time in alerting media that she was the mystery woman and Alex Baxter's girlfriend. One of them immediately called the newspaper tip line:

克里斯蒂娜所在组织中的两个人嫉妒克里斯蒂娜的绝色容貌，也对克里斯蒂娜得到的升职感到不满，于是他们立即向媒体透露，克里斯蒂娜就是那位神秘女子，也是亚历克斯·巴克斯特的女友。其中一人立即拨打了报纸的举报热线：

COWORKER
Christina Garrison is the woman in the photograph

with Alex Baxter and she is my coworker shown in the gossip section news article.

同事

克里斯蒂娜·加里森是照片中与亚历克斯·巴克斯特在一起的女人，她是我八卦新闻文章中出现的同事。

NEWSPAPER REP
Do you have any pictures to substantiate your claim?

报纸代表
你有照片来证实你的说法吗？

COWORKER

I do have several good office party photographs from the Holidays, but if I share them with you, then you must agree not to use them or my name. I want it to be totally anonymous.

同事

我确实有几张假期办公室聚会的精彩照片，但如果我与你分享，那么你必须同意不使用它们或我的名字。我希望它是完全匿名的。

NEWSPAPER REP

We have several protected news source contributors we never disclose their identity. It's the only way we can stay in business.

报纸代表

我们有几位受保护的新闻来源撰稿人，我们绝不会透露他们的身份。这是我们能继续经营下去的唯一方法。

COWORKER

Alright, I'll text you a couple pictures. Call me back to let me know if you got them and what you think.

同事

好的，我会给你发几张照片。给我回电话，告诉我你收到了，以及你的想法。

Sadly, the only piece of paper that gets as many viewers as the front page and the editorial page, is the gossip section. Several million people were now curious as to who is the beautiful almost movie star quality woman shown in the picture with the filthy rich, *Dome Guy*.

可悲的是，报纸上唯一能像头版和社论版一样吸引大量读者的是八卦版。现在有数百万人好奇，照片中那位几乎是电影明星般美丽的女人是谁，她和那个富得流油的圆顶男在一起。

Sadly, for Christina's family, the yellow journalists were already starting to invade her Queens New York area of her residence trying to track her down and corner her for an interview or questions.

可悲的是，对于克里斯蒂娜的家人来说，黄色记者已经开始入侵她位于纽约皇后区的住所，试图追踪她，并将她逼入角落，进行采访或提问。

Christina now starting to see this all unfold, knew going out in a Limo would only create opportunities for the news bloodhounds to find her easier. Privacy was becoming a problem. Things were certainly getting a lot more complicated.

克里斯蒂娜现在开始看到这一切的展开，她知道乘坐豪华轿车出行只会让新闻侦探更容易找到她。隐私正在成为一个问题。事情肯定变得更加复杂。

Once Christina was in the cab, she Text Messaged Alex to let him know she was on the way and five minutes away.

克里斯蒂娜一上车，就给亚历克斯发短信，告诉他她已经在路上，五分钟后就到了。

Alex was in a coffee shop adjacent to the hotel lobby and suddenly with the help of the caffeine shot in his drink and the thought of Christina arriving, caused his endorphins to flow and he achieved a moment of happiness and tranquility not too unlike one of his better periods of meditation.

亚历克斯在酒店大堂旁边的一家咖啡店里，突然间，在饮料中加了咖啡因，想到克里斯蒂娜就要来了，他的内啡肽开始分泌，他感到了片刻的幸福和宁静，这与他冥想时的感觉很相似。

Alex proceeded to walk to the side entrance as he discussed with Christina and shortly a cab pulled up. Alex could easily spot Christina and quickly approached the cab. Christina had told the cabbie her friend was going to get in the cab, and they would drive to a nice movie theater she knew was clean and comfortable and easy to get to and from with a cab.

亚历克斯一边和克里斯蒂娜讨论着，一边向侧门走去，不一会儿，一辆出租车停了下来。亚历克斯很容易就认出了克里斯蒂娜，于是迅速走近出租车。克里斯蒂娜告诉司机，她的朋友要上车，然后他们会开车去一家不错的电影院，她知道这家电影院干净、舒适，打车来回都很方便。

With Alex's semi disguise, and Christina's somewhat modest dress, it's unlikely anyone would spot them or figure out who they were, so the prospect for a good evening existed.

由于亚历克斯的半伪装和克里斯蒂娜相对朴素的着装，不太可能有人会发现他们或猜出他们是谁，因此他们有望度过一个美好的夜晚。

They agreed in the cab since neither of them was hungry they would go see the movie first.

他们在出租车上同意，因为他们都不饿，所以先去看电影。

ALEX
What movie would you like to see?

亚历克斯
你想看什么电影？

CHRISTINA
How about Mufasa, the Lion King?

克里斯蒂娜
《狮子王穆法沙》怎么样？

ALEX
That sounds interesting, sure let's go see it.

亚历克斯
听起来很有趣，我们去看看吧。

The cabbie soon pulled up to the curb of the theater Christina suggested. The Cabbie didn't get out, the street was busy, and Alex understood instinctively and gave him a $20 tip anyway.

出租车司机很快就停在了 克里斯蒂娜 建议的剧院路边。出租车司机没有下车，街道上很繁忙，亚历克斯本能地明白了，还是给了他 20 美元的小费。

The seemingly grouchy cabbie suddenly came alive, as Alex made his day.

看似脾气暴躁的出租车司机突然活跃起来，因为 亚历克斯 让他度过了愉快的一天。

In a short period of time, they were seated with popcorn and drinks and watched the spell binding movie.

不一会儿，他们就坐在爆米花和饮料旁观看了这部引人入胜的电影。

Alex whispered in Christina's ear:

亚历克斯 在 Christina 耳边低声说：

ALEX
The cinematography just keeps getting better and better.

亚历克斯
电影摄影越来越好了。

Christina whispered back feeling Alex's warmth and affection:

克里斯蒂娜低声回应，感受到了 亚历克斯 的温暖和爱意:

CHRISTINA
It's amazing, so life like.

克里斯蒂娜
太神奇了，太逼真了。

The movie ended at perfect time. They were both hungry.

电影结束的时间恰到好处。他们都饿了。

Christina and Alex soon walked out of the movie theater, and nobody knew who they were, nor did they care.

克里斯蒂娜和亚历克斯很快就走出了电影院，没有人知道他们是谁，也没有人关心。

ALEX
Are there any good places to eat around here?

亚历克斯
这附近有什么好吃的地方吗？

CHRISTINA
Yes, across the street is a good Greek Restaurant if you like that kind of food.

克里斯蒂娜
是的，如果你喜欢希腊菜的话，街对面就有一家不错的希腊餐厅。

ALEX
Sure, that works for me.

亚历克斯
当然，对我来说没问题。

The two had a nice Greek dinner.

两人吃了一顿美味的希腊晚餐。

ALEX
Christina, what do you like doing in your spare time?

亚历克斯
克里斯蒂娜，你闲暇时喜欢做什么？

CHRISTINA
I would say my favorite past time is reading books. I do watch TV now and then and watch the evening news to catch up on what's happening in the world.

克里斯蒂娜
我想说我过去最喜欢的时间就是读书。我偶尔会看电视，看晚间新闻，了解世界正在发生的事情。

ALEX
I kind of do that too.

亚历克斯
我也会这么做。

CHRISTINA
Since I work for a non-profit organization, I do some traveling and meet a lot of interesting people. Sometimes I must travel to foreign countries just like many NGO REPS and check out the recipients of the money we generate to verify it's legitimate and set up good accounting principles on how the money is spent.

克里斯蒂娜
因为我在一家非营利组织工作，所以我会去旅行，遇到很多有趣的人。有时我必须像许多非政府组织代表一样前往国外，检查我们筹集的资金的接收者，以验证资金是否合法，并制定良好的会计原则来处理资金的使用。

ALEX
May I ask you a question and I will hold your answer in the strictest of confidence.

亚历克斯
我可以问您一个问题吗？我会严格保密您的答案。
CHRISTINA
Sure.

克里斯蒂娜
当然可以。

ALEX
Do you uncover fraud in these dealings?

亚历克斯
您发现这些交易中存在欺诈行为吗？

CHRISTINA
In my opinion, there is always a potential for fraud even if the representatives to the recipients are model citizens and have the best in mind for them. Corruption can come in many forms and sometimes people with impecable backgrounds get corrupt for many reasons. In some of the areas we serve, there are wretched conditions which multiply the chances of these officials becoming corrupt.

克里斯蒂娜
我个人认为，即使接收者的代表是模范公民，并且对他们抱有最好的期望，也总是存在欺诈的可能性。腐败有多种形式，有时背景无可挑剔的人会因为多种原因而腐败。在我们服务的某些地区，恶劣的环境使这些官员腐败的可能性成倍增加。

ALEX
Is that because the flow of cash starts feeding their machinations?

亚历克斯
是因为现金流开始助长他们的阴谋吗？

CHRISTINA
Sure, money has a way of corrupting people and unfortunately, when we discover it, the person has often disappeared with the loot, and nobody hears from he or she again. With the levels of money, we sometimes transfer to big projects such as building a school or a hospital, in parts of the world that person can live well.

克里斯蒂娜
当然，金钱可以腐蚀人，不幸的是，当我们发现它时，这个人往往已经带着赃物消失了，再也没

有人听到他或她的消息。我们有时会将资金转移
到大型项目，例如建造学校或医院，在世界某些
地方，这个人可以过上好日子。

ALEX

Did you run into any people like that?

亚历克斯
你遇到过这样的人吗？

CHRISTINA

I had one such person who left Sudan and ended up in
Egypt where he lived well until he spent all the money.
His problem is he could never come back because after
we filed complaints with the government, they would
immediately arrest him if he returned and life in their
prisons is very harsh.

克里斯蒂娜

我遇到过这样一个人，他离开苏丹，最终来到埃
及，在那里他过得很好，直到他把所有的钱都花
光了。他的问题是他再也回不来了，因为在我们
向政府提出投诉后，如果他回来，他们会立即逮
捕他，监狱里的生活非常艰苦。

ALEX

I do not envy you. I know you probably have some
tough times dealing with all this.

亚历克斯

我并不羡慕你。我知道你可能在处理这一切时会
遇到一些困难。

CHRISTINA

I received a good education quickly after I was hired
and coached on how not to get psychologically worked
up about it, because in our business such nefarious
activities can and will happen. We give the donors
copies of the police files and make apologies. They
are disappointed their money was wasted. But they
know it was out of our control when a person becomes
corrupt and evil.

克里斯蒂娜
我被聘用后很快就接受了良好的教育，并被指导
如何不对此产生心理上的激动，因为在我们的行

业中，这种邪恶的活动是可能发生的，也会发生。我们向捐赠者提供了警方档案的副本并表示道歉。他们很失望他们的钱被浪费了。但他们知道，当一个人变得腐败和邪恶时，这是我们无法控制的。

ALEX
I would assume so.

亚历克斯
我想是这样。

CHRISTINA
Alex, what do you do for fun?

克里斯蒂娜
亚历克斯，你有什么消遣方式？

ALEX,
I like to travel now and then. I have a second home in Switzerland I visit now and then. I like symphonies and sometimes operas. I love hearing Aida Garifullina sing opera songs. And of course there are many other singers, male and female I like hearing.

亚历克斯，
我喜欢时不时地旅行。我在瑞士有第二个家，我时不时会去那里。我喜欢交响乐，有时也喜欢歌剧。我喜欢听阿依达·加里弗利娜演唱歌剧歌曲。当然，还有很多其他歌手，我喜欢听男歌手和女歌手。

CHRISTINA
Who are some of them?

克里斯蒂娜
他们中有些是谁？

ALEX
I love hearing Carly Paoli sing. Her concerts in Rome were outstanding. The Pope chose her to sing at his Jubilee.

亚历克斯
我喜欢听卡莉·保利唱歌。她在罗马的音乐会非常精彩。教皇选择她在他的禧年庆典上演唱。

CHRISTINA
Nice.


克里斯蒂娜
很好。


ALEX
A lot of people who love the opera enjoy Andrea Bocelli. I've heard Andrea Bocelli sing with Sara Brightman, Carly Paoli, Aida Garifullina, and Laura Pausini.


亚历克斯
很多喜欢歌剧的人都喜欢安德烈·波切利。我听过安德烈·波切利和萨拉·布莱曼、卡莉·保利、阿依达·加里弗琳娜和劳拉·普西尼一起演唱。

FLASHBACK (MUSIC)

https://www.youtube.com/watch?v=zLmFEIksvh8

Andrea Bocelli, Laura Pausini - *Dare To Live* (Live From Teatro Del Silenzio, Italy / 2007)

END FLASHBACK

闪回（音乐）

https://www.youtube.com/watch?v=zLmFEIksvh8

安德烈·波切利、劳拉·普西尼 - 敢于生存（意大利寂静剧院现场演唱 / 2007）

闪回结束


CHRISTINA
Would you take me to the symphony?


克里斯蒂娜
你能带我去听交响乐吗？


ALEX
Definitely. The symphony with you would be a joyous occasion for me.


亚历克斯
当然。和你一起听交响乐对我来说是一件快乐的事。

Christina was smiling, feeling the wonderful feelings Alex was giving her. She knew he just pressed her button, and she might have reached the point of no return.

克里斯蒂娜微笑着，感受到亚历克斯给她的美妙感觉。她知道他只是按下了她的按钮，她可能已经到了无法挽回的地步。

CHRISTINA
(Thought)
*I hope Alex doesn't use me and toss me aside. I don't
know if I could live then.*

克里斯蒂娜
(想)
我希望亚历克斯不要利用我，然后把我抛弃。我
不知道那时我是否还能活下去。

After dinner they hopped back in a cab and by mutual agreement went back to Alex's hotel. It was around 11:00 p.m.

晚餐后，他们跳上出租车，按照双方的约定回到了亚历克斯的酒店。当时大约是晚上 11 点。

ALEX
Would you like to come up to my room for a little bit?

亚历克斯
你愿意到我房间来待一会儿吗？

CHRISTINA
I can't stay too long; I have to work in the morning,
and I need to get my beauty sleep.

克里斯蒂娜
我不能待太久；我早上要上班，我需要睡个美容
觉。

ALEX
Understand.

亚历克斯
明白。

Anticipating a romantic intrigue that might lead to a transcendental splendid euphoria, Christina was getting moist and almost wanting to be submissive. She didn't know if it was love or lust, the attraction was real and genuine.

克里斯蒂娜期待着一场浪漫的阴谋，这可能会导致一种超然的极致欣快感，她开始湿润，几乎想要顺从。她不知道这是爱还是欲望，但这种吸引力是真实的。

Alex was sincerely a nice guy, not demanding, and fully understanding and accommodative. Christina felt that Alex is a true gentleman, rare and unique, and somewhat protective yet private.

亚历克斯真的是一个好人，不要求太多，完全理解和包容。克里斯蒂娜觉得亚历克斯是个真正的绅士，罕见而独特，有点保护欲但又很私密。

There was no mistake in their intentions. It very well could quickly end in some intensive love making. Christina was now adamant about letting the cards lie where they fell. Despite the admonition from her mother to be extra careful and delay the inevitable as long as possible, the pressure was building, and Christina was looking forward to the release.

他们的意图没有错。这很可能很快就会以激烈的做爱结束。克里斯蒂娜现在坚持让牌落在地上。尽管母亲告诫她要格外小心，尽可能拖延不可避免的事情，但压力越来越大，克里斯蒂娜期待着释放。

Just as the taxi pulled up to the side entrance Alex spotted the bitch reporter that put his picture in the paper the other day.

就在出租车停在侧门时，亚历克斯发现了前几天在报纸上登照片的那个婊子记者。

ALEX
We have a problem, Christina.

亚历克斯
我们遇到麻烦了，克里斯蒂娜。

CHRISTINA
What Alex.

克里斯蒂娜
什么，亚历克斯。

ALEX
Remember the woman at the Broadway show the other
night who came up to me and asked me how I liked the
show and wanted to know what my name was?

亚历克斯
还记得前几天晚上在百老汇演出时，那个女人走
到我面前，问我是否喜欢这个演出，并想知道我
的名字吗？

CHRISTINA
Sort of?

克里斯蒂娜
有点？

ALEX
That's her over there.

亚历克斯
那边就是她。

CHRISTINA
I remember her now.

克里斯蒂娜
我现在记得她了。

ALEX
Christina, I can't let you get out of the cab, if you do,
your picture will be in tomorrow's newspaper.

亚历克斯
克里斯蒂娜，我不能让你下车，如果你这么做，
你的照片就会出现在明天的报纸上。

CHRISTINA
Damn.

克里斯蒂娜
该死的。

亚历克斯
我很抱歉。

CHRISTINA
It's getting so complicated.

克里斯蒂娜
事情变得太复杂了。

ALEX
We'll have to work out some way to get alone together,
but we are not going to be able to do it tonight and
protect your reputation.

亚历克斯
我们必须想办法单独相处，但我们今晚无法做到
这一点并保护你的名誉。

CHRISTINA
I'm ready.

克里斯蒂娜
我准备好了。

ALEX
Go home and get a good night's sleep, let me work on
it. Call me when you get home so I know you are safe.

亚历克斯
回家睡个好觉，让我来处理。你到家后给我打电
话，这样我就知道你安全了。

CHRISTINA
I want to be frank with you.

克里斯蒂娜
我想对你坦诚相待。

ALEX
Sure.

亚历克斯
当然。

CHRISTINA
You have no idea how ready I was tonight.

克里斯蒂娜
你不知道我今晚准备得有多充分。

ALEX
I was just as ready. And nothing has changed. We are
just delayed.

亚历克斯
我也准备好了。什么都没有改变。我们只是延误
了。

The cabbie was getting very interested and wrote to memory everything he heard now
as the car set idling waiting for the passengers to get out.

出租车司机非常感兴趣，他把听到的一切都记在了脑子里，车子停了下来，等待乘客下车。

Alex pulled out a crisp pair of $100 bills and gave them to the cabbie and announced:

亚历克斯拿出一对崭新的 100 美元钞票，递给出租车司机，并宣布：

ALEX
Here, take her home and make sure she's safe.

亚历克斯
来，送她回家，确保她安全。

CAB DRIVER
You can count on it, Mr.

出租车司机
你可以放心，先生。

The cab driver never got tips like this before. He was also getting excited because he was hearing some interesting things going on.

出租车司机以前从来没有得到过这样的小费。他也兴奋起来，因为他听到了一些有趣的事情。

Alex softly kissed Christina on the forehead and said some nice words.

亚历克斯轻轻地吻了吻克里斯蒂娜的额头，说了一些好听的话。

ALEX
I miss you already.

亚历克斯
我已经想你了。

Before Christina came out of her trance from the sweet words, Alex hopped out of the cab, shut the door, and the cab drove off. Alex slipped on his sunglasses as he was getting out of the cab and promptly walked to the side entrance of the hotel.

克里斯蒂娜还没从甜言蜜语的恍惚中清醒过来，亚历克斯就跳下车，关上车门，车子开走了。亚历克斯下车时戴上太阳镜，迅速走到酒店的侧门。

The news reporter didn't recognize Alex until he was right at the door to the hotel. If she made the mistake of bird dogging him into the hotel, he would have sued the crap out of her paper the first thing in the morning for harassment and invasion of privacy.

新闻记者直到亚历克斯走到酒店门口才认出他。如果她犯了跟踪他进酒店的错误，他明天一早就起诉她的报纸，指控她骚扰和侵犯隐私。

If Alex knew he could get away with chicken choking the female reporter, he would have, but he humbly and quietly continued his way to his hotel room.

如果亚历克斯知道他可以逃脱用鸡掐女记者的惩罚，他就会这么做，但他谦虚而安静地继续走向他的酒店房间。

The woman was upset with herself, she had let down her vigilance just for a moment asking nonsense questions to one of the valet parking guys who didn't know *Jack Shit from Shinola* about her target.

女人对自己很生气，她一时放松了警惕，问了一个对她的目标一无所知的代客泊车员一些无稽之谈。

In the reporter's self-criticism she realized that if she had she just kept her mouth shut and not pestered the dummy valet parking guys who didn't know anything about Mr. Baxter, she would have seen him arrive in the cab and even more tantalizing, his new girlfriend might have been in the CAB! But she didn't know and now it's too late, her quarry was gone.

在记者的自我批评中，她意识到如果她闭上嘴巴，不去骚扰那些对巴克斯特先生一无所知的笨蛋代客泊车员，她就会看到他乘坐出租车到达，更诱人的是，他的新女友可能就在出租车里！但她不知道，现在已经太晚了，她的猎物已经不见了。

As soon as Alex got to his room, he texted Christina.

亚历克斯一到他的房间，就给克里斯蒂娜发短信。

ALEX
(Text Message)
I've figured out where I can take you to get some privacy and enjoy ourselves. Is your passport up to date?

亚历克斯
（短信）
我已经想好可以带你去哪里玩了，这样你就可以有隐私了。你的护照是最新的吗？

Christina didn't know if she should cry or pout or both, then suddenly the ringer on her iPhone alerted she had the message which she promptly read.

克里斯蒂娜不知道自己是应该哭还是生气，或者两者兼而有之，然后突然她的苹果手机铃声提醒她收到了信息，她立即阅读了信息。

Even though the end of the evening felt unpleasant because some newspaper person was hell bent on invading their privacy, this text suddenly made Christina suddenly feel a lot better.

尽管**晚**上结束时感觉不愉快，因为有些报社的人执意要侵犯他们的隐私，但这条短信突然让克里斯蒂娜感觉好多了。

CHRISTINA
(Text Message)
Yes, my passport is up to date.

克里斯蒂娜
（短信）
是的，我的护照是最新的。

ALEX
(Text Message)

Good, I'll tell you what I have in mind after I do some checks. Be prepared to leave work on Friday afternoon. Be prepacked for a couple days and I'll send Rodriguez to pick you up at work then drive you home to get your luggage and take you to the airport where we'll meet up.

亚历克斯
（短信）

很好，我检查完后会告诉你我的想法。准备周五下午下班。提前收拾好几天的行李，我会派罗德里格斯去公司接你，然后开车送你回家拿行李，送你去机场，我们会在那里见面。

CHRISTINA
(Text Message)
Ok.

克里斯蒂娜
（短信）
好的。

ALEX
(Text Message)
What time can you leave?

亚历克斯
（短信）
你什么时候可以离开？

CHRISTINA
(Text Message)
3:00 P.M. would work out.

克里斯蒂娜
（短信）
下午 3 点可以。


ALEX
(Text Message)
Rodriguez will pull up exactly at 3:00, as soon as you walk out of the building you will see him roll down his window so you can see him.

亚历克斯
（短信）

罗德里格斯会在　3：00　准时到达，你一走出大楼，就会看到他摇下车窗，这样你就能看到他了。


CHRISTINA
(Text Message)
Okay.

克里斯蒂娜
（短信）
好的。


Alex sadly flew back to Minnesota in the morning. He was deprived that splendid euphoria with a woman that enamored his soul by a corrupt and crummy newspaper witch.

亚历克斯早上伤心地飞回了明尼苏达州。他被一个腐败而卑鄙的报纸女巫剥夺了与一个让他心动的女人在一起的那种美妙的快感。


ALEX
(Thought)
*It's time to give her a taste of her own medicine.*
亚历克斯
（想）
是时候让她尝尝她的苦头了。


Alex decided to send private detectives after the reporter and the management of her paper. He was going to pay good money to dig deep to get dirt.

亚历克斯决定派私家侦探去追踪记者和她所在报纸的管理层。他打算付钱深挖以找到真相。

***

*Hans Jespersen* was putting his plan together. Working every day, seven days a week as a stevedore, he was starting to build up some disposable income. He was eating better, saving up some cash for a rainy day and now he could buy things that would be useful to more effectively take out Alex Baxter and Nuuk Dome Inc.

汉斯·杰斯帕森正在制定计划。他每周七天每天做码头工人，开始积累一些可支配收入。他吃得更好，攒了一些现金以备不时之需，现在他可以买些有用的东西，以便更有效地消灭亚历克斯·巴克斯特和努克圆顶公司。

Because of the end of shift, walking to the liquor store at a certain time of day, he realized he was able to do some surveillance on Nuuk Dome Inc. and in a period discovered as he started walking by later and later in the evenings that by 9:00 p.m. the facility was almost a ghost town and only a couple people typically remained. The day would come when only one of them was left and he would make his move. There was no security; the place could easily be penetrated.

由于轮班结束，他在一天中的某个时间步行到酒铺，他意识到他能够对努克圆顶公司进行一些监视，在一段时间内，当他开始在晚上越来越晚地走过时，他发现到晚上 9 点，该设施几乎成了一座鬼城，通常只剩下几个人。总有一天，只剩下一个人，他就会采取行动。这里没有安全保障；很容易被渗透。

***

The Greenland Dome Pillars were slowly rising. Alex would be back soon for another look. Bringing Christina along with him saved his life. Had he not been in a hurry to get her someplace where he knew they could have privacy and some tender moments alone; *Hans Jespersen* would have carried out a supreme sacrifice if necessary to take Alex Baxter out.

格陵兰圆顶柱正在慢慢升起。亚历克斯很快就会回来再看一眼。带上克里斯蒂娜救了他的命。如果他不急着把她带到一个他知道他们可以有隐私和一些温柔时刻的地方；汉斯·杰斯珀森会在必要时做出最大的牺牲来除掉亚历克斯·巴克斯特。

Alex had made the arrangements, stopped in as usual to check in with Claude and get reports and discussed the progress had Brad pick him up in his rental car as to reduce visibility and throw off the newspaper bird-dogs if there were any.

亚历克斯已做好安排，像往常一样停下来与克劳德核对并获取报告，并讨论进展情况，让布拉德开着租来的车来接他，以降低能见度并甩掉报纸的追捕者（如果有的话）。

At 2:55 p.m. Christina walked out of her office, five minutes ahead of the crowd who feared getting fired by leaving early, watching Christina glide out of the office with a smile. By the time they made it down to the ground floor, Christina was long gone.

下午 2:55，克里斯蒂娜走出办公室，比那些担心提前离开被解雇的人群早了五分钟，他们面带微笑地看着她从办公室里溜出来。当他们下到一楼时，克里斯蒂娜早已不见踪影。

Because of the timing, Christina stood inside the building until the Limo pulled up exactly at 3:00, then she walked out and just as Alex had said, Rodriguez rolled down the window, whom she instantly recognized, and Leroy knew by now the rumors opened the car door and she got in and Rodriguez drove her home, where her mother was waiting with her suitcase, at the curb.

由于时间原因，克里斯蒂娜一直站在大楼里，直到豪华轿车在 3:00 准时停下，然后她走了出来，正如亚历克斯所说的，罗德里格斯摇下了车窗，她立刻认出了他，勒罗伊现在也知道谣言了，他打开了车门，她上了车，罗德里格斯开车送她回家，她的母亲拿着行李箱在路边等着。

CHRISTINA'S MOTHER
Be careful and don't make any mistakes.

克里斯蒂娜的母亲
要小心，不要犯任何错误。

CHRISTINA
Thank you, mother, I know Alex's sincere.

克里斯蒂娜
谢谢你，妈妈，我知道亚历克斯是真诚的。

CHRISTINA'S MOTHER
Alex's a complicated man and has a lot of issues because who he is. You already know how your privacy has been destroyed. It's only going to get worse.

克里斯蒂娜的母亲
亚历克斯是个复杂的人，因为他的身份，他有很多问题。你已经知道你的隐私是如何被破坏的。情况只会变得更糟。

CHRISTINA
Well, if it works out, then it will be worth it.
克里斯蒂娜
如果成功了，那就值得了。

CHRISTINA'S MOTHER
Okay Christina, text me, let me know where you go and that you're safe.

克里斯蒂娜的母亲

好的克里斯蒂娜，给我打电话，告诉我你去哪里了，是否安全。

CHRISTINA
Alex will keep me safe. I'm sure of that.

克里斯蒂娜
亚历克斯会保护我的安全。我相信这一点。

CHRISTINA'S MOTHER
Okay Christina, have a good time.

克里斯蒂娜的母亲
好的克里斯蒂娜，玩得开心。

They hugged and then Rodriguez had her luggage in the trunk, and Christina climbed into the Limo, then Rodriguez shut the door, then got in and drove off.

他们拥抱了一下，然后罗德里格斯把行李放进了后备箱，克里斯蒂娜爬进了豪华轿车，然后罗德里格斯关上了车门，然后上车开车走了。

About a half a block away, a private detective in a car parked, taking notes, called the reporter who paid him.

大约半个街区外，一个停在车里做笔记的私家侦探打电话给付钱给他的记者。

PRIVATE DETECTIVE
Limo just picked up Christina Garrison, she had luggage, they're going somewhere.

私家侦探
豪华轿车刚刚接走了克里斯蒂娜·加里森，她有行李，他们要去某个地方。

NEWSPAPER REPORTER
Get the license plate number?

报纸记者
拿到车牌号了吗？
PRIVATE DETECTIVE
Yes.

私家侦探
是的。

NEWSPAPER REPORTER
Great.

报纸记者
太好了。

In 35 minutes, the Limo pulled up to the curb of the hanger, Rodriguez got out, opened the trunk and pulled out Christina's luggage. Alex was right there with John Black and they both grabbed her luggage and walked into the office space adjacent to the hanger down the hallway and out into the hanger where Brad was standing next to the plane.

35 分钟后，豪华轿车停在机库边上，罗德里格斯下车，打开后备箱，拿出克里斯蒂娜的行李。亚历克斯和约翰·布莱克就在那里，他们俩都抓起她的行李，沿着走廊走进机库旁边的办公室，从隔壁的门走进机库，布拉德正站在飞机旁边。

Few women can say their lover took them too Greenland on their first romantic sojourn. But this was just a temporary stopover, and it was on the way to Europe. Alex sat in his seat on the starboard side with the view of the cockpit and pilot and Christina was seated next to him across the aisle.

很少有女人能说她们的爱人在她们的第一次浪漫之旅中就带她们去了格陵兰岛。但这只是一次短暂的停留，而且是在前往欧洲的途中。亚历克斯坐在右舷的座位上，可以看到驾驶舱和飞行员，克里斯蒂娜坐在过道对面的旁边。

There was essentially no way under the circumstances that Alex could have Stephanie aboard with her past role as administrative assistant and flight attendant. Neither woman would be comfortable and would probably have put a damper on things.

在这种情况下，亚历克斯根本不可能让斯蒂芬妮上飞机，因为她过去担任行政助理和空乘。这两个女人都不会舒服，而且可能会给事情带来不利影响。

But to help make Christina more comfortable, Alex used a professional flight attendant who worked for a major airline from time to time, mainly to allow Stephanie a lot of time off but also to sustain operations for multiple flights over numerous days because sometimes he would have to send his plane places with special guests without him or Stephanie.

但为了让克里斯蒂娜更舒服，，亚历克斯不时聘请了一位在一家大型航空公司工作的专业空乘人员，主要是为了让斯蒂芬妮有很多休息时间，同时也是为了在数天内维持多个航班的运营，因为有时他不得不在没有他或斯蒂芬妮的情况下将他的飞机派往载有特殊客人的地方

In some cases, people in the INTEL business paid Alex to fly their agents places they could not get to otherwise. It was best that Stephanie never knew of those missions for her own safety.

在某些情况下，英特尔公司的人付钱给亚历克斯，让他飞到他们代理人无法到达的地方。为了她自己的安全，斯蒂芬妮最好不要知道这些任务。

The flight attendant Gladys was very cheerful, she wasn't beautiful and had seen her better days, but few flight attendants were better. She was a very polite and intelligent person who got along well with Brad.

空乘人员格拉迪斯非常开朗，她并不漂亮，也曾有过辉煌的日子，但很少有空乘人员比她更好。她是一个非常有礼貌和聪明的人，和布拉德相处得很好。

BRAD
He's taking his new girlfriend to Switzerland.

布拉德
他要带他的新女友去瑞士。

GLADYS
Does Stephanie know about it.

格拉迪斯
斯蒂芬妮知道吗？

BRAD
The word is Stephanie knows. Alex was photographed with Christina and that picture showed up in the gossip section of a New York newspaper. Kind of hard to hide it now.

布拉德
据说斯蒂芬妮知道。亚历克斯和克里斯蒂娜合影，那张照片出现在纽约一家报纸的八卦栏目上。现在很难掩盖它了。

GLADYS
Why the stop in Greenland?

格拉迪斯
为什么在格陵兰停留？

BRAD
Alex wants to see the progress on the dome, the pillars are slowly growing and in May they are scheduled to install the first roof sections.

布拉德
亚历克斯想看看圆顶的进展情况，柱子正在慢慢长大，他们计划在五月安装第一批屋顶部分。

Alex and Christina arrived moments later and climbed aboard the jet.

片刻之后，亚历克斯和克里斯蒂娜抵达并登上飞机。

Alex helped Christina up into the Gulfstream 650, meanwhile Brad tied down her luggage in the cargo bay and latched it shut. He then shook John Black's hand, and climbed up the ladder then pulled it up and shut the plane's door and proceeded to the cockpit.

亚历克斯帮助克里斯蒂娜登上湾流 650 飞机，与此同时，布拉德把她的行李绑在货舱里，用闩锁锁好。然后他握了握约翰·布莱克的手，爬上梯子，拉起梯子，关上飞机门，走进驾驶舱。

ALEX
Gladys, let me introduce you to my special friend Christina.

亚历克斯
格拉迪斯，让我向你介绍我的好朋友克里斯蒂娜。

GLADYS
Pleased to meet you, Christina.

格拉迪斯
很高兴见到你，克里斯蒂娜。

CHRISTINA
Thank you. Good to meet you as well.

克里斯蒂娜
谢谢你。我也很高兴见到你。

BRAD
Christina, I promise not to jet jockey the plane today. Alex likes it nice and smooth.

布拉德
克里斯蒂娜，我保证今天不会在飞机上操纵飞机。亚历克斯喜欢平稳的飞行。

CHRISTINA
I appreciate that.

克里斯蒂娜
我很感激。

Brad had tipped off Gladys that Alex was madly in love with Christina in a discussion they had before Alex arrived.

在亚历克斯到达之前，布拉德曾与格拉迪斯讨论过亚历克斯疯狂地爱着克里斯蒂娜。

Thanks to Gladys, who took care of them very nicely, Christina was put to ease and felt welcome and important.

感谢格拉迪斯对他们的悉心照顾，克里斯蒂娜感到轻松自在，感到受欢迎且受重视。

As soon as Brad sat down and put on the headphones, he told the Plane-Tug driver to go ahead and pull the plane out of the hanger. In a short while the preflight checks were completed, the engines were brought up online and the jet was given permission to taxi to the runway for takeoff.

布拉德一坐下戴上耳机，就告诉飞机拖船司机继续把飞机从机库里拖出来。不一会儿，飞行前检查就完成了，发动机启动，飞机获准滑行到跑道起飞。

INT. DAY. ALEX'S GS650 READY TO DEPART.

白天内景。亚历克斯的 GS650 准备起飞。

Everyone was soon in their seats ready for take-off. Alex was in a swivel seat facing aft looking at Christina smiling and happy. The chitchat would not begin until they were airborne, Gladys served them coffee and snacks which Alex liked on these long flights.

很快，每个人都坐到座位上准备起飞。亚历克斯坐在面向后方的旋转座椅上，面带微笑，开心地看着克里斯蒂娜。直到他们起飞后，他们才开始闲聊，格拉迪斯为他们端上了咖啡和零食，亚历克斯在长途飞行中很喜欢这些零食。

EXT. DAY. JFK-NYC. ALEX'S GS650 TAKEOFF. (15 SECONDS).

白天外景。肯尼迪机场飞往纽约。亚历克斯的 GS650 起飞。（15 秒）。

During the climb up to cruising altitude, it was quiet, nobody was talking. Most aircraft disasters happen during takeoff or landing. Out of that knowledge Alex conducted himself like a song he once heard:

THE TREMELOES - "SILENCE is GOLDEN" 1971 & 1983

在爬升至巡航高度的过程中，一切都很安静，没有人说话。大多数飞机事故都发生在起飞或降落期间。亚历克斯意识到这一点，他表现得就像他曾经听过的一首歌：

颤音乐团 (THE TREMELOES) - "沉默是金" 1971 年和 1983 年

INT. DAY ALEX'S GS650 PASSENGER CABIN UP AT CRUISING ALTITUDE

白天内景 亚历克斯的 GS650 客舱处于巡航高度

GLADYS
Christina, would you like some coffee and snacks?

格拉迪斯
克里斯蒂娜，你要喝点咖啡和吃点零食吗？

CHRISTINA
Sure, that sounds good.

克里斯蒂娜
当然，听起来不错。

Gladys served Christina and Alex, then walked into the cockpit and asked Brad if he wanted some coffee. Brad was more than happy to have the coffee.

格拉迪斯为克里斯蒂娜和亚历克斯服务，然后走进驾驶舱，问布拉德是否想要喝咖啡。布拉德非常乐意喝咖啡。

Time passed quickly and the plane was starting its descent down to Nuuk airport. Alex asked Christina:

时间过得很快，飞机开始降落到努克机场。亚历克斯问克里斯蒂娜：

ALEX
Christina, would you like to sit up in the Copilot's chair while we land?

亚历克斯
克里斯蒂娜，我们降落的时候你想坐在副驾驶的椅子上吗？

CHRISTINA
Sure, that would be kind of fun.

克里斯蒂娜
当然，那会很有趣。

ALEX
Go ahead and go up there, Brad will enjoy the company.

亚历克斯
去那里吧，布拉德会喜欢你的陪伴的。

CHRISTINA
Okay.

克里斯蒂娜
好的。

ALEX
And be sure to put the headphones on and listen to the
air traffic controller, you might be amused.

亚历克斯
一定要戴上耳机，听听空中交通管制员的话，你
可能会觉得很有趣。

CHRISTINA
Alright.

克里斯蒂娜
好吧。

Christina was a welcome member of the cockpit crew. It didn't bother Brad one bit to
have a very beautiful woman sitting in the co-pilot seat. Eyeball liberty is always good.

克里斯蒂娜是机舱乘务员中很受欢迎的成员。布拉德一点也不介意副驾驶座位
上坐着一位非常漂亮的女人。视线自由总是好的。

The plane soon touched down, and Christina enjoyed the bird's eye view from the
cockpit.

飞机很快就降落了，克里斯蒂娜从机舱欣赏着鸟瞰的景色。

The plane was not pulled into the hanger because they would not be in Greenland very
long. Brad and Gladys stayed with the plane and the customs official easily checked
Alex and Christina thru because they left their luggage on the plane.

飞机没有被拉进机库，因为他们在格陵兰岛停留的时间不长。布拉德和格拉迪
斯留在飞机上，海关官员很容易就检查了亚历克斯和克里斯蒂娜，因为他们把
行李留在了飞机上。

Limo was waiting for them outside the hanger building, which they quickly got in.

豪华轿车在机库大楼外等着他们，他们很快就上了车。

ALEX
Take us over to Nuuk Dome Inc. offices.

亚历克斯
带我们去努克圆顶公司办公室。

LIMO DRIVER
Yes sir, Mr. Baxter.

豪华轿车司机
是的，巴克斯特先生。

In about five minutes they pulled into the parking lot and a reserved spot right in front of the main entrance. Alex took Christina into the building and introduced her to Jeff Sinclair who then asked:

大约五分钟后，他们驶入停车场，在正门前有一个预留车位。亚历克斯把克里斯蒂娜带进大楼，把她介绍给杰夫·辛克莱，然后杰夫问道：

JEFF SINCLAIR
Would you like to go look at the pillars?

杰夫·辛克莱
你想去看看柱子吗？

ALEX
Definitely.

亚历克斯
当然。

JEFF SINCLAIR
Let's go up in the Range Rover; the road is rough in places.

杰夫·辛克莱
我们坐路虎上去吧；这条路有些地方很崎岖。

ALEX
Sure.

亚历克斯
当然。

五分钟后，他们就到了工作现场。

In five minutes, they were at the work site.

Alex got out, and not too far from him were stevedores moving materials in and out of containers just offloaded from a ship. *Hans Jespersen* for a few minutes was 30 meters away from Alex and he spotted him with Jeff Sinclair. *Hans Jespersen's* passions elevated and if he had a weapon with him that moment, he would have *risked life in prison for the chance to kill Alex and his girlfriend bimbo with him.*

亚历克斯下了车，离他不远的地方有装卸工在把材料从船上卸下来的集装箱里搬进搬出。几分钟后，汉斯·杰斯珀森就在离亚历克斯 30 米远的地方，他发现他和杰夫·辛克莱在一起。汉斯·杰斯珀森怒不可遏，如果当时他手里有武器，他会冒着终身监禁的风险，杀死亚历克斯和他身边的花瓶女友。

In the 2 weeks since Alex had last seen the pillars a lot of work had been done. They were now sticking up almost 200 feet. It looked kind of eerie. Also, the hill was about half its original height and a lot of material had been removed and from a distance, Alex could see rock piles formed from the debris of the explosions and earth moving operations going on.

自从亚历克斯上次看到柱子以来的两周里，已经做了很多工作。它们现在几乎有 200 英尺高。看起来有点怪异。此外，这座山的高度只有原来的一半，很多材料都被移走了，从远处，亚历克斯可以看到爆炸和土方工程的碎片形成的岩石堆。

The sight of the pillars and the construction site had a huge psychological impact on Christina. Seeing all this in person was so much different than reading about it in the newspaper or looking at internet stories.

看到这些柱子和施工现场对克里斯蒂娜产生了巨大的心理影响。亲眼目睹这一切与在报纸上读到或在网上看到的故事大不相同。

Alex and Christina watched the cranes lifting buckets of concrete on the six different pillars going up in parallel. All this incredible development drew Christina closer to Alex.

亚历克斯和克里斯蒂娜看着起重机将一桶桶混凝土吊到六根平行竖立的柱子上。这一切令人难以置信的进展让克里斯蒂娜与亚历克斯的关系更加亲密。

Christina felt Alex's awesome contribution to a very rare and incredible development, unlike society had experienced before.

克里斯蒂娜认为亚历克斯为社会做出了前所未有的罕见和令人难以置信的贡献。

ALEX
Looks good, Jeff.

亚历克斯
看起来不错，杰夫。

JEFF SINCLAIR
Right on schedule Alex. We will be transitioning to the
20-foot diameter sections soon.

杰夫·辛克莱
亚历克斯，一切按计划进行。我们很快就会过渡
到直径 20 英尺的部分。

ALEX
Ok, keep me posted, I might want to make a visit soon. Keep the emails coming; I enjoy looking at the pictures you send me.

亚历克斯
好的，请随时通知我，可能想尽快拜访一下。继续发邮件；我喜欢看你发给我的照片。

JEFF SINCLAIR
No problem, Alex.

杰夫·辛克莱
没问题，亚历克斯。

Jeff drove Alex and Christina back to the Greenland Dome Inc. offices. They transferred to the Limo and went back to the airport.

杰夫开车送亚历克斯和克里斯蒂娜回到格陵兰穹顶公司办公室。他们换乘豪华轿车返回机场。

Soon the Gulfstream 650 heading to Switzerland was back up in the air, with additional fuel taken on.

很快，飞往瑞士的湾流 650 又重新起飞，并加满了燃料。

Alex had a beautiful mansion in Switzerland. It overlooked a lake and was located next to a couple cottages once owned by Charles A. Lindbergh and the great psychoanalyst Carl Jung.

亚历克斯在瑞士有一座美丽的豪宅。它俯瞰着湖泊，毗邻查尔斯·A·林德伯格和伟大的心理分析学家卡尔·荣格曾经拥有的几间小屋。

Even though Alex didn't spend a lot of time in his mansion in Switzerland, a butler and a maid and a cook lived full time there as their secondary role was security of the home.

尽管亚历克斯并没有花很多时间在他位于瑞士的豪宅里，但一名管家、一名女仆和一名厨师全职住在那里，因为他们的次要职责是家庭安全。

Most of the time, the staff at Alex's mansion in Switzerland didn't have much to do but look out for each other. They enjoyed Alex visiting because life was boring without him.

大多数时候，亚历克斯瑞士豪宅的工作人员除了互相照顾外，没有太多事情可做。他们喜欢亚历克斯的来访，因为没有他，生活很无聊。

Alex's GS650 arrived at Geneva's Airport at an Aircraft Services company he used when he was in Geneva. They provided him jet fuel, push back service, passenger steps, luggage handlers, toilet and water service, ground power unit, air start unit, and hangarage, especially during the winter.

亚历克斯的 GS650 抵达日内瓦机场，由他在日内瓦时使用的一家航空服务公司提供服务。他们为他提供喷气燃料、后推服务、乘客台阶、行李搬运工、卫生间和供水服务、地面电源装置、空中启动装置和机库，尤其是在冬天。

Alex and Christina breezed through the air services company building with prefilled out customs forms that were merely stamped and they were soon out to curb side with Alex's employee loading up their small amount of luggage into the trunk of the Rolls Royce purple Spectre.

亚历克斯和克里斯蒂娜拿着预先填好的海关表格轻松地穿过航空服务公司大楼，这些表格只是盖了章，他们很快就到了路边，亚历克斯的员工把他们少量的行李装进了劳斯莱斯紫色幽灵的后备箱。

This Rolls Royce Spectre was a stretch model about six feet longer than a normal production Spectre allowing the amenities of a Limo.

这辆 劳斯莱斯幽灵 (Rolls Royce Spectre) 是一款加长版车型，比普通量产版 幽灵(Spectre) 长约 六英尺，可提供豪华轿车的舒适设施。

The drive to Alex's mansion wasn't long and Christina got to see a little of the countryside and Lake Geneva that seemed huge for such a small country.

开车去亚历克斯的豪宅没多久，克里斯蒂娜看到了乡村和日内瓦湖的景色，对于这样一个小国来说，日内瓦湖似乎很大。

A man named Grant was driving and called ahead to tell the staff when they were ab out five minutes away.

一个名叫格兰特的男人在开车，他提前打电话告诉工作人员他们还有五分钟就到了。

When the Rolls Royce pulled into the circular driveway, the staff was outside waiting to meet and greet the beautiful princess Alex was bringing. They had seen some of the Yellow Journalism reports and high-fidelity pictures that were published and were mildly impressed by Alex's fantastic taste in women, even more so Alex was bringing Christina here for a quick stopover.

当劳斯莱斯驶入环形车道时，工作人员正在外面等着迎接亚历克斯带来的美丽公主。他们看过一些黄色新闻报道和高保真图片，对亚历克斯对女人的绝妙品味印象深刻，亚历克斯带克里斯蒂娜来这里短暂停留更是令人难忘。

The maid, Mary is a beautiful blonde German lady 24 years old who feared she would become an old maid and had a fantasy that someday Alex would pick her. The Butler was Grant, and the cook Chris.

女仆玛丽是一位 24 岁的金发美女德国女士，她担心自己会成为老处女，幻想有一天亚历克斯会选择她。管家是格兰特，厨师是克里斯。

To Christina's surprise she had her own private bedroom.

令克里斯蒂娜惊讶的是，她有自己的私人卧室。

Mary led Christina to her private bedroom to show her a few things and allow her to freshen up if she needed from the long flight and drive to the mansion.

玛丽把克里斯蒂娜带到她的私人卧室，给她看了几件东西，让她在长途飞行和开车去豪宅后梳洗一番。

MARY<br>
Alex wants you to feel you will always have privacy<br>
and never feel any kind of pressure.

玛丽<br>
亚历克斯希望你永远有隐私，永远不会感到任何<br>
压力。

CHRISTINA<br>
Alex keeps proving to me he's a true gentleman.

克里斯蒂娜<br>
亚历克斯一直向我证明他是一位真正的绅士。

MARY<br>
I doubt we will meet many men like Alex who is kind<br>
and gentle.

玛丽<br>
我怀疑我们不会遇到很多像亚历克斯这样善良温<br>
柔的男人。

The staff were professionals and did their jobs quite well. They were happy, paid well, and allowed a lot of time off if Alex wasn't in Switzerland. The only requirement is, at least one of the 3 had to be always at the mansion for security reasons.

工作人员都很专业，工作做得相当好。他们很开心，薪水很高，如果亚历克斯不在瑞士，他们有很多休假时间。唯一的要求是，出于安全原因，这三个人中至少有一个人必须一直在豪宅里。

If the two men were going to be gone at the same time, Alex wanted them to have a security guy there, who was former French Foreign Legion Special Forces guy, Maurice.

如果这两个人要同时离开，亚历克斯希望他们有一个保安在那里，这个人是前法国外籍军团特种部队的莫里斯。

Probably one third of the year, Maurice was staying there. Mary preferred Maurice to be there as she felt safer when he was available. She had low confidence that Grant and Chris could protect her as well as Maurice.

一年中大概有三分之一的时间，莫里斯都住在那里。玛丽更希望莫里斯在那里，因为当他在的时候，她会觉得更安全。她对格兰特和克里斯能否像保护莫里斯一样保护她没有信心。

It was getting late so after showing Christina around they all decided it was bedtime.

天色已晚，所以在带克里斯蒂娜四处参观后，他们都决定该睡觉了。

Soon everyone was sleeping. Alex's bedroom was right across from Christina's. To make Christina feel safer, Mary was in the room next to her. Christina, like all the rooms had their own private bathrooms.

很快大家都睡着了。亚历克斯的卧室就在克里斯蒂娜的卧室对面的走廊上。为了让克里斯蒂娜感到更安全，玛丽住在她旁边的房间里。克里斯蒂娜喜欢所有的房间都有自己的私人浴室。

Christina laid there sleepless for a few minutes and knew she was too wound up to sleep any time soon. She was in her pajamas. Finally, she had enough. Christina got up quietly and shut her door behind her as she left her room and went across the hall.

克里斯蒂娜在那里躺了几分钟，一夜未眠，她知道自己太紧张了，一时半会儿睡不着。她穿着睡衣。最后，她受够了。克里斯蒂娜悄悄地起身，关上身后的门，离开了房间，穿过走廊。

Mary heard the unmistakable door latch click when Christina closed it. Then she heard the door open to Alex room. Mary smiled.

玛丽听到克里斯蒂娜关门时门闩发出的咔哒声。然后她听到亚历克斯房间的门打开了。玛丽笑了。

The room was dark but there was a little light given off from a digital clock radio, just enough for her to see the bed ahead.

房间里很暗，但数字时钟收音机发出一点光亮，刚好够她看清前面的床。

As Christina slowly approached Alex's bed she had surreal thoughts.

克里斯蒂娜慢慢走近亚历克斯的床，她产生了超现实的想法。

CHRISTINA
(Thought)
*Oh God I hope I'm not making a mistake.*

克里斯蒂娜

(想)

哦，天哪，我希望我没有弄错。

It must have been intuition that Alex had that she would come to him and could feel her come to the bed. He reached up and touched her as she climbed onto the bed and slid under the blankets with him.

亚历克斯一定是直觉让她来到他身边，能感觉到她来到床上。他伸手触摸她，她爬上床，和他一起钻进毯子里。

The electricity was floating in the air; the caldrons of emotions were overflowing. Anticipation was gripping Christina and Alex as they soon embraced.

空气中飘荡着电流；情感的漩涡四溢。克里斯蒂娜和亚历克斯很快就拥抱在一起，期待之情油然而生。

Finally in the privacy, the security, and the presence of each other, they didn't even think about sex, they just embraced and held each other like old friends for a long time, then when Alex could no longer hold back, he kissed Christina.

最后，在私密、安全、彼此陪伴的情况下，他们甚至没有想到性爱，只是像老朋友一样拥抱在一起，久久不散，然后当亚历克斯再也忍不住时，他吻了克里斯蒂娜。

Christina kissed Alex back. Their affection and mutual attraction soon ascended into splendid euphoria with an explosive release of pent-up demand.

克里斯蒂娜也吻了亚历克斯。他们的感情和相互吸引很快就上升为极度的兴奋，压抑的需求得到了爆发性的释放。

Mary had a few run-ins with Stephanie in the past. Mary wasn't making any attempts on Alex but Stephanie, who was so extremely paranoid and selfish, treated Mary as if she were a bitter rival.

玛丽过去曾与斯蒂芬妮发生过几次冲突。玛丽并没有试图对亚历克斯下手，但斯蒂芬妮非常偏执和自私，她对待玛丽就像对待自己的死对头一样。

Mary had no designs on Alex, because she came from a background where a class system existed and knew her boundaries, she never made any effort to cross.

玛丽对亚历克斯没有任何企图，因为她来自一个存在阶级制度的背景，知道自己的界限，她从未试图跨越。

Mary also had good hearing, and her bitterness towards Stephanie blossomed in sheer delight when as quiet as the couple tried to be, the sound of love and joy could not be fully disguised or hidden. Mary smiled throughout. Tomorrow would be a great day for Mary knowing Stephanie lost Alex.

玛丽的听力也很好，当这对夫妇试图保持安静时，她对斯蒂芬妮的怨恨在纯粹的喜悦中绽放，爱和喜悦的声音无法完全掩饰或隐藏。玛丽一直面带微笑。知道斯蒂芬妮失去了亚历克斯，明天对玛丽来说将是美好的一天。

The staff knew better than disturbing Alex or interfering with his current situation. And thus, they made no effort to wake him, nor did they allow anyone to call or disturb him in any way.

工作人员知道最好不要打扰亚历克斯或干涉他的现状。因此，他们没有试图叫醒他，也不允许任何人打电话或以任何方式打扰他。

Somehow Stephanie discovered Alex had gone to Switzerland and she had already called this morning and wanted to talk to him. She was put on ice for several hours.

不知怎么的，斯蒂芬妮发现亚历克斯去了瑞士，她今天早上已经打电话想和他谈谈。她被冰敷了几个小时。

Eventually the two lovebirds awoke, and it was a new and glorious day.

最终，这对情侣醒了，这是崭新的、美好的一天。

Mary waited until Christina was taking a bath before she had a private moment to inform Alex:

玛丽等到克里斯蒂娜洗澡时才有时间告诉亚历克斯：

MARY
Stephanie called and wanted to talk to you.

玛丽
斯蒂芬妮打电话来想和你谈谈。

ALEX
I wonder how the hell she found out I was here.

亚历克斯
我不知道她是怎么知道我在这里的。

MARY
Obviously, you have got someone working for you
who has a big mouth.

玛丽
显然，你雇了一个大嘴巴的人为你工作。

ALEX
I'll have to find out.

亚历克斯

我得去查一下。

One thing Alex had figured out, Mary always sided with him. She was definitely on his side, and he had heard some rumors that Mary and Stephanie didn't get along.

亚历克斯发现有一件事，玛丽总是站在他一边。她肯定站在他那边，他听到一些传言说玛丽和斯蒂芬妮相处不融洽。

Alex suspected he knew what Stephanie wanted to talk to him about, she would be angry if he didn't take her to Greenland the day scheduled to start installing the roof starting sometime in May. And that was right around the corner.

亚历克斯怀疑他知道斯蒂芬妮想和他谈什么，如果他不在计划于 5 月开始安装屋顶的那一天带她去格陵兰，她会生气的。而那就在眼前。

That was going to be a logistical problem. As it turned out Christina still wanted to work and was going to be busy during that week, so taking Stephanie there would not be a problem other than any possible confrontation that might come up if Stephanie was to ask: "Why am I not good enough?"

这将是一个后勤问题。事实证明，克里斯蒂娜仍然想工作，而且那一周会很忙，所以带斯蒂芬妮去那里不会有问题，除非斯蒂芬妮问："为什么我不够好？" 可能会发生冲突。

Alex put all that out of his mind for now as he had a surprise he was going to spring on Christina, since they had such a short time and would have to go back to New York in time for her to go to work on Monday.

亚历克斯暂时把这些都抛在脑后，因为他要给克里斯蒂娜一个惊喜，因为他们的时间很短，周一必须赶回纽约，让她上班。

Alex had rented a private rail car, equipped with a 2nd car with staff and in a few hours, they were going to the train station where the private car would be hooked to a passenger train rear end, and Christina was going to get a tour by rail of Switzerland for the day, then be back in the evening. Alex was going to take Christina to the symphony after the train sight-seeing.

亚历克斯租了一辆私人火车车厢，车厢里有第二节车厢和工作人员，几个小时后，他们就要去火车站，在那里，私人车厢将被挂在客运列车的尾部，克里斯蒂娜将乘坐火车游览瑞士，然后晚上返回。亚历克斯打算在火车观光后带克里斯蒂娜去听交响乐。

Alex requested Mary's help:

亚历克斯请求玛丽的帮助：

ALEX

Mary, I want you to go with Christina and get her size

and go out and get a couple evening gowns for her to wear tonight. Get four or five couture dresses and maybe you'll pick one she will like and wear. Also bring in a hair stylist so she can change her hair to however she wants; maybe put it up in a bun in the back.

亚历克斯
玛丽，我想让你和克里斯蒂娜一起去量一下她的尺码，然后出去买几件晚礼服让她今晚穿。买四五件高级定制礼服，也许你会选一件她会喜欢并穿上的。还要带上一位发型师，这样她就可以随心所欲地改变发型；也许可以把头发在后面扎成一个发髻。

Alex's staff was wonderful; he knew he could count on them.

亚历克斯的员工很棒；他知道他可以信赖他们。

CHRISTINA
Alex, is it ok if I take a few pictures during our trip?

克里斯蒂娜
亚历克斯，我在旅途中拍几张照片可以吗？

ALEX
Take all you want; you're my sweetheart now.

亚历克斯
想拍多少就拍多少，你现在是我的爱人了。

Christina loved the way Alex said that and smiled.

克里斯蒂娜喜欢亚历克斯说这话的方式，并微笑着。

CHRISTINA
Can I text some pictures to my mother? She's very discreet.

克里斯蒂娜
我可以给我妈妈发几张照片吗？她很谨慎。

ALEX
I don't mind you taking a lot of pictures and sending them to your mother but remember you and I have a security problem and if those pictures get out it might get rough for you at work and elsewhere.

亚历克斯
我不介意你拍很多照片并发给你妈妈，但请记
住，你和我都有安全问题，如果这些照片泄露出
去，可能会给你的工作和其他地方带来麻烦。

CHRISTINA
Don't worry, my mom will only show my dad.

克里斯蒂娜
别担心，我妈妈只会给我爸爸看。

They rode to the train station in the Rolls Royce. The car pulled up right next to the private cars they would board. Fifteen minutes later the train left, and Christina now got to see the picturesque countryside of Switzerland.

他们乘坐劳斯莱斯前往火车站。车停在他们要乘坐的私家车旁边。十五分钟后，火车开动了，克里斯蒂娜看到了风景如画的瑞士乡村。

The train pulled through many villages and passed a lot of other trains on the double track mainline.

火车穿过许多村庄，在双轨干线上与许多其他火车擦肩而过。

One quickly got the notion the Swiss were proud people, and they took care of their properties. The entire Swiss rail system was fully integrated into everyday life.

人们很快就意识到瑞士人是骄傲的民族，他们非常爱护自己的财产。整个瑞士铁路系统完全融入了日常生活。

Commuting by rail in Switzerland was one of the major methods of transportation to work as well as vacationers going on a Holiday.

在瑞士，乘火车上下班是上班和度假的主要交通方式之一。

In Switzerland because of the early and late year skiing, the small country was a tourist mecca year-round.

由于早年和晚年滑雪的兴起，瑞士这个小国全年都是旅游胜地。

Many Americans and Europeans spent Christmas in Switzerland because the Christmas decorations were spectacular and the craftsmanship story book quality. And many tourists purchased the fabulous Swiss Christmas decorations back with them and decorated their own trees in years to come.

许多美国人和欧洲人在瑞士过圣诞节，因为瑞士的圣诞装饰非常壮观，工艺精湛，堪比故事书。许多游客购买了精美的瑞士圣诞装饰，并在几年后装饰了自己的圣诞树。

In a way Alex felt sorry for Christina. If she ever rode trains in America in the future, she would be seriously disappointed because of these special memories she now obtained.

在某种程度上，亚历克斯为克里斯蒂娜感到难过。如果她将来在美国坐火车，她会因为现在获得的这些特殊记忆而感到非常失望。

After the train pulled back into the station in the late afternoon, they got back into the Rolls-Royce and went back to the mansion, where they changed their clothes, and prepared themselves for the symphony playing that evening.

火车在傍晚回到车站后，他们回到劳斯莱斯，回到豪宅，换了衣服，为当晚的交响乐做好准备。

The Orchestre de la Suisse Romande (OSR) is the Swiss symphony orchestra, based in Geneva at Victoria Hall.

瑞士罗曼德管弦乐团 (OSR) 是瑞士交响乐团，总部位于日内瓦维多利亚音乐厅。

The hairdresser pulled Christina's hair up into a bun in the back and Mary put diamonds on Christina's ears, a bracelet, and a necklace.

理发师将克里斯蒂娜的头发在后面扎成发髻，玛丽为克里斯蒂娜的耳朵镶上钻石，并戴上手镯和项链。

CHRISTINA
Thank you for loaning me this lovely jewelry.

克里斯蒂娜
谢谢你借给我这些漂亮的珠宝。

Mary smiled and responded.

玛丽微笑着回答道。

MARY
Christina, that is not my jewelry, it's your jewelry.

玛丽
克里斯蒂娜，那不是我的珠宝，是你的珠宝。

CHRISTINA
You must be mistaken.

克里斯蒂娜
你肯定搞错了。

MARY
No, I'm certain that Mr. Baxter bought all that for you.
He just forgot to tell you.

玛丽
不，我敢肯定这些都是巴克斯特先生给你买的。
他只是忘了告诉你。

Christina was stunned; she was probably wearing a million dollars' worth of diamonds.

克里斯蒂娜惊呆了；她戴的钻石可能价值一百万美元。

Soon, Christina was ready, and Alex was notified as Mary brought out his beautiful date.

很快，克里斯蒂娜准备好了，玛丽带出他美丽的约会对象，亚历克斯也收到了通知。

MARY
Isn't Christina so beautiful?

玛丽
克里斯蒂娜不是很漂亮吗？

ALEX
Mary, could you do me a favor and take a couple pictures for us?

亚历克斯
玛丽，你能帮我个忙，帮我们拍几张照片吗？

Alex handed Mary his cell phone.

亚历克斯把手机递给玛丽。

After the pictures were taken, Alex looked at them and commented.

拍完照片后，亚历克斯看着它们，评论道。

ALEX
Christina looks very beautiful in these pictures. Now I have pictures of her I can look at during private moments.

亚历克斯
克里斯蒂娜在这些照片里看起来很漂亮。现在我有了她的照片，可以在私人时间看看。

Alex then text messaged the pictures to Christina who had her cell phone in the little purse that came with the evening gown she had on for the symphony.

随后，亚历克斯将这些照片发短信给克里斯蒂娜，克里斯蒂娜将手机放在了她参加交响乐会时穿的晚礼服的小钱包里。

ALEX
Christina, I sent those pictures to your cell phone so you can share them with your mother.

亚历克斯
克里斯蒂娜，我把这些照片发到你的手机上了，这样你就可以和你的妈妈分享了。

CHRISTINA
Thank you, Alex. Give me a minute so I can look at them.

克里斯蒂娜
谢谢你，亚历克斯。给我一分钟时间，我看看它们。

Grant drove the Stretch Rolls Royce Spectre taking Christine and Alex to the Geneva Victoria Concert Hall to watch the performance of Orchestre de la Suisse Romande (OSR) Swiss symphony orchestra Perform a Rachmaninoff's Piano Concerto Number Two followed by a Tchaikovsky Violin concerto.

格兰特开着加长版劳斯莱斯幽灵载着克里斯汀和亚历克斯前往日内瓦维多利亚音乐厅观看瑞士罗曼德管弦乐团（OSR）的演出。瑞士交响乐团演奏了拉赫玛尼诺夫的第二钢琴协奏曲，随后演奏了柴可夫斯基的小提琴协奏曲。

While they were traveling in the Stretch Rolls Royce Spectre, Christina looked at the pictures just taken of her all dressed up. The pictures were indeed lovely, and she then forwarded them to her mother.

当他们乘坐加长版劳斯莱斯幽灵旅行时，克里斯蒂娜看着刚刚拍下的自己盛装打扮的照片。这些照片确实很可爱，然后她把照片转发给了她的母亲。

Christina's mother was now getting concerned for her baby daughter, fearing she could one day soon get her heart crushed if the billionaire suddenly put his affection somewhere else.

克里斯蒂娜的母亲现在开始担心她的宝贝女儿，担心如果这位亿万富翁突然把他的感情放在别的地方，她有一天会心碎。

This was a trying time for Christina's mother, and equally concerned was her father, because his baby girl was so sweet he didn't want anyone to hurt her.

这对克里斯蒂娜的母亲来说是艰难的时刻，她的父亲也同样担心，因为他的宝贝女儿太可爱了，他不想让任何人伤害她。

The concert hall was one of the best in Europe. The acoustics were phenomenal, and the crowd had great expectations. Alex reserved one of the best sets of balcony seats in the concert hall. He bought the tickets for all six seats in that mini balcony, just to make sure they had complete privacy. Alex also could move the seats around to have a better angle at the stage.

音乐厅是欧洲最好的音乐厅之一。音响效果非常好，观众对音乐厅寄予厚望。亚历克斯预订了音乐厅最好的一组阳台座位。他买了那个小阳台上所有六个座位的票，以确保他们有完全的隐私。亚历克斯还可以移动座位，以便更好地观看舞台。

MUSIC FOR THE NEXT SECTION:

Yuja Wang: Rachmaninov Piano Concerto No. 2 in C minor Op. 18

下一节的音乐：

王羽佳：拉赫玛尼诺夫 C 小调第 2 号钢琴协奏曲，作品 18 ［高清］

Yuja Wang: Rachmaninov Piano Concerto No. 2 in C minor Op. 18 [HD]

Tonight, the first performance will be Rachmaninov Piano Concerto Number Two, one of Alex's favorites. Since that was a relatively short performance, the orchestra would also perform Tchaikovsky violin concerto afterwards.

今晚，第一场演出将是 亚历克斯 最喜欢的拉赫玛尼诺夫第二号钢琴协奏曲。由于这是一场相对较短的演出，乐团随后还将演奏柴可夫斯基的小提琴协奏曲。

Both performances had world class performers. The lights eventually dimmed and with the orchestra seated, the conductor and the pianist walked out on stage the female pianist, an Asian lady looked incredibly beautiful, and her glittery long dress added to the ambience and accelerated her persona especially the way she smiled and bowed.

两场演出都有世界级的表演者。灯光渐渐暗了下来，乐队成员就座，指挥和钢琴师走上舞台，女钢琴师是一位亚洲女士，看起来非常漂亮，她闪亮的长裙增添了气氛，增强了她的个性，尤其是她微笑和鞠躬的方式。

The conductor took his position in the middle of the stage on a platform with hand grabs around waste high in the event he wanted to steady himself. The noise in the concert hall slowly died down and when the conductor raised his baton, the silence had reached the point one could hear a pin drop, except for an occasional cough once every minute or two. Coughers at concerts terribly annoyed Alex who thought they should not be here distracting the audience.

指挥家站在舞台中央的平台上，双手高高地抓住腰部，以防他想稳住自己。音乐厅里的噪音慢慢消失了，当指挥举起指挥棒时，寂静到了可以听到针落地的程度，除了每隔一两分钟偶尔会咳嗽一次。音乐会上的咳嗽声让亚历克斯非常恼火，他认为他们不应该在这里分散观众的注意力。

The Rachmaninoff Piano Concerto performance began, and it conveyed a moment of blackness and bleakness that transcends towards a reflective passivity, then a delicate passage followed by a crescendo, sets the mood for the following discerning melody. One could remember old acquaintances and lovers about three minutes into the piece.

拉赫玛尼诺夫钢琴协奏曲开始演奏，它传达出一瞬间的黑暗和凄凉，然后超越反思的被动，然后是一段细腻的乐段，然后是高潮，为接下来的挑剔旋律奠定了基调。大约三分钟后，人们就会想起旧识和恋人。

The heavily stuffed chairs were very comfortable and with Christina to Alex's right, she was at the perfect angle for him to first touch her hand, then he held it in a most lovingly fashion.

厚厚的软垫椅子非常舒适，克里斯蒂娜坐在亚历克斯的右边，她的角度非常完美，他先是触摸她的手，然后以最深情的方式握住她的手。

The music poured through Alex's soul as he felt the essence of Christina in ways she could hardly imagine he felt.

当亚历克斯感受到克里斯蒂娜的本质时，音乐涌入他的灵魂，而克里斯蒂娜几乎无法想象他的感受。

VOICEOVER

*Alex knew he was falling in love with Christina. His psyche was drenched with ethereal orbs of passion that he had never experienced in his life.*

画外音

亚历克斯知道他爱上了克里斯蒂娜。他的心灵充满了他一生中从未经历过的空灵的激情。

*With all the money and opportunity, Alex had for lovely women, movie stars, and fashion models, he had yet to encounter desires and emotions like this. Cristina's magic had engulfed Alex's psyche completely, rendering him almost spellbound*

尽管亚历克斯拥有这么多金钱和机会，可以结识美丽的女人、电影明星和时装模特，但他还没有遇到过这样的欲望和情感。克里斯蒂娜的魔力完全吞噬了亚历克斯的心灵，让他几乎着迷。

*Alex cherished these euphoric moments that eclipsed his senses with a new foundation of splendor and surreal gratification.*

亚历克斯珍惜这些令人欣喜的时刻，这些时刻让他的感官被一种新的辉煌和超现实的满足感所淹没。

*As the music played on, Alex couldn't help but to look at Christina with many glances. Her dress, the diamonds, her hair arrangement, and the professional makeup that had been applied by one of the best makeover persons in Switzerland who specialized in making ultra-wealthy women more appealing to their suitors.*

随着音乐的播放，亚历克斯忍不住多看克里斯蒂娜一眼。她的礼服、钻石、发型，以及由瑞士最好的化妆师之一化的专业妆，这些化妆师专门让超级富婆对追求者更有吸引力。

The makeup designer had taken a beautiful woman, and with incredible precision multiplied her beauty 10-fold. Christina's co-workers would be utterly impressed if they witnessed this moment.

化妆师把一个美丽的女人，以令人难以置信的精准度让她的美丽增加了 10 倍。克里斯蒂娜的同事们如果目睹这一刻，一定会大为惊叹。

### VOICEOVER
*At the thirteen or so minute mark, when the soft clarinet rarified the piano in a lovely passage, Alex almost felt so overjoyed he had to work hard to restrain himself from allowing tears to escape his eyes.*

### 画外音
在 十三分钟左右的时候，当柔和的单簧管在一段优美的乐段中使钢琴变得稀疏时，亚历克斯几乎感到欣喜若狂，他不得不努力克制自己不让泪水流出眼眶。

*Alex was thus emotionally erupting, not to dissimilar to when you see major athletes at the Olympics win a gold medal or ice-skating championship and tear up and fight to not break down and cry. It was a very somber moment. Alex totally humbled by this woman, would never be the same person again for the rest of his life.*

亚历克斯因此情绪爆发，就像你看到奥运会上的
主要运动员赢得金牌或滑冰冠军时，泪流满面，
努力不哭出来一样。那是一个非常悲伤的时刻。
亚历克斯完全被这个女人折服了，在他的余生中
再也不会是同一个人了。

Christina was having the time of her life. She was utterly touched when Mary informed her, those were now her diamonds, worth more than her home.

克里斯蒂娜正在享受她一生中最美好的时光。当玛丽告诉她，那些现在是她的钻石，比她的家更值钱时，她完全被感动了。

Though she thought Alex was being a bad boy by delegating the responsibility to Mary to inform her of this delicate arrangement. Then with a wicked grin she said to herself:

虽然她认为亚历克斯把这个微妙的安排的责任委托给玛丽，这是个坏孩子。然后她带着邪恶的笑容对自己说：

CHRISTINA (Thought)
*I might just have to spank Alex tonight.*

克里斯蒂娜（想道）
今晚我可能得打亚历克斯的屁股了。

Then Christina asked herself:

然后克里斯蒂娜问自己：

CHRISTINA
(Thought)
*Is this really happening or am I dreaming?*

克里斯蒂娜
（想）
这是真的吗，还是我在做梦？

At around the 21-minute mark, when the performance very tenderly faded, Christina glanced towards Alex and saw him looking at her, he was smiling, and his smile was so cute. She suddenly felt moist, and her emotions suddenly gushed within her. She felt an incredible sensation and she couldn't help but squeeze his hand which he felt and responded.

大约 21 分钟时，当表演非常温柔地淡出时，克里斯蒂娜瞥了一眼亚历克斯，看到他在看着她，他在微笑，他的笑容太可爱了。她突然感到湿润，情绪突然涌上心头。她有一种难以置信的感觉，忍不住握紧了他的手，他感觉到了，并做出了回应。

Mary who was very sophisticated and had spent a lot of time being around and serving rich women, was an expert on their perfumes.

玛丽非常老练，花了很多时间与有钱的女人相处，为她们服务，是香水方面的专家。

The French made some of the very best perfumes. Mary took it upon herself to get several bottles of perfume to give Christina an aroma she knew would help seal the deal. And nothing would please Mary more than anything than help Christina ace Stephanie McFarland.

法国人制作了一些最好的香水。玛丽自告奋勇买了几瓶香水，给克里斯蒂娜一种她知道有助于达成交易的香味。没有什么比帮助克里斯蒂娜赢得斯蒂芬妮·麦克法兰更让玛丽高兴的了。

Christina didn't know this quite yet, but she had a team routing for her, the entire staff wanted Christina to win.

克里斯蒂娜还不知道这一点，但她有一个团队在为她加油，全体员工都希望克里斯蒂娜获胜。

As far as they were concerned, Christina is the most beautiful and friendly woman that ever came to the mansion.

在他们看来，克里斯蒂娜是来过这栋豪宅的最美丽、最友善的女人。

Christina was unassuming and not full of herself like the bimbo's Alex had invited over, and unfortunately for Stephanie, she was too pushy and wrongfully assumed her role with Alex was more than what it really was.

克里斯蒂娜谦逊，不像亚历克斯邀请来的花瓶那样自以为是，不幸的是，对于斯蒂芬妮来说，她太咄咄逼人，错误地认为她与亚历克斯的关系比实际更重要。

To some extent, that also may have played a factor in why Alex never crossed the line with Stephanie and consummated the relationship. And now with these developing events and future events, Alex knew how lucky he was that did not happen.

在某种程度上，这也可能是亚历克斯从未越过与斯蒂芬妮的界限并实现关系的原因之一。现在，随着这些事件的发展和未来的事件，亚历克斯知道他是多么幸运，没有发生这种事。

The strong passage at the 32-minute mark not only elevated the audience, but it was like the exclamation point on the emotions Alex and Christina now embraced.

32 分钟处的强劲段落不仅让观众兴奋不已，而且就像是亚历克斯和克里斯蒂娜现在所拥抱的情感的感叹号。

Then shortly the performance ended, the crowd was ecstatic. After all the applause and the pianist and conductor leaving the stage and coming back several times, the applause and the noise died down and one of the stagehands came out with a display board on a presentation easel that said: *Intermission*.

演出很快结束，观众欣喜若狂。在掌声雷动、钢琴师和指挥家离开舞台又回来几次之后，掌声和噪音渐渐平息，一位舞台工作人员拿着展示架上的展示板走出来，上面写着：中场休息。

Alex, suddenly feeling invigorated, suggested:

亚历克斯突然感到精神振奋，建议道：

ALEX
Would you like to get a glass of champagne?

亚历克斯
你想喝杯香槟吗？

Christina already feeling naturally high loved the idea, thinking it would add to the sensation she was feeling responded.

克里斯蒂娜自然而然地兴奋起来，她很喜欢这个主意，认为这会让她感觉更兴奋。

CHRISTINA
Sure, that would be great.

克里斯蒂娜
当然，那太好了。

The immaculately dressed waitresses walking thought the crowd took orders, and it would be a 20-minute intermission so some of them would have as many as two possibly three drinks, some being mixed cocktails.

穿着整洁的女服务员走来走去，以为观众在点菜，中间会有 20 分钟的休息时间，所以有些人会喝两杯甚至三杯，有些是混合鸡尾酒。

ALEX
Excuse me Miss, I would like a couple glasses of Dom
Perignon.

亚历克斯
对不起，小姐，我想要几杯唐培里侬香槟王。

WAITRESS
Yes, sir, right away.

女服务员
是的，先生，马上就来。

The waitress who had served Alex Baxter at numerous symphony performances knew he was a VIP and perhaps the wealthiest person present.

这位曾在多次交响乐表演中为亚历克斯·巴克斯特服务的女服务员知道他是贵宾，也许是在场最富有的人。

Alex was holding Christina's right hand with his left hand, they were probably the only people holding hands, but there were a couple women in Mink Coats with their arms wrapped around the arm of their Daddy Warbucks partners. It was plain to see that Alex and Christina were a couple and there seemed more to it than what met the naked eye.

亚历克斯用左手牵着克里斯蒂娜的右手，他们可能是唯一牵着手的人，但有几个穿着貂皮大衣的女人，胳膊搂着她们的爸爸沃巴克伙伴的胳膊。很明显，亚历克斯和克里斯蒂娜是一对情侣，而且似乎还有比肉眼所见更深刻的东西。

*Michelle Montez* the editor of *Magazine Femmes Réelles Exigeantes*, was prowling, the crowd sniffing a story and right in front of her about 20 feet away in a semi unobstructed view was none other than Mr. Dome, Alex Baxter.

《真实女性杂志》的主编米歇尔·蒙特兹正在四处走动，人群嗅到了这个故事，就在她面前大约 20 英尺远的地方，半无遮挡的视野中，正是圆顶先生亚历克斯·巴克斯特。

*MICHELLE MONTEZ*
(Thought)
*Here's the man who was creating an international stir*
*by the most expensive boondoggle in human history,*
*or so it was said.*

*If one collected all the media outlets commentary on*
*the subject matter it was easy to conclude the world*
*was betting against Alex.*

*He is simply lavishly wasting his money, which he had*
*plenty of only because he could and was doing it for*
*publicity it seems.*

米歇尔·蒙特兹
（想法）
据说，这个人通过人类历史上最昂贵的浪费引起
了国际轰动。

如果收集所有媒体对这个主题的评论，很容易得
出结论，全世界都在与亚历克斯作对。

他只是在挥霍他有很多钱，只是因为他可以这样
做，而且似乎是为了宣传。

At first *Michelle Montez* wondered if this glamorous woman with Mr. Dome a movie starlet gold digger or a new fashion model?

起初，米歇尔·蒙特兹想知道这位与圆顶先生在一起的迷人女人是电影明星淘金者还是新时装模特？

*MICHELLE MONTEZ*
(Thought)
*I will have to find out the details.*

米歇尔·蒙特兹
（想）
我得弄清楚细节。

*Michelle Montez* smelled a magazine cover coming up. The woman was so beautiful, that alone would sell copies, and all she had to do is add the salacious and scandalous details in the magazine article.

米歇尔·蒙特兹　嗅到了杂志封面的气味。这个女人太漂亮了，光是这一点就能卖出好几本，她所要做的就是在杂志文章中添加一些淫秽和丑闻的细节。

The rush was sitting in, as *Michelle Montez* knew she had just hit pay-dirt!

热潮正在袭来，因为 米歇尔·蒙特兹 知道她刚刚找到了宝藏！

But the first thing *Michelle Montez* had to do is to get some photos without pissing off a lot of people. *Michelle Montez* had become an expert of faking Text messaging and phone calls while clicking away pictures on a specially modified phone that had a camera mounted on the edge instead of the front and back like most phones these days.

但　米歇尔·蒙特兹 要做的第一件事是拍几张照片，但又不能惹恼很多人。米歇尔·蒙特兹　已经成为伪造短信和电话的专家，她用一部经过特殊改装的手机拍照，这种手机的摄像头安装在手机边缘，而不是像现在大多数手机一样安装在手机的正面和背面。

*Michelle Montez* could be texting away and clicking pictures, and nobody would ever know. In the span of several minutes, *Michelle Montez* managed to get 50 shots from a few angles. And to add fuel to the fire, those had to be real diamonds because Alex Baxter never did anything fake. If his girlfriend was wearing diamonds, they were real diamonds.

米歇尔·蒙特兹　可以发短信和点击照片，没有人会知道。在几分钟的时间里，

米歇尔·蒙特兹设法从几个角度拍摄了 50 张照片。更糟糕的是，那些必须是真正的钻石，因为亚历克斯·巴克斯特从不做任何假事。如果他的女朋友戴的是钻石，那一定是真钻石。

*Michelle Montez* made a dash to the lady's room, which only had a small line compared to usual and since she was at the back of the line, she was able to thumb through the pictures in an element of privacy with nobody else observing what she was checking.

米歇尔·蒙特兹　冲进女厕所，那里的排队人数比平时少，而且由于她排在队伍的最后面，所以她可以私密地翻看照片，不会有其他人看到她在看什么。

The high-resolution pictures with 8 million pixels had extreme detail. *Michelle Montez* could pan or expand and get just the woman's face.

800　万像素的高分辨率照片细节极其丰富。米歇尔·蒙特兹　可以平移或扩大镜头，只拍到女人的脸。

*MICHELLE MONTEZ*
(Thought)
*Oh, wow that woman is a beautiful, exotic creature.*
*Alex sure knows how to find them.*

米歇尔·蒙特兹
（想）
哦，哇，那个女人真是个美丽而奇异的生物。亚
历克斯肯定知道如何找到她们。

After *Michelle Montez* sent the pictures to her photograph department with instructions to put a photographic piece together on the woman and more to follow, she turned around and left the ladies room and then started the next phase of her activity.

米歇尔·蒙特兹　将照片发给她的摄影部门，并指示她将这名女子的照片拼凑起来，然后再拍更多照片。之后，她转身离开了女厕所，开始下一个阶段的活动。

*Michelle Montez* slyly approached Christina from her flanks as to avoid spooking the prey. Then when the opportunity arose approached by only a couple feet and announced:

米歇尔·蒙特兹　狡猾地从克里斯蒂娜的侧面接近她，以免惊吓到猎物。然后，当机会出现时，她只走近几英尺，宣布：

*MICHELLE MONTEZ*
Oh, that is such a beautiful dress, you are so lovely!

米歇尔·蒙特兹
哦，这件衣服真漂亮，你真可爱！

Christina was beaming with excitement and expectations, and Alex was temporarily distracted by the waitress paying her and taking possession of the 2 glasses of champagne, otherwise he would have studied who the woman was and remembered it was the wicket Witch of the West that no smart guy would ever let near their date.

克里斯蒂娜兴奋不已，满怀期待，而亚历克斯则被女服务员付钱给她并拿走两杯香槟分散了注意力，否则他会研究一下这个女人是谁，并记得这是西方的女巫，没有一个聪明的男人会让这个女巫接近他们的约会对象。

Unfortunately, before Alex could get reoriented and in command of the situation *Michelle Montez* said:

不幸的是，在亚历克斯重新调整并掌控局面之前，米歇尔·蒙特兹说：

*MICHELLE MONTEZ*
Hi, I'm *Michelle Montez*, what's your name dear?

米歇尔·蒙特兹

嗨，我是米歇尔·蒙特兹，亲爱的，你叫什么名字？

*Michelle Montez* didn't need to write anything down or take notes because her iPhone had a surveillance AP on it that was recording all sound real time and before Alex could intervene, Christina Garrison gave her full name.

米歇尔·蒙特兹不需要写下任何东西或做笔记，因为她的 iPhone 上有一个监控 AP，可以实时记录所有声音，在亚历克斯介入之前，克里斯蒂娜·加里森报出了她的全名。

CHRISTINA
I'm Christina Garrison.

*MICHELLE MONTEZ*
Where are you from Christina?

米歇尔·蒙特兹
克里斯蒂娜，你来自哪里？

CHRISTINA
I live in New York City. How about yourself?

克里斯蒂娜
我住在纽约市。你呢？

*MICHELLE MONTEZ*
I live in Paris France.

米歇尔·蒙特兹
我住在法国巴黎。

CHRISTINA
What brings you to Switzerland?

克里斯蒂娜
你来瑞士干什么？

*MICHELLE MONTEZ*
On a holiday by myself.

米歇尔·蒙特兹
独自度假。

CHRISTINA
Oh, that's nice.

克里斯蒂娜
哦，太好了。

As Alex started realizing what was happening and that he was standing next to none other than *Michelle Montez*, he announced:

当亚历克斯开始意识到发生了什么，他正站在米歇尔·蒙特兹旁边时，他宣布：

ALEX
Miss, could you please excuse us for a moment or two
if I want to show my friend something.

亚历克斯
小姐，你能不能让我们休息一会儿，我想给我的
朋友看点东西。

Alex, then took starstruck Christina away to a private corner where he explained.

然后，毒枭亚历克斯把克里斯蒂娜带到一个私人角落，在那里他解释了一下。

ALEX
I wanted to toast you, but that obnoxious woman was
invading our space.

亚历克斯
我想为你干杯，但那个讨厌的女人侵犯了我们的
空间。

CHRISTINA
Oh, that's alright.

克里斯蒂娜
哦，没关系。

ALEX
Here's to you Christina, a lovely lady whom I adore.

亚历克斯
为你干杯，克里斯蒂娜，我崇拜的一位可爱的女
士。

CHRISTINA
And here's to you Alex, a charming man.

克里斯蒂娜
为你干杯，亚历克斯，一个迷人的男人。

ALEX
Thank you.

亚历克斯
谢谢你。

CHRISTINA
You are more than welcome.

克里斯蒂娜
非常欢迎你。

ALEX
Christina, another reason why I pulled you over here
is to warn you, that you were talking to a muckraker
gossip person that puts salacious information in her
magazine.

亚历克斯
克里斯蒂娜，我把你拦下来的另一个原因是警告
你，你正在和一个在她的杂志上发布淫秽信息的
揭丑八卦者交谈。

CHRISTINA
Really?

克里斯蒂娜
真的吗？

ALEX
You gave away too much information when you told
*Michelle Montez* your last name. Which I don't mind,
because I want you, but on Monday morning a lot of
people around the world are going to know who you
are.

亚历克斯
当你告诉米歇尔·蒙特兹你的姓氏时，你透露了太
多信息。我不介意，因为我想要你，但周一早上
全世界很多人都会知道你是谁。

CHRISTINA
Damn.

克里斯蒂娜
该死。

ALEX
Christina, if you are willing to give up your freedom
and privacy, then don't hesitate to answer their
questions.

But if you think it's been uncomfortable up to now, where we had to fly all the way to
Switzerland to get some privacy, in the future it will get tough.

I had to warn you that next week expect a lot of things because that woman is going to
try to dig up anything she can on you. I'll try to protect you as much as I can.

亚历克斯
克里斯蒂娜, 如果你愿意放弃你的自由和隐私, 那
么不要犹豫, 回答他们的问题。

但是如果你觉得到目前为止我们一直很不舒服，我们不得不一路飞到瑞士才能
获得一些隐私，那么将来会变得艰难。

我不得不警告你，下周要做好很多准备，因为那个女人会试图挖出任何她能挖
到的关于你的信息。我会尽我所能保护你的。

CHRISTINA
That's okay Alex, I'm a big girl, and if you still want
me, none of the rest bothers me.

克里斯蒂娜
没关系，Alex，我是个大女孩了，只要你还想要
我，其他的都不是困扰我的。

ALEX
Christina, as long as we have that understanding I'm
fine with that, but don't come crying to me later when
you feel like you no longer have any privacy. And I'm
sorry I put you in this position, but you touched me so
deeply, I let my selfishness probably go too far.

亚历克斯
克里斯蒂娜，只要我们有这种理解，我就可以接
受，但是当你觉得你不再有任何隐私时，不要哭
着来找我。我很抱歉让你处于这种境地，但你深
深地触动了我，我的自私可能太过分了。

CHRISTINA
Does that mean you love me?

克里斯蒂娜
这是否意味着你爱我？

ALEX
More than you can imagine.

亚历克斯
比你想象的还要多。

The combination of Champagne and the heightened emotions hit Christina all at once.
She couldn't hold back, nor did she care, and threw her arms around Alex and Kissed
him.

香槟和高涨的情绪同时袭上克里斯蒂娜的心头。她无法抑制，也不在乎，张开
双臂拥抱亚历克斯并亲吻他。

Alex didn't mind that one bit and reciprocated and that sealed the deal for Christina.

亚历克斯对此毫不介意，并给予了回应，这对克里斯蒂娜来说就是板上钉钉的
事。

Christina, she could give a dam what the Wicket Witch of the West *Michelle Montez*
published. She was in love and the moment now is all that mattered.

克里斯蒂娜，她不在乎西方女巫米歇尔·蒙特兹发表的内容。她坠入爱河，现
在才是最重要的。

Even though they were away from the crowd and slightly isolated by 5 or 10 feet from the nearest person, there were a few people in the crowd astonished, some of them knew who Alex was. None other than *Michelle Montez* though and her Cell Phone was on overdrive with more pictures being taken, and *it was pay dirt time.*

尽管他们远离人群，与最近的人相距 5 到 10 英尺，但人群中仍有一些人感到惊讶，他们中的一些人知道亚历克斯是谁。不过，正是米歇尔·蒙特兹，她的手机超速行驶，拍了更多照片，这是收获的时刻。

*The dome man's* kiss was front cover material. *Michelle Montez's* article out next week would make a National Inquirer or the New York Times Newspaper reporter's blush.

圆顶男子的吻是封面材料。米歇尔·蒙特兹下周发表的文章会让《国家询问报》或《纽约时报》记者脸红。

CHRISTINA
Shall we go back to our seats and enjoy the rest of the
performance?

克里斯蒂娜
我们回到座位上，享受剩下的表演吧？

Alex responded, feeling uplifted and totally enamored by Christina. She had just turned him on so much the past moment he knew he had a reaction.

亚历克斯回应道，他感到振奋，完全被克里斯蒂娜迷住了。克里斯蒂娜刚才让他兴奋不已，他知道自己会有反应。

ALEX
Alright.

亚历克斯
好吧。

It was more than a pleasant reaction, but it was a shame they could not have been alone that moment to christen the passion with evocative and transcendental eagerness to please each other.

这不仅仅是一个愉快的反应，但遗憾的是，他们当时不能单独在一起，用令人回味和超然的渴望来取悦对方，来宣告激情。

Christina and Alex re-entered their balcony seats.

克里斯蒂娜和亚历克斯重新进入他们的阳台座位。

Now *Michelle Montez* was searching for Alex Baxter and his girlfriend Christina Garrison out in the concert hall.

现在，米歇尔·蒙特兹 正在音乐厅里寻找亚历克斯·巴克斯特和他的女友克里斯蒂娜·加里森。

The lights were still on making her cell phone camera quite capable. *Michelle Montez* had noticed in the first performance that most of the balcony seats along the right side of the concert hall facing the Orchestra were empty.

灯光还亮着，使她的手机相机非常实用。米歇尔·蒙特兹在第一场演出中就注意到，音乐厅右侧面向管弦乐队的阳台座位大部分都是空的。

Either people didn't want to pay the high cost, or they wanted to be down in the middle where they could get the best musical projections in a more symmetrical fashion. Acoustics is one of the drawbacks of balcony seating, but you must give up privacy to do so. Which means you can't have a chicken sandwich in your pocket (joke).

要么人们不想支付高昂的费用，要么他们想坐在中间，这样他们就能以更对称的方式获得最好的音乐投影。声学效果是阳台座位的缺点之一，但你必须放弃隐私才能这样做。这意味着你不能在口袋里放一个鸡肉三明治（开玩笑）。

<u>MUSIC FOR THIS NEXT SCENE:</u>

<u>Janine Jansen performs Tchaikovsky's violin concerto live in 2013</u>

<u>下一幕的音乐：</u>

<u>Janine Jansen 于 2013 年现场演奏柴可夫斯基的小提琴协奏曲</u>

The violinist and the conductor came out on the stage. The performer was wearing a long red dress, which meshed well with her attractive body.

这位美国小提琴家和指挥家登上了舞台。这位表演者穿着一条红色长裙，与她迷人的身材相得益彰。

The Tchaikovsky violin concerto was a little more exciting than the Rachmaninov piano concerto, which was more reflective, and helped to shift the emotions a little.

柴可夫斯基的小提琴协奏曲比拉赫玛尼诺夫的钢琴协奏曲更令人兴奋，后者更具反思性，有助于稍微转移情绪。

Had concertos been in the opposite order of performance, it's likely *Michelle Montez's* sudden appearance would have left them a little depressed at the end of the evening, knowing the consequences of what she can do and they would soon learn how much.

如果协奏曲的表演顺序相反，米歇尔·蒙特兹的突然出现可能会让他们在晚上结束时感到有些沮丧，因为他们知道她能做什么，他们很快就会知道她能做多少。

Tchaikovsky violin concerto helped to build the fire and even though it also has some delicate passages, they are more existential in nature, and the preponderance of the melody fortified Alex's sudden recent outpour of passion upon the revelation that Christina triggered when she asked that frank question concerning Alex's feelings for her.

柴可夫斯基小提琴协奏曲助长了这股激情，尽管它也有一些微妙的段落，但它们本质上更具存在感，旋律的优势强化了亚历克斯最近突然爆发的激情，克里斯蒂娜在坦率地问了亚历克斯对她的感情时引发了启示。

Once Alex answered Christina question *if he loved her* in the affirmative, he could never take it back, otherwise he would be a liar and provocateur.

一旦亚历克斯回答了克里斯蒂娜他是否爱她的问题，他就永远不会收回这句话，否则他就是一个骗子和挑衅者。

Christina would never have asked that question before today. There was never a man she had met that ever came this close to her to the point she would entertain wanting to ask such a question.

克里斯蒂娜在今天之前绝不会问这个问题。她从未遇到过一个男人如此接近她，以至于她会想问这样的问题。

If Christina had been talking to her friends just a week ago and they had asked her if she would ever ask a man that question: "Do you love me?" she would have responded:

如果克里斯蒂娜一周前和她的朋友聊天时，他们问她是否会问男人这个问题："你爱我吗？" 她会回答：

CHRISTINA
Don't be ridiculous.

克里斯蒂娜
别这么荒唐。

However, now reality strikes home and because of the unplanned encounter that led to this changed all the rules. Christina was thinking while the violin was being manipulated with such great precision.

然而，现在现实打击了亚历克斯，因为一场意外的邂逅导致了这一切，改变了所有的规则。克里斯蒂娜一边思考，一边用如此精确的方式操纵小提琴。

CHRISTINA
(Thought)
*Am I in over my head?*

克里斯蒂娜
(思考)
我是不是有点不知所措了？

Christina had unwittingly, and in a purposeful and seemingly accidental and spontaneous manner got a lot of answers quickly and efficiently. And just as the melody implied at around the 28-minute mark, nothing is apparent in life as situations like she now experienced were accidental, and she had to live for today for tomorrow may never come.

克里斯蒂娜不知不觉地、有目的地、看似偶然、自发地迅速有效地得到了很多答案。正如 28 分钟左右的旋律所暗示的那样，生活中没有什么是显而易见的，因为她现在所经历的情况都是偶然的，她必须活在当下，因为明天可能永远不会到来。

With nobody around observing what *Michelle Montez* was doing, she sent more pictures she captured of the two lovebirds. She had much to do to research who and what was Christina Garrison of New York City. And she had a deadline, if she hustled and got the story done in 48 hours it could be in the next edition which the way things were shaping up started to smell delicious.

由于没有人在观察米歇尔·蒙特兹在做什么，她发送了更多她拍摄的这对情侣的照片。她有很多工作要做，要研究纽约市的克里斯蒂娜·加里森是谁，是什么。而且她有一个最后期限，如果她赶在 48 小时内完成这个故事，它可能会出现在下一期，事情的发展开始散发出美妙的味道。

It was Saturday evening in Paris, and she was lucky she got in touch with some of the editorial staff before they left for the day. Otherwise, she would have to push this off another week, by then someone else may have broken the story.

那是巴黎的星期六晚上，她很幸运在编辑人员下班前联系上了他们。否则，她就得再推迟一周，到那时其他人可能已经报道了这个故事。

By the time the Tchaikovsky Violin Concerto was completed, information started rolling in. The first was a New York Newspaper report with Christina Garrison's picture recently that didn't really identify who the woman was, because they didn't know her name. Only *Michelle Montez* had the whole enchilada, name, romantic pictures and a pathway to the treasure trove.

当柴可夫斯基小提琴协奏曲完成时，信息开始涌入。第一个是纽约报纸最近刊登的克里斯蒂娜·加里森的照片，但并没有真正确定这名女子是谁，因为他们不知道她的名字。只有米歇尔·蒙特兹知道全部细节，包括名字、浪漫照片和通往宝藏的途径。

Fifteen minutes later *Michelle Montez* received a text message.

十五分钟后，她收到了一条短信。

> Christina Garrison of Queens New York identified as
> the mystery woman with Alex Baxter.

杂志工作人员
（短信）
纽约皇后区的克里斯蒂娜·加里森被确认为与亚历
克斯·巴克斯特在一起的神秘女子。

*MICHELLE MONTEZ*
(Text Message)
Oh wow, nice progress.

米歇尔·蒙特兹
（短信）
哇，进展不错。

And just as she started to smile it got better.

就在她开始微笑的时候，情况变得更好了。

MAGAZINE STAFF
(Text Message)
Christina Garrison works for a non-profit organization that happens to be located at 120 Wall Street, in the same building that Alex Baxter's Dome Building construction company contractor, Reardon, Construction Company resides.

杂志工作人员
（短信）
克里斯蒂娜·加里森在一家非营利组织工作，该组织恰好位于华尔街 120 号，与亚历克斯·巴克斯特的圆顶建筑公司承包商 里尔登建筑公司位于同一栋大楼里。

Then the salacious materials started arriving.

然后，淫秽材料开始到达。

MAGAZINE STAFF
(Text Message)
Christina's father is of African descent, she's half black.

杂志工作人员
（短信）
克里斯蒂娜的父亲是非洲裔，她有一半黑人血统。

*MICHELLE MONTEZ*
(Text Message)
Dig, Dig, Dig! We need more information about her father. Does he have a criminal background?

米歇尔·蒙特兹
（短信）
挖，挖，挖！我们需要更多关于她父亲的信息。
他有犯罪背景吗？

A few minutes later:

几分钟后：

MAGAZINE STAFF
(Text Message)
Mother and dad are retired schoolteachers, father is former US Army Green Beret, heavily decorated for deployments and missions to Vietnam in the late 1960's.

杂志工作人员
（短信）
母亲和父亲是退休的学校教师，父亲是前美国陆军绿色贝雷帽，在 20 世纪 60 年代末因在越南的部署和任务而获得多项荣誉。

Even though some would think it was a smear campaign, now suddenly Christina Garrison has an interesting family.

尽管有些人认为这是一场诽谤运动，但现在克里斯蒂娜·加里森突然有一个有趣的家庭。

MAGAZINE STAFF
(Text Message)
WOW! We got a winner!

杂志工作人员
（短信）
哇！我们赢了！

*MICHELLE MONTEZ*
(Text Message)
This is better than mana from heaven God sent to Moses!

米歇尔·蒙特兹<br>
（短信）<br>
这比上帝赐给摩西的天赐法力还要好！

The managing editor of the magazine then texted Michelle.

该杂志的主编随后给米歇尔发了短信。

Note to cinematographer:

Kindly remember during text messages, the image of the cell phone display is shown. French could be substituted for display text between the French Magazine characters. Also note VOICE OVER of stating the context of the text message is done with the actor's voice.

摄影师须知：

请记住，在发送短信时，手机显示屏的图像会显示出来。法语杂志字符之间的显示文本可以用法语代替。还请注意，说明短信内容的画外音是用演员的声音完成的。

MANAGING EDITOR<br>
(Text Message)<br>
We have called writers in to work tomorrow, we've looked over the pictures you have sent, we are making this a priority story. We need you in the office tomorrow if we are going to meet the Monday deadline.

总编辑<br>
（短信）<br>
我们已经叫作家明天来上班，我们看过你发来的图片，我们正在把这作为优先报道。如果我们要在周一的最后期限前完成，明天就需要你来办公室。

*MICHELLE MONTEZ*<br>
(Text Message)<br>
I'll try to get back to Paris as soon as I can get there.

米歇尔·蒙特兹<br>
（短信）<br>
我会尽快赶回巴黎。

MANAGING EDITOR<br>
(Text Message)<br>
Special request: Can you take a night train or a red eye flight and be here tomorrow morning? This is quickly

turning into a huge project; it's going to take some time to put it together.

总编辑
（短信）

特别要求：你能坐夜班火车或红眼航班明天早上来吗？这很快就会变成一个巨大的项目；需要花些时间才能完成。

*MICHELLE MONTEZ*
(Text Message)
I'll try my best.

米歇尔·蒙特兹
（短信）
我会尽力的。

Michelle Montez thought she would try to get in one more clandestine interview with Christina.

米歇尔·蒙特兹想再和克里斯蒂娜进行一次秘密采访。

*MICHELLE MONTEZ*
(Thought)

I pray Christine must use the bathroom before she leaves.

米歇尔·蒙特兹
（想法）
我祈祷克里斯蒂娜在离开前必须上厕所。

Alex fearing the crowd, traffic, and wanted to avoid the Wicked Witch of the West, *Michelle Montez* approaching them again said to Christina:

亚历克斯害怕人群和交通，想避开西方邪恶女巫，米歇尔·蒙特兹再次走近他们，对克里斯蒂娜说：

ALEX
Let's leave now, while the end of the concerto is playing, we can get out of here much quicker then.

亚历克斯
我们现在就走吧，趁着协奏曲快要结束的时候，
我们可以更快地离开这里。

CHRISTINA
Good idea.

克里斯蒂娜
好主意。

*Michelle Montez* saw Christina and Alex move out of their balcony and figured they might be heading for the exit, she then followed their queue, but wasn't walking nearly as brisk as Alex and Christina were.

米歇尔·蒙特兹看到克里斯蒂娜和亚历克斯从阳台上走出来，她猜想他们可能正朝着出口走去，然后她跟着他们的提示，但走得没有亚历克斯和克里斯蒂娜快。

By the time *Michelle Montez* got to the entrance she saw Christina and Alex go out the door and Alex, being a bright planner, had Grant drive his Rolls Royce up to be the front entrance right as the Performance was scheduled to end.

当米歇尔·蒙特兹到达入口时，她看到克里斯蒂娜和亚历克斯出了门，而亚历克斯是一位聪明的计划者，他让格兰特在表演结束时开着他的劳斯莱斯停在前门。

Alex only had to walk 20 feet to the car, which had the doors open. Christina and Alex got into the Rolls Royce on the passenger side and attendants shut their door for them.

亚历克斯只需走 20 英尺就到了车前，车门是开着的。克里斯蒂娜和亚历克斯坐在乘客一侧上了劳斯莱斯，服务员为他们关上了车门。

*Michelle Montez* got one last shot and a clear picture of Christina and Alex together in his Rolls Royce.

米歇尔·蒙特兹　最后拍了一张清晰的照片，克里斯蒂娜和亚历克斯坐在他的劳斯莱斯里。

*Michelle Montez* then said to herself:

然后　米歇尔·蒙特兹 对自己说：

***MICHELLE MONTEZ***
(Thought)
*It can't get any better than this.*

米歇尔·蒙特兹
(想)
没有比这更好的了。

Grant drove Christina and Alex back to Alex's mission and covered the distance quickly and was soon home.

格兰特开车送克里斯蒂娜和亚历克斯回到亚历克斯的任务地点，很快就到了家。

ALEX
Christina, I have got a few things I need to take care of, why don't you take a bath, freshen up a bit and I'll ask Chris if he can get us something to eat in a few minutes.

亚历克斯
克里斯蒂娜，我有几件事要处理，你为什么不洗个澡，梳洗一下，我会问克里斯几分钟后能不能给我们弄点吃的。

CHRISTINA
Okay thanks.

克里斯蒂娜
好的，谢谢。

Mary overheard the conversation and knew that Christina was probably in over her head and needed some help from her team, and said to Christina:

玛丽偷听到了他们的谈话，她知道克里斯蒂娜可能有点不知所措，需要团队的帮助，于是她对克里斯蒂娜说：

MARY
May I help you get ready Christina?

玛丽
克里斯蒂娜，我可以帮你准备好吗？

CHRISTINA
Sure.

克里斯蒂娜
当然可以。

Mary led Christina up the circular stone stairs to the next floor to the hallway that led to some of the bedrooms including Christina's and Alex.

玛丽领着克里斯蒂娜走上圆形的石阶，来到下一层，来到通往一些卧室的走廊，包括克里斯蒂娜和亚历克斯的卧室。

Mary and Christina went into Christina's bedroom and shut the door.

玛丽和克里斯蒂娜走进克里斯蒂娜的卧室并关上了门。

MARY
Christina, how hot do you like your bathwater?

玛丽
克里斯蒂娜，你喜欢多热的洗澡水？

CHRISTINA
Oh about ninety-five degrees, I guess.

克里斯蒂娜
哦，我想大概是九十五度吧。

MARY
It's digitally controlled. I can make it whatever you like so if you want to change the temperature, I'll show you the controls.

玛丽
它是数字控制的，我可以把它调成你喜欢的任何温度，所以如果你想改变温度，我会给你看控制按钮。

Mary turned on the water and showed Christina the simple controls which were very intuitive and logical.

玛丽打开水龙头，向克里斯蒂娜展示了简单的控制按钮，这些按钮非常直观和合乎逻辑。

MARY
Let me help you take off your jewelry and your dress.

玛丽
让我帮你脱下你的珠宝和衣服。

CHRISTINA
Okay.

克里斯蒂娜
好的。

MARY
Alex asked me to inform you that your diamonds will be sent to the Chase Manhattan bank near where you work and placed in a safety deposit box for you which he will arrange for you, so that you can get them when you need or want to wear them in the future.

玛丽
亚历克斯让我通知你，你的钻石将被送到你工作地点附近的大通曼哈顿银行，并放在一个保险箱里，他会帮你安排，这样你以后需要或想戴的时候就可以拿到。

CHRISTINA
Alex's so thoughtful.

克里斯蒂娜
亚历克斯很体贴。

MARY
That's because he really adores you.

玛丽
那是因为他真的很崇拜你。CHRISTINA

CHRISTINA
I believe he does too.

克里斯蒂娜
我相信他也爱你。

MARY
Christina, I'll let you alone now so you can take your bath, there is an intercom box right there on the side of the bathtub, if you need me for anything just press the big red button on top and speak into it and I'll come right in to assist you as required.

玛丽
克里斯蒂娜, 现在我让你一个人呆着，你可以去洗澡了，浴缸边上有一个对讲机，如果你需要我做什么，只要按一下上面的大红色按钮，对着它说话，我就会马上进来帮助你。

CHRISTINA
Thank you.

克里斯蒂娜
谢谢。

Christina didn't need any further help, took her hot bath, freshened up, took off her makeup, and had a clean but sparkling face. Her skin was so beautiful, the perfect tone and dimensions fit for a top movie star.

克里斯蒂娜不需要任何进一步的帮助，洗了个热水澡，精神焕发，卸掉了妆容，脸色干净却闪闪发光。她的皮肤太漂亮了，肤色和身材都完美，适合顶级电影明星。

Christina didn't dress to impress, she put on some casual and comfortable clothes then went downstairs thinking that she would be eating with Alex real soon.

克里斯蒂娜并没有打扮得漂漂亮亮，她穿了件休闲舒适的衣服，然后下楼去想她很快就会和亚历克斯一起吃饭。

Nobody was in the dining room, so Christina went into the Kitchen. It too was void of people, then suddenly, Christina heard voices. It was Alex talking to Mary in the Pantry adjacent to the kitchen.

餐厅里没人，克里斯蒂娜就走进了厨房。厨房里也没有人，突然，克里斯蒂娜听到了声音。是亚历克斯在厨房旁边的餐具室里和玛丽说话。MARY

Mary<br>
Did you have a good time, Mr. Baxter.


玛丽<br>
你玩得开心吗，巴克斯特先生。


ALEX<br>
Oh yes, I cherished every moment with Christina.


亚历克斯<br>
哦，是的，我珍惜和克里斯蒂娜在一起的每一刻。


MARY<br>
You really like her?


玛丽<br>
你真的喜欢她吗？


ALEX<br>
Yes, I think I've fallen in love with Christina.


亚历克斯<br>
是的，我想我已经爱上 克里斯蒂娜了。


MARY<br>
Does Christina know this?


玛丽<br>
克里斯蒂娜知道这件事吗？

ALEX

We might have had some special words, but I need to
find the words so that I can tell Christina how much
she means to me.

亚历克斯

我们可能说过一些特别的话，但我需要找到合适
的词来告诉 克里斯蒂娜， 她对我有多重要。

MARY

Just tell Christina you love her dummy.

玛丽

直接告诉克里斯蒂娜你喜欢她的假奶嘴就行了。

ALEX

I'm not sure I know how to do exactly that. All I know
is I doubt now that I could live without her.

亚历克斯

我不确定我是否知道该怎么做。我只知道我现在
怀疑如果没有她我是否能活下去。

MARY

Did she touch you deeply?

玛丽

她对你的影响这么深吗？

ALEX

Yes, I am very attached to her. I want her in my life.

亚历克斯

是的，我非常依恋她。我希望她能成为我生命中
的一部分。

Christina, feeling slightly embarrassed eavesdropping on the conversation quietly
exited the Kitchen, walked through the dining room, and into the huge open front
entrance that had as much room as a hotel lobby. The fifty foot wide Persian Rug
had brilliant blues and reds. The Persian Rug was finely woven, and no doubt cost a
fortune.

克里斯蒂娜偷听着他们的谈话，感到有点尴尬，于是她悄悄地走出厨房，穿过
餐厅，走进宽敞的前门，那里的空间和酒店大堂一样大。五十英尺宽的波斯地
毯有着鲜艳的蓝色和红色。它编织得很精细，毫无疑问价值不菲。

Christina never paid much attention to Alex's artwork while she had been at his mansion and regretted having her head in the clouds. But now Christina made an assertive effort to get real and not be so temporally detached with reality. Christina knew it was time to take a step back and do some simple things like enjoy Alex's paintings for a few minutes.

克里斯蒂娜在亚历克斯的豪宅时从未关注过他的艺术作品，她后悔自己不切实际。但现在克里斯蒂娜做出了坚定的努力，回归现实，不再那么脱离现实。克里斯蒂娜知道是时候退后一步，做一些简单的事情，比如花几分钟欣赏亚历克斯的画作。

Some of Alex's oil paintings were rare and expensive famous artist's works Christina recognized that would be fitting art museum piece.

亚历克斯的一些油画是著名艺术家的稀有且昂贵的作品，克里斯蒂娜认出它们适合作为艺术博物馆的藏品。

Over to the side was an adjacent room, stood a Steinway grand piano.

旁边是一个相邻的房间，放着一架 施坦威 (Steinway)大钢琴。

Suddenly Alex approached Christina from the dining room hallway.

突然，亚历克斯从餐厅走廊向克里斯蒂娜走来。

ALEX
Christina, Grant and Mary are setting us a place to eat,
if you would please care to join me.

亚历克斯
克里斯蒂娜、格兰特和玛丽正在为我们安排吃饭
的地方，如果你愿意和我一起去的话。

CHRISTINA
I would be delighted.

克里斯蒂娜
我很乐意。

Just like on the train today, the food was exquisite. Alex suggested:

就像今天在火车上一样，食物非常精致。亚历克斯建议：

ALEX
Why don't we have a glass of wine with dinner?

亚历克斯
我们晚餐时喝杯葡萄酒好吗？

The mansion staff member Grant was standing by him to assist. He was more than pleased to pour glasses of wine for Christina and Alex. That's because Christina and Alex brought with them an amount of pleasantness in their personalities and the curiosity of Christina that took away the boredom for the mansion.

大厦工作人员　格兰特（Grant）在一旁待命，他非常乐意为克里斯蒂娜和亚历克斯倒酒。因为克里斯蒂娜和亚历克斯的性格中带着一丝愉悦，而克里斯蒂娜的好奇心也为大厦扫除了一丝沉闷。

CHRISTINA

Alex, I noticed a piano in the room adjacent to the front room, do you play?

克里斯蒂娜

亚历克斯，我注意到前厅旁边的房间里有一架钢琴，你会弹钢琴吗？

ALEX

A little and I compose music, would you like me to play you a song?

亚历克斯

我会作曲，你想让我给你弹首歌吗？

CHRISTINA

I would love that.

克里斯蒂娜

我很乐意。

Alex, feeling satisfied with his meal and observing Christina had about half of her meal but had slowed down and appeared to be finished, responded:

亚历克斯对自己的饭菜感到满意，他看到克里斯蒂娜吃了大约一半的饭，但已经放慢了速度，似乎吃完了，于是回答道。

ALEX

Christina, bring your wine glass, Let's go to the piano.

亚历克斯

克里斯蒂娜，拿上你的酒杯，我们去钢琴那里。

Then Alex requested:

然后亚历克斯要求：

ALEX
Grant, would you please move a bar stool next to the
piano so Christina can watch me play.

亚历克斯
格兰特，你能把一个酒吧凳子搬到钢琴旁边吗，
这样克里斯蒂娜就能看我弹琴了。

Grant responded energetically as he also loved to hear Alex perform.

格兰特热情地回应，因为他也喜欢听亚历克斯的表演。

GRANT
I would be delighted, sir.

格兰特
我很高兴，先生。

Christina was seated with her wine glass on a little place mat covered with extremely fine linen, with markings from Poland when Alex sat down and began to play.

克里斯蒂娜坐在一块铺着极细亚麻布的小餐垫上，餐垫上有波兰的标记，这时亚历克斯坐下开始演奏。

In a few seconds Christina was enthralled and joyous by the performance. Just like his sweet love making, Alex's fingers glided along the piano like it was a natural part of his body.

几秒钟后，克里斯蒂娜就被表演迷住了，感到很高兴。就像他甜蜜的做爱一样，亚历克斯的手指在钢琴上滑动，就像它是他身体的自然部分一样。

Alex played for thirty minutes. Christina was now feeling blessed, she didn't know why she deserved all this, but she would return the love in different ways. One of which is loyalty and devotion.

亚历克斯演奏了三十分钟。克里斯蒂娜现在感到很幸福，她不知道为什么她值得拥有这一切，但她会以不同的方式回报爱。其中之一就是忠诚和奉献。

Alex must have sensed that, as now he was in the process of rearranging his life, and for the future, Christina would be the focus of his daily life. Soon it would be time to move to another more permanent situation, where he would be better able to protect her, as well as facilitate their cohesive migration towards a unity and a lifelong partnership to devote their lives towards.

亚历克斯一定感觉到了这一点，因为现在他正在重新安排他的生活，而未来，克里斯蒂娜将成为他日常生活的焦点。很快，他就要换一个更稳定的环境，在那里，他能更好地保护她，并促进他们团结一致，建立终生伴侣关系，为之奉献一生。

The music tonight was a special treat for the staff. Everyone was joyous because they knew Alex was falling in love and it only took them a few minutes to size up Christina.

今晚的音乐是员工们的特别享受。每个人都很高兴，因为他们知道亚历克斯坠入爱河，他们只花了几分钟就了解了克里斯蒂娜。

Aside from Christina being a very beautiful and pretty lady, her demure and casual sweetness positively affected them all.

克里斯蒂娜是一位非常漂亮漂亮的女士，她端庄而随意的甜美也对他们所有人都产生了积极的影响。

Alex finished playing the Steinway then announced.

亚历克斯弹完斯坦威钢琴后宣布。

ALEX
Christina and I would now like to be by ourselves for
a while, you guys' *carryon.*

亚历克斯
克里斯蒂娜和我现在想独处一会儿，你们继续。

The staff then withdrew to their private quarters to enjoy themselves and not be concerned about performing any functions unless Alex called upon them, which was unlikely for the rest of the night.

然后，工作人员撤退到他们的私人住处享受生活，不用担心执行任何功能，除非亚历克斯召唤他们，而这在当晚的剩余时间里不太可能发生。

ALEX
Christina, you were looking at a painting before I
invited you over to the piano.

亚历克斯
克里斯蒂娜，在我邀请你去弹钢琴之前，你正在
看一幅画。

Christina
Yes, it's a beautiful painting.

克里斯蒂娜
是的，这是一幅美丽的画。

ALEX
The artist wasn't appreciated until long after his death.

亚历克斯
这位艺术家直到他去世很久之后才得到赞赏。

CHRISTINA
You know what that means?

克里斯蒂娜
你知道这意味着什么吗？

ALEX
What?

亚历克斯
什么？

CHRISTINA
Don't wait until you die to have fun.

克里斯蒂娜
不要等到你死了才找乐子。

Alex then grabbed Christina's hand and guided her towards the stairway where they went to his room.

然后亚历克斯抓住克里斯蒂娜的手，领着她走向楼梯，他们去了他的房间。

Within minutes Christina and Alex transcended into a physical embrace full of love and appreciation on many levels.

几分钟之内，克里斯蒂娜和亚历克斯就超越了身体上的拥抱，充满了多层次的爱和欣赏。

Alex took Mary's recent advice and during the rarified coitus, Alex said some very special words that Christina knew came from his heart because of what she accidentally overheard that Alex was unaware. These were thus validated admissions of real love.

亚历克斯听从了玛丽最近的建议，在一次罕见的性交中，亚历克斯说了一些非常特别的话，克里斯蒂娜知道这些话来自他的内心，因为她无意中听到了亚历克斯不知道的事情。因此，这些都是真爱的认可。

During this special moment when love blossoms and all ambiguities are resolved, Christiana had a psychophysical response and strongly wrapped her legs around Alex who was on top of her doing conventional intercourse and squeezed him hard and bucked him like a bronco throwing her thrusts into him like he had no idea was possible. That created a chain reaction and spontaneous super gratification for both Alex and Christina orgasming precisely at the same time.

在这个爱情绽放、所有歧义都得到解决的特殊时刻，克里斯蒂娜产生了心理物理反应，用力用腿缠住亚历克斯，亚历克斯正压在她上面进行常规性交，用力挤压他，像野马一样把他撞倒，把她的力道猛地推入他的身体，就像他不知道可能发生的那样。这产生了连锁反应，让亚历克斯和克里斯蒂娜同时达到了高潮，自发获得了极大的满足感。

Splendid euphoria swept through Alex and Christina as the chemical's dopamine, oxytocin, serotonin, and testosterone pumped into their brains within the couple as their mutual attraction and affection created that moment of ecstasy that transcends time and space.

随着化学物质多巴胺、催产素、血清素和睾丸激素注入这对情侣的大脑，亚历克斯和克里斯蒂娜感到无比的幸福，他们之间的相互吸引和爱慕创造了超越时空的狂喜时刻。

Multiple spatially remote parts of their brains were achieving this massive pleasure. Genital sensory cortex, motor areas, hypothalamus, thalamus, and substantia nigra all lit up during their simultaneous orgasms with elevated dopamine pumped into the pleasure center of the brain creating a super orgasm they achieved by the psychological responses triggered by discovering *real love.*

他们大脑中多个空间上相距遥远的部分正在获得这种巨大的快感。生殖器感觉皮层、运动区、下丘脑、丘脑和黑质在他们同时达到高潮时都亮了起来，高浓度的多巴胺被泵入大脑的快感中心，创造了一种超级高潮，他们通过发现真爱引发的心理反应实现了这种高潮。

Just like the gratification of the concerto performed at the symphony earlier that left Christina and Alex spellbound for a few moments, they slowly slid into that mental state creating slumber and joyful happiness, they were the purveyors of joy for each other.

就像早些时候在交响乐团演奏的协奏曲让克里斯蒂娜和亚历克斯着迷了片刻一样，他们慢慢地进入了那种精神状态，创造了沉睡和快乐的幸福，他们是彼此的欢乐的传播者。

Alex and Christina were not sound conscious or aware or even cared if somehow their activity leaked out of the room even though it was very well soundproof.

亚历克斯和克里斯蒂娜没有声音意识或意识，甚至不在乎他们的活动是否会以某种方式泄露到房间里，尽管这个房间的隔音效果很好。

Mary was in her room reading a *loquacious* and *garrulous novel* that paralleled what was going on in Alex's bedroom, overheard enough of it to fully understand why Alex wanted *some privacy.* Some of Christina's words escaped the room and her outpour of emotional sound effects left no doubt in Mary's mind that Alex might have taken her recommendation and leveled most genuinely with Christina about their state of affairs.

玛丽在她的房间里读着一本喋喋不休的小说，这与亚历克斯卧室里发生的事情相似，她偷听到了足够多的内容，完全理解了亚历克斯为什么想要一些隐私。克里斯蒂娜的一些话传到了房间里，她情绪激动的声音效果让玛丽毫不怀疑亚历克斯可能采纳了她的建议，并真诚地向克里斯蒂娜坦白了他们的状况。

Hence Christina's response further conveyed success which Mary was happy about meaning, Christina had fully aced Stephanie. The race was over, and Christina was a strong contender and victor in the quest for Alex.

因此，克里斯蒂娜的回应进一步传达了成功，玛丽对此感到高兴，这意味着克里斯蒂娜完全击败了斯蒂芬妮。比赛结束了，克里斯蒂娜在争夺亚历克斯的比赛中成为了强有力的竞争者和胜利者。

Alex and Christina woke late in the morning. After they bathed and dressed casually, they made their way to the dining room where they could smell the staff patiently waited for them and had a stupendous breakfast, not heavy but enough to make them quite comfortable.

亚历克斯和克里斯蒂娜早上很晚才醒来。洗完澡，换上休闲装，他们走到餐厅，在那里他们闻到了工作人员耐心等待他们并享用丰盛早餐的味道，早餐不多，但足以让他们感到很舒服。

ALEX

Christina, we are going to have to leave in a little while and start to make our way back to the USA so that you will be ready to go to work on Monday morning and on the way back I want to fly into Greenland and get a good gauge on how close they are to finishing up those first six pillars.

亚历克斯

克里斯蒂娜，我们过一会儿就要离开了，开始返回美国，这样你就可以在周一早上准备好去上班了，在回来的路上，我想飞往格陵兰岛，好好评估一下他们距离完成前六根支柱还有多远。

CHISTINA

Alex, I'll be ready when you are.

克里斯蒂娜

亚历克斯，我会为你做好准备。

ALEX

Mary will help you get everything ready; we'll probably leave in an hour so do whatever you need to do by then.

亚历克斯
玛丽会帮你准备好一切；我们可能在一小时内出
发，所以到那时你需要做的一切都做好。

CHRISTINA
Ok Alex.

克里斯蒂娜
好的，亚历克斯。

It was a bittersweet moment as the staff lined up to see Alex and Christina leave to return to America. Christina and Alex's brief stay brought a lot of joy and happiness, and their sudden departure created the feeling of change of season to fall, and winter was quickly approaching, after a glorious spring and summer blossoms.

当工作人员排队送亚历克斯和克里斯蒂娜返回美国时，这是一个苦乐参半的时刻。克里斯蒂娜和亚历克斯的短暂停留带来了许多欢乐和幸福，他们的突然离去让人感觉季节转入秋季，在春光明媚、夏日繁花盛开之后，冬天很快就要来临了。

Grant drove Christina and Alex to the airport in the Rolls Royce. Brad and Gladys were waiting for them at the GS650 jet. They too had their own adventures in Switzerland and the hotel accommodations that Alex provided them, more than made up for the fact they were stuck here for the weekend. It was apparent; everyone was leaving in a very happy mood.

格兰特开着劳斯莱斯把克里斯蒂娜和亚历克斯送到机场。布拉德和格拉迪斯在GS650 喷气式飞机旁等着他们。他们在瑞士也有自己的冒险经历，亚历克斯为他们提供的酒店住宿弥补了他们被困在这里度过周末的遗憾。显然，每个人都带着非常愉快的心情离开。

Jeff Sinclair, Nuuk Dome General On-site Construction Manager, was informed that Alex was arriving in Greenland to take a quick look at the pillars to make a determination about when he should fly back to be sure he was going to be there when the first roof sections were installed.

努克圆顶现场总施工经理杰夫·辛克莱 (Jeff Sinclair) 获悉，亚历克斯 (Alex) 将抵达格陵兰，快速查看一下柱子，以确定他应该何时飞回来，确保自己能在第一批屋顶部分安装完成时到达现场。

The stopover in Greenland was going to be a very short stop, probably thirty minutes, airport to the work site and back. Jeff would meet Alex and Christina at the airport in the Range Rover, take a quick ride up to the pillars, and then take him back to the airport so he could leave right away.

在格陵兰岛的停留时间很短，大概三十分钟，从机场到工作地点再返回。Jeff 会驾驶路虎揽胜在机场接 亚历克斯和 克里斯蒂娜，然后快速登上这些柱子，然后送他回机场，让他马上离开。

Flying west in a fast jet made for a long day, the sun was barely beating them by a few hundred miles per hour. In eight hours, they landed in Greenland but because of the time zone difference they had only lost four hours, so it was early afternoon when they touched down at Nuuk airport.

乘坐高速喷气式飞机向西飞行，这一天非常漫长，太阳的光照速度仅比他们每小时快几百英里。八小时后，他们抵达格陵兰岛，但由于时区差异，他们只损失了四个小时，所以当他们抵达努克机场时，已经是下午早些时候了。

True to his words, Jeff Sinclair was waiting for Alex at the airport with the Land Rover and drove Alex and Christina up to the pillars.

杰夫·辛克莱 (Jeff Sinclair) 信守诺言，开着路虎在机场等候亚历克斯 (Alex)，并载着亚历克斯 (Alex) 和克里斯蒂娜 (Christina) 来到柱子前。

CHRISTINA
Oh my god they look huge and tall.

克里斯蒂娜
天哪，它们看起来又大又高。

ALEX
Yes, and they must support the heavy weight of the
roof.

亚历克斯
是的，而且它们必须支撑屋顶的重量。

JEFF SINCLAIR
Already the Nuuk people are somewhat stunned by the
size of those pillars.

杰夫·辛克莱
努克人已经对这些石柱的大小感到有些震惊。

ALEX
And when the roof goes on more so. I've seen enough,
Let's head to the airport.

亚历克斯
屋顶建好后更是如此。我看够了，我们去机场吧。

Soon Alex and Christina were airborne and heading for New York City JFK Airport.

很快亚历克斯和克里斯蒂娜就空降并前往纽约市 （New York City） 肯尼迪机场 （JFK Airport）

It was sundown as they were landing at JFK in New York City. Rodriguez was there to meet them. Alex was taking Christina to her home when she suddenly asked:

当他们降落在纽约市肯尼迪机场时，日落时分。罗德里格斯在那里迎接他们。亚历克斯正带克里斯蒂娜回家，她突然问道：

Christina
Since it's still a little early, would you mind stopping
in and meeting my parents for a few minutes?

克里斯蒂娜
因为时间还早，你介意过来见我父母几分钟吗？

ALEX
Sure, I'd love it too.

亚历克斯
当然，我也很乐意。

Alex didn't know to the extent Christina had communicated with her mother. It seemed to Christina her mother was starting to come around and appear more positive about Alex.

亚历克斯不知道克里斯蒂娜与她母亲沟通了多少。克里斯蒂娜觉得她母亲开始转变态度，对亚历克斯的态度也更加积极了。

The pictures Christina sent to her mother were astounding. Her mother knew her baby daughter Christina had grown into incredible attractiveness but knew how to conduct her affairs. Christina was proving to her parents their fears were placed in the wrong direction.

克里斯蒂娜寄给母亲的照片令人震惊。她的母亲知道她的宝贝女儿克里斯蒂娜已经长得非常漂亮，但她知道如何处理自己的私事。克里斯蒂娜向她的父母证明了他们的担心是错误的。

Christina texted her parents and asked them to park one of the cars on the street so the limo could pull into the driveway since they might be there for a while.

克里斯蒂娜给她的父母发短信，让他们把一辆车停在街上，这样豪华轿车就可以停进车道，因为他们可能会在那里待一会儿。

<u>INT. EVENING. QUEENS NEW YORK. CHRISTINA GARISON PARENT'S HOME.</u>

<u>内景，晚上。纽约皇后区·克里斯蒂娜·加里森父母的家。</u>

By the time they arrived at Christina's parents' home, the driveway was clear, and Christina informed Alex that Rodriguez could pull in there while he waited.

当他们到达克里斯蒂娜父母家时，车道上已经畅通无阻，克里斯蒂娜告诉亚历克斯，罗德里格斯可以在车道上停车，而他则在车道上等候。

Alex was a little apprehensive at first, he of course wanted to make a good first impression, but the hundred pictures that Christina had already sent made a good pictorial record on how the two appeared ideal for each other.

亚历克斯一开始有点担心，他当然想给人留下一个好的第一印象，但克里斯蒂娜已经发来的一百张照片很好地记录了两人看起来多么相配。

Christina's mother knew her daughter had not smiled like that in a long time. Alex had caused her metamorphism, unparalleled any in her life. The change was extraordinary. Christina was beaming with self-confidence and happiness that seemed to evade her in the past.

克里斯蒂娜的母亲知道她的女儿已经很久没有这样笑过了。亚历克斯让她发生了蜕变，这是她一生中前所未有的。这种变化是非凡的。克里斯蒂娜满脸自信和幸福，这在过去似乎一直没有。

Christina and Alex approached the front door and just as Christina was pressing the doorbell, her mother opened the door.

克里斯蒂娜和亚历克斯走到前门，就在克里斯蒂娜按门铃的时候，她的母亲打开了门。

**MRS. GARRISON**
(Christina's Mother)
Please come in.

加里森夫人
（克里斯蒂娜的母亲）
请进来。

Mr. Garrison was there standing a few feet back. He had a respectful gaze and immediately began to size up his potential future son-in-law, based on what his wife had informed him.

加里森先生站在几英尺远的地方。他带着尊重的目光，立即开始根据妻子告诉他的情况来评估他未来的潜在女婿。

Spending a lot of time with guys in combat situations in Vietnam, Mr. Garrison could spot a chickenshit a mile away. Mr. Garrison was now analyzing Alex to decide: what kind of person is Alex?

在越南与战友们相处了很长时间，加里森先生一眼就能看出胆小鬼。加里森先生现在正在分析亚历克斯，以确定：亚历克斯是什么样的人？

Having studied Christina's one hundred plus pictures with his wife, Mr. Garrison has drawn some conclusions.

在研究了克里斯蒂娜和妻子的一百多张照片后，加里森先生得出了一些结论。

Of course, Christina, with her very private discussions texting her mother, could not inform her father of the things that only she and her mother could discuss.

当然，克里斯蒂娜与母亲的私下谈话内容非常私密，她无法将只有她和母亲才能讨论的事情告诉父亲。

Christina's mother knew that Christina had just gone through a lot and she was very vulnerable now and prayed that Alex remained true to his word of the type of relationship they were entering.

克里斯蒂娜的母亲知道克里斯蒂娜刚刚经历了很多，现在非常脆弱，她祈祷亚历克斯能够信守承诺，他们正在建立这种关系。

Christina and her mother went to the kitchen to make some coffee, which Alex was more than happy to receive, leaving him alone with Mr. Garrison for a few minutes.

克里斯蒂娜和她的母亲去厨房煮咖啡，亚历克斯非常高兴，只留下他和加里森先生单独呆了几分钟。

The two chatted and quickly found they had similar interests as Alex was a history buff. Their political leanings were similar.

两人聊着聊着，很快发现他们有相似的兴趣，因为亚历克斯是个历史迷。他们的政治倾向也相似。

MR. GARRISON
Alex, tell me, how do you feel about my daughter?

加里森先生
亚历克斯，你觉得我女儿怎么样。

ALEX
Mr. Garrison, I want you to know I'm very attached
to Christina.

亚历克斯
加里森先生，我想让你知道，我非常依恋克里斯
蒂娜。

MR. GARRISON
What does that mean exactly?

加里森先生
这到底是什么意思？

ALEX
It means I want her in my life.

亚历克斯
这意味着我希望她出现在我的生命中。

MR. GARRISON
Does she know this?

加里森先生
她知道吗？

ALEX
I hope so, and I'll do the best I can to make sure she does.

亚历克斯
我希望如此，我会尽我所能确保她知道。

MR. GARRISON
Alex, Christina is a very special lady.

加里森先生
亚历克斯，克里斯蒂娜是一位非常特别的女士。

ALEX
I know Mr. Garrison. That's one of the reasons why I'm very attracted to Christina.

亚历克斯
我认识加里森先生。这也是我非常喜欢克里斯蒂娜的原因之一。

MR. GARRISON
Alex, what qualities in Christina do you like the best?

加里森先生
亚历克斯，你最喜欢克里斯蒂娜的哪些品质？

ALEX
Mr. Garrison, I'm convinced Christina will be loyal to me and always try to help me as much as she can.

亚历克斯
加里森先生，我相信克里斯蒂娜会忠于我，并总是尽其所能帮助我。

MR. GARRISON
Alex, a man of your means probably doesn't need much help from anyone.

加里森先生
亚历克斯，像你这样有钱的人可能不需要任何人
的太多帮助。

ALEX

On the contrary, Mr. Garrison, her emotional support
and companionship is that tangible asset I can't get
anywhere else nor desire to obtain elsewhere.

亚历克斯

相反，加里森先生，她的情感支持和陪伴是我在
其他地方得不到的，也不想在其他地方得到的有
形资产。

MR. GARRISON

That's interesting to know Alex. What are your plans
with Christina?

加里森先生

很高兴认识亚历克斯。你对克里斯蒂娜有什么计
划？

ALEX

I'm involved in building these domes, that will keep
me busy for quite some time, but with Christina's help,
I'll try to learn to take more time off so I can be with
her, and we can build a family together.

亚历克斯

我参与了这些圆顶的建造，这会让我忙上好一阵
子，但在克里斯蒂娜的帮助下，我会试着学会抽
出更多的时间，这样我就可以和她在一起，我们
可以一起建立一个家庭。

MR. GARRISON

Alex, are you truly attached to Christina?

加里森先生
她知道这个会很高兴的。

ALEX

Yes, Mr. Garrison, I believe Christina and I have
reached the point of no return. I've made up my mind,
I will always want to be with your daughter.

亚历克斯
是的，加里森先生，我相信克里斯蒂娜和我已经

到了无法挽回的地步。我下定了决心，我会一直
和你的女儿在一起。

MR. GARRISON
She'll be happy to know that.

加里森先生
我希望如此。

ALEX
I hope so.

亚历克斯
我希望如此。

About that time the coffee arrived, and the chatter became a lot less heavy. Christina was very happy about the way her parents treated Alex.

大约在那个时候，咖啡来了，闲聊变得不那么沉重了。克里斯蒂娜对父母对待亚历克斯的方式非常满意。

As educators, Christina's parents had learned long ago how to size up someone quick, and their research on Alex had turned up mostly positives.

作为教育工作者，克里斯蒂娜的父母早就学会了如何快速评估一个人，他们对亚历克斯的研究大多是积极的。

Alex wasn't the rich playboy type and seemed to be aloof in the past and never had much of a public record of involvement with any women and her mother's secret communique with Christina well explained he was a healthy male, who would most likely be a good partner. Christina reported Alex had a sweet demeanor, and the trajectory was obvious.

亚历克斯不是有钱的花花公子类型，过去似乎很冷漠，从未公开与任何女性交往过，她母亲与克里斯蒂娜的秘密交流很好地解释了他是一个健康的男性，很可能是一个好的伴侣。克里斯蒂娜说亚历克斯举止温柔，轨迹显而易见。

In a while when Alex finished his cup of coffee, he announced:

过了一会儿，亚历克斯喝完咖啡，他宣布：

ALEX
I need to get back to Minnesota tonight, we have some
big events coming up and I need to make a lot of
preparations. So, I must say good night.

亚历克斯
我今晚需要回明尼苏达州，我们有一些大活动要
参加，我需要做很多准备。所以，我必须说晚
安。

MRS. GARRISON
(Christina's Mother)
Alex, thank you for stopping in.

加里森夫人
（克里斯蒂娜的母亲）
亚历克斯，谢谢你的来访。

They all stood up and escorted Alex to the front door. Christina's mother and father were somewhat struck when Christina grabbed Alex and hugged him and kissed him and he held her for a brief while hugging her with his eyes closed. It was apparent something deep and lasting had developed between them. Alex then left.

他们都站起来，护送亚历克斯到前门。当克里斯蒂娜抓住亚历克斯，拥抱他、亲吻他，而亚历克斯闭着眼睛拥抱了她一会儿时，克里斯蒂娜的父母有些震惊。显然，他们之间已经产生了某种深刻而持久的感情。亚历克斯随后离开了。

***

## INT. DAY. ALEX BAXTER'S HOME IN MINNESOTA.

白天，亚历克斯·巴克斯特在明尼苏达州的家。

Two days later, all hell broke loose. Alex was home doing work, planning a trip for the first roof installation as the six pillars were almost complete. *Magazine Femmes Réelles Exigeantes* did the nuclear option. Alex and Christina were on the front cover.

两天后，一切都乱套了。亚历克斯在家工作，计划去安装第一个屋顶，因为六根柱子几乎已经完工。《真实女性》杂志采取了核选项。亚历克斯和克里斯蒂娜上了封面。

*Michelle Montez* had done a complete expose.

米歇尔·蒙特兹 做了一个完整的揭露。

*Magazine Femmes Réelles Exigeantes* research department had dug deeply into every nook and cranny for information on Christina and her family.

《真实女性》杂志 (Magazine Femmes Réelles Exigeantes) 研究部门深入挖掘了克里斯蒂娜及其家人的每一个角落。

Luckily for Christina, her father was a national hero and lived such an exemplary life, they couldn't get wicked with him even though he was black, but actually ½ Cherokee Indian.

克里斯蒂娜很幸运，她的父亲是一位民族英雄，过着模范的生活，他们无法对他恶毒，尽管他是黑人，但实际上是半个切诺基印第安人。

Christina's mother was also a pillar of society so there wasn't much Magazine Femmes Réelles Exigeantes could do to defame her.

克里斯蒂娜的母亲也是社会支柱，因此《真实女性外出杂志》无法对她进行太多诽谤。

Christina had no record or history of anything they could find, but the way the article was written, she was portrayed as the gold digger from Queens and was helped by a non-profit organization by providing her with some employment she probably couldn't find elsewhere. Nowhere did it mention she had a master's degree and an MBA working in management for the non-profit.

克里斯蒂娜没有任何记录或历史，但文章的写作方式将她描绘成来自皇后区的淘金者，并得到了一家非营利组织的帮助，为她提供了一些她可能在其他地方找不到的工作。文章中没有提到她拥有硕士学位和工商管理硕士学位，在非营利组织从事管理工作。

The New York newspapers somehow got wind of the Magazine Femmes Réelles Exigeantes story and plagiarized the hell out of it and there was Christina in just about every newspaper on multiple pages.

纽约的报纸不知怎么地得到了《真实女性外出杂志》的故事，并大肆抄袭，克里斯蒂娜几乎出现在每份报纸的多个版面上。

The newspaper mentioned the Magazine Femmes Réelles Exigeantes which was easy to find internet links to get the electronic copy for a small fee.

报纸提到了《真实女性外出杂志》，很容易找到互联网链接，只需支付少量费用即可获得电子版。

Tuesday morning someone brought the paper into the office, but that really didn't start the gossip to heavy. It was when they got online to Magazine Femmes Réelles Exigeantes web site, and those glorious high-resolution pictures of the two love birds that got everyone talking. One thing was certain, Christina certainly looked glamorous.

星期二早上有人把报纸带到办公室，但这并没有真正引起流言蜚语。当他们出现在《真实女性》杂志（Magazine Femmes Réelles Exigeantes）网站上时，这对情侣的高清照片引起了大家的热议。有一点是肯定的，克里斯蒂娜看起来确实很迷人。

Stephanie's friend Barbara called her and having paid the fee for the download from *Magazine Femmes Réelles Exigeantes* emailed the link to Stephanie. Now it was clear and apparent, Stephanie's worst nightmare just came true. Alex had fallen in love with the woman she saw in the elevator.

斯蒂芬妮的朋友芭芭拉给她打了电话，并支付了《真实女性杂志》下载费用，通过电子邮件将链接发送给了斯蒂芬妮。现在一切都很清楚了，斯蒂芬妮最可怕的噩梦成真了。亚历克斯爱上了她在电梯里看到的那个女人。

Alex was informed by a phone call from Claude Reardon about the New York newspapers reporting on the *Magazine Femmes Réelles Exigeantes* article that *Michelle Montez* had wrote.

亚历克斯接到克劳德·里尔登的电话，得知纽约报纸报道了米歇尔·蒙特兹撰写的《真实女性杂志》文章。

Alex called Christina immediately.

亚历克斯立即打电话给克里斯蒂娜。

ALEX

Christiona, I'm very sorry I put you through all this, but I want you to know you are still very special to me.

亚历克斯

克里斯蒂娜，我很抱歉让你经历了这一切，但我想让你知道，你对我来说仍然很特别。

CHRISTINA

Thank you, Alex, you have no idea how important it is to me because of what you just said.

克里斯蒂娜

谢谢你，亚历克斯，你不知道你刚才说的话对我有多重要。

ALEX

Christina, this changes nothing, it just makes it a little more inconvenient because we will have to put up with a lot more BS from the public.

亚历克斯

克里斯蒂娜，这什么也没改变，只是让事情变得更加不方便，因为我们将不得不忍受更多来自公众的胡说八道。

CHRISTINA

Don't worry Alex, you warned me about this. I'm a big girl, I can take it. I know I'll have to be more careful in the future, but so will you.

克里斯蒂娜

别担心，亚历克斯，你警告过我了。我是个大女孩，我能承受。我知道我以后要更加小心，但你也一样。

ALEX

Christina, I must go to Greenland in a couple days, Stephanie will be traveling with me. Your relationship with me upsets Stephanie greatly but she is a big part of getting this dome project moving.

亚历克斯

克里斯蒂娜，几天后我必须去格陵兰，斯蒂芬妮会和我一起去。你和我的关系让斯蒂芬妮非常难过，但她是推动这个圆顶项目的重要因素。

Alex knew Christina was not going to like hearing what he had to say but he had to be frank with her to make sure there were no misunderstandings.

亚历克斯知道克里斯蒂娜不会喜欢听他说的话，但他必须坦诚相待，以确保没有误会。

ALEX

Christina, I must take Stephanie with me to make the public appearances and the ceremony we'll have up there for the milestone, then when I finish up there, I will fly down to see you.

亚历克斯

克里斯蒂娜，我必须带斯蒂芬妮一起去公开露面，参加我们在那里举行的里程碑仪式，然后当我在那里完成任务后，我会飞过去见你。

CHRISTINA

Ok Alex, you must do what you need to do. I look forward to seeing you then.

克里斯蒂娜

好的亚历克斯，你必须做你需要做的事。我期待到时候见到你。

ALEX

Christina, one other thing. I'm concerned about your safety. I've hired a firm to provide security for you and your parents.

亚历克斯
克里斯蒂娜，还有一件事。我担心你的安全。我
已经聘请了一家公司为你和你父母提供安全保
障。

CHRISTINA
When do they start?

克里斯蒂娜
他们什么时候开始？

ALEX
They're going to visit you and your parents today
and introduce you to some agents who will be doing
physical security around your homes.

亚历克斯
他们今天要拜访你和你的父母，并向你介绍一些
负责你家周围人身安全的特工。

CHRISTINA
How will we know when they are present?

克里斯蒂娜
我们怎么知道他们什么时候到场？

ALEX
They will have a parked car in your block until further
notice. We may have a problem keeping some of the
press away from you.

亚历克斯
他们会把车停在你的街区，直到另行通知。我们
可能很难阻止一些媒体骚扰你。

CHRISTINA
What about reporters harassing me at work?

克里斯蒂娜
记者在工作中骚扰我怎么办？

ALEX
I've contacted Leroy, the building security manager,
there at 120 Wall Street and you will be picked up at
work every day by Rodriguez and in the mornings
driven to work. Pinkerton's will help you get to and
from the building and the Limo.

亚历克斯
我已经联系了华尔街 120 号大楼的保安经理，勒
罗伊 (Leroy)，罗德里格斯 (Rodriguez) 每天上
班都会来接你，早上会开车送你去上班。平克顿
(Pinkertons)　会帮助你往返于大楼和豪华轿车之
间。

CHRISTINA
Understand Alex. I'll be looking forward to seeing you
when you get back.

克里斯蒂娜
明白了，亚历克斯。我期待着你回来后见到你。

ALEX
Christina, I miss you terribly.

亚历克斯
克里斯蒂娜，我非常想念你。

CHRISTINA
Alex, I miss you as well.

克里斯蒂娜
亚历克斯，我也想念你。

Alex and Stephanie flew to Greenland. Conversations like in the past were nonexistent. Alex could tell she was taking it real hard. Alex assumed Stephanie might have overstated the relationship between them to her friends and family.

亚历克斯和斯蒂芬妮飞往格陵兰岛。他们之间再也没有像过去那样交谈过。亚历克斯看得出她非常难过。亚历克斯认为斯蒂芬妮可能对她的朋友和家人夸大了他们之间的关系。

With the Magazine Femmes Réelles Exigeantes revelations and that passionate embrace caught on film, it was now a foregone conclusion Alex and Christina were lovers. Anyone with the slightest sophistication knew that where there is smoke there is usually fire.

随着《真实女性》杂志的曝光和那次激情拥抱被拍下来，现在亚历克斯和克里斯蒂娜是情侣已成定局。任何稍微有点见识的人都知道，无风不起浪。

Alex knew the room arrangements were different now. Even though he still had lingering fear of safety from that recent attack a few months back, there would be too much sensationalism if one of the wicked media types discovered they had adjoining rooms. As an added measure, his pilot Brad as put in a room between them.

亚历克斯知道现在房间的安排不同了。尽管他仍然对几个月前那次最近的袭击感到担忧，但如果某个邪恶的媒体发现他们住在相邻的房间，那也太耸人听闻了。作为额外的措施，他的飞行员布拉德被安排在他们中间的一个房间里。

Alex was just getting settled in his hotel room and there was a knock at the door. He got up and walked over and looked through the security eye piece and saw police officer Rodney Hansen standing outside. He quickly opened the door.

亚历克斯刚在酒店房间安顿下来，就听到了敲门声。他起身走过去，透过安全目镜看到警官罗德尼·汉森站在外面。他赶紧打开了门。

ALEX
Good evening, Rodney, what can I do for you?

亚历克斯
晚上好，罗德尼，有什么可以帮你的吗？

RODNEY HANSEN
May I come in I need to speak privately with you.

罗德尼·汉森
我可以进来吗？我需要和你私下谈谈。

ALEX
Sure. What do you want to discuss Rodney?

亚历克斯
当然可以。你想讨论什么，罗德尼？

RODNEY HANSEN
Mr. Baxter, I got some bad news for you. Jeff Sinclair,
the General Manager for Nuuk Dome Inc. was found
dead a little while ago.

罗德尼·汉森
巴克斯特先生，我有个坏消息要告诉你。努克圆
顶公司总经理杰夫·辛克莱不久前被发现死亡。

ALEX
How did he die?

亚历克斯
他是怎么死的？

RODNEY HANSEN
An autopsy has not yet been performed, but initial

indications are from a blunt strike to the head and several knife wounds.

罗德尼·汉森
尸检尚未进行，但初步迹象表明他头部受到钝器打击，身上还有几处刀伤。

ALEX
Jesus. Who the hell could have done this?

亚历克斯
天啊。到底是谁干的？

RODNEY HANSEN
The investigation is still preliminary; we do not currently have a person of interest. We are still collecting information at the crime scene.

罗德尼·汉森
调查仍处于初步阶段；我们目前还没有嫌疑人。我们仍在犯罪现场收集信息。

ALEX
I see.

亚历克斯
我明白了。

RODNEY HANSEN
Based on what you experienced last time, it's evident someone doesn't want this dome to get built. We'll have a detective to keep an eye on you in case there is a threat for your life.

罗德尼·汉森
根据你上次的经历，显然有人不想建造这个圆顶。我们会派一名侦探监视你，以防你的生命受到威胁。

ALEX
I appreciate that.

亚历克斯
我很感激。

Rodney Hansen left Alex's room. Alex, worrying about Stephanie, called her immediately.

罗德尼·汉森离开了亚历克斯的房间。亚历克斯担心斯蒂芬妮，立即给她打了电话。

ALEX

Hey Stephanie, I'm going to dinner in a few minutes, to a restaurant about a block away. Would you like to go?

亚历克斯

嘿，斯蒂芬妮，几分钟后我要去吃饭，去一个街区外的一家餐馆。你想去吗？

STEPHANIE
Sure.

史蒂芬妮
当然。

ALEX

Good, I'm going to call Brad and have him come with us because there is something I want to tell you both.

亚历克斯

很好，我要打电话给　布拉德，让他和我们一起去，因为我想告诉你们两个一些事情。

Fifteen minutes later the three of them left the hotel and walked a block to a restaurant for dinner. Nothing out of the ordinary, but Alex informed them on the situation with Jeff Sinclair and warned them to be careful.

十五分钟后，他们三人离开酒店，步行一个街区到一家餐厅吃饭。没有什么不寻常的，但亚历克斯告诉他们杰夫辛克莱的情况，并警告他们要小心。

Brad, who could not drink a lot of the time since he was under FAA scrutiny before flights took advantage of the situation, knowing he would not be flying for 36 hours, decided he wanted to stay at the restaurant/bar they were at. Alex and Stephanie opted to go back to the hotel and take care of business.

布拉德不能喝酒，因为他在航班利用这一情况之前受到联邦航空管理局的审查，知道自己 36 小时后不会飞行，所以决定留在他们所在的餐厅/酒吧。亚历克斯和斯蒂芬妮选择回到酒店处理事情。

*Hans Jespersen* had gotten away with the first crime. He thought he was invincible after cracking the head of Jeff Sinclair, then stabbing him with a long stiletto type knife. The knife punctured his heart from behind and killed him quickly.

汉斯·杰斯珀森　在第一次犯罪后逃脱了惩罚。他以为自己无敌了，因为他打碎了杰夫辛克莱的头，然后用一把长剑刺伤了他。刀从后面刺穿了他的心脏，很快就杀死了他。

*Hans Jespersen* had gone to work that day and tried to appear as normal, he went to the liquor store and bought more vodka and pickled herring.

汉斯 杰斯珀森 那天去上班了，他试图表现得像正常人一样，他去了酒铺买了更多的伏特加和腌鲱鱼。

*Hans Jespersen* had his stiletto on him and suddenly as he was walking home there was the target of opportunity. Alex Baxter walking along with that woman he had seen before.

汉斯·杰斯珀森拿着细高跟鞋，在回家的路上，他突然发现了一个机会目标。亚历克斯·巴克斯特和他以前见过的那个女人一起走着。

*Hans Jespersen* walked up to them and as he got near, he dropped the bottle of vodka in the snow slid the knife out and yelled:

汉斯·杰斯珀森走到他们面前，走近后，他把伏特加酒瓶扔在雪地里，拔出刀子，大喊：

*HANS JESPERSEN*
You die you motherfucker.

汉斯·杰斯珀森
你去死吧，混蛋。

As he lunged for Alex, *Hans Jespersen* got lucky and got one poke in the rib cage, it was quite painful, but not life threatening.

当他向亚历克斯扑过去时，汉斯·杰斯珀森很幸运，肋骨被刺了一下，很疼，但不会危及生命。

Stephanie screamed and not knowing what to do did the best she could and grabbed the Vodka bottle and attempted to hit Hans over the head with it. It didn't do enough damage and all it did was piss off *Hans Jespersen* more who was already high on dope turned and stabbed Stephanie giving her a mortal wound.

斯蒂芬妮尖叫起来，不知道该怎么做，她尽了最大的努力，抓起伏特加酒瓶，试图用它砸汉斯的头。这并没有造成足够的伤害，反而让已经吸毒成瘾的汉斯·杰斯珀森更加恼火，转身刺伤了斯蒂芬妮，给她造成了致命伤。

Even though Stephanie didn't disable Hans, she distracted him just barely enough where Alex could deliver a well-placed hit. Alex receiving some training in martial arts, aimed and hit Hans in the face right on the nose as hard as he could which semi knocked him unconscious, then Alex kicked him a couple times for good measure, thinking he had disabled him.

尽管斯蒂芬妮没有打倒汉斯，但她分散了他的注意力，使亚历克斯能够精准地击中他。亚历克斯接受了一些武术训练，瞄准汉斯的脸，用尽全力击中他的鼻子，将他打晕了，然后亚历克斯踢了他几脚，以为自己已经打倒了他。

Rodney Hansen had observed this all unfold about a block away was quick on his heels, running up to the fight.

罗德尼·汉森在一个街区外看到了这一切，他迅速跟上，跑向打斗现场。

Alex was concerned about Stephanie being bent down. She was coughing up blood and looked at Alex and said:

亚历克斯担心斯蒂芬妮，弯下腰。她咳血，看着亚历克斯说：

STEPHANIE
I do not feel too good Alex.

斯蒂芬妮
我感觉不太好，亚历克斯。

Alex grabbed his cell phone and was dialing 911 for an ambulance.

亚历克斯抓起手机，拨打 911 叫救护车。

*Hans Jespersen* regained his composure, grabbed the knife lying on the ground next to him suddenly got up lunged for Alex with every intent to kill him.

罗德尼·汉森恢复了镇静，抓起躺在他旁边地上的刀，突然站起来，向亚历克斯扑去，一心想杀了他。

Rodney Hansen was an excellent shot and as he realized what was about to happen, grabbed his gun out of his shoulder holster, steadied his and let off three fast bursts cutting *Hans Jespersen* down.

罗德尼·汉森是个神枪手，当他意识到即将发生什么时，他从肩部皮套中掏出枪，稳住身形，快速连射三枪，将汉斯·杰斯帕森击倒。

*Hans Jespersen* died momentarily with his eyes open and a glazed look. Within a minute Stephanie grasped her last breath and died in Alex's arms. Alex was immediately devastated, as he bore responsibility.

汉斯·杰斯帕森双眼睁开，目光呆滞，当场死亡。不到一分钟，斯蒂芬妮就咽下了最后一口气，死在了亚历克斯的怀里。亚历克斯立刻崩溃了，因为他负有责任。

In short order an ambulance and police cars arrived.

很快，救护车和警车就到了。

Hearing all the commotion word spread in the bar quickly and the customers filed out quickly to take a look. Brad went outside and saw that Alex and Stephanie were involved and Alex sat there until the ambulance people removed Stephanie's body with her head in his lap.

听到所有的骚动，酒吧里迅速传开了消息，顾客们迅速出来看一看。布拉德走到外面，看到亚历克斯和斯蒂芬妮也参与其中，亚历克斯坐在那里，直到救护车的人把斯蒂芬妮的尸体抬出来，她的头靠在他的腿上。

Brad suddenly started feeling an amount of guilt because had he gone back to the hotel with Alex and Stephanie, this probably would not  have happened.

布拉德突然开始感到内疚，因为如果他和亚历克斯和斯蒂芬妮一起回到酒店，这一切可能就不会发生了。

The first roof section going up on the dome was the worst day of Alex's life.

圆顶上的第一个屋顶部分被安装上去是亚历克斯一生中最糟糕的一天。

After spending some time at the Emergency Room getting X-rays and stitches and a few pain killers, Alex was then taken by Detective Rodney Hansen to the police station where he was asked a few questions.

在急诊室待了一段时间，做了 X 光检查、缝了针，还吃了一些止痛药后，侦探罗德尼·汉森 (Rodney Hansen) 把亚历克斯带到了警察局，问了他几个问题。

RODNEY HANSEN<br>
(Detective)<br>
Have you ever met the assailant?

罗德尼·汉森<br>
(侦探)<br>
你见过袭击者吗？

ALEX<br>
No.

RODNEY HANSEN<br>
(Detective)<br>
Do you know who he is?

罗德尼·汉森<br>
(侦探)<br>
你知道他是谁吗？

ALEX<br>
No.

亚历克斯
没有。

RODNEY HANSEN
(Detective)
Do you know anyone who knows him or of him.

罗德尼·汉森
(侦探)
你认识任何认识他或知道他的人吗？

ALEX
No.

亚历克斯
没有。

RODNEY HANSEN
(Detective)
Any idea why he attacked you and Stephanie McFarland?

罗德尼·汉森
(侦探)
知道他为什么袭击你和斯蒂芬妮·麦克法兰吗？

ALEX
He was only going after me, but Stephanie tried to stop him from stabbing me again, she simply was an innocent bystander.

亚历克斯
他只是在追我，但斯蒂芬妮试图阻止他再次刺伤我，她只是一个无辜的旁观者。

RODNEY HANSEN
(Detective)
I was a block away and saw this all begin and immediately ran your way. This is the type of an attack one doesn't expect until it all unfolds.

罗德尼·汉森
(侦探)
我当时离你只有一个街区远，看到这一切开始了，然后立即朝你跑去。这是一场人们在事情发生之前无法预料的袭击。

ALEX
Have you identified who he is?

亚历克斯
你确定他是谁了吗？

RODNEY HANSEN
(Detective)
Yes, he's a local person. Apparently according to his neighbors has recently worked as a Stevedore for Nuuk Dome Inc.

罗德尼·汉森
（侦探）
是的，他是当地人。据邻居说，他最近在 努克圆顶公司 (Nuuk Dome Inc.) 担任码头工人。

ALEX
Any connection to the Jeff Sinclair murder?

亚历克斯
与杰夫·辛克莱谋杀案有什么关系？

RODNEY HANSEN
(Detective)
We have forensics working the case, and yes there is a good possibility he's the killer in that case as well.

罗德尼·汉森
（侦探）
我们有法医在调查此案，是的，他很有可能也是那起案件的凶手。

There were no further questions, as Detective Hansen was already starting to develop a picture in his mind as to what it was all about and feared that others in the community may not be happy about the Dome construction hence this could be just the beginning of more trouble.

没有进一步的问题，因为汉森侦探已经开始在脑海中勾勒出这一切是怎么回事，他担心社区里的其他人可能对圆顶建筑不满意，因此这可能只是更多麻烦的开始。

RODNEY HANSEN
(Detective)
I'll give you a ride to your hotel now Mr. Baxter.

罗德尼·汉森
（侦探）
我现在就送你回酒店，巴克斯特先生。

ALEX
Thank you, I appreciate that.

亚历克斯
谢谢，我很感激。

As Alex walked outside Rodney Hansen's office into the police station waiting room, there was Shelley Bergman of the *North Ice News* who saw the bloody shirt and approached Alex.

当亚历克斯走出罗德尼·汉森的办公室，走进警察局候诊室时，北方冰雪新闻的雪莱·伯格曼看到了那件血淋淋的衬衫，走近了亚历克斯。

SHELLEY BERGMAN
Mr. Baxter, were you wounded in the fight outside the bar?

雪莱·伯格曼
巴克斯特先生，你在酒吧外的打斗中受伤了吗？

ALEX
No comment.

亚历克斯
无可奉告。

SHELLEY BERGMAN
Mr. Baxter, you are a public figure who's having a big impact on Nuuk Greenland, don't you think you owe the public an explanation?

雪莱·伯格曼
巴克斯特先生，你是一位公众人物，对格陵兰努克有着很大的影响，你不觉得你欠公众一个解释吗？

ALEX
My lawyer will make a statement shortly.

亚历克斯
我的律师很快就会发表声明。

Alex then proceeded to leave with Detective Hansen and went back to his hotel room and when he was alone in his room, cried. Alex shortly regained his self-control so that he could begin to make arrangements to ship Stephanie's body to Denver, her hometown and where her parents lived.

然后亚历克斯和汉森侦探一起离开，回到他的酒店房间，当他独自一人在房间里时，哭了起来。亚历克斯很快恢复了自我控制，开始安排将斯蒂芬妮的遗体运回丹佛，那是她的家乡，也是她父母居住的地方。

This startling event could not be hidden from Christina. This sensational story would be immediately in the news because Alex was involved. No doubt Shelley Bergman reporter for North Ice News has already interviewed on American, Canadian, Greenland, and Denmark news channels.

这件令人震惊的事情无法瞒过克里斯蒂娜。这个轰动一时的故事会立即成为新闻，因为亚历克斯参与其中。毫无疑问，《北方冰雪新闻》的记者雪莱·伯格曼已经在美国、加拿大、格陵兰和丹麦的新闻频道上接受过采访。

Alex called Christina after he regained his composure and asked her to go somewhere that they could talk privately and thought it was best she went home for the rest of the day.

亚历克斯恢复镇定后打电话给克里斯蒂娜，让她去一个可以私下谈谈的地方，并认为她最好回家度过这一天的剩余时间。

Christina informed her boss she needed to go home and might not be back for the rest of the day. Her boss was very understanding and was amazed she was holding up as good as she was considering the almost scandalous *Magazine Femmes Réelles Exigeantes* story that was now starting to circulate around the office.

克里斯蒂娜告诉老板她需要回家，可能一整天都不会回来。她的老板非常理解，并惊讶于她能坚持到现在，考虑到《杂志真实女性紧急救援》的报道几乎是丑闻，该报道现在开始在办公室里流传。

Rodriguez picked Christina up a short time later and drove her home. Rodriguez was happy about this arrangement because his income rose significantly with all the Limo Service he now provided for Christina at Alex's doings. But going home early with the look on Christina's face left Rodriguez with the notion that something bad might be going on.

不久之后，罗德里格斯接克里斯蒂娜回家。罗德里格斯对这种安排很满意，因为他现在为克里斯蒂娜提供的所有豪华轿车服务都让他的收入大幅增加。但是，看到克里斯蒂娜脸上的表情，罗德里格斯早早回家，觉得可能有什么不好的事情发生了。

When Christina got home, she called Alex not knowing what had occurred, but she knew something big was up and the fact Stephanie was with him, and it appears there was a history between the two.

克里斯蒂娜回到家后，她打电话给亚历克斯，不知道发生了什么，但她知道一定有什么大事发生了，而且斯蒂芬妮和他在一起，看来他们之间有一段历史。

CHRISTINA
Hello Alex.

克里斯蒂娜
你好，亚历克斯。

ALEX
Christina, thanks for calling me back. We have got something I need to discuss.

亚历克斯
克里斯蒂娜，谢谢你给我回电话。我们有事要谈。

Fearing the worst, even possibly a breakup or change of heart, Christina was just about ready for anything other than what Alex was just about to inform her.

克里斯蒂娜担心情况会更糟，甚至可能是分手或改变主意，她几乎准备好接受亚历克斯即将告诉她的任何事情。

Alex explained what just happened in Nuuk Greenland.

亚历克斯解释了格陵兰努克刚刚发生的事情。

亚历克斯
这有点沉重，你很快就会知道我有点震惊。

ALEX
This is kind of heavy duty, and you will soon know I'm kind of shook up.

CHRISTINA
I'm all ears Alex. Please let me know.

克里斯蒂娜
我洗耳恭听，亚历克斯。请告诉我。亚历克斯

ALEX
Christina, Stephanie was murdered while saving my life.

亚历克斯
克里斯蒂娜，斯蒂芬妮在救我的时候被谋杀了。

CHRISTINA
Oh my God.

克里斯蒂娜
哦，天哪。

Christina sat stunned and felt so terrible for Alex. She instantly knew that because of the kind of person Alex was, he personally would bear full responsibility for Stephanie's death. And what made it even more painful was Stephanie's last act was to save his life.

克里斯蒂娜惊呆地坐在那里，为亚历克斯感到难过。她立刻意识到，因为亚历克斯是这样的一个人，他个人将对斯蒂芬妮的死负全部责任。更让人痛苦的是，斯蒂芬妮的最后一件事是救他一命。

This far away, there wasn't much Christina could do for Alex, but she suggested:

这么远的地方，克里斯蒂娜为亚历克斯做不了什么，但她建议：

CHRISTINA
Alex, when you get finished there in Greenland, why don't you just come back to New York and stay a few days with me at my house. My parents will understand and help keep people away plus the security guys are here now.

克里斯蒂娜
亚历克斯，当你在格陵兰岛完成任务后，为什么不回到纽约，在我家和我一起住几天呢。我的父母会理解并帮助阻止人们靠近，而且安全人员现在就在这里。

ALEX
Yes, I would like that. It will be a couple days; we are going to have a memorial for Jeff Sinclair.

亚历克斯
是的，我希望如此。过几天，我们会为杰夫·辛克莱举行追悼会。

CHRISTINA
Their deaths were so close together.

克里斯蒂娜
他们的死亡时间非常接近。

ALEX
The perpetrator who killed Stephanie most likely killed Jeff since the knife wounds were from the same type of knife. The police are doing forensics now, should know more soon.

亚历克斯
杀害斯蒂芬妮的凶手很可能杀死了杰夫，因为刀
伤是同一种刀造成的。警方目前正在进行法医鉴
定，很快就会有更多线索。

As it was, *Hans Jespersen* didn't do a very good job cleaning up and they found traces of Jeff's DNA in his apartment, which confirms he was the killer in both cases.

事实上，汉斯·杰斯帕森没有很好地清理现场，他们在杰夫的公寓里发现了杰夫的 DNA 痕迹，这证实了他在两起案件中都是凶手。

Alex had Brad fly down to New York where a company that worked on his jet had the technicians that could remove enough seats to get Stephanie's casket aboard the Jet which they flew back to Denver and turned over to representatives of her family.

亚历克斯让布拉德飞到纽约，一家为他的飞机提供服务的公司有技术人员可以拆下足够的座椅，把斯蒂芬妮的棺材装上飞机，然后他们飞回丹佛，交给了她家人的代表。

Stephanie's family wasn't that well off and only Alex knew he had given her money to buy the company which he immediately forgave.

斯蒂芬妮的家庭并不富裕，只有亚历克斯知道他给了她钱来买下这家公司，亚历克斯立即原谅了她。

The family then inherited a viable company with no debt. A funeral was set for a few days later.

然后，这个家庭继承了一家没有债务的可行公司。几天后安排了葬礼。

Meanwhile Alex flew back to New York and when it was dark to avoid public exposure, went to Christina's home arriving after dark, where he could commiserate his emotions with Christina's help.

与此同时，亚历克斯飞回纽约，天黑后为了避免被公众曝光，他去了克里斯蒂娜的家，在天黑后他才到达，在克里斯蒂娜的帮助下，他可以抚慰自己的情绪。

Christina took some vacation time, which was good because Alex's involvement in the murder became big news as the public had developed a fascination with the story.

克里斯蒂娜休了一段时间假，这很好，因为亚历克斯参与谋杀案成了大新闻，因为公众对这个故事产生了浓厚的兴趣。

*Magazine Femmes Réelles Exigeantes* was selling out their entire magazine production over this story. *Michelle Montez* had her golden achievement. As one American Tabloid Magazine Reporter stated:

《真实女性》杂志因为这个故事卖光了他们所有的杂志。米歇尔·蒙特兹获得了她的黄金成就。正如一位美国小报杂志记者所说：

American Tabloid

Magazine Reporter

*Michelle Montez* DOME MAN report in *Magazine Femmes Réelles Exigeantes* even made us blush.

美国小报

杂志记者

米歇尔·蒙特兹在《真实女性》杂志上发表的 穹顶

人 (DOME MAN) 报道甚至让我们脸红。

The Dome had lost its luster with Alex, but he didn't give up. Christina's parents were notably alarmed but understood two things: there wasn't much they could do about it and that Christina and Alex had bonded entirely.

圆顶屋对亚历克斯来说已经失去了光彩，但他没有放弃。克里斯蒂娜的父母非常惊慌，但他们明白两件事：他们对此无能为力，克里斯蒂娜和亚历克斯已经完全团结在一起。

Christina's love for Alex made it very easy for her to cope with any inconvenience and disruption in her profession and her personal life. She was being tested like never before.

克里斯蒂娜对亚历克斯的爱使她能够非常轻松地应对职业和个人生活中的任何不便和干扰。她正在接受前所未有的考验。

Christina's inner strength was now the foundation that Alex leaned on so they could cope with the developments together as a couple. For Claude Rearden, it was extremely tough, because Jeff Sinclair was a dynamic individual and big shoes to fill in his absence.

克里斯蒂娜的内在力量现在是亚历克斯依靠的基础，这样他们就可以作为一对夫妻共同应对事态的发展。对于克劳德·里尔登来说，这是极其艰难的，因为杰夫·辛克莱是一个充满活力的人，在他不在的时候，很难填补。

In the panic phone calls between him and Alex and the other partners, Claude stepped up to the plate and offered to cover the temporary shortcomings and flew to Greenland to be temporary General Manager, at the same time hired a new General Manager and started teaching him on the job to one day take it all over.

在他和亚历克斯以及其他合伙人之间惊慌失措的电话中，克劳德挺身而出，主动承担起弥补暂时不足的责任，飞往格陵兰担任临时总经理，同时聘请了一位新总经理，并开始在工作中教他如何有朝一日接管一切。

That was actually a brilliant move because only an individual like Claude Rearden could cope with the sudden impact by losing the previous General Manager on such a huge project.

这实际上是一个绝妙的举动，因为只有像 克劳德·里尔登来 这样的人才能应对突然失去如此庞大项目的前任总经理所带来的影响。

Later in the week Alex recovered emotionally and physically feeling better after having 35 stitches for his knife wound removed and his bruised ribs were healing, and he found that if he slept on his other side he could cope if he had sufficient pain killers.

本周晚些时候，亚历克斯情绪和身体都恢复了，他拆掉了 35 针刀伤，肋骨受伤正在愈合，感觉好多了，他发现如果睡在另一侧，只要服用足够的止痛药，他就能应付。

When Christina saw Alex's knife wounds it became crystal clear to her that Alex was a victim and came close to being killed himself. Doctors informed Alex just a few inches over and he would be dead. Alex was such an ideal person he would wish he died, and Stephanie lived. But he realized it was all out of his control.

当 克里斯蒂娜看到亚历克斯的刀伤时，她清楚地意识到 亚历克斯是一个受害者，差点被自己杀死。医生告诉 亚历克斯，只要再多几英寸，他就会死。亚历克斯是一个如此理想的人，他希望自己死去，而斯蒂芬妮活着。但他意识到这一切都超出了他的控制范围。

Alex then flew to Denver for Stephanies' funeral, which marked the end of one phase of his life.

随后，亚历克斯飞往丹佛参加斯蒂芬妮的葬礼，这标志着他生命中一个阶段的结束。

At the funeral Stephanie's friend Barbara requested a private meeting, and in that discussion, it became apparent that Stephanie had told a lot of people their relationship was far more than it was. Stephanie's impression of what their relationship stood for was diabolically different to what Alex considered to be the case.

在葬礼上，斯蒂芬妮的朋友芭芭拉要求举行一次私人会面，在那次讨论中，很明显 斯蒂芬妮告诉很多人他们的关系远不止于此。斯蒂芬妮对他们的关系的印象与亚历克斯认为的完全不同。

ALEX

I assure you, I never had sex with Stephanie, and I believe as I was taught, never stick your pen in company ink.

亚历克斯

我向你保证，我从未与斯蒂芬妮发生过性关系，而且我相信正如我被教导的那样，永远不要将你的钢笔沾上公司墨水。

Barbara kind of figured that out and informed Alex:

芭芭拉大概明白了这一点，并告诉亚历克斯：

BARBARA
Stephanie might have embellished a bit.

芭芭拉
斯蒂芬妮可能有点夸大其词。

ALEX
It doesn't matter now, Stephanie is gone and will be missed by a lot of people.

亚历克斯
现在没关系，斯蒂芬妮走了，很多人都会想念她。

Barbara then warned Alex:

芭芭拉随后警告亚历克斯：

BARBARA
Stephanie's family isn't too happy with you because of the *Magazine Femmes Réelles Exigeantes* business and you breaking her heart.

芭芭拉
斯蒂芬妮的家人对你不太满意，因为《真实女性》杂志的事情和你伤了她的心。

Alex responded in a terse manner:

亚历克斯简短地回答道：

ALEX
All I can do now is simply leave and put it out of my mind because trying to set the record straight would be counterproductive.

亚历克斯
我现在能做的就是离开，忘掉这件事，因为试图澄清事实只会适得其反。

BARBARA
I suppose it's time to move on and put this behind us the best way we can.

芭芭拉
我想是时候继续前进并以最好的方式把这件事抛在脑后了。

***

## EXT. DAY. NYC. MANHATTAN JEWELER DISTRICT.

第二天。纽约•曼哈顿珠宝区。

Alex flew back to New York the following day. He had a few ideas about how just to do that. But first thing was first, he had Rodriguez drop him off at a Jeweler in Manhattan. There was a dozen of them close together; he could just walk to the others if they didn't have what he wanted. He had to guess on her ring size, as it could always be altered and from his recollection it would be about the size of his pinky finger or a little smaller.

第二天，亚历克斯飞回了纽约。他有几个想法。但首先，他让罗德里格斯把他送到曼哈顿的一家珠宝店。那里有十几家珠宝店，彼此很近；如果没有他想要的，他可以步行去其他的。他不得不猜测她的戒指尺寸，因为它随时可以改变，而且在他的记忆中，戒指的尺寸大约是小指的大小，或者更小一点。

JEWELRY STORE
(Employee)
What may I do for you sir?

珠宝店
（员工）
先生，我能为您做些什么？

ALEX
I would like to buy my girlfriend a ring.

亚历克斯
我想给我女朋友买一枚戒指。

JEWELRY STORE
(Employee)
Any particular style?

珠宝店
（员工）
有什么特别的款式吗？

ALEX
Something like one of these.

亚历克斯
像这个一样。

Alex pointed to one of the most expensive trays of diamonds locked up in a display case that would no doubt go into a vault during the night closed store hours.

亚历克斯指着陈列柜里锁着的最昂贵的钻石托盘之一，毫无疑问，在夜间关门营业时，它会被放进保险库。

JEWELRY STORE
(Employee)
Are there one of those you would like to look at.

珠宝店
（员工）
有没有哪一款是你特别想看的？

ALEX
Yes, the one in the upper corner with a square face to it.

亚历克斯
是的，就是上角的那个方形的。

JEWELRY STORE
(Employee)
Sir, that ring is $185,000.00.

珠宝店
（员工）
先生，那枚戒指价值 185,000.00 美元。

ALEX
I just spent $1 million on diamond jewelry for her, so
$185,000 for an engagement ring is a bargain.

亚历克斯
我刚为她花了 100 万美元买钻石首饰，所以
185,000 美元买一枚订婚戒指很划算。

The salesman sized up Alex who was well dressed and most likely the real deal responded:

销售员打量了一下穿着考究、很可能是真货的 亚历克斯，然后回答道：

JEWELRY STORE
(Employee)
Ok sir, one minute please.

珠宝店
（员工）
好的先生，请稍等片刻。

The Jewelry Store Employee then punched in a series of numbers on a security lock and suddenly a noise sounded and the bullet proof glass door on the salesman side slid open. The salesman then pulled the little case that held the ring out of the display case and put it up on the counter.

珠宝店员工随后在安全锁上输入了一串数字，突然响起一声响声，销售员一侧的防弹玻璃门滑开了。销售员随后将装着戒指的小盒子从展示柜中取出，放在柜台上。

ALEX
My girlfriend will probably have to come back to get it sized but if you can try putting it on my little pinky up an inch or so, then that's probably the right size.

亚历克斯
我的女朋友可能得回来量一下尺寸，但如果你试着把它戴在我小指上，向上一英寸左右，那么这可能是合适的尺寸。

JEWELRY STORE
(Employee)
There you go.

珠宝店
（员工）
就这样。

The salesman slid the ring on Alex's finger.

销售员将戒指戴在亚历克斯的手指上。

ALEX
That will work, I'll buy it.

亚历克斯
这样就行了，我会买的。

JEWELRY STORE
(Employee)
Ok sir, how do you intend to pay for it?

珠宝店
（员工）
好的，先生，您打算怎么付款？

Alex pulled out his wallet and a credit card and handed it to the salesman who then shut the display case door and punched in a security code and Alex could then hear the mechanism making noise as it locked the display case door.

亚历克斯掏出钱包和信用卡，递给销售员，销售员关上展示柜门，输入安全代码，然后亚历克斯听到机械装置锁上展示柜门时发出的声音。

The salesman took the credit card and the ring to a small table about five feet behind the counter where he fed the credit card into a reader connected to a terminal and within a minute a receipt printed out. The salesman handed it to Alex with a gold pen.

销售员拿着信用卡和戒指走到柜台后面约五英尺的一张小桌子上，将信用卡插入连接到终端的读卡器，一分钟内就打印出一张收据。销售员用一支金笔将收据递给亚历克斯。

JEWELRY STORE
(Employee)
Please sign this copy.

珠宝店
（员工）
请签署此副本。

Alex signed it and handed the receipt and pen back to the salesman. The salesman had a little booklet which was some kind of an assay book for the diamond mounted on the ring and the ring plus the ring box and put it and the receipt in the bag and handed it to Alex.

亚历克斯签了字，将收据和笔交还给销售员。销售员有一本小册子，是戒指上镶嵌的钻石和戒指以及戒指盒的化验书，他把小册子和收据放进袋子里，递给了亚历克斯。

JEWELRY STORE
(Employee)
Sir, your receipt is in the bag, bring that in if you come back and we'll adjust the ring to fit her finger at no additional charge.

珠宝店
（员工）
先生，您的收据在袋子里，您回来时请带上它，我们会调整戒指以适合她的手指，不收取额外费用。

ALEX
Thank you.

ALEX
谢谢。

JEWELRY STORE
(Employee)
And thank you sir, I hope she likes the ring.

珠宝店
（员工）
谢谢先生，我希望她喜欢这枚戒指。

ALEX
I'm sure she will.

亚历克斯
我相信她会喜欢的。

Alex then put the ring box in his pocket and pulled out his cell phone and called Rodriguez.

亚历克斯随后将戒指盒放进口袋，掏出手机给 罗德里格斯打电话。

ALEX
I'm ready to leave now.

亚历克斯
我现在准备离开了。

RODRIGUEZ
I'll be pulling up in one minute Alex.

罗德里格斯
我马上就来，亚历克斯。

And about one minute later Alex walked out as the Limo pulled up next to the curb, then Rodriguez got out, walked over and quickly opened the door just in time for Alex to move inside the Limo. Rodriguez then got into the Limo and drove it to Queens and Christina's home. He had a small suitcase; the rest was left in the plane back at the airport.

大约一分钟后，亚历克斯从车里出来，豪华轿车停在路边，罗德里格斯也下了车，走过去迅速打开车门，亚历克斯正好进入了豪华轿车。罗德里格斯随后上了豪华轿车，开车去了皇后区克里斯蒂娜的家。他带了一个小行李箱，其余的东西留在了机场的飞机上。

Alex informed Rodriguez:

亚历克斯告诉罗德里格斯：

ALEX
It's just a small suitcase, I can handle it, and you can
take off now.

亚历克斯
这只是一个小行李箱，我可以拿，你现在可以走
了。

RODRIGUEZ
Thanks Alex.

罗德里格斯
谢谢亚历克斯。

ALEX
I do not expect any to go anywhere until the morning;
you can leave and go home.

亚历克斯
我预计明天早上你不会去任何地方；你可以离开
回家了。

RODRIGUEZ
See you tomorrow, Alex.

罗德里格斯
明天见，亚历克斯。

ALEX
Have a good night.

亚历克斯
祝你晚安。

RODRIGUEZ
Thanks.

罗德里格斯
谢谢。

Alex walked up the sidewalk and could see lights were on in the house and it was
occupied with people inside. Out of habit he rang the doorbell which was opened right
away by Christina's father.

亚历克斯走上人行道，看到房子里灯亮着，里面有人。出于习惯，他按响了门铃，克里斯蒂娜的父亲马上就开了门。

MR. GARRISON
Welcome home Alex.

加里森先生
欢迎回家，亚历克斯。

ALEX
Thank you, Mr. Garrison.

亚历克斯
谢谢你，加里森先生。

Mrs. Garrison and another lady whom Alex had never met were there and something smelled good.

加里森夫人和另一位亚历克斯从未见过的女士在那里，闻起来很香。

Christina approached Alex and put her arms around him and the two hugged each other for a brief period. It gave Alex a sense of relief that he was back after some turmoil. Christina suddenly broke free of Alex and announced:

克里斯蒂娜走近亚历克斯，搂住他，两人短暂地拥抱在一起。经过一番折腾，亚历克斯终于回来了，这让他松了一口气。克里斯蒂娜突然挣脱了亚历克斯，宣布：

CHRISTINA
Let me introduce you go my good friend Jann.

克里斯蒂娜
让我向你介绍我的好朋友詹恩。

A nice lady about Christina's age stepped forward and said hello and held out her hand which Alex shook.

一位和克里斯蒂娜年龄相仿的好心女士走上前来打招呼，并伸出手与亚历克斯握了握。

JANN
Nice to meet you.

詹恩
很高兴见到你。

ALEX
Likewise.

亚历克斯
同样。

## CHRISTINA
Jann is a great cook and my best friend for many years.
We had not seen each other for a few weeks because
I've been busy.

克里斯蒂娜
詹恩是一位很棒的厨师，也是我多年来最好的朋
友。由于我一直很忙，我们已经有几个星期没见
面了。

## ALEX
Sounds like fun getting together with your friend.

亚历克斯
和你的朋友聚在一起听起来很有趣。

Alex then smiled.

亚历克斯笑了。

Alex already knew a little about Jann from the private detective report on Christina.
She was a nice lady and worked at 120 Wall Street for another company and had
developed a friendship with Christina when they were both interns there several years
ago.

亚历克斯已经从私人侦探对克里斯蒂娜的报告中对詹恩有了一点了解。她是一
位好心的女士，在华尔街 120 号的另一家公司工作，几年前她们都是那里的实
习生，与克里斯蒂娜建立了友谊。

Christina's mother broke into the conversation.

克里斯蒂娜的母亲打断了谈话。

## MRS. GARRISON
Dinner is ready if you all would like to take a seat.

夫人加里森
如果你们想坐下的话，晚餐已经准备好了。

Soon they were all enjoying dinner which Jann helped make.

很快，他们都开始享用詹恩帮忙做的晚餐。

Jann had noticed recently after Christina met Alex how she had blossomed. Her smile was more constant, she just seemed to be always in a more cheerful mood.

詹恩最近注意到克里斯蒂娜在遇到亚历克斯后变得容光焕发。她更加经常微笑，似乎总是心情愉快。

Then suddenly, there was the news spectacle, and Christina didn't show up for work a couple days, and while Alex was away handling matters, Jann had called and asked to come by.

然后突然出现了新闻奇闻，克里斯蒂娜几天没有出现在上班，而当亚历克斯外出处理事务时，詹恩打来电话要求过来。

Christina was feeling bad at the time, fearing something was happening with Alex and the stress of the tabloids and gossip columns creating havoc, thought she could use a friend about then and asked her to come over.

克里斯蒂娜当时心情非常糟糕，担心亚历克斯出了什么事，小报和八卦专栏带来的压力让她心烦意乱，她想找个朋友谈谈，于是就请她过来。

Christina's mother, also concerned, came over and offered to cook dinner because she was concerned her daughter might skip eating and endanger her health.

克里斯蒂娜的母亲也很担心，她过来主动提出做晚饭，因为她担心女儿可能会不吃饭，危害她的健康。

Alex sat next to Christina and across from her parents. Jann sat at the end of the table next to Christina and her mother who were facing each other.

亚历克斯坐在克里斯蒂娜旁边，对面是她的父母。詹恩坐在桌子的尽头，克里斯蒂娜和她的母亲面对面。

The food was essentially a vegetarian meal as Christina's mother was really keen on health issues from being a teacher. That was just fine for Alex, and it was very tasty.

食物基本上是素食，因为克里斯蒂娜的母亲非常关心作为一名教师的健康问题。这对亚历克斯来说很好，而且非常美味。

Alex was kind of quiet and everyone knew he was going through a lot, so they didn't try to engage him too much and gave him plenty of space. He often smiled and tried to appear cheerful despite these recent events. Nobody at the table expected what he was going to do.

亚历克斯有点安静，每个人都知道他经历了很多事情，所以他们没有试图过多地打扰他，给了他足够的空间。尽管最近发生了这些事情，但他经常微笑，并试图表现出开朗的样子。餐桌上没有人预料到他会做什么。

MRS. GARRISON
Would anyone like some coffee and dessert?

加里森夫人
有人想喝点咖啡和甜点吗？

Alex
Yes, I would like some.

亚历克斯
是的，我想要一些。

Soon Alex had a cup of coffee and some apple pie dessert, which was delicious and commented:

很快亚历克斯就喝了一杯咖啡，吃了一些苹果派甜点，味道很好，他评论道：

ALEX
This pie must have been made by someone who knew
how to bake well.

亚历克斯
这个派一定是由一个知道如何烘焙的人做的。

MRS. GARRISON
Christina made the apple pie.

加里森夫人
克里斯蒂娜做了苹果派。

Alex used that as a segue to do what he wanted to do tonight and as far as he was concerned it didn't matter if all present observed it as he reached into his suit coat jacket pocket and pulled out the little box and announced:

亚历克斯利用这个机会做了他今晚想做的事情，就他而言，当他把手伸进西装外套口袋，掏出小盒子并宣布时，在场的所有人都看到了，这并不重要：

ALEX
Christina, there is something I want to give you to
show you my sincerity of my intentions with you.

亚历克斯
克里斯蒂娜，我想给你一件东西，向你展示我对
你的诚意。

Christina's mother saw the ring box before anyone else by several seconds and they only realized what was going on by the tenor of Alex's voice as he very softly and delicately continued.

克里斯蒂娜的母亲比其他人早几秒钟看到了戒指盒，他们只是从亚历克斯非常轻柔而细腻地继续说的声音中意识到发生了什么。

Christina sitting on Alex's right had her left hand exposed, which Alex reached for and about that time a few tears were now in her mother's eye corners. Jann quickly observed Christina's mother's response and her eye's now watering and then gasped almost when she spotted the little ring box now open with a huge diamond sparkling against the blue felt surface of the ring holder.

克里斯蒂娜坐在亚历克斯的右边，露出了左手，亚历克斯伸手去抓她的手，就在这时，克里斯蒂娜母亲的眼角已经流下了几滴泪水。詹恩很快注意到了克里斯蒂娜母亲的反应，她的眼睛已经开始流泪，当她看到小戒指盒已经打开，一颗巨大的钻石在戒指盒的蓝色毡面上闪闪发光时，她几乎倒吸了一口凉气。

As if he had practiced it a few times Alex had set the little box on the table and removed the ring and momentarily proceeded to slide it on Christina's ring finger.

仿佛已经练习过几次一样，亚历克斯将小盒子放在桌子上，取下戒指，然后立即将其戴在克里斯蒂娜的无名指上。

Christina instantly saw and felt what was going on and her eyes also watered. She smiled beautifully and struggled not to break down and cry.

克里斯蒂娜立刻看到并感受到了正在发生的事情，她的眼睛也湿润了。她露出了美丽的笑容，努力不让自己哭出来。

Christina's nose was already watering up slightly as her emotions were pumping through her body almost at the level she experienced when she bravely walked into Alex's bedroom in Switzerland thus changing irrevocably the nature of their relationship forever.

克里斯蒂娜的鼻子已经有点湿润了，因为她的情绪在她体内翻腾，几乎达到了她勇敢地走进瑞士亚历克斯卧室时所经历的水平，从而永远不可逆转地改变了他们的关系。

Christina's father was also slightly emotional and after having a few private conversations with her, had learned much about Alex, and her description of him perfectly expressed an acute observation that only someone with extraordinary focus would exert.

克里斯蒂娜的父亲也有点情绪化，在与她进行了几次私人谈话后，对亚历克斯有了更多的了解，她对他的描述完美地表达了只有专注力超群的人才能做出的敏锐观察。

Christina from the very beginning had decided that she would allow Alex to pursue her, but she also would pursue him, in a careful way as to gently allow him to evolve into this new situation to avoid any possible discomfort.

克里斯蒂娜从一开始就决定让亚历克斯追求她，但她也会小心翼翼地追求他，让他慢慢适应这种新情况，避免任何可能的不适。

Christina's accommodation and reactions to him in every action Alex took reinforced his attraction for her. And now before her parents, her best friend, not knowing she would be there when he arrived, he was spontaneously exposing his real intentions which were along the line that Christina sensed he had evolved towards.

克里斯蒂娜对他的包容和对亚历克斯的每一个举动的反应都增强了他对她的吸引力。现在，当着亚历克斯父母和她最好的朋友的面，亚历克斯不知道亚历克斯会在他到达时在场，他自发地暴露了自己的真实意图，而亚历克斯也感觉到他已经朝着这个方向发展了。

Christina looked down at the ring that magically fit almost perfectly, then looked up into Alex's eyes and with no warning she threw her arms around him and held on for a long time as her face was buried into his neck as she sobbed slightly with tears of joy with her emotions not completely released in torrents of sensations.

克里斯蒂娜低头看着那枚神奇地几乎完美贴合的戒指，然后抬头看着亚历克斯的眼睛，毫无预兆地，她伸出双臂拥抱了他，久久地抱住了他，将脸埋在他的脖子里，她微微抽泣着，喜极而泣，情绪尚未完全释放，而是汹涌澎湃。

By now the tears of her mother had a steady stream all the way down her cheeks as she too had incredible feelings of happiness for her daughter. Jann too was affected by the sight and the events unfolding and could not hold back as hard as she tried, she was also touched in a rather magnificent way.

此时，母亲的泪水已顺着脸颊流淌，因为她也为女儿感到无比幸福。Jann 也被眼前的景象和正在发生的事情所感动，她再怎么努力也抑制不住自己的情绪，她也受到了极大的感动。

Mr. Garrison's eyes had watered up and no matter how tough he was as a Green Beret; his daughter's emotions had completely disarmed him. He was proud of Alex for being so genuine and real, and now all that was unfolding was exactly the way Christina had described him in their private discussions when they were alone grocery shopping or doing errands for mother.

加里森先生的眼睛湿润了，无论他作为一名绿色贝雷帽有多么强硬，他女儿的情绪都完全让他放下了戒备。他为亚历克斯的真诚和真实而感到自豪，而现在发生的事情和克里斯蒂娜在他们单独购物或为母亲办事时的私人谈话中对他的描述一模一样。

In a few minutes everyone regained their composure, and Christina pulled her face away from Alex so she could talk.

几分钟后，每个人都恢复了镇静，克里斯蒂娜把脸 亚历克斯身上移开，这样她就可以说话了。

CHRISTINA
It's very beautiful, just like you are.

克里斯蒂娜<br>
非常漂亮，就像你一样。

Alex smiled back at Christina.

亚历克斯对 克里斯蒂娜笑了笑。

ALEX<br>
You make me feel cherished and loved.

亚历克斯<br>
你让我感觉到被珍惜和被爱。

Christina's father came up with an excuse to get everyone out of the house so that the love birds could have a tender moment, stood up.

克里斯蒂娜的父亲找了个借口让所有人都离开房子，以便这对情侣可以享受片刻温情，然后站了起来。

MR. GARRISON<br>
Let me carry a few of these dishes to the Kitchen.

加里森先生<br>
让我把这些盘子拿去厨房。

JANN<br>
I want to help too.

詹恩<br>
我也想帮忙。

Christina's mother stood up without saying a word.

克里斯蒂娜的母亲一言不发地站了起来。

MRS. GARRISON<br>
I'm going to put the dishes in the dishwasher.

加里森夫人<br>
我要把碗碟放进洗碗机。

Jann helped to quickly clean off the table and then came back in the room.

詹恩帮忙快速清理桌子，然后回到房间。

JANN<br>
Christina, thanks for letting me come over for dinner.

I need to get home and take my dogs out for a walk.
They're probably going nuts now.

詹恩
克里斯蒂娜，谢谢你让我过来吃晚饭。我需要回
家带我的狗出去散步。它们现在可能疯了。

Christina told a *white lie* as now she knew there was something she really wanted to
do.

克里斯蒂娜说了一个善意的谎言，因为她现在知道她真正想做的事情。

CHRISTINA
Oh, I'm so sorry you must leave so soon.

克里斯蒂娜
哦，我很遗憾你这么快就要走了。

Christina's mother saw her body language and knew it was time to give her daughter
and future son-in-law a little privacy for their tender moment and came into the room.

克里斯蒂娜的母亲看到了她的肢体语言，知道是时候给她的女儿和未来女婿一
点隐私来享受这温柔的时刻了，于是她走进了房间。

MRS. GARRISON
Dishes are being washed and I put the leftovers in the
refrigerator in case you want a snack later.

加里森夫人
我正在洗碗，把剩菜放进冰箱，以防你一会儿想
吃零食。

CHRISTINA
Thanks Mother.

克里斯蒂娜
谢谢妈妈。

Mrs. Garrison walked over and gave her daughter a hug, then walked over to Alex and
gave him a hug too and very softly said:

加里森夫人走过去给了女儿一个拥抱，然后走到亚历克斯身边，也给了他一个
拥抱，轻声说道：

MRS. GARRISON
Thank you, Alex.

加里森夫人
谢谢你，亚历克斯。

Mrs. Garrison then smiled and then she and Mr. Garrison departed with him saying:

加里森夫人笑了，然后和加里森先生一起离开了，说道：

MR. GARRISON
I'll see you tomorrow, Alex, I want to get home and
watch the boxing match tonight on pay per view.

加里森先生
明天见，亚历克斯，我想回家看今晚的付费拳击
比赛。

ALEX
Ok Mr. Garrison, have good night.

亚历克斯
好的，加里森先生，晚安。

MR. GARRISON
You too Alex.

加里森先生
你也是，亚历克斯。

Everyone soon was gone except Christina and Alex, leaving them some privacy.

除了克里斯蒂娜和亚历克斯，其他人很快就走了，给他们留下了一些私人空间。

Christina was feeling more than ready.

克里斯蒂娜感觉已经做好了充分的准备。

CHRISTINA
Excuse me for just a minute Alex.

克里斯蒂娜
抱歉，亚历克斯，请稍等片刻。

Christina went into her bedroom and slipped out of her clothes and into a very sexy negligee that Jann helped her pick out for such a moment. Christina then dabbed a slight amount of perfume in a couple of places to make Alex happy then walked over to the bedroom door, opened it and asked Alex:

克里斯蒂娜走进卧室，脱下衣服，换上詹恩帮她为这一刻挑选的性感睡衣。克里斯蒂娜在几个地方喷了一点香水，让亚历克斯高兴，然后走到卧室门口，打开门问亚历克斯：

CHRISTINA
Alex, could you please come here.

克里斯蒂娜
亚历克斯，你能过来一下吗？

Alex stood up and walked over and put his arms around her and they kissed then she tugged him into the room and shut the door in case someone like her parents came unexpectedly into the house.

亚历克斯站起来走过去，用手臂搂住她，两人接吻，然后她把他拉进房间，关上了门，以防像她父母这样的人突然闯进屋子。

Christina quickly helped Alex get out of his clothes and as they stood beside the bed, she dropped her lingerie to the floor then crawled onto the bed holding Alex hand and guided him towards a Celestial Feast.

克里斯蒂娜迅速帮助亚历克斯脱下衣服，当他们站在床边时，她将内衣扔到地板上，然后爬到床上，牵着亚历克斯的手，带他去参加天体盛宴。

Afterwards Christina and Alex fell into a very restful sleep with Christina's head on Alex's chest.

之后，克里斯蒂娜和亚历克斯都进入了非常安稳的睡眠，克里斯蒂娜的头靠在亚历克斯的胸口上。

In the morning around 9:00 Alex's cell phone rang. It was Claude who was reporting on a milestone accomplishment Alex had asked to be informed of.

早上 9 点左右，亚历克斯的手机响了。是克劳德打来的，他正在汇报亚历克斯想要通报的一个里程碑式的成就。

CLAUDE REARDEN
The hill is mostly reduced to half its original height
and has conical terraces which after June you will see
some of the early trees and Dome plant life.

克劳德·里尔登
山丘的高度基本下降到原来的一半，呈现出圆锥
形的台地，六月之后，台地上会长出一些早熟的
树木和圆顶植物。

ALEX
How soon will the North End and wind break get
finished?

亚历克斯
北端和防风墙多久能完工？

CLAUDE REARDEN
Probably at the end of the month.

克劳德·里尔登
可能在月底。

ALEX
Do you think it would then be warm enough to start planting trees along the hill?

亚历克斯
你认为天气会暖和到可以开始在山边种树吗？

CLAUDE REARDEN
I see why not, if they freeze and die, we'll just replant those that don't make it.

克劳德·里尔登
我明白为什么不行，如果它们冻死了，我们就重新种植那些没能存活下来的。

ALEX
I really want to make that a priority, because I've read in the North Ice News which I now subscribe to that Shelley Bergman, their reporter, is making a lot of noise about us destroying the hill and the view. If we get those trees up and turn the modified hill into the parkland we promised, it might shut her up.

亚历克斯
我真的想把这件事放在首位，因为我在现在订阅的《北方冰雪新闻》上看到，他们的记者 雪莱·伯格曼 正在大声疾呼我们破坏了山丘和风景。如果我们把那些树拔起来，把改造后的山丘变成我们承诺的公园，她可能会闭嘴。

CLAUDE REARDEN
Understand.

克劳德·里尔登
明白。

ALEX
One other thing, I might be coming up there in a few days to see you and plan to bring someone special along. I'll be bringing up a security detail with me just in case.

亚历克斯

另一件事，我可能会在几天后去那里看你，并计
划带一个特别的人一起去。为了以防万一，我会
带上一名保安人员。

CLAUDE REARDON

How long will you be staying.

克劳德·里尔登
你会待多久？

ALEX

We will not be staying overnight, just want to take
a quick look, then we'll be on our way to another
location.

亚历克斯

我们不会过夜，只是想快速浏览一下，然后我们
将前往另一个地点。

CLAUDE REARDON

We'll be ready for you.

克劳德·里尔登
我们会为您做好准备。

ALEX

I'll have a few people with me and my security detail,
so I'll call ahead and let you know what time we
expect to land.

亚历克斯

我会有几个人和我的安保人员陪同，所以我会提
前打电话告诉您我们预计降落的时间。

CLAUDE REARDON

We'll be waiting.

克劳德·里尔登
我们会等待。

Claude Reardon hung up and Alex turned to Christina.

ALEX

Christina, are your parents busy for the next few days?

亚历克斯
亚历克斯挂了电话，然后问克里斯蒂娜：

CHRISTINA
Not really, they are retired people and have a daily routine, but they're not tied down with any responsibilities.

克里斯蒂娜
其实不然，他们都是退休人员，有自己的日常生活，但没有任何责任的束缚。

ALEX
Good.

ALEX
很好。

CHRISTINA
Why do you ask?

克里斯蒂娜
你为什么问这个？

ALEX
I want to take them to some place special.

亚历克斯
我想带他们去一些特别的地方。

CHRISTINA
I'm sure they will be willing to go.

克里斯蒂娜
我相信他们会愿意去的。

ALEX
Ask them to pack their bags for a trip for 4 or 5 days.

亚历克斯
让他们收拾好行李，进行 4 或 5 天的旅行。

CHRISTINA
Are we going somewhere warm?

克里斯蒂娜
我们要去暖和的地方吗？

ALEX
No, it will be winter weather, dress warm.

亚历克斯
不，现在是冬天了，穿得暖和点。

CHRISTINA
Are we going back to Switzerland?

克里斯蒂娜
我们要回瑞士吗？

ALEX
We'll stop there for a couple days, but I have some special place I want to take your father.

亚历克斯
我们会在那里停留几天，但我有个特别的地方想带你父亲去。

CHRISTINA
Any place in particular you wish me to tell my father?

克里斯蒂娜
你希望我告诉我父亲什么具体的地方吗？

ALEX
No. I want this to be a surprise.

亚历克斯
不。我想给你们一个惊喜。

CHRISTINA
Good thing I have not taken any vacation time in a while, my boss can't get too upset with me taking time off.

克里斯蒂娜
幸好我已经有一段时间没有休假了，我的老板不会因为我休假而太生气。

ALEX
No pressing needs back at the office?

亚历克斯
办公室里没什么紧急需求吗？

CHRISTINA
Not really, most of the paperwork I needed to do for

tax season is finished, my co-worker Gary Alan, can take care of any urgent matter.

克里斯蒂娜
不是，纳税季我需要做的大部分文书工作都已经完成了，我的同事加里·艾伦可以处理任何紧急事宜。

ALEX
Take a week off and tell your parents I would like to leave this afternoon.

亚历克斯
请一周假并告诉你的父母我想今天下午离开。

CHRISTINA
Okay.

克里斯蒂娜
好的。

After one more soiree down the path to splendid euphoria and transcendental gratification, the two got out of bed and showered and played with each other as if they were children with new toys at Christmas time.

在经历了又一次极度兴奋和超然满足之后，两人起床、洗澡，然后一起玩耍，就像圣诞节时孩子们得到了新玩具一样。

Christina was now starting to feel fulfilled for the first time in her life. Nothing before even comes close to the excitement, thrill, and satisfaction that Alex brought to her life. As she pondered the irreducible, she realized how pathetically boring her life was until out of sheer coincidence Alex walked into her domain.

克里斯蒂娜现在开始有生以来第一次感到满足。之前没有任何东西能与亚历克斯给她的生活带来的兴奋、激动和满足感相提并论。当她思考这个无法简化的问题时，她意识到自己的生活是多么无聊，直到亚历克斯偶然走进了她的领域。

Christina scrambled packing and Alex thought she was going overboard and suggested:

克里斯蒂娜忙着收拾行李，亚历克斯认为她太过分了，并建议道：

ALEX
Pack light, it will be a good excuse to take your mother shopping. We'll be going someplace where you will want to do a lot of that.

亚历克斯
轻装上阵，这是带妈妈去购物的好借口。我们会
去一个你会想做很多事情的地方。

Alex was fully dressed and ready to depart then announced:

亚历克斯穿戴整齐，准备出发，然后宣布：

ALEX
Oh, by the way I forgot to give you this.

亚历克斯
哦，顺便说一句，我忘了给你这个。

Alex then reached into his pocket and pulled out a credit card that had Christina's name on it.

然后亚历克斯伸手到口袋里，掏出一张写着克里斯蒂娜名字的信用卡。

ALEX
In case I'm not around while you are shopping, this
will have satisfactory funds to purchase anything you
want, it's prepaid.

Alex handed the pre-paid credit card to Christina, who started tearing up because reality started to strike her. Alex's love was no longer fantasy, it was now transcending to what every little girl ever dreamed about: *finding her prince*.

亚历克斯把预付信用卡递给了克里斯蒂娜，克里斯蒂娜开始流泪，因为现实开始打击她。亚历克斯的爱情不再是幻想，而是超越了每个小女孩的梦想：找到她的王子。

Christina spontaneously threw her arms around Alex and held him close and started crying.

克里斯蒂娜自发地伸出双臂拥抱了亚历克斯，并将他紧紧抱住，然后开始哭泣。

Feeling Christina's sobbing, Alex, who by now was very sensitive to her ever mood, responded.

感受到克里斯蒂娜的哭泣，亚历克斯现在对她的情绪非常敏感，做出了回应。

ALEX
Christina, what's wrong?

亚历克斯
克里斯蒂娜，怎么了？

After sucking the moisture from her nose and clearing her emotions for a moment so she could respond very softly, Christina answered:

CHRISTINA
Alex, you make me feel so happy, I suddenly felt like
crying.

克里斯蒂娜
亚历克斯，你让我感觉很开心，我突然想哭。

Christina held on to Alex for a long time as she slowly calmed from her emotional spike, her grip slowly eased and soon gave one last strong hug and kissed Alex on the forehead, and whispered because she could hardly talk:

克里斯蒂娜紧紧抱住亚历克斯许久，慢慢从情绪的波动中平静下来，她慢慢放松手，很快给了亚历克斯最后一次坚定的拥抱，亲吻了亚历克斯的额头，因为几乎说不出话而低声说道：

CHRISTINA
You mean so much to me Alex.

克里斯蒂娜
亚历克斯，你对我来说很重要。

VOICEOVER
*For a few fleeting moments Alex felt the love that Christina bestowed upon him, and now knew choosing her as his partner was one of the most astute decisions he had made in his life.*

画外音
在那短暂的片刻中，亚历克斯感受到了克里斯蒂娜给予他的爱，现在他知道选择她作为他的伴侣是他一生中最明智的决定之一。

At first Mr. Garrison was reluctant to go. Even though he was a tough *Green Beret Hombre*, the fact was beyond a shadow of a doubt, Mrs. Garrison wore the pants in the family.

起初，加里森先生不愿意去。尽管他是一名强悍的绿色贝雷帽士兵，但毫无疑问，加里森太太才是这个家庭的掌权者。

Mrs. Garrison was the type to be president of the PTA or Soccer Mom's association. All through her life as a teacher working in the New York School system, she had maintained her image as a strict disciplinarian, including her micromanagement of her daughter. She was not going to leave anything to change then or now.

加里森女士属于那种适合担任家长教师协会或足球妈妈协会主席的人。在纽约教育系统当老师的整个生涯中，她一直保持着严谨的形象，包括对女儿的微观管理。她不会让任何事情听天由命，无论是过去还是现在。

Mrs. Garrison knew the world was full of unpleasant surprises and Alex recent experience where one bad thrust by *Hans Jespersen* meant the difference between Alex being in the pine box verses Stephanie. Now was the time for her daughter. Her daughter was not asking for help, nor had Christina ever, but intuitively, Christina's mother knew it was a role she must fulfill, being a strong supporter of Alex, her future son-in-law, and assisting Christina in any way possible.

加里森夫人知道这个世界充满了不愉快的意外，亚历克斯最近也经历了一次汉斯·杰斯帕森的猛烈攻击，这意味着亚历克斯是被关进监狱还是被斯蒂芬妮抓获。现在是她女儿的时间了。她的女儿没有寻求帮助，克里斯蒂娜也没有寻求帮助，但克里斯蒂娜的母亲凭直觉知道这是她必须履行的职责，她要坚定地支持她未来的女婿亚历克斯，并尽一切可能帮助克里斯蒂娜。

This whole business with Alex caught Garrison's by surprise and Mr. Garrison was indeed having a chore evolving into this new very complicated situation.

亚历克斯的整个事情让加里森一家措手不及，加里森先生确实遇到了一件越来越复杂的新情况。

Mr. Garrison almost invisible life, where he was just part of the backdrop of society, allowed him to exist with no pain. He didn't like to stand out and just wanted a peaceful retirement living on his teacher's pension and savings plus his military pension, gave him the ability to take care of all his necessities.

加里森先生的生活几乎是隐形的，他只是社会背景的一部分，这让他可以毫无痛苦地生活。他不喜欢引人注目，只想过上平静的退休生活，靠教师退休金和积蓄加上军人退休金生活，这让他有能力照顾好自己的一切必需品。

As Mr. Garrison looked to the future, he bought his home and with a triple income was able to pay off his mortgage on his home well in advance of his retirement. When the neighbor's husband suddenly died from a heart attack and the house was put up for sale, looking towards his daughter's future, Mr. Garrison jumped on the chance to buy it.

加里森先生着眼于未来，于是他买了自己的房子，收入增加了三倍，能够在退休前提前还清抵押贷款。当邻居的丈夫突然心脏病发作去世，房子挂牌出售时，为了女儿的未来，加里森先生抓住机会买下了它。

Even though Mr. Garrison had to take out another mortgage which he would have to pay for well into retirement, that would diminish his lifestyle a bit, including foregoing vacations and spending like most middle-class families, he felt satisfied that he had made sure Christina had a decent home to live in the future.

尽管加里森先生不得不再背上一笔抵押贷款，而且直到退休后还要继续偿还，这会稍微降低他的生活方式，包括放弃假期和像大多数中产阶级家庭一样消费，但他感到很满意，因为他确保了克里斯蒂娜将来有一个舒适的家。

Christina was a very good daughter. She loved her daddy beyond words.

克里斯蒂娜是个好女儿。她对爸爸的爱无以言表。

Mr. Garrison cherished life after leaving the hells of the Vietnam jungles and hair-raising Studies and Observation Group (SOG) ventures into Cambodia with the likes of Colonel Plaster who was also a Sargent back in those days.

离开越南丛林地狱，与当时也是一名中士的普拉斯特上校等人一起进入柬埔寨进行惊心动魄的特种部队冒险后，加里森先生珍惜生命。

When Mr. Garrison's little baby girl Christina was born, Mr. Garrison had a conduit to reality, one that Christina would never know how important it was.

当加里森先生的小女儿克里斯蒂娜出生时，加里森先生有了与现实的沟通渠道，而克里斯蒂娜永远不会知道这有多么重要。

FLASHBACK:
Those five-minute emergency extractions behind enemy territory where 33% of the time SOG guys were either wounded or killed came close to Sargent Garrison many times. Sargent Garrison was a *Triple Purple Heart Recipient*, and just like Colonel Plaster volunteered to remain beyond his 11-month tour, just to make sure a bunch of the new guys didn't end up in the hands of the Vietcong.

闪回：
在敌方领土后方的五分钟紧急撤离行动中，33% 的 SOG 人员受伤或死亡，这多次接近中士加里森的水平。中士加里森曾三次获得紫心勋章，就像普拉斯特上校一样，他自愿在 11 个月的任期结束后继续留守，只是为了确保一群新人不会落入越共之手。

And just like Colonel Plaster stayed there for three years. Sargent Garrison only left because he was kicked out of Vietnam. When the Pentagon issued him his 5th silver star, the Army now extremely politically correct under President Nixon, could not allow an African American national hero to be killed in Vietnam. Orders came down from the Secretary of the Army:

就像普拉斯特上校在那里待了 3 年一样。加里森中士离开只是因为他被赶出了越南。当五角大楼向他颁发第五颗银星勋章时，在尼克松总统领导下，军队在政治上极其正确，不能允许一位非裔美国民族英雄在越南被杀。陆军部长下达命令：

**SECRETARY OF THE ARMY**
Get Sargent Garrison the hell out of Vietnam NOW!

陆军部长
立即让加里森中士滚出越南！

Sargent Garrison's SOG-team got whacked their next time out without him. Team cohesion was critical and there should have been a few missions where they sent out four guys instead of the regular three Green Beret (along with 5 Vietnamese Montagnard Mercenaries) so that the team would be able to fully cope with Sargent Garrison's departure.

在没有加里森中士的情况下，他的　SOG小组在下一次行动中遭受重创。团队凝聚力至关重要，他们应该在几次任务中派出四个人，而不是通常的三个绿色贝雷帽（以及 5 名越南山地雇佣兵），这样团队才能完全应对加里森中士的离开。

As it was, Sargent Garrison wasn't even out of the country yet, getting ready to board a plane destined to San Francisco when some of his platoon buddies met him at the Airport to say goodbye and sadly reported, two of his best friends and SOG-team partners had been killed in the most recent mission.

事实上，加里森中士还没有出国，正准备登上飞往旧金山的飞机，他的一些排战友在机场与他告别，并悲伤地报告说，他的两个最好的朋友和 SOG　小组伙伴在最近的一次任务中阵亡了。

Per SOG Team tradition, Sargent Garrison and his buddies had a Budweiser Beer together they had brought in a bag from the camp. That's how SOG teams honored their fallen comrades, a final toast and salute.

按照 SOG　小队的传统，中士加里森和他的伙伴们一起喝了他们从营地带回来的百威啤酒。SOG 小队就是这样向阵亡战友致敬的，最后举杯敬礼。

Sargent Garrison felt responsible because he had not been there to save his team. It might have been bad luck, or it might have been timing. This mission failure could have been nothing more than the new guy who was incompetent and didn't have enough missions under his belt to cope with the dynamics of the hair-raising extraction.

加里森中士觉得自己有责任，因为他没能拯救他的团队。可能是运气不好，也可能是时机不对。这次任务失败可能只是因为新人能力不足，没有足够多的任务经验来应对令人毛骨悚然的撤离行动。

Most of the SOG extractions from Cambodia and Laos were of the type of extraordinary action that movie studios would be playing Wagner's "Flight of the Valkyries" in feature films depicting similar combat activities.

从柬埔寨和老挝撤离的大多数特种作战部队都属于那种非同寻常的行动，电影制片厂会在描述类似战斗活动的故事片中播放瓦格纳的《女武神的飞行》。

The SOG-teams were not extracted until they had to be. In most of the SOG extractions, they were lifting off with the North Vietnamese shooting at them. It took two fighter bombers, and a half dozen helicopters to emergency extract the typical eight member SOG team.

SOG 小队只有在万不得已的情况下才会撤离。在大多数 SOG 撤离行动中，他们都是趁着北越军队开火时起飞的。通常需要两架战斗轰炸机和六架直升机才能紧急撤离一支由八名成员组成的 SOG 小队。

The fighter bombers would usually lay down napalm which by now the North Vietnamese knew was the procedure and they had to stay far enough away from the landing zone to not be incinerated.

战斗轰炸机通常会投下凝固汽油弹，现在北越人知道了这是程序，他们必须远离着陆区，以免被烧毁。

Four of the helicopters laid down continuous machine gun and rocket fire to force the North Vietnamese pursuers to keep their heads down as the two extraction choppers swooped in and extracted the team. Most often half the team was wounded and some dead. They never left the dead behind; they always carried them out.

四架直升机连续发射机枪和火箭弹，迫使北越追击者低头，两架撤退直升机则飞来，将队伍撤出。大多数时候，队伍中有一半人受伤，有些人死亡。他们从不抛弃死者，总是把他们抬出去。

Furthermore, if they were captured or killed, a special group was flown in to either attempt rescue or extract or retrieve the dead bodies. In most cases it was dead bodies, who the North Vietnamese soldiers had severely tortured as they were killing them. Only rarely when a North Vietnamese officer was nearby, they survived and were taken prisoner so they could be interrogated.

此外，如果他们被俘或被杀，就会有专门的小组飞往营救他们，或者试图将尸体取出或找回。在大多数情况下，尸体都是北越士兵在杀死他们时对他们施以酷刑的。只有在极少数情况下，当北越军官在附近时，他们才会幸存下来并被俘虏，以便接受审讯。

END FLASHBACK.

结束闪回。

Christina's birth snapped Mr. Garrison out of his Vietnam nightmares forever. There was no doubt of why Mr. Garrison protected Christina and would never stand for anyone hurting her.

克里斯蒂娜的出生让加里森先生永远摆脱了越南战争的噩梦。毫无疑问，加里森先生会保护克里斯蒂娜，绝不容忍任何人伤害她。

Even though Mr. Garrison was now old and no longer the tough Green Beret that he once was, no doubt he would travel to the ends of the earth to track down anyone who hurt his daughter. And now as it was becoming crystal clear how much Alex meant to Christina, hurting him would constitute hurting her.

尽管加里森先生现在已经老了，不再是曾经的绿色贝雷帽战士，但毫无疑问，他会走遍天涯海角去追捕伤害他女儿的人。现在，亚历克斯对克里斯蒂娜的重要性已经变得一清二楚，伤害他就等于伤害她。

Mr. Garrison wasn't interested in travel and was satisfied to stay home and watch sports coverage around the clock. Mr. Garrison loved sports and often went to games.

加里森先生对旅行不感兴趣，他满足于待在家里，全天候观看体育报道。加里森先生热爱体育运动，经常去观看比赛。

Soon Mr. Garrison would be watching games from a private suite not far from the owners during the baseball and football games thanks to Alex. His front row seats at the basketball games would also impact on some of his friends, who absolutely never otherwise would get to see all those fabulous players up close, sitting next to their lifelong friend.

很快，在亚历克斯的帮助下，加里森先生就可以在棒球和足球比赛期间坐在离老板不远的私人包厢里观看比赛了。他在篮球比赛中坐在前排的座位也会影响到他的一些朋友，否则他们绝对不可能坐在他们一生的朋友旁边近距离看到这些出色的球员。

Luckily for Mr. Garrison there were two SOG team survivors in Queens New York, who he had served in the same camps together and once or twice went on missions behind enemy lines.

对加里森先生来说幸运的是，纽约皇后区有两名 SOG 小组幸存者，他们曾和他在同一个营地服役，还曾一两次执行过敌后任务。

Before all the trappings of being part of Alex's new family evolved, Mr. Garrison was slow in getting with the program. You just can't remold a black Archie Bunker overnight. As a staunch Republican, the liberal agenda drove Mr. Garrison nuts, and one may say opposites attract, his wife was a staunch Democrat!

在成为亚历克斯新家庭一员的所有条件都成熟之前，加里森先生对该计划的适应很慢。你不可能在一夜之间重塑一个黑人阿奇·邦克。作为一名坚定的共和党人，自由主义议程让加里森先生抓狂，而且人们可能会说，异性相吸，他的妻子是一位坚定的民主党人！

MR. GARRISON
I really don't want to go on the trip.

加里森先生
我真的不想去旅行。

MRS. GARRISON
You must go; it's for Christina.

加里森夫人
你必须走了，这是给克里斯蒂娜的。

MR. GARRISON
With all this latest commotion, I'm not sure I want to
be out there in public.

加里森先生
鉴于最近发生的这一切骚乱，我不确定自己是否
想出现在公众面前。

MRS. GARRISON
Don't worry, you'll be safe, we now have a top security
company guarding us 7/24.

加里森夫人
别担心，你会很安全的，我们现在有一家顶级保
安公司全天候保护我们。

Mr. Garrison knew most explicitly that if he didn't quickly agree with his wife, that she
would be pounding him for weeks.

加里森先生非常清楚，如果他不迅速与妻子达成一致，她就会对他进行数周的
殴打。

Going along with Mrs. Garrison was the easiest path towards peace and harmony.
Otherwise, life would become difficult, which it always did if he didn't go along with
Mrs. Garrison's plans. So, as he was in his SOG team in his head he quickly calculated
the tradeoff of his action, and the solution was simply to say:

与加里森夫人合作是实现和平与和谐的最简单途径。否则，如果他不按照加里
森夫人的计划行事，生活就会变得困难，而情况总是如此。因此，当他在脑
海中与 SOG 团队合作时，他很快就计算了自己的行动的利弊，解决方案很简
单：

MR. GARRISON
Ok honey, I'll go.

加里森先生
好的亲爱的，我走了。

Some of the romantic atmosphere that Alex brought into Christina's life now rubbed
off on Mr. Garrison, as Mrs. Garrison blossomed, and a little bit of that expressive
emotion quickly paved the way to a narrative that rewarded him for his choice of
action.

随着加里森夫人的成长，亚历克斯为克里斯蒂娜的生活带来的一些浪漫气氛也影响到了加里森先生，而这种表达情感的一点点迅速铺平了故事情节，奖励了他所选择的行动。

Early in the afternoon the doorbell rang, it was Rodriguez, and he was double parked in the street with the security company guys standing by his car, expecting Alex and his new family to be leaving soon.

下午很早的时候，门铃响了，是罗德里格斯来的，他把车停在街上，保安公司的人站在他的车旁边，等着亚历克斯和他的新家人很快就要离开。

As planned, there would be a security guard in each house, guarding them until they returned and then they would migrate back outside to spending time in their cars and walking around the street with the whole block now very happy since they quickly learned they had the best physical security in all of New York with nonexistent crime.

按照计划，每家每户都会有一名保安，守护着他们直到他们回来，然后他们就会回到外面，在车里消磨时光，在街上散步，整个街区现在都非常高兴，因为他们很快就知道他们拥有全纽约最好的物理安全，不存在犯罪。

Alex had instructed Christina to ask them to pack light, because they could get whatever they needed at the destinations. So, there wasn't much luggage, and everyone had been staged in Christina's home.

亚历克斯曾指示克里斯蒂娜让他们轻装上阵，因为到目的地就可以买到所需的一切。所以，行李并不多，大家都被安排在克里斯蒂娜的家里。

Rodriguez reached to grab both suitcases, when Mr. Garison who was still very physically fit even though he was now in his early 70's announced:

罗德里格斯伸手去拿两个行李箱，这时虽然已经 70 多岁了但身体依然很健康的加里森先生宣布道：

**MR. GARRISON**
I'll carry my suitcase.

加里森先生
我会带着我的行李箱。

Mr. Garrison then he picked it up the suitcase carrying his wife and his articles.

加里森先生随后拿起了装有他妻子和物品的手提箱。

**ALEX**
Why don't you let me carry that Mr. Garrison.

亚历克斯
加里森先生，你为什么不让我拿着它呢？

MR. GARRISON
Don't worry Alex, I need the exercise.

加里森先生
别担心，亚历克斯，我需要锻炼。

ALEX
As you wish Mr. Garrison.

亚历克斯
如你所愿，加里森先生。

Soon Rodrigeuz drove Alex and the Garrisons to the airport. Just like clockwork, John Black met the group and escorted them to Alex's Gulfstream 650.

很快，罗德里格斯就开车送亚历克斯和加里森一家去了机场。约翰·布莱克准时接见了他们，并护送他们上了亚历克斯的湾流 650 飞机。

Brad was standing by the ladder and with Alex and Mr. Garrison carrying the 2 suitcases, they sat them down by the ladder as Christina and her mother were being led up towards the jet's ladder.

布拉德站在梯子旁边，亚历克斯和加里森先生拿着两个行李箱，他们把行李箱放在梯子旁边，而克里斯蒂娜和她的母亲则被带上飞机的梯子。

ALEX
Mr. Garrison, Brad will take care of our luggage. After
you Mr. Garrison.

亚历克斯
加里森先生，布拉德会帮我们照看行李。加里森
先生，您先请。

Alex then moved his arm to the signal *to go up the stairway*.

然后亚历克斯挥动手臂，示意上楼梯。

Mr. and Mrs. Garrison went up first, followed by Christina and Alex. Shortly after stowing the luggage, Brad came aboard and walked up to the cockpit and began completing his preflight checkoffs and started the jet engines.

加里森夫妇首先登机，克里斯蒂娜和亚历克斯紧随其后。收拾好行李后不久，布拉德登上飞机，走到驾驶舱，开始完成飞行前检查，并启动了喷气发动机。

Gladys was the flight attendant today, like usual since Stephanie's departure, and said to them:

格拉迪斯今天担任空乘，自从斯蒂芬妮离开后，她照常担任空乘，她对他们说：

GLADYS
Sit where you would like.

格拉迪斯
想坐哪儿就坐哪儿。

Gladys operated the controls that folded the stairway into the plane's body and shut the cabin door and walked up to the cockpit.

格拉迪斯操作控制装置，将舷梯折叠到机身内，关闭机舱门，然后走上驾驶舱。

GLADYS
Brad, we are ready to depart when you are ready.

格拉迪斯
布拉德，只要你准备好，我们就可以出发了。

ALEX
Mr. Garrison, if you would like, you can sit in the Copilot's seat and watch the takeoff.

亚历克斯
加里森先生，如果您愿意，您可以坐在副驾驶座位上观看起飞。

Mr. Garrison now starting to take it all in and just going with the flow saw the covert signal his wife often gave him that he had learned a long time ago meant: "*Just do it.*"

加里森先生现在开始接受这一切，并顺其自然，他看到了妻子经常给他的隐秘信号，他很久以前就知道这个信号的含义是："只管去做。"

MR. GARRISON
Yes, I would like to

加里森先生
是的，我想

Mr. Garrison walked up to the CO pilot's chair where Brad held out his hand.

加里森先生走到机长座椅前，布拉德向他伸出了手。

BRAD
I'm Brad.

布拉德
我是布拉德。

**MR. GARRISON**
I'm William.

加里森先生
我是威廉。

**BRAD**
Pleased to meet you, William.

布拉德
很高兴认识你，威廉。

**WILLIAM (a.k.a. Mr. Garrison)**
Thank you, Brad.

威廉（又名加里森先生）
谢谢你，布拉德。

Soon the plane took off and was heading to Minnesota. Alex was going there to do a couple things, show Christina her new home and let the Garrison's know they are invited to live there with them in the future if they would like. One thing was for certain, Alex would not be seeing them in Minnesota much in the wintertime as the weather there was far too harsh for the Garrisons.

飞机很快就起飞前往明尼苏达州。亚历克斯去那里做几件事，带克里斯蒂娜参观她的新家，并让加里森夫妇知道，如果他们愿意的话，将来可以和他们一起住在那里。有一件事是肯定的，亚历克斯在冬天不会经常在明尼苏达州见到他们，因为那里的天气对加里森夫妇来说太恶劣了。

The plane touched down on Alex's private runway and pulled next to the hanger as was the standard procedure. Shortly the engines were shut down and the plane tug moved the jet into the hanger, then the door to the hanger closed. People in the cabin of the plane could feel a little vibration and noise as the cargo bay was opened and the workers removed their suitcases.

飞机降落在亚历克斯的私人跑道上，并按照标准程序停在机库旁边。不久，发动机关闭，飞机牵引机将飞机移入机库，然后机库门关闭。当货舱打开，工人们卸下行李箱时，机舱里的人们能感觉到一点震动和噪音。

As soon as Brad saw the signal indicating the hanger was sufficiently warm enough for them to get out of the plane without being confronted with serious cold just like they left New York, Brad opened the jet's door and lowered the stairway, and the passengers deplaned.

当布拉德看到信号表明机库已经足够温暖，他们可以下飞机而不必像离开纽约那样面临严重的寒冷时，布拉德打开了飞机的门，放下了舷梯，乘客们下了飞机。

Alex led the group to the elevator. Their luggage was already in the golf cart as Alex directed them to it and got in on the driver's side with Christina following him into the passenger side and her parents tucked themselves into the back.

亚历克斯带领大家来到电梯前。亚历克斯带他们来到电梯前，行李已经放在高尔夫球车里，亚历克斯坐在驾驶座上，克里斯蒂娜跟着他坐在副驾驶座上，她的父母则坐在后座上。

ALEX
To the house please.

ALEX
请进屋。

The voice recognition sofware in the electric cart's *Artificial Intelligence* control system as well as the security team which could have directed the cart, soon set it moving and within a minute or so, pulled into the turnaround area next to the elevator up to his home.

电动车人工智能控制系统中的语音识别软件以及可以指挥电动车的保安团队很快就让电动车移动，并在一分钟左右的时间内驶入通往他家的电梯旁边的转弯区。

Mr. Garrison marveled at the tunnel decorations that gave anyone a sense of adventure. Soon they were up the elevator into Alex's home.

加里森先生对隧道装饰感到惊叹，它给人一种冒险的感觉。很快他们就乘电梯来到了亚历克斯的家。

As soon as they stepped out of the elevator, Sam the butler met them.

两人刚走出电梯，管家萨姆就迎接了他们。

SAM
Welcome home Alex.

萨姆
欢迎亚历克斯回家。

The maid, Marilynn was standing there also and wearing a elegant uniform. Sam and Marilyn were both very attractive people.

女仆玛丽莲也站在那里，穿着优雅的制服。萨姆和玛丽莲都是很有魅力的人。

ALEX
Sam and Marilynn this is Christina, and her parents
Mr. and Mrs. Garrison.

亚历克斯<br>
萨姆和玛丽莲，这是克里斯蒂娜，还有她的父母<br>
加里森先生和夫人。

After Stephanie's death, Sam and Marilyn had some concern about Alex because Stephanie had overstated her significance in their relationship.

斯蒂芬妮去世后，萨姆和玛丽莲对亚历克斯有些担心，因为斯蒂芬妮夸大了她在他们的关系中的重要性。

Alex slowly exposed his relationship with Christina, and when he informed Sam and Marilyn, he was taking Christina to his mansion in Switzerland, they knew she was someone special in his life. When Sam and Marilyn were notified, Alex was bringing Christina's parents to his home in Minnesota, they understood the significance of that involvement.

亚历克斯慢慢地暴露了他与克里斯蒂娜的关系，当他告诉萨姆和玛丽莲，他要带克里斯蒂娜去他在瑞士的豪宅时，他们知道她是他生命中特别的人。当萨姆和玛丽莲得知亚历克斯要带克里斯蒂娜的父母去他在明尼苏达州的家时，他们明白了这种参与的重要性。

Mary who worked in Alex's Switzerland mansion knew Marilyn quite well coordinating trips, sent Marilyn some pictures of Christina wearing a million dollars' worth of diamond Jewelry Alex bought her and how she looked dressed up for the symphony.

在亚历克斯瑞士豪宅工作的玛丽非常了解玛丽莲，负责安排行程，她给玛丽莲发了一些照片，照片中克里斯蒂娜戴着亚历克斯给她买的价值一百万美元的钻石首饰，还有她盛装出席交响乐会的样子。

Marilyn was impressed because Christina looked just as beautiful now as she did in the pictures. Her evaluation of Alex just rose a few notches.

玛丽莲很感动，因为克里斯蒂娜现在看起来和照片上一样漂亮。她对亚历克斯的评价又提高了几个档次。

Marilyn (Thought)<br>
*Pictures are worth a thousand words.*

玛丽莲（思想）<br>
图片胜过千言万语。

Sam reached out to shake Mr. Garrison's hand.

萨姆伸出手去和加里森先生握手。

SAM<br>
It's an honor to meet you Mr. and Mrs. Garrison.

萨姆
加里森先生和夫人，我很荣幸见到你们。

Simultaneously Marilyn who stood in front of Mrs. Garrison, reached out to shake her hand and announced:

与此同时，站在加里森夫人面前的玛丽莲伸出手来和她握手，并宣布：

MARILYN
Mrs. Garrison, I'm so happy to get a chance to meet
you.

玛丽莲
加里森夫人，我很高兴有机会见到你。

Marilyn shook Mrs. Garrison's hand then turned to Christina.

玛丽莲握了握加里森夫人的手，然后转向克里斯蒂娜。

MARILYN
Christina, you are just as beautiful as Alex described
you. I'm so very happy to meet you.

玛丽莲
克里斯蒂娜，你就像亚历克斯描述的一样漂亮。
我很高兴见到你。

Christina blushed slightly and responded.

克里斯蒂娜微微红着脸回答道。

CHRISTINA
It's good to meet you too.

克里斯蒂娜
我也很高兴认识你。

ALEX
Let me show you around.

亚历克斯
让我带你参观一下。

Sam and Marilyn stood aside as the group walked into a hallway leading to the front room and a side family room area that was about the size of a hotel lobby.

当一行人走进通往前厅和侧面家庭活动室的走廊时，萨姆和玛丽莲站在一旁，这个家庭活动室的大小与酒店大堂差不多。

Marilyn and Sam Grabbed the two suitcases and carried them to the elevator, and then up to the next floor to the bedrooms they would be staying in.

玛丽莲和萨姆抓起两个行李箱，把它们抬到电梯里，然后到了下一层，到了他们将要住的卧室。

The Garrisons would soon learn their bedrooms were better than any luxury hotel they had ever stayed in.

加里森夫妇很快就会发现，他们的卧室比他们曾经住过的任何豪华酒店都要好。

Walking through the living room, there were incredible paintings and furniture. Van Gogh's, Rembrandt's, Picasso's, Monet, and even Red Skelton paintings blistered the walls and set up an impression that would no doubt, stay with the Garrisons forever.

穿过客厅，映入眼帘的是令人惊叹的画作和家具。梵高、伦勃朗、毕加索、莫奈，甚至雷德·斯克尔顿的画作都挂满了墙壁，给加里森一家留下了深刻的印象，毫无疑问，这种印象将永远留在他们心中。

In the family room like his Switzerland home was a grand piano. The gold-plated Steinway looked more like a toy than an operational piano.

就像瑞士的家一样，客厅里摆放着一架三角钢琴。这架镀金的施坦威钢琴看起来更像是一个玩具，而不是一架可以操作的钢琴。

VOICEOVER (WILLIAM GARRISON)
THOUGHT
*A guy could get used to this real fast.*

画外音（威廉·加里森）
想法
一个人可以很快适应这一点。

They were all somewhat overwhelmed as this all unfolded. With his immense wealth and the ability to crush Christina's heart, Ethel Garrison was suddenly relieved as she realized, Alex had certified his emotional bond to Christina before all this was exposed, otherwise she would be filled with fear of a terrible let down Christina could experience because Alex could have just about any woman he wanted.

随着这一切的展开，他们都有些不知所措。凭借亚历克斯巨大的财富和击碎克里斯蒂娜心的能力，埃塞尔·加里森突然松了一口气，因为她意识到，亚历克斯在这一切曝光之前已经证明了他与克里斯蒂娜的感情纽带，否则她会充满恐惧，担心克里斯蒂娜会经历可怕的失望，因为亚历克斯几乎可以拥有他想要的任何女人。

Alex selecting Christina seemed like a miracle. But what Mrs. Garrison didn't quite understand was, Alex was more in need of Christina than the other way around.

Christina was genuine, a real person, not a gold digger, and as far as Alex was concerned, he was the one who pursued Christina and not the other way around.

亚历克斯选择克里斯蒂娜似乎是一个奇迹。但加里森夫人还不太明白的是，亚历克斯需要克里斯蒂娜，而不是克里斯蒂娜需要他。克里斯蒂娜是一个真诚的人，不是一个拜金女，而且对亚历克斯来说，是他追求克里斯蒂娜，而不是克里斯蒂娜追求他。

Christina would have gone on with her life with or without Alex just fine. And as beautiful and demure as Christina was, it would have only been a matter of time before another suitable suitor had pursued her.

不管有没有亚历克斯，克里斯蒂娜都会过得很好。克里斯蒂娜美丽而娴静，另一位合适的追求者追求她只是时间问题。

Such a scenario was already beginning just before Alex met Christina, as a Saudi Prince had laid his eyes upon her and didn't yet have four wives. The prince was only a few days away from starting an official introduction when his private detectives sadly informed him, she was already taken.

在亚历克斯遇见克里斯蒂娜之前，这样的情况已经开始了，因为一位沙特王子看上了她，而她当时还没有四个妻子。王子距离正式介绍只有几天的时间了，但他的私人侦探却悲伤地告诉他，克里斯蒂娜已经被人带走了。

When it was learned, Alex Baxter was pursuing Christina, the Prince backed out on the other side of valor, because Alex had never pursued many women, and had a reputation of being aloof, so if he was displaying overt signs of interest in this woman, he would pursue her most vigorously, so the prince would be wasting his time pursuing her. Plus, he didn't know for sure Christina would tolerate being wife number four.

当得知亚历克斯·巴克斯特正在追求克里斯蒂娜时，王子出于勇气而退缩了，因为亚历克斯从未追求过很多女人，而且以冷漠著称，所以如果他对这个女人表现出明显的兴趣，他会最积极地追求她，所以王子追求她是在浪费时间。另外，他不确定克里斯蒂娜是否能接受成为第四任妻子。

The five-hour flight had left them all hungry since everyone was so busy getting ready that morning, they had skipped breakfast and missed lunch. Snacks on the jet were not enough.

五个小时的飞行让他们都饿了，因为早上大家都忙着准备，没吃早餐，也没吃午餐。飞机上的零食根本不够吃。

As soon as Sam and Marilyn had delivered their suitcases to the respective bedrooms, Marilyn got busy and unpacked for them and by the time the Garrisons and Christina got up to their rooms they were amazed, all their clothes were hanging in the walk-in closet that Marilyn showed them. Also, what they didn't know was Marilyn's assistant had been busy ironing and taking care of any wrinkles in their clothes.

山姆和玛丽莲把行李箱送到各自的卧室后，玛丽莲就开始忙着帮他们打开行李。等到加里森夫妇和克里斯蒂娜回到房间时，他们惊讶地发现，他们所有的衣服都挂在玛丽莲带他们参观的步入式衣橱里。而且，他们不知道的是，玛丽莲的助手一直在忙着熨烫和整理他们衣服上的褶皱。

Alex feeling some slight hunger pains shortly after showing them the indoor heated pool and explaining the private dressing rooms and swimsuits were available to them to change into, suggested:

在向他们展示了室内温水游泳池并解释可供他们更换的私人更衣室和泳衣后不久，亚历克斯感到有些饥饿，他建议道：

ALEX
Why don't we get something to eat, I'm starving.

亚历克斯
我们为什么不去吃点东西呢，我饿坏了。

Everyone was most sympathetic to the suggestion as they too were starting to feel like they were in a similar hunger condition.

每个人都对这个建议深表同情，因为他们也开始感觉自己处于类似的饥饿状态。

Alex led them to the dining room.

亚历克斯带领他们去了餐厅。

The dining room table was twenty feet long and about six feet wide. It had the best Polish tablecloth money could buy. The glasses on the table were from the Edwardian period and no doubt collectors would envy Alex using them for ordinary everyday use.

餐桌长二十英尺，宽约六英尺。餐桌上铺着最好的波兰桌布。桌上的玻璃杯是爱德华时期的，收藏家们肯定会羡慕亚历克斯在日常生活中使用这些玻璃杯。

The table sets had period cut glass, intricately cut with geometric patterns and prisms. The strawberry diamond patterns included Aztec, Panel, and Trellis designs.

餐桌套装采用老式切割玻璃，上面雕刻着复杂的几何图案和棱镜。草莓钻石图案包括阿兹特克、面板和格子设计。

Mrs. Garrison recognized some of this as she had seen it in a few places in her travels and usually only in museums or special decorations for exhibits. And now in a few minutes she would be using it along with the gold flatware silverware on French placemats, added greatly to the ambience.

加里森夫人认出了其中的一些，因为她在旅行中曾在一些地方见过它，而且通常只在博物馆或展览的特殊装饰中看到。现在，几分钟后，她将把它与法式餐垫上的金色餐具和银器一起使用，大大增添了氛围。

Sam came in and seated everyone and shortly started serving.

萨姆进来让大家坐下并很快就开始上菜。

Alex sat at the end of the table, and each placemat had a little gold name plate with a printed name. The staff knew in advance who was coming and had them printed up and inserted into the holder.

亚历克斯坐在桌子的尽头，每张餐垫上都放着一块金色的小铭牌，上面印着名字。工作人员事先知道了谁会来，并把名字打印出来，放在餐垫上。

Christina was seated to Alex right side. That was symbolic and an indication to everyone her purpose in life now had changed.

克里斯蒂娜坐在亚历克斯的右侧。这具有象征意义，也向所有人表明她现在的人生目标已经改变了。

Mr. Garrison was seated next to Alex on his left with Mrs. Garrison sitting next to Christina.

加里森先生坐在亚历克斯左边，加里森夫人坐在克里斯蒂娜旁边。

Sam appeared with a large silver tray and sat it down next to the table, left and came back shortly with four bottles of wine. A cabernet, a blush, and white wine. They were all $1000 bottles, from France.

萨姆很快就端着一个大银托盘出现了，把它放在桌子旁边，然后离开，不久又带着 四 瓶葡萄酒回来了。一瓶赤霞珠、一瓶红葡萄酒和一瓶白葡萄酒。它们都是来自法国的，每瓶售价 1000 美元。

SAM
Does anyone want wine?

萨姆
有人要酒吗？

Sam soon had three of the four bottles opened and pouring, first for Christina, the new woman of the house, whom the staff quickly began to adore, then Mrs. Garrison followed by Mr. Garrison and finally Alex was poured a glass of cabernet sauvignon.

萨姆很快就打开了四瓶酒中的三瓶，倒了第一瓶给家里的新女主人克里斯蒂娜，员工们很快就开始喜欢上她，然后是加里森夫人，接着是加里森先生，最后是亚历克斯，也倒了一杯赤霞珠。

Alex then made a toast:

然后亚历克斯举杯祝酒：

ALEX

To my dearest Christina and may your parents have
good health and happiness.

亚历克斯

致我最亲爱的克里斯蒂娜，祝你的父母身体健
康，幸福快乐。

Everyone joined in with the toast: Cheers.

大家一起举杯：干杯。

A beautiful salad was then served, with fresh baked bread and then entrées were served.
Knowing Mrs. Garrison was a vegetarian, and she imposed that on her husband she
was provided with a vegetarian meal.

然后，一份漂亮的沙拉和新鲜出炉的面包端上了餐桌，然后是主菜。加里森太
太知道她是个素食主义者，于是她强迫丈夫给她提供一顿素食餐。

At the same time on another silver plate set to the side of the table, the Chef carried out
what looked like perhaps a small baked Turkey.

与此同时，厨师在桌子一侧的另一个银盘上端出了看起来像是一只小烤火鸡的
东西。

Alex feared he might receive a negative reaction since he didn't quite yet know enough
about the Garrison's didn't want to tell them it was roasted Peacock flown in from
Thailand.

亚历克斯担心他可能会收到负面反应，因为他对加里森的情况还不够了解，不
想告诉他们这是从泰国空运来的烤孔雀。

Nor did Alex inform the Garrison's the "*beef*" they were eating was Tiger meat flown
in from India. The vegetables served with the main course were steamed and utterly
delicious as they were cooked in special garlic oil that made an incredible taste.

亚历克斯也没有告诉加里森一家他们吃的 "牛肉" 是从印度空运过来的虎肉。
主菜上的蔬菜是蒸的，非常美味，因为它们用特制的蒜油烹制而成，味道好极
了。

Even though Mrs. Garrison was a vegetarian, she asked to be served a small portion of
the Turkey and Beef, because she was curious of the taste knowing a world class chef
just made their dinner.

尽管加里森夫人是素食主义者，她还是要求提供一小部分火鸡和牛肉，因为她
很好奇这些食物的味道，知道一位世界级的厨师刚刚为他们做了晚餐。

Soon they all had deserts of various choices, some preferring just ice cream others
baked Alaska or a cheesecake with an incredible French sauce on it.

很快，他们都有各种各样的甜点可供选择，有些人只喜欢冰淇淋，其他人则喜欢烤阿拉斯加或上面涂有令人难以置信的法式酱汁的芝士蛋糕。

When it appeared, everyone had finished eating, Alex suggested:

等到大家都吃完饭了，亚历克斯建议道：

ALEX
Everyone, take some time to freshen up then let's all meet downstairs in a while. I wanted to show a power point of the Greenland construction that Claude Rearden just emailed me showing a time lapsed photography of all the Greenland Dome events coming together.

亚历克斯
大家先花点时间梳洗一下，一会儿就到楼下集合。我想展示一下格陵兰建设的幻灯片，克劳德·里尔登刚刚给我发了一封电子邮件，展示了格陵兰穹顶所有活动聚集在一起的延时摄影。

The Garrisons were escorted by Marilyn up to their room where she informed them:

玛丽莲陪同加里森夫妇来到他们的房间，并告诉他们：

Marilyn
I unpacked for you. Let me show you the walk-in closet where your garments were professionally hanging.

玛丽莲
我帮你打开了行李。让我带你参观一下步入式衣橱，你的衣服都挂在那里，很专业。

All of Mrs. Garrisons items were arranged on a Napoleon heirloom dresser, that Alex had spent over $1 million purchasing it.

加里森夫人的所有物品都摆放在一个拿破仑传家宝梳妆台上，亚历克斯花了100 多万美元购买它。

The Garrison's room had a king size bed with a canopy over it and the forty-foot-wide Persian rug covering the wood floor had amazing colors and design to it, made the room look fabulously beautiful.

加里森的房间里有一张带天篷的特大号床，木地板上铺着四十英尺宽的波斯地毯，颜色和图案都很好看，让整个房间看起来美不胜收。

The huge ten-foot-tall glass window had a view showing Alex's private twenty-four-acre lake and had a boat dock with a sailboat on one side and a motorboat on the other.

巨大的十英尺高的玻璃窗外是亚历克斯的私人二十四英亩湖泊，湖泊的一侧停着一艘帆船，另一侧停着一艘摩托艇。

Mrs. Garrison noticed her clothes were hanging with sufficient space between each garment so that she could easily pick out one item. She also noticed there were no wrinkles in any of her clothes which often happen when you pack them in a suitcase.

加里森女士注意到她的衣服挂起来时每件衣服之间都留有足够的空间，这样她可以轻松地挑选一件衣服。她还注意到她的衣服上没有任何褶皱，而当你把衣服装进行李箱时，褶皱经常会出现。

                    MARILYN
The bedroom has two separate toilets, and one had a shower, the other shower and bathtub about the size of a Jacuzzi.

                    玛丽莲
开室里有两个独立的卫生间，一个有淋浴，另一个有淋浴和大约按摩浴缸大小的浴缸。

                MRS. GARRISON
That's good because William spends too much time in the bathroom, I will not have to wait on him.

                   加里森夫人
这样很好，因为威廉在浴室里待的时间太长了，我不用等他了。

Mrs. Garrison then chuckled slightly.

加里森夫人随后轻轻笑了笑。

                    MARILYN
When you want to take a bath, just hit the red button on the call box here, which has an intercom, and I will come pour your bath Mrs. Garrison.

                    玛丽莲
如果你想洗澡，只要按下这里带对讲机的呼叫器上的红色按钮，我就会来给你放洗澡水，加里森女士。

                MRS. GARRISON
How about now, I'm ready.

                   加里森夫人
现在怎么样，我准备好了。

MARILYN

Mrs. Garrison, would you like me to bring you a glass
of champagne while you can enjoy your bath?

玛丽莲
加里森夫人，您泡澡的时候，需要我给您拿一杯
香槟吗？

MRS. GARRISON
Why not?

加里森夫人
为什么不呢？

MARILYN
Would you also like a bubble bath Mrs. Garrison?

玛丽莲
加里森女士，您也想泡个泡泡浴吗？

MRS. GARRISON
Absolutely.

加里森夫人
当然。

Marilyn looked at Mr. Garrison's facial expression and understanding of older people
announced.

玛丽莲看着加里森先生的表情，理解了长辈们的宣告。

MARILYN

Mr. Garrison over here is another bathroom with a
shower if you would like to freshen up.

玛丽莲
加里森先生，如果你想洗个澡，这边还有另一间
带淋浴的浴室。

Marilyn then opened the door to the second bathroom and showed Mr. Garrison, then
walked back to the other bathroom and turned the water on and started filling it.

玛丽莲随后打开了第二间浴室的门，给加里森先生看，然后走回另一间浴室，
打开水龙头开始注水。

MARILYN

Mrs. Garrison, this control here sets the temperature, it

defaults to 98 degrees, you can change it to whatever you want, and if you want the Jacuzzi jets turned on, just press this button.

玛丽莲
加里森女士，这里的控制器用于设置温度，默认温度为 98 度，您可以根据需要进行更改，如果您想打开按摩浴缸喷头，只需按下这个按钮即可。

MRS. GARRISON
Thank you, I think I can handle it from here.

加里森夫人
谢谢，我想我可以从这里处理这件事。

Marilyn then walked across the room to Alex's bedroom and looked in, the door was open, and the room was empty, but momentarily Christina and Alex came walking up the stairs.

玛丽莲随后穿过房间，来到亚历克斯的卧室，往里看了一眼，门开着，房间里空无一人，但克里斯蒂娜和亚历克斯很快就走上楼梯。

MARILYN
Christina, let me show you your bedroom. It has a private entry to Alex's room which will be available for you should you wish to go to Mr. Baxter's room at night in case you get scared or for other reasons.

玛丽莲
克里斯蒂娜，让我带你看看你的卧室。它有一个通往亚历克斯房间的私人入口，如果你晚上害怕或出于其他原因想去巴克斯特先生的房间，你可以使用这个入口。

Christina responded as Marilyn escorted her down the hallway to the next door which entered her private bedroom.

当玛丽莲陪着克里斯蒂娜穿过走廊，来到通往她私人卧室的隔壁门时，克里斯蒂娜回应了。

CHRISTINA
Thank you.

克里斯蒂娜
谢谢。

Christina and Marilyn walked into the Christina's bedroom, and it was almost as big as Christina's home.

克里斯蒂娜和玛丽莲走进克里斯蒂娜的卧室，这个卧室几乎和克里斯蒂娜的家一样大。

### MARILYN
Here is the walk-in closets and your dresses from Switzerland were shipped here and are hanging in the closet in case you wish to wear them.

### 玛丽莲
这里是步入式衣橱，您从瑞士寄来的裙子已经运到这里，挂在衣橱里，以备您随时穿着。

Christina saw the dress she wore to the symphony and the others separated in space with enough room so she could easily see and evaluate each dress to pick from. The fact Alex had done that touched her deeply.

克里斯蒂娜看到她参加交响乐会时穿的那条裙子和其他裙子之间有足够的空间，这样她就可以轻松地看到和评估每一条裙子，以便挑选。亚历克斯这样做让她深受感动。

### CHRISTINA (THOUGHT)
*Mother did not pack for any extravagant event and just in case she needs to dress up, her size was identical to mine, which might come in handy.*

### 克里斯蒂娜（想）
妈妈没有为任何奢华的活动准备任何行李，为了以防万一需要盛装打扮，她的尺寸和我的一样，这可能会派上用场。

Alex, who followed them in the room, suddenly spoke up.

跟随他们进入房间的亚历克斯突然开口说道。

### ALEX
Christina, we are going to have some music performers later this evening, I think it would be marvelous if you wouldn't mind putting on one of those dresses for me.

### 亚历克斯
克里斯蒂娜，今晚晚些时候我们将有一些音乐表演者，我想如果你不介意为我穿上一件这样的衣服那就太好了。

CHRISTINA

I would love to and one other thing I want my mother
to dress up.

克里斯蒂娜

我也非常想，还有一件事我想让我妈妈穿上。

MARILYN

Alright Christina. I will help.

玛丽莲

好的，克里斯蒂娜。我会帮忙的。

CHRISTINA

I'll keep these two dresses, one I wore in Switzerland
and the other one I want to wear tonight, please take
the other dresses to my mother's room and ask her to
pick one to wear tonight as I want her to dress up with
me.

克里斯蒂娜

我会保留这两条裙子，一条是我在瑞士穿过的，
另一条是我今晚想穿的，请把其他裙子拿到我妈
妈的房间，让她挑选一条今晚穿的，因为我想让
她和我一起穿。

MARILYN

Excellent idea.

玛丽莲

好主意。

Marilyn smiled, then walked over and grabbed the other 5 dresses, all of which were
very beautiful couture designer dresses. She then walked down the hallway and
knocked on the Garrison's room and asked:

玛丽莲笑了笑，走过去拿了另外五件裙子，都是非常漂亮的高级定制设计师礼
服。然后她沿着走廊走下去，敲了敲加里森的房间，问道：

MARILYN

Mrs. Garrison, may I come in?

玛丽莲

加里森夫人，我可以进来吗？

Ethel Garrison was wearing a bathrobe ready to take her bath and happened to be near
the door and opened it.

519

埃塞尔·加里森穿着浴袍准备洗澡，碰巧站在门口，于是打开了门。

MRS. GARRISON (a.k.a. Ethel)
Yes, please come in.

加里森夫人（又名埃塞尔）
是的，请进。

MARILYN

Mrs. Garrison, Christina asked that I bring these dresses and asked me to request you consider wearing one of them tonight, we'll be having some music performers in a couple hours.

玛丽莲
加里森夫人，克里斯蒂娜让我带上这些裙子，并让我请您考虑今晚穿其中一件，几个小时后我们会有一些音乐表演者。

MRS. GARRISON (a.k.a. Ethel)
Sure, hang them up in the closet and let's take a look at the dresses.

加里森夫人（又名埃塞尔）
好的，把它们挂在衣柜里，我们来看看这些裙子。

Just like her other clothes, Marilynn hung them up on the garment rack spaced out so Mrs. Garrison could see each dress and pick one she liked.

就像她的其他衣服一样，玛丽莲把它们隔开一些距离挂在衣架上，以便加里森夫人可以看到每件衣服并挑选一件她喜欢的。

MRS. GARRISON (a.k.a. Ethel)
Those dresses look very expensive.

加里森夫人（又名埃塞尔）
那些裙子看上去很贵。

MARILYN

They are all *couture designer dresses* and one of a kind. No one else anywhere has seen these dresses nor do they have one.

玛丽莲
它们都是高级定制礼服，独一无二。其他地方没有人见过这些礼服，他们也没有。

Example of couture designs to select for this film sequence:

<u>Embroidered Long Dress Black Silk Knit | DIOR</u>

<u>Cady Couture embroidered gown in pink - Valentino | Mytheresa</u>

<u>Carolina Herrera Floral Embroidered Cap Sleeve Midi Dress - Bergdorf Goodman</u>

<u>Dolce & Gabbana Elegant Crystal Embellished Silk Women's Gown – Bluefly</u>

MRS. GARRISON (a.k.a. Ethel)
You mean they're one of a kind?

加里森夫人（又名埃塞尔）
你的意思是她们是独一无二的？

MARILYN
Yes, personally designed and crafted by the world's best designers. You should have no fear of seeing another woman anywhere wearing a copy. Also, if you look on the garments there is a label and autographed by the designer.

玛丽莲
是的，由世界顶级设计师亲自设计和制作。你不必担心在任何地方看到其他女性穿着仿制品。此外，如果你看看这些服装，你会发现上面有设计师的标签和亲笔签名。

MRS. GARRISON (a.k.a. Ethel)
I think I might like to wear this blue dress.

加里森夫人（又名埃塞尔）
我想我可能喜欢穿这件蓝色连衣裙。

MARILYN
Mrs. Garrison, that dress was designed with a *Cobalt Blue Pigment* which is rare and expensive. Would you like to try it on now so we can see if it needs any tailoring?

玛丽莲
加里森女士，这件裙子是用稀有且昂贵的钴蓝色颜料设计的。你现在想试穿一下吗，这样我们就能看看它是否需要裁剪？

MRS. GARRISON (a.k.a. Ethel)
Sure, why not.

加里森夫人（又名埃塞尔）
当然，为什么不呢。

Mrs. Garrison, the retired schoolteacher, looked like a different person with the *Cobalt Blue Pigment* dress, and it fit perfectly.

退休教师加里森夫人穿上这件蓝色连衣裙后看起来就像换了一个人，而且非常合身。

MRS. GARRISON (a.k.a. Ethel)
It makes me look so good.

加里森夫人（又名埃塞尔）
这让我看起来很漂亮。

Marilyn, who was helping Mrs. Garrison put the dress on responded:

正在帮加里森夫人穿裙子的玛丽莲回答道：

MARILYN
Mrs. Garrison, you are very pretty, and you make the dress look good.

玛丽莲
加里森夫人，您太漂亮了，而且您穿的这件裙子也很漂亮。

MRS. GARRISON (a.k.a. Ethel)
Oh, you are such a darling, Marilynn; help me take this off so that I can take my bath now.

加里森夫人（又名埃塞尔）
玛丽莲，哦，你真是个可爱的人。请帮我脱掉这件裙子，这样我现在就可以洗澡了。

Mrs. Garrison quickly took the dress off and went into the bathroom, and as she was walking into the bathroom, Marilyn followed her announcement:

加里森夫人迅速脱下衣服，走进浴室，玛丽琳走进来时宣布：

MARILYN
Mrs. Garrison, I will be back in a couple of minutes with your champagne.

玛丽莲
加里森夫人，我过几分钟就带着您的香槟回来。

MRS. GARRISON (a.k.a. Ethel)
Alright.

加里森夫人（又名埃塞尔）
好的。

By the time Marilynn was back, Mrs. Garrison was in the bathtub enjoying her bubble bath and Marilynn in one hand had a portable table just like restaurants use to hold meals as they serve their customers. In the other hand, just like an experienced waiter, she had a sparkling silver tray with a bottle of opened Dom Perignon in an intricately designed silver ice bucket, and a beautiful *Cut Crystal Champagne Glass.*

玛丽莲回来时，加里森夫人正在浴缸里享受泡泡浴，玛丽莲一只手拿着一张便携式桌子，就像餐厅为顾客服务时用来放置餐点的桌子一样。另一只手就像一位经验丰富的服务员一样，拿着一个闪闪发光的银托盘，托盘上放着一瓶打开的唐培里侬香槟王，盛在一个设计精巧的银冰桶里，还有一个漂亮的切割水晶香槟杯。

Marilyn then poured a glass of champagne and handed it to Mrs. Garrison who looked very satisfied. Marilyn then placed a small black box with a red button on top near Mrs. Garrison.

玛丽莲随后倒了一杯香槟，递给了看上去非常满意的加里森夫人。随后，玛丽莲将一个上面有一个红色按钮的小黑盒子放在了加里森夫人身边。

MARILYN
Mrs. Garrison, if you need my help press that red button on the box. It's an intercom. Also, I will come back in a few minutes and pour you another glass of champagne.

玛丽莲
加里森女士，如果您需要我的帮助，请按盒子上的红色按钮。这是对讲机。另外，我几分钟后会回来再给您倒一杯香槟。

<u>MUSIC FOR THE NEXT SEQUENCE:</u>

Dohnányi: Symphony No. 1 in D Minor, Op. 9 & Symphonic Minutes, Op. 36

下一个片段的音乐：

多赫南伊：D小调第一交响曲，作品。9 & 交响分钟，作品。36、

## <u>Symphony No. 1 in D Minor, Op. 9: I. Allegro ma non troppo</u>

Alex and Christina had shut her bedroom door and kissed like newlyweds, then Alex asked:

亚历克斯和克里斯蒂娜关上了卧室的门，像新婚夫妇一样亲吻，然后亚历克斯问道：

ALEX
Would you like to go for a swim?

亚历克斯
你想去游泳吗？

CHRISTINA
Sure, why not?

克里斯蒂娜
当然可以，为什么不呢？

ALEX
I guessed on your swimsuit size, but there are several sizes in your walk-in closet to choose from. Find one that you want to wear, and we'll go swim when you are ready.

亚历克斯
我猜到了您的泳衣尺码，但您的步入式衣橱里有多种尺码可供选择。找一件你想穿的，等你准备好了，我们就去游泳。

CHRISTINA
Okay.

克里斯蒂娜
好的。

Then, Alex walked through their adjoining room door into his bedroom and quickly changed into swim trunks and a tee shirt and walked back into Christina's room about the same time she walked out of her dressing room.

然后，亚历克斯穿过隔壁的房门，进入自己的卧室，迅速换上泳裤和 T 恤，在克里斯蒂娜走出更衣室的同时，走回了克里斯蒂娜的房间。

Alex noted how stunning she looked in a swimming suit.

亚历克斯在心里记着克里斯蒂娜穿着泳衣看起来多么惊艳。

ALEX
There also is a robe in there you can wear down to the
swimming pool.

亚历克斯
里面还有一件浴袍，你可以穿着它去游泳池。

Alex showed Christina the specially designed bathrobe and had the Baxter logo on it.

亚历克斯向克里斯蒂娜展示了专门设计的带有巴克斯特标志的浴袍。

Christina put the white robe on and walked out of the dressing room.

克里斯蒂娜穿上白色的长袍，走出了化妆室。

ALEX
Over there are slippers you can wear.

亚历克斯
那边有拖鞋你可以穿。

Alex pointed to a shoe rack loaded with female shoes and slippers.

亚历克斯指着一个摆满女鞋和拖鞋的鞋架。

While Alex stayed in Christina's home a few days he noticed her shoe size and text messaged his new administrative aid, Gladys, to get a couple dozen pairs of designer shoes and slippers for Christina.

当亚历克斯在克里斯蒂娜家住了几天时，他注意到了克里斯蒂娜的鞋子尺码，并给他的新行政助理格拉迪斯发短信，让她为克里斯蒂娜买几十双名牌鞋和拖鞋。

ALEX
Those are your shoes as well.

亚历克斯
那也是你的鞋子。

Christina looked briefly and saw some very beautiful shoes.

克里斯蒂娜匆匆看了一眼，看到了一双非常漂亮的鞋子。

Shortly Christina and Alex made their way down to the indoor heated pool where they quickly walked down the steps in the pool to deeper water. The water was nice and warm and the pool room which had a door entry from the major hallway leading to the family room, had a chlorine-like smell probably from the chemicals they treated the pool with to keep it clean.

克里斯蒂娜和亚历克斯很快就来到了室内温水游泳池，他们沿着游泳池的台阶快速走到更深的水域。水很温暖，游泳池房间有一扇门从通往家庭室的主要走廊进入，里面有一股氯气的味道，可能是他们用化学药剂处理游泳池以保持其清洁。

Christina and Alex swam a little then Alex grabbed Christina and put his arms around her and pulled her close. Christina, feeling so invigorated, wrapped her legs around him and pressed herself against Alex. She could feel he was having a reaction which she suddenly enjoyed, and the feedback made her feel a strange desire.

克里斯蒂娜和亚历克斯游了一会儿，然后亚历克斯抓住克里斯蒂娜，用手臂搂住她，把她拉近。克里斯蒂娜感到精神抖擞，用双腿缠住他，紧紧贴着亚历克斯。她能感觉到他的反应，她突然很享受，这种反应让她感到一种奇怪的欲望。

Christina and Alex embraced and kissed, and Alex, who had never said these words before, even though he used other words, felt compelled and whispered in Christina's ear:

克里斯蒂娜和亚历克斯紧紧相拥亲吻，从来没有说过这句话的亚历克斯，虽然用的是其他的词语，却也情不自禁地在克里斯蒂娜耳边低声说道：

ALEX
Christina, I'm in love with you.

亚历克斯
克里斯蒂娜，我爱你。

Christina's emotion was flooding, just like when Alex gave her the ring and she reciprocated by strongly applying pressure with her arms and legs in an emotional embrace and kissed him in the most passionate manner, then responded:

克里斯蒂娜的情绪如潮水般涌来，就像亚历克斯给她戒指时，她用力地用胳膊和腿给他一个深情的拥抱，用最热情的方式亲吻他，然后回答道：

CHRISTINA
I want to go back to the bedroom now.

克里斯蒂娜
我现在想回卧室。

Alex knew what Christina wanted, he wanted it too, held her hand and guided her into his bedroom as they stood next to his bed looking into each other's eyes, Christina removed her bathing suit fully exposing herself to Alex who took no time dropping his swimming trunks on the floor and they crawled in bed together and made passionate love.

亚历克斯知道克里斯蒂娜想要什么，他也想要，他握住她的手，领她走进他的卧室，他们站在床边，互相看着对方的眼睛，克里斯蒂娜脱下泳衣，将自己完全暴露在亚历克斯面前，亚历克斯很快就把泳裤脱到地板上，他们一起爬到床上，热情地做爱。

They took their time and completely exhausted each other and then Alex suggested:

他们慢慢地聊着，直到筋疲力尽，然后亚历克斯建议道：

ALEX
Let's take a bath.

亚历克斯
我们去洗澡吧。

Alex and Christina slid out of bed then Alex led Christina over to the bathroom that had a Jacuzzi size bath and controls temperature and water flow. In moments the water filled up quickly and Alex poured the ingredients for a rejuvenating bubble bath which they soon enjoyed, holding each other as if there were no tomorrow.

亚历克斯和克里斯蒂娜从床上滑下来，然后亚历克斯带着克里斯蒂娜来到浴室，浴室里有一个按摩浴缸，可以控制温度和水流。一会儿，水就很快满了，亚历克斯倒了泡泡浴的材料，他们很快就享受了泡泡浴，拥抱在一起，仿佛没有明天一样。

After the bath, Christina and Alex dressed, Alex announced:

洗完澡后，克里斯蒂娜和亚历克斯穿好衣服，亚历克斯宣布：

ALEX
In a short while, a hairdresser is arriving to give you and your mother a hair design for tonight. There will also be a top Hollywood makeup artist to doll you ladies up.

亚历克斯
不一会儿，理发师就来了，为你和你妈妈设计今晚的发型。还有好莱坞顶级化妆师来为你们化妆。

Christina, recalling how the makeup artist had made her look like a princess in Switzerland, started smiling thinking *how beautiful mother would look for daddy tonight.*

克里斯蒂娜回想起在瑞士化妆师把她打扮得像个公主一样，想到妈妈今晚在爸爸面前会显得多么漂亮，她不禁笑了起来。

***

Mr. Garrison. went into the second bathroom to sit on the throne and looked around and saw a couple dozen books, all the kind he liked to read, plus a small box labeled, *"book markers."*

加里森先生走进第二间浴室，坐在宝座上，环顾四周，看到几十本书，都是他喜欢读的那种，还有一个标有"书签"的小盒子。

**WILLIAM GARRISON**
(Thought.)
*Good thing we have separate bathrooms,*

威廉·加里森
（想了想。）
幸好我们有独立的浴室，

Christina and Mrs. Garrison had dressed after their bath and shower when suddenly Marilynn knocked on the Garrison's bedroom door and asked if she may come in.

克里斯蒂娜和加里森夫人洗完澡后穿好衣服，玛丽莲突然敲加里森卧室的门，问她是否可以进来。

Mrs. Garrison opened the door and then Marilynn reported:

加里森夫人打开了门，然后玛丽琳报告说：

**MARILYN**

Mrs. Garrison, the hair designer is downstairs and ready to give you a hair design for tonight if you like.

玛丽莲

加里森夫人，发型设计师就在楼下，如果你愿意的话，她可以为你设计今晚的发型。

**MRS. GARRISON (a.k.a. Ethel)**

That sounds like it might be interesting. Sure, maybe the hair designer can do something with my hair to make it look better.

加里森夫人（又名埃塞尔）

听起来可能很有趣。当然，也许发型设计师可以对我的头发做点什么，让它看起来更好。

Mrs. Garrison followed Marilynn down to a room downstairs that looked like a den of some sort, with a lot of books, a telescope and other gadgets. Luigi was there patiently waiting. There was also a nail technician.

加里森夫人跟着玛丽莲来到楼下的一个房间，房间看起来像是书房，里面放着很多书、望远镜和其他小玩意。路易吉在那里耐心地等待着。房间里还有一位美甲师。

MARILYN
Mrs. Garrison, this is Luigi who will make some
suggestions for your hair, and this is Ms. Suzuki who
can do your fingernails.

玛丽莲
加里森女士，这位是路易吉，她会为您的头发提
出一些建议，这位是铃木女士，她会为您修指
甲。

MRS. GARRISON (a.k.a. Ethel)
Pleased to meet you,

加里森夫人（又名埃塞尔）
很高兴认识你，

Mrs. Garrison held out her hand and shook Luigi then Ms. Suzuki's hands in the most
cordial fashion.

加里森夫人伸出手，以最热情的方式与路易吉握手，然后又与铃木女士握手。

LUIGI
(Hairdresser/Designer)
We can both work at the same time, we've learned to
work around each other.

路易吉
（美发师/设计师）
我们可以同时工作，我们学会了围绕彼此工作。

Mrs. Garrison was facing a large flat screen which was connected up to a laptop.

加里森夫人正面对着一台连接着笔记本电脑的大型平板屏幕。

LUIGI
(Hairdresser/Designer)
I'm going to show you some pictures of women with
my hair styles. Tell me when you see one you like.

路易吉
（美发师/设计师）
我要给你们看一些女性发型的照片。当你看到喜
欢的发型时告诉我。

The *PowerPoint Slide Show* began, and women were sequentially shown, who were
clients of Mr. Luigi, who agreed to let them be photographed. Mr. Luigi's *PowerPoint
Slide Show* presented before and after images, results were rather stunning.

幻灯片放映开始，依次展示了一些女性，她们是路易吉先生的客户，路易吉先生同意让她们拍照。路易吉先生的微软幻灯片软件幻灯片放映展示了拍摄前后的图像效果，效果相当惊人。

LUIGI
(Hairdresser/Designer)
We can apply hair color if you like as well.

路易吉
（美发师/设计师）
如果您愿意，我们也可以为您涂发色。

Mrs. Garrison's hair was sandy brown but was sprinkled with a lot of grey hairs. Mrs. Garrison's hair was below her shoulders currently in a ponytail.

加里森女士的头发呈沙棕色，但夹杂着许多白发。加里森女士的头发扎在肩膀以下，扎成马尾辫。

MRS. GARRISON (a.k.a. Ethel)
I would like to try number seven with the wavy hair
style and add some hair coloring to hide the grey.

加里森夫人（又名埃塞尔）
我想尝试七号波浪发型，并添加一些染发剂来遮
盖白发。

LUIGI
(Hairdresser/Designer)
Just like Rameses II, the Pharaoh of Egypt during the
time of Exodus once said: *So, let it be written, so let
it be done.*

路易吉
（美发师/设计师）
就像出埃及时的埃及法老拉美西斯二世曾经说过
的那样：所以，让它写下来，让它完成。

Next Ms. Suzuki then plugged the cable from the large screen display into her iPhone and showed Mrs. Garrison a variety of *Gel Nail Products*.

接下来，铃木女士将大屏幕显示器上的电缆插入她的 苹果手机 (iPhone)，并向加里森女士展示了各种凝胶指甲产品。

MS. SUZUKI
These are the latest innovations in temporary
fingernails including 3D designs with diamonds,
gems, and rubies mounted.

铃木女士
这些是临时指甲的最新创新，包括镶嵌有钻石、
宝石和红宝石的 3D 设计。

MRS. GARRISON (a.k.a. Ethel)
I would like the blue 3D set of nails you just passed by.
They will go great with my Cobalt Blue designer dress
I'm going to wear this evening.

加里森夫人（又名埃塞尔）
我想要你刚刚路过的那套蓝色三维指甲。它们与
我今晚要穿的钴蓝色设计师连衣裙很相配。

MS. SUZUKI
Good choice. The average movie star might be jealous
of your nails tonight.

铃木女士
不错的选择。今晚普通的电影明星可能会嫉妒你
的指甲。

MRS. GARRISON (a.k.a. Ethel)
I like it!

加里森夫人（又名埃塞尔）
我喜欢它！

MS. SUZUKI
Those are rare Cobalt Blue Spinel Gems from Vietnam
mounted prefabricated on the gel nails.

铃木女士
这些是来自越南的稀有钴蓝色尖晶石宝石，预制
在凝胶指甲上。

MRS. GARRISON (a.k.a. Ethel)
Very interesting!

MS. SUZUKI
Under the right lighting conditions those Cobalt Blue
Spinel Gems will give off spectacular Cobalt Blue
light reflections. Your fingers will come alive, and
people will notice.

加里森夫人（又名埃塞尔）
非常有趣！

Over the next hour the two designers did magic and suddenly Mrs. Garrison looked twenty years younger. That's even before the makeup artist started. When Hollywood Makeup Artist Gabriel finished Mrs. Garrison makeover, she was given a mirror and looked at the results.

接下来的一个小时里，两位设计师施展了魔法，突然间加里森夫人看起来年轻了　二十岁。这还是在化妆师开始化妆之前。好莱坞化妆师加布里埃尔为加里森夫人完成化妆后，她拿到了一面镜子，看着化妆效果。

Mrs. Garrison almost wanted to cry. It's as if she was transported twenty-five years in time. Mr. Garrison was going to be shocked in a few minutes.

加里森女士几乎想哭。她仿佛穿越到了二十五年前。几分钟后，加里森先生就会大吃一惊。

While Mrs. Garrison was getting her makeover, Sam knocked on the Garrison bedroom door and asked permission to go in. Mr. Garrison answered the door, then was informed by Sam:

加里森女士几乎想哭。她仿佛穿越到了二十五年前。几分钟后，加里森先生就会大吃一惊。

SAM<br>
Mr. Garrison, we have a barber here if you would<br>
like a haircut, we have a room downstairs where he's<br>
waiting for you.

山姆<br>
加里森先生，如果您想理发的话，我们这里有一<br>
位理发师，他在楼下的一个房间里等您。

Mr. Garrison liked it short on the sides, almost a Marine high and tight Cut, responded:

加里森先生喜欢两侧剪短的发型，几乎是海军陆战队的那种高而紧的发型，他回答说：

MR. GARRISON<br>
Sure, I wouldn't mind a haircut.

加里森先生<br>
当然，我不介意剪头发。

SAM<br>
Please, follow me, Mr. Garrison.

山姆<br>
请跟我来，加里森先生。

Sam led Mr. Garrison down to a multipurpose room which was used for Alex to get haircuts and manicured. There was also a table/bed that looked like what would be in a doctor's office.

山姆带着加里森先生来到一间多功能室，亚历克斯在这里理发和修指甲。房间里还有一张桌子/床，看起来像是医生办公室里的。

The barber, a Portuguese man named Virgil was waiting. He knew William Garrison's name in advance.

理发师维吉尔正在等候，他是一位葡萄牙人，他事先知道了威廉·加里森的名字。

VIRGIL<br>
Mr. Garrison, how would you like your hair cut?

维吉尔<br>
加里森先生，您想剪什么发型？

MR. GARRISON<br>
Short on the sides and a little off the top would be good.

加里森先生<br>
两侧剪短，顶部留长一点就好了。

Virgil then opened a box of *Cuban Cigars* and held it out in front of Mr. Garrison.

维吉尔随后打开了一盒古巴雪茄并将其拿到加里森先生面前。

VIRGIL<br>
Mr. Garrison, would you like a cigar?

维吉尔<br>
加里森先生，您要抽雪茄吗？

MR. GARRISON<br>
Sure, why not.

加里森先生<br>
当然可以，为什么不呢。

Virgil cut the cigar tip off for Mr. Garrison then held out a cigar lighter and asked:

维吉尔为加里森先生剪掉了雪茄烟头，然后拿出一个雪茄打火机问道：

VIRGIL<br>
Would you like me to light your cigar for you sir?

533

维吉尔
先生，您要我为您点根雪茄吗？

MR. GARRISON
Yes. Please.

加里森先生
是的。请讲。

Sam was standing about ten feet from Mr. Garrison observing the haircut and ready to take care of any requests Mr. Garrison asked.

萨姆站在距加里森先生约十英尺的地方观察着他的发型，并准备满足加里森先生的任何要求。

MR. GARRISON
Sam, what's the table/bed was used for?

加里森先生
山姆，这张桌子/床是用来做什么的？

SAM
Mr. Garrison, that's a massage table. As soon as your hair cut is complete to your satisfaction, if you would like a message, the Masseuse is here ready to give you a massage if you would like one.

山姆
加里森先生，那是一张按摩床。当你的发型剪得让你满意后，如果你想要按摩，按摩师随时准备为你按摩。

MR. GARRISON
That sounds good.

加里森先生
听起来不错。

Because of the nature of Mr. Garrison's haircut, it didn't take the barber Virgil long to finish. After Virgil vacuumed up all the hair trimmings and applied some lotion and powder on Mr. Garison's neck, he excused himself and left.

由于加里森先生的发型比较特殊，理发师维吉尔很快就剪完了。维吉尔用吸尘器吸走了所有头发，并在加里森先生的脖子上抹了一些润肤露和粉末后，他就告辞离开了。

Immediately a very attractive Thai woman came in and asked:

马上就有一个非常漂亮的泰国女人进来询问：

THAI MASSUESE
(a.k.a. Chuenchai)
Mr. Garrison would you like a message?

泰国按摩师
（又名：春柴）
加里森先生，您需要留言吗？

MR. GARRISON
Certainly.

加里森先生
当然可以。

Thai Masseuse (a.k.a. Chuenchai) tapped on the massage bed/table as she spoke:

泰国按摩师（又名 春柴）一边敲着按摩床/按摩台一边说道：

THAI MASSUSE
(a.k.a. Chuenchai)
Mr. Garrison, could you please strip down to your
underwear, then set up on the massage table. Sam will
take care of your clothes.

泰国按摩师
（又名：春柴）
加里森先生，请你脱得只剩下内衣，然后坐在按
摩床上。山姆会帮您整理衣服。

After Mr. Garrison undressed and set up on the massage table Thai Masseuse (a.k.a.
Chuenchai) announced:

当加里森先生脱掉衣服并躺在按摩床上后，泰式按摩师（又名 春柴）宣布：

CHUENCHAI
My name is Chuenchai, I'm from Thailand.

春柴
我的名字是 春柴，我来自泰国。

MR. GARRISON
Pleased to meet you, I'm William.

加里森先生
很高兴认识你，我是威廉。

CHUENCHAI
Ok William, please lay down on the massage table on your stomach.

春柴
好的，威廉，请趴在按摩床上。

Chuenchai then she went to work but wished she could give Mr. Garrison a Nuru Massage. But a Nuru Massage is only done in privacy where the client and the Masseuse are both nude with special oils and full body contact.

春柴随后去上班，但她希望能给 加里森先生做一次 努鲁按摩。但 努鲁按摩只能在私密的环境下进行，顾客和按摩师都裸体，使用特殊精油，全身接触。

Sam then informed Mr. Garrison:

萨姆随后告诉加里森先生：

SAM
Mr. Garrison, I wanted to let you know, I've hung a tuxedo in your room for tonight's performance, we believe it will fit you, as a tailor checked some of your clothes, and will alter it as necessary after you try it on when you are done here.

山姆
加里森先生，我想让你知道，我在你的房间里挂了一套燕尾服，用于今晚的演出，我们相信它会适合你，因为裁缝检查了你的一些衣服，当你在这里演出结束后试穿后，他会根据需要对其进行修改。

MR. GARRISON
Are we going to dress up tonight?

加里森先生
我们今晚要盛装打扮吗？

SAM
Yes sir, Mr. Baxter is having a dinner party in honor of your daughter, we are going to first have a musical performance, then we'll have dinner with more music as you eat.

山姆
是的，先生，巴克斯特先生正在为您的女儿举办
晚宴，我们将首先进行音乐表演，然后在您用餐
时播放更多音乐。

MR. GARRISON
That sounds delightful.

SAM
Mr. Baxter also invited a couple of neighbors and
friends over who he wants to introduce to Christina.

山姆
巴克斯特先生还邀请了一对邻居和朋友过来，他
想把他们介绍给克里斯蒂娜。

MR. GARRISON
I'm glad to see Alex bring Christina into his inner
circle. It demonstrates that he's committed to Christina.

SAM
Mr. Garrison, as you probably understand, is
committed to protect Mr. Baxter's reputation and look
out for his well-being. As such we get informed often
about Mr. Baxter's desires. I can assure you Christina
is the chosen one.

山姆
加里森先生，您可能知道，这里的工作人员致力
于保护巴克斯特先生的名誉并照顾他的福祉。因
此，我们经常会了解巴克斯特先生的愿望。我可
以向您保证，克里斯蒂娜是被选中的人。

Mr. Garrison suddenly, was starting to feel very good from the message. Knowing
the staff was convinced Christina was Alex's number one girl also added an amount
of happiness. Mr. Garrison already sensed that to be the case, but independent
confirmation is always nice.

加里森先生突然开始因为按摩而感觉非常好。得知工作人员确信克里斯蒂娜是
亚历克斯的头号女孩，也让他更加高兴。加里森先生已经感觉到了这一点，但
独立的确认总是好的。

Christina and Alex were next in line for their makeovers. And the results were rather
spectacular. Later in his Tuxedo, Alex looked like the prince that Christina always
dreamed of having.

接下来是克里斯蒂娜和亚历克斯接受改造。改造后的效果相当惊人。亚历克斯
穿上燕尾服后，看起来就像克里斯蒂娜一直梦想的王子。

Just as soon as Alex was finished with his makeover, Sam reported:

亚历克斯 (Alex) 的装扮一完成，萨姆 (Sam) 就报告说：

SAM
The musicians have arrived, and I've had them set up
in the family room precisely the way you drew the
map.

山姆
音乐家们已经到了，我已经让他们按照你画的地
图在家庭娱乐室里安顿下来了。

ALEX
Thank you, Sam.

亚历克斯
谢谢你，萨姆。

This concert musical group of some of the finest performers had strings, including
violins, cello, base, as well as clarinet, oboe, a Harp (using Alex's own Harp which
was on display in the corner and tuned for this event), and a few pieces of brass, and a
set of drums. There were also 3 guitarists.

这个音乐会音乐团体由一些最优秀的表演者组成，他们有弦乐，包括小提琴、
大提琴、低音提琴，以及单簧管、双簧管、竖琴（使用　　亚历克斯自己的竖
琴，该竖琴在角落里展出，并针对本次活动进行了调音），几件铜管乐器和一
套鼓。还有 三名吉他手。

ALEX
Inform the musicians they can warm up if they wish.

亚历克斯
告诉音乐家们，如果他们愿意的话，他们可以热身。

SAM
Certainly sir.

山姆
当然可以，先生。

In a while everyone was ready for prime time. Marilyn and a temporary assistant
helped Mrs. Garrison and Christina put on their evening gowns.

一会儿，大家就准备好迎接黄金时段了。玛丽莲和一名临时助理帮助加里森夫
人和克里斯蒂娜穿上晚礼服。

As such when they were ready, Marilyn escorted Christina and Mrs. Garrison downstairs where Mr. Garrison and Alex, were standing by the fireplace with an actual fire going sipping on some Louis 13th Cognac and looking at a Japanese sword and talking about it.

因此，当他们准备好时，玛丽莲护送克里斯蒂娜和加里森夫人下楼，加里森先生和亚历克斯正站在壁炉旁，壁炉里燃着熊熊的火，他们一边喝着路易十三干邑，一边看着一把日本刀谈论着它。

ALEX
This is General Yamashita's Sword he surrendered to General Krueger on the Philippines at the end of the war.

亚历克斯
这是山下将军在战争结束时在菲律宾向克鲁格将军投降的剑。

MR. GARRISON (a.k.a. William)
No kidding.

加里森先生（又名威廉）
不是开玩笑。

ALEX
It has a letter from General Krueger's widow to the person who purchased it thanking them for the generous amount of money which she used from the auction to help pay for a school she was building in the Philippines back in the 1960's. I obtained it from that family.

亚历克斯
里面有一封克鲁格将军遗孀写给购买者的信，感谢他们慷慨地捐赠了她在 1960 年代在菲律宾建造的一所学校的拍卖所得资金。我从那个家庭那里得到了它。

MR. GARRISON
It looks impressive.

加里森先生
看起来令人印象深刻。

ALEX
Do you like it?

亚历克斯
你喜欢它？

MR. GARRISON
Sure.

加里森先生
当然了。

Alex pulled General Yamashita's Sword off the fireplace still in the display box and handed it to Mr. Garrison.

亚历克斯从壁炉里取出仍在展示盒中的山下将军之剑，并将其递给了加里森先生。

ALEX
Mr. Garrison, I would like to give General Yamashita's Sword to you. I want you to know you deserve a lot more for your courage and sacrifice you made in Vietnam.

亚历克斯
加里森先生，我想把山下将军的剑送给你。我想让你知道，你在越南的勇气和牺牲值得更多。

Mr. Garrison appeared astonished.

加里森先生显得很惊讶。

MR. GARRISON
Alex, I don't know what to say.

加里森先生
亚历克斯，我不知道该说什么。

Sam was walking by about then.

那时萨姆正好走过。

ALEX
Sam, would you please take this sword up to Mr. Garrison's room and when he leaves, wait about three or four days, then FEDEX to his address in New York.

亚历克斯
萨姆，你能把这把剑拿到加里森先生的房间吗？等他离开后，等三四天，然后通过联邦快递寄到他在纽约的地址。

SAM
That will be my pleasure, Mr. Baxter.

山姆
巴克斯特先生，我非常荣幸。

Mr. Garrison almost speechlessly handed the sword to Sam who took it up to his bedroom. As a History Teacher who studied the Battles on Luzon, Mr. Garrison knew the significance of General Yamashita sword.

加里森先生几乎说不出话来，轻轻地把剑递给了萨姆，萨姆把它带到了自己的卧室。作为一名研究过吕宋岛战役的历史老师，加里森先生知道山下将军剑的意义。

Mr. Garrison a former Green Beret SOG operator studied WWII and knew General Yamashita and his forces on Luzon had not been defeated and moved into the mountains where fighting them would cost a lot of American lives, probably as bad as what was experienced in Okinawa.

加里森先生曾是绿色贝雷帽特种作战部队的队员，他研究过二战，他知道山下将军和他在吕宋岛的部队并没有被击败，他们转移到了山区，在那里作战将耗费大量美国人的生命，其惨烈程度可能不亚于冲绳的惨烈程度。

General Yamashita surrendered only because the War was over, and it was more of a ceremonial action than what one would think is a surrender.

山下将军投降只是因为战争结束了，这更多的是一种仪式性的行为，而不是人们所认为的投降。

The invited guests were slowly trickling in with numerous introductions to Mr. Garrison.

受邀的嘉宾们慢慢地进来，并向加里森先生作了多次介绍。

Christina and her mother were announced by Sam a few minutes later as they walked down the circular stairway.

几分钟后，当克里斯蒂娜和她的母亲走下圆形楼梯时，萨姆通知了她们的到来。

SAM
Ladies and gentlemen, my I announce Mrs. Garrison
and Christina Garrison.

山姆
女士们，先生们，我宣布加里森夫人和克里斯蒂
娜·加里森到场。

The band members and a half dozen local people that Alex had invited over, well dressed and obviously wealthy all clapped in unity.

乐队成员和亚历克斯邀请的六个当地人，衣着考究，显然很有钱，都齐声鼓掌。

Alex was once again stunned at Christina's beauty and demure as she was movie starlet quality in image that moment.

亚历克斯再一次被克里斯蒂娜的美丽和娴静所震惊，那一刻，她的形象就像电影明星一样。

The guests were also stunned at how beautiful Christina was in real life, and even though they had already got a glimpse of her when they heard the rumors swirling around caused by the *Magazine Femmes Réelles Exigeantes* expose and saw some of the internet media reports. The guests knew Christina was a good-looking woman from the internet pictures, but now, in real life, Christina Garrison was stunning.

客人们也为克里斯蒂娜在现实生活中的美貌而震惊，尽管他们在听到《真实女性》杂志曝光的谣言和看到一些网络媒体报道时就已经对她有所了解。客人们从网上的照片中知道克里斯蒂娜是个漂亮的女人，但现在，在现实生活中，克里斯蒂娜·加里森真是令人惊艳。

Christina and Mrs. Garrison blushed as they walked into the room. Alex signaled Sam who came and removed his Cognac glass and asked Mr. Garrison:

克里斯蒂娜和加里森夫人走进房间时脸红了。亚历克斯向山姆打了个手势，山姆过来，拿出白兰地酒杯，问加里森先生：

SAM
Mr. Garrison, would you like a refill?

山姆
加里森先生，您要再来一杯吗？

Mr. Garrison, knowing his wife would not approve of him drinking a lot, replied.

加里森先生知道妻子不会同意他喝酒，于是回答道。

MR. GARRISON
No thank you, I need to wait for dinner later.

加里森先生
不用了，谢谢，我需要等一会儿再吃晚饭。

Alex walked up and grabbed Mrs. Garrison's hand.

亚历克斯走上前去，握住了加里森夫人的手。

ALEX
Let me take you to your seat, Mrs. Garrison.

亚历克斯
加里森女士，我带您去座位吧。

Alex led Mrs. Garrison next to the piano on the right side and then announced to Mr. Garrison:

亚历克斯带着加里森夫人来到右侧的钢琴旁，然后对加里森先生宣布道：

ALEX
Mr. Garrison, please sit here with Mrs. Garrison,

亚历克斯
加里森先生，请和加里森夫人一起坐在这里，

Alex then walked over and took Christina by her hand and took her over to a chair by itself very close to the piano on the side by the pianist chair.

然后亚历克斯走过去，牵着克里斯蒂娜的手，把她带到钢琴师椅子旁边一张离钢琴很近的椅子上。

The makeshift orchestra was behind the piano and the guests saw their names on little cards on the backs of each chair and were invited:

临时乐队在钢琴后面，客人们在每张椅子的背面的小卡片上看到自己的名字，并被邀请：

SAM
Everyone, *please have a seat.*

山姆
各位，请就座。

Alex stood by the piano next to Christina, looking at the six guests and her parents.

亚历克斯站在克里斯蒂娜旁边的钢琴旁，看着六位客人和她的父母。

ALEX
I want to thank you all for coming. We are going to have a little performance, then we shall go into the dining room and have dinner, and we'll have some performances during dinner, and if you have any requests afterwards, I'm sure the orchestra wouldn't mind playing.

亚历克斯

我要感谢大家的到来。我们会进行一些小型表演，然后去餐厅吃晚饭，晚餐期间我们会进行一些表演，如果你们之后有什么要求，我相信乐团不会介意演奏。

Alex looked around the room at the guests and the staff and the Garrisons knowing his next statements would confirm the speculations in the media.

亚历克斯环顾房间内的客人、工作人员和加里森一家，他知道他的接下来的言论将证实媒体的猜测。

ALEX

We'll all get to know each other a little better during dinner, but first I wanted to introduce you to my significant other, Christina Garrison from New York City. She's a remarkable woman and I truly adore her, and hope that she will agree to stay with me for the rest of my life.

ALEX

晚餐时我们会更进一步了解彼此，但首先我想向你们介绍我的另一半，来自纽约的克里斯蒂娜·加里森。她是一位了不起的女性，我真的很爱她，希望她能同意和我共度余生。

Christina's eyes watered up and she fought hard not to cry and messed up her world class makeup. Alex was aware something like that could happen, so the makeup artist was asked to stay though the evening just in case he was needed. Sam and Marilyn were in the back, ready to refill drinks that some of them had or show them to the restroom or be of assistance.

克里斯蒂娜的眼睛湿润了，她努力忍住不哭，不弄乱她那世界级的妆容。亚历克斯知道可能会发生这样的事情，所以要求化妆师留到晚上，以防万一需要他。萨姆和玛丽莲在后面，准备给一些人续杯饮料，带他们去洗手间，或者提供帮助。

Alex then continued as it appeared Christina was getting control of herself:

当克里斯蒂娜似乎已经控制住自己时，亚历克斯继续说道：

ALEX

As soon as I saw Christina for the first time in the elevator as I was going up to Claude Rearden's office at the 120 Wall Street building, I was immediately captivated by Christina, and thus immediately pursued her.

亚历克斯
当我前往克劳德·里尔登位于华尔街120号大楼的
办公室时，在电梯里第一次看到克里斯蒂娜时，
我立刻就被克里斯蒂娜迷住了，于是立即追求了
她。

The guests and Christina's parents were now transfixed on every statement Alex made.

现在，客人们和克里斯蒂娜的父母都全神贯注地听着亚历克斯说的每句话。

ALEX
Christina and I are now very close, and I hope that one
day I will prove to her that I'm worthy of her love.

亚历克斯
克里斯蒂娜和我现在非常亲密，我希望有一天我
能向她证明我值得她的爱。

Alex walked over to the piano seat and sat down and was soon prepared to start performing with orchestra backup. Before he gave the signal to the orchestra, Alex had one more comment he wished to make.

阿历克斯走到钢琴椅旁坐下，很快就准备好在乐团的伴奏下开始演奏。在向乐团发出信号之前，阿历克斯还有一句话想说。

ALEX
I know the song I'm just about to play may not be
all that great, but I wrote this song for Christina. It's
an expression of my love for Christina and I hope it
conveys what's in my heart for her.

ALEX
我知道我即将演奏的这首歌可能不是那么好，但
这首歌是我为克里斯蒂娜写的。这是我对克里斯
蒂娜的爱的表达，我希望它能传达我对她的心
声。

Alex had sent a tape recording of the piano music to the Orchestra group so they could practice it without him. He managed to get together with them one time and practice it. He knew it might be rough, but at least the piano part of it he would play his heart out for Christina.

亚历克斯将钢琴曲的录音带寄给了管弦乐队，这样他们就可以在没有他的情况下练习。他设法和他们聚在一起练习了一次。他知道这可能很难，但至少钢琴部分他会为克里斯蒂娜倾尽全力演奏。

Alex then sat down and nodded at the orchestra, then a violinist started playing a very soft and sweet passage, then Alex began playing.

然后亚历克斯坐下来，朝着管弦乐队点点头，然后一位小提琴手开始演奏一段非常柔和甜美的乐段，然后亚历克斯开始演奏。

One might think Alex was a reincarnation of Rachmaninoff as the chords were exclusively Rachmaninov like. Soon the other instruments were added, and if Alex had any doubt, it was quickly dispelled as the music resonated the persona of everyone in the room.

人们可能会认为亚历克斯是拉赫玛尼诺夫的转世，因为这些和弦完全是拉赫玛尼诺夫式的。很快其他乐器也加入了进来，如果亚历克斯有任何疑虑，那么这种疑虑很快就会被打消，因为音乐引起了房间里每个人的共鸣。

In a surprising twist to it all, a man and a woman stepped forward after a minute or so and began singing the vocalist portion of the piece with the wonderful sound of the Steinway and the Orchestra combining for the quintessential effect.

令人惊讶的是，大约一分钟后，一男一女走上前来，开始演唱这首曲子的声乐部分，斯坦威钢琴和管弦乐队的美妙声音交织在一起，产生了典型的效果。

The words of the love song finally pushed Christina over the line, and she could no longer hold back the tears, nor could her mother, the three women guests, and Marilynn standing in the back. Even Sam's eyes were watering up a bit.

情歌的歌词终于让克里斯蒂娜忍不住流下了眼泪，她妈妈、三位女嘉宾和站在后面的玛丽莲也忍不住流下了眼泪，就连萨姆的眼睛也有些湿润了。

The song lasted about 15 minutes; it had a rather profound effect on everyone including the performers.

这首歌大概持续了15分钟，对包括表演者在内的所有人都产生了比较深远的影响。

As soon as the song ended, Alex stood up, so did everyone and applauded. Alex then stepped aside while another person sat down at the piano and started playing other songs for almost 30 minutes. The fantastic sounds enthralled the guests, which made a huge impact.

一曲终了，亚历克斯起身，大家也起身鼓掌，亚历克斯退到一旁，另一个人坐到钢琴前，继续弹奏其他歌曲，持续近三十分钟，美妙的音效让在场嘉宾沉醉其中，震撼不已。

And then right on cue after a song finished, Alex announced:

然后，一首歌一结束，亚历克斯就宣布：

ALEX
Everyone, please follow Sam to the dining room.

亚历克斯
各位，请跟着山姆去餐厅。

Everyone then stood and relocated to the dining room.

然后**每**个人都站起来并走向餐厅。

MUSIC FOR THE NEXT SEQUENCE:

Gino Marinuzzi (1882-1945) : Symphony in A major (1943)

下一幕的音乐：

吉诺·马里努齐 (1882-1945)：A 大调交响曲 (1943)

Marilynn walked up to Christina and advised her:

玛丽莲走到克里斯蒂娜面前并告诉她：

MARILYNN
Christina, please come with me for a minute.

玛丽莲
克里斯蒂娜，请跟我来一下。

Mary took Christina upstairs to her bedroom.

玛丽带克里斯蒂娜上楼到她的卧室。

MARILYN
The makeup artist is ready to perform his miracles by
fixing the damage your tears have done.

玛丽莲
化妆师已准备好施展奇迹，修复你泪水造成的伤
害。

CHRISTINA
Marilyn, thank you so much I appreciate this.

克里斯蒂娜
玛丽莲，非常感谢你，我很感激。

Christina's makeup was quickly repaired, and Christina was so very happy that it
could be taken care of so quickly. The makeup artist also stated:

克里斯蒂娜的妆容很快就修好了，克里斯蒂娜自己也非常开心，能这么快就修
好，化妆师还表示：

MAKEUP ARTIST
I'm going to be there for several more hours at the
request of Alex, in case Christina you need another
*makeup refresh.*

化妆师
应亚历克斯的要求，我将在那里多待几个小时，
以防克里斯蒂娜需要再次化妆。

Little did Christina know or suspect, those moments would come again. Marilynn
dismissed the makeup artist for a while and then said to Christina:

克里斯蒂娜根本不知道，也没想到，这样的时刻会再次出现。玛丽琳让化妆师
休息了一会儿，然后对克里斯蒂娜说：

MARILYN
The red dress you have on is beautiful, but you
are keeping the guests waiting, so you need to do
something special for them and change your dress.

玛丽莲
你穿的红裙子很漂亮，但是你让客人等得太久
了，所以你需要为他们做点特别的事，换上你的
裙子。

CHRISTINA
That's a great idea.

克里斯蒂娜
这是个好主意。

MARILYN
Try on this purple dress, I think it will capture your
magic.

玛丽莲
试穿这件紫色连衣裙，我想它会捕捉到你的魅力。

Marilynn had Christina redressed in the purple in just a couple minutes, then she
looked at the mirror.

玛丽琳只用了几分钟就让克里斯蒂娜重新穿上了紫色的衣服，然后她看向镜
子。

CHRISTINA
Isn't the slit on the side of the dress too revealing?

克里斯蒂娜
裙子侧面的开衩是不是太暴露了？

MARILYN
Absolutely yes, but in fact that's what you want. Alex
made you cry with the piano, now you need to make
him whimper with this dress.

玛丽莲
当然，但事实上这正是你想要的。亚历克斯用钢
琴让你哭了，现在你需要用这件衣服让他呜咽。

The two women chuckled a little and then Marilynn announced:

两个女人笑了笑，然后玛丽琳宣布：

MARILYN
We had better go downstairs now, or they may think
something is wrong. Now it's time to put on that big
smile to go along with your beautiful dress.

玛丽莲
我们最好现在就下楼，不然他们可能会觉得有什
么不对劲。现在是时候露出灿烂的笑容来搭配你
漂亮的裙子了。

CHRISTINA
I hope Alex likes my change of dresses.

克里斯蒂娜
我希望亚历克斯会喜欢我换的衣服。

MARILYN
Christina, I promise one glance at you and Alex will
feel Cupid just shot an arrow through his heart.

玛丽莲
克里斯蒂娜，我保证，只要看你一眼，亚历克斯
就会感觉丘比特之箭射穿了他的心脏。

Alex was slightly panicking because nobody had seen Christina for fifteen minutes
or more and the Chef as duly waiting to start the service but, didn't want to offend
Christina by starting before she arrived.

亚历克斯有点惊慌，因为十五分钟内没人见过克里斯蒂娜，而厨师也在等着开
始服务，但他不想在克里斯蒂娜到达之前就开始服务而冒犯她。

Alex was hoping Christina had calmed down by now and was at the foot of the stairway when the two women suddenly appeared and were heading down the circular stairway.

亚历克斯希望克里斯蒂娜现在已经冷静下来，并正走到楼梯脚下时，那两个女人突然出现并正沿着圆形楼梯走下去。

This new dress took Alex's breath away. He was stunned by Christina's exquisite beauty. Christina was beautiful before wearing the red dress, but now in this reddish purple, Christina's imagery transcended to a new dimension.

这件新裙子让亚历克斯惊叹不已。克里斯蒂娜的绝色美貌让他震惊不已。克里斯蒂娜在穿这件红裙子之前就很漂亮，但现在穿上这件红紫色裙子，克里斯蒂娜的形象超越了一个新的维度。

Alex was so astounded he became speechless and knew what to say other than:

亚历克斯震惊得说不出话来，除了说：

ALEX<br>
Let me escort you to the dining room.

亚历克斯<br>
让我护送您去餐厅。

As Alex and Christina appeared with the orchestra already playing a lovely piece, Christina's entry once again captivated the guests as well as her parents.

当亚历克斯和克里斯蒂娜出现时，管弦乐队已经在演奏一首优美的乐曲，克里斯蒂娜的出场再一次吸引了在场嘉宾和她的父母的注意。

Christina's mother was learning from her daughter, the change of dress had a surreal effect on everyone in the room. Christina was definitely the princess they knew Alex had always wished to meet.

克里斯蒂娜的妈妈正在向女儿学习，换衣服对房间里的每个人都产生了超现实的影响。克里斯蒂娜绝对是他们知道亚历克斯一直希望见到的公主。

Alex walked holding hands with Christina and took her to her chair to his right side at the end of the table. Once again, Mr. Garrison was to his left and Mrs. Garrison right side of Christina.

阿历克斯牵着克里斯蒂娜的手走过去，把她带到桌子末端他右侧的椅子上。加里森先生再次在他左边，加里森夫人则在克里斯蒂娜的右边。

The wine glasses had already been filled and about one second after Alex bowed then sat down and gave a Buddhist hands together momentary prayer.

酒杯已斟满，大约一秒钟后，亚历克斯鞠躬并坐下来，双手合十，做了一个佛教祈祷。

The Chef served Mrs. Garrison first, followed by Mr. Garrison, then Christina, and then the guests and last was Alex smiling at them all. This was the arrangement Alex had stipulated earlier in preparation for this dinner to convey respect to Christina's parents.

厨师首先为加里森夫人服务，然后是加里森先生，然后是克里斯蒂娜，然后是宾客，最后是微笑着看着大家的亚历克斯。这是亚历克斯之前为这顿晚餐规定的安排，以表达对克里斯蒂娜父母的尊重。

Mr. Garrison was just starting to come to grips with his wife, suddenly looking 25 years younger, enjoyed talking to Alex and the guests also chimed in from time to time including talking to each other.

加里森先生刚刚开始接受这个事实：他的妻子突然看起来年轻了 25 岁，他很喜欢和亚历克斯聊天，客人们也时不时地插话，包括互相交谈。

The woman sitting next to Mrs. Garrison whispered to her:

坐在加里森夫人旁边的女人低声对她说道：

FEMALE GUEST
At first, I thought you two ladies were sisters, you look
so good.

女嘉宾
一开始, 我以为你们两个是姐妹，你们看起来真好看。

MRS. GARRISON
It's the Irish in me.

加里森夫人
这是我身上的爱尔兰血统。

FEMALE GUEST
I wish I looked as pretty as you.

女嘉宾
我希望自己能像你一样漂亮。

MRS. GARRISON
You look fine.

加里森夫人
你看上去很好。

FEMALE GUEST
Thank you for your sweet lies.

女嘉宾<br>
谢谢你的甜蜜谎言。

The Female guest and Mrs. Garrison giggled in an instantaneous release of humility.

女客人和加里森夫人瞬间释放出谦卑之情，咯咯地笑了起来。

The man sitting next to Mr. Garrison is a history buff and asked Mr. Garrison:

坐在加里森先生旁边的男人是一位历史爱好者，他问加里森先生：

HISTORY BUFF<br>
(a.k.a. Walter - Guest)<br>
Mr. Garrison, what do you do in New York?

历史爱好者<br>
（又名沃尔特 - 嘉宾）<br>
加里森先生，您在纽约做什么？

MR. GARRISON<br>
I'm a retired teacher.

加里森先生<br>
我是一名退休教师。

HISTORY BUFF<br>
(a.k.a. Walter - Guest)<br>
That's nice, what did you teach.

历史爱好者<br>
（又名沃尔特 - 嘉宾）<br>
很好，你教了什么。

MR. GARRISON<br>
I was a history teacher.

加里森先生<br>
我是一名历史老师。

HISTORY BUFF<br>
(a.k.a. Walter - Guest)<br>
That's great, did you teach students about WW2,
Korea, or Vietnam?

历史爱好者<br>
（又名沃尔特 - 嘉宾）<br>
太好了，您教过学生关于二战、朝鲜战争或越南战争的知识吗？

MR. GARRISON
I taught high school history, so we touched upon those wars.

加里森先生
我教高中历史，所以我们谈到了那些战争。

HISTORY BUFF
(a.k.a. Walter - Guest)
I'm glad we are teaching our kids History; I think it's important.

历史爱好者
（又名沃尔特 - 嘉宾）
我很高兴我们教孩子们历史；我认为这很重要。

MR. GARRISON
So, do I.

加里森先生
我也是。

Alex knowing his guest a banker was a history buff and would really be interested, announced:

亚历克斯知道他的客人是一位银行家，是个历史爱好者，而且非常感兴趣，于是他宣布道：

ALEX
Walter, Mr. Garrison served in the Green Beret in Vietnam.

亚历克斯
沃尔特，加里森先生曾在越南的绿色贝雷帽部队服役。

WALTER
No kidding, wow!

沃尔特
别开玩笑了，哇！

MR. GARRISON
Yes, I did a good job of forgetting most of that.

加里森先生
是的，我把大部分事情都忘得一干二净了。

Walter the history buff who had met Colonel Plaster at a book signing asked:

历史爱好者沃尔特在一次签售会上遇见了普拉斯特上校，他问道：

WALTER

Mr. Garrison, did you know a Green Beret guy in Vietnam named Plaster?

沃尔特

加里森先生，您认识越南的一个名叫普拉斯特的绿色贝雷帽士兵吗？

MR. GARRISON

Yes, I was at the SOG camp with Sargent Plaster who later was promoted to a full colonel. I didn't go out on many missions with him specifically, but I know based on the reports a lot of what he did.

加里森先生

是的，我和普拉斯特中士一起在　特种部队(SOG)营地，他后来晋升为上校。我并没有和他一起执行过很多任务，但根据报告，我知道他做过很多事情。

WALTER

Did Colonel Plaster operate behind enemy lines like he says in his books?

沃尔特

普拉斯特上校是否像他在书中所说的那样在敌后行动？

MR. GARRISON

Definitely. Every mission Colonel Plaster went on while he was a Sargent and team leader on an SOG Team was behind enemy lines. Most of Sargent Plaster's SOG missions took place in Cambodia, though I do know he made a couple missions into Laos.

加里森先生

当然。普拉斯特上校在担任特种作战大队中士和队长期间执行的每项任务都是在敌后。普拉斯特中士的大多数特种作战大队任务都在柬埔寨进行，但我知道他曾执行过几次进入老挝的任务。

WALTER

So, all that business about being extracted with no time to spare is how it really was?

沃尔特
那么，所有那些关于没有时间被提取的事情，事
实是这样的吗？

VOICEOVER (WILLIAM
GARRISON) THOUGHT

*I hoped I never thought about Vietnam again, but Walter's questions and comments seemed to have caused a temporal hallucination (Flashback).*

画外音（威廉·
加里森）思考
我希望我再也不会想到越南，但沃尔特的问题和
评论似乎引起了暂时的幻觉（闪回）。

People who experienced severe Trauma sometimes experience temporal hallucinations in vivid video and sound and psychiatrists work hard to help them forget about it.

经历过严重创伤的人有时会在生动的视频和声音中出现暂时性幻觉，精神科医生会努力帮助他们忘记这些幻觉。

FLASHBACK

倒叙

Sargent Garrison and his Studies and Observation Group (SOG) team were spotted by an entire North Vietnamese Army (NVA) Regiment.

加里森中士和他的 研究与观察组 （SOG） 团队被整个北越陆军 （NVA） 团发现。

The Green Beret didn't know it at the time, but an American Army Warrant Officer in Europe was selling America's military's Crypto to the Soviets, which Studies and Observation Group (SOG) and Military Assistance Command, Vietnam (MACV) in Saigon used.

当时，绿色贝雷帽并不知道，驻扎在欧洲的美国陆军准尉正在向苏联出售美国军方的密码，而西贡的 研究和观察组 (SOG) 和越南军事援助司令部 (MACV) 正在使用这种密码。

John Walker was also selling Crypto the Navy used for Navy Seals sometimes used in task forces with SOG Teams. 50% of all SOG missions were compromised by traitors which almost got Sargent Garrison killed multiple times.

约翰·沃克还出售海军使用的密码，海豹突击队有时会在特遣部队中使用 研究和观察组 (SOG) 小组。50% 的 SOG 任务都遭到叛徒破坏，这差点导致加里森中士多次丧命。

Sargen Garrison's SOG team was found within three days after arrival on-station.

加里森中士的 研究和观察组 (SOG)小队在抵达驻地三天后就被找到。

Like many compromised SOG missions, Sargent Plaster an OV-10 back seater happened to be supporting the mission monitoring SOG team communications in case they called for an emergency extraction.

和许多受损的 SOG 任务一样，坐在 OV-10 后座上的普拉斯特中士恰好在支持任务，监控 SOG 小队的通信，以防他们呼叫紧急撤离。

**OV-10 SOG RECON SUPPORT AIRCRAFT**
哦维十 (OV-10) SOG 侦察支援飞机

This was a complicated SOG extraction because the signals compromise allowed the North Vietnamese Army (NVA) to move in anti-aircraft batteries that had to be dealt with. The extraction took about four times as long and a lot of NVA soldiers surrounded the landing zone which had to be offset, or emergency extraction could not be accomplished.

这是一次复杂的 SOG 撤离行动，因为信号泄露使北越军得以调动防空炮台，而防空炮台必须加以应对。撤离行动耗时大约是原来的四倍，而且许多北越军士兵包围了必须撤离的着陆区，否则紧急撤离就无法完成。

NVA Type 63 anti-aircraft gun.
NVA 63 式防空炮。

As soon as the SOG Team was directed to get down low, the fighter bombers dropped their entire load of napalm on the Southwest corner and called in for more air strikes.

当 SOG 小队接到降低高度的命令时，战斗轰炸机立即将全部凝固汽油弹投向西南角，并呼叫更多空袭。

FORWARD AIR CONTROLLER
SARGENT PLASTER
(OV-10 Back-seater)
The helicopter gunships were taking a few hits from NVA Type 63 anti-aircraft guns and had to back away until more Napalm arrives.

前线空中管制员
萨金特·普拉斯特
（哦维十 (OV-10) 后座）
武装直升机遭到北越 63 式高射炮的几次射击，不得不后退，直到更多凝固汽油弹抵达。

SARGENT GARRISON
(SOG Team Leader)
I'm not sure how much longer we can hold out. We are almost out of ammunition.

加里森中士
（SOG 小队队长 ）
我不确定我们还能坚持多久。我们的弹药快用完了。

FORWARD AIR CONTROLLER
SARGENT PLASTER

(OV-10 Back-seater)
There are two more F4 Fantoms and two A1 Sky
Raiders inbound – five minutes out.

前线空中管制员
萨金特·普拉斯特
（哦维十 (OV-10) 后座）
另外两架 艾弗四 幻影战斗机和两架 甲一 天空袭
击者战斗机正在进港 – 五分钟后。

SARGENT GARRISON
(SOG Team Leader)
This extraction will be cutting it close.

加里森中士
（SOG 小队队长）
这次撤离行动将非常紧急。

F4 PHANTOM
F4 幻影

The F4's had only about 30 minutes of on station time, whereas the propeller driven
A1's could loiter for almost two hours if they dropped most of their bombs.

艾弗四的 (F4's) 停留时间仅有 30 分钟左右，而螺旋桨驱动的 甲一的 (A1's) 如
果投下大部分炸弹则可以盘旋近两个小时。

A1 Sky Raider
甲一 天袭者

The OV-10 gave good coordinates to where the NVA Type 63 anti-aircraft guns were located and after 20 minutes, they were all silenced, allowing the helicopters to get in closer.

OV-10 提供了北越 63 型高射炮位置的准确坐标，20 分钟后，所有高射炮都安静下来，以便直升机可以更靠近。

By now the NVA Infantry had crawled up to almost a charging location and had to be dealt with. Thanks to the A1's the crawlers quickly turned into runners heading backwards and half of them were cut down by SOG fire or from their Cadres who made examples out of cowards.

此时，北越步兵已爬到几乎可以冲锋的位置，必须予以应对。多亏了甲一的，爬行者迅速变成了向后逃跑的逃兵，其中一半被 艾丝哦吉 (SOG) 的火力或他们的干部击倒，他们以懦夫为榜样。

During this SOG Team emergency extraction is where Sargent Garrison earned one of his purple hearts as he was wounded in an arm and in the chest that didn't do too much damage thanks to his new Kevlar Vest. But it still hurt like hell.

在这次 SOG 小队的紧急撤离中，加里森中士获得了一枚紫心勋章，因为他的手臂和胸部受伤，但由于穿着新凯夫拉防弹衣，所以没有造成太大伤害。但还是很疼。

Every member of the eight-member SOG team was wounded. A couple of the Montagnard's very seriously and had to be carried and loaded up on one of the evacuation helicopters.

这支由八名队员组成的 SOG 小队中，每个人都受了伤。有几名山地人伤势严重，不得不被抬上一架撤离直升机。

Secretly back at Military Assistance Command, Vietnam (MACV) whether the SOG team was rescued or not, this turned out to be a great American elaborate trap that did a lot of damage to the NVA Regiment.

秘密返回越南军事援助司令部 (MACV)，无论 SOG 小组是否获救，这都被证明是美国精心策划的一次陷阱，对北越军团造成了巨大的伤害。

The NVA officers got *Buck Fever* and wanted to capture the SOG team at all costs and in the process lost almost a regiment plus the destruction of all their self-propelled NVA Type 63 anti-aircraft guns.

北越军官们患上了巴克热，不惜一切代价想要抓住 SOG 小组，结果他们几乎损失了一个团，而且所有北越 63 式自行高射炮也被毁。

> Note: an example of *Buck Fever* is when Texans go Deer Hunting in Colorado and shoot a farmer's COW because they think it's a Buck Deer. The term *Pareidolia* describes *Buck Fever* perfectly.

注：雄鹿热的一个例子是，德克萨斯人在科罗拉多州猎鹿时，误以为一头农民的牛是雄鹿，结果射杀了它。 "空想性错视" 这个术语完美地描述了雄鹿热。

> Pareidolia - Wikipedia

The mindset at MACV was the lives of eight SOG men was a good price for an entire NVA regiment destroyed. On top of all that the SOG Team completed their mission taking pictures of tank tracks proving this was the axis of invasion that eventually came in 1975.

MACV 的想法是，八名 SOG 队员的生命足以换来一整个北越军团的覆灭。最重要的是，SOG 小队完成了拍摄坦克履带照片的任务，证明这是最终在 1975 年到来的入侵轴心。

North Vietnam T-54 Tank
北越T-54坦克

Without the anti-aircraft artillery provided by the NVA Type 63 anti-aircraft guns, the remnants of the NVA Regiment were now at a disadvantage allowing the extraction force to systematically widen the landing zone to get the choppers down safely and pick up the SOG Team.

由于没有北越军 63 式高射炮的防空火力，北越军团的残余部队现在处于不利地位，这使得撤离部队可以系统地扩大着陆区，以使直升机安全降落并接走 SOG 小队。

As soon as the SOG team was airborne flying out of the landing zone, the A1's and F4's came down and unloaded the remainder of the Napalm around the perimeter to smoke out NVA hiding leaving behind a couple hundred more dead enemy soldiers.

当 SOG 小队飞出着陆区后，甲一的 (A1's) 和 艾弗四的 (F4's) 便降落并在边界发射了剩余的凝固汽油弹，以熏出北越军队的藏身之处，留下数百名敌军的尸体。

Not all the choppers flew back to base. The two evacuation helicopters were flown directly to a military hospital in Saigon, where all eight SOG Team members went through emergency surgeries, with some terrible wounds. Sargent Garrison was not in as bad shape as some of the other team members, but he sure hurt like hell and had surgery on his arm and stitches where some skin lacerations happened under the Kevlar vest.

并非所有直升机都飞回了基地。两架撤离直升机直接飞往西贡的一家军医院，所有八名 SOG 队员都在那里接受了紧急手术，伤势严重。加里森中士的情况没有其他队员那么糟糕，但他确实伤得很重，手臂接受了手术，凯夫拉背心下的一些皮肤裂伤也缝合了。

END FLASHBACK

结束闪回

MR. GARRISON

Yes, the extractions were due to the fact the North Vietnamese had detected us and were coming in to capture us.

加里森先生

是的，撤离的原因是北越人发现了我们，并准备进来抓捕我们。

WALTER
Did you ever get wounded?

MR. GARRISON
I received three purple hearts from three battles.

沃尔特
你受过伤吗？

WALTER
Mr. Garrison, I'm very honored to have met you.

沃尔特
加里森先生，我很荣幸见到您。

Walter then pulled out his business card and offered:

沃尔特随后拿出了自己的名片并说道：

WALTER

Mr. Garrison, when you come back to visit Alex, I would like to invite you over to my home for dinner and visit.

沃尔特

加里森先生，当你回来看望亚历克斯时，我想邀请你来我家吃饭和拜访。

MR. GARRISON (a.k.a. William)
I would enjoy that, Walter. Please call me William.

加里森先生（又名威廉）
沃尔特，我很乐意。请叫我威廉。

Six different meat entrées were served.

供应六种不同的肉类主菜。

Another guest, who everyone called Max, asked Alex:

另一位大家都叫麦克斯的客人问亚历克斯：

MAX
Alex, are you feeding us Peacock again?

马克斯
亚历克斯，你又在给我们喂孔雀吗？

Alex grinned and replied:

亚历克斯笑着回答道：

ALEX
No Max, maybe a little Giraffe and Lion.

亚历克斯
没有马克斯，也许有一点长颈鹿和狮子。

The guests' thought Alex was joking and chuckling, but the fact is Alex had both types of meat flown in just for this occasion.

客人们以为亚历克斯在开玩笑，并笑了起来，但事实上亚历克斯为了这次活动特意空运了这两种肉。

The lion had been killing cattle, so the Kenyan Park Ranger was ordered to kill the lion. After the lion was shot, there were immediate bids for the carcass, which ended up in Alex's hands.

这头狮子一直在捕杀牲畜，于是肯尼亚公园管理员奉命杀死这头狮子。狮子被射杀后，立即有人竞拍狮子尸体，最后落入了亚历克斯手中。

The next day, as the lion was flown to Minnesota and a local butcher quickly prepared the carcass for Alex and the butcher was allowed to keep the hide and head which he turned over to a taxidermist to make into a lion figure he put as a decoration in his store with the label:

第二天，狮子被空运到明尼苏达州，当地的一名屠夫迅速为亚历克斯准备了狮子尸体，屠夫被允许保留狮子皮和头，并将其交给动物标本剥制师制成狮子雕像，放在商店里作为装饰，并贴上标签：

## BUTCHER LABEL
We'll butcher lions and tigers if you bring them in.

屠夫标签
如果您带狮子和老虎来，我们就会屠宰它们。

After dinner and dessert were finished the group went back out to the family room where they found comfortable seats and continued their conversation as a pianist performed playing soft music. The dining room was quickly cleaned up and the table was reset for the musicians who gorged themselves on Lion, Giraffe, Peacock, Alaskan wild Salmon, and Kobe beef.

晚餐和甜点吃完后，大家回到家庭室，找到舒适的座位，一边听钢琴师演奏轻柔的音乐，一边继续聊天。餐厅很快就打扫干净，餐桌也重新摆好，音乐家们大快朵颐，享用了狮子、长颈鹿、孔雀、阿拉斯加野生鲑鱼和神户牛肉。

After their dinner, the musicians went back to the piano and played as an orchestra. The female guests approached and talked with Christina. They were very much focused on her and as they got close and shook hands and got to know each other, these women, who were all about Christina's mother's age, could see her exquisite beauty up front.

晚餐后，音乐家们回到钢琴前，像乐队一样演奏。女客们走上前来和克里斯蒂娜交谈。她们非常关注她，随着她们走近、握手和互相认识，这些与克里斯蒂娜母亲年龄相仿的女性可以一眼看出她精致的美貌。

One of the couples talked to each other in Russian for a moment. Christina understood what they were saying, much was about her so she didn't want them to feel embarrassed later interrupted them briefly so they wouldn't go too far before discovering her Russian ability, said to them:

其中一对夫妇用俄语交谈了一会儿。克里斯蒂娜听懂了他们在说什么，大部分内容都是关于她的，所以她不想让他们感到尴尬，后来她短暂地打断了他们，以免他们在发现她的俄语能力之前说得太远，然后对他们说：

### CHRISTINA
Я так рад, что встретил тебя, я могу практиковать
мой русский Когда я бываю с вами.

[YA tak rad, chto vstretil tebya, ya mogu praktikovat'
moy russkiy Kogda ya byvayu s vami.]

{I'm so happy to have met you; I can practice my
Russian when I visit with you.}

克里斯蒂娜
我很高兴见到你；和你见面时我可以练习俄语。

The couple was astonished, and the wife spoke:

夫妻俩非常惊讶，妻子说道：

VISITING WIFE

Ты меня удивляешь, Кристина, ты такая красивая и к тому же очень умная.

[Ty menya udivlyayesh', Kristina, ty takaya krasivaya i k tomu zhe ochen' umnaya.]

{You amaze me Christina, you're so very beautiful and you're also quite intelligent.}

探望妻子

你让我很惊讶，克里斯蒂娜，你非常漂亮，而且你也很聪明。

CHRISTINA

Почему спасибо. Я думаю, хотя, я просто средний. [Pochemu spasibo. YA dumayu, khotya, ya prosto sredniy.]

{Why thank you. I think though, I'm just average.}

克里斯蒂娜

谢谢你。不过我觉得我只是个普通人。

The lady walked over and put her arms on Christina and hugged her and spoke:

那位女士走过去，搂住克里斯蒂娜，拥抱了她，说道：

VISITING WIFE

Кристина, ты такая красивая, милая леди. Мне повезло познакомиться с тобой.

[Kristina, ty takaya krasivaya, milaya ledi. Mne povezlo poznakomit'sya s toboy.}

{Christina, you are such a beautiful, sweet lady. I'm privileged to have met you.}

来访的妻子

克里斯蒂娜，你真是一个美丽、可爱的女士。我很荣幸能见到你。

The night continued in such a friendly manner and eventually it was time for the guests to slowly filter out.

565

夜晚在如此友好的氛围中继续进行，最终客人们都慢慢散去了。

Alex had one last surprise for all of them. The orchestra had recorded Alex's piano performance as well as another 60 minutes of performances and during the evening, downloaded the recordings on to CD's and as they were lined up at the door to bid their farewells, Alex handed them the CD, with a professional looking label on it with Christina's picture titled, *"Cristina B."*

亚历克斯还为他们所有人准备了最后一个惊喜。乐团录制了亚历克斯的钢琴演奏以及另外 60 分钟的表演，并在当晚将录音下载到 CD 上，当他们在门口排队道别时，亚历克斯将 CD 递给他们，CD 上贴着一张看起来很专业的标签，上面印着克里斯蒂娜的照片，标题是 "克里斯蒂娜 B" 。

Later, when Christina's parents were also given a CD, Mrs. Garrison asked:

后来，当克里斯蒂娜的父母也收到一张 CD 时，加里森女士问道：

MRS. GARRISON<br>
Alex, why the B?

加里森夫人<br>
亚历克斯，为什么是 B ？


ALEX<br>
That's my last name initial and soon will be Christina's<br>
as well.

亚历克斯<br>
这是我姓氏的首字母，很快也会是克里斯蒂娜的。

Mrs. Garrison suddenly threw her arms around Alex and hugged him.

加里森夫人突然张开双臂拥抱了亚历克斯。

MRS. GARRISON<br>
Alex, we will love you as if you are our own son.

加里森夫人<br>
亚历克斯，我们会爱你，就像爱你自己的儿子一<br>
样。

Alex responded in a respectful manner which enamored Ethel Garrison, Christina's mother.

亚历克斯以尊重的方式回应，这让克里斯蒂娜的母亲埃塞尔·加里森(Ethel Garrison) 非常喜爱。

ALEX<br>
Thank you, mother.

亚历克斯
谢谢你，妈妈。

Mr. Garrison was impressed with how Alex made it clear what his intentions were.

亚历克斯明确表达自己的意图给加里森先生留下了深刻的印象。

As a leader of men in life and death situations, Mr. Garrison could size up people real fast and had determined, Alex was a natural born leader and had the qualities that would make his daughter and excellent husband. He was so happy for his daughter living a good life and waiting to meet the right man before any entanglements.

作为生死攸关时刻的领导者，加里森先生能够快速地评估人，并确定亚历克斯是天生的领导者，具备成为他女儿和优秀丈夫的品质。他很高兴他的女儿过着好日子，等待着遇到合适的男人，以免陷入任何纠葛。

Soon after all the guests were gone, Alex announced:

所有客人都离开后不久，亚历克斯宣布：

ALEX
We'll be traveling tomorrow and suggest we all get some rest.

亚历克斯
我们明天要旅行，建议大家休息一下。

A while later they were all in their bedrooms and in the morning Christina's bed would not need to be remade up.

过了一会儿，他们都回到了自己的卧室，第二天早上，克里斯蒂娜的床就不需要重新整理了。

Alex slept on his side still having some slight pains where his injury was. When he was getting the 36 stitches the doctor told him:

亚历克斯侧卧着，受伤的地方仍然有些疼痛。当他缝上　36　针时，医生告诉他：

DOCTOR
Today is your lucky day.

医生
今天是你的幸运日。

ALEX
Why so, doctor?

亚历克斯
医生，为何如此？

DOCTOR
Had that knife been just one more inch over, it would have sliced your pancreas, and you would have probably died.

医生
如果那把刀再多一英寸，它就会切开你的胰腺，你可能会死。

Since then, Alex no longer took anything for granted, especially concerning Christina.

从此以后，亚历克斯不再将任何事视为理所当然，尤其是对克里斯蒂娜而言。

On this splendid night Christina wrapped her arms around Alex and the calming she did for him placed him quickly into a very restful sleep. Christina laid there for over an hour looking into his face in the thin light provided by a night light on the wall.

在这个美妙的夜晚，克里斯蒂娜用双臂拥抱着亚历克斯，她安抚着他，让他很快进入了非常安稳的睡眠。克里斯蒂娜躺在那里一个多小时，在墙上一盏夜灯发出的微弱光线下看着他的脸。

CHRISTINA (THOUGHT)
*Alex is such a handsome man.*

克里斯蒂娜（心里想）
亚历克斯真是个英俊的男人。

*Christina* then she slowly fell asleep.

克里斯蒂娜随后慢慢睡着了。

In the morning Alex was awaken with a soft knock on the door. He could hear Sam's voice.

早上，亚历克斯被一阵轻轻的敲门声吵醒。他听见了萨姆的声音。

SAM
Mr. Baxter, it's time for you to wake up.

山姆
巴克斯特先生，你该醒醒了。

Sam repeated this procedure until he heard Alex say from behind the door:

萨姆重复了这个过程，直到他听到亚历克斯在门后说：

ALEX
Thanks for waking me up, Sam, I'm getting up now.

亚历克斯
谢谢你叫醒我，萨姆，我现在要起床了。

Alex then shook Christina, and informed her:

然后亚历克斯摇了摇克里斯蒂娜，告诉她：

ALEX
Christina, sweet love, you need to get up and get ready.
We are now on our way to France.

ALEX
克里斯蒂娜，亲爱的，你该起床准备一下了。我
们现在要去法国了。

Christina got up did her morning activity, and dressed in some very hot looking tight jeans and a very sexy top that would no doubt cause every man she would pass on the street in New York turn their heads and take a second look. Christina's legs and breast size were ideal. Her hips were perfect for jeans commercials.

克里斯蒂娜起床后做了早间活动，穿上了一条非常性感的紧身牛仔裤和一件非常性感的上衣，毫无疑问，纽约街头遇到的每个男人都会回头多看她一眼。克里斯蒂娜的腿和胸部尺寸非常理想。她的臀部非常适合牛仔裤广告。

While they were down having a light breakfast with Christina's parents, Marilynn and Sam were busy packing for them. They were expert packers and as soon as they finished eating, Sam arrived and announced:

当他们和克里斯蒂娜的父母一起吃早餐时，玛丽琳和萨姆正忙着帮他们打包行李。他们是打包专家，他们刚吃完饭，萨姆就来了，并宣布：

SAM
Mr. Baxter, everyone's suitcases are packed up and
have been sent to the Gulfstream 650.

山姆
巴克斯特先生，大家的行李都打包好了，并被送
到了湾流飞机上。

ALEX
After everyone uses the bathroom and freshens up, we
are ready to leave.

亚历克斯
每个人都使用完浴室并梳洗完毕后，我们就准备离开。

The Garrisons went up to their room, and as expected all their belongings were gone and presumably on the airplane.

加里森夫妇回到他们的房间，正如他们预料的那样，他们的所有物品都不见了，很可能都在飞机上了。

MR. GARRISON
I wish I had kept my toothbrush.

加里森先生
我希望我能保留我的牙刷。

MRS. GARRISON
Look in your bathroom.

加里森夫人
看看你的浴室。

MR. GARRISON
Why?

加里森先生
为什么？

MRS. GARRISON
You will find a toothbrush, toothpaste, and mouth wash.

加里森夫人
您将找到牙刷、牙膏和漱口水。

MR. GARRISON
Really?

加里森先生
真的吗？

MRS. GARRISON
Alex thinks of everything. He's always five steps ahead.

加里森夫人
亚历克斯考虑周全。他总是领先 五步。

MR. GARRISON
I wonder why did, Alex picked our daughter?

加里森先生
我想知道亚历克斯为什么会选择我们的女儿？

MRS. GARRISON
In my opinion it's because Christina is very intelligent
as well as beautiful.

加里森夫人
在我看来，这是因为克里斯蒂娜不仅漂亮，而且
非常聪明。

MR. GARRISON
Yes, she is.

加里森先生
是的，她是。

After Mr. and Mrs. Garrison finished using the restroom and brushed their teeth and
used mouthwash, the same brand they used, they went downstairs, and Christina and
Alex were waiting for them.

加里森夫妇上完厕所，刷完牙，用了同一个牌子的漱口水后，就下楼了，克里
斯蒂娜和亚历克斯已经在等他们了。

*** 

INT. DAY. GS650 PASSENGER COMPARTMENT.

内部。白天。GS650 乘客舱。

In a few minutes they were back on the Gulfstream 650 as it was being pulled out of
the hanger with a plane tug. In moments they were airborne. This flight was different.
There were two men aboard in suits, wearing sunglasses.

几分钟后，他们回到了湾流 650 飞机上，飞机牵引车正将其从机库中拖出。不
一会儿，他们就飞上了天空。这次飞行不同。机上有两名男子身着西装，戴着
墨镜。

Gladys was there to take care of them, and Brad was flying. One of the men sat in the
cockpit with Brad, the other out in the cabin with the group.

格拉迪斯在那里照顾他们，布拉德则负责驾驶飞机。其中一个男人和布拉德一
起坐在驾驶舱里，另一个男人则和其他人一起坐在机舱里。

Alex had introduced these men who could pass for spooks.

亚历克斯介绍了这些可能被当成间谍的人。

ALEX

This is Trevor Morgan and Buster Francher, of my
security detail.

亚历克斯

这是我的保安特工特雷弗·摩根和巴斯特·弗兰彻。

MR. GARRISON.
Pleased to meet you.

加里森先生。
很高兴见到你。

TREVOR

Mr. Garrison, the pleasure is mine.

特雷弗
加里森先生，我很荣幸。

ALEX

Mr. Garrison, Trever and Buster are both former Navy
Seals.

亚历克斯

特雷弗和巴斯特都是前海豹突击队队员。

ALEX

Mr. Garrison is a retired Army Green Beret.

亚历克斯

加里森先生是一名退役陆军绿色贝雷帽队员。

BUSTER
No kidding.

巴斯特
别开玩笑了。

ALEX

Mr. Garrison led SOG teams in Vietnam.

亚历克斯
加里森先生在越南领导 SOG 队伍。

TREVER

Those SOG guys earned their pay that's for sure. I never had it as rough as those SOG guys.

特雷弗

那些SOG的人确实赚到了他们的薪水。我从来没有像那些 SOG 的人那样艰难。

MR. GARRISON

It was different times and circumstances.

加里森先生

那是不同的时代和环境。

TREVER

Mr. Garrison, you probably don't need our protection, you can no doubt hold your own, but we'll be along for the ride if you need any help.

特雷弗

加里森先生，你可能不需要我们的保护，你肯定能自己保护自己，但如果你需要任何帮助，我们会陪你一起去。

MR. GARRISON

Maybe in my younger days, but now I'm an old, retired guy.

加里森先生

也许在我年轻的时候是这样，但现在我已经是个退休老人了。

TREVER

Don't worry Mr. Garrison; we got your 6:00 O'clock.

特雷弗

别担心，加里森先生；我们掌握了你的六点钟时间。

MR. GARRISON

I appreciate that.

加里森先生

我很感激。

Alex had said it was a big surprise and didn't tell them where they were going. Five hours later Alex asked Mr. Garrison:

阿历克斯说这是个大惊喜，并没有告诉他们要去哪里。五个小时后，阿历克斯
问加里森先生：

ALEX

Mr. Garrison, would you like to go to the cockpit and
watch us land?

亚历克斯

加里森先生，您愿意去驾驶舱看我们着陆吗？

MR. GARRISON

Yea that would be fun.

加里森先生

是的，那会很有趣。

Alex got up and walked to the cockpit and said to Buster:

亚历克斯起身走到驾驶舱，对巴斯特说道：

ALEX

Buster, Mr. Garrison wants to sit in the co-pilot's seat,
come back and sit next to me.

亚历克斯

巴斯特，加里森先生想坐在副驾驶座位上，回来
坐在我旁边。

Ten minutes later, they were on the ground and taxied up to the same hanger they had
used before.

十分钟后，他们落地并滑行到他们之前使用过的同一个机库。

Alex

We are making a short stop to show the Garrisons my
project and will be back in about forty-five minutes.
Brad and Gladys will stay on the plane.

亚历克斯

我们短暂停留，向加里森一家展示我的项目，大
约四十五分钟后回来。布拉德和格拉迪斯将留在
飞机上。

***

EXT. DAY. NUUK GREENLAND INTERNATIONAL AIRPORT BY PRIVATE
AIRCRAFT OWNERS HANGERS.

<u>外景。白天。努克格陵兰国际机场由私人飞机所有者的机库组成。</u>

The Limo Driver was patiently waiting out in front of the hanger office. Behind him was Claude Rearden in a Land Rover. When Claude spotted Alex, he got out of the Land Rover and walked up to Alex, and they shook hands.

豪华轿车司机在机库办公室门前耐心等候。他身后是开着路虎的克劳德·里尔登。克劳德看到亚历克斯后，便下了路虎，走到亚历克斯面前，两人握了握手。

CLAUDE REARDEN

Let's drive over to our offices and pick up another Land Rover. The ground is too ruff up there for that Limo.

克劳德·里尔登

我们开车去办公室，再开一辆路虎。那里的地面太崎岖了，开不了那辆豪华轿车。

ALEX
Okay.


亚历克斯
好的。

<u>EXT. DAY. NUUK GREENLAND DOME CONSTRUCTION SITE.</u>

<u>外景。白天。努克格陵兰穹顶建筑工地。</u>

Alex and Claude were in the front seat. Christina and her parents were in the back seat as they drove over to the complete roof section. 1000 feet up in the air, it all looked incredible. They got out of the car and walked a few feet next to the supervisor's trailer where on site management worked, constantly watching, checking, and making reports. The Garrisons were utterly amazed.

亚历克斯和克劳德坐在前排，克里斯蒂娜和她的父母坐在后排，他们开车来到已完工的屋顶部分。在 1000 英尺的高空，一切看起来都令人难以置信。他们下了车，走到主管拖车旁边几英尺处，现场管理人员正在那里工作，不断观察、检查和做报告。加里森夫妇完全惊呆了。

MR. GARRISON
So, this is your project, Alex?


加里森先生
那么，亚历克斯，这是你的项目吗？


ALEX
Yes Mr. Garrison, the world's first domed city.

亚历克斯
是的，加里森先生，这是世界上第一个圆顶城市。

CLAUDE REARDEN
Mr. Garrison, if you look over at that hill which will be
under the dome, you will see we have already started
planting trees. In a few more years that hill will look a
lot better than it did with all the rock.

克劳德·里尔登
加里森先生，如果你看看圆顶下的那座小山，你
会发现我们已经开始种树了。再过几年，那座小
山就会比以前满是岩石时好看多了。

ALEX
We took the hill down 500 feet.

亚历克斯
我们把山往下推了 500 英尺。

MR. GARRISON
What did you do with all the dirt and rock?

加里森先生
你把这些泥土和石头如何处理了？

CLAUDE REARDEN
We have it situated in a couple places; we plan
on building one, possibly two sea walls and pier
complexes with it.

克劳德·里尔登
我们在几个地方进行了展示；我们计划用它建造
一两座海堤和码头综合体。

MR. GARRISON
How soon will that start?

加里森先生
什么时候开始？

CLAUDE REARDEN
Most likely this year. We are waiting on approval from
Denmark and Greenland's government.

克劳德·里尔登
今年很有可能。我们正在等待丹麦和格陵兰政府
的批准。

ALEX
More pillars are going up now and more roof sections
will be added soon.

亚历克斯
现在正在竖起更多的柱子，很快就会添加更多的
屋顶部分。

After Claude Reardon drove Alex and the Garrison's around a little while longer, it appeared everyone was satisfied with what they saw, so Alex announced:

克劳德·里尔登载着亚历克斯和加里森一家人又转了一会儿，看起来大家都对他们所看到的景象感到满意，于是亚历克斯宣布：

ALEX
I think we saw enough time to head back to Greenland Dome Inc. Offices and we'll all hop in the Limo and head back to the airport.

艾力克斯
我想我们已经看够了，是时候返回格陵兰圆顶公司办公室了，我们都会跳上豪华轿车返回机场。

***

## INT. DAY. NUUK GREENLAND AIRPORT. GULFSTREAM 650 PASSENGER CABIN.

内景。白天。努克格陵兰机场。湾流 650 客舱。

Shortly Alex and the Garrisons were back at the airport and onboard the Gulfstream 650 and taking off again.

不久之后，亚历克斯和加里森一家回到了机场，登上湾流 650 飞机再次起飞。

The next stop would be a tearful surprise to Mr. Garrison. He would soon be at General Patton's grave site.

下一站将是让加里森先生惊喜不已的。他很快就会到达巴顿将军的墓地。

Because the departure was in Greenland, the flight to Luxembourg was not long like everyone expected. Alex and his guests were lucky the 200-mph tail wind of the jet stream was blowing from directly behind allowing 800 mph over the ground speed, allowing them to arrive a couple hours early.

因为从格陵兰岛出发，所以飞往卢森堡的航程并不像大家预期的那样漫长。亚历克斯和他的客人很幸运，时速 200 英里的急流尾风从正后方吹来，使飞机速度比地面速度高出 800 英里，使他们提前几个小时到达。

<u>**EXT. DAY. LUXEMBOURG. GENERAL PATTON'S GRAVE SITE.**</u>

<u>白天。卢森堡。巴顿将军墓地。</u>

The Gulfstream landed at Luxembourg's airport which was a short distance by Limo to General Patton's grave site.

这架湾流客机降落在卢森堡机场，乘坐豪华轿车从这里出发不远便可到达巴顿将军的墓地。

The Limo Driver notified Alex:

豪华轿车司机通知亚历克斯：

**LIMO DRIVER**
The flowers you requested are in the car trunk.

豪华轿车司机
您要的花在汽车后备箱里。

The Limo pulled up into a parking area not far from Patton's grave.

豪华轿车停在了距离巴顿坟墓不远的停车场。

The Limo driver then opened the Limo door and the 4 adults plus security man Trevor Morgan got in the passenger section of the Limo while the other security man, Buster Fancher, sitting up front with the driver got out of the Limo. Both security men were packing weapons.

随后，豪华轿车司机打开车门，四名乘客和保安特雷弗·摩根 (Trevor Morgan) 进入了豪华轿车的乘客区，而坐在司机前面的另一名保安巴斯特·范彻 (Buster Fancher) 则从豪华轿车中走出来。两名保安都携带武器。

The American Military Cemetery in Luxembourg is a somber place. Most Americans alive today, have little knowledge of all the Americans who never came home.

卢森堡的美国军人公墓是一个阴郁的地方。如今活着的大多数美国人都对那些再也没有回家的美国人知之甚少。

When the American Battle Monuments Commission began its Program of repatriating soldiers killed in combat, 68 percent of the American soldiers were sent back to the US.

当美国战争纪念碑委员会启动遣返战斗中阵亡士兵的计划时，68%的美国士兵被送回美国。

But Patton remained because his wife Beatrice was upset about a plan to move her husband and the Luxembourg Grand Duchess Charlotte, a friend of Beatrice Patton stepped forward and offered a place in the Grand Ducal crypt in Luxembourg's "Notre Dame" Cathedral.

但巴顿仍留下来，因为他的妻子比阿特丽斯对于搬家计划感到不满，而卢森堡大公爵夫人夏洛特，比阿特丽斯·巴顿的朋友站出来，为他提供了一个在卢森堡"巴黎圣母院"大公墓中的座位。

When the US government found out, they finally acquiesced and allowed Patton's grave to stay as it was on its own, behind the 5,075 other graves, where it remains today.

当美国政府发现后，他们最终默许并允许巴顿墓保留原样，与其他 5,075 个坟墓一起，至今仍在那里。

LIMO DRIVER
Buster, can you please help me carry some flowers to
Patton's grave.

豪华轿车司机
巴斯特，你能帮我把一些花送到巴顿的墓前吗？

BUSTER FRANCHER
I feel honored to carry flowers we'll put on General
Patton's grave.

巴斯特·范彻
我很荣幸能带着鲜花献到巴顿将军的墓前。

The group was surprised when Mr. Garrison kneeled and kissed Patton's grave stone in a somber display of respect.

当加里森先生跪下并亲吻巴顿的墓碑以示尊重时，大家感到很惊讶。

VOICEOVER (ALEX)
THOUGHT
*Patton would have been proud of Mr. Garrison in
Vietnam. Patton hated chickenshits but he loved brave
men like Mr. Garrison.*

画外音（亚历克斯）
想法
巴顿会为越南战争中的加里森先生感到骄傲。巴
顿讨厌胆小鬼，但他喜欢像加里森先生这样的勇
敢的人。

Some of the other visitors there, surprisingly Chinese Military Officers approached and looked at the wreath and flowers, and one of them who spoke perfect English, spoke:

在场的其他一些游客中，令人惊讶的是中国军官们走近并看着花圈和鲜花，其中一位能说一口流利英语的军官说道：

**CHINESE ARMY OFFICER**
The Chinese military admires Patton. He's America's
Sun Tzu.

中国军官
中国军方钦佩巴顿。他是美国的孙子。

In short while, Alex introduced himself and the group to the Chinese Officers who were wearing civilian clothes.

不一会儿，亚历克斯就向穿着便装的中国军官们介绍了自己和这群人。

**ALEX**
I'm Alex Baxter.

亚历克斯
我是亚历克斯·巴克斯特。

The older Chinese man in the group had no hesitation of exposing his PLAN (People's Liberation Army Navy) affiliation.

该团伙中的一名中国老年男子毫不犹豫地公开了他与中国人民解放军海军的联系。

**CHINESE ARMY OFFICER**
I'm Liu Zhenli an officer in China's People Liberation
Army.

中国陆军军官
我是刘振利，中国人民解放军军官。

Alex knowing Chinese do not like to touch hands in general during greets bowed.

亚历克斯知道中国人一般不喜欢在鞠躬打招呼时触摸手。

**ALEX**
It's a pleasure to meet you Liu Zhenli.

亚历克斯
很高兴认识你，刘振利。

CHINESE ARMY OFFICER
(a.k.a. Liu Zhenli)
Alex Baxter, what brings you to Brussels?

中国陆军军官
（又名刘振利）
亚历克斯·巴克斯特，您来布鲁塞尔有什么事吗？

ALEX
I'm with my future father-in-law a retired American
Army Green Beret giving General Patton our respect.

亚历克斯
我和我未来的岳父、退役美国陆军绿色贝雷帽一
起向巴顿将军表示敬意。

CHINESE ARMY OFFICER
(a.k.a. Liu Zhenli)
What do you do for a living Alex?

中国陆军军官
（又名刘振利）
亚历克斯，你是做什么工作的？

ALEX
I'm financing the new *Nuuk Greenland Dome City* and
part of the management team.

亚历克斯
我为新努克格陵兰穹顶城提供资金，也是管理团
队的一部分。

Chinese Army Officer Liu Zhenli knew a lot about the Nuuk Greenland Dome under
construction and was part of a group sent there to do a survey and see if such a
construction model would be practical and possible to build in the Gobi Desert.

中国陆军军官刘振利对正在建设中的努克格陵兰穹顶建筑非常了解，他是被派
往那里进行勘察的小组成员之一，目的是了解这种建筑模式是否实用，是否可
在戈壁沙漠中建造。

The jury was still out as far as Chinese Army Officer Liu Zhenli was concerned, but
the progress up to date showed a lot of promising.

就中国陆军军官刘振利而言，目前尚无定论，但迄今为止的进展显示出很大的
希望。

As the Nuuk Greenland Dome construction advanced, the Chinese Government took
further interest.

随着努克格陵兰穹顶建设的推进，中国政府对此产生了进一步的兴趣。

Suddenly, here was Chinese Army Officer Liu Zhenli standing face to face with Mr. Dome guy Alex Baxter himself. Talk about coincidences!

突然，中国陆军军官刘振利与圆顶先生亚历克斯·巴克斯特本人面对面站着。真是巧合啊！

CHINESE ARMY OFFICER
(a.k.a. Liu Zhenli)
What an amazing opportunity to meet such a person here.


中国陆军军官
（又名刘振利）
能在这里遇见这样的人真是难得的机会。


ALEX
Same for me meeting a Chinese People's Liberation Army Officer at Patton's grave here today.

亚历克斯
今天我在巴顿墓前见到了一位中国人民解放军军官，感觉也一样。

CHINESE ARMY OFFICER
(a.k.a. Liu Zhenli)
I'm a science fiction reader. I would like to one day see China build a Dome City.

中国陆军军官
（又名刘振利）
我是一名科幻小说读者。我希望有一天能看到中国建造一座穹顶城市。


ALEX
So, would I. I would love to build a Dome City in the Gobi Desert.

亚历克斯
那么，我会吗？我很想在戈壁沙漠建造一座圆顶城市？

CHINESE ARMY OFFICER
(a.k.a. Liu Zhenli)
Why the Gobi Desert? We have a lot of nice areas nestled in beautiful mountains?

中国陆军军官
（又名刘振利）
为什么是戈壁沙漠？我们有很多美丽的地区坐落
在美丽的山脉中？

ALEX
By building comfortable Dome Cities in places like
Greenland, Gobi Desert, Sahara Desert, and places
where crops seldom survive, we can avoid turning
farmland into cities.

亚历克斯
通过在格陵兰岛、戈壁沙漠、撒哈拉沙漠以及农
作物很少成活的地方建设舒适的穹顶城市，我们
可以避免农田变成城市。

CHINESE ARMY OFFICER
(a.k.a. Liu Zhenli)
What kind of Dome City in the Gobi Desert would you
visualize?

中国陆军军官
（又名刘振利）
您能想象出戈壁沙漠中什么样的穹顶城市？

ALEX
Mr. Liu Zhenli as an officer in the Peoples Liberation
Army, you know size and scale matters on efficiency
and success.

亚历克斯
刘振利先生作为中国人民解放军的一名军官，您
知道规模和规模对效率和成功至关重要。

CHINESE ARMY OFFICER
(a.k.a. Liu Zhenli)
True.

中国陆军军官
（又名刘振利）
没错。

ALEX
I would like to see the first China Gobi Dome built 25
miles in diameter with Alternating rings of greenhouses
and solar panels surrounding it.

亚历克斯
我希望看到中国第一个戈壁穹顶建成，直径为 25
英里，周围有交替的温室和太阳能电池板环。

CHINESE ARMY OFFICER
(a.k.a. Liu Zhenli)
Mr. Baxter, I like your idea.

中国陆军军官
（又名刘振利）
巴克斯特先生，我喜欢你的想法。

ALEX
China's Gobi Dome City should be built adjacent to
an international airport with underground commuter
trains between the airport and the Dome City and
high-speed rail connections to the rest of the country.

亚历克斯
中国的戈壁巨蛋城应该建在国际机场附近，在机
场和巨蛋城之间有地下通勤列车，并有高铁连接
到中国其他地区。

CHINESE ARMY OFFICER
(a.k.a. Liu Zhenli)
What about backup power for nights?

中国陆军军官
（又名刘振利）
夜间的备用电源怎么样？

ALEX
Two types of backup power could be implemented:
Underground nuclear power plants and hydrogen used
to power gas turbines with secondary steam turbines
operating off exhaust gases.

亚历克斯
可以实施两种类型的备用电源：地下核电站和用
于为燃气轮机提供动力的氢气，以及利用废气运
行的二级蒸汽轮机。

CHINESE ARMY OFFICER
(a.k.a. Liu Zhenli)
True. Sounds like you have this well thought out.

中国陆军军官
（又名刘振利）
没错。听起来你已经深思熟虑了。


ALEX
We had to solve all these issues in the design of the
Nuuk Greenland Dome City.


亚历克斯
我们必须在努克格陵兰圆顶城的设计中解决所有
这些问题。亚历克斯

CHINESE ARMY OFFICER
(a.k.a. Liu Zhenli)
Great conversation Alex Baxter. When I get back to
China, I'm going to discuss this with some of my
relatives who are in the construction business building
our new cities and high-speed rail network.


中国陆军军官
（又名刘振利）
亚历克斯·巴克斯特，谈话很精彩。我回国后会和
一些从事建筑行业的亲戚讨论这个问题，他们正
在建设我们的新城市和高速铁路网络。

Alex gave one of his business cards to the Chinese Army Officer Liu Zhenli.

亚历克斯将自己的一张名片递给了中国陆军军官刘振利。


ALEX
I wish all of you a safe flight home.


亚历克斯
祝大家乘飞机安全回家。


Alex bowed again and this time, all the Chinese men bowed back in great respect.
They could also understand English and felt good that Alex Baxter would have such
positive ideas about China.

亚历克斯再次鞠躬，这一次，所有的中国男人都以极大的敬意回礼。他们也能
听懂英语，很高兴亚历克斯·巴克斯特对中国有如此积极的看法。

Alex led his group got back into the Limo and went back to the Airport. The driver got
a tip equal to his monthly salary.

亚历克斯带领一行人坐上豪华轿车返回机场，司机得到了相当于他一个月薪水
的小费。

***

## EXT. EVENING. PARIS FRANCE BEAUVAIS AIRPORT.

外景。晚上。法国巴黎博韦机场。

The next surprise to the group was they now flew to Paris Beauvais Airport. Paris' Beauvais airport is also less than an hour's drive from Normandy.

令该团惊喜的是，他们现在飞往巴黎博韦机场。巴黎博韦机场距离诺曼底也只有不到一小时的车程。

As prearranged by Alex's staff, A Limo was waiting for them when they arrived. Again, as if practiced, Buster rode shotgun up in the front seat with the driver and Trevor rode with the rest in the back of the Limo. It was evening when they arrived, so there would not be much to see until in the morning.

按照　亚历克斯工作人员的安排，他们到达时，一辆豪华轿车正在等着他们。同样，就像练习过一样，巴斯特坐在司机旁边的前排座位上，特雷弗和其他人一起坐在豪华轿车的后排座位上。他们到达时已经是晚上了，所以直到早上才有太多可看的东西。

> ALEX
> We'll check into a hotel and visit the beach in the morning.

> 亚历克斯
> 早上我们将入住酒店并参观海滩。

Alex knew they would run out of time if they went to the beach now and wanted Mr. Garrison the opportunity to see Normandy. It was the least he could do for a national hero and his future father-in-law.

阿历克斯知道，如果他们现在去海滩，时间就不够了，他想让加里森先生有机会去看看诺曼底。这是他能为一位民族英雄和他未来的岳父做的最起码的事情。

***

## INT. EVENING. LE CHATEAU D'AUDRIEU RESORT.

内景。晚上。奥德里城堡度假村。

Le Chateau d'Audrieu is an older building, but its décor was terrifically European.

奥德里厄城堡 (Le Chateau d'Audrieu) 是一座较古老的建筑，但其装饰却极具欧式风格。

Alex reserved 4 adjacent rooms in the Le Chateau d'Audrieu.

<u>Hôtel 5 étoiles à Bayeux | Château d'Audrieu *****</u>

亚历克斯在奥德里城堡（Le Chateau d'Audrieu）预订了4间相邻的房间。

贝叶 5 星级酒店奥德里城堡 *****

The door between Buster and Alex room was unlocked and Buster could come into Alex's room immediately if trouble occurred. Likewise, Trevor's room was adjacent to the Garrison's and set up the same way for security.

巴斯特和亚历克斯房间之间的门没有锁，如果发生麻烦，巴斯特可以立即进入亚历克斯的房间。同样，特雷弗的房间与　加里森的房间相邻，并且以相同的方式设置以保证安全。

Brad and Gladys had hotel rooms near the Airport so they could get to the plane earlier and prepare for immediate departure. Brad had been to Normandy before as well as Gladys, so it was not necessary for them to go.

布拉德和格拉迪斯住在机场附近的酒店房间，所以他们可以早点上飞机，为立即出发做准备。布拉德和格拉迪斯以前都去过诺曼底，所以他们没必要去。

The rooms had plenty of room. The plush blue carpet was very warm and appealing. The bar was perfect for socializing. It also had a flush blue carpet just like in the hotel rooms.

房间空间很大。柔软的蓝色地毯非常温暖，很有吸引力。酒吧非常适合社交。它也有和酒店房间一样的蓝色地毯。

The restaurant in Le Chateau d'Audrieu had tiled floors and adjacent lounge area where one could read a book and sip on wine or liquors. The fireplace in the lounge added to the ambience of the late winter and early spring. After settling into their rooms, the plan was to meet in an hour for dinner.

奥德里城堡 (Le Chateau d'Audrieu) 的餐厅铺着瓷砖地板，毗邻休息区，人们可以在那里看书、品尝葡萄酒或烈酒。休息室的壁炉增添了冬末春初的氛围。入住房间后，他们计划一小时后一起吃晚饭。

Upon the agreed time, Alex, the Garrisons, and their bodyguards made their way to the Le Chateau d'Audrieu restaurant dining room. Passing the bar and the lounge.

到了约定的时间，亚历克斯和加里森一家以及他们的保镖们一起前往了奥德里城堡餐厅的餐厅。他们经过了酒吧和休息室。

The bar with its wood paneling felt European. The dining room with the red walls felt like France. The French food was delightful, and it was an early night for everyone as they were all somewhat suffering from jet lag.

酒吧的木质镶板给人一种欧洲的感觉。餐厅的红墙给人一种法国的感觉。法国菜很美味，大家都很早就睡了，因为他们都有点时差反应。

Alex awoke early in the morning and by 06:30, against some of their wishes, they were assembled in a dining room with a more distinct European taste. The yellow walls and paneling gave a sense of workmanship.

亚历克斯一大早就醒了，6:30，他们不顾部分人的反对，来到一间欧式风格的餐厅。黄色的墙壁和镶板给人一种工艺感。

Hot freshly baked French bread and fresh butter was really appealing. Then the jams and French poached eggs and potatoes, went well with the French style coffee.

热腾腾的新鲜出炉的法式面包和新鲜黄油确实很诱人。然后是果酱和法式荷包蛋和土豆，与法式咖啡搭配得很好。

Soon Alex and his group were all fortified and headed to Normandy beaches where they drove around and stopped and looked.

很快，亚历克斯和他的团队就聚集起来，前往诺曼底海滩，他们在那里四处转悠，停下来观赏。

<u>EXT. DAY. NORMANDY FRANCE WW2 MUSEUM AND BEACH AREA.</u>

<u>外部。白天。诺曼底法国二战博物馆和海滩区。</u>

The Limo driver was selected for his knowledge of the area, and he rolled down his service window so that he could talk to everyone and answer questions. Trevor could speak French, so any language difficulties were easily overcome.

之所以选择豪华轿车司机，是因为他熟悉当地环境，他摇下车窗，以便与每个人交谈并回答问题。特雷弗会说法语，因此任何语言障碍都很容易克服。

Eventually they came to an abandoned bunker.

最后他们来到了一个废弃的掩体。

TREVER

This is the spot where the Army rangers climbed up this tall hill to take out four 155-millimeter guns that were in this bunker.

特雷弗

陆军游骑兵就是在这里爬上这座高山，摧毁了掩体中的四门 155 毫米火炮。

MR. GARRISON

Had the Army Rangers not taken out those 155 MM Guns, a lot of ships could have been sunk.

加里森先生
如果陆军游骑兵没有摧毁那些 155 毫米火炮，很
多船只都可能被击沉。

VOICEOVER
*Mr. Garrison, steep in military tradition and history
as a teacher, was fully absorbed in all this Normandy
visit. It was a special moment for Mr. Garrison. In all
his years and for whatever reason, Mr. Garrison had
never made the effort to get to Normandy.*

*Now Mr. Garrison had a growing respect for Alex,
who had the thoughtfulness to take him here, knowing
how important WWII History was to Mr. Garrison.*

画外音
作为一名教师，加里森先生深谙军事传统和历
史，他完全沉浸在这次诺曼底之行中。这对加里
森先生来说是一个特殊的时刻。加里森先生一生
中从未努力去过诺曼底，无论出于什么原因。

现在，加里森先生对亚历克斯越来越敬佩，亚历
克斯知道二战历史对加里森先生有多重要，所以
他很体贴地带他来这里。

Mrs. Garrison as a teacher and well read, had a somber experience as she gauged the
coastline and pondered that day many years ago when one of the most important days
in World History occurred.

加里森夫人是一位博览群书的教师，当她测量海岸线并思考多年前世界历史上
最重要的一天的那一天时，她有过一次忧郁的经历。

MRS. GARRISON
12,000 young Americans died on Normandy Beaches
the day of the invasion.

加里森夫人
入侵当天，12,000 名美国青年在诺曼底海滩丧生。

MR. GARRISON
Depending on which Historian you read, you get the
impression that most of those deaths all happened
before noon.

加里森先生
根据你读过哪位历史学家的著作，你会觉得大多
数死亡事件都发生在中午之前。

TREVER
Until 10:30 in the morning it was starting to look like Rommel's plan was working and Americans would be pushed back into the sea and the invasion defeated.

特雷弗
直到早上　10:30，隆美尔的计划才开始奏效，美国人将被赶回海里，入侵将被击败。

ALEX
Such a defeat would be instrumental in setting up for a different world, possibly an armistice that would have led to WW3 20 years later.

亚历克斯
这样的失败将有助于建立一个不同的世界，可能会导致 20 年后第三次世界大战的停战。

MR. GARRISON
According to historian Steven Ambrose, thanks to a half dozen Naval destroyers who risked hitting mines, they came in close and started slowly taking out the beach defenses, saving the invasion.

加里森先生
据历史学家史蒂文·安布罗斯说，多亏有六艘海军驱逐舰冒着触雷的危险，靠近并开始慢慢摧毁海滩防御工事，才挽救了入侵。

ALEX
I read Gordan Harrison's Cross Channel Attack once I decided to visit Normandy in the future like now. Gordan Harrison does not mention those destroyers.

亚历克斯
当我决定将来像现在一样访问诺曼底时，我读了戈丹·哈里森的《跨海峡攻击》。戈登·哈里森没有提到那些驱逐舰。

TREVER
Being a former Navy Seal, I can tell you the Army never likes to give the Navy Credit for anything.

特雷弗
作为一名前海豹突击队队员，我可以告诉你，陆军从来不喜欢把任何事情归功于海军。

MR. GARRISON

Sadly, one of the destroyers with a Polish Crew hit a mine which detonated the magazine setting off a horrible explosion and killing all hands. Another destroyer with an American crew was also destroyed losing about 170 people.

加里森先生

不幸的是，一艘载有波兰船员的驱逐舰触雷，弹药库爆炸，船员全部遇难。另一艘载有美国船员的驱逐舰也被摧毁，约 170 人丧生。

FLASHBACK

EXT. DAY. NORMANDY BEACH. MONTAGE OF D-DAY SCENES. (ONE MINUTE).

References to build the montage:

https://www.youtube.com/watch?v=FTAW1PvEcAk

CMH Pub 7-4-1 Cross-Channel Attack: Harrison, Gordon A: Free Download, Borrow, and Streaming: Internet Archive

D-Day June 6, 1944: The Climactic Battle... book by Stephen E. Ambrose

闪回

外景。诺曼底海滩。诺曼底登陆日场景的蒙太奇。（一分钟）。

制作蒙太奇的参考资料：[See above]

By noon, it appeared the Garrison's had seen enough.

到了中午，驻军似乎已经看够了。

ALEX

Is it ok to go back to the airport so we can continue onto our next stop?

艾力克斯

可以返回机场以便继续前往下一站吗？

By 3:00 p.m. they were in Switzerland and two cars were at the airport to pick them up.

下午三点他们到达瑞士，两辆车在机场接他们。

Alex, Christina, and Buster rode in the Rolls Royce. The Garrisons and Trevor rode in a Jaguar to Alex's Swiss mansion.

亚历克斯、克里斯蒂娜和巴斯特乘坐劳斯莱斯。加里森一家和特雷弗乘坐捷豹前往亚历克斯的瑞士豪宅。

***

Alex asked the Garrisons:

亚历克斯向加里森一家询问：

**ALEX**
Would everyone like to attend the symphony tonight?

亚历克斯
每个人都想参加今晚的交响乐吗？

The Garrisons were more than happy to attend the symphony. Soon everyone was dressed up appropriately.

加里森一家人非常高兴能去听交响乐。很快，每个人都穿得漂漂亮亮。

Christina was pleasantly surprised to discover Alex had prearranged a half dozen dresses there for her and her mother along with a dozen pairs of expensive shoes, so they were ready to go in a short time.

克里斯蒂娜惊喜地发现，亚历克斯已经为她和她的母亲预先安排了六套礼服和十几双昂贵的鞋子，所以她们很快就准备出发了。

Mary, who was delighted to see Christina again and still somewhat shocked over Stephanie's death, was happy to help Christina put her diamonds on again. When they were alone, and Mary was helping Christina she noticed the large diamond ring and asked:

玛丽很高兴再次见到克里斯蒂娜，但对斯蒂芬妮的死仍有些震惊，她很乐意帮助克里斯蒂娜重新戴上钻石。当她们独处时，玛丽正在帮助克里斯蒂娜，她注意到了那枚大钻戒，并问道：

**MARY**
Did Alex propose?

玛丽
亚历克斯求婚了吗？

**CHRISTINA**
Alex's not officially asked my father's permission yet,
but that I think the question is coming soon.

克里斯蒂娜
亚历克斯还没有正式向我父亲征求许可，但我认
为这个问题很快就会出现。

***

<u>INT. EVENING. GENEVA SWITZERLAND. SYMPHONY HALL.</u>

<u>内部。晚上。瑞士日内瓦。交响乐大厅。</u>

<u>MUSIC FOR THIS SECTION:</u>

<u>Smetana: Vltava (The Moldau) - Stunning Performance</u>

<u>本部分音乐：</u>

<u>斯美塔那：伏尔塔瓦河（摩尔达河）- 精彩表演</u>

In due time Alex, Christina and her parents were seated with the bodyguards in the concert hall balcony.

准时，亚历克斯、克里斯蒂娜和她的父母与保镖一起坐在音乐厅的阳台上。

The program started with Vltava (The Moldau) by Bedrich Smetana. The lights were soon dimmed, and the concert began. Alex observed a woman in the balcony directly across. It only took a few minutes to recognize it was none other than *Michelle Montez*.

节目以贝德里奇·斯美塔那的《伏尔塔瓦河》拉开序幕。灯光很快暗了下来，音乐会开始了。亚历克斯看到对面阳台上有一位女士。没过几分钟，他就认出了她就是米歇尔·蒙特兹。

Alex's blood began to boil when he recognized the *Wicked Witch of The West*.

当亚历克斯认出西方邪恶女巫时，他的血液开始沸腾。

*Michelle Montez* was quickly rewarded for hijacking the balcony she didn't pay for. There he was, none other than *Mr. Dome*, Alex Baxter and again with that glamorous lady, Christina Garrison.

米歇尔·蒙特兹很快就因劫持了她没有付钱的阳台而得到了回报。他在那里，正是圆顶先生、亚历克斯·巴克斯特，还有那位迷人的女士克里斯蒂娜·加里森。

Just like before, Michelle's modified cell phone was back in *picture-taking-paradise*.

和以前一样，米歇尔改装后的手机又回到了拍照天堂。

Just as the crescendo to *The Moldau* manifested, those sweet pictures rolled in and just like before they came across the wire to the editor's desk before he let everyone go home for the day. It was going to be another long couple of days, with another looming deadline.

就在《莫尔道河》的高潮出现时，那些可爱的照片滚滚而来，就像之前一样，它们通过电线送到了编辑的办公桌上，然后他让大家回家了。这将是又漫长的几天，又一个迫在眉睫的截止日期。

MICHELLE MONTEZ

(Thought)

*Magazine Femmes Réelles Exigeantes will sellout another week's production. Now it's just getting the story.*

米歇尔·蒙特兹

（想法）

真正要求高的女性杂志《*Magazine Femmes Réelles Exigeantes*》下一周的票房将全部售罄。现在只是在讲故事。

*The Moldau* finished soon since it was a relatively short piece, another short piece was performed: Smetana ~ *From Bohemia's Woods and Fields*. Another short piece was performed: Bedrich Smetana - *The Bartered Bride – Overture*. Then there was an intermission.

莫尔道河很快就结束了，因为这是一首相对较短的曲子，之后又表演了另一首短曲：斯美塔那～来自波西米亚的森林和田野。表演的另一首短曲是：贝德里奇·斯美塔那——《被出卖的新娘》序曲。然后是中场休息。

MORE MUSIC CLIPS TO CARRY INTO THE NEXT SCENE:

Smetana ~ From Bohemia's Woods and Fields

Smetana: Die verkaufte Braut – Ouvertüre · hr-Sinfonieorchester · Andrés Orozco-Estrada

更多音乐片段将带入下一个场景：

斯美塔那～来自波西米亚的森林和田野

斯美塔那：《卖身新娘》– 序曲 · hr-Sinfonieorchester · 安德烈斯·奥罗斯科-埃斯特拉达

Alex and the Garrison's went to the lobby and the waitress who really enjoyed the last time Alex was here by the size of her tip, bypassed a dozen concert goers and walked up to Alex to take his order. His security staff who took their job seriously and trained and gamed just like they did when they were seals operating in the enemies back yard, did not drink on duty. Duty meant up to the point where they delivered Mr. Baxter back to Minnesota safely.

亚历克斯和加里森来到大厅，女服务员非常高兴亚历克斯上次来这里，因为她给了他很多小费，她绕过十几个音乐会观众，走到亚历克斯面前，为他点菜。

他的安保人员工作认真，接受的训练和游戏方式就像他们在敌后执行任务时的海豹突击队一样，而且值班时不喝酒。责任意味着他们将把巴克斯特先生安全送回明尼苏达州。

ALEX
I would like four glasses of Dom Perignon.

亚历克斯
我想要四杯唐培里侬香槟王。

WAITRESS
Cash or Credit Card?

女服务员
现金还是信用卡？

ALEX
Cash.

亚历克斯
现金。

WAITRESS
I will be right back with your drinks.

女服务员
我马上就回来给您送饮料。

The waitress was back in a flash with four Champaign glasses filled with Dom Perignon near the top.

女服务员很快就回来了，手里拿着四个香槟酒杯，杯中倒满了唐培里侬香槟王。

Alex paid the waitress with a number of $100.00 dollar bills.

亚历克斯用几张 100 美元的钞票付给了女服务员钱。

Alex feeling a little celebratory, having a great time with his future in-laws, felt generous and gave the waitress a $200 tip.

亚历克斯感到有点高兴，与他未来的岳父岳母度过了愉快的时光，他感到非常慷慨，给了女服务员 200 美元的小费。

A couple women who knew Alex approached him and Christina. Alex was holding Christina's right hand with his left hand when the women approached.

几个认识亚历克斯的女人走近了他和克里斯蒂娜。当那两名女子走近时，亚历克斯正用左手握着克里斯蒂娜的右手。

ALEX'S GENEVA
FEMALE ACQUAINTANCE
Hello Mr. Baxter.

亚历克斯的日内瓦
女性熟人
你好，巴克斯特先生。

ALEX
Good evening, ladies.

亚历克斯
女士们，晚上好。

ALEX'S GENEVA
FEMALE ACQUAINTANCE
This must be your glamorous girlfriend we hear so
much now about in the press.

亚历克斯的日内瓦
女性熟人
这肯定就是我们现在在媒体上经常听到的你的迷
人女友。

ALEX
Christina's much more than a girlfriend.

亚历克斯
克里斯蒂娜不仅仅是一位女朋友。

ALEX'S GENEVA
FEMALE ACQUAINTANCE
Oh, how sweet!

亚历克斯的日内瓦
女性熟人
噢，多甜蜜啊！

SECOND GENEVA
FEMALE ACQUAINTANCE
You are so beautiful Christina. Alex is a lucky man.

第二届日内瓦
女性熟人
克里斯蒂娜，你太美丽了。亚历克斯是一个幸运
的人。

Christina responded and smiled, showing her perfect beautiful teeth.

克里斯蒂娜回答道，并微笑着露出她完美美丽的牙齿。

CHRISTINA
I'm a lucky woman.

克里斯蒂娜
我是一个幸运的女人。

Just like the last time Christina was here with Alex; her dress was immaculate and very thought-provoking.

就像上次克里斯蒂娜和亚历克斯来这里一样，她的衣着整洁，引人深思。

Other women were focused on Christina, the subject of that scandalous *Magazine Femmes Réelles Exigeantes*.

其他女性的注意力都集中在克里斯蒂娜身上，她是那本丑闻杂志《真实的女性追求者》的主角。

Here Christina Garrison was front and center. Most recently all these women gawking on Christina didn't know who she was. Christina Garrison was a stranger to Geneva Switzerland.

克里斯蒂娜·加里森 (Christina Garrison) 站在最中央。最近，所有这些围观克里斯蒂娜的女人都不知道她是谁。克里斯蒂娜·加里森 (Christina Garrison) 对瑞士日内瓦来说是一个陌生人。

Now this beautiful woman, Christina Garrison was someone they all wanted to meet and become friendly. Some of these women were gold diggers and had no doubt Christina Garrison would soon be part of Alex Baxter's financial empire.

现在，这位美丽的女人，克里斯蒂娜·加里森 (Christina Garrison) 是他们都想认识并结交朋友的人。其中一些女人是淘金者，她们毫不怀疑克里斯蒂娜·加里森很快就会成为亚历克斯·巴克斯特金融帝国的一部分。

*Michelle Montez* was working the crowd pumping them for information, but none of them knew much about the other woman also dressed up nicely. Michelle's research staff could not identify her, so they did the dumbest thing possible, *Magazine Femmes Réelles Exigeantes* made up a sleezy story about the pretty woman and went with it.

米歇尔·蒙特兹 (Michelle Montez) 正在向人群打探信息，但没有人对另一位同

样衣着光鲜的女子有太多了解。米歇尔的研究人员无法辨认出她，所以他们做了最愚蠢的事情，《真实女性追求者》杂志编造了一个关于这位漂亮女人的低俗故事并顺其自然。

The ushers came into the lobby and asked people to return to their seats:

引座员走进大厅，请人们回到座位上：

USHER
The performance would continue in a few minutes.

亚瑟小子
演出几分钟后继续。

## MUSIC FOR THIS SEGMENT:

### Richard Wagner - Ride of The Valkyries

本部分音乐：

### 理查德·瓦格纳-女武神的骑行

Richard Wagner - Ride of the Valkyries, then Prelude, followed by Lohengrin (Prelude to Act. III) and several other short pieces were performed next by the symphony.

理查德·瓦格纳——《女武神的骑行》，然后是《前奏曲》，接着是《罗恩格林》（第三幕前奏曲），接下来交响乐团演奏了其他几首短曲。

***

## INTERNAL. DAY. GENEVA SWITZERLAND. ALEX BAXTER'S MANSION.

内部。白天。瑞士日内瓦。亚历克斯·巴克斯特的豪宅。

Music for this segment:

### (1) Bruch: 1. Violinkonzert · hr-Sinfonieorchester · Hilary Hahn · Andrés Orozco-Estrada - YouTube

A couple days later Christina's mother was shown the article in *Magazine Femmes Réelles Exigeantes* exclaiming:

几天后，克里斯蒂娜的母亲看到了《现实女性》杂志上的一篇文章，她惊呼道：

*EXIGEANTES MAGAZINE FEMMES RÉELLES*
*(Headline)*
Dome guy Alex Baxter's bride to be future father-in-
law seen in Switzerland with a younger woman and
Alex with his bride to be Christina Garison.

要求真正的女性杂志
（标题）
穹顶人亚历克斯·巴克斯特的新娘将成为未来的
岳父，他与一名年轻女子在瑞士相见，亚历克
斯还和他的新娘克里斯蒂娜·加里森　　(Christina
Garison) 在一起。

Alex got permission from the Garrison's to have his lawyer file a libel suit against *Michelle Montez*, demanding a retraction and an explanation. OOPS.

亚历克斯获得加里森的许可，让他的律师对米歇尔蒙特兹提起诽谤诉讼，要求其撤回声明并做出解释。哎呀。

Since this family was starting to get some notoriety, the neighbors back in Queens NY were somewhat moved in how much younger Mrs. Garrison looked! At least 25 years younger, and she really did look very pretty.

自从这个家族开始出名以来，纽约皇后区的邻居们都对这位年轻得多的夫人感到感动。加里森看了！至少年轻25岁，而且她确实看起来非常漂亮。

***

EXT. DAY. GENEVA SWITZERLAND TRAIN STATION AND TRAIN RIDE.

外面。白天。瑞士日内瓦火车站和火车之旅。

The day after the symphony Alex took the Garrison family on a train ride. Again, Alex had two private cars hooked to the rear of a passenger train.

交响乐演奏结束后的第二天，亚历克斯带着加里森一家坐火车。再次，亚历克斯将两辆私家车挂在了客运列车的尾部。

The end car had a platform Alex, and the Garrisons could sit at and get fresh air and have unobstructed views.

The extra passenger car in front of them had the kitchen and crews' quarters in case they took a long trip. Alex purchased these two Pullman Cars because of the enthusiasm his friend Paul had towards trains. Paul would be Alex's best man at his wedding, and it might be on this train.

末端车厢有一个平台，加里森一家可以站在那里呼吸新鲜空气，并享有一览无余的视野。他们前面的额外客车里设有厨房和机组人员的宿舍，以备他们长途旅行时使用。由于朋友保罗 (Paul) 对火车的热爱，亚历克斯 (Alex) 获得了这两辆普尔曼车厢。保罗将会在亚历克斯的婚礼上担任他的伴郎，他也可能会在这列火车上。

Spring was turning everything green. The Swiss countryside was spring green now.

春天使万物复苏，万物复苏。瑞士的乡村此刻春意盎然。

The beauty and splendor of the forests and streams they passed added to the ambience of the trip. Compared to American railroads, the Swiss had much smoother track, and the trains were far more comfortable. The Garrisons were enjoying the sightseeing immensely.

他们经过的森林和溪流的美丽和壮丽为这次旅行增添了氛围。与美国铁路相比，瑞士的铁路轨道更加平坦，火车也更加舒适。驻军非常享受这次观光。

Note to the cinematographer:

Imagery from such a Switzerland Swiss *Alps Train Ride* can be found on various Youtube videos that could be licensed for the movie. The railcar scene would have to be shot separately and integrated into the video stream:

Switzerland • Swiss Alps Train Rides | Relaxation Film | Relaxing Music | Nature 4k Video UltraHD - YouTube

摄影师须知：

在各种可获得电影授权的 YouTube 视频中都可以找到瑞士阿尔卑斯山火车之旅的图像。火车车厢场景必须单独拍摄并集成到视频流中：

瑞士 • 瑞士阿尔卑斯山火车之旅 |放松电影 |轻松的音乐 |自然 4k 视频超高清 - YouTube

Just like before, Alex and Christina returned home in the evening all rested up. Christina's parents were very pleased with the trip as the high-speed Pullman Cars were very comfortable with thickly padded chairs and sofas.

和以前一样，亚历克斯和克里斯蒂娜晚上休息好后就回家了。克里斯蒂娜的父母对这次旅行非常满意，因为高速的普尔曼车厢非常舒适，配有厚厚的软垫椅子和沙发。

**INT. DAY. PARIS FRANCE. ALEX'S THREE BEDROOM APARTMENT.**

室内日。法国巴黎。亚历克斯的三居室公寓。

In the morning, after they got dressed, Alex and the Garrisons flew to Paris. Alex wanted Christina to take her mother shopping and do some other things.

早上，穿好衣服后，亚历克斯和加里森一家飞往巴黎。亚历克斯希望克里斯蒂娜带她妈妈购物并做一些其他的事情。

Alex also had the desire to make love with Christina in Paris.

亚历克斯也渴望与克里斯蒂娜在巴黎做爱。

Alex owned a three-bedroom apartment in Paris overlooking the La Seine River. Just like his other homes this was well furnished.

亚历克斯在巴黎拥有一套三居室的公寓，可以俯瞰塞纳河。正如他的其他住所一样，这间住所装修精良。

The security detail had one room, Garrisons, another room, and Alex and Christina would sleep together in the master bedroom.

安全部门有一间房间，加里森有另一间房间，亚历克斯和克里斯蒂娜会一起睡在主卧室。

At this point in time, it was a foregone conclusion Christina and Alex were a couple, so there was no point in hiding it. Alex intended to secretly marry Christina at the Cathedral of Notre Dame de Paris.

此时，克里斯蒂娜和亚历克斯是一对已成定局，没有必要隐瞒。亚历克斯打算在巴黎圣母院与克里斯蒂娜秘密结婚。

Not even Christina's parents would know, since this was not the official wedding. Alex was moving forward on it because he had reached the point that if something happened to him, he wanted to make sure Christina inherited his fortune since he had no relatives and grew up as a gypsy.

由于这不是正式的婚礼，甚至连克里斯蒂娜的父母都不知道。亚历克斯正在继续前进，因为他已经到了这样的地步：如果他发生什么事，他想确保克里斯蒂娜继承他的财产，因为他没有亲戚，而且是在吉普赛人的家庭中长大的。

Gladys had been sent to Notre Dame de Paris to arrange the marriage with a Catholic Priest who at first did not want to perform the marriage on grounds neither were Catholic and Alex had never been baptized. But when Gladys texted Alex and he instructed her to indicate to the Priest of the substantial contribution he would privately make and the Priest could either feed a lot of homeless people or expand his personal bank account or a little bit of both, the Priest had a change of heart.

格拉迪斯被派往大教堂与牧师进行安排，但牧师起初并不想主持这场婚礼，理由是他们俩都不是天主教徒，而且亚历克斯从未受过洗礼。但是当格拉迪斯给亚历克斯发短信，亚历克斯指示她向神父表明他将私下做出的大量捐赠，而神父则可以为许多无家可归的人提供食物，或者扩大他的个人银行账户，或者两者兼而有之时，神父改变了主意。

Brad and Gladys would be witnesses, since they were trusted employees and sworn to secrecy. One of his lawyers was immediately flown to Paris with a dozen pieces of legal paperwork, which would be in force immediately in case something happened unexpectedly to Alex, because the two Greenland murders had been a wakeup call.

布拉德和格拉迪斯将担任证人，因为他们是值得信赖的员工，并宣誓保守秘密。他的一名律师立即带着十几份法律文件飞往巴黎，如果亚历克斯遇到意外情况，这些文件将立即生效，因为格陵兰的两起谋杀案已经敲响了警钟。

At first Christina, when presented with the plan responded:

当克里斯蒂娜得知这个计划时，她最初是这样回应的：

### CHRISTINA
I'm adamantly against it; I want my parents present.

### 克里斯蒂娜
我坚决反对，我希望我的父母在场。

Alex then explained very effectively.

然后亚历克斯非常有效地进行了解释。

### ALEX
For your own safety and security, we need to keep this matter extremely private, and nobody will know, until we have the official wedding back in Queens, New York, so that all your friends can be there.

### 亚历克斯
为了您自己的安全，我们需要对此事严格保密，在我们在纽约皇后区举行正式婚礼之前，没有人会知道，这样您所有的朋友都可以参加。

### CHRISTINA
Why do we have to do this now? Why can't we wait until we get back to New York?

### 克里斯蒂娜
为什么我们现在必须这么做？为什么不能等到我们回到纽约后再做呢？

### ALEX
This will demonstrate I'm serious to the commitment, and you will never have to worry about me ever wanting to split up with you.

### 亚历克斯
这表明我对承诺是认真的，你永远不必担心我会想和你分手。

Christina thought about it long and hard, and then reluctantly agreed to the Paris secret wedding.

克里斯蒂娜深思熟虑后，才勉强答应了在巴黎秘密结婚。

Alex was always a great thinker and planner.

ALEX

This will be okay because only you and the two witnesses sworn to secrecy and my lawyer will know there will be no fear of hurting your parents' feelings, since the big event will be scheduled soon, which we must do if we are going to do much international travel together on this trip.

亚历克斯

没关系，因为只有你和两位宣誓保密的证人以及我的律师知道，不用担心会伤害你父母的感情，因为大型活动将在不久的将来安排，如果我们要在这次旅行中一起进行很多国际旅行，我们就必须这样做。

Before they split up because the men hate going shopping with women, they would first take in the Louvre and see the artworks and do a few other events.

在他们分手之前，因为男人讨厌和女人一起购物，他们会先去卢浮宫看艺术品并参加一些其他活动。

Next, they went to the Eiffel Tower for Lunch.

接下来，他们去埃菲尔铁塔吃午餐。

ALEX

This restaurant sure has a great view of Paris. It has great food too.

亚历克斯

这家餐厅确实可以欣赏到巴黎的美景，食物也很棒。

Mr. Garrison

It does have a great view. Thanks for taking us here.

加里森先生

这里的景色确实很棒。谢谢你带我们来这里。

Suddenly Alex said to the group:

突然，亚历克斯对大家说道：

ALEX

I want to take Christina to some private place for a few minutes. We'll all meet over at the Napoleon Austerlitz memorial, say in about an hour?

亚历克斯
我想带克里斯蒂娜去一个私密的地方待几分钟。
我们将在拿破仑·奥斯特里茨纪念馆那边见面，大
约一小时后？

Christina's parents were thinking what Alex really wanted was a few minutes of romantic ambience and transcendence to ethereal plateaus on a theme from Paganini.

克里斯蒂娜的父母认为亚历克斯真正想要的是几分钟的浪漫氛围和在帕格尼尼主题下超越空灵的高原。

If this helped cement their daughter's cause, they were all for it. The parties split up; Buster accompanied the almost newlywed couple while Trevor remained with the Garrisons.

如果这种水泥能帮助他们女儿的事业，他们就会全力支持。双方分道扬镳；巴斯特陪伴着这对即将结婚的夫妇，而特雷弗则留在了加里森一家。

The drive from the Eiffel tower to the Notre Dame Cathedral about a mile away as a crow flies, took 30 minutes because of the traffic congestion that time of day. Buster remained outside at the steps of the church curbside and was amused this took place in all the locations. *Perhaps they're going to confession?*

从埃菲尔铁塔到大教堂直线距离大约一英里，由于当时交通拥堵，需要 30 分钟。巴斯特一直站在教堂路边的台阶外面，对所有地方发生的这种事情感到很有趣。也许他们要去忏悔？

**INT. DAY. PARIS FRANCE NOTRE DAME CATHEDRAL.**

国际日。法国巴黎圣母院。

There were a few Parisians in the church praying and no church services were scheduled for several hours, so there was a degree of privacy.

教堂里有少数巴黎人在祈祷，而且几个小时内没有安排教堂礼拜，因此有一定程度的隐私。

The priest had been advised by Brad, the couple was on the way, and he was patiently waiting for pay day. The priest looked slightly frustrated they were delayed fifteen minutes, but just as he was starting to get agitated, the couple strolled into the Church.

牧师已得到布拉德的建议，这对夫妇已经在路上，他正在耐心等待发薪日。由于他们迟到了十五分钟，牧师看起来有些沮丧，但就在他开始焦躁起来时，这对夫妇漫步走进了教堂。

Nobody would have guessed it was Alex Baxter because they were in blue jeans and dressed casually to avoid any unnecessary exposure while out enjoying Paris.

没有人会猜到那是亚历克斯·巴克斯特，因为他们穿着蓝色牛仔裤，穿着休闲服，以避免在外出游览巴黎时出现不必要的暴露。

The Catholic Priest Father Marion had paperwork made out and Alex's lawyer was there as well.

天主教神父马里恩已经准备好了文件，亚历克斯的律师也在场。

Father Marion quickly performed the marriage, with Brand and Gladys as witnesses. The priest was asked if they could use a room to record some other legal documents, and the priest invited them into his office, mainly for intelligence gathering purposes.

马里昂神父很快主持了婚礼，布兰德和格拉迪斯是他们的证婚人。神父被问及是否可以使用一间房间来记录其他法律文件，神父邀请他们到他的办公室，主要是为了收集情报。

The Vatican would be informed within the hour that one of the Richest men in the world had secretly been married in his church in Paris.

梵蒂冈将在一小时内收到通知，世界上最富有的人之一已在巴黎的教堂秘密结婚。

There was a table in front of Father Marion's desk, which was used for conferences, he suggested they could do the work there, as he sat at his desk using the internet and the word processor for work, he had in progress.

马里恩神父的办公桌前面有一张桌子，用于开会，他建议他们可以在那里工作，而他则坐在办公桌前使用互联网和文字处理器处理他正在进行的工作。

The lawyer had a total of fifteen documents, which Alex signed, and a couple which he asked Christina sign, which simply acknowledged that in the event of Alex death she would resume fiduciary responsibility for all his business activities.

律师总共有十五份文件，亚历克斯都签署了，还有几份他要求克里斯蒂娜签署的文件，这些文件只是承认，如果亚历克斯死亡，她将恢复对他所有商业活动的受托责任。

CHRISTINA
I'm scared to sign.


ALEX
Christina, you will have a staff to advise you and that
you do not have to make any decisions on your own if
it comes to that.

起初，克里斯蒂娜害怕签字，亚历克斯向她解释说，会有工作人员为她提供建议，如果真的需要签字，她不必自己做任何决定。

Christina reluctantly signed all the documents.

克里斯蒂娜不情愿地签署了所有文件。

ALEX'S LAWYER
Alex, I'm carrying all the signed documents including the marriage certificate back to New York on the private jet you arranged for me.

亚历克斯的律师
亚历克斯，我会带着所有签好字的文件，包括结婚证，乘坐你为我安排的私人飞机回纽约。

ALEX
Where will they be stored?

亚历克斯
它们将被存储在哪里？

ALEX'S LAWYER
All these documents will be placed in your safety deposit box at Chase Manhattan Bank we can access since you gave the law firm the key and permissions to place documents. Copies will be retained at the law office in our vault as a backup.

亚历克斯的律师
所有这些文件都将存放在您在大通曼哈顿银行的保险箱中，我们可以访问，因为您向律师事务所提供了存放文件的钥匙和权限。副本将保留在律师事务所的保险库中作为备份。

ALEX
Thanks.

亚历克斯
谢谢。

Alex's attorney turned and looked at Christine and made the point that he hit home and exemplified the necessity of this unprecedented activity.

亚历克斯的律师转过身看着克里斯汀，指出他的观点一针见血，并举例说明了这一前所未有的活动的必要性。

ALEX'S ATTORNEY
Christina, I know this is probably stressful for you, but you are now Alex's executor of his estate and in Alex's

*Living Will* you have medical executorship in case Alex is incapacitated by a stroke or some other reason.

亚历克斯的律师
克里斯蒂娜，我知道这对你来说可能很有压力，但你现在是亚历克斯的遗产执行人，而且在亚历克斯的生前遗嘱中，你拥有医疗执行权，以防亚历克斯因中风或其他原因丧失行为能力。

CHRISTINA
I understand.

ALEX'S ATTORNEY
Should something bad happen to Alex, you do not need to fear being swamped with requirements. Our law firm stands by in the event of tragedy strikes to assist you in all the activities you need help with under those circumstances. I know you have your parents for help for now, so you do not have to deal with it alone. We are poised to also help.

亚历克斯的律师
如果亚历克斯发生了不好的事情，你不必担心被各种要求淹没。我们律所随时待命，在悲剧发生时为您提供协助，协助您处理所有需要帮助的活动。我知道您现在有父母的帮助，所以您不必独自面对这一切。我们也随时准备提供帮助。

CHRISTINA
Thank you, I appreciate that.

克里斯蒂娜
谢谢，我很感激。

ALEX'S ATTORNEY
Here's my business card in case you need to contact me. Congratulations on your wedding and the new chapter in your life.

亚历克斯的律师
这是我的名片，以便您需要时与我联系。祝贺您的新婚燕尔，开启人生新篇章。

CHRISTINA
Thank you.

克里斯蒂娜
谢谢。

Just before Father Marian said goodbye to the newlywed couple, Alex on his cell phone, texted his accountant who was standing by to wire the money to the priest.

就在玛丽安神父与新婚夫妇告别之前，亚历克斯用手机给正待命的会计师发了短信，让他把钱汇给神父。

Because Father Marion thought the best way to handle the transaction would be to send it to his private Swiss Bank Account, that's where the money went. However, much money the Church received in the transaction would never be known.

因为马里昂神父认为处理这笔交易的最佳方式是将其转入他的私人瑞士银行账户，所以钱就转到了那里。然而，教会在这笔交易中收到了多少钱却不得而知。

***

EXT. DAY. PARIS FRANCE. NOTRE DAME CATHEDRAL.

外部。白天。法国巴黎。巴黎圣母院。

There is always a matter of luck that enters in everyone's life. The odds were billions to one this would ever happen.

每个人的一生中总会有运气的成分。这种事情发生的几率只有十亿分之一。

*Michelle Montez* happened to be driving by Paris Notre Dame Cathedral and Alex was the last person in the world she would ever see coming out of a church with his girlfriend Christina Garrison.

米歇尔·蒙特兹 (Michelle Montez) 碰巧开车经过大教堂，亚历克斯是她这辈子见过的最不可能看到他和女友克里斯蒂娜·加里森从教堂走出来的人。

*Michelle Montez* drove ahead and pulled over and watched Alex and Christina Garrison get in a Limo through the rear-view mirror.

米歇尔·蒙特兹开车上路并靠边停车，通过后视镜看到亚历克斯和克里斯蒂娜·加里森上了一辆豪华轿车。

Christina was so caught up in emotion that it turned out Alex was true to his word, and he was really in love with her, could no longer hold back the flood gates of emotion. As she hit the church door on her way out, the crocodile tears started flowing.

克里斯蒂娜陷入了深深的感情之中，原来亚历克斯信守了自己的诺言，他真的爱上了她，再也无法抑制内心的情感。当她走出教堂时撞到门，鳄鱼的眼泪开始流淌。

> *MICHELLE MONTEZ*
> (THOUGHT)
> *Not knowing a lot about Christina Garrison, including her religious affiliation, since I had never learned of it, assumed she might have been a Catholic.*
>
> *The fact she is crying leaving the church is probably related to something really good or really bad.*
>
> *Either way it didn't matter. I have another story!*

> 米歇尔·蒙特兹
> （想法）
> 我对克里斯蒂娜·加里森了解不多，包括她的宗教信仰，因为我从未听说过，所以假设她可能是天主教徒。
>
> 她哭着离开教堂，这可能与一些非常好或非常糟糕的事情有关。
>
> 不管怎样都无所谓。我还有另一个故事！

Alex Baxter had become *Michell Montez* supreme benefactor even though *Magazine Femmes Réelles Exigeantes* had to recently print a retraction or face a grueling legal procedure.

尽管《真实女性杂志》(Magazine Femmes Réelles Exigeantes) 最近不得不刊登撤回声明，否则将面临严格的法律程序，但亚历克斯·巴克斯特 (Alex Baxter) 已成为米歇尔·蒙特兹 (Michell Montez) 的最大赞助人。

*Michell Montez* waited until the Limo was long gone, got out of the car and went into the Paris Notre Dame Cathedral. *Michell Montez* a Catholic knew the priests that worked at the Cathedral and when she went inside and saw a nun walking down the outer isle, approached the nun and inquired:

米歇尔·蒙特兹一直等到豪华轿车开走后，才下车走进大教堂。米歇尔·蒙特兹是一名天主教徒，她认识在大教堂工作的牧师，当她走进去时，看到一位修女走在外岛上，她走近修女并询问道：

> MICHELL MONTEZ
> Is there a priest here now?

> 米歇尔·蒙特兹
> 现在这里有牧师吗？

> CATHOLIC NUN
> Yes, Father Marian is here now and will be conducting services in about an hour.

天主教修女
是的，玛丽安神父现在就在这里，大约一小时后
将主持礼拜。

*MICHELLE MONTEZ*
I need to talk with Father Marian, it's very important.

米歇尔·蒙特兹
我需要和玛丽安神父谈谈，这很重要。

CATHOLIC NUN
I'll see if he's available, wait here one minute please.

天主教修女
我看看他有没有空，请在这里等一下。

A few minutes later the nun returned and announced:

几分钟后，修女回来宣布：

CATHOLIC NUN
I will take you to see Father Marian.

天主教修女
我会带你去见玛丽安神父。

A moment later Michelle Montez was in Father Marian's office and the priest vaguely recognized Michelle Montez but didn't quite remember who she was or what she did.

一会儿，米歇尔·蒙特兹就来到了玛丽安神父的办公室，神父隐约认出了米歇尔·蒙特兹，但不太记得她是谁，也记不清她做什么。

*MICHELLE MONTEZ*
Thank you for seeing me, Father Marian.

米歇尔·蒙特兹
感谢您来看望我，马里安神父。

FATHER MARIAN
What can I do for you, Ms. Montez?

玛丽安神父
蒙特兹女士，我能为您做些什么？

*MICHELLE MONTEZ*
Father Marian, as you may or may not be aware; I
publish *Magazine Femmes Réelles Exigeantes*.

米歇尔·蒙特兹
玛丽安神父，你可能知道也可能不知道；我出版
杂志令人兴奋的女人《Magazine *Femmes Réelles
Exigeantes*》。

FATHER MARIAN
Go on.

玛丽安神父
继续说。

*MICHELLE MONTEZ*
One of the subjects of my recent editorials, Alex
Baxter was just here with his girlfriend, Christina
Garrison, can you tell me a little about their visit here?

米歇尔·蒙特兹
我最近社论的主角之一亚历克斯·巴克斯特刚刚和
他的女友克里斯蒂娜·加里森来到这里，你能告诉
我他们来此参观的一些情况吗？

FATHER MARIAN
I'm sorry Ms. Montez, but that was strictly a private
matter.

玛丽安神父
很抱歉，蒙特兹女士，但这完全是私事。

*MICHELLE MONTEZ*
Nothing that you can tell me?

米歇尔·蒙特兹
你没什么可以告诉我的吗？

FATHER MARIAN
No, I'm sorry.

玛丽安神父
不，我很抱歉。

*MICHELLE MONTEZ*
Ok father Marian, I understand, thank you for taking
the time to see me.

米歇尔·蒙特兹
好的，玛丽安神父，我明白了，感谢您抽出时间
来见我。

FATHER MARIAN
You're welcome Ms. Montez. Will I be seeing you
at Sunday's Services, and will you be coming into
confession again real soon?

玛丽安神父
不客气，蒙特兹女士。我会在周日的礼拜仪式上
见到您吗？您很快就会再次忏悔吗？

*MICHELLE MONTEZ*
I will Father Marian.

米歇尔·蒙特兹
我愿意，玛丽安神父。

FATHER MARIAN
Very well, I'm looking forward to seeing you then.

玛丽安神父
很好，我期待着到时候见到你。

*MICHELLE MONTEZ*
Thank you, Father Marian.

米歇尔·蒙特兹
谢谢您，马里安神父。

FATHER MARIAN
You're welcome.

玛丽安神父
别客气。

Ms. Montez stood up and walked to the door and opened it herself before Father
Marion could assist and departed.

蒙特兹女士站起来走到门口，在马里恩神父帮忙离开之前亲自打开了门。

Father Marion watched *Michelle Montez* leave and turned around and went back into
his office and sat down and immediately was looking at some *travel brochures to
Bangkok Thailand.*

马里恩神父目送米歇尔·蒙特兹离开，转身回到办公室坐下，立即翻看去泰国
曼谷的旅游手册。

*Michelle Montez,* walked out the church, was outside about two seconds then smiled and turned around and hustled back into the church, she went up to a couple elderly women who were on their knees praying.

米歇尔·蒙特兹走出教堂，在外面待了大约两秒钟，然后微笑着转身匆匆跑回教堂，她走向一对跪着祈祷的老年妇女。

*MICHELLE MONTEZ*

Excuse me, I think I'm late for the wedding, did I miss it?

米歇尔·蒙特兹

不好意思，我想我已经迟到了，我错过了婚礼吗？

ELDERLY WOMAN

Oh, I'm terribly sorry, you missed it. Father Marian married the couple fifteen minutes ago.

老年妇女

哦，非常抱歉，你错过了。玛丽安神父十五分钟前为这对新人主持了婚礼。

*MICHELLE MONTEZ*

That's terrible, I feel so bad.

米歇尔·蒙特兹

这太糟糕了，我感觉很糟糕。

Michelle then turned and walked out the church and went back to her offices and she now had a Pulitzer's prize story.

然后米歇尔转身走出教堂，回到她的办公室，现在她有一篇获得普利策奖的故事。

Michelle Montez had the scoop on a story probably worth millions one way or the other. She now had leverage, like nobody's dream. She called her lawyer who had been dealing with the messy business of the retraction.

米歇尔·蒙特兹 (Michelle Montez) 掌握了价值数百万美元的独家新闻。她现在拥有了无人能及的优势。她打电话给了一直在处理撤稿事宜的律师。

MICHELLE MONTEZ

I need you to set up a meeting with Alex Baxter.

米歇尔·蒙特兹

我需要你安排与亚历克斯·巴克斯特的会面。

**MICHELLE MONTEZ'S LAWYER**
(a.k.a. Elliot Rubenstein)
What for?

米歇尔·蒙特兹的律师
（又名艾略特·鲁宾斯坦）
为什么？


**MICHELLE MONTEZ**
I got some real juicy stuff on Alex Baxter now.

米歇尔·蒙特兹
我现在得到了一些关于亚历克斯·巴克斯特的真正
有趣的东西。

**MICHELLE MONTEZ'S LAWYER**
(a.k.a. Elliot Rubenstein)
Sounds like a major event. We can't discuss it over the
phone in case someone is listening, we'll have to talk
privately.

米歇尔·蒙特兹的律师
（又名埃利奥特·鲁宾斯坦）
听起来像是一件大事。我们不能通过电话讨论，
以防有人听到，我们只能私下谈。

**MICHELLE MONTEZ**
Okay, I can be in your office in 30 minutes.

米歇尔·蒙特兹
好的，我 30 分钟后就能到你的办公室。

Michelle had been brainstorming and what Alex would have to do for her to keep the story out of the magazine might require millions, which he could easily afford. Her meal ticket just came in on her ship.

米歇尔一直在绞尽脑汁，亚历克斯要怎么做才能让她的故事不被杂志刊登出来，可能需要数百万美元，而亚历克斯可以轻松负担得起。她的餐券刚刚从船上寄来。

***

<u>EXT. DAY. PARIS FRANCE AUSTERLITZ MEMORIAL.</u>

<u>第二天。法国巴黎奥斯特里茨纪念馆。</u>

Christina appeared emotionally shaken and felt terrible that her parents did not attend the wedding as she and Alex were going to meet her parents at Napoleon's Austerlitz Memorial. Alex was quite insistent when he commented:

ALEX
Christina: you need to get ahold of herself and put on a little makeup; otherwise, we will be forced to explain to your parents why they were not invited to the wedding.

亚历克斯
克里斯蒂娜：你需要控制住自己，化个淡妆； 否则，我们将被迫向您的父母解释为什么他们没有被邀请参加婚礼。

CHRISTINA
I was just very happy; I'll be ok now.

克里斯蒂娜
我非常高兴；现在我会没事的。

ALEX
You can cry all you want at our official wedding later.

亚历克斯
稍后在我们正式的婚礼上，你想哭就哭吧。

CHRISTINA
Remind me to spank you later.

克里斯蒂娜
提醒我稍后打你屁股。

ALEX
I know I probably earned a spanking.

亚历克斯
我知道我可能挨了打屁股。

The Limo pulled up to the Austerlitz memorial and they got out. Christina and her mother went shopping together with Trevor escorting them from a distance as to not intrude on their conversation, but close enough to protect them.

豪华轿车停在奥斯特里茨纪念碑前，他们下了车。克里斯蒂娜和她的母亲一起去购物，特雷弗远远地护送着他们，既不打扰他们的谈话，又足够保护他们。

Alex and Mr. Garrison were going to do some History Buff things together, exploring Napoleon and planning to visit some of the fabulous Paris military museums.

亚历克斯和加里森先生打算一起做一些历史爱好者的事情，探索拿破仑，并计划参观一些神奇的巴黎军事博物馆。

Alex and Mr. Garrison got back into the Limo which drove them to the Musée de l'Armée (Army Museum) the military museum of France located at Les Invalides in the 7th Arrondissement of Paris.

亚历克斯和加里森先生回到豪华轿车，车子把他们送到了法国军事博物馆（Musée de l'Armée），这是位于巴黎第七区荣军院的法国军事博物馆。

***

<u>EXT./INT. DAY. MUSÉE DE L'ARMÉE (ARMY MUSEUM) THE MILITARY MUSEUM OF FRANCE</u>

<u>军事博物馆 (MUSÉE DE L'ARMÉE) – (ARMY MUSEUM: 陆军博物馆 ) 法国军事博物馆</u>

Out front of the museum were French special forces soldiers brandishing machine guns.

博物馆前面是挥舞着机枪的法国特种部队士兵。

ALEX (THOUGHT)<br>Oh, how the world had changed because of Terrorism.

亚历克斯（心想）<br>哦，世界因为恐怖主义而发生了多大的变化。

This was one time that Buster was extremely happy to be with Alex, because of his military service and interests.

这一次，巴斯特因为亚历克斯的军事服务和兴趣而感到非常高兴。

The three men walked through the museum as if they were all old friends. Buster of course had bonded with Mr. Garrison right away.

三人走过博物馆，仿佛都是老朋友。巴斯特当然很快就和加里森先生打成一片。

The Navy Seals have a tough job, but what Mr. Garrison performed in Vietnam going behind enemy lines in Cambodia on almost 200 missions, was about 10 times more than Buster ever did.

海豹突击队的任务很艰巨，但加里森先生在越南、柬埔寨敌后执行了近 200 次任务，比巴斯特执行的任务多 10 倍左右。

In Buster's training they had read about Green Beret missions which showcased the milestone in extraction techniques. Penetration is easy; getting the hell out of there while surrounded by the enemy took extraordinary skill and daring.

在　巴斯特的训练中，他们学习了绿色贝雷帽任务，这些任务展示了撤离技术的里程碑。渗透很容易；在被敌人包围的情况下逃脱需要非凡的技巧和勇气。

200 years of French field artillery history showcased the museum. Napoleon, who was the first General to integrate massive artillery into his major plan changed the nature of warfare.

博物馆展示了法国200年的野战炮兵历史。拿破仑是第一位将大规模火炮纳入其主要计划的将军，他改变了战争的性质。

Colorful uniforms on display showed the stylish nature of French military.

展出的色彩鲜艳的制服展现了法国军队的时尚气质。

French designed Army Tanks which the Japanese's copied for World War II engrossed viewers.

法国设计的陆军坦克被日本在第二次世界大战中仿制，引起了观众的着迷。

Guns, toy soldiers, and vast numbers of military paraphernalia decorated the museum. It was a surreal experience as Alex, Mr. Garrison and Buster walked past Napoleon's tomb.

博物馆里摆满了枪支、玩具士兵和大量军事装备。当亚历克斯、加里森先生和巴斯特走过拿破仑的坟墓时，这是一种超现实的体验。

As they were looking at pictures, and paintings on display, Buster commented, "Those guys on bicycles saved Paris in WW1.

当他们观看展出的图片和绘画时，巴斯特评论道：　"那些骑自行车的人在第一次世界大战中拯救了巴黎。

**ALEX**
Plus, the Taxi drivers,

亚历克斯
另外，出租车司机，

**MR. GARRISON**
This museum contains artifacts going all the way back
to the Middle Ages.

加里森先生
这座博物馆收藏着可追溯至中世纪的文物。

ALEX
The military artwork is the best in the world.

亚历克斯
军事艺术是世界上最好的。

Alex and the other two men took it all in. None of the three men had ever been here before.

亚历克斯和其他两名男子都看到了这一切。这三个人之前都没有来过这里。

MR. GARRISON
Alex, had it not been for you, I would never have come here.

加里森先生
亚历克斯，要不是因为你，我就不会来这里。

Father, there are many places I wish to take you to some day.

爸爸，有很多地方我希望有一天能带您去。

Mr. Garrison was taken back by the label Alex had just used. And it all came about after his private departure with Christina. He then knew something was up. One of his concerns was: *What if Christina's pregnant?*

加里森先生被亚历克斯刚刚使用的标签吓了一跳。这一切都发生在他与克里斯蒂娜私下离开之后。然后他知道有些事情发生了。他担心的一个问题是：如果克里斯蒂娜怀孕了怎么办？

Mr. Garrison consoled himself.

加里森先生安慰自己。

MR. GARRISON (THOUGHT)
With that huge ring on Christina's finger, *it's evident that Alex is moving along in an honorable fashion.*

加里森先生 （思考）
克里斯蒂娜手指上戴着那枚巨大的戒指，显然亚历克斯正以一种光荣的方式前进。

***

The women were not too far from the major tourist shopping area. And money was not an issue.

这两个女人住的地方距离主要的旅游购物区并不太远。而且钱也不是问题。

The first store they went into where they looked at a few souvenirs to buy for friends back home, Christina asked the store owner:

她们走进第一家商店，想买一些纪念品送给家乡的朋友，克里斯蒂娜问店主：

### CHRISTINA

If we buy some merchandise, can you send it to New York for us or to our apartment here in Paris?

### 克里斯蒂娜

如果我们买些东西，你能帮我们寄到纽约或者我们巴黎的公寓吗？

### STORE OWNER

Why certainly madam, whichever destination you prefer. I would warn you, however, if we send it to New York, it will cost quite a bit more than if we ship it to a local address.

### 店主

当然可以，女士，无论您想寄到哪里都可以。不过，我要提醒您，如果我们寄到纽约，费用会比寄到本地地址贵很多。

Trevor had come into the store and overheard part of the conversation and interjected:

特雷弗走进商店，听到了部分谈话，便插话说：

### TREVOR

Christina, just have them deliver it to the apartment, Alex will make all the arrangements to ship it home if it all doesn't fit on the airplane.

### 特雷弗

克里斯蒂娜，让他们把东西送到公寓就行了，如果飞机装不下，亚历克斯会安排把东西运回家。

### CHRISTINA

That sounds like a good plan.

### 克里斯蒂娜

这听起来是个不错的计划。

### TREVOR

The cargo bay on that plane is large. The plane can carry a lot and since we will be flying from Europe to New York on the way home, the plane probably doesn't need a full fuel tank, so we can carry a lot more extra cargo than normal.

特雷弗
那架飞机的货舱很大。飞机可以载很多东西，而且由于我们将在回家的途中从欧洲飞往纽约，飞机可能不需要满油箱，所以我们可以携带比平时多得多的额外货物。

CHRISTINA
I see.

克里斯蒂娜
我明白了。

After a dozen stores, Christina declared:

逛了十几家商店后，克里斯蒂娜宣布：

CHRISTINA
I think we've bought enough souvenirs, let's go look at some clothes.

克里斯蒂娜
我想我们已经买够纪念品了，我们去看看衣服吧。

MRS. GARRISON
Good idea.

加里森夫人
好主意。

In a short while, Christina and her mother ended up and a lingerie shop, which gave Trevor a good excuse to wait outside.

不一会儿，克里斯蒂娜和她的母亲来到了一家内衣店，这给了特雷弗一个在外面等候的好借口。

Inside the store, Christina picked out a dozen very sexy articles and wanted to try them on.

在商店里，克里斯蒂娜挑选了十几件非常性感的物品，想试穿一下。

STORE CLERK
I'm sorry, madam, because of sanitary requirements, if you try it on you must buy it first.

店员

对不起女士，出于卫生要求，如果您试穿，必须
先购买。

CHRISTINA

Okay no problem, I can always give them to friends if
they don't work out.

克里斯蒂娜

好的，没问题，如果它们不合适，我可以把它们
送给朋友。

Moments later the store clerk charged Christina's credit card and stated:

过了一会儿，店员从克里斯蒂娜的信用卡中扣款，并说：

STORE CLERK

You now own all those garments; you may take them
into the changing room and try them on.

店员

现在这些衣服都归你所有了；你可以把它们带进
更衣室试穿。

CHRISTINA

Mother, please come with me into the changing room.

克里斯蒂娜
妈妈，请跟我去更衣室。

Christina decided she needed to confide in her mother and even though Alex had told
her not to divulge it for their own security, she felt bad her parents were not present
during the marriage and wanted to explain it.

克里斯蒂娜决定她需要向她的母亲吐露心声，尽管亚历克斯告诉她为了他们自
己的安全不要泄露这件事，但她还是为她的父母在婚礼期间不在场而感到难
过，并想解释这件事。

Christina had a dozen pieces of lingerie, so it would be natural it would take her a
while to try them out. She tried on one outfit to check the sizes, it matched perfectly,
she didn't need to try on the rest in the store but took the time to talk to her mother
privately.

克里斯蒂娜有十几件内衣，所以她自然需要花点时间试穿。她试穿了一套衣服
检查尺寸，尺寸非常合适，她不需要在店里试穿其余的衣服，而是花时间和她
妈妈私下交谈。

CHRISTINA

Mom, I know you are going to be extremely upset at me for what I did, but there was a reason for it.

克里斯蒂娜

妈妈，我知道你会因为我的所作所为而对我非常生气，但这是有原因的。

MRS. GARRISON

What did you do, honey?

加里森夫人

你做了什么亲爱的？

CHRISTINA

Alex and I were secretly married when we left you guys for a while earlier today?

克里斯蒂娜

今天早些时候我们离开你们一段时间的时候，亚历克斯和我就已经秘密结婚了？

MRS. GARRISON

Why were we not invited?

加里森夫人

为什么我们没有受到邀请？

CHRISTINA

It's supposed to be kept as a big secret for our personal security. Alex said he will plan a big wedding for Queens New York, where all our friends and relatives can attend.

克里斯蒂娜

这应该作为我们人身安全的大秘密来保守。亚历克斯说他将在纽约皇后区策划一场盛大的婚礼，我们所有的朋友和亲戚都可以参加。

MRS. GARRISON

Why was it necessary to rush to get married?

加里森夫人

为什么要这么急着结婚？

CHRISTINA

Alex had a lawyer there with a bunch of documents for me to sign. He wanted to make sure that if something happened to him, that I would inherit his fortune. I'm now his designated heir to his estate.

克里斯蒂娜

亚历克斯请了一位律师，给我准备了一堆文件。他想确保如果他出了什么事，我能继承他的财产。我现在是他指定的遗产继承人。

MRS. GARRISON

But why the big secret?

加里森夫人

但为什么要有这么大的秘密呢？

CHRISTINA

With all the recent sensational news, Alex felt we would be safer delaying the news until we got back to America and had the big wedding.

克里斯蒂娜

鉴于最近这些轰动性的消息，亚历克斯觉得我们最好等到回到美国举行盛大婚礼后再公布这个消息。

MRS. GARRISON

But why the pressing need to do it now?

加里森夫人

但为什么现在必须这么做呢？

CHRISTINA

After the murder incidents in Greenland, Alex's slightly paranoid that something could happen to him, and wanted to make sure I would be taken care of for the rest of my life under those circumstances. He did it strictly for me.

克里斯蒂娜

格陵兰发生谋杀事件后，亚历克斯有点担心自己会出事，他想确保在这种情况下我的余生都能得到照顾。他这么做完全是为了我。

MRS. GARRISON

I see, I think we should tell your father.

加里森夫人
我明白了，我觉得我们应该告诉你父亲。

CHRISTINA
Please mother, I needed to confide in you and I'm
afraid daddy will be very upset if he finds out.

克里斯蒂娜
妈妈，拜托了，我需要向你吐露心声，我担心爸
爸如果知道了会非常难过。

MRS. GARRISON
He will be, what do you expect?

加里森夫人
他将会是，你所期望的那样吗？

CHRISTINA
I know mother, please, just help me now with this, I
desperately need your support.

克里斯蒂娜
我知道，妈妈，请你现在就帮助我，我迫切需要
你的支持。

Christina's mother a shrewd woman knew it was best not to argue with her daughter,
even though she told her a white lie, she had no intentions of hiding it from her
husband. Plus, Christina didn't have faith in her father who would be very supportive,
but he was entitled to know. And the Wedding in Queens for the official version wasn't
such a bad idea after all.

克里斯蒂娜的母亲是个精明的女人，她知道最好不要和女儿争吵，尽管她说了
一个善意的谎言，但她无意向丈夫隐瞒。此外，克里斯蒂娜不相信她的父亲会
非常支持她，但他有权知道。而且，官方版本的皇后区婚礼毕竟不是一个坏主
意。

Christina's mother was also very pleased because now she knew for a fact; Alex's
intentions towards her daughter were real and permanent, not of risk of falling apart
before a wedding since they were now already married.

克里斯蒂娜的母亲也很高兴，因为现在她知道了一个事实；亚历克斯对她女儿
的心意是真实而永久的，而不会冒着婚前分手的风险，因为他们现在已经结婚
了。

MRS. GARRISON (THOUGHT)
*It's apparent Christina needs some quality time with*
*Alex tonight, so William and I will have to come up*

*with some excuse to get away from the apartment so that the honeymooners can have some emotional bonding in private.*

加里森夫人 （想法）
显然，克里斯蒂娜今晚需要和亚历克斯共度一段美好时光，所以威廉和我必须找个借口离开公寓，这样度蜜月的情侣们才能私下里进行一些情感交流。

***

<u>INT. DAY. PARIS FRANCE. MICHELLE MONTEZ'S LAWYER, ELLIOT RUBENSTEIN'S OFFICE.</u>

<u>法国巴黎，白天。米歇尔·蒙特兹的律师，埃利奥特·鲁宾斯坦的办公室。</u>

Michelle Montez's lawyer, Elliot Rubenstein arrived punctually 30 minutes later as promised in his office.

米歇尔·蒙特兹的律师埃利奥特·鲁宾斯坦按照对他办公室的承诺，在 30 分钟后准时到达。

ELLIOT RUBENSTEIN
What is so earth shattering you had to drag me in here today?

埃利奥特·鲁宾斯坦
今天有什么惊天动地的事要把我拖到这里来？

MICHELLE MONTEZ
What I'm about to disclose is extremely confidential. I need your legal advice as well as you may have to make contact and negotiate with Alex Baxter over the matter.

米歇尔·蒙特兹
我即将披露的信息属于高度机密。我需要你的法律建议，而且你可能需要就此事与亚历克斯·巴克斯特联系并进行谈判。

ELLIOT RUBENSTEIN
Ok, what is it?

埃利奥特·鲁宾斯坦
好的，是什么？

MICHELLE MONTEZ
Alex Baxter secretly married Christina Garrison at the Notre Dame Cathedral earlier today.

米歇尔·蒙特兹
亚历克斯·巴克斯特今天早些时候在巴黎圣母院与克里斯蒂娜·加里森秘密结婚。

ELLIOT RUBENSTEIN
So, what's the big deal about that?

埃利奥特·鲁宾斯坦
那么，这有什么大不了的？

MICHELLE MONTEZ
Alex Baxter's gone way overboard in keeping it secret. No family members were present.

米歇尔·蒙特兹
亚历克斯·巴克斯特在保守秘密方面做得过分了。没有家人在场。

ELLIOT RUBENSTEIN
That's no different than a Las Vegas drive through wedding.

埃利奥特·鲁宾斯坦
这和拉斯维加斯的驾车婚礼没什么不同。

MICHELLE MONTEZ
Oh, but it gets juicier.

米歇尔·蒙特兹
哦，但事情会变得更加有趣。

ELLIOT RUBENSTEIN
Is she's knocked up?

埃利奥特·鲁宾斯坦
她怀孕了吗？

MICHELLE MONTEZ
Not that I know of, but that's possible too.

米歇尔·蒙特兹
据我所知没有，但这也是有可能的。

ELLIOT RUBENSTEIN
Then what's the information that led to this meeting?

埃利奥特·鲁宾斯坦
那么，促成这次会面的信息是什么呢？

MICHELLE MONTEZ
Christina's parents are in Paris staying at Alex's apartment.

米歇尔·蒙特兹
克里斯蒂娜的父母在巴黎，住在亚历克斯的公寓里。

ELLIOT RUBENSTEIN
And what's the big deal about that?

埃利奥特·鲁宾斯坦
那这有什么大不了的？

MICHELLE MONTEZ
It apparently is such a big secret; Christina Garrison's parents were not invited to the wedding!

米歇尔·蒙特兹
这显然是一个天大的秘密；克里斯蒂娜·加里森的父母没有被邀请参加婚礼！

ELLIOT RUBENSTEIN
So, you think they kept it secretly away from her parents for some reason.

埃利奥特·鲁宾斯坦
所以，你认为他们出于某种原因，秘密地向她的父母隐瞒了这件事。

MICHELLE MONTEZ
Yes. I got a private detective following them around, the mother and daughter are out shopping together acting as if nothing happened. I'm sure the mother doesn't know.

米歇尔·蒙特兹
是的。我派了一名私家侦探跟踪她们，母女俩一起出去购物，假装什么事都没发生过。我敢肯定母亲不知道。

### ELLIOT RUBENSTEIN
Ok then what do you want me to do?

艾略特·鲁宾斯坦
好吧，那么你想让我做什么？

### MICHELLE MONTEZ
Contact Alex Baxter and tell him we'll keep the story out of the magazine for $5 million.

米歇尔·蒙特兹
联系亚历克斯·巴克斯特，告诉他我们会以 500 万美元的价格将这个故事保密。

### ELLIOT RUBENSTEIN
You realize what you are asking me to do is black male Mr. Baxter.

埃利奥特·鲁宾斯坦
你知道你要求我做的是黑人男性巴克斯特先生。

### MICHELLE MONTEZ
No, you are just the messenger; I'm the one blackmailing Mr. Baxter.

米歇尔·蒙特兹
不，你只是个信使；我才是敲诈巴克斯特先生的人。

### ELLIOT RUBENSTEIN
I suppose under the attorney client privilege I can be a message passer, but I will warn you that if I get a court summons and interrogated, I will be compelled to admit I gave Mr. Baxter the message at your request.

埃利奥特·鲁宾斯坦
我想，根据律师客户特权，我可以成为信息传递者，但我要警告你，如果我收到法庭传票并接受审讯，我将被迫承认我是按照你的要求向巴克斯特先生传递信息的。

### MICHELLE MONTEZ
I doubt seriously Mr. Baxter is going to litigate you over this matter. I feel confident he will simply pay me off and that will be the end of it.

米歇尔·蒙特兹
我非常怀疑巴克斯特先生会就此事起诉你。我相信他只会付钱给我，然后事情就结束了。

**ELLIOT RUBENSTEIN**
Ok, but I warn you that if this blows up in your face,
I'm not taking any responsibility for your actions. I will
be cooperative with the courts and the investigation if
one happens.

埃利奥特·鲁宾斯坦
好吧，但我警告你，如果这件事让你大吃一惊，
我不会为你的行为承担任何责任。如果发生这种
情况，我会配合法院和调查。

**MICHELLE MONTEZ**
I would not expect you to do otherwise.

米歇尔·蒙特兹
我不会指望你做其他事。

**ELLIOT RUBENSTEIN**
Okay as long as we have that understanding.

埃利奥特·鲁宾斯坦
好的，只要我们有这种理解。

***

Trevor was greatly appreciative when Christina announced:

当克里斯蒂娜宣布时，特雷弗显得非常感激：

**CHRISTINA**
We have done enough shopping and are ready to go
back to the apartment.

克里斯蒂娜
我们已经买够了东西，准备回公寓了。

Trevor, then phoned the Limo driver who arrived in five minutes to pick them up and
drive them back to the apartment.

特雷弗随后打电话给豪华轿车司机，司机在五分钟内赶到，接他们并将他们送
回公寓。

INT. DAY. PARIS FRANCE. MUSÉE DE L'ARMÉE (ARMY MUSEUM)

INT。天。法国巴黎。陆军博物馆 (MUSEE DE L'ARMÉE)

Alex had seen enough of the Musée de l'Armée (Army Museum) after two hours when
suddenly, he got a text message from his lawyer.

两个小时后，亚历克斯参观够了军事博物馆，突然，他收到了律师的短信。

ALEX'S LAWYER
(Text Message)
A meeting is being set up with you and Elliot Rubenstein, Michelle Montez's attorney.

亚历克斯的律师
（短信）
正在安排您和米歇尔·蒙特兹的律师埃利奥特·鲁宾斯坦见面。

ALEX
(Text Message)
I do not want to meet with him.

亚历克斯
（短信）
我不想和他见面。

ALEX'S LAWYER
(Text Message)
You have too. Otherwise, you will greatly regret it.

亚历克斯的律师
（短信）
你也必须这么做。否则，你会后悔莫及。

ALEX
(Text Message)
What do they have that would possess me to want to attend a meeting.

亚历克斯
（短信）
他们有什么能让我想参加会议呢？

ALEX'S LAWYER
(Text Message)
Apparently, *Michelle Montez* claims you got married today.

亚历克斯的律师
（短信）
显然，米歇尔·蒙特兹的声称你们今天结婚了。

Alex was stunned and felt even more animosity towards *Michelle Montez*. There was no person in the world that got under Alex's skin as badly as *Michelle Montez* did.

阿历克斯大吃一惊，对米歇尔·蒙特兹的仇恨也更加深了。世界上没有人像米歇尔·蒙特兹那样让阿历克斯如此恼火。

ALEX
(Text Message)
When does he want to meet?

亚历克斯
（短信）
他什么时候想见面？

ALEX'S LAWYER
(Text Message)
In two hours.

亚历克斯的律师
（短信）
两小时后。

ALEX
(Text Message)
Where?

ALEX
（短信）
在哪里？

ALEX'S LAWYER
(Text Message)
In his office. He said that it must be a private meeting, he's just providing information.

亚历克斯的律师
（短信）
在他的办公室。他说这一定是一次私人会议，他只是提供信息。

ALEX
(Text Message)
Ok, but I want you to find a local attorney to meet me there and represent me in case I need legal assistance.

亚历克斯
（短信）
好的，但我希望您找到一位当地律师在那里与我
会面，并在我需要法律援助时代表我。

ALEX'S LAWYER
(Text Message)
You read my mind. I already have an attorney standing
by who will meet you at *Michelle Montez's attorney
office* and has signed a non-disclosure statement.

亚历克斯的律师
（短信）

你读懂了我的心思。我已经安排了一位律师，他
会在米歇尔·蒙特兹的律师办公室与你会面，并签
署了一份保密声明。

ALEX
(Text Message)
What's his name?

亚历克斯
（短信）
他叫什么名字？

ALEX'S LAWYER
(Text Message)
The attorney I hired to represent you is Pierre
Goldstein, he's one of the best attorneys in Paris.

亚历克斯的律师
（短信）
我聘请的代表您的律师是皮埃尔·戈德斯坦，他是
巴黎最好的律师之一。

***

Two hours later, after Alex informed the Garrison's back at his apartment, he had some urgent business to attend to, and would be back in about an hour, left with Buster, hopped in a Limo that drove about 15 minutes away to *Michelle Montez's attorney* Elliot Rubenstein's office.

两个小时后，亚历克斯通知加里森一家回到他的公寓，他有些紧急的事情要处理，大约一小时后回来，和巴斯特一起，跳上一辆豪华轿车，开了大约 15 分钟的车程，到了米歇尔·蒙特兹的律师艾略特·鲁宾斯坦的办公室。

***

<u>INT. DAY. PARIS FRANCE. *MICHELLE MONTEZ'S ATTORNEY* ELLIOT RUBENSTEIN'S OFFICE.</u>

法国巴黎，白天，米歇尔·蒙特兹的律师埃利奥特·鲁宾斯坦的办公室。

A well-dressed man was waiting for Alex at the entrance of Elliot Rubenstein's law office building.

一位衣着考究的男子正在艾略特·鲁宾斯坦律师事务所大楼门口等候亚历克斯。

PIERRE GOLDSTEIN
You are Mr. Baxter, I presume?

皮埃尔·戈德斯坦
我想您是巴克斯特先生吧？

ALEX,
Yes, that's me.

亚历克斯，
是的，那就是我。

PIERRE GOLDSTEIN
I'm representing you, my name is Pierre Goldstein, sir.
I will take you to Mr. Rubenstein's office.

皮埃尔·戈德斯坦
我代表您，我的名字是皮埃尔·戈德斯坦，先生。
我会带您去鲁宾斯坦先生的办公室。

The office building had great furnishings, including famous paintings on the wall. It was getting late in the day; the offices were mostly empty.

办公楼内摆设精美，墙上挂着名画。天色已晚，办公室里几乎空无一人。

Alex and his new temporary lawyer, Pierre Goldstein took an elevator up to the 3^rd floor and followed a man waiting for them at the elevator.

亚历克斯和他的新临时律师皮埃尔·戈德斯坦乘电梯到了三楼，跟着一名在电梯里等候他们的男子。

WELL DRESSED MAN
I will escort you to Elliot Rubenstein's office.

衣着得体的男人
我将护送您到埃利奥特·鲁宾斯坦的办公室。

The man led Alex and his attorney down a short hallway to an office that appeared to belong to someone rather affluent by the statues and paintings and other decorations.

该名男子带着亚历克斯和他的律师穿过一条短短的走廊，来到一间办公室，从里面的雕像、绘画和其他装饰品来看，这间办公室的主人似乎相当富有。

A secretary was still there, and she knew already what she was required to do, stood up and announced:

一位秘书还在那里，她已经知道自己需要做什么，站起来宣布：

ELLIOT RUBENSTEIN'S SECRETARY
This way gentlemen.

埃利奥特·鲁宾斯坦的秘书
先生们，这边请。

The well-dressed man remained in the secretary's office as she led Alex and Pierre Goldstein into a small conference room where Rubenstein sat with a laptop. On it he had photographs that Michelle Montez and taken with her modified cellphone.

这位衣着考究的男子留在秘书办公室，秘书将亚历克斯和皮埃尔·戈德斯坦带入一间小会议室，鲁宾斯坦坐在那里，手里拿着一台笔记本电脑。电脑上有米歇尔·蒙特兹的照片，以及她用改装过的手机拍摄的照片。

Elliot Rubenstein stood up and spoke:

艾略特·鲁宾斯坦站起来发言：

ELLIOT RUBENSTEIN
Welcome Mr. Baxter.

埃利奥特·鲁宾斯坦
欢迎您，巴克斯特先生。

Elliot Rubenstein then looked at Pierre Goldstein who he knew and had battled a few times in the court room, and said:

随后，埃利奥特·鲁宾斯坦看着他认识并在法庭上交手过几次的皮埃尔·戈德斯坦，说道：

ELLIOT RUBENSTEIN
I thought my instructions were *Mr. Baxter was to appear alone.*

埃利奥特·鲁宾斯坦
我以为我的指示是巴克斯特先生要单独出现。

Alex then immediately responded:

亚历克斯随即回应：

ALEX
Mr. Goldstein has signed a nondisclosure agreement,
what is said between us today, will be of confidentiality
by all parties.

亚历克斯
戈尔茨坦先生已经签署了一份保密协议，我们今
天所说的内容将由各方保密。

ELLIOT RUBENSTEIN
Very well.

埃利奥特·鲁宾斯坦
很好。

Elliot Rubenstein knew that Alex Baxter would probably never reveal it for the reason
it might prove to be severely embarrassing if he did.

艾略特·鲁宾斯坦 (Elliot Rubenstein) 知道亚历克斯·巴克斯特 (Alex Baxter) 可能
永远不会透露这一点，因为如果他透露的话，可能会让他非常尴尬。

ELLIOT RUBENSTEIN
Please have a seat.

埃利奥特·鲁宾斯坦
请坐。

Ellio Rubenstein then nodded to the secretary who then left and shut the door behind
her.

埃利奥·鲁宾斯坦随后向秘书点点头，秘书随后离开并关上了门。

ALEX
So, what's this all about?

亚历克斯
那么，这到底是怎么回事？

ELLIOT RUBENSTEIN
For starters, Ms. Montez has stated she hasn't liked the
way you recently treated her, with all the threats and
you went heavy- handed when you forced her to put
out a retraction.

埃利奥特·鲁宾斯坦
首先，蒙特兹女士表示她不喜欢你最近对待她的
方式，不喜欢你对她进行各种威胁，也不喜欢你
强迫她撤回声明的强硬手段。

ALEX
Well, she earned it.

亚历克斯
好吧，她值得拥有它。

ELLIOT RUBENSTEIN
That's beside the point.

埃利奥特·鲁宾斯坦
这不是重点。

ALEX
No, it's not.

亚历克斯
不，不是。

ELLIOT RUBENSTEIN
Okay, Mr. Baxter, let's move on to the bottom line.

埃利奥特·鲁宾斯坦
好的，巴克斯特先生，我们来谈谈底线问题。

ALEX
Yes, that's what I want to hear.

亚历克斯
是的，这就是我想听的。

ELLIOT RUBENSTEIN
I'm just the messenger Mr. Baxter; I have no personal
involvement or opinion in this matter.

埃利奥特·鲁宾斯坦
我只是个信使，巴克斯特先生，我对此事没有任
何个人参与或意见。

ALEX
Alright.

亚历克斯
好吧。

ELLIOT RUBENSTEIN
Mrs. Montez took these pictures of you leaving the church with your new bride.

埃利奥特·鲁宾斯坦
蒙特兹夫人拍了这些照片，照片中你和新娘一起离开了教堂。

Elliot Rubenstein then turned the laptop around and started the power point showing almost 30 pictures including some close-ups showing Christina crying.

随后，艾略特·鲁宾斯坦转动笔记本电脑并开始播放幻灯片，其中展示了近 30 张照片，其中包括一些克里斯蒂娜哭泣的特写镜头。

ALEX
Leaving the church together after prayers doesn't prove anything.

亚历克斯
祈祷后一起离开教堂并不能证明任何事情。

ELLIOT RUBENSTEIN
We have eyewitnesses, two elderly ladies who were sitting in the church who watched Father Marian perform the wedding ceremony for you.

埃利奥特·鲁宾斯坦
我们有目击证人，两位老太太坐在教堂里，看着玛丽安神父为您主持婚礼。

ALEX
Is that so.

亚历克斯
是这样吗。

Elliot Rubenstein then turned the laptop around and played the voice recording of the questions and answers with Michelle Montez and the two elderly women.

随后，艾略特·鲁宾斯坦将笔记本电脑翻转，播放了米歇尔·蒙特兹与两位老年妇女问答的录音。

ALEX
Okay, suppose all that's true, what does Ms. Montez want?

亚历克斯
好吧，假设这一切都是真的，蒙特兹女士想要什么？

ELLIOT RUBENSTEIN
Your permission to print the story, with a few questions
and answers from you, or $5 million to withhold the
story.

埃利奥特·鲁宾斯坦
您允许刊登该报道，并提出一些问题和答案，否
则将支付 500 万美元以保留该报道。

ALEX
That sounds like blackmail to me.

亚历克斯
这对我来说听起来像是敲诈勒索。

ELLIOT RUBENSTEIN
I'm just the messenger, tell that to Ms. Montez.

亚历克斯
这对我来说听起来像是敲诈勒索。

ALEX
I think we may have a good case that you are party to
the crime.

亚历克斯
我想我们可能有充分的理由证明你是犯罪的一方。

ELLIOT RUBENSTEIN
I warned Ms. Montez I would cooperate with any
investigation including testifying that I was used as a
messenger.

埃利奥特·鲁宾斯坦
我警告过蒙特兹女士，我会配合任何调查，包括
作证说我被当作了信使。

Pierre Goldstein then jumped in and responded:

皮埃尔·戈德斯坦随后插话回应：

PIERRE GOLDSTEIN
I think your law license is in jeopardy.

皮埃尔·戈德斯坦
我认为你的律师执照岌岌可危。

ELLIOT RUBENSTEIN
I considered that when I agreed to communicate with you. I just want to avoid a nasty court case is all. Ms. Montez will most likely publish the story otherwise. For Mr. Baxter, $5 million is chump change.

埃利奥特·鲁宾斯坦
当我同意与您沟通时，我就考虑到了这一点。我只是想避免一场棘手的诉讼。否则，蒙特兹女士很可能会发表这个故事。对于巴克斯特先生来说，500 万美元只是小数目。

Alex, thinking five chess moves ahead of the attorneys responded:

亚历克斯比律师们领先思考了五步，然后回答道：

ALEX
I will probably agree to Michelle Montez's demands, but I would like the opportunity to reach out to my wife and her parents before I move forward for, I fear this matter could get out of control real fast.

亚历克斯
我可能会同意米歇尔·蒙特兹的要求，但我希望在继续之前有机会联系我的妻子和她的父母，因为我担心这件事可能很快就会失控。

ELLIOT RUBENSTEIN
That's only reasonable, but under the circumstances with a looming deadline for the next magazine production, I was advised we need to conclude this arrangement by noon tomorrow in order to meet the deadline in case the story must be printed.

埃利奥特·鲁宾斯坦
这很合理，但考虑到下一期杂志的制作截止日期迫在眉睫，我被告知我们需要在明天中午之前完成这项安排，以便在需要印刷该故事的情况下赶上截止日期。

ALEX
I understand, you will have your answer later today, there will be no reason to wait until tomorrow.

亚历克斯
我明白，今天**晚**些时候你就会得到答案，没有理
由等到明天。

ELLIOT RUBENSTEIN
That's great, Mr. Baxter that you are being reasonable.

埃利奥特·鲁宾斯坦
巴克斯特先生，您说得真好，您讲道理。

ALEX
I always am.

亚历克斯
我一直都是。

Pierre Goldstein wanted to talk privately with Alex to see what he really was up to, announced:

皮埃尔·戈尔茨坦想与亚历克斯私下交谈，看看亚历克斯的真正计划是什么，他宣布：

PIERRE GOLDSTEIN
On that note, we must leave now.

皮埃尔·戈德斯坦
说到这里，我们必须离开了。

They all stood shook hands, Alex had no animosity towards Rubenstein, and he was as he said, *I'm just the messenger.*

他们都站起来握手，亚历克斯对鲁宾斯坦没有任何敌意，就像他所说的那样，我只是一个信使。

Elliot Rubenstein on the other hand suddenly had a lot of growing respect for Alex who remained civil throughout the discussion and did not hold him personally responsible for what a greedy woman was hell bent on doing.

另一方面，艾略特·鲁宾斯坦突然对亚历克斯产生了越来越深的敬意，因为亚历克斯在整个讨论过程中都保持着礼貌的态度，并没有因为一个贪婪的女人一心想做的事而追究他个人的责任。

Pierre Goldstein suggested he give Alex a ride back to his apartment to discuss their business and Alex responded:

皮埃尔·戈尔茨坦建议他载亚历克斯回公寓讨论他们的生意，亚历克斯回应道：

ALEX
I want my bodyguard, Buster, to ride up front with the
driver in case something bad happens.

亚历克斯
我希望我的保镖巴斯特和司机一起骑在前面，以
防发生什么不好的事情。

PIERRE GOLDSTEIN
Of course.

皮埃尔·戈德斯坦
当然。

***

In the car, Alex laid out his plan. Pierre Goldstein agreed to all Alex planned and felt
it was the smartest move Alex could make.

在车里，亚历克斯阐述了他的计划。皮埃尔·戈德斯坦同意亚历克斯的所有计
划，并认为这是亚历克斯能做出的最明智的举动。

Alex got back to the apartment and then asked Buster and Trevor:

ALEX
Buster and Trever I want you guys to wait outside
for a few minutes. I needed to talk privately with the
Garrison family.

亚历克斯
巴斯特和特雷弗，我希望你们在外面等几分钟。
我需要和加里森一家人私下谈谈。

Alex had decided he was going to beat *Michelle Montez* at her own game.

阿历克斯决定要用米歇尔·蒙特兹自己的方法打败她。

***

<u>INT. DAY. PARIS FRANCE. ALEX'S APPARTMENT.</u>

<u>室内图·白天·法国巴黎·亚历克斯的公寓。</u>

What Alex did not know was as soon as Mr. Garrison got home, Mrs. Garrison called
William into the bedroom as she preferred to call her husband.

亚历克斯不知道的是，加里森先生一回到家，加里森夫人就把威廉叫进了卧
室，因为她更喜欢这样叫她的丈夫。

MRS. GARRISON

William, please come into the bedroom for a private conversation with me and we have something to discuss.

加里森夫人

威廉，请到卧室来和我私下谈谈，我们有些事要讨论。

Inside the bedroom alone with his wife Ethel, William Garrison asked:

威廉·加里森和妻子埃塞尔独自在卧室里，他问道：

MR. GARRISON

What do you want to discuss Ethel?

加里森先生

埃塞尔，你想讨论什么？

MRS. GARRISON

Christina and Alex were married today.

加里森夫人

克里斯蒂娜和亚历克斯今天结婚了。

William of course was angry and hurt at first, then the educator part of him prevailed with Ethel's brow beating of course and accepted the new reality for what it was worth.

威廉一开始当然是生气和受伤的，但是随后，他身上作为教育者的一面当然战胜了埃塞尔的威吓，接受了新的现实。

MRS. GARRISON

Alex is just trying to protect our daughter and wanted to make sure she was taken care of in case something happened to him. The plan is to have the "official wedding" back in New York so all our friends can attend.

加里森夫人

亚历克斯只是想保护我们的女儿，并希望确保她得到照顾，以防他发生意外。计划是在纽约举行"正式婚礼"，以便我们所有的朋友都能参加。

For that reason, William immediately forgave Alex.

因此，威廉立刻原谅了亚历克斯。

Then Alex suddenly appeared and told the family, what had happened and apologized.

然后亚历克斯突然出现并告诉家人发生的事并道歉。

ALEX
I've changed his mind and Christina, and I are going to get married again immediately so you can attend and invite a member of the press there to record the event.

亚历克斯
我改变了他的想法，我和克里斯蒂娜马上就要再婚了，这样你就可以参加婚礼，并邀请媒体来记录婚礼。

Alex then called Father Marian, who was in the process of booking a three-week vacation to Bangkok Thailand leaving in a few days from now.

ALEX
Father Marian, this is Alex Baxter.

亚历克斯
玛丽安神父，我是亚历克斯·巴克斯特。

FATHER MARIAN
Alex, I'm surprised to hear from you. Are you calling to annul the wedding or something?

玛丽安神父
亚历克斯，我很惊讶收到你的来信。你打电话是想取消婚礼还是什么？

ALEX
Father Marian, no, I have an important request, I would like to come over to the church right away and have you to perform another wedding ceremony again, so that Christina's parents can observe the *marriage*.

亚历克斯
玛丽安神父，不，我有一个重要的请求，我想马上去教堂，让您再举行一次婚礼，以便克里斯蒂娜的父母可以见证婚礼。

FATHER MARIAN
Well, I'm kind of busy now.

玛丽安神父
嗯，我现在有点忙。

ALEX
I will make it worth your while just like the last time
with some extra money to help Catholic Charities.

亚历克斯
我会像上次一样，给你一些额外的钱来帮助天主
教慈善机构，让你觉得值得。

FATHER MARIAN
Come right over.

玛丽安神父
快过来。

Alex then called the Associated Press in Paris and got in touch with a reporter. When Alex announced he was Alex Baxter the reporter didn't wish to believe it.

随后，亚历克斯打电话给巴黎美联社，联系上了一名记者。当亚历克斯宣布自己就是亚历克斯·巴克斯特时，这位记者不愿相信。

AP REPORTER
I do not believe you are Dome Man - Alex Baxter.

美联社记者
我不相信你是穹顶人-亚历克斯·巴克斯特。

ALEX
Alright, you can come by my apartment right away to
meet me here then go somewhere with my family and
you will have the story of the century.

亚历克斯
好吧，你可以马上到我的公寓来见我，然后和我
的家人一起去某个地方，你就会听到这个世纪的
故事。

When the reporter saw the caller I.D. had the name *Baxter*, he suddenly had a quick change of heart and responded:

当记者看到来电显示时 名叫巴克斯特的他突然改变了主意，回答道：

AP REPORTER
I'll be right over; can you text me the address?

美联社记者
我马上就来；你能把地址发给我吗？

ALEX
Certainly.

亚历克斯
当然了。

Alex then explained to everyone who had been observing and listening.

然后亚历克斯向所有观察和聆听的人解释道。

ALEX
As soon as the reporter gets here, we are all going to drive over to the Notre Dame Cathedral and get married again, Father Marian is expecting us.

亚历克斯
记者一到，我们就要开车去巴黎圣母院再次结婚，玛丽安神父正在等我们。

William (a.k.a. Mr. Garrison) was now having a lot better feeling about this marriage and was glad his son-in-law Alex was coming to his senses. But William (a.k.a. Mr. Garrison) understood why Alex did what he did. Had he been in Alex's shoes William knew he might have done the same thing.

威廉（又名加里森先生）现在对这段婚姻的感觉好多了，很高兴他的女婿亚历克斯恢复了理智。但威廉（又名加里森先生）理解亚历克斯为什么这么做。如果他处在亚历克斯的境地，威廉知道他可能会做同样的事情。

In about 15 minutes the doorbell rang. There was a reporter and 2 others with a camera, microphone and a few other devices.

大约15分钟后，门铃响了。一名记者和另外两名记者带着摄像机、麦克风和其他一些设备进来了。

PHILLIP MARCONI
(AP Reporter)
I'm Phillip Marconi of the AP; you called me a while ago.

菲利普·马可尼
（美联社记者）
我是美联社的菲利普·马可尼，您刚才给我打过电话。

Phillip had looked up Alex on the internet and seen numerous pictures on the way over and read some information so that he would know what questions to ask.

菲利普在互联网上查找了亚历克斯的信息，在途中看过无数的照片，还阅读了一些资料，以便知道要问什么问题。

ALEX
Phillip, we are all going over to the Notre Dame
Cathedral for the big event, can you meet us there?

亚历克斯
菲利普，我们要去巴黎圣母院参加大型活动，你
能在那里见我们吗？

Now Phillip was getting excited, because this could very well turn out to be a big story responded:

现在菲利普开始兴奋起来，因为这很可能成为一个大新闻。他回答道：

PHILLIP MARCONI
(AP Reporter)
No problem Mr. Baxter, how soon will you be there?

菲利普·马可尼
（美联社记者）
没问题，巴克斯特先生，您什么时候能到？

ALEX
Not sure but I'll tell the Limo driver to beat you there!

亚历克斯
不确定，但我会让豪华轿车司机先你到那里！

Alex then put on a *Cheshire Cat Smile* [ cheshire cat smile - Search Images ]

然后，亚历克斯露出了柴郡猫般的微笑 [ 柴郡猫般的微笑 - 搜索图片 ]

Alex turned to everyone and announced:

亚历克斯转向大家宣布：

ALEX
Let's go!

亚历克斯
我们走吧！

CHRISTINA
Shouldn't we change our clothes?

克里斯蒂娜
我们不应该换衣服吗？

ALEX
Nope, we'll dress up for the next wedding!

亚历克斯
不，我们会盛装出席下一场婚礼！

WILLIAM
(a.k.a. Mr. Garrison)
I like the way you are thinking son.

威廉
（又名加里森先生）
儿子，我喜欢你的想法。

The group and the bodyguards all departed the apartment and got into the Limo that was waiting for them. The AP news van waited and followed them to Notre Dame Cathedral.

一行人和保镖离开公寓，坐上等候的豪华轿车。美联社新闻车一直等着他们，并跟随他们前往巴黎圣母院。

<u>INT. DAY. PARIS FRANCE NOTRE DAME CATHEDRAL</u>

<u>内景白天法国巴黎巴黎圣母院</u>。

Father Marian was there all smiles because this time he would have Alex wire the money to the Vatican Bank in his name. The Pope would never know all the other money went into his personal Swiss bank account.

玛丽安神父满脸笑容，因为这次他会让亚历克斯以他的名义把钱汇到梵蒂冈银行。教皇永远不会知道其他钱都汇入了他的私人瑞士银行账户。

Alex informed Father Marian:

亚历克斯通知了玛丽安神父:

ALEX
Father Marian, if you don't mind, I've invited these news people along; they will film the wedding ceremony.

亚历克斯
玛丽安神父，如果你不介意的话，我已经邀请了
这些新闻界人士一起来；他们将拍摄婚礼仪式。

Father Marian who suddenly knew he would be on a lot of Paris TVs responded:

玛丽安神父突然意识到自己将出现在巴黎很多电视台的节目中，他回答道:

**FATHER MARIAN**
That's not a problem, Mr. Baxter.

玛丽安神父
这不是问题，巴克斯特先生。

Father Marion then smiled at the prospects of his few moments of fame.

马里恩神父对自己即将迎来的短暂名声笑了笑。

Mr. Garrison was after all given the opportunity to give away his daughter, and said when asked responded:

加里森先生毕竟得到了送出女儿的机会，当被问及时，他回答道：

**WILLIAM (a.k.a. Mr. Garrison)**
It will be my pleasure to give my daughter to Alex Baxter in holy matrimony.

威廉（又名加里森先生）
我非常高兴能将我的女儿嫁给亚历克斯·巴克斯特，让他们结为神圣的婚姻。

Mrs. Garrison was delighted because Christina no longer had tears, she was beaming with happiness. She knew she married a good man who loved her tenderly.

加里森夫人很高兴，因为克里斯蒂娜不再流泪，她满脸幸福。她知道自己嫁给了一个温柔爱着她的好男人。

It did not take the film crew long to skedaddle out of Notre Dame Cathedral back to their offices with such a hot story.

带着这样一个热门故事，摄制组很快就从巴黎圣母院赶回办公室了。

Alex was soon informed by his temporary attorney Pierre Goldstein:

亚历克斯的临时律师皮埃尔·戈德斯坦很快告知他：

**PIERRE GOLDSTEIN**
(Text Message)
I just seen the AP report of the marriage on the internet.
Good job!

皮埃尔·戈德斯坦
（短信）
我刚刚在网上看到了美联社对这场婚礼的报道。
干得好！

ALEX
(Text Message)
Mr. Goldstein, you have my permission to now call *Michelle Montez's* attorney Elliot Rubenstein to inform him he needed to advise his client, *Michelle Montez* just lost out on the story because she got too greedy,

亚历克斯
（短信）
戈德斯坦先生，我允许你现在打电话给米歇尔·蒙特兹的律师埃利奥特·鲁宾斯坦，告诉他他需要为他的客户提供建议，米歇尔·蒙特兹只是因为太贪婪而失去了这个故事，

PIERRE GOLDSTEIN
(Text Message)
Anything you want me to say about the $5 million *Michelle Montez* demanded?

皮埃尔·戈德斯坦
（短信）
关于米歇尔·蒙特兹要求的 500 万美元，你想让我说什么？

ALEX
(Text Message)
Inform Elliot Rubenstein I might have considered $4 million but was not able to consider $5 million. Then share with him the AP report.

亚历克斯
（短信）
告诉埃利奥特·鲁宾斯坦（Elliot Rubenstein），我可能考虑过 400 万美元，但无法考虑 500 万美元。然后与他分享美联社的报道。

PIERRE GOLDSTEIN
(Text Message)
Alex, I like the way you think.

皮埃尔·戈德斯坦
（短信）
亚历克斯，我喜欢你的想法。

ALEX
Thanks for your help.

亚历克斯
谢谢你的帮助。

***

Jann Peters, Christina's close friend, saw the Internet article as it popped up as a major story in the international press. She then immediately called Christina.

克里斯蒂娜的密友詹恩·彼得斯看到互联网上的这篇文章后，立即给克里斯蒂娜打了电话。

JANN PETERS
Christina, wow, I'm so excited for you!

詹·彼得斯
克里斯蒂娜，哇，我为你感到非常兴奋！

CHRISTINA
Oh, thank you, I'm happy too.

克里斯蒂娜
哦，谢谢你，我也很高兴。

JANN PETERS
I'm sorry you didn't have a big wedding back here.

詹·彼得斯
很抱歉你没有在这里举办盛大的婚礼。

CHRISTINA
That's going to happen. We are going to have another wedding in Queens so that all our family and friends can attend the "Official Wedding." We just got married here because Alex wanted to marry me in Paris.

克里斯蒂娜
这一定会发生的。我们将在皇后区再举行一次婚礼，这样我们所有的家人和朋友都可以参加"正式婚礼"。我们在这里结婚是因为亚历克斯想在巴黎娶我。

JANN PETERS
How romantic, but your next wedding will not feel the same.

詹·彼得斯
多么浪漫，但你的下一场婚礼将不会有同样的感
觉。

CHRISTINA
It will, it will have all the trimmings, and you will be
my maid of honor.

克里斯蒂娜
是的，一切都很完美，你将成为我的伴娘。

JANN PETERS
Why thank you.

詹·彼得斯
为什么要谢谢你。

Shortly after they all made it back to the apartment after the wedding, the Garrisons
insisted on checking into a hotel or kick the newlyweds out for a couple days.

婚礼结束后不久，他们回到公寓，加里森夫妇坚持要入住酒店或将新婚夫妇赶
出去几天。

Alex responded:

亚历克斯回应：

ALEX
Okay, I get it you want some privacy.

亚历克斯
好的，我明白你想要一些隐私。

Alex then proceeded to pack a few items.

然后亚历克斯开始打包一些物品。

CHRISTINA
I don't know what to bring.

克里斯蒂娜
我不知道该带什么。

ALEX
I'll go talk to your father a bit, I'll have your mother
come in and help you pack.

亚历克斯
我去和你父亲谈谈，然后让你母亲进来帮你收拾
行李。

Alex stepped out of the bedroom and walked into the living room and announced:

亚历克斯走出卧室，走进客厅，宣布：

ALEX
Mother, Christina, would like you to help her in the
bedroom.

亚历克斯
妈妈，克里斯蒂娜想让你去卧室帮她。

Mrs. Garrison was mildly taken back by hearing Alex call her mother, but reality was sitting in, she was now in fact his mother-in-law, so it fit nicely.

听到亚历克斯叫她妈妈，加里森夫人稍微吃了一惊，但现实是，她现在实际上
已经成为了他的岳母，所以这很合适。

ETHEL (a.k.a. Mrs. Garrison)
Ok Alex.

埃塞尔（又名加里森夫人）
好的，亚历克斯。

Mrs. Garrison then went into the bedroom and shut the door.

然后加里森夫人走进卧室并关上了门。

In a few minutes the two emerged and the small handbag is all Christina had, and announced:

几分钟后，两人走了出来，克里斯蒂娜只带着一个小手提包，并宣布：

CHRISTINA
Okay, I'm ready to go.

克里斯蒂娜
好的，我准备好了。

Alex commented:

亚历克斯评论：

ALEX
Looks like you didn't pack much.

亚历克斯
看来你带的东西不多。

CHRISTIAN
We will not need many clothes where we'll be going.

克里斯蒂娜
我们去的地方不需要很多衣服。

Mr. Garrison raised his eyebrows a bit but knew better than to pursue that conversation. He also knew they needed a little motivation to leave and so he stated:

加里森先生微微扬起眉毛，但他知道最好不要继续这个话题。他也知道他们需要一点动力才能离开，于是他说：

WILLIAM (a.k.a. Mr. Garrison)
You guys need to hurry up and leave, your mother and
I have plans.

威廉（又名加里森先生）
你们得赶紧走，我和你妈妈有事要办。

CHRISTIAN
Okay, I got the message.

克里斯蒂安
好的，我明白了。

Christina hugged her mother and father, then she and Alex departed.

克里斯蒂娜拥抱了她的父母，然后和亚历克斯离开了。

As they walked towards the Limo, Alex asked Christina:

当他们走向豪华轿车时，亚历克斯问克里斯蒂娜：

ALEX
Where would you like to go, Christina?

亚历克斯
克里斯蒂娜，你想去哪里？

CHRISTINA
Why not Switzerland, I feel safe there.

克里斯蒂娜
为什么不去瑞士呢？我觉得那里很安全。

ALEX
Great idea.

亚历克斯
好主意。

Alex then called up Brad who had just changed his clothes and was about to take Gladys out to dinner when Alex called.

亚历克斯随后给布拉德打了电话，布拉德刚刚换好衣服，正准备带格拉迪斯出去吃饭，亚历克斯打来了电话。

ALEX
Brad sorry to bug you but I'm heading to the airport,
you need to fly me to Switzerland tonight.

亚历克斯
布拉德（Brad）很抱歉打扰您，但我要去机场，
您今晚需要带我飞往瑞士。

Brad, who was paid well, replied:

薪水丰厚的布拉德回答道：

BRAD
No problem, how soon do you want to leave?

布拉德
没问题，你想什么时候离开？

ALEX
Right away.

亚历克斯
马上。

BRAD
I'm about ten minutes from the airport; I'll probably
be there before you get there.

布拉德
我离机场大约十分钟路程；我可能比你到得更早。

ALEX
Call Gladys and ask her to go as well.

亚历克斯
打电话给格拉迪斯并请她也去。

BRAD
Sure, but I have one request?

布拉德
当然可以，但我有一个要求？

ALEX
What's the request?

亚历克斯
有什么要求？

BRAD
Can we wear the clothes we have on now instead of
our uniforms since we are dressed up to go out.

布拉德
既然我们要盛装出门，我们可以穿现在的衣服而
不是制服吗？

ALEX
Sure, no problem.

亚历克斯
当然，没问题。

The flight to Switzerland took one hour. The staff at the mansion were advised Alex
would be arriving and to make them something to eat, they were hungry.

飞往瑞士的航班耗时一小时。豪宅的工作人员被告知亚历克斯即将抵达，并让
他们准备一些吃的，因为他们饿了。

The staff was delighted to see them and by then Mary had been informed Alex and
Christina were married.

工作人员很高兴见到他们，那时玛丽已经得知亚历克斯和克里斯蒂娜已经结婚
了。

Alex and Christina soon arrived to the Geneva mansion with Buster along to protect
them. Buster was moved into a spare bedroom for a couple days. His life of luxury was
just what the doctor ordered as he was informed, they might not be going many places.

亚历克斯和克里斯蒂娜很快就来到了日内瓦的豪宅，巴斯特也随行保护他们。
巴斯特被安排在一间空余的卧室里住了几天。他的奢华生活正是医生建议的，
因为他被告知，他们可能不会去很多地方。

Christina's mother was correct on what to pack, just the lingerie. Mary broke into hysterical laughter when she unpacked. And by the time they finished eating Christina and Alex were more than ready to go play newlyweds.

克里斯蒂娜的母亲打包的东西是正确的，只带了内衣。玛丽打开行李时歇斯底里地大笑起来。等他们吃完饭，克里斯蒂娜和亚历克斯已经准备好去扮演新婚夫妇了。

Christina had clothes and shoes to wear in her walk-in closet. What she didn't have took Mary no difficulty and quickly obtaining.

克里斯蒂娜的步入式衣橱里有衣服和鞋子可以穿。玛丽没有的衣服和鞋子也毫不费力地很快就弄到了。

Christina and Alex finally came out of hibernation love noon the next day, only because they were seriously hungry.

第二天中午，克里斯蒂娜和亚历克斯终于从冬眠中醒来，只是因为他们真的饿了。

The following evening when Alex inquired what Christina would like to do, she indicated:

第二天晚上，当亚历克斯询问克里斯蒂娜想做什么时，她表示：

### CHRISTINA
I would love to go to the symphony again, since now I
will be going as Mrs. Baxter.

克里斯蒂娜
我很想再次去听交响乐，因为现在我将扮演巴克
斯特夫人。

After another professional makeup and hairdo and wearing another couture evening gown, Christina appeared glamorous once again.

经过又一次专业的化妆和发型设计并穿上另一件高级定制晚礼服后，克里斯蒂娜再次显得光彩夺目。

Tonight, the orchestra performed the Sibelius violin concerto. The beautiful young Asian violinist from America captivated the audience.

今晚，乐团演奏了西贝柳斯小提琴协奏曲，这位来自美国的美丽年轻亚裔小提琴家征服了观众。

**MUSIC FOR THIS SEQUENCE:**

**Sarah Chang plays Sibelius Violin Concerto in D minor (full)**

本片段音乐：

莎拉·张演奏西贝柳斯 D 小调小提琴协奏曲（完整版）

In the middle of the performance, Alex felt the buzzer on his cell phone. It was Claude Reardon who was taking care of the business while Alex was vacationing and now on his honeymooning.

表演进行到一半的时候，亚历克斯感觉到手机铃声响了。是克劳德·里尔登打来的,亚历克斯去度假了，现在正在度蜜月，他正在处理公司事务。

Note:

 During this next sequence there is quite a few TEXT MESSAGES on their cell phones. This will be handled like a VOICE OVER. The image of the cellphone TEXT will be shown, and at the same time the actor's voice will read the text.

注意：

 在接下来的这个片段中，他们的手机上会有很多短信。这将像画外音一样处理。手机文本的图像将会显示出来，同时演员的声音会朗读文本。

CLAUDE REARDEN
(Text Message)
Congratulations.

克劳德·里尔登
（短信）
恭喜。

ALEX
(Text Message)
Thank you.

亚历克斯
（短信）
谢谢。

Text messages were becoming more and more popular because you could text someone without another person eavesdropping or hearing the conversation such as in a public forum like a concert.

短信变得越来越流行，因为你可以给某人发短信而其他人不会窃听或听到你的谈话，例如在音乐会等公共场合。

CLAUDE REARDEN
(Text Message)
Vladimir Putin called me and wanted a meeting up in
Moscow this week.

克劳德·里尔登
（短信）
弗拉基米尔·普京打电话给我，希望本周在莫斯科
会面。

ALEX
(Text Message)
Doesn't he realize I just got married?

亚历克斯
（短信）
难道他不知道我刚结婚吗？

CLAUDE REARDEN
(Text Message)
Yes, he's duly informed.

克劳德·里尔登
（短信）
是的，他已收到通知。

ALEX
(Text Message)
You know Vladimir Putin's very demanding; I do not
think we can avoid a delay. He may discover other
options.

亚历克斯
（短信）
你知道弗拉基米尔·普京的要求非常高；我认为我
们无法避免延误。他可能会发现其他选择。

CLAUDE REARDEN
(Text Message)
You mean some other outfit like Bechtel?

克劳德·里登
（短信）
你是指像柏克德这样的其他公司吗？

ALEX
(Text Message)
Certainly, they probably could do the job.

亚历克斯
（短信）
当然，他们可能能胜任这项工作。

CLAUDE REARDEN
(Text Message)
Yes, that's what I was thinking too.

克劳德·里尔登
（短信）
是的，我也是这么想的。

Alex fast thinking announced:

亚历克斯快速思考宣布：

ALEX
(Text Message)
Alright. Inform Vladimir Putin I will go there, but I'm bringing my new wife and her parents as we extend the honeymoon to St. Petersburg and Moscow.

亚历克斯
（短信）
好的。告诉弗拉基米尔·普京我会去那里，但我会带上我的新婚妻子和她的父母，因为我们的蜜月将延长到圣彼得堡和莫斯科。

CLAUDE REARDEN
(Text Message)
I'm sure he'll understand if you bring your wife and her parents along for a vacation.

克劳德·里尔登
（短信）
我相信如果你带着你的妻子和她的父母一起去度假，他会理解的。

ALEX
(Text Message)
Okay, when do we have to be there?

亚历克斯
（短信）
好的，我们什么时候必须到那里？

CLAUDE REARDEN
Day after tomorrow.

克劳德·里尔登
后天。

ALEX
(Text Message)
I suppose that will work, since I have no other choices.

亚历克斯
（短信）
我想这可行，因为我没有其他选择。

CLAUDE REARDEN
I'll let the Russians know.

克劳德·里尔登
我会通知俄罗斯人的。

ALEX
(Text Message)
Thanks.

亚历克斯
（短信）
谢谢。

During the intermission, Christina was feeling so good getting complements from several women in the lobby who now knew who she was and simply was kissing her ass, for future business opportunities with her husband.

中场休息时，克里斯蒂娜感觉非常好，大厅里几个女人都夸她好，现在她们知道她是谁了，并且都在拍她的马屁，希望将来能与她的丈夫有商机。

Christina didn't quite understand it yet, but she would soon become the back door for enterprising businessmen to try to get to Alex for deals through their wives. And it didn't take long for Christina to discover how conniving these women were. And how they would spread vicious gossip if she stood in the way of their husbands' efforts to secure deals.

克里斯蒂娜当时还不太明白，但她很快就成了那些有进取心的商人的后门，他们试图通过他们的妻子与亚历克斯达成交易。克里斯蒂娜很快就发现这些女人是多么狡猾。如果克里斯蒂娜妨碍了她们的丈夫达成交易，她们就会散布恶意的流言蜚语。

The next morning Alex broke the news to Christina.

第二天早上，亚历克斯把这个消息告诉了克里斯蒂娜。

ALEX
We are going to fly to Moscow and St. Petersburg the following day for a business meeting. Your parents can either go with us or simply stay in Paris for a few days.

亚历克斯
第二天我们将飞往莫斯科和圣彼得堡参加商务会
议。你的父母可以和我们一起去，也可以在巴黎
呆几天。

CHRISTINA

I'll contact my parents and ask them what they want
to do.

克里斯蒂娜
我会联系我的父母，问他们想做什么。

Christina sent a text message to her mother explaining the plans. Christina was surprised how her mother responded.

克里斯蒂娜给妈妈发了一条短信，解释了这个计划。克里斯蒂娜对妈妈的回应感到惊讶。

ETHEL (a.k.a. Mrs. Garrison)
(Text Message)
Your father and I will be happy to go to Moscow with
you if you and your husband do not make too much
noise at night <wink>.

埃塞尔（又名加里森夫人）
（短信）
只要你和你丈夫晚上不制造太多噪音，你父亲和
我很乐意和你一起去莫斯科<眨眼>。

Christina broke into a mild laugh and responded.

克里斯蒂娜轻轻笑了一声并回答道。

CHRISTINA
(Text Message)
Did we do something that tipped you off?

克里斯蒂娜
（短信）
我们做了什么让你知道的事情了吗？

Christina's mother with a sense of humor responded with a joke:

克里斯蒂娜的妈妈幽默地回应了一个笑话：

ETHEL (a.k.a. Mrs. Garrison)
(Text Message)
Your father said he wished to hell he had a set of ear plugs, and it was a damn good thing he lost some hearing in Vietnam.

埃塞尔（又名加里森夫人）
（短信）
你父亲说他真希望自己有一副耳塞，幸好他在越南失去了一些听力。

Christina chuckled again and sent back a text message.

克里斯蒂娜再次轻笑一声，回复了一条短信。

CHRISTINA
(Text Message)
I'm sorry mom, but Alex makes me feel like a little girl again.

克里斯蒂娜
（短信）
对不起妈妈，但亚历克斯让我感觉自己又回到了小女孩的状态。

ETHEL (a.k.a. Mrs. Garrison)
(Text Message)
Are you enjoying yourself?

埃塞尔（又名加里森夫人）
（短信）
你玩得开心吗？

CHRISTINA
(Text Message)
Yes, I asked Alex to take me to the symphony last evening, and the women there came onto me like magnets.

克里斯蒂娜
（短信）
是的，昨晚我让亚历克斯带我去听交响乐，那里的女人像磁铁一样吸引着我。

ETHEL (a.k.a. Mrs. Garrison)
(Text Message)
That AP press report left no doubt in anyone's mind. Including your father.

埃塞尔（又名加里森夫人）
（短信）
美联社的报道让所有人都心生疑虑。包括你的父亲。

CHRISTINA
(Text Message)
There's no more speculation or rumors now.

克里斯蒂娜
（短信）
现在没有更多的猜测或谣言了。

ETHEL (a.k.a. Mrs. Garrison)
(Text Message)
Just among us girls, your father says nice things about
your husband.

埃塞尔（又名加里森夫人）
（短信）
我们几个女孩之间，你父亲对你丈夫说了很多好
话。

CHRISTINA
(Text Message)
Well Alex's a nice guy. He's always soft and gentle to
me and I can tell he likes me as much as I like him.

克里斯蒂娜
（短信）
嗯，亚历克斯是个好人。他对我总是温柔体贴，
我能感觉到他喜欢我，就像我喜欢他一样。

ETHEL (a.k.a. Mrs. Garrison)
(Text Message)
Yes, I could see that in Alex when he's around you.

埃塞尔（又名加里森夫人）
（短信）
是的，当亚历克斯在你身边时，我能看出这一点。

CHRISTINA
(Text Message)
Ok, we'll see you tomorrow.

克里斯蒂娜
（短信）
好的，我们明天见。

ETHEL (a.k.a. Mrs. Garrison)
(Text Message)
Love you.

埃塞尔（又名加里森夫人）
（短信）
爱你。


CHRISTINA
(Text Message)
I love you too mom. Thanks for everything you did for me.

克里斯蒂娜
（短信）
妈妈，我也爱你。谢谢你为我做的一切。

***

Alex and Christina boarded the GS650 the following morning to go pick up her parents in Paris.

第二天早上，亚历克斯和克里斯蒂娜登上 GS650 去巴黎接她的父母。

Alex felt bad he called Brad at the last minute, rewarded him by putting him up in the best hotel in Geneva with Gladys staying in the same hotel.

亚历克斯感到很抱歉，他在最后一刻打电话给布拉德，作为奖励，他安排布拉德住在日内瓦最好的酒店，格拉迪斯也住在同一家酒店。

ALEX
How was your hotel last night?

亚历克斯
昨晚你住的酒店怎么样？

BRAD
Thanks for you allowing us to wear our street clothes, we quickly got checked into our rooms and the manager of the hotel told us to charge our meals and drinks on the room.

布拉德
感谢您允许我们穿便装，我们很快就入住了房间，酒店经理告诉我们餐饮费用计入房费中。

ALEX
That certainly was my instructions to him.

亚历克斯
这当然是我对他的指示。

BRAD
Alex, the bar bill will probably upset you, Gladys is a
heavy drinker.

布拉德
亚历克斯，酒吧账单可能会让你不高兴，格拉迪
斯是个酒鬼。

Alex chuckled and responded:

亚历克斯笑了笑并回答道：

ALEX
I know you're pulling my leg, but under the
circumstances that's okay.

亚历克斯
我知道你在开我的玩笑，但在这种情况下没关系。

Gladys and Christina were having such a good time talking about the wedding that
Alex decided he would go up to the cockpit and spend the hour flying back to Paris
chatting with Brad in his spare time.

格拉迪斯和克里斯蒂娜谈论婚礼时玩得很开心，亚历克斯决定到驾驶舱，利用
飞回巴黎的一个小时的空闲时间和布拉德聊天。

AIR TRAFFIC CONTROLLER
N80973 you are clear for takeoff on runway 28. Wind
8 knots, 170 degrees. No inbound traffic.

空中交通管制员
N80973 您已获准在 28 号跑道起飞。风速 8 节，
风向 170 度。禁止入境交通。

BRAD
Tower this is N80973. Understand cleared to take off
on runway 28.

布拉德
塔台，这是 N80973。了解已获准在 28 号跑道起飞。

Brad advanced the throttles forward which revved up the GS650 jet engines and with very little luggage and only four passengers plus the pilot, the fuel tanks half full, the plane was light and gained altitude very rapidly. They would only climb to 35,000 feet and would start their descent in only fifteen minutes afterwards.

布拉德将油门向前推, GS650　喷气式发动机加速运转。由于行李很少，只有四名乘客和飞行员，油箱半满，飞机很轻，爬升非常快。他们只能爬升到 35,000 英尺，然后十五分钟后就开始下降。

Soon they were on final approach to Runway 27 right at Paris Charles de Gaulle Airport (CDG). Many farm fields were near the airport and since it was spring in the area, the fields were either green with this year's wheat and corn crops or being plowed.

很快，他们就进入了巴黎戴高乐机场 (CDG) 27　号跑道的最后进近。机场附近有很多农田，由于当时正值春天，田地里要么长满了今年的小麦和玉米，要么正在耕作。

Since they were stopping only to pick up Mr. and Mrs. Garrison and take on a little more fuel, they did not have to clear customs. That customs nightmare would not begin until they landed in Moscow. No doubt the FSB (KGB) would thoroughly search the aircraft. Alex was expecting to pay some official standard bribe to allow a speedy departure when the time came.

由于他们只是停下来接加里森夫妇并加点油，所以他们不需要办理海关手续。海关的噩梦要等到他们降落在莫斯科时才会开始。毫无疑问，联邦安全局（克格勃）会彻底搜查飞机。亚历克斯原本打算向某位官员支付标准贿赂，以便在时间到时迅速离开。

Alex paid the gate fee for one of the airlines at Terminal number one that would be empty for about two hours, which would be more than plenty of time to take on the fuel and collect the Garrisons as well as Trevor.

亚历克斯支付了 一 号航站楼其中一家航空公司的登机费，该航站楼大约有两个小时的空闲时间，足够加满燃料并接回加里森一家和特雷弗了。

Trevor took Christina's parents in a Limo to the airport where they would soon meet up with Alex and Christina.

特雷弗乘坐豪华轿车将克里斯蒂娜的父母送到机场，他们很快就会在那里与亚历克斯和克里斯蒂娜会合。

Since they were going into Russia, because of the gun laws, all their weapons were put in a box and stored in the cargo bay and left there. Should the FSB find the guns which were not going to be removed from the plane to keep everyone out of trouble, Alex would have to pay a $50,000 fine to get the plane released so they could depart.

由于他们要前往俄罗斯，根据枪支法，他们所有的武器都被装在一个盒子里，存放在货舱里，然后就留在那里。如果联邦安全局发现这些枪支，而这些枪支并没有被从飞机上移走，以防止大家惹上麻烦，亚历克斯将不得不支付　五万美元的罚款，才能让飞机放行，这样他们才能离开。

Since Trevor and Buster would not be apprehended with guns, they would not face any criminal prosecution. As owner of the plane, all consequences would then fall upon Alex.

由于特雷弗和巴斯特不会因携带枪支被抓，因此他们不会面临任何刑事起诉。作为飞机的主人，所有后果都将落在亚历克斯身上。

Alex didn't fear so much going into Russia since they would be monitored and watched every second on the ground. Christina and her parents were indoctrinated by Trevor who was a Russian expert and a former officer in the U.S. Navy Seals, on what to do or not do while in Russia.

亚历克斯并不怎么害怕进入俄罗斯，因为他们在当地会受到监视和时刻监视。特雷弗是俄罗斯专家，曾是美国海豹突击队军官，他告诉克里斯蒂娜和她的父母在俄罗斯应该做什么和不应该做什么。

TREVOR
Despite the end of the cold war, espionage has not ended. You must be constantly vigilant and have no dealings with any locals.

特雷弗
尽管冷战已经结束，但间谍活动并未结束。你必须时刻保持警惕，不要与任何当地人打交道。

MR. GARRISON
What if Vladimir Putin or some of his associates attempt to socialize with us?

加里森先生
如果弗拉基米尔·普京或他的一些同伙试图与我们交往怎么办？

TREVOR
Those are the only people you should meet and socialize with. Avoid all others.

特雷弗
这些人是你唯一应该见面和交往的人。避开其他人。

MR. GARRISON
Anything else we should know?

加里森先生
还有什么我们应该知道的吗？

TREVOR
Yes, never travel alone. Moscow can be a very
dangerous place for a lone woman.

特雷弗
是的，永远不要独自旅行。莫斯科对单身女性来
说可能是一个非常危险的地方。

The plane took on extra fuel and soon it was on runway 9 left starting take off. The flight to Moscow was uneventful.

飞机加了油，很快就在左侧9号跑道上起飞。飞往莫斯科的航程很顺利。

***

**EXT. DAY MOSCOW SHEREMETYEVO INTERNATIONAL AIRPORT (KHIMKI) GS650 LANDING. (15 SECONDS).**

外景。莫斯科谢列梅捷沃国际机场（希姆基）GS650 着陆。（15 秒）。

AIR TRAFFIC CONTROLLER
N80973 you are cleared to land on runway 7 left, wind
speed 6 knots 330 degrees.

空中交通管制员
N80973 您获准在跑道 7 左侧降落，风速 6 节 330
度。

BRAD
KHIMKI Tower this is N80973 understand cleared to
land on runway 7 left.

布拉德
希姆基塔台，这是 N80973，了解已获准在 7 号
跑道左侧降落。

Soon Alex's GS650 pulled into their designated parking area and two Zil Limousines pulled up followed by airport security cars. The jet engines were shut down.

很快，亚历克斯的　GS650　驶入指定停车区，两辆　齐尔　豪华轿车 （Zil Limousines）也停了下来，后面跟着机场安保车。喷气式发动机已关闭。

Gladys
Everyone put on your winter coats. It is cold outside.

格拉迪斯
大家穿上冬衣吧。外面很冷。

When everyone was buttoned up, Gladys opened the door and lowered the built-in stairs so that people could exit the aircraft.

当所有人都穿好衣服后，格拉迪斯打开了舱门，放下了内置楼梯，以便人们可以离开飞机。

Gennady Alexeyev got out of the first Zil Limousine and approached Alex's GS650 jet and reached a few feet from the steps when Alex the first person off the plane stepped down on the concrete tarmac.

根纳季·阿列克谢耶夫从第一辆　齐尔　豪华轿车　中走出来，走近阿列克谢的 GS650 喷气式飞机，当第一个下飞机的阿列克谢踏上水泥停机坪时，他已经到达了距离舷梯几英尺远的地方。

**GENNADY ALEXEYEV**
Glad you could make it on such short notice, Mr. Baxter.

根纳季·阿列克谢耶夫
很高兴您能在这么短的时间内赶到，巴克斯特先生。

**ALEX**
I want to get these Dome Cities built so I must put
forth the effort.

亚历克斯
我想要建造这些圆顶城市，所以我必须付出努力。

**GENNADY ALEXEYEV**
(Text Message)
Mr. Baxter, I will provide transportation.

根纳季·阿列克谢耶夫
（短信）
巴克斯特先生，我会提供交通工具。

Even though they had never met, Alex while in flight looked over an information package on the plane provided by Claude Rearden that showed Gennady Alexeyev's picture.

尽管他们从未见过面，但阿历克斯在飞行途中查看了克劳德·里尔登提供的飞机上的信息包，上面有根纳季·阿列克谢耶夫的照片。

**ALEX**
Thanks for meeting me here, Gennady. I'm glad to be
here if it will result in building a *Domed City*.

亚历克斯

谢谢你在这里见到我，根纳迪。如果能建造一座圆顶城市，我很高兴来到这里。

GENNADY ALEXEYEV

As you should know, Mr. Baxter, Vladimir Putin is fond of the idea of building *Domed Cities* and I'm sure he will want to get something moving soon.

根纳季·阿列克谢耶夫

巴克斯特先生，您应该知道，弗拉基米尔·普京很喜欢建造圆顶城市的想法，我相信他很快就会开始行动。

ALEX

That's good to hear because I believe Siberia would be an ideal place for *Domed Cities*.

亚历克斯

很高兴听到这个消息，因为我相信西伯利亚将是圆顶城市的理想之地。

GENNADY ALEXEYEV

Not that many people in Siberia vote, that's why we have other ideas which we'll present to you in a while.

根纳季·阿列克谢耶夫

西伯利亚投票的人并不多，这就是为什么我们有其他想法，稍后会向大家介绍。

ALEX

Gennady, I made our reservations for the hotel you recommended.

亚历克斯

根纳迪，我预订了你推荐的酒店。

GENNADY ALEXEYEV

Alex, we contacted the hotel and made sure you were booked and will have rapid check-in for your family, your security detail, and your flight crew.

根纳季·阿列克谢耶夫

亚历克斯，我们联系了酒店并确保您已预订，并将为您的家人、安保人员和机组人员快速办理入住。

ALEX
Thank you.

亚历克斯
谢谢。

GENNADY ALEXEYEV
We'll take everyone now except your flight crew to the hotel, then when they get done with locking down the plane, we have a car that will wait here to take them.

根纳季·阿列克谢耶夫
我们现在会把除了机组人员之外的所有人送往酒店，等他们锁好飞机后，我们会有一辆车在这里等着接他们。

ALEX
Thanks. I appreciate that.

亚历克斯
谢谢。我很感激。

A couple men approached, then Gennady announced:

一对男子走了过来，然后根纳迪宣布道：

GENNADY ALEXEYEV
These men are here to unload your luggage and will take it to your hotel.

根纳迪·阿列克谢耶夫
这些人来这里是为了卸下您的行李并将其运送到您的酒店。

ALEX
My pilot Brad will soon open the cargo bay, and they can get the luggage out then.

亚历克斯
我的飞行员布拉德很快就会打开货舱，然后他们就可以把行李拿出来了。

GENNADY ALEXEYEV
Alright.

根纳季·阿列克谢耶夫
好的。

ALEX
Gennady, this is my wife, Christina.

亚历克斯
根纳迪，这是我的妻子克里斯蒂娜。

GENNADY ALEXEYEV
Mrs. Baxter, you are very beautiful, I'm so happy to meet you.

根纳季·阿列克谢耶夫
巴克斯特女士，您非常漂亮，我很高兴见到您。

Gennady held out his hand to shake Christina's.

根纳迪伸出手来和克里斯蒂娜握手。

CHRISTINA
Eto bol'shaya chest' vstretit'sya s vami Gennadiya.
[Это большая честь встретиться с вами Геннадия.]
{It is an honor to meet you Gennady.}

克里斯蒂娜
很荣幸见到你根纳迪。

GENNADY ALEXEYEV
Mrs. Baxter, you speak Russian?

根纳季·阿列克谢耶夫
巴克斯特女士，您会说俄语吗？

CHRISTINA
Yes, I majored in both Russian and Economics at the University.

克里斯蒂娜
是的，我在大学主修俄语和经济学。

GENNADY ALEXEYEV
(Thought)
*Russian Intelligence hates to miss out on big information such as Mrs. Baxter's ability to speak Russian; someone will have to answer for this.*

根纳季·阿列克谢耶夫
（思考）
俄罗斯情报部门不愿错过重要信息，例如巴克斯特夫人会说俄语；总得有人对此负责。

ALEX
Gennady, this is my mother and father-in-law, Ethel
and William Garrison.

亚历克斯
根纳迪，这是我的岳母和岳父埃塞尔和威廉·加里
森。

GENNADY ALEXEYEV
Please to meet you Ethel and William.

根纳季·阿列克谢耶夫
很高兴见到埃塞尔和威廉。

Gennady shook the Garrison's family hands.

根纳迪与加里森一家人握手。

ALEX
Very well why don't we get in the cars and drive to
the hotel.

亚历克斯
好吧，我们为什么不上车去酒店呢？

GENNADY ALEXEYEV
I would like Mr. and Mrs. Baxter to ride with me in
the first car, The Garrisons and your security detail in
the second car.

根纳季·阿列克谢耶夫
我希望巴克斯特先生和夫人和我一起乘坐第一辆
车，加里森一家和您的保镖乘坐第二辆车。

Everyone understood and took their positions in the cars. The two Limousines
immediately departed the parked GS650 and made their way to the hotel.

大家都明白了，各自坐上车，两辆豪华轿车立刻驶离停在路边的 GS650，朝酒
店驶去。

FLASHBACK
倒叙

Before they left Switzerland Alex warned Christina:

在他们离开瑞士之前，亚历克斯警告克里斯蒂娜：

ALEX

We will be under severe scrutiny and every move we
make in Russia will be observed and espionage is alive
and well, so be careful what you do.

亚历克斯
我们将受到严格的审查，我们在俄罗斯的一举一
动都将受到观察，间谍活动依然存在，所以要小
心你的所作所为。

Mr. Garrison a former Green Beret was also well versed on Russian espionage and
privately told his wife back in Paris the same thing.

前绿色贝雷帽队员加里森先生也熟悉俄罗斯的间谍活动，他私下里向远在巴黎
的妻子透露了同样的事情。

<u>END FLASHBACK</u>

结束闪回

At the edge of the Airport a police car moved in front of the Zil Limo's, and one pulled
into the rear and followed them to the center of Moscow where they pulled up to *the
Baltschug Kempinski Hote*l. This five-star Hotel has spectacular views of the Kremlin
and St. Basil's Cathedral.

在机场边缘，一辆警车停在 齐尔 豪华轿车 前面，另一辆警车停在后面，跟随
它们前往莫斯科市中心，然后停在巴尔舒格凯宾斯基酒店 (Baltschug Kempinski
Hotel)　。这家五星级酒店可以欣赏到克里姆林宫和圣巴西尔大教堂的壮丽景
色。

GENNADY ALEXEYEV

After you and your wife have a chance to freshen up
you will be taken somewhere for a preliminary meeting
with Putin. Bring your bride because Vladimir Putin is
eager to meet her.

根纳季·阿列克谢耶夫
您和您的妻子梳洗完毕后，将被带往某处与普京
进行初步会晤。带上您的新娘，因为弗拉基米尔·
普京非常渴望与她见面。

ALEX
Sure, we'll get ready, and I'll contact you.

*Baltschug Kempinski Hotel* is located next to the Moskva River, and a nice park to
walk along. The Hotel was originally built in 1898 and as the oil money flowed in
during the twentieth century and Moscow got a facelift, the Hotel was renovated by

eager investors and each one of its 227 rooms is elegant and pleasing to the eye. It has a couple restaurants, a bar, and health club.

巴尔舒格凯宾斯基酒店毗邻莫斯科河，旁边还有一座适合散步的公园。酒店最初建于 1898 年，随着 20 世纪石油资金的涌入和莫斯科的改建，酒店被热切的投资者翻新，其 227 间客房每一间都优雅而赏心悦目。酒店设有几家餐厅、一间酒吧和健身俱乐部。

The event that Mr. Garrison would never dream of experiencing in his lifetime was now unfolding as he opened the curtain to his hotel room and was staring directly at *Moscow's Red Square.*

当加里森先生拉开酒店房间的窗帘，直视莫斯科红场时，他一生中做梦也想不到的事情正在发生。

And in all his wildest imagination, it never occurred to William Garrison he would be with his daughter on her honeymoon staring directly at St. Basil's Cathedral from a the *Baltschug Kempinski Hotel.*

即使威廉·加里森 (William Garrison) 想象得再疯狂，他也没有想到自己会和女儿一起度蜜月，在巴尔舒格凯宾斯基酒店直视圣巴西尔大教堂。

William Garrison smiled at Ethel Garrison then announced:

威廉·加里森对埃塞尔·加里森笑了笑，然后宣布：

WILLIAM GARRISON<br>
This is where we should have had the wedding!

威廉·加里森<br>
我们应该在这里举行婚礼！

ETHEL GARRISON<br>
Oh, but Paris was the ideal romantic place. Christina<br>
can tell her children she was married in Paris.

埃塞尔·加里森<br>
哦，但巴黎是理想的浪漫之地。克里斯蒂娜可以<br>
告诉她的孩子们，她是在巴黎结婚的。

Christina and Alex were getting settled into their hotel room.

克里斯蒂娜和亚历克斯正在安顿酒店房间。

CHRISTINA<br>
It's a good thing you made me bring all those dresses along.

克里斯蒂娜和亚历克斯正在安顿酒店房间。

ALEX
Christina, I love to see you dressed up.

亚历克斯
克里斯蒂娜，我喜欢看到你盛装打扮。

CHRISTINA
But I do not have a makeup artist here.

克里斯蒂娜
但我这里没有化妆师。

ALEX
Let's check with the hotel, don't make any assumptions.

亚历克斯
我们先跟酒店确认一下，不要做任何假设。

Alex picked up the phone and called the front desk. The person could not speak English very well, so Alex responded:

亚历克斯拿起电话给前台打电话。前台的工作人员英语不太好，于是 亚历克斯回答道：

ALEX
Excuse me for one minute.

亚历克斯
请稍等片刻。

Alex then handed the phone to Christina.

然后亚历克斯把手机递给了克里斯蒂娜。

ALEX
Christina, you talk to them, because I can't understand Russian.

亚历克斯
克里斯蒂娜，你和他们说话，因为我听不懂俄语。

Christina got on the phone.

克里斯蒂娜接了电话。

CHRISTINA
(KRISTINA)
Privet, eto missis Bakster. Mne interesno, yest' li u vas v otele sotrudniki, kotoryye zanimayutsya makiyazhem i kosmetikoy?

[Привет это миссис Бакстер, мне было интересно, если у вас какие-либо работники в гостинице, которые делают макияж и косметику?]

{Hello this is Mrs. Baxter; I was wondering if you had any workers in the hotel that do makeup and cosmetics?}

克里斯蒂娜
您好，我是巴克斯特女士，我想知道酒店里是否有化妆和美容的工作人员？

The response from the front desk was positive.

前台的回应是积极的。

CHRISTINA
Вы делаете? Это замечательно!
[Вы делаете? Это прекрасно!]
{You do? That's wonderful!

克里斯蒂娜
你真的这么做吗？太棒了！

FRONT DESK
Yesli vam nuzhna vizazhist, ona seychas dostupna.
[*Если вам нужна визажист, она сейчас доступна.*]
The makeup artist is available now if you need her.

前台
如果您需要，化妆师现在就可以为您服务。

CHRISTINA
Ne mogli by vy seychas prislat' ko mne v komnatu vizazhista?
[Не могли бы вы сейчас прислать ко мне в комнату визажиста?]
{Could you please send the makeup artist to my room now?}

克里斯蒂娜
{您现在可以派化妆师来我的房间吗？}

FRONT DESK
Vizazhist seychas pridet k vam v nomer.
[Визажист сейчас придет к вам в номер.]
{The makeup artist will be sent to your room now.}


前台
{化妆师现在将被派往您的房间。}


CHRISTINA
O, spasibo vam ogromnoye!
[О, спасибо вам большое!]
{Oh, thank you so very much!}


克里斯蒂娜
哦，非常感谢！


The beautiful young blonde Russian lady arrived within five minutes to do Christina's makeup. Christina wanted to be alone with the girl while she was getting all made up.

这位年轻漂亮的金发俄罗斯女士在五分钟内就赶到了，为克里斯蒂娜化妆。克里斯蒂娜想在化妆时和女孩单独相处。


CHRISTINA
Alex, would you mind taking my father for a walk
and ask my mother if she wouldn't mind coming over
because she might like to get made-up too.


克里斯蒂娜
亚历克斯，你介意带我爸爸出去走走吗？然后问
问我妈妈是否愿意过来，因为她可能也想化妆。


Alex smiled when he said the white lie. But love does that to a man. Just like Mrs. Garrison, it wasn't long before Christina wore the pants in the family.

亚历克斯在撒谎时面带微笑。但爱情对男人来说就是这样。就像加里森夫人一样，克里斯蒂娜很快就成了家里的掌权者。


ALEX
I would be delighted too.


亚历克斯
我也会很高兴。


Alex walked out of hotel room where there his security detachment of two former navy seals sitting in chairs facing two Russian FSB (KGB) agents, barely tolerating each other.

亚历克斯走出酒店房间，他的安全支队由两名前海豹突击队员组成，他们坐在椅子上，对面是两名俄罗斯联邦安全局 (KGB) 特工，几乎无法容忍对方。

The two former Soviet Spetsnaz soldiers may have traded gunfire with the seals sometime in the past. But they would never know for sure.

这两名前苏联特种部队士兵可能在过去某个时候与海豹突击队交火过。但他们永远无法确定。

Alex ignored the security men and walked down to the next room and knocked on the door and announced:

阿历克斯无视保安人员，走到隔壁房间，敲门并宣布：

ALEX
Mr. Garrison, it's Alex.

亚历克斯
加里森先生，我是亚历克斯。

In about 30 seconds the door opened, and Mr. Garrison asked:

大约 30 秒后，门开了，加里森先生问道：

MR. GARRISON
What's up Alex?

加里森先生
亚历克斯，怎么了？

ALEX
Papa, Christina wants me to take you for a walk and
she would like her mother to go to our room for a
while she gets her makeup done by a professional.

亚历克斯
爸爸，克里斯蒂娜想让我带你去散步，她想让她
妈妈去我们房间一会儿，让专业人士帮她化妆。

Mr. Garrison was just about ready to say he didn't feel like going for a walk when his wife suddenly appeared and announced:

加里森先生刚要说他不想出去散步，他的妻子突然出现并宣布：

MRS. GARRISON
That's an excellent idea honey; you two guys need to
go get to know each other a little better.

加里森夫人
亲爱的，这是个好主意；你们两个需要多了解一
下彼此。

MR. GARRISON
Yes dear, let me grab my jacket.

加里森先生
是的，亲爱的，让我拿一下我的夹克。

Alex and Mr. Garrison walked down the hallway to the elevator and as they approached it, a Navy Seal and a Spetsnaz followed along. As it turned out the Spetsnaz guy would get into a lot more trouble if something happened to Alex than the Seal would have.

亚历克斯和加里森先生沿着走廊走向电梯，当他们接近电梯时，一名海豹突击队队员和一名特种部队队员跟在后面。事实证明，如果亚历克斯出了什么事，特种部队队员会比海豹突击队队员惹上更大的麻烦。

They took the elevator down to the ground floor and when they stepped out of the elevator Alex asked Mr. Garrison:

他们乘电梯来到一楼，走出电梯后，亚历克斯问加里森先生：

ALEX
Papa, where would you like to walk to?

亚历克斯
爸爸，您想步行去哪里吗？

MR. GARRISON
Why don't we walk across the street and visit St. Basil's Cathedral?

加里森先生
我们何不走过马路去参观圣巴西尔大教堂？

ALEX
Sure.

亚历克斯
当然了。

<u>MUSIC FOR THE NEXT SEGMENT:</u>

<u>11 SHOSTAKOVICH Symph No 11 The Year 1905 in G min Op 103 Dir Valery Gergiev Mariinsky Orchestra - YouTube</u>

下一乐段的音乐：

11 肖斯塔科维奇 第 11 号交响曲 1905 年，G 小调，作品 103，指挥：瓦列里·捷杰耶夫 马林斯基管弦乐团 – YouTube

They crossed the street and went to the Cathedral and walked up to the reception area and asked where they could buy a ticket.

他们穿过马路来到大教堂，走到接待处询问在哪里可以买票。

In poor English the Russian Receptionist got the point across:

俄罗斯人用蹩脚的英语表达了他们的观点：

RECEPTIONIST
I'm sorry we are sold out.

接待员
很抱歉，我们的票已经卖完了。

The former Russian Spetsnaz guy now an FSB Agent following along heard Alex's request and receptionist statements. The FSB Agent walked up to the Russian clerk spoke a couple sentences in Russian.

这位前俄罗斯特种部队成员，现为联邦安全局特工，跟在后面听了亚历克斯的请求和接待员的陈述。联邦安全局特工走到俄罗斯职员面前，用俄语说了几句话。

The only words Alex recognized were *Vladimir Putin*. As soon as the FSB Agent showed the receptionist his ID, the receptionist issued all of them tickets.

阿历克斯唯一听得懂的词是弗拉基米尔·普京。联邦安全局特工向接待员出示他的身份证后，接待员立即向他们所有人发放了机票。

FSB AGENT
Please follow me Mr. Baxter and Mr. Garrison.

联邦安全局代理
请跟我来，巴克斯特先生和加里森先生。

<u>INT. DAY. MOSCOW RUSSIA. INSIDE ST. BASIL'S CATHEDRAL</u>

The group then went inside St. Basil's Cathedral.

随后，一行人进入了圣巴西尔大教堂。

FSB AGENT
Instead of you following the tourists around I will give you the guided tour.

联邦安全局代理
你不用跟着游客到处走，我会带你参观。

ALEX
We appreciate that.

亚历克斯
我们对此表示赞赏。

The former Spetznez FSB agent got into a little of the history of St. Basil's Cathedral:

这位前联邦安全局特种部队特工介绍了一些圣巴西尔大教堂的历史：

FSB AGENT
This Cathedral was built from 1555–1561 on orders from Ivan the Terrible and commemorates the capture of Kazan and Astrakhan. It was the city's tallest building until the completion of the Ivan the Great Bell Tower in 1600.

联邦安全局代理
这座大教堂于 1555 年至 1561 年根据伊凡雷帝的命令建造，旨在纪念攻克喀山和阿斯特拉罕。在 1600 年伊凡大帝钟楼建成之前，它一直是这座城市最高的建筑。

Note:

Siege of Kazan - Wikipedia

Kazan - Wikipedia

笔记：

喀山围攻 - 维基百科

喀山 - 维基百科

FSB AGENT
As part of the program of state atheism, the church was confiscated from the Russian Orthodox community as part of the Soviet Union's antitheist campaigns and has operated as a division of the State Historical Museum since 1928.

联邦安全局特工
作为国家无神论计划的一部分，这座教堂在苏联反神论运动中被从俄罗斯东正教社区没收，自

1928 年以来一直作为国家历史博物馆的一个部门运营。

It is not actually within the Kremlin but often served as a visual symbol for Russia in American media throughout the Cold War.

它实际上并不在克里姆林宫内，但在整个冷战期间，它经常在美国媒体上作为俄罗斯的视觉象征。

The identity of the architect is unknown. Tradition held that the church was built by two architects, Barma and Postnik.

建筑师的身份不详。传统认为这座教堂是由两位建筑师巴尔玛 (Barma) 和波斯特尼克 (Postnik) 建造的。

The official Russian cultural heritage register lists Barma and Postnik Yakovlev as the St. Basil's Cathedral architects.

俄罗斯官方文化遗产登记册将巴尔马和波斯特尼克·雅科夫列夫列为圣巴西尔大教堂的建筑师。

The four men walked around for a while, observing the beauty of all the artwork that went into the building of St. Basil's Cathedral.

四个人走了一会儿，观察着圣巴西尔大教堂内所有艺术品的美丽。

Note:  St Basil's Cathedral Inside - Search Images

注：圣巴西尔大教堂内部 - 搜索图片

ALEX
St. Basil's Cathedral is very beautiful.

亚历克斯
圣瓦西里大教堂非常漂亮。

MR. GARRISON
Yes, incredible artists were at work here.

加里森先生
是的，这里有着令人惊叹的艺术家。

Alex turned to the FSB agent.

亚历克斯转向联邦安全局特工。

ALEX
Are you a Russian Orthodox?

亚历克斯
您是俄罗斯东正教徒吗？

FSB AGENT
Yes, I am.

联邦安全局代理
我是。

After walking around a while inside St. Basil's Cathedral, Alex suddenly announced:

在圣瓦西里大教堂内走了一会儿后，亚历克斯突然宣布道：

ALEX
Let's walk around Red Square and see some of the sights.

亚历克斯
让我们在红场周围走走，看看一些景点。

FSB AGENT
Let me show you the way.

联邦安全局代理
让我给你指路。

The Russian FSB Agent was being very polite and courteous. Alex would extend his appreciation at the proper time.

俄罗斯联邦安全局特工非常有礼貌和谦恭。亚历克斯会在适当的时候表达他的谢意。

The men walked around RED SQUARE and saw the monument to Kusma Minin.

Note: Kuzma Minin - Wikipedia

这些人绕着红场走了一圈，看到了库兹马·米宁的纪念碑。

注：库兹马·米宁 - 维基百科

Since it was next to Kusma Minin's monument Alex and Mr. Garrison were shown and briefed about the Lobnoye Mesto and its history.

Note: Lobnoye Mesto - Wikipedia.

由于它紧邻库斯马·米宁 (Kusma Minin) 的纪念碑，亚历克斯 (Alex) 和加里森先生参观了洛布诺耶梅斯托，并听取了关于它的历史的简要介绍。

注：洛布诺耶梅斯托 - 维基百科。

Next, they came up to Lenin's Mausoleum.

Note: Lenin's Mausoleum - Wikipedia

接下来，他们来到了列宁陵墓。

注：列宁陵墓 - 维基百科

There were Japanese tourists there taking pictures of Lenin.

有日本游客在那里拍摄列宁的照片。

Then the FSB Agent took them inside the State Historical Museum.

Note: State Historical Museum - Wikipedia

Note: Inside pictures of Russia's Red Square State Historical Museum:

Inside the Russian State Historical Museum - Search Images

随后，联邦安全局特工将他们带入国家历史博物馆。

注：国家历史博物馆 - 维基百科

注：俄罗斯红场国家历史博物馆内部图片：

俄罗斯国家历史博物馆内部 - 搜索图片

In due time their Russian handler led them inside the State Historical Museum despite protests from an anxious clerk who feared she might be stuck in traffic if she did not leave soon.

她们准时到达了俄罗斯管理员所在地，尽管一名焦虑的工作人员担心她如果不尽快离开，可能会被困在交通堵塞中，但仍将她们带入了国家历史博物馆。

Alex soon was staring at Carlo Rastelli's silver death mask of Peter the Great:

Death Mask of Peter I - Virtual Russian Museum

亚历克斯很快就盯着卡洛·拉斯特利的彼得大帝银质死亡面具：

彼得一世死亡面具 - 虚拟俄罗斯博物馆

Red Square's State Historical Museum displays a rich collection of artifacts that tell the history of the Russian lands from the Paleolithic period to the present day.

红场的国家历史博物馆展示了丰富的文物，讲述了俄罗斯从旧石器时代到现在的历史。

### MR. GARRISON
Look at these paintings. This is rather incredible. As a
history teacher I'm truly humbled looking at all this.
Alex, you made my day many times over.

### 加里森先生
看看这些画。这真是太不可思议了。作为一名历
史老师，看到这一切，我真的很谦卑。亚历克
斯，你让我的心情好了很多倍。

### ALEX
Papa, you produced Christina the love of my life. You
made my day many times over as well.

### 亚历克斯
爸爸，您让克里斯蒂娜成为我一生的挚爱。您也
让我的心情无比愉悦。

Mr. Garrison was suddenly glad he listened to his wife Ethel and went on this
astonishing walk with Alex.

加里森先生突然很高兴他听了妻子埃塞尔的话，和亚历克斯一起进行了这次令
人惊奇的散步。

### FSB AGENT
Mr. Baxter, we also have another State History
Museum in St. Petersburg along with the Hermitage
you should see. They also have fabulous paintings.

### 联邦安全局代理
巴克斯特先生，我们在圣彼得堡还有另一个国家
历史博物馆以及您应该参观的艾尔米塔什博物
馆。他们也有精美的画作。

### ALEX
I want to take my wife and her parents to St. Petersburg
and see all that.

### 亚历克斯
我想带我的妻子和她的父母去圣彼得堡看看这一切。

Being mindful of the young lady who needed to leave soon, Alex announced:

考虑到这位年轻女士很快就要离开了，亚历克斯宣布：

### ALEX
I think it's time we left and let the young lady go home
for the day.

亚历克斯
我想我们该离开了，让这位年轻女士回家休息一天。

FSB AGENT
You are very considerate, Mr. Baxter.

联邦安全局代理
你很体贴，巴克斯特先生。

ALEX
Thank you.

亚历克斯
谢谢。

As they walked by GUM Department Store (Glavny Universalny Magazin), Alex announced:

当他们走过 GUM 百货商店（Glavny Universalny Magazine）时，亚历克斯宣布：

ALEX
Let's go inside here.

亚历克斯

我们进去看看吧。

**GUM (department store) - Wikipedia**

GUM（百货公司）- 维基百科

The four men walked around inside the GUM department store for a while looking at a lot of interesting items for sale when Alex suddenly saw some delicious snacks. Alex knew they were well beyond the financial reach of the two Russian security guys, so he decided to buy enough snacks for all the security men including the two left behind to protect Mrs. Garison and Christina.

四个人在 GUM 百货商场里逛了一会儿，看着很多有趣的商品，亚历克斯突然看到一些美味的零食。亚历克斯知道这些零食远远超出了两个俄罗斯保安的财力，所以他决定给所有保安买足够的零食，包括留下来保护加里森夫人和克里斯蒂娜的那两个保安。

Thinking ahead Alex bought Russian Rubbles in Paris so that he could buy things without any trouble. Alex reached into his pockets and pulled out double the amount for the cost of the delicious snacks.

亚历克斯深思熟虑后，在巴黎买了俄罗斯卢布，这样他就可以毫无障碍地买东西了。亚历克斯伸手到口袋里，掏出双倍的钱来买这些美味小吃。

ALEX
Keep the change.

亚历克斯
留着零钱吧。

The clerk slightly broke down crying because this one generous gift just paid her rent for the next two months, and her family would be far more content for a while.

店员有些失声痛哭，因为这一份慷慨的礼物刚好够她支付接下来两个月的房租，她的家庭暂时会过得幸福很多。

ALEX
Let's take these snacks back to the hotel and see if the
women are ready.

亚历克斯
我们把这些零食带回酒店，看看女人们准备好了吗？

As they were approaching GUM's entrance Alex noticed a place that sold canned sodas and ordered half a dozen of them and asked Buster to help carry them. Soon he was back at the hotel and handed the snacks and sodas to the Russians and his two security men.

当他们接近 GUM 的入口时，亚历克斯注意到一家卖罐装苏打水的地方，于是他订购了六罐，并让巴斯特帮忙搬运。很快他就回到了酒店，把零食和苏打水递给了俄罗斯人和两名保安人员。

ALEX
Thank you for protecting me, here's some drinks and
snacks in case you get hungry or thirsty.

亚历克斯
谢谢你保护我，这里有一些饮料和零食，以防你
饿了或渴了。

FSB AGENT
Sir, it's not professional for us to drink or snack on duty.

联邦安全局代理
先生，我们值班时喝酒或吃零食是不专业的。

ALEX
Don't you guys take smoke breaks or use the restroom?

亚历克斯
你们不抽烟或上厕所吗？

FSB AGENT
Certainly.

联邦安全局代理
当然。

ALEX
Well, take a snack and drink break at the same time.

亚历克斯
我们可以同时吃点零食和喝点饮料。

The Russian smiled.

俄罗斯人笑了。

FSB AGENT
Yes sir, we will,

联邦安全局代理
是的，先生，我们会的，

Alex knocked on the door and announced:

亚历克斯敲了敲门，宣布道：

ALEX
Christina, it's me Alex.

亚历克斯
克里斯蒂娜，我是亚历克斯。

Mrs. Garrison stuck her face through a small opening in the door after she opened the door and responded:

加里森女士打开门后，把脸探进门上的一个小缝隙，回答道：

MRS. GARRISON
Alex, we are not done yet, please come back in about
a half an hour.

加里森夫人
亚历克斯，我们还没说完，请半小时后再来。

Alex then heard some laughter in the background.

然后亚历克斯听到背景中传来一些笑声。

ALEX
Ok, mother.

亚历克斯
好的，妈妈。

After Mrs. Garrison closed the hotel room door, Mr. Garrison asked:

加里森女士关上酒店房间门后，加里森先生问道：

MR. GARRISON
Where too now, Alex?

加里森先生
亚历克斯现在在哪里？

ALEX
I have a really good idea.

亚历克斯
我有一个非常好的主意。

Alex had an evil thought:
亚历克斯心里有一个邪恶的想法：

ALEX (Thought)
*I would love to get this Russian FSB handler intoxicated.*

亚历克斯（思考）
我很想让这位俄罗斯联邦安全局的管理人员喝醉。

Alex led Mr. Garrison, and two security men went down to the hotel bar located by the main entrance. In a few minutes the four were sitting at the hotel bar and Alex knew how to prime the pump.

阿历克斯带着加里森先生和两名保安来到位于正门旁的酒店酒吧。几分钟后，他们四个人就坐在了酒店的酒吧里，阿历克斯知道如何启动水泵。

ALEX
I know you guys are not supposed to drink on duty,
but I'm going to order you a drink so that it looks like
you're my friend, so nobody gets suspicious.

亚历克斯
我知道你们不应该在值班时喝酒，但我会请你们
喝一杯，这样看起来你们是我的朋友，这样就不
会引起任何人的怀疑。

FSB AGENT
Okay.

联邦安全局代理
好的。

Alex then ordered a round of vodka shots and demanded the bartender have one with them. But after Alex left a huge tip after paying for the round of drinks the bar tender had a change of heart and so the four men toasted.

随后，亚历克斯点了一轮伏特加，并要求酒保再给他们一杯。但亚历克斯付完酒钱后留下了一大笔小费，酒保改变了主意，于是四个人干杯。

ALEX
Here's to your health.

联邦安全局代理
好的。

BARTENDER
Vot dlya vashego zdorov'ya.
[вот для вашего здоровья.]
{Here's for your health.}

调酒师
这是为了您的健康。

In a short while the Russian FSB agent excused himself and went to the restroom.

没过多久，这名俄罗斯联邦安全局特工就去洗手间了。

ALEX (Thought)
I wonder if he's calling his office or something.

亚历克斯（思考）
不知道他是不是在给他的办公室打电话或者做别的事。

While the FSB Agent was gone Alex said to the bartender:

当联邦安全局特工离开时，亚历克斯对调酒师说：

ALEX
Keep his glass full. Here's another tip.

亚历克斯
把他的杯子装满。这是另一个提示。

The bartender who spoke English had almost a Chesshire Cat smile after looking at the size of the tip.

说英语的酒保看到小费的数额后，脸上露出了近乎柴郡猫般的微笑。

When the FSB Agent came back Alex reported:

当 联邦安全局代理回来时，亚历克斯报告说：

ALEX
We toasted again while you were gone.

亚历克斯
你不在的时候我们又举杯了。

The Russian unwittingly fell for the trick and quickly swallowed the full shot. Russian shot glasses are about double the size of Americans, so just two shots is already a lot of booze.

俄罗斯人无意中中计，很快就喝光了整杯酒。俄罗斯人的酒杯大约是美国人的两倍大，所以两杯酒就已经是不少了。

Alex then decided it was about time for another shot and since the Russian had been "primed," this time it didn't take too much time for him to decide to down the Vodka. The vodka he was drinking was about 20 times more expensive than what he normally drank and tasted that much better as well.

亚历克斯决定再来一杯，由于俄罗斯人已经 "喝醉了"，这次他没花太多时间就决定喝下伏特加。他喝的伏特加比他平时喝的伏特加贵 20 倍左右，而且味道也好得多。

Alex kept a close look on his watch and about the 25-minute mark announced:

亚历克斯密切关注着他的手表，大约 25 分钟后他宣布：

ALEX
Ok, let's go back and see the ladies.

亚历克斯
好吧，我们回去看看女士们。

Alex had just enough to get a nice buzz off the vodka, but as nowhere near a level of intoxication as the FSB Agent now experienced. Unfortunately, the Russian FSB Agent had drunk significantly more and was now feeling it.

亚历克斯喝了足够的伏特加，但醉意远不及　联邦安全局代理现在所经历的程度。不幸的是，俄罗斯 联邦安全局代理喝得更多，现在感觉很好。

This time when Alex knocked on the door, Mrs. Garrison opened it and said you may come in now and then she left and the young blonde girl carrying her pouch did as well.

这次当亚历克斯敲门时，加里森夫人打开门并说你可以进来，然后她就离开了，带着小袋子的金发小女孩也走了。

Mrs. Garrison looked good too.

加里森夫人看上去也不错。

Alex went inside, shut the door and called for Christina, who yelled back:

亚历克斯走进去，关上门，叫了克里斯蒂娜，克里斯蒂娜喊道：

CHRISTINA
I'm getting dressed; I'll be out in a minute.

克里斯蒂娜
我正在穿衣服；一会儿就出去。

Alex walked over and sat down on the sofa thinking if he should change or just wear the business suit he had on.

亚历克斯走过去，坐在沙发上，考虑是否应该换衣服，或者就穿他身上的西装。

Christina suddenly appeared and she looked spectacular.

克里斯蒂娜突然出现，看上去非常美丽。

ALEX
Wow you look gorgeous.

亚历克斯
哇你看起来很漂亮。

CHRISTINA
Why thank you.

克里斯蒂娜
谢谢你。

Suddenly there was a knock at the door, Alex opened the door. Buster was there and reported:

突然，门外传来一阵敲门声，亚历克斯开了门。巴斯特当时就在那里并报告说：

BUSTER
Mr. Baxter, Gennady Alexeyev is here to see you.

巴斯特
巴克斯特先生，根纳迪·阿列克谢耶夫来见您了。

Alex opened the door a little more and Gennady Alexeyev explained:

阿历克斯把门打开了一点，根纳季·阿历克斯耶夫解释道：

GENNADY ALEXEYEV
Alex, we have two Limo's downstairs, and we are ready to take you to the meeting. Please bring your wife and in-laws with you.

根纳季·阿列克谢耶夫
亚历克斯，我们楼下有两辆豪华轿车，我们已经准备好带您去参加会议。请带上你的妻子和公婆。

ALEX
I really didn't have time to change my clothes.

亚历克斯 (
我真的没有时间换衣服。

GENNADY ALEXEYEV
Alex, your appearance is very distinguished sir, I recommend you come as you are.

根纳季·阿列克谢耶夫
亚历克斯，您的相貌非常尊贵，先生，我建议您就这样来吧。

Thanks to the Vodka, Alex was somewhat disarmed psychologically.

喝了伏特加之后，阿历克斯的心理防线稍微放松了一些。

ALEX (Thought)
*Sure, what the heck.*

亚历克斯（思考）
当然，管他呢。

ALEX
Sure, let me get everyone, I'll meet you in the Hotel lobby.

亚历克斯
当然，让我来召集大家，我会在酒店大堂与您见面。

GENNADY ALEXEYEV
We'll be waiting.

根纳季·阿列克谢耶夫
我们会等待。

ALEX
Thank you.

亚历克斯
谢谢。

Alex closed the door of the hotel room then turned to Christina. Since Christina was just a few feet away from Alex, she smelled the Vodka on his breath, and asked:

亚历克斯关上酒店房间的门，然后转向克里斯蒂娜。克里斯蒂娜离亚历克斯只有几英尺远，她闻到了他嘴里伏特加的味道，于是问道：

CHRISTINA
Did you buy my daddy drinks?

克里斯蒂娜
你给我爸爸买饮料了吗？

ALEX
Only a couple.

亚历克斯
只有一对。

CHRISTINA
Don't make a habit of it, he shouldn't drink too much
at his age.

克里斯蒂娜
别养成这种习惯，他这个年纪不应该喝太多酒。

Alex right then and there realized there was much more to Christina than he imagined and now understood she was a woman of principals and expectations. It was too late to back out now. He would slowly have to learn how to get along with Christina and avoid any more mine fields.

亚历克斯当时就意识到克里斯蒂娜远比他想象的要复杂得多，现在他明白了她是一个有原则、有期望的女人。现在退缩已经太晚了。他现在必须慢慢学会如何与克里斯蒂娜相处，避免更多的雷区。

ALEX
Understand dear.

亚历克斯
理解亲爱的。

Christina threw her arms around Alex and hugged him and announced:

克里斯蒂娜张开双臂拥抱了亚历克斯并宣布：

CHRISTINA
I'm ready, my mother will get ready quickly, I'll go get them.

克里斯蒂娜
我准备好了，我妈妈很快就会准备好，我去接他们。

ALEX
Thank you.

亚历克斯
谢谢。

Christina went next door to her parents' room and knocked on the door. Mr. Garrison opened the door for Christina. She didn't smell the booze on her daddy and asked him:

克里斯蒂娜走到隔壁父母的房间，敲了敲门。加里森先生为克里斯蒂娜开了门。她没有闻到爸爸身上的酒味，问他：

CHRISTINA
Didn't you have drinks with Alex?

克里斯蒂娜
你没有和亚历克斯一起喝酒吗？

WILLIAM (a.k.a. Mr. Garrison)
Yes, when Alex wasn't looking, I told the bartender to give me just water, I don't really care for Vodka.

威廉（又名加里森先生）
是的，当亚历克斯没注意的时候，我告诉酒保只给我水，我不太喜欢伏特加。

Christina threw her arms around her daddy.

克里斯蒂娜张开双臂拥抱了她的爸爸。

CHRISTINA
Daddy, you are so smart.

克里斯蒂娜
爸爸，你真聪明。

Christina looked at her mother who wasn't dressing fast enough for her desires, and spoke:

克里斯蒂娜看着母亲那没有按照她的意愿快速穿衣服的样子，说道：

CHRISTINA
Mother, hurry up, we must go now.

克里斯蒂娜
妈妈，快点，我们必须走了。

A moment later Mrs. Garrison walked out of the bathroom looking spectacular.

一会儿之后，加里森夫人从浴室走了出来，看上去美极了。

While Christina was at her parents' hotel room, Alex quickly cleaned up. Alex quickly brushed his teeth and used some mouthwash to eliminate the smell of alcohol.

当克里斯蒂娜回到父母的酒店房间时，亚历克斯迅速打扫了一下房间，喷上了一瓶好闻的古龙水。亚历克斯迅速刷了牙，用漱口水消除了酒味。

Alex applied Clive Christian cologne which shortly had an immediate effect on his wife. Just like Christina's transcendence and metamorphosis, Alex also changed without doing much.

亚历克斯喷上克莱夫·克里斯蒂安香水后，很快就对妻子产生了立竿见影的效果。就像克里斯蒂娜的超越和蜕变一样，亚历克斯也无需付出太多努力就发生了改变。

Alex then took an aspirin to reduce the effects of alcohol. That was a trick Alex learned a long time ago because in many business deals, he was forced to toast and needed a way to get his equilibrium back quickly.

随后，亚历克斯服用了一片阿司匹林来减轻酒精的影响。这是亚历克斯很久以前学会的诀窍，因为在许多商业交易中，他被迫举杯庆祝，需要一种方法来迅速恢复平衡。

Alex, Christina, her parents and security men went to the Hotel Lobby and met

Gennady Alexeyev who was designated to take them to Vladimir Putin's Dacha 25 miles northwest of Moscow.

亚历克斯、克里斯蒂娜、她的父母和保安人员来到酒店大堂，会见了根纳季·阿列克谢耶夫，后者受命带他们前往莫斯科西北 25 英里的弗拉基米尔·普京的别墅。

The two Zil Limousines turned off the main hiway to a road that had many trees on both sides of the road and nothing much else to see. The Limo's then drove past an area with a tall wall, that Alex estimated must have been 16 feet tall.

两辆 齐尔 豪华轿车 驶离主干道，驶向一条道路，道路两旁有很多树木，没有什么可看的。随后，豪华轿车驶过一处有高墙的区域，亚历克斯估计这堵墙一定有 16 英尺高。

Eventually the Zil Limousines came to a gate with armed guards and what appeared to be a guard house. There were a couple men standing outside the guard house with sub machine guns. These soldiers' reminded Alex of the soldiers in front of the French Military Museum.

最后，齐尔 豪华轿车的来到一扇有武装警卫的大门前，那里似乎是一间警卫室。警卫室外站着几名手持冲锋枪的士兵。这些士兵让 亚历克斯想起了法国军事博物馆前的士兵。

The Alex Baxter group escorted by Gennady Alexeyev were expected and had been observed on hidden video cameras the entire five miles up the private road. The two security cars leading and following the big Zil Limousines had called ahead and informed the security detail their progress up the road. About the time they reached the gate, the door started sliding open, and then they drove into the compound.

亚历克斯·巴克斯特 (Alex Baxter) 小组由根纳季·阿列克谢耶夫 (Gennady Alexeyev) 护送，他们已经到达了私路上，整个五英里路程都被隐藏的摄像机拍到。齐尔 豪华轿车的大车的前后两辆安保车提前打电话通知了安保人员他们的进展。他们到达大门的时候，门开始滑开，然后他们驶进了大院。

Vladimir Putin's Dacha was nothing like anything Alex ever saw in Russia before. Whoever lived here was fabulously rich.

弗拉基米尔·普京的别墅与亚历克斯在俄罗斯见过的任何别墅都不一样。住在这里的人一定非常富有。

The white building with two large wings was as ornate as anything in La Jolla or Rancho Santa Fe near San Diego, California.

这座带有两个大翼的白色建筑与加利福尼亚州圣地亚哥附近的拉霍亚或圣菲牧场的任何建筑一样华丽。

ALEX (THOUGHT)
The ten-foot-tall glass windows on the 2nd floor must
have an incredible view.

亚历克斯（心想）
二楼十英尺高的玻璃窗一定有令人惊叹的美景。

In a short while when Alex was sampling the view it was confirmed.

不久之后，当亚历克斯欣赏这一景色时，这一点得到了证实。

The Zil Limousine drove along a long cobblestone driveway that had a big circle near the mansion. Inside the circular driveway arch were decorative plants and bushes now green with the springtime weather. The ground keepers obviously had a lot of work to do every day to keep up this fine-looking place.

齐尔豪华轿车沿着一条长长的鹅卵石车道行驶，这条车道在豪宅附近绕了一个大圈。圆形车道拱门内是装饰性植物和灌木丛，春天的天气让它们变得绿意盎然。显然，园丁每天都要做很多工作来维护这个美丽的地方。

The first Zil Limousine pulled up and stopped in front of the mansion's main entrance.

第一辆 齐尔豪华轿车驶来，停在了豪宅正门前。

A man in a crisp dress military uniform immediately opened the passenger door to the Zil Limousine, and Alex got out.

一名身着笔挺军装的男子立即打开了 齐尔豪华轿车的乘客侧车门，亚历克斯走了出来。

Gennady Alexeyev
This way Alex.

根纳季·阿列克谢耶夫
阿列克谢，这边走。

Gennady Alexeyev led Alex and the Garrisons into the front entrance of the Dacha. As soon as they opened the door, there was a very beautiful lady standing inside waiting.

根纳季·阿列克谢耶夫领着阿列克谢和驻军走进别墅的正门。他们一打开门，就看到里面站着一位非常漂亮的女士。

ALEX (Thought)
*Wow, she's smoking hot.*

亚历克斯（想道）
哇，她太性感了。

The woman greeted Alex and Christina and her Parents who were closely behind.

这位女士向紧随其后的亚历克斯、克里斯蒂娜和她的父母打了招呼。

**ALINA KABAYEVA**
Thank you all for coming, I'm Alina Kabayeva.

阿丽娜·卡巴伊娃
谢谢大家的到来，我是阿丽娜·卡巴耶娃。

**ALEX**
Good evening, Alina. I'm Alex Baxter. This is my wife
Christina, and her parents, Mr. and Mrs. Garrison.

亚历克斯
晚上好，阿丽娜。我是亚历克斯·巴克斯特。这是
我的妻子克里斯蒂娜，以及她的父母加里森先生
和夫人。

Vladimir Putin being a smart guy, former head of the KGB, Double Black Belt in martial arts, and proficient in seven languages suddenly appeared at the top of the stairway.

弗拉基米尔·普京是一个聪明人，曾任克格勃局长，武术双黑带，精通七种语言，突然出现在楼梯顶端。

**VLADIMIR PUTIN**
Alina, bring the guests up here.

弗拉基米尔·普京
阿丽娜，把客人带上来。

**ALINA KABAYEVA**
Alright Vladimir.

阿丽娜·卡巴耶娃
好吧，弗拉基米尔。

Vladimir Putin tasked the FSB to check out Alex Baxter extensively. They knew everything about Alex and were slowly getting all the facts on his new bride Christina and the Garrison family.

Note: Federal'naya Sluzhba Bezopasnosti, [Федеральная служба безопасности] (FSB) was formerly called KGB before the merger with the Russian Border Guards. FSB is also referred to as Federal Security Service (FSS).

<u>Federal Security Service - Wikipedia</u>

弗拉基米尔·普京委托联邦安全局对亚历克斯·巴克斯特进行全面调查。他们了解亚历克斯的一切，并慢慢地了解了他的新娘克里斯蒂娜和加里森家族的所有事实。

注：联邦安全局（FSB）在与俄罗斯边防卫队合并前曾被称为克格勃。FSB 也称为联邦安全局 (FSS)。

<u>联邦安全局 - 维基百科</u>

Knowing Christina's father was former Green Beret and thanks to John Walker and others who sold the KGB considerable amounts of American Crypto during the cold war, Vladimir Putin knew a lot about secret SOG missions William Garrison led into Cambodia behind enemy lines.

弗拉基米尔·普京知道克里斯蒂娜的父亲是前绿色贝雷帽，并且由于约翰·沃克和其他人在冷战期间向苏联克格勃出售了大量美国加密货币，弗拉基米尔·普京对威廉·加里森领导的深入柬埔寨敌后秘密 SOG 任务了解很多。

Its guys like Mr. Garrison and the two former Spetsnaz troops protecting Alex and the Garrisons, that Putin respected.

正是像加里森先生和两名保护亚历克斯和加里森一家的前特种部队士兵这样的人，才赢得了普京的尊敬。

Even before Vladimir Putin met Mr. Garrison, he had a fondness towards him. No matter what Vladimir Putin's negative feelings towards Obama might have been at the time, had no effect on his viewpoints of William Garrison, a multiple Silver Star recipient who most likely deserved the American Congressional Medal of Honor as much as anyone else who didn't die in the process.

甚至在弗拉基米尔·普京遇见加里森先生之前，他就对他有好感。无论弗拉基米尔·普京当时对奥巴马的负面情绪有多大，都不会影响他对威廉·加里森的看法。威廉·加里森曾多次获得银星勋章，他很可能和其他没有在勋章授予过程中牺牲的人一样，应该获得美国国会荣誉勋章。

After shaking Alex's hand and welcoming Christina, Vladimir Putin walked over to Mr. Garrison.

与亚历克斯握手并欢迎克里斯蒂娜后，弗拉基米尔·普京走向了加里森先生。

**VLADIMIR PUTIN**
Mr. Garrison, it is a special honor for me to meet you.
Few men have ever displayed the courage as you did
as a Green Beret in Vietnam.

弗拉基米尔·普京
加里森先生，能见到您是我的荣幸。很少有人能像您作为越南绿色贝雷帽部队的一员那样表现出勇气。

### MR. GARRISON
Thank you, sir, for your kind words.

加里森先生
先生，谢谢您的善意言辞。

### VLADIMIR PUTIN
Mr. Garrison even though we were once enemies, during the Vietnam war, we can't ignore the fact that men such as you accomplished far more than what most people are aware. Your missions, according to my INTEL experts, involved incredible daring and efforts that are legendary.

弗拉基米尔·普京
加里森先生，尽管我们在越南战争期间曾是敌人，但我们不能忽视这样一个事实：像你这样的人所取得的成就远远超出了大多数人的认知。根据我的情报专家的说法，你的任务需要令人难以置信的勇气和传奇般的努力。

### MR. GARRISON
Thank you, President. Putin.

加里森先生
谢谢普京总统。

### VLADIMIR PUTIN
Mr. Garrison, someone is here who requested to meet you.

弗拉基米尔·普京
加里森先生，有人要求见您。

Vladimir Putin nodded at Russian Anatoly Vyacheslavovich Lebed wearing a lot of medals on his dress uniform who then stepped forward.

普京向身着锦旗佩戴多枚勋章的俄将军阿纳托利·维亚切斯拉沃维奇·列别德点头致意，随后列别德走上前来。

**ANATOLY VYACHESLAVOVICH LEBED**
Hello, Mr. Garison, I'm Anatoly Vyacheslavovich Lebed.

阿纳托利·维亚切斯拉沃维奇·列贝德
你好，加里森先生，我是阿纳托利·维亚切斯拉沃维奇·列贝德。

**VLADIMIR PUTIN**
Mr. Garrison, Anatoly Vyacheslavovich Lebed served on combat operations in Afghanistan in 1986–87 as an aircrew member in a helicopter regiment. You both have a lot in common, fighting a losing cause but remaining eternally vigilant.

弗拉基米尔·普京
加里森先生，阿纳托利·维亚切斯拉沃维奇·列别德于 1986-87 年在阿富汗担任直升机团机组人员。
你们有很多共同之处，都在为必败的事业而战，
但始终保持警惕。

Colonel Anatoly Vyacheslavovich Lebed's also highly decorated like you, and his actions during the 2008 South Ossetia war earned him the honour of becoming only the second Knight of the Order of St. George 4th class.

阿纳托利·维亚切斯拉沃维奇·列别德上校也像您一样功勋卓著，他在 2008 年南奥塞梯战争中的表现为他赢得了第二位四级圣乔治骑士勋章获得者称号。

**WILLIAM GARRISON (Thought.)**
*With his skin head haircut, he looks the part as well.*

威廉·加里森（沉思）
他的光头发型看起来也很像这个角色。

Note: A few months later after this meeting, Lebed was killed in a motorcycle accident in Moscow.

注：这次会面几个月后，列别德在莫斯科的一场摩托车事故中丧生。

**WILLIAM GARRISON**
It's a pleasure to meet you Mr. Lebed.

威廉·加里森
很高兴见到您，莱贝德先生。

**VLADIMIR PUTIN**
Everyone, let me show you my favorite view.

弗拉基米尔·普京
各位，让我带你们看看我最喜欢的风景。

Vladimir Putin led Alex right to the spot with the excellent view Alex was thinking about just a few minutes before.

弗拉基米尔·普京领着亚历克斯来到了几分钟前亚历克斯还在想着的那个可以欣赏到绝美风景的地方。

Alina Kabayeva approached Christina.

阿丽娜·卡巴耶娃走近克里斯蒂娜。

ALINA KABAYEVA
Mrs. Baxter, you are very beautiful.

阿丽娜·卡巴耶娃
巴克斯特夫人，你非常美丽。

CHRISTINA
Please call me Christina.

克里斯蒂娜
请叫我克里斯蒂娜。

Christina then put her hand out to shake Alina's.

然后克里斯蒂娜伸出手和阿丽娜握手。

ALINA KABAYEVA
Certainly, Christina.

阿丽娜·卡巴耶娃
当然，克里斯蒂娜。

CHRISTINA
Alina, this is my mother, Ethel Garrison.

克里斯蒂娜
阿丽娜，这是我的母亲，埃塞尔·加里森。

ALINA KABAYEVA
Mrs. Garrison, you look so pretty and young, you could be your daughter's sister!

阿丽娜·卡巴耶娃
加里森夫人，你看起来又漂亮又年轻，可以当你女儿的妹妹了！

MRS. GARRISON (a.k.a. Ethel)
Oh, thank you for the kind words, Alina, but you are
very beautiful.

加里森夫人（又名埃塞尔）
哦，谢谢你的赞美，阿丽娜，不过你真的非常漂
亮。

Alina's hair was flowing down and wavy. Her gold glittery dress showed ample
cleavage. Her thick eyebrows were perfect, her teeth were jewels, and her smile was
infectious.

阿丽娜的头发垂落而卷曲。她那件闪闪发亮的金色连衣裙露出了丰满的乳沟。
她的浓眉完美无瑕，牙齿洁白如宝石，笑容极具感染力。

Alina Kabayeva, an athlete and conscious of her body, kept in wonderful condition.
Her seduction of Vladimir Putin was perfect. She was undoubtedly the best-looking
partner of any world leader. It was not until President Trump was elected that America
ever had such a beautiful princess role model.

阿丽娜·卡巴耶娃是一名运动员，她很注重自己的身材，保持着极佳的状态。
她对弗拉基米尔·普京的诱惑堪称完美。她无疑是任何世界领导人中最漂亮的
伴侣。直到特朗普总统当选，美国才有了如此美丽的公主榜样。

In a few moments, Alina remembered her FSB briefing about Christina; she was fluent
in Russian and naturally shifted to speaking in Russian. And when Christina naturally
flowed in Russian, Alina became even more appreciative of Christina.

过了一会儿，阿丽娜想起了联邦安全局对克里斯蒂娜的简报；她能说一口流利
的俄语，于是自然而然地开始用俄语交谈。当克里斯蒂娜自然而然地说出俄语
时，阿丽娜对克里斯蒂娜更加欣赏了。

ALINA KABAYEVA (Thought)
*Kristina — nastoyashchaya nakhodka: skromnaya,
ekzoticheskaya, napolovinu chernokozhaya, krasivaya
i gorazdo umneye bol'shinstva amerikanok, kotorykh
ya vstrechal.*

[Кристина — настоящая находка: скромная,
экзотическая, наполовину чернокожая, красивая и
гораздо умнее большинства американок, которых
я встречал.]

{Christina is the real deal, unassuming, exotic half
black and beautiful, and far more intelligent than most
American women that I have met.}

阿丽娜·卡巴耶娃 （思考）
克里斯蒂娜是货真价实的、谦逊的、充满异国情
调的、一半黑人血统、美丽动人的女人，而且比
我见过的大多数美国女人聪明得多。

Vladimir Putin well dressed and mannered servants were highly paid FSB agents playing the double role, to spy on Vladimir, to protect him, and if necessary, kill him.

弗拉基米尔·普京的衣着考究、举止优雅的仆人都是高薪的联邦安全局特工，他们扮演着双重角色，既监视弗拉基米尔，又保护他，必要时甚至杀死他。

Vladimir Putin understood the fundamentals of how that worked and understood in the twentieth century, six Russian leaders left office in death, and two others were removed without killing them.

弗拉基米尔·普京了解其中的原理，也知道在二十世纪，有六位俄罗斯领导人在任职期间去世，还有两位领导人是在没有被处死的情况下被免职的。

In a couple minutes, one of the servants arrived with two trays of glasses, and asked each if they would like some refreshments.

几分钟后，一名仆人端着两盘杯子过来，询问他们是否想喝点茶点。

Christina and her mother asked for some white wine and Alina Kabayeva followed their lead and asked for the same.

克里斯蒂娜和她的母亲要了一些白葡萄酒，阿丽娜也效仿她们要了同样的酒。

**VLADIMIR PUTIN**
Alex, William, and Gennady, would you like some Cognac?

弗拉基米尔·普京
亚历克斯、威廉和根纳迪，你们想来点干邑白兰地吗？

**ALEX**
Yes, that would be nice. Thank you.

亚历克斯
是的，那就太好了。谢谢。

Mr. Garrison knew there would soon be a toast.

加里森先生知道很快就会有人举杯祝酒。

**MR. GARRISON (a.k.a. William)**
Just a little for me. Half a shot.

加里森先生（又名威廉）
我只要一点。半杯。

GENNADY ALEXEYEV
I would love some Cognac.

根纳季·阿列克谢耶夫
我想喝点干邑白兰地。

Vladimir Putin nodded to the servant who left momentarily and returned with a bottle of Rémy Martin Louis XIII Cognac.

弗拉基米尔·普京向仆人点点头，仆人不久后离开，拿回了一瓶人头马路易十三干邑白兰地。

And as expected right after their glasses were filled by a very handsome and distinguished looking servant who had killed his fair share number of people in Chechnya and Afghanistan as part of a Spetsnaz Regiment, they soon toasted:

正如所料，在一位英俊而杰出的仆人给他们倒酒后，他们很快就举杯敬酒：这位仆人曾作为特种部队的一员在车臣和阿富汗杀死了相当多的人：

VLADIMIR PUTIN
To the successful building of Dome Cities.
Za uspeshnoye stroitel'stvo gorodov-kupolov.
[За успешное строительство городов-куполов.]

弗拉基米尔·普京
祝圆顶城市建设成功。

Christina toasted to Alina in Russian who responded likewise.

Alina Kabayeva
Za vashe zdorov'ye.
[За ваше здоровье.]
{To your health.}

阿琳娜·卡巴耶娃
祝您健康。

After they socialized for a while, Vladimir feeling some hunger sensations of his own, and mindful his guests probably had not eaten since they arrived, suggested:

他们聊了一会儿之后，弗拉基米尔也感觉饿了，想到客人到达后可能还没有吃过东西，于是他建议道：

## VLADIMIR PUTIN
I would like to invite all of you into the dining room
for a meal prepared for this special occasion.

弗拉基米尔·普京
我邀请大家到餐厅来享用为这个特殊时刻准备的
晚餐。

## ALEX
Sounds good to me.

亚历克斯
对我来说听起来不错。

Alex responded and soon they all followed Vladimir Putin's lead as he led Alex, Christina, and the Garrison's into the large dining room that could easily seat 100 people if they put out the extra tables. Vladimir Putin could also have concerts there for a small crowd with a scaled down symphony orchestra or have ballroom dancing.

亚历克斯回应道，很快他们都跟着弗拉基米尔·普京走，他带着亚历克斯、克里斯蒂娜和加里森一家走进了大餐厅，如果他们把额外的桌子摆出来，这个餐厅很容易就能容纳 100 人。弗拉基米尔·普京还可以在这里为一小群人举办音乐会，配有一个规模较小的交响乐团，或者举行交谊舞。

Not too different than Alex's home, Vladimir Putin's dinner table settings had gold-plated silverware and expensive Russian crystal. Alex recognized the Royal Copenhagen *Flora Danica* porcelain settings on the table.

与亚历克斯的家没什么不同，弗拉基米尔·普京的餐桌上摆放着镀金银器和昂贵的俄罗斯水晶。亚历克斯认出了桌上摆放的是皇家哥本哈根的丹麦花神瓷器。

The meal served was impressive and delicious. The dessert was one that would be hard to forget. Throughout the meal everyone socialized.

餐点令人印象深刻，美味可口。甜点令人难以忘怀。用餐期间，每个人都在交流。

Alina began to like Christina more as it was very easy for her to communicate with Christina.

由于阿丽娜和克里斯蒂娜交流起来非常容易，所以她开始越来越喜欢克里斯蒂娜。

Unlike many official visits that often required the need of a cumbersome translator when they had to be careful what they said, Alina and Christina could talk freely. However, Vladimir Putin tuned into and monitored their conversation.

与许多官方访问不同，阿丽娜和克里斯蒂娜可以自由交谈，因为官方访问通常需要借助繁琐的翻译，因为她们必须小心谨慎地说出自己想说的话。然而，弗拉基米尔·普京却监听并监视着她们的谈话。

With Christina's charm, Alina quickly was disarmed and by the end of the evening and knew Christina would be a tremendous social asset for Alex in the future.

在克里斯蒂娜的魅力下，阿丽娜很快就被迷住了，到了晚上结束时，她知道克里斯蒂娜将来会成为亚历克斯巨大的社交财富。

The Garrison's socialized equally as well and being retired teachers could hold a very intelligent conversation.

加里森一家的社交能力也同样出色，而且作为退休教师，他们可以进行非常有深度的对话。

Vladimir Putin later remarked to one of his associates:

弗拉基米尔·普京后来对他的一位同事说：

### VLADIMIR PUTIN

This is one of the best well rounded families I've met. Perhaps through them we could do more to improve relations with Americans.

弗拉基米尔·普京

这是我见过的最全面家庭之一。也许通过他们我们可以做更多的事情来改善与美国人的关系。

Vladimir Putin observed everyone finished eating and announced:

普京观察大家是否吃完饭后宣布：

### VLADIMIR PUTIN

We have some entertainment. In the drawing room, let's all go there.

弗拉基米尔·普京

我们有一些娱乐活动。在客厅里，我们都去那里吧。

## MUSIC FOR THIS SEGMENT:

Mozart String Quartet in C major, K.465 'Dissonance'

本片段的音乐：

莫扎特 C 大调弦乐四重奏，K.465"不和谐音"

<u>https://www.youtube.com/watch?v=97Rry5cs2Gc</u>

A quartet was playing some Mozart pieces low enough in volume to where a casual conversation could be conducted on the far side of the room.

一个四重奏组正在演奏一些莫扎特的曲子，音量很低，房间另一边的人可以进行随意的交谈。

Vladimir and Alex were on the side of the room talking about Nuuk Greenland's dome, when Vladimir suddenly announced to Alex:

弗拉基米尔和亚历克斯在房间的一侧谈论努克格陵兰岛的穹顶，这时弗拉基米尔突然对亚历克斯宣布：

### VLADIMIR PUTIN
Alex, please come with me for a minute to my private study, I want to talk to you a little about *Chita Dome* project and not disturb the performance.

弗拉基米尔·普京
亚历克斯，请跟我到我的私人书房来一会儿，我想跟你谈谈赤塔穹顶项目，但不要打扰演出。

Note full name: Chita Zabaykalsky Krai, Russia. <u>Chita, Zabaykalsky Krai - Wikipedia</u>

注全名：赤塔后贝加尔边疆区，俄罗斯。
后贝加尔边疆区赤塔 - 维基百科

Alex nodded and followed Vladimir down the hallway, into the large room that was loaded with books, pictures, and objects.

亚历克斯点点头，跟着弗拉基米尔穿过走廊，走进一个堆满书籍、图片和物品的大房间。

Vladimir Putin had a wide taste of many subjects, topics, and scenarios that played out. His personal library in this room was expansive and articulated why he was a master chess player always beating the West in their own games.

弗拉基米尔·普京对许多主题、话题和情景都涉猎广泛。这间房间里的私人藏书丰富，充分说明了他为何是一位棋艺高超、总能在西方人的棋局中战胜他们。

Once inside the room Vladimir shut the door. An FSB guard stood outside to prevent any entry.

一进房间，弗拉基米尔就关上了门。一名联邦安全局的警卫站在外面，防止任何人进入。

VLADIMIR PUTIN
Alex, I wanted to tell you how I want to proceed with
Dome Cities in Russia.

弗拉基米尔·普京
亚历克斯，我想告诉你我想如何推进俄罗斯的圆
顶城市计划。

ALEX
Okay, Vladimir what do you have in mind?

亚历克斯
好吧，弗拉基米尔，你有什么想法？

VLADIMIR PUTIN
I want you to start in Moscow.

弗拉基米尔·普京
我希望你从莫斯科开始。

Alex appeared stunned and repeated the word:

亚历克斯看上去很震惊，重复了一遍这句话：

ALEX
Moscow?

亚历克斯
莫斯科？

VLADIMIR PUTIN
Yes absolutely.

弗拉基米尔·普京
是的，绝对是。

ALEX
Moscow is a huge Vladimir. Moscow must be twenty-
five miles across.

亚历克斯
莫斯科是一个巨大的弗拉基米尔。莫斯科肯定有
二十五英里宽。

VLADIMIR PUTIN
Yes Alex, Moscow's twenty miles East to West and
twenty-five miles North to South. It's a large city.

弗拉基米尔·普京
是的，亚历克斯，莫斯科东西长二十英里，南北
长二十五英里。这是一座大城市。

ALEX
Do you want to cover the entire city with a dome?

亚历克斯
你想用穹顶覆盖整个城市吗？

VLADIMIR PUTIN
No, I realize that would be too costly and take too
long, I'm thinking of a ten-mile diameter dome in the
middle of Moscow. But after we do an analysis, I'm
willing to cut it down to a two-point five-mile radius.

弗拉基米尔·普京
不，我知道那会花费太多，而且耗时太长，我考
虑在莫斯科市中心建造一个直径十英里的圆顶。
但在我们进行分析后，我愿意将其半径缩小到两
点五英里。

ALEX
Including the Moskva River running through the
middle of it?

亚历克斯
包括中间穿过的莫斯科河吗？

VLADIMIR PUTIN
Yes.

弗拉基米尔·普京
是的。

ALEX
If that's possible, the river will waste a lot of space.

亚历克斯
如果可以的话，但是河流会浪费很多空间。

VLADIMIR PUTIN
True but I have an idea for a work around to regain space.

弗拉基米尔·普京
没错，但我有一个办法可以重新获得空间。

ALEX
Such as?

亚历克斯
例如？

VLADIMIR PUTIN
Since you have shown that building the dome eliminates the need to build lateral strength in buildings allowing us to build much higher without fear of wind issues, we'll just build taller buildings.

弗拉基米尔·普京
既然你已经证明，建造圆顶建筑就无需在建筑物中增加横向强度，让我们可以建造更高的建筑而不用担心风的问题，那么我们就会建造更高的建筑。

ALEX
It will not take much to fill up 1000 feet, it will still lose a lot of land being built over the river.

亚历克斯
填满 1000 英尺并不需要太多，但仍然会损失大量在河上建造的土地。

VLADIMIR PUTIN
I considered that too, I want the dome built a mile tall.

弗拉基米尔·普京
我也考虑过这一点，我想把圆顶建到一英里高。

Alex was astonished and felt compelled to ask:

亚历克斯很惊讶，不禁问道：

ALEX
Vladimir, do you want the dome 5280 feet up in the air?

亚历克斯
弗拉基米尔, 你想要建一个 5280 英尺高的圆顶吗？

VLADIMIR PUTIN
In Russia we prefer to say 1609 meters.

弗拉基米尔·普京
在俄罗斯我们更喜欢说 1609 米。

ALEX
I like the idea, but I still think we should concentrate on less habitable regions such as Siberia.

亚历克斯
我喜欢这个想法，但我仍然认为我们应该集中精力于西伯利亚等不太适宜居住的地区。

VLADIMIR PUTIN
I have a proposal to make.

弗拉基米尔·普京
我有一个建议。

ALEX
Such as?

亚历克斯
例如？比如？

VLADIMIR PUTIN
I will let you build a second dome in Siberia which you will pay for as our agreement we are negotiating. If you will build the Moscow Dome with Russian help and Russia will pay for most of it.

弗拉基米尔·普京
我会让你在西伯利亚建造第二个穹顶，按照我们正在谈判的协议，你得付钱。如果你在俄罗斯的帮助下建造莫斯科穹顶，俄罗斯将支付大部分费用。

ALEX
I will talk to my partners in the morning when they arrive, and we can then meet and discuss it further. I can't commit without their concurrence.

亚历克斯
早上我的合作伙伴到达时我会和他们谈谈，然后我们可以见面并进一步讨论。如果没有他们的同意，我无法做出承诺。

VLADIMIR PUTIN
Who will that be?

弗拉基米尔·普京
那个人会是谁？

ALEX

James Walker, CEO Hercules Steel, Howard Grady, the Cement King, and Claude Reardon, the Construction Company Guru, would all be arriving in Moscow in the morning ready to negotiate the final details of the Chita Dome.

亚历克斯

赫拉克勒斯钢铁公司首席执行官詹姆斯·沃克、水泥大王霍华德·格雷迪和建筑公司大师克劳德·里尔登将于早上抵达莫斯科，准备就赤塔穹顶的最后细节进行谈判。

ALEX (Thought)

*Vladimir Putin's Moscow Dome stands in the way, though probably it's feasible to build.*

*I fear doing three dome projects overlapping might tax the system far more than we can cope with.*

*Plus, doing two domes in Russia simultaneously would no doubt open the door for Bechtel to come in and take at least one of the contracts away from us.*

*If Bechtel won the contract to build the Moscow Dome, it would be detrimental to us long term.*

亚历克斯（思考）

弗拉基米尔·普京的莫斯科穹顶阻碍了这一进程，尽管建造它可能是可行的。

我担心三个穹顶项目重叠可能会给系统带来比我们所能应付的更多的负担。

此外，同时在俄罗斯建造两个穹顶无疑会为贝克泰尔公司打开大门，从我们手中夺走至少一份合同。

如果贝克泰尔公司赢得建造莫斯科穹顶的合同，从长远来看，这将对我们不利。

Alex felt a sinking sensation and he felt he was being backed into a corner.

亚历克斯感到一种沉重的感觉，他觉得自己被逼到了墙角。

ALEX (Thought)

*One thing I do know, with a guy like Vladimir Putin forcibly backing a project with a difficult construction like Moscow, and over the top of a river, there was a chance we could be successful.*

*It all comes down to how much Vladimir Putin was willing to shell out for the costs and how enough steel could get produced. There are many questions left to answer.*

亚历克斯（思考）
有一件事我确实知道，像弗拉基米尔·普京这样的人强行支持像莫斯科这样建设难度大、而且要越过河流的项目，我们还是有机会成功的。

这一切都取决于弗拉基米尔·普京愿意为这些成本付出多少钱，以及如何生产出足够的钢铁。还有很多问题有待解答。

VLADIMIR PUTIN
What will you advise your business associates?

弗拉基米尔·普京
您会给您的商业伙伴什么建议？

ALEX
I will tell them I have no reservations about the *Chita Dome* since it's a similar design to what we are doing in Nuuk Greenland, but a mile up in Moscow makes it the modern-day wonder for mankind.

亚历克斯
我会告诉他们，我对奇塔圆顶没有保留，因为它的设计与我们在格陵兰岛努克所做的类似，但距莫斯科一英里远，使它成为人类的现代奇迹。

VLADIMIR PUTIN
That's true, nobody ever before would have thought it feasible, or has the nerve to attempt it.

弗拉基米尔·普京
没错，以前没人认为这是可行的，也没人有勇气去尝试。

ALEX
I will tentatively go along with it until we do structural analysis and weigh the risk. The Dome may have to be shorter due to the high risk.

亚历克斯

我会暂时同意它，直到我们进行结构分析并权衡风险。由于风险较高，穹顶可能不得不缩短。

VLADIMIR PUTIN

So, would you be willing to attempt it if your partners agree?

弗拉基米尔·普京

那么，如果您的合作伙伴同意的话，您愿意尝试一下吗？

ALEX

Yes, with the engineer's concurrence we can build that high and you are willing to have a shorter dome if engineering analysis indicates we cannot build *Moscow Dome* that high.

亚历克斯

是的，经过工程师的同意，我们可以建造那么高，如果工程分析表明我们无法建造那么高的莫斯科圆顶，您愿意拥有更短的圆顶。

VLADIMIR PUTIN

That's a reasonable approach. I understand.

ALEX

Also, it will help move the project forward if you assist us with dealing with local rules and regulations.

亚历克斯

此外，如果你协助我们处理当地的法规，这将有助于推进项目。

VLADIMIR PUTIN

You will have carte blanche. I will put together a team of city planners and experts to identify any rules or regulations that could get in your and have all those regulatory issues resolved before construction starts.

弗拉基米尔·普京

您将拥有全权委托权。我将组建一支由城市规划师和专家组成的团队，以找出可能影响您的任何规则或法规，并在施工开始之前解决所有这些监管问题。

ALEX

With that understanding, it allows us to think in terms of building two *Dome Cities* in Russia in parallel.

亚历克斯

有了这种理解，我们就可以考虑在俄罗斯并行建设两个圆顶城市。

VLADIMIR PUTIN

I think the public will get behind you once they start enjoying just the wind break you will create like you did in Greenland.

弗拉基米尔·普京

我认为，一旦公众开始享受你们在格陵兰岛创造的防风屏障，他们就会支持你们。

ALEX

We studied the Weather History of Moscow and would start construction on the North Side of the planned dome for that reason.

亚历克斯

我们研究了莫斯科的天气历史，因此将在计划圆顶的北侧开始施工。

VLADIMIR PUTIN

What did your weather analysis show?

弗拉基米尔·普京

你的天气分析显示了什么？

ALEX

The prevailing winds in Moscow are southwesterly and southerly. The wind speed varies between 6 and 11 mph with gusts up to 20 mph.

亚历克斯

莫斯科盛行风为西南风和南风。风速在 6 至 11 英里/小时之间，阵风最高可达 20 英里/小时。

VLADIMIR PUTIN

That sounds about right. Also, with solar and wind power with baseline nuclear power, we can reduce coal generators and associated smog in the region.

弗拉基米尔·普京

听起来不错。此外，利用太阳能和风能以及基础核能，我们可以减少该地区的燃煤发电和相关雾霾。

ALEX

In Greenland, under the dome there will be no polluters. Also, only electric vehicles will be permitted inside *Greenland's Dome*.

亚历克斯

在格陵兰岛，穹顶之下不会有污染者。此外，格陵兰岛穹顶内只允许使用电动汽车。

VLADIMIR PUTIN

We can do the same in Moscow and Chita. We've studied your Greenland plan. There is a lot of sound judgement going into that project.

弗拉基米尔·普京

我们可以在莫斯科和赤塔做同样的事情。我们研究了你们的格陵兰计划。这个项目经过了很多合理的判断。

ALEX

I've suggested to China developers they build a Dome City in the Gobi Desert. Part of the planning for that would be to install rings of solar panels and greenhouses around *Gobi Dome City*.

亚历克斯

我建议中国开发商在戈壁沙漠建造一座穹顶城。计划的一部分是在戈壁穹顶城周围安装一圈太阳能电池板和温室。

VLADIMIR PUTIN

How does that pertain to Russia?

弗拉基米尔·普京

这与俄罗斯有什么关系？

ALEX

Even though we would only be building a *Moscow Dome City* with a radius of 2.5 miles, there is no reason why not redevelop areas outside the *Moscow Dome* to include rings of outdoor parks, greenhouses, and solar panels.

亚历克斯
尽管我们只会建造一个半径为 2.5 英里的莫斯科
圆顶城市，但没有理由不重新开发莫斯科圆顶以
外的区域，包括室外公园、温室和太阳能电池板
环。

## VLADIMIR PUTIN

Solar would only be good for about six months of the
year.

弗拉基米尔·普京
太阳能一年只能使用六个月左右。

## ALEX

That's true but during those six months is when you
can plan for heavy industry since you have long days
in the summer and maximum solar power output.

亚历克斯
确实如此，但在这六个月里，您可以规划重工
业，因为夏天的白天很长，太阳能输出也最大。

## VLADIMIR PUTIN

How soon will you make the decision to move forward
on the project.

弗拉基米尔·普京
您什么时候会决定继续推进这个项目？

## ALEX

Vladimir, I can't promise you anything until I talk with
the management team tomorrow.

亚历克斯
弗拉基米尔, 在明天与管理团队交谈之前，我无法
向您保证任何事情。

## VLADIMIR PUTIN

I understand that, but your positive attitude towards
building the *Moscow Dome* is a huge step in the right
direction.

弗拉基米尔·普京
我理解这一点，但你对建造莫斯科圆顶体育场的
积极态度是朝着正确方向迈出的一大步。

ALEX

We do not know the engineering requirements yet, so you need to be aware, we may have to scale the *Moscow Dome* height down to say 2,500 feet verses the mile you want.

亚历克斯

我们还不知道工程要求，所以您需要注意，我们可能必须将莫斯科穹顶的高度缩小到 2,500 英尺，而不是您想要的英里。

VLADIMIR PUTIN

Alex, the fact you indicated you are willing to proceed is a big step forward, we'll see what your partners have to say tomorrow.

弗拉基米尔·普京

亚历克斯，你表示愿意继续下去，这是一大进步，我们明天看看你的合作伙伴会怎么说。

ALEX

Vladimir, that's the best I can promise you now. But you should know I'm passionate about saving farmland from Urban Spral.

I want to see the world building cities where crops would not grow well in places such as Greenland and Chita Russia, unless we build greenhouses.

亚历克斯

弗拉基米尔，这是我现在能向你做出的最好承诺。但你应该知道，我热衷于拯救 城市扩张的农田。

我希望看到世界在格陵兰岛和俄罗斯赤塔等地建设城市，除非我们建造温室，否则农作物无法很好地生长。

VLADIMIR PUTIN

Alex, I've studied you with the help of the FSB. You are idealistic, and I agree with your sentiments on ending the irrational behavior of turning farmland into urban sprawl just because the land is cheaper.

弗拉基米尔·普京

亚历克斯，我在联邦安全局的帮助下研究了你。你很理想主义，我同意你的观点，即结束仅仅因

为土地更便宜而将农田变成城市扩张的不合理行
为。

## ALEX

Thank you for that comment, Vladimir. It means a lot
to me because I know you understand my motives.

亚历克斯

谢谢你的评论，弗拉基米尔。这对我来说意义重
大，因为我知道你理解我的动机。

## VLADIMIR PUTIN

Alex, why don't we go out and join the lovely ladies
and the other guests?

弗拉基米尔·普京

亚历克斯，我们为什么不出去和这些可爱的女士
们以及其他客人聚一聚呢？

## VLADIMIR PUTIN

After you sir.

弗拉基米尔·普京

先生，您先请。

Vladimir Putin opened the door to his Den, and Alex followed him out as they went back to the musical performance for the guests.

弗拉基米尔·普京打开了他的书房门，亚历克斯跟着他出去，一起回去为客人们欣赏音乐表演。

The three women were all semi-huddled talking and smiling and enjoying each other.

三个女人半挤在一起，一边聊天，一边微笑，很开心。

Other guests and staff watched Vladimir Putin and Alex come back into the room wondering why they had departed for a few minutes. Many wondered if in a few days a possibility existed they might hear a pronouncement that changed the world.

其他客人和工作人员看到弗拉基米尔·普京和亚历克斯回到房间，想知道他们为什么离开了几分钟。许多人想知道几天后他们是否有可能听到一个改变世界的声明。

Vladimir Putin acted very friendly to his guests all the time. Vladimir Putin's intelligence was superb as he was always calculating, and never took bets he didn't think were wise if he intended on winning.

弗拉基米尔·普京一直对他的客人表现得非常友好。弗拉基米尔·普京的智商非常高，他总是在深思熟虑，从不接受他认为不明智的赌注，只要他想赢。

Vladimir Putin led Alex to the far side of the room where they could continue Moscow Dome discussions that included Gennady Alexeyev. William Garrison was following along in the conversation but had been absorbed in discussions with Colonel Anatoly Vyacheslavovich Lebed and Gennady Alexeyev when Vladimir Putin and Alex approached them.

弗拉基米尔·普京将亚历克斯带到房间的另一边，在那里他们可以继续讨论莫斯科圆顶，其中包括根纳季·阿列克谢耶夫。威廉·加里森一直在关注谈话，但当弗拉基米尔·普京和亚历克斯走近他们时，他正全神贯注于与阿纳托利·维亚切斯拉沃维奇·列别德上校和根纳季·阿列克谢耶夫的讨论。

### VLADIMIR PUTIN
The notion of a mile high *Moscow Dome* is breath-taking.

### 弗拉基米尔·普京
莫斯科穹顶高达一英里，这一想法令人叹为观止。

### GENNADY ALEXEYEV
*The Moscow Dome* will also set an example for the rest of the world as a daring but majestic project.

### 弗拉基米尔·普京
莫斯科穹顶高达一英里，这一想法令人叹为观止。

### VLADIMIR PUTIN
Later additions to the Moscow Dome could be built as well as additional domes just like Alex is planning that will soon change Greenland quite profoundly.

### 弗拉基米尔·普京
莫斯科穹顶以后可能会增建，还会建造额外的穹顶，就像亚历克斯计划的那样，这将很快给格陵兰带来深刻的变化。

### ALEX
Once the *Moscow Dome* initial construction is completed and internal building implemented, even if only half mile high buildings could be built at this time.

### 亚历克斯
一旦莫斯科圆顶初始建设完成并实施内部建筑，即使此时只能建造半英里高的建筑物。

### VLADIMIR PUTIN
Why is that?

弗拉基米尔·普京
为什么呢？

ALEX
These very tall buildings can be more easily built since wind would not be a factor in designing building lateral strength.

亚历克斯
这些非常高的建筑物可以更容易建造，因为风不会成为设计建筑物横向强度的因素。

VLADIMIR PUTIN
Any other insights that promote good building construction?

弗拉基米尔·普京
还有其他可以促进良好建筑施工的见解吗？

ALEX
The pillars that support the rooftop could be utilized as parts of buildings creating vast stabilization and hiding their existence for ambience.

亚历克斯
支撑屋顶的柱子可以用作建筑物的一部分，创造巨大的稳定性并隐藏其存在以营造氛围。

VLADIMIR PUTIN
After looking at some of the buildings built in Dubai and Shanghai, it seems almost certainly possible.

弗拉基米尔·普京
看过迪拜和上海建造的一些建筑后，我觉得这几乎是完全有可能的。

ALEX
Not having wind inside the dome also means that besides subways there could be airways of tube trains traveling at staggering heights between buildings. People could spend long periods at altitudes and never go to the surface of the planet.

亚历克斯
圆顶内没有风也意味着除了地铁之外，建筑物之间还可能存在以惊人高度行驶的地铁通道。人们可以在高空待很长时间，而永远不会到达地球表面。

### VLADIMIR PUTIN
Dome top observation platforms and a restaurant at the pinnacle of the dome would no doubt usher in countless customers.

弗拉基米尔·普京
圆顶观景台和圆顶顶端的餐厅无疑会吸引无数顾客。

Alex Baxter had a lot of plans and by contract, he would own the Dome Top Moscow Restaurant.

亚历克斯·巴克斯特有很多计划，根据合同，他将拥有莫斯科圆顶餐厅。

### GENNADY ALEXEYEV
The initial cost of the dome is staggering, but if it lasts for 5,000 years, it will pay for itself many times over.

根纳季·阿列克谢耶夫
圆顶的初始成本令人震惊，但如果它能维持5,000年，其成本将翻几倍。

### VLADIMIR PUTIN
Eventually because of snow and temperature intervention, the eventual energy savings would quickly pay for the dome.

弗拉基米尔·普京
最终，由于降雪和温度干预，最终节省的能源将很快支付圆顶的费用。

### ANATOLY VYACHESLAVOVICH LEBED
How will you purify the air in the dome?

阿纳托利·维亚切斯拉沃维奇·列别德
你将如何净化圆顶内的空气？

### ALEX
Air purification mandating electric cars, trucks and trains changes the internal climate a lot. It would be expected that eventually, air inside the dome would be many times purer than air outside the dome.

亚历克斯
电动汽车、卡车和火车需要进行空气净化，这极大地改变了内部气候。预计最终穹顶内的空气将比穹顶外的空气纯净许多倍。

## VLADIMIR PUTIN

Anatoly, I think there will be concentric circles of greenhouses and solar panels outside the dome that would help purify the air.

## 弗拉基米尔·普京

阿纳托利，我认为圆顶外面会有同心圆的温室和太阳能电池板，这将有助于净化空气。

## ALEX

The Greenland Dome plans have forced air blowers to move Dome air into one end of a string of Greenhouses that feed air cleaned by the Greenhouses into the HVAC plant that adjusts the Dome environment.

## 亚历克斯

格陵兰圆顶计划迫使鼓风机将圆顶空气输送到一系列温室的一端，这些温室将温室净化后的空气输送到调节圆顶环境的暖通空调设备中。

## ANATOLY VYACHESLAVOVICH LEBED

Why do you not just put a lot of green plants and trees inside Moscow Dome City?

## 阿纳托利·维亚切斯拉沃维奇·列别德

为什么你们不在圆顶城市里种植很多绿色植物和树木呢？

## ALEX

China did that with one of their developments and now they have a lot of insect problems. We designed it to be comfortable. Nuuk Greenland Dome has parks and green areas and trees.

But based on China's attempt, we do not want to create an insect problem by building buildings where buildings are integrated with a lot of plant life.

## 亚历克斯

中国在其中一个开发项目中就这么做了，现在他们面临很多昆虫问题。我们设计它是为了舒适。努克格陵兰穹顶有公园、绿地和树木。

但基于中国的尝试，我们并不想在建筑中融入大量植物，从而造成昆虫问题。

## ANATOLY VYACHESLAVOVICH LEBED

If you do not put a lot of green plants and trees inside *Moscow Dome,* then what's going to purify the air?

阿纳托利·维亚切斯拉沃维奇·列别德

如果你不在莫斯科穹顶内种植大量绿色植物和树
木，那用什么来净化空气呢？

ALEX

The greenhouses outside the dome can do the job, and
we will install air filters and dump some air out into
the atmosphere while filtering some of it.

亚历克斯

圆顶外的温室可以完成这项工作，我们将安装空
气过滤器，将一些空气排入大气，同时过滤部分
空气。

The music was outstanding since the best musicians in Russia loved to perform for
Vladimir Putin if they had the opportunity. But the end of the evening came too quickly.

音乐非常出色，因为俄罗斯最好的音乐家如果有机会就愿意为弗拉基米尔·普
京演奏。但晚会结束得太快了。

In the morning, Christina announced to Alex:

早上，克里斯蒂娜向亚历克斯宣布：

CHRISTINA

Alina Kabaeva is going to pick up mother and I and
take us shopping and sightseeing.

克里斯蒂娜

阿丽娜·卡巴耶娃要来接我和妈妈，带我们去购物
和观光。

Alex pleasantly thought, those three women going together will be eye candy for sore
eyes in Moscow.

阿历克斯心里愉快地想，这三个女人一起去，一定会成为莫斯科的一道亮丽风
景。

ALEX

Ok, but be careful. Trevor or Buster will go with you.

亚历克斯

好的，但是要小心。特雷弗或巴斯特会和你一起去。

CHRISTINA

There will be lots of security for Alina, do I need them?

克里斯蒂娜

阿丽娜会有很多保安人员，我需要他们吗？

ALEX
I want my sets of eyes and ears there in case something
happens.

亚历克斯
我希望我的眼睛和耳朵能一直在那里, 以防万一。

CHRISTINA
Ok honey but I don't think anything is going to happen.

克里斯蒂娜
好的亲爱的，但我认为不会发生任何事情。

Alex then thought about Christina's father who would have nothing to do for a while.

亚历克斯接着想到了克里斯蒂娜的父亲，他将会暂时无事可做。

ALEX
What about your dad?

亚历克斯
你爸爸呢？

CHRISTINA
I'm sure he can find something to do.

克里斯蒂娜
我相信他能找到事做。

Alex had a thought:

亚历克斯有一个想法：

ALEX
Perhaps you could ask Alina to arrange for that Russian
Special Forces guy, Anatoly Vyacheslavovich Lebed,
we met last night, to take your father to the Moscow
Military Museum?

亚历克斯
也许你可以请阿丽娜安排我们昨晚见过的俄罗斯
特种部队人员阿纳托利·维亚切斯拉沃维奇·列贝德
带你父亲去莫斯科军事博物馆？

CHRISTINA
That's a great idea.

克里斯蒂娜
这是个好主意。

In a few minutes after Christina's phone call to Alina, she received a call back saying that Colonel Lebed, would be arriving in about an hour to take her father to the museum.

克里斯蒂娜给阿丽娜打电话几分钟后，她就接到了回电，说列别德上校将在大约一小时后抵达，带她父亲去博物馆。

Christina scheduled the Russian makeup artist to come up again to take care of her makeup, fingernails, and her hair. To some extent Alex as relieved to have to leave for the meeting and happy that her father would have something to do as well. He was soon on his way. After a knock at the door with Buster announcing a Limo was out front waiting, Alex kissed Christina then departed.

克里斯蒂娜安排俄罗斯化妆师再次上门为她化妆、修指甲和做头发。从某种程度上来说，亚历克斯很高兴自己可以离开去参加会议，也很高兴她的父亲也有事要做。他很快就上路了。巴斯特敲门后宣布有一辆豪华轿车在前面等着，亚历克斯亲吻了克里斯蒂娜，然后离开了。

James Walker, CEO Hercules Steel, Howard Grady, the Cement King, Claude Reardon, the Construction Company owner met with Alex at the American Embassy where they received special treatment.

赫拉克勒斯钢铁公司首席执行官詹姆斯·沃克、水泥大王霍华德·格雷迪、建筑公司老板克劳德·里尔登在美国大使馆会见了亚历克斯，并受到了特殊的待遇。

The U.S. Ambassador was seriously looking into the proposed *Russian Dome* business. To some extent the American Government was jealous but due to their incompetence in this matter, just like the initial space race, the Russians were going to take the lead in *the Dome City Race*.

美国大使正在认真研究俄罗斯提出的穹顶城项目。美国政府在某种程度上对此感到嫉妒，但由于他们在这件事上的无能，就像最初的太空竞赛一样，俄罗斯人将在穹顶城竞赛中占据领先地位。

Alex explained to Ambassador Watson, the Grandson of Thomas Watson, and the son of a former Russian Ambassador:

亚历克斯向托马斯·沃森的孙子、前俄罗斯大使的儿子沃森大使解释道：

ALEX
I'm on record for wanting to build an American Dome
and have proposed two Domes at Twenty-Nine Palms
which would help the U.S. Marine Corp.

亚历克斯
我曾公开表示想建造一座美国穹顶建筑，并已提
议在二十九棕榈村建造两座穹顶建筑，这将有助
于美国海军陆战队。

AMBASSADOR WATSON
What's the delay and how come we never heard about
it?

沃森大使
为什么延误了？我们怎么没听说过？

ALEX
There is too much resistance by locals there.

亚历克斯
那里当地人的抵抗太大了。

AMBASSADOR WATSON
Afraid to screw up their view of Desert Land, I get it.

沃森大使
我明白，他们害怕破坏他们对沙漠之地的看法。

ALEX
Environmentalists are fighting it as well.

亚历克斯
环保主义者也在与之斗争。

AMBASSADOR WATSON
As they fight everything.

沃森大使
他们与一切抗争。

Alex needed to hold this urgent conversation in a SKIF where the four dome management members could discuss the deal without Russians prying.

亚历克斯需要在 斯基尔夫（SKIF）上进行这场紧急对话，以便四名穹顶管理成员能够在不受俄罗斯人窥探的情况下讨论这笔交易。

Ambassador Watson wanted to monitor the four dome builder men so the American State Department would know what they were up to. The Embassy CIA detachment was more than happy to assist Ambassador Watson bugging the SKIF in advance of this meeting.

沃森大使想监视这四名圆顶建造者，以便美国国务院知道他们在做什么。大使馆的 中央情报局 (CIA) 分遣队非常乐意在这次会议之前协助沃森大使窃听 斯基尔夫 (SKIF) 。

Butts Are Us (BAU), a cyberwarfare contractor working for the Cash in Advance boys came in and installed all the surveillance equipment necessary so Ambassador Watson could hear recordings of everything Dome Inc Management said in the SKIFF.

屁股是我们 (BAU) 是一家为 预付现金 (Cash in Advance) 男孩工作的网络战承包商，他们进来安装了所有必要的监控设备，以便大使沃森可以听到 圆顶公司管理(Dome Inc Management) 在 斯基尔夫 (SKIF)上所说的一切录音。

Alex realizing the room could be bugged didn't care, he just wanted consensus between the four men before they committed to the Russians.

亚历克斯意识到房间可能被窃听，但他并不在意，他只是想让四个人在向俄罗斯人做出承诺之前达成共识。

ALEX

Ok Gentlemen, that's the deal. Do we take it or leave it?

亚历克斯

好的，先生们，事情就是这样。我们接受还是拒绝？

Claude also feared their own government was listening announced:

克劳德还担心自己的政府会听到以下消息：

CLAUDE REARDEN

Let's take a secret vote. I'll write yes or no on eight pieces of paper hand each of you a yes and a no paper. I'll pass my hat around and you put back into it one of the two pieces then I will count it out in front of you.

克劳德·里尔登

我们来秘密投票吧。我会在八张纸上写下赞成或反对，然后给你们每人一张赞成和反对的纸。我会把我的帽子传给大家，你们把其中一张放回帽子里，然后我会当着你们的面数数。

ALEX

Fair enough.

亚历克斯

公平地说。

James Walker, CEO Hercules Steel, announced a concern before Claude passed around the vote papers.

在克劳德分发选票文件之前，赫拉克勒斯钢铁公司首席执行官詹姆斯沃克就表达了自己的担忧。

JAMES WALKER

But with the caveat that if our engineering analysis shows we can't do a mile up, we'll agree to attempt just half a mile on the *Moscow Dome* so that we can evaluate whether a full mile up is achievable. I think even 2500 feet up will challenge our abilities.

詹姆斯·沃克

但是，如果我们的工程分析表明我们无法爬升一英里，我们将同意尝试爬升莫斯科穹顶半英里，以便评估是否可以爬升一英里。我认为，即使是 2500 英尺的高空也会挑战我们的能力。

Soon the vote was taken was unanimous. Claude gave the thumbs up. Everyone was positive since each one voted yes. Claude then put all eight pieces of paper in the wastepaper basked, which conveyed no direction of vote.

很快，投票结果一致通过。克劳德竖起了大拇指。每个人都投了赞成票，所以大家都很积极。克劳德随后把所有八张纸都扔进了废纸篓，这表示没有投票方向。

As the men left the SKIF and met Ambassador Watson in the hallway, he appeared readily upset about something. If the truth be known, it was the Russian Government and Vladimir Putin would know the results of that vote before the American Government.

当这些人离开 斯基尔夫（SKIF）并在走廊上遇见沃森大使时，他似乎对某事感到不安。如果事实真相大白，那应该是俄罗斯政府，而弗拉基米尔·普京会比美国政府更早知道投票结果。

That afternoon, the four men were whisked to Putin's Dacha where he met with them in his study sitting at a table large enough for the group.

当天下午，四人被迅速带到普京的别墅，普京在书房与他们会面，桌子足够大，可以容纳四人。

Two Russian English translators were present sitting next to Alex and Vladimir Putin, just to make sure there were no discrepancies in the Language translations.

两名俄语/英语翻译坐在亚历克斯和弗拉基米尔·普京旁边，以确保语言翻译中没有差异。

It was a hard bargain, but Putin agreed that after 1/3 of the Moscow roof structures were installed, they would be allowed to start building Chita Dome.

这是一笔很难的交易，但普京同意，在莫斯科三分之一的屋顶结构安装完成后，他们就可以开始建造赤塔穹顶体育场了。

For Alex, Chita Russia was more important in that it was far more desolate and out of the way, hence it had the most promise for future expansion and growth.

对于阿历克斯来说，俄罗斯赤塔更重要，因为它地处更为荒凉的地区，而且偏僻，因此最有希望进行未来的扩张和发展。

Land in Chita was about 1/20$^{th}$ the cost of Moscow land. So, the initial outlay in buying up the real estate would be far cheaper. Plus, Vladimir Putin did not stipulate a mile high dome. The one-thousand-foot dome would be best for Chita Russia since the design and engineering had been fully tested with a real example being built in Nuuk Greenland.

赤塔的土地价格约为莫斯科土地价格的二十分之一。因此，购买房地产的初始支出将便宜得多。此外，弗拉基米尔·普京并没有规定要建造一英里高的圆顶。一千英尺高的圆顶最适合俄罗斯赤塔，因为设计和工程已经通过格陵兰努克建造的真实样板进行了充分测试。

Putin asked his servant:

普京问仆人：

**VLADIMIR PUTIN**
Dmitri, can you please bring a bottle of Belver Bears Belvedere Vodka and serve them all in my Swarovski Regina Vodka glasses for a toast with these fine gentlemen?

德米特里，你能带一瓶　贝尔弗熊队贝尔维德雷 (Belver Bears Belvedere) 伏特加酒并用我的施华洛世奇 里贾纳 (Regina) 伏特加酒杯为他们倒上一杯，与这些绅士们干杯吗？

**DMITRI**
Mr. President I would be delighted.

德米特里
总统先生，我非常高兴。

At $7,200 a bottle Belver Bears Belvedere vodka tasted distinctively better than most other Vodka's and it naturally seemed to have a bigger kick.

每瓶售价 7,200 美元的 贝尔弗熊队贝尔维德雷 (Belver Bears Belvedere) 伏特加的口感明显优于大多数其他伏特加，而且劲道自然更大。

Moments later Dmitri returned with a tray and a bottle of Belver Bears Belvedere vodka and in front of the guests poured the large size Regina vodka glasses a double shot and systematically handed each to the principal guests near Vladimir Putin followed by the last one going to the Russian President.

片刻之后，德米特里端着托盘和一瓶 贝尔弗熊队贝尔维德雷 (Belver Bears Belvedere) 伏特加回来了，他当着宾客的面用大号 里贾纳 (Regina) 伏特加酒杯倒了双份酒，并有条不紊地递给弗拉基米尔·普京附近的主要宾客，最后把最后一杯递给了俄罗斯总统。

**VLADIMIR PUTIN**
To your health

弗拉基米尔·普京
祝您健康

The guests all gave a similar toast.

来宾们都发出了类似的祝酒声。

**VLADIMIR PUTIN**
This vodka is named after Belweder, the Polish Presidential Palace in Warsaw.

弗拉基米尔·普京
这款伏特加以位于华沙的波兰总统府贝尔韦德 贝
尔韦德(Belweder) 命名。

The Toast was over, and the project was a go. And soon it will be the 8th wonder of the world.

祝酒仪式结束，项目顺利启动。很快它将成为世界第八大奇迹。

***

Anatoly Vyacheslavovich Lebed stepped out of the Zil Limo that Putin sent for him. He was wearing a suit and tie, out of respect for Mr. Garrison.

阿纳托利·维亚切斯拉沃维奇·列别德从普京派来的 齐尔豪华轿车 (Zil Limo) 轿车里走出来。出于对加里森先生的尊重，他穿着西装，打着领带。

The FSB (KGB) provided Colonel Lebed with a Microsoft PowerPoint presentation derived from their dossier on Sargent Garrison, former Green Beret.

俄罗斯联邦安全局（克格勃）向列别德上校提供了一份 微软幻灯片 (Microsoft PowerPoint) 演示文稿，该演示文稿源自他们关于前绿色贝雷帽中士加里森的档案。

Like many Pentagons and OPM records, the KGB hacked long ago. Sargent Garrison's dossier was over two inches thick printed out all the hard copy. Colonel Lebed speed read the dossier and had read books by Colonel Plaster and others on the SOG operations in Cambodia.

就像五角大楼和 OPM 的许多记录一样，克格勃早就入侵了。加里森中士的档案厚达两英寸，所有硬拷贝都打印出来了。列别德上校快速阅读了这份档案，并阅读了普拉斯特上校和其他人撰写的有关 SOG 在柬埔寨行动的书籍。

With Colonel Lebed's Spetsnaz Military indoctrination, and time in Afghanistan, he understood vividly the critical timing required for insertion and extraction of special forces, *especially extraction*. Shoulder launched missiles was a game changer in Afghanistan.

列别德上校曾接受过特种部队的军事训练，并在阿富汗待过一段时间， 他清楚地了解特种部队的插入和撤离（尤其是撤离）所需的关键时间。肩射导弹改变了阿富汗的局势。

Colonel Lebed (Thought)
*Americans were lucky the North Vietnamese only had triple-A, machine guns and rifles to shoot at the helicopters.*

列别德上校 (思想)
美国人很幸运，因为北越只有三 A 机关枪和步枪
来射击直升机。

Anatoly Vyacheslavovich Lebed knows he's lucky to be alive due to the shoulder launched missiles the Americans gave the Mujahideen in Afghanistan.

阿纳托利·维亚切斯拉沃维奇·列别德知道，自己能够活下来是非常幸运的，因为美国向阿富汗圣战者提供了肩射导弹。

On the other hand, Anatoly knew the Russians and all the *Soviet Bloc Countries* provided the North Vietnamese missiles and technology during the Vietnam War.

另一方面，阿纳托利知道俄罗斯和所有苏联集团国家在越南战争期间都向北越提供了导弹和技术。

Colonel Lebed (Thought)
*Looking back at it, Afghanistan was payback time. Iraq was payback multiplied.*

莱贝德上校（思考）
回想起来，阿富汗是报应的时候。伊拉克是报应
成倍增加的时候。

Trevor knocked on the Garrison's room door and announced:

特雷弗敲开了驻军的房间门，宣布道：

TREVOR
Mr. Garrison, your visitor, is down in the hotel lobby
waiting.

特雷弗
您的访客加里森先生正在酒店大堂等候。

William Garrison opened the door, had his winter coat on and was looking forward to the trip.

威廉·加里森 打开门, 穿上冬衣, 期待着这次旅行。

Moscow's Museum of the Armed Forces is located north of Moscow and takes a little while to get there. As they approached, William Garrison could see military devices around the outside of the building including tanks, aircraft, and missiles.

莫斯科武装部队博物馆位于莫斯科北部，需要一段时间才能到达。当他们走近时，威廉·加里森可以看到建筑外围摆放着各种军事设备，包括坦克、飞机和导弹。

Moscow's Museum of the Armed Forces (Wikipedia)
莫斯科武装部队博物馆（维基百科）

The museum was established at the end of World War I and was initially more of a propaganda venue. It was not until the 1990s that it gradually evolved into a true museum and no longer had to do with politics.

该博物馆成立于一战结束后，最初更多的是一个宣传场所，直到20世纪90年代才逐渐演变成一个真正的博物馆，不再与政治扯上关系。

The really only political things there now is the victory banner raised over the Berlin Reichstag in 1945, which is kept here alongside the swathes of captured Nazi standards that were trampled on Red Square during victory celebrations. Old soviet propaganda is simply displays of relics of the past, with no real state sponsorship.

现在，这里唯一真正具有政治意义的东西就是 1945 年在柏林国会大厦上空升起的胜利旗帜，它与在胜利庆典期间被踩踏在红场上的缴获的纳粹旗帜一起保存在这里。旧苏联宣传只是过去遗物的展示，没有真正的国家支持。

Gary Powers U2 SPY PLANE
加里·鲍尔斯 U2 间谍飞机

As William Garrison walked through the museum he saw the remains of US pilot Gary Powers' U-2 spy plane, brought down over the Urals in 1960.

当威廉·加里森走过博物馆时，他看到了美国飞行员加里·鲍尔斯的 U-2 间谍飞机的残骸，该飞机于 1960 年在乌拉尔山脉上空坠毁。

Mr. Garrison a former High School History Teacher knew the rare opportunity he now experienced as he came across a copy of Hitler's Barbarossa Plans to invade Russia.

加里森先生曾是一名高中历史老师，当他偶然发现一份希特勒入侵俄罗斯的巴巴罗萨计划时，他知道自己现在面临一个难得的机会。

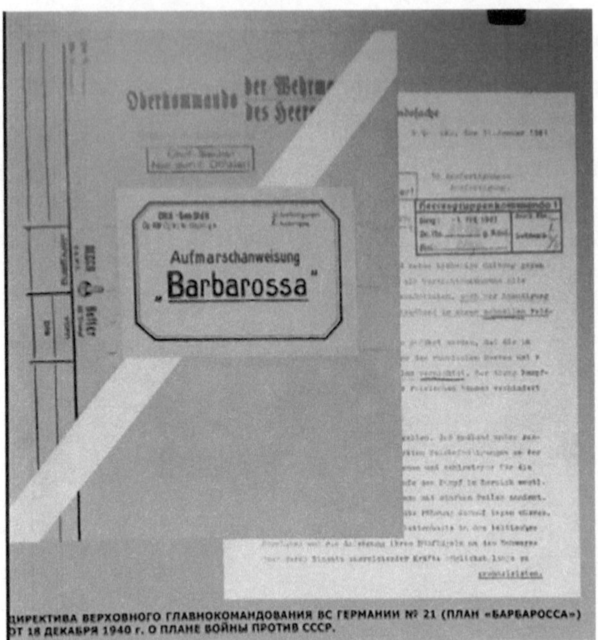


Hitler's Barbarossa Plans
希特勒的巴巴罗萨计划

What struck William Garrison more than anything compared to American Museums was the number of tanks, missiles, and airplanes on exhibit outside the main display building.

与美国博物馆相比，最让威廉·加里森震惊的是主展览楼外展出的坦克、导弹和飞机的数量。

NOTE to the cinematographer: There are a lot of YouTube videos of the museum that could possibly be licensed to use portions to avoid a lot of onsite filming for this sequence. In this video as an example near the end it shows a lot of the aircraft and military hardware located outdoors adjacent to the exhibit hall:

RU (4K) MOSCOW /23.02.2023/Central Museum of the Armed Forces of Russia. - YouTube

摄影师须知：YouTube 上有很多博物馆的视频，可能获得授权使用其中的部分内容，以避免在现场拍摄此片段。在此视频中，作为示例，视频末尾展示了位于展厅附近户外的许多飞机和军事硬件：

RU (4K) 莫斯科 /23.02.2023/俄罗斯武装部队中央博物馆。- YouTube

Today, two conversations were not going to occur about SOG in Vietnam, and about the Mujahedeen blasting a lot of Soviet helicopters out of the sky in Afghanistan.

今天，不会再有两场谈话，关于越南的特种作战大队，以及圣战者在阿富汗空中击落大量苏联直升机。

Brave men on horses carrying shoulder launched missiles on their shoulders, what a concept; the world didn't see it coming.

勇敢的士兵骑在马上，肩扛肩射导弹，这是多么神奇的创意啊；世界从未料到会有这样的事情发生。

The blending of ancient technology with recent technology provided synergism that took down the largest Army in the world.

古代技术与现代技术的结合产生了协同效应，摧毁了世界上规模最大的军队。

Anatoly Vyacheslavovich Lebed had been trained to do sabotage in America if necessary for WW3. He would either be involved in dam busting with suitcase nukes or taking out nuclear power plants to turn America dark again.

阿纳托利·维亚切斯拉沃维奇·列别德曾接受过训练，如果第三次世界大战需要的话，他会在美国进行破坏活动。他要么参与用手提箱核弹摧毁水坝，要么摧毁核电站，让美国再次陷入黑暗。

For Anatoly Vyacheslavovich Lebed to accomplish sabotage during wartime, he was trained in English and sent to America to their consulates at various locations to learn the lay of the land and mingle with the people to get better versed at the language skills.

为了在战争期间完成破坏活动，阿纳托利·维亚切斯拉沃维奇·列别德接受了英语培训，并被派往美国各地的领事馆，了解当地情况，与当地人民交流，以提高语言技能。

Sometimes Anatoly Vyacheslavovich Lebed was used as a watcher for Soviet Spies dealing with American Traitors like John Walker. He was like many other Spetsnaz Officers detailed to the KGB for the special training and operations.

有时，阿纳托利·维亚切斯拉沃维奇·列别德被用作苏联间谍的监视者，监视与约翰·沃克等美国叛徒打交道的苏联间谍。他和其他许多特种部队军官一样，被派往克格勃进行特殊训练和行动。

Allowing many spies to float around America helped poison the well for the Soviets. Several defections and vast dissension occurred as those who traveled to America quickly learned how much propaganda their government put out.

允许大量间谍在美国四处游荡，有助于毒害苏联。前往美国的人很快了解到他们的政府进行了多少宣传，因此发生了数起叛逃事件和巨大的分歧。

A lot of Russian Spies who got caught often sought to defect to the west.

许多被抓获的俄罗斯间谍经常试图叛逃到西方。

The way America punished these spies for their past sins was to send them back to Russia where they got to explain why they got caught. Soviet Officials were tipped off by double agents these highly placed spies attempted to defect.

美国惩罚这些间谍过去所犯下的罪行的方式是将他们遣返回俄罗斯，让他们解释自己被抓的原因。苏联官员得到了双重间谍的情报，这些高级间谍试图叛逃。

At the end of the *Cold War*, many KGB agents who offered to defect were turned away unless they brought with them new INTEL CIA or FBI viewed as important.

冷战结束时，许多提出叛逃的克格勃特工都被拒之门外，除非他们能带来中央情报局或联邦调查局认为重要的新情报。

Since the cold war had ended and neither the Russians nor the Americans truly knew how to proceed. Hawks in both countries continuously threw monkey wrenches into peaceful transcendence.

冷战结束后，美俄双方都不知道下一步该如何走，两国鹰派势力不断给和平超越设置障碍。

International bankers, who stood to lose vast fortunes if the *Cold War* ended, went unmercifully after any progressive thought about ending the antagonism towards Russia. Hence Anatoly Vyacheslavovich Lebed knew soldiers such as Sargent Garrison, had nothing to do with the prevention of peace.

如果冷战结束，国际银行家将损失巨额财富，他们毫不留情地追究任何关于结束与俄罗斯对抗的进步思想。因此，阿纳托利·维亚切斯拉沃维奇·列别德知道，像萨金特·加里森这样的士兵与阻止和平无关。

Sargent Garrison had one other element that Anatoly Vyacheslavovich Lebed felt set him apart from others as he went where few ever had gone in the most arduous manner possible.

阿纳托利·维亚切斯拉沃维奇·列别德认为，加里森中士的另一个与众不同之处在于，他以最艰苦的方式到达了很少有人到达的地方。

Sleeping on a slope tied to tree so that North Vietnamese Night patrols couldn't find you is one of those many rare capabilities that soldiers like the Green Beret Sargent Garrison did unquestioningly for 10 years of war, then the Americans simply left and went home, wasting that huge sacrifice.

睡在斜坡上，绑在树上，这样北越的夜间巡逻队就找不到你，这是众多罕见能力之一，像绿色贝雷帽驻军中士这样的士兵在 10 年的战争中毫不犹豫地做到了这一点，然后美国人就直接离开回家了，浪费了巨大的牺牲。

Anatoly Vyacheslavovich Lebed could not understand why Americans did what they did, then 10 years later the Russians copied their folly and stayed in an unpopular war for 10 years, with far more casualties, plus in the end the Russians also simply drove out of Afghanistan an equal lost cause.

阿纳托利·维亚切斯拉沃维奇·列别德无法理解为什么美国人会做出那样的举动，而十年之后，俄国人也效仿了他们的愚蠢行为，在这场不受欢迎的战争中坚持了十年之久，伤亡人数也更多，而且最后俄国人还干脆把同样失败的军队赶出了阿富汗。

Anatoly Vyacheslavovich Lebed analyzed the two of them simply were champions caught up in lost causes, and the day his Helicopter Squadron Departed Afghanistan, he then knew exactly how William Garrison felt after being sent home from years of fighting and SOG operations, where over half of his buddies didn't make it.

阿纳托利·维亚切斯拉沃维奇·列别德 (Anatoly Vyacheslavovich Lebed) 分析说，他们两个只不过是陷入失败事业的斗士，而当他的直升机中队离开阿富汗的那天，他便完全理解了威廉·加里森 (William Garrison) 在结束多年的战斗和 SOG 行动后被送回国后的感受，在这些行动中，他的一半以上的战友都没有活下来。

The average SOG survival rate was about 18 missions. Sargent Garrison did approximately 200. And thanks to superb KGB operations, Anatoly knew the exact details of some of those missions that had been compromised long ago.

SOG 的平均存活率约为 18 次任务。加里森中士大约执行了 200 次任务。得益于克格勃的出色行动，阿纳托利知道一些早已被泄露的任务的确切细节。

William Garrison managed to get extracted under the most arduous scenarios because in many cases the enemy was tipped off, they were coming in advance through espionage.

威廉·加里森在最艰苦的情况下成功撤离，因为在许多情况下，敌人得到了通风报信，他们通过间谍活动提前到来。

The depth of the penetration was magnified almost a million times when an inept administration simply allowed the North Koreans to grab the Spy Ship Pueblo and all the CRYPTO equipment aboard.

当无能的政府允许朝鲜人夺取间谍船 "普韦布洛号" 和船上所有加密设备时，渗透的深度被放大了近一百万倍。

Coupled with and Army Warrant Officer who sold the CRYPTO to the Russians in Germany, and having the actual hardware to run it on, was taken from the Pueblo, which made the war in Vietnam suddenly get nasty in 1968. The blunder was the President should have ordered the Pueblo sunk by American forces to prevent one of the greatest compromises of national security in American History.

再加上一名陆军准尉将 CRYPTO 卖给了在德国的俄罗斯人，并且拥有运行它的实际硬件，却被从普韦布洛号上夺走，这导致 1968 年越南战争突然变得严峻。错误在于总统本应命令美军击沉普韦布洛号，以防止美国历史上最大的国家安全危机之一。

The Army Warrant Officer should have been executed since the espionage happened during war time.

由于该间谍活动发生在战争时期，这名陆军准尉应该被处决。

Through their Vietnam War, Afghanistan Blunder, the two old cold warriors bonded in a silent way out of mutual respect and knowing what the other had been through. They were just soldiers following orders.

通过越南战争和阿富汗战争，这两位冷战老战士出于相互尊重和了解对方经历过的事情，默默地建立了联系。他们只是服从命令的士兵。

These former war heroes survived to come back to forget the memories of events they would never divulge. They wanted to put behind them the experiences and never wanted to think about them again.

这些前战争英雄们幸存下来，回来是为了忘记那些他们永远不会透露的记忆。他们想把这些经历抛在身后，再也不想想起它们。

***

Christina and her mother were notified by Trevor that Alina Kabaeva was in the hotel lobby waiting for them.

特雷弗通知克里斯蒂娜和她的母亲，阿丽娜·卡巴耶娃正在酒店大堂等候她们。

All three women left with Trevor who was ordered to stay with Christina at all costs.

三名女子都和特雷弗一起离开了，特雷弗被命令不惜一切代价和克里斯蒂娜呆在一起。

**EXT./INT. DAY. MOSCOW RUSSIA. GUM SHOPPING CENTER.**

外景/内景。白天。俄罗斯莫斯科。口香糖购物中心。

The first thing Alina did was take them across the street to GUM, the department store building. It was turning into a tourist trap, but they could afford it and most of the products or souvenirs they might need were located there.

阿丽娜做的第一件事就是带他们穿过马路来到 GUM 百货大楼。那里正变成一个旅游陷阱，但他们负担得起，而且他们可能需要的大多数产品或纪念品都在那里。

Alex had schooled Christina not to use her credit card in Moscow because she didn't need too and because it allowed such large amounts of transactions, if the Russian Mafia got the number, they would tap it real fast. As such he brought along a lot of Russian Rubles. The benefits of flying in on a personal Jet are your luggage is not subject to inspections; hence it's much easier to carry a lot of cash around.

亚历克斯告诉克里斯蒂娜不要在莫斯科使用信用卡，因为她不需要，而且信用卡允许进行大额交易，如果俄罗斯黑手党得到这个号码，他们会很快盗刷。因此他带了很多俄罗斯卢布。乘坐私人飞机的好处是你的行李不受检查；因此随身携带大量现金要容易得多。

Should they need any more cash, Alex would simply make a call and send Brad and Gladys to one of the large banks in Moscow where an amount of Rubles would be provided, but that wasn't expected.

如果他们需要更多现金，亚历克斯只需打个电话，让布拉德和格拉迪斯去莫斯科的一家大银行，那里会提供一定数量的卢布，但这并不在亚历克斯的预料之中。

Christina took note of several items that she would arrange to obtain later when she and her mother would come back in their spare time.

克里斯蒂娜记下了几件物品，她准备等她和母亲有空回来时买下来。

Alina was touched by the numerous positive comments that Christina made about a lot of the merchandise.

克里斯蒂娜对许多商品的积极评价让阿丽娜很感动。

ALINA KABAYEVA
You do not want to buy anything now?

阿丽娜·卡巴耶娃
(ALINA KABAYEVA)

您现在不想买任何东西吗？

CHRISTINA
No, we'll come back later where we can spend a few
hours when Alex is busy with his partners which will
give us something to do.

克里斯蒂娜
不，我们稍后再回来，等亚历克斯和他的伙伴们
忙完后，我们就可以花几个小时做点事情了。

ALINA KABAYEVA
Good idea.

阿丽娜·卡巴耶娃
好主意。

After the three women walked around for about 15 minutes, Christina noticed, a growing crowd was starting to follow them. The expected pictures were starting to be taken by a wide spectrum of individuals.

三个女人走了大约 15 分钟后，克里斯蒂娜注意到，越来越多的人开始跟随她们。正如预料的那样，各种各样的人开始拍照。

Most of the people following the three women were just curious tourists who had overheard Vladimir Putin's special friend (mistress) Alina Kabayeva was walking through GUM, and she was also in the company of the DOME GUY Alex Baxter's exotic looking wife Christina Garrison and her mother!

跟随这三名女子的大多数人只是好奇的游客，他们无意中听到弗拉基米尔·普京的密友（情妇）阿琳娜·卡巴耶娃 (Alina Kabayeva) 走过 GUM，而和她在一起的还有 穹顶人 (DOME GUY) 亚历克斯·巴克斯特 (Alex Baxter) 的异国妻子克里斯蒂娜·加里森 (Christina Garrison) 和她的母亲！

Some of the individuals taking pictures of the three very well-dressed women put the pictures on their Facebook accounts. In five5 minutes, a couple of the pictures went viral.

一些为这三名衣着考究的女子拍照的人将照片上传到了自己的 脸书 (Facebook) 账户上。五分钟内，其中几张照片就传遍了网络。

Before long Google Search Engines had one of sudden posts going viral as one of the top 20 topics trending.

不久之后，谷歌搜索引擎中的一篇帖子突然成为最热门的 20 个话题之一。

It didn't take long for that information to find its way to *Magazine Femmes Réelles Exigeantes*. As soon as one of the staff writers saw it, he emailed the link to Charles Denning, the head of the editorial board. A few minutes later Charles Denning contacted *Michelle Montez* and asked her to come into his office.

这条信息很快就传到了《真实女性杂志》上。一名编辑看到后，立即将链接通过电子邮件发送给了编辑委员会主席查尔斯·丹宁 (Charles Denning)。几分钟后，查尔斯·丹宁联系了 米歇尔·蒙特兹 (*Michelle Montez*)，请她到他的办公室来。

*Michell Montez* arrived in somewhat an excited manner because usually the only time she was called into Charles Denning's office was to get an assignment to a hot story.

米歇尔·蒙特兹 (*Michell Montez*) 来的时候显得有些兴奋，因为通常她被叫到查尔斯·丹宁 (Charles Denning) 办公室的唯一一次目的就是接到一个热门报道的任务。

NOTE to Director/Cinematographer: this next sequence with Michell Montez talking with Charles Denning can be filmed in French with English and Chinese subtitles:

*MICHELLE MONTEZ*
*De quoi veux-tu me parler?*
What do you want to talk to me about?


米歇尔·蒙特兹
你想跟我谈什么？


CHARLES DENNING
*Regarde ça.*
Take a look at this.


查尔斯·丹宁
看看这个。


Charles Denning rotated his laptop around so that *Michelle Montez* could see the screen.

查尔斯·丹宁 (Charles Denning) 旋转了他的笔记本电脑，以便米歇尔·蒙特兹 (*Michelle Montez*) 可以看到屏幕。


*MICHELLE MONTEZ*
*Qu'allons-nous faire à ce sujet?*
What are we going to do about it?


米歇尔·蒙特兹
我们该怎么办？


CHARLES DENNING
*Il y a peut-être une histoire là-bas. Avez-vous encore*
*des contacts à Moscou?*

There might be a story there. Do you still have contacts
in Moscow?


查尔斯·丹宁
那里可能有个故事。你在莫斯科还有联系人吗？


*MICHELLE MONTEZ*
*J'ai un bon contact, mais il attend toujours une*
*contrepartie pour m'aider.*

I have one good contact, but he is always expecting
some quid pro quo to help me.

米歇尔·蒙特兹
我有一个很好的联系人，但他总是希望得到一些
回报来帮助我。

**CHARLES DENNING**
*Il est tard dans la matinée; je parie que M. Baxter et Vladimir Poutine sont peut-être en train de socialiser ce soir puisque la maîtresse de Vladimir Poutine, Alina Kabayeva, est en public en ce moment avec la femme d'Alex Baxter.*

It's late in the morning; I would bet that Mr. Baxter and Vladimir Putin may be socializing tonight since Vladimir Putin's mistress Alina Kabayeva is in public right now with Alex Baxter's wife.

查尔斯·丹宁
现在已经是上午晚些时候了；我敢打赌，巴克斯
特先生和弗拉基米尔·普京今晚可能在社交，因为
弗拉基米尔·普京的情妇阿丽娜·卡巴耶娃现在正和
亚历克斯·巴克斯特的妻子一起出现在公众面前。

*MICHELLE MONTEZ*
*Alors, qu'allons-nous faire?*
So, what are we going to do?

米歇尔·蒙特兹
现在，我们该怎么办？

**CHARLES DENNING**
*Avez-vous préparé votre sac de voyage?*
Do you have a travel bag packed?

查尔斯·丹宁
你的旅行包准备好了吗？

*MICHELLE MONTEZ*
*Vous savez que j'ai toujours un sac d'urgence pour des moments comme celui-ci.*

You know I always have an emergency bag pack for moments like this.

米歇尔·蒙特兹
你知道，我总是带着一个应急包，以备不时之需。

**CHARLES DENNING**
*Rentrez chez vous, prenez votre sac, rendez-vous à l'aéroport, le personnel prendra les dispositions nécessaires pour votre vol et votre chambre d'hôtel. Nous organiserons une prise en charge en limousine à l'aéroport de Moscou et vous conduirons à votre hôtel.*

Go home, grab your bag, get to the airport, the staff will make arrangements for your flight and hotel room. We'll arrange for Limo to pick you up at the Airport in Moscow and take you to your hotel.

查尔斯·丹宁
回家，拿上行李，前往机场，工作人员会为您安排航班和酒店房间。我们会安排豪华轿车在莫斯科机场接您，然后送您到酒店。

*MICHELLE MONTEZ*
*Bon, je vais quitter le bureau tout de suite.*
Alright, I shall be leaving the office right away.

米歇尔·蒙特兹
好的，我马上就离开办公室。

**CHARLES DENNING**
*Une autre chose, arrêtez-vous au bureau de Pierre, je l'appellerai dans un instant. Pierre doit avoir quelques roubles à vous transférer pour certaines de vos dépenses et au cas où vous devriez soudoyer quelqu'un.*

One other thing, stop over at Pierre's desk, I'll call him momentarily. Pierre should have some Rubles to transfer to you for some of your expenses and in case you must bribe someone.

查尔斯·丹宁
还有一件事，你去皮埃尔的办公桌那边等一下，我马上就给他打电话。皮埃尔应该有一些卢布可以转给你，以支付你的一些费用，以防你需要贿赂某人。

*MICHELLE MONTEZ*
*Ça ira.*
Will do.

米歇尔·蒙特兹
会的。

**CHARLES DENNING**
*Un hôtel particulier dans lequel vous aimeriez séjourner?*
Any particular hotel you want to stay at?

查尔斯·丹宁
你想住哪家特定的酒店？

*MICHELLE MONTEZ*
*Réservez-moi à l'hôtel Kempinski dans le quartier de
la Place Rouge.*

Book me at the Kempinski Hotel in the Red Square
area.

米歇尔·蒙特兹
为我预订红场区的凯宾斯基酒店。

*Michelle Montez* gave the cab a nice tip to get her home and to the airport as fast as
possible.

米歇尔·蒙特兹 (Michelle Montez) 给了出租车司机一笔丰厚的小费，以便尽快
送她回家并去机场。

*Michelle Montez* made it to the airport in time to get on the next Air France flight to
Moscow.

米歇尔·蒙特兹及时赶到机场，搭乘下一班法航航班飞往莫斯科。

With a four-hour flight that would get her there in time to be in position to arrive at
a social location where Vladimir Putin would likely take Alex and Christina. If her
hunch was right, it would be a symphony or ballet.

经过四个小时的飞行，她可以及时到达弗拉基米尔·普京可能会带亚历克斯和
克里斯蒂娜去的一个社交场所。如果她的直觉没错的话，那将是一场交响乐或
芭蕾舞。

***

Alina Kabaeva could tell it was time to depart GUM and take Christina somewhere
else before the crowd got out of control. Her itinerary included Cathedral of the
Annunciation (Blagoveshchensk Sobor), which was nearby, then they would go to a
nice restaurant for lunch.

阿丽娜·卡巴耶娃知道是时候离开古姆百货商场，带克里斯蒂娜去别的地方，

以免人群失控。她的行程包括参观附近的天使报喜大教堂（布拉戈维申斯克大教堂），然后她们会去一家不错的餐厅吃午饭。

Cathedral of the Annunciation (Blagoveshchensk Sobor)

When Alina Kabaeva and her guests arrived at the Cathedral of the Annunciation (Blagoveshchensk Sobor), Patriarch Kirill, who was a close friend to Vladimir Putin, was waiting to give them a personal tour.

当阿丽娜·卡巴耶娃和她的客人抵达天使报喜大教堂（布拉戈维申斯克大教堂）时，普京的密友基里尔大牧首正在等候，并亲自带领他们参观。

Note: for internal view of Cathedral of the Annunciation (Blagoveshchensk Sobor):

注：天使报喜大教堂（布拉戈维申斯克大教堂）的内部景观：

<u>Moscow church of the annunciation blagoveshchensk sober interior pictures - Search Images</u>

PATRIARCH KIRILL
(a.k.a. Vladimir Mikhailovich Gundyayev)
Dobroye utro, Alina Kabayeva, missis Garrison i missis Bakster.

[Доброе утро, Алина Кабаева, миссис Гаррисон и миссис Бакстер.]

{Good morning, Alina Kabaeva, Mrs. Garrison and Mrs. Baxter.}

基里尔大主教
（又名 弗拉基米尔·米哈伊洛维奇·贡佳耶夫）
早上好，阿琳娜·卡巴耶娃和巴克斯特夫人。

**ALINA KABAEVA**
Dobroye utro, Patriarkh Kirill.
[Доброе утро, Патриарх Кирилл.]
{Good morning, Patriarch Kirill}

阿丽娜·卡巴伊娃
早上好，基里尔宗主教

**PATRIARCH KIRILL**
Pozvol'te mne pokazat' vam okrestnosti.
[Позвольте мне показать вам окрестности.]
{Let me show you around.}

基里尔大主教
让我带你四处看看。

**ALINA KABAEVA**
Nam by eto ochen' ponravilos'.
[Нам бы это очень понравилось.]
{[We would love that.]

阿丽娜·卡巴伊娃
我们会喜欢的。

**PATRIARCH KIRILL**
Eta tserkov' byla zavershena v 1489 godu, no byla sozhzhena, perestroyena i pozzhe razgrablena armiyey Napoleona, byla tsentrom mnozhestva intrig i imela neveroyatnuyu istoriyu. Yeye zolotyye kupola imeli osobuyu arkhitekturu, kotoraya imeyet vechnuyu privlekatel'nost'.

[Эта церковь была завершена в 1489 году, но была сожжена, перестроена и позже разграблена армией Наполеона, была центром множества интриг и имела невероятную историю. Ее золотые купола имели особую архитектуру, которая имеет вечную привлекательность.]

{This church was completed in 1489, but had been burned down rebuilt and later, looted by Napoleon's Army, had been the center of a lot of intrigue and had an incredible history. Its gold domes had a distinct architecture that has an everlasting appeal.}

基里尔大主教
这座教堂于 1489 年建成，但被烧毁重建，后来被拿破仑军队洗劫一空，成为众多阴谋的中心，有着令人难以置信的历史。它的金色圆顶具有独特的建筑风格，具有永恒的吸引力。

## ALINA KABAEVA

V inter'yere Blagoveshchenskogo sobora predstavleno krupnoye proizvedeniye iskusstva.

[В интерьере Благовещенского собора представлено крупное произведение искусства.]

{The Blagoveshchensk Sobor interior exhibits a major work of art.}

阿丽娜·卡巴伊娃
布拉戈维申斯克索博尔的内部展示了一件重要的艺术品。

## PATRIARCH KIRILL

Seychas eta tserkov' bol'she turisticheskaya dostoprimechatel'nost'. No ona prodemonstrirovala ustoychivost' Russkoy pravoslavnoy tserkvi, i s prinyatiyem tserkvi Vladimirom Putinym yeye budushcheye vyglyadit namnogo svetleye.

[Сейчас эта церковь больше туристическая достопримечательность. Но она продемонстрировала устойчивость Русской православной церкви, и с принятием церкви Владимиром Путиным ее будущее выглядит намного светлее.]

{Now this church is more of a tourist attraction. But it demonstrated the resiliency of the Russian Orthodox Church and with Vladimir Putin embracing the church, its future looks a lot brighter.}

基里尔大主教
现在这座教堂更像是一个旅游景点。但它展示了

俄罗斯东正教的韧性，随着弗拉基米尔·普京对这
座教堂的支持，它的未来看起来更加光明。

Patriarch Kirill was the subject of a lot of media attention and had been recently in the news. His relationship with Vladimir Putin significantly elevated his status, and at the same time the Russian Orthodox Church was now becoming a new member of the power brokers in Russia.

基里尔大牧首是媒体关注的焦点，最近频频登上新闻头条。他与普京的关系大大提升了他的地位，与此同时，俄罗斯东正教会也成为俄罗斯权力掮客的新成员。

Lenin and Stalin are turning over in their graves. The atheist communists had lost their grip on the country. The heavenly father Patriarch Kirill now had more influences over the masses.

列宁和斯大林在坟墓里翻身了。无神论共产主义者已经失去了对国家的控制。天父基里尔大牧首现在对群众的影响力更大了。

## PATRIARCH KIRILL

Posle 1992 goda vozobnovilis' otdel'nyye bogosluzheniya, v tom chisle bogosluzheniye v prazdnik Blagoveshcheniya, kotoroye provodil Patriarkh Moskovskiy. Zdaniye tserkvi bylo otrestavrirovano v 2009 godu.

[После 1992 года возобновились отдельные богослужения, в том числе богослужение в праздник Благовещения, которое проводил Патриарх Московский. Здание церкви было отреставрировано в 2009 году.]

{After 1992, occasional religious services resumed, including a service on the Feast of the Annunciation, conducted by the Patriarch of Moscow. The church building underwent a restoration in 2009.}

### 基里尔大主教

1992 年后，教堂恢复了偶尔举行的宗教仪式，包括由莫斯科牧首主持的圣母领报节仪式。教堂建筑于 2009 年进行了修复。

## CHRISTINA

Vyglyadit velikolepno, mastera prodelali bol'shuyu rabotu po yego vosstanovleniyu.

[Выглядит великолепно, мастера проделали большую работу по его восстановлению.]

{It looks wonderful the craftsmen did a great job renovating it.}

克里斯蒂娜
它看起来棒极了，工匠们把它翻新得非常好。

PATRIARCH KIRILL
Kak vam Moskva, missis Bakster?
[Как вам Москва, миссис Бакстер?]
{How do you like Moscow so far, Mrs. Baxter?}

基里尔大主教
巴克斯特夫人，您觉得莫斯科怎么样？

CHRISTINA
Patriarkh Kirill, ya poka malo chto videl, tak chto, chestno govorya, ya ne tak uzh mnogo znayu o Moskve, izvinite.

[Патриарх Кирилл, я пока мало что видел, так что, честно говоря, я не так уж много знаю о Москве, извините.]

[Patriarch Kirill I've not seen a lot of it yet, so to be honest I don't know much about Moscow, I'm sorry.]

克里斯蒂娜
我还没有看过很多，所以说实话我对莫斯科不太了解，很抱歉。

PATRIARCH KIRILL
Ne izvinyaytes', i ya nadeyus', chto vashe prebyvaniye budet priyatnym.

[Не извиняйтесь, и я надеюсь, что ваше пребывание будет приятным.]

{Don't be sorry, and I hope you have an enjoyable stay.}

基里尔大主教
不要感到遗憾，希望您在这里过得愉快。

CHRISTINA
Spasibo.
Спасибо.
[Thank you.]

克里斯蒂娜
谢谢。

It did not take long to see the Cathedral's interior, and Patriarch Kirill was pleasantly pleased that Christina would want to visit the Cathedral since she had many other options.

没过多久，他们就参观完了大教堂的内部，基里尔大主教很高兴克里斯蒂娜愿意参观大教堂，因为她还有很多其他的选择。

Christina's visit would help build a foundation for future support from the Church. And when she engaged Patriarch Kirill in Russian language, she touched him deeply, as her persona and demeanor though very respectful, also was delightful.

克里斯蒂娜的来访为教会未来提供支持奠定了基础。当她用俄语与基里尔牧首交谈时，她深深地打动了他，因为她的性格和举止虽然非常尊重，但也令人愉快。

Christina was glad to leave the Cathedral since she felt a little hungry and figured her mother was too, even though she was a good trooper and conducted herself in the most dignified manner.

克里斯蒂娜很高兴离开大教堂，因为她觉得有点饿，而且她认为她的母亲也是如此，尽管她是一名好士兵，并且举止得体。

One other aspect of Alex Baxter's visit, which Patriarch Kirill did not fail to notice and hear about from several sources, was the unique nature of Alex taking his in-laws along on his working honeymoon. That would be unheard of in Russia!

亚历克斯·巴克斯特此次访问的另一个特点是，基里尔大主教注意到了这一点，并从多个消息来源听说了这一情况，那就是亚历克斯带着他的姻亲一起度工作蜜月，这在俄罗斯是闻所未闻的！

The three women didn't have far to walk. Soon they were at the Bosco Bar, which had fantastic service, and the food looked and tasted as it should when a top world chef was in charge of the Kitchen.

三位女士不用走多远，很快就到了 博斯科 酒吧 (Bosco Bar) 。酒吧的服务非常棒，食物看起来和尝起来都像是世界顶级厨师掌勺的。

Typically, this time of day, Bosco Bar usually wasn't full of customers, because the prices were a little expensive for the high quality and thus was more of a dinner restaurant and fashionable bar.

通常这个时间，博斯科酒吧一般不会挤满顾客，因为这里的价格相对于品质来说有点贵，因此更像是一家晚餐餐厅和时尚酒吧。

Since the visit to Bosco Bar was on Alina's official itinerary, several of the customers sitting in there filling up the restaurant were FSB (KGB) agents (males and females). Neither Christina nor Alina really understood the level of security present this day. And they were all good actors. Nobody would know the tables surrounding their reserved table for 4 (the 3 women and Trevor), were inhabited exclusively by FSB personnel.

由于博斯科酒吧之行是阿丽娜的官方行程，餐厅里坐满了几位顾客，他们其实是联邦安全局 (KGB) 的特工（男性和女性）。克里斯蒂娜和阿丽娜都不太清楚今天的安保程度。而且他们都是演技高超的人。没人会知道，他们预订的四人桌（三名女性和特雷弗）周围的桌子都是联邦安全局的工作人员。

The manager suspected that was the case, but since this large crowd for this time of day was filling his cash registers, he didn't care. Ivan also enjoyed the view of the two gorgeous women that were seated. He knew who Alina was since she was locally a famous person because of the rumors swirling around her relationship with Vladimir Putin.

经理怀疑情况确实如此，但由于这个时间段人潮汹涌，收银机已经满了，所以他也不介意。伊万也欣赏着坐在那里的两位美女的风景。他知道阿丽娜是谁，因为她在当地很有名，因为有传言说她和弗拉基米尔·普京有关系。

IVAN<br>
What would you ladies like to drink?

伊万<br>
各位女士想喝什么？

Ivan pretty much ignored Trevor since it was obvious he was part of the security team only sitting at the table so that it didn't look awkward.

伊万几乎忽略了特雷弗，因为很明显他是保安团队的一员，只是坐在桌边，以免显得尴尬。

ALINA KABAEVA<br>
I'll have white wine.

阿丽娜·卡巴耶娃<br>
我要白葡萄酒。

MRS. GARRISON<br>
So, will I.

加里森夫人<br>
我也是。

CHRISTINA<br>
Make that three.

克里斯蒂娜
一共有三个。

IVAN
Sir?

伊万
奶酪？

TREVER
I'll just have hot tea please.

特雷弗
请给我一杯热茶。

No sooner than after Ivan departed the table, Alina Kabaeva shocked Christina with a question:

伊万刚离开餐桌，阿琳娜·卡巴耶娃就问了克里斯蒂娜一个令她震惊的问题：

ALINA KABAYEVA
Tell me Christina, is Alex a good lover?

阿丽娜·卡巴耶娃
告诉我克里斯蒂娜，亚历克斯是个好情人吗？

Somewhat in shock, Christina didn't know how to respond but said some things that surprised Alina.

克里斯蒂娜有些震惊，不知道该如何回应，但却说了一些让阿丽娜感到惊讶的话。

CHRISTINA
Alina, my husband, is very gentle and very kind. I could not ask for a better partner.

克里斯蒂娜
我的丈夫阿丽娜非常温柔、善良。我找不到比她更好的伴侣了。

ALINA KABAYEVA
Christina, I understand you are newlyweds?

阿丽娜·卡巴耶娃
克里斯蒂娜，我知道你们是新婚夫妇？

CHRISTINA
Yes, we are.


克里斯蒂娜
是的，我们是。


ALINA KABAEVA
How does your husband feel about your parents tagging along during your honeymoon, its unheard of here in Russia?


阿丽娜·卡巴伊娃
你丈夫对于你父母在蜜月期间跟着你有什么看法，这在俄罗斯是闻所未闻的？


CHRISTINA
Alex loves my parents. He invited them along. He's now a member of the family. We are very close.


克里斯蒂娜
亚历克斯爱我的父母。他邀请他们一起来。他现在是我们家的一员。我们关系非常亲密。


ALINA KABAYEVA
Very close?


阿丽娜·卡巴耶娃
信仰接近吗？


Mrs. Garrison emphasized:

加里森女士强调：


MRS. GARRISON
We are.


加里森夫人
是的。


ALINA KABAYEVA
But how do you handle moments of passion if mom and dad are around, they're almost certain to hear something?


阿丽娜·卡巴耶娃
但是，如果爸爸妈妈在身边，他们几乎肯定会听到一些事情，你该如何处理激情时刻呢？

CHRISTINA
We just wait till we hear them snoring, then we proceed!

克里斯蒂娜
我们只要等到听到他们打呼噜，然后我们就可以
继续了！

There was huge laughter. Some of the agents nearby who were not only recording the conversation but listening to it in their camouflaged ear buds cracked up giving away their cover.

现场爆发出一阵大笑。附近的一些特工不仅录下了他们的对话，还戴着伪装的耳塞听着他们的对话，他们忍不住哈哈大笑起来，暴露了他们的身份。

After lunch Alina walked with Christina and her Mrs. Garrison back to their hotel where she bid them goodbye and expected to catch up with them again in a day or two up in St. Petersburg where they would stop next. Alex decided it would be important for his teacher-in-laws to see the Hermitage and the Bolshoi.

午饭后，阿丽娜和克里斯蒂娜以及加里森夫人一起步行回酒店，向她们道别，并希望一两天后在圣彼得堡再次见到她们，她们下一站就是圣彼得堡。亚历克斯认为，让岳父岳母参观冬宫和莫斯科大剧院很重要。

The Spetsnaz Colonel, Anatoly Vyacheslavovich Lebed, brought Mr. Garrison back to the hotel where he went directly up to his room. Mr. Garrison was alone for a while.

特种部队上校阿纳托利·维亚切斯拉沃维奇·列别德将加里森先生带回酒店，他直接上楼回房间。加里森先生独自待了一会儿。

Christina and her mother went to Christina's room because Christina wanted to take a bubble bath, but didn't want to be in the room alone during the bath. If Alex had been there she would have been comfortable, but having her mother there was also satisfactory as it made her feel safe from possible intruders.

克里斯蒂娜和她的母亲去了克里斯蒂娜的房间，因为克里斯蒂娜想泡个泡泡浴，但又不想在洗澡时一个人待在房间里。如果亚历克斯在场，她会感到很舒服，但有母亲在场也让她感到很满意，因为这让她感到安全，不会有入侵者。

Eventually Alex returned and scared his mother-in-law slightly when he opened the door because they didn't expect him back at that moment.

最后亚历克斯回来了，当他打开门时，他的岳母有点被吓到了，因为她们没想到他会在那一刻回来。

MRS. GARRISON
Alex, you scared me.

加里森夫人
亚历克斯，你吓到我了。

ALEX
I'm sorry.

亚历克斯
对不起。

MRS. GARRISON
Hey Alex, since you are back, I'm going to our room
to see if Mr. Garrison is back.

加里森夫人
嘿，亚历克斯，既然你回来了，我要去我们房间
看看威廉回来了吗。

ALEX
Mother, where's Christina?

亚历克斯
妈妈，克里斯蒂娜在哪儿？

MRS. GARRISON
Alex, after I leave, you can explore and try to find out
where she is.

加里森夫人
亚历克斯，我走后，你可以去探索一下，看看她
在哪里。

Mrs. Garrison put on a wicked smile then left.

加里森夫人露出一丝邪恶的笑容，然后离开了。

Alex made a good guess and walked up to the bathroom door and knocked.

亚历克斯猜对了，他走到浴室门口敲了敲门。

ALEX
Christina, I'm home.

亚历克斯
克里斯蒂娜，我回来了。

CHRISTINA
Is mother still here?

克里斯蒂娜
妈妈还在吗？

ALEX
No, she just left, wanted to go see if your father was back yet.

亚历克斯
不，她刚刚离开，想去看看你爸爸回来没。

CHRISTINA
Ok.

克里斯蒂娜
好的。

ALEX
May I come in?

亚历克斯
我可以进来吗？

CHRISTINA
Only if you are properly prepared.

克里斯蒂娜
只有你做好了充分的准备才行。

ALEX
Room for two?

亚历克斯
两人间？

CHRISTINA
I think so.

克里斯蒂娜
我想是的。

ALEX
I need to get something to help prepare, give me a couple minutes.

亚历克斯
我需要准备一些东西，给我几分钟。

CHRISTINA
Hurry up, I don't want to shrivel like a fish.

克里斯蒂娜
快点，我不想像鱼一样枯萎。

Alex called room service and asked for a bottle of Dom Perignon and announced:

亚历克斯打电话给客房服务部，要了一瓶唐培里侬香槟王，然后宣布：

ALEX
If the Champagne is in this room in five minutes, the
deliverer will get $100.00 tip.

亚历克斯
如果香槟在五分钟内到达这个房间，送货员将获
得 100.00 美元的小费。

In four minutes, Alex was giving the young Russian lady $100 tip a moment before
she departed the hotel room.

四分钟后，在这位俄罗斯年轻女士离开酒店房间之前，亚历克斯给了她 100 美
元小费。

After the hotel employee left, Alex poured two glasses of Dom Perignon Champagne,
then walked into the bathroom sat them on the edge of the tub that had a large surface
area to lay objects then announced:

酒店工作人员离开后，亚历克斯倒了两杯唐培里侬香槟王，然后走进浴室，把
杯子放在了浴缸边缘，浴缸的面积很大，可以放东西，然后宣布道：

ALEX
I'll be back in a minute.

亚历克斯
我一会儿就回来。

True to his words, Alex was climbing in the tub with Christina and handed her one of
the champagne glasses he took the other and they toasted. Christina took a deep drink,
put the glass down on the edge of the bathtub.

亚历克斯果然和克里斯蒂娜一起爬进浴缸，递给她一只香槟酒杯，然后拿起另
一只，两人举杯庆祝。克里斯蒂娜喝了一大口，把杯子放在浴缸边上。

Christina took control of Alex's champagne glass, sat it down next to her glass.
Christina then put her arms around Alex and pulled him close to where they got into
a good loving position. The newlywed couple kissed most passionately and enjoyed
the bath together.

克里斯蒂娜接过亚历克斯的香槟酒杯，把它放在她的酒杯旁边。克里斯蒂娜用手臂搂住亚历克斯，把他拉近，两人摆出一个亲密的姿势。这对新婚夫妇热情地接吻，一起享受沐浴。

Mr. Garrison noticed how beautiful his wife Ethel looked when she arrived back in their hotel room. The 70-year-old had a sudden flash of romance. This trip had suddenly rekindled a fire that had slowly been burning out in recent years, and now the flames were shooting high as if someone had put new fuel on the fire.

加里森先生回到酒店房间时，注意到妻子埃塞尔看起来多么美丽。这位 70 岁老人突然闪现出浪漫的火花。这次旅行突然重新点燃了近年来慢慢熄灭的爱情之火，现在火焰越来越旺，就像有人在火上加了新的燃料一样。

After newlywed recreation in the bathtub was completed and the next door hotel room elderly sojourn back in time and space to temporal ecstasy, the couples understood it would soon be time to prepare for their evening events.

新婚夫妇在浴缸中结束娱乐活动后，隔壁酒店房间里的老人回到了时空，享受着暂时的狂喜，夫妻俩明白很快就该为他们晚上的活动做准备了。

More makeup, hair design, and fingernails, and then Christina and her mother were looking exceptionally good. Alex was proud of his bride and Mr. Garrison appreciated all this activity and made his wife appear 25 years younger.

化妆、做发型、修指甲，克里斯蒂娜和她的母亲看起来都特别漂亮。亚历克斯为他的新娘感到骄傲，加里森先生很欣赏这一切，让妻子看起来年轻了　25 岁。

Note: <u>Moscow symphony orchestra - Search Images</u>

注：莫斯科交响乐团 - 搜索图片

### ALEX
Christina, we have reservations for the Moscow Symphony and will meet my business partners there so let's have dinner in the hotel restaurant, then we can leave the hotel and go to the symphony.

### 亚历克斯
克里斯蒂娜，我们预订了莫斯科交响乐团的演出，并将在那里与我的商业伙伴见面，所以我们在酒店餐厅吃晚饭，然后我们可以离开酒店去听交响乐。

### CHRISTINA
That sounds good.

### 克里斯蒂娜
听起来不错。

Christina informed her parents of the plan soon after they arrived dressed and ready to head out.

当他们到达并穿好衣服准备出发时，克里斯蒂娜很快就将这个计划告知了父母。

<u>INT. EVENING. MOSCOW RUSSIA. BALTSCHUG KEMPINSKI HOTEL. ALEX, CHRISTINA, THE GARRISONS AND ONE OF THE SECURITY MEN GO TO THE HOTEL'S RESTAURANT AND HAVE A MEAL. SIX SEQUENCES TOTAL. (30 SECONDS COMBINED).</u>

Note: this is a quick video segment showing a nice dinner in a luxurious restaurant fit for a wealthy person and the family enjoying the time together.

内景。晚上。俄罗斯莫斯科。巴尔舒格凯宾斯基酒店。亚历克斯、克里斯蒂娜、驻军和一名保安人员前往酒店餐厅用餐。共六个片段。（合计 30 秒）。

注意：这是一个简短的视频片段，展示了在一家豪华餐厅享用美味晚餐，适合富人和家人一起享受时光。

After a quick meal at the hotel restaurant, Alex and the family went back to their rooms to freshen up then get ready to travel to the Moscow Symphony.

在酒店餐厅快速吃完饭后，亚历克斯和家人回到房间梳洗一番，然后准备前往莫斯科交响乐团。

***

When Alex got out of the elevator and walked past the front desk, he was looking at his wife and the Garrisons waiting for him in the lobby and thus missed detecting the woman who was checking in the hotel.

当亚历克斯走出电梯，走过前台时，他正看着大厅里等待他的妻子和加里森一家，因此没有注意到正在酒店办理入住手续的女人。

*Michelle Montez* had just given her credit card to the hotel clerk as she was checking in, and in the mirror directly ahead could see people passing by, who were mostly speaking Russian.

米歇尔·蒙特兹 (*Michelle Montez*) 在办理入住手续时刚刚将她的信用卡交给酒店工作人员，从正前方的镜子里可以看到路过的人，他们大多说俄语。

Then suddenly someone was speaking English directly behind her, and in the mirror, she saw a pleasant surprise. *Michelle Montez's* target Alex Baxter had just stepped out of the elevator.

突然，有人在她身后说英语，镜子里，她看到了一个惊喜。米歇尔·蒙特兹的目标亚历克斯·巴克斯特刚刚从电梯里走出来。

*MICHELLE MONTEZ* (Thought)
*What a pleasant surprise. Alex Baxter is probably a*
*hotel guest here at the* Baltschug Kempinski Hotel.

米歇尔·蒙特兹（心想）
真是个惊喜。亚历克斯·巴克斯特可能是巴尔舒格
凯宾斯基酒店的客人。

Timing is everything. The hotel clerk handed *Michelle Montez* back her credit card and gave her a digital room key.

时机就是一切。酒店工作人员将信用卡还给了米歇尔·蒙特兹，并给了她一把数字房间钥匙。

*MICHELLE MONTEZ*
Would you please have a porter take my luggage up to
my room? I need to go somewhere now.

米歇尔·蒙特兹
请你叫一个搬运工帮我把行李送到我的房间好
吗？我现在需要去个地方。

HOTEL RECEPTIONIST
We'll take care of that right away, Ms. Montez.

酒店接待员
我们会立即处理，蒙特兹女士。

Alex led Christina and the Garrisons out the main entrance and walked to the curb. A Limo was waiting and the driver expecting four English speaking people dressed up.

亚历克斯带着克里斯蒂娜和加里森夫妇走出大门，走到路边。一辆豪华轿车正在等候，司机期待着四个打扮得漂漂亮亮的说英语的人。

LIMO DRIVER
Excuse me sir, are you Mr. Baxter?

豪华轿车司机
对不起先生，您是巴克斯特先生吗？

ALEX
Yes, that's me.

亚历克斯
是的，那就是我。

LIMO DRIVER
I'm your driver.

豪华轿车司机
我是您的司机

The Limo driver then opened the passenger door.

然后豪华轿车司机打开了乘客侧车门。

There were two additional people, Buster and one FSB agent. Even so Alex suspected there would be an FSB car behind them.

另外还有两个人，巴斯特FSB和一名 FSB 特工。即便如此，亚历克斯还是怀疑他们身后会有一辆 联邦安全局（FSB）赛车。

ALEX
Buster, why don't you get in the front seat with the driver, and Mr. Anatoly will ride with us in the back.

亚历克斯
巴斯特，你为什么不和司机一起坐在前座，阿纳托利先生会和我们一起坐在后面呢。

BUSTER
Sure thing Mr. Baxter.

巴斯特
当然可以，巴克斯特先生。

Alex looked at the Limo Driver while he inquired:

亚历克斯一边看着豪华轿车司机，一边询问道：

ALEX
Is it okay that Buster rides up front with you?

亚历克斯
巴斯特和你一起骑在前面可以吗？

LIMO DRIVER
Not a problem sir.

豪华轿车司机
没问题，先生。

The driver in some way was happy because he would have someone to talk with because usually, he's alone and only had the radio turned down low most of the time.

司机在某种程度上感到高兴，因为他可以有人聊天，因为通常他都是独自一人，而且大多数时候收音机的音量都调得很低。

The *Greenland Dome* construction partners and their wives and girlfriends were to meet Alex at the Tchaikovsky Concert Hall. Alex, who was asked not to disclose to anyone for security reasons, was informed there was a possibility that Vladimir Putin and Alina Kabaeva might arrive and enjoy the symphony with them.

格陵兰穹顶的施工方及其妻子和女友们将在柴可夫斯基音乐厅与阿历克斯见面。出于安全原因，阿历克斯被要求不向任何人透露这一消息，并被告知弗拉基米尔·普京和阿琳娜·卡巴耶娃可能会到场与他们一起欣赏交响乐。

The Limo turned on Tverskaya St. and drove several blocks to Bol'shaya Sadovaya ul where it turned into an obscure entrance. The driver was obviously prepared in advance for this trip. The driver stopped the Limo, got out and opened the car doors, and everyone exited the car. An emergency exit was manned by FSB agents waiting for their arrival.

豪华轿车驶上特维尔大街，驶过几个街区后，来到了 大萨多瓦亚路（Bol'shaya Sadovaya ul）街，然后拐进了一个不起眼的入口。司机显然提前为这次行程做好了准备。司机停下豪华轿车，下车打开车门，所有人都下了车。紧急出口处有联邦安全局特工在等着他们。

Buster was briefed on the plan by the security officials announced:

安全官员向巴斯特通报了该计划并宣布：

**BUSTER**
This way Mr. Baxter.

巴斯特
这边走，巴克斯特先生。

Buster led Alex and the group to the emergency exit entrance. The Russian escort just ahead of them walked forward and Buster and the rest simply followed. They were led up some slight stairs and then into the private entrance to balcony seats that were somewhat shielded from the audience and looked directly down on the symphony hall.

巴斯特带着亚历克斯等人来到紧急出口。前面的俄罗斯护卫队走上前去，巴斯特等人则紧随其后。他们被带上一段不长的楼梯，然后进入私人入口，进入阳台座位，那里与观众隔开，可直接俯瞰交响乐厅。

The concert hall had been refurbished in recent years while the Tchaikovsky Symphony was relocated to another venue during the reconstruction. A lot of Russian oil money poured into the rehabilitation of the cold war artifact.

音乐厅近年经过整修，柴可夫斯基交响乐团在重建过程中被转移到另一个场地。俄罗斯投入了大量石油资金来修复这个冷战时期的遗迹。

The seating is elevated like a sports stadium and aligned in a slightly more than a half circle arrangement with the curved stage. The essential layout was the same as it was during the 1960's, but the paint and gloss and new modern comfortable seats added a lot of comfort.

座位像体育场一样高，与弧形舞台呈略大于半圆形的排列。基本布局与 20 世纪 60 年代相同，但油漆和光泽以及新的现代舒适座椅增加了许多舒适感。

Moscow Symphony Hall received redesigning of the acoustics, which helped make the sound performance much better in projection and reduced echoes or any interfering reflections.

莫斯科交响乐厅重新进行了声学设计，使得投射的声音效果更加出色，并减少了回声或任何干扰反射。

Thanks to the arrangement of the circular stage and seating, the music performed sounded symphonic and the quality of the symphony sounded very good despite where you sat.

由于圆形舞台和座位的布置，演奏的音乐听起来像交响乐，而且无论你坐在哪里，交响乐的质量都非常好。

The closeness of their balcony seats, aside from having the best signal levels, also complete observation of the performers without a lot of exposure to the audience below

阳台座位距离较近，除了信号水平最好之外，还可以完全观察表演者，而不会过多地暴露在楼下的观众面前

Most of the audience was already sitting as Alex's group arrived with about five minutes left before the symphony orchestra performance started.

当亚历克斯的乐队到达时，距离交响乐团表演开始还有大约五分钟，大多数观众已经就座。

The business partners all thought they would see Mr. Putin one more time before they left to go back to America or Greenland in the case of Claude Rearden who was currently acting general manager on site.

这些商业伙伴都认为，在他们返回美国之前，他们还能再见一见普京先生或者在目前担任现场代理总经理的克劳德·里尔登看来，他们还能再见一见格陵兰。

The seats that Alex had reserved were adjacent to his business partners who were invited with the expectations of meeting with Vladimir Putin.

亚历克斯预订的座位与他的商业伙伴相邻，这些商业伙伴受邀前来与弗拉基米尔·普京会面。

***

When Alex's group left the Baltschug Kempinski Hotel *Michelle Montez* was about twenty seconds behind Alex and hopped in a waiting cab.

当亚历克斯 (Alex) 的团队离开巴尔舒格凯宾斯基酒店 (Baltschug Kempinski Hotel) 时，米歇尔·蒙特兹 (Michelle Montez) 落后亚历克斯 (Alex) 大约二十秒，跳上了一辆等候的出租车。

**MICHELLE MONTEZ**
Follow the Limo right in front of us.


米歇尔·蒙特兹
跟着我们前面的那辆豪华轿车。


CAB DRIVER
I'm not sure I want to do that lady.


出租车司机
我不确定我是否想和那位女士做爱。


*MICHELLE MONTEZ*
Here's a couple hundred extra Rubles if you don't lose
that car.


米歇尔·蒙特兹
如果你没有丢失那辆车的话，我会给你额外的几
百卢布。


CAB DRIVER
I'll do my best.


出租车司机
我会尽力的。

Little did *Michelle Montez* know the distance that Limo would go would not be far. As soon as Alex's Limo pulled into the side entrance to the Symphony, she knew where they were going. She hated herself for not guessing.

米歇尔·蒙特兹根本不知道豪华轿车要开的距离不会太远。亚历克斯的豪华轿车一驶进交响乐团的侧门，她就知道他们要去哪里了。她恨自己没猜到。

When Alex's Limo pulled in the driveway the cab driver in Michelle Montez's cab knew better than to follow them and continued down *Bol'shaya Sadovaya ul* until he could exit and get turned around.

当亚历克斯的豪华轿车驶入车道时，米歇尔·蒙特兹的出租车司机知道最好不要跟着他们，而是继续沿着 大萨多瓦亚街（*Bol'shaya Sadovaya ul*）行驶，直到他可以下车并掉头。

> *MICHELLE MONTEZ*
> Why did they pull in there?

> 米歇尔·蒙特兹
> 他们为什么停在那里？

> CAB DRIVER
> The main entrance to the symphony is on Tverskaya St. but VIP's sometimes get taken to the back entrance for security reasons.

> 出租车司机
> 交响乐团的主入口位于特维尔大街，但出于安全原因，贵宾的 (VIP's) 有时会被带到后门。

> *MICHELLE MONTEZ*
> OK, drop me off at the Tverskaya St. entrance to the Moscow Symphony.

> 米歇尔·蒙特兹
> 好的，请把我送到特维尔大街莫斯科交响乐团入口处。

Moments later, *Michelle Montez* got out of the Limo in front of the Moscow Symphony. She was dressed in attractive clothes, not super exorbitant to her, but very stylish for Moscow women who were often six months behind Paris fashions.

片刻之后，米歇尔·蒙特兹从莫斯科交响乐团前的豪华轿车中走出来。她穿着漂亮的衣服，对她来说不算特别昂贵，但对于莫斯科女性来说非常时尚，因为她们的时尚潮流往往比巴黎时尚潮流落后六个月。

Looking at clothing other women were wearing left *Michelle Montez* with the impression she would she fit in and was more attractive compared to most of the women that were arriving.

看着其他女人穿的衣服，米歇尔·蒙特兹觉得她很合群，而且比大多数到达的女性更有魅力。

*Michelle Montez* went inside the Moscow Symphony main entrance and approached the concierge and ticket agent.

米歇尔·蒙特兹走进莫斯科交响乐团正门，走近礼宾部和售票员。

> MICHELLE MONTEZ
> I would like to buy a ticket to the symphony.

> 米歇尔·蒙特兹
> 我想买一张交响乐的票。

TICKET AGENT
I'm sorry we are sold out.

售票员
很抱歉，我们的票已经卖完了。

*MICHELLE MONTEZ*
How about this I will give you some extra money and
I'll wait for a few minutes after the symphony starts
playing and I will go find an empty seat?

米歇尔·蒙特兹
这样吧，我给你一些额外的钱，等交响乐开始演
奏后我再去找一个空座位，怎么样？

No other people were around the ticket booth and the ticket agent figured this westerner
was just about to give him the bribe he expected.

售票亭周围没有其他人，售票员猜想这个西方人正要给他他所期望的贿赂。

TICKET AGENT
That will be 11750 Rubles ($200 USD on current
rate of exchange).

售票员
费用为 11750 卢布（按当前汇率计算为 200 美
元）。

*Michelle Montez* pulled out 15,000 Rubles, handed it to the clerk.

米歇尔·蒙特兹 拿出 15,000 卢布，递给店员。

MICHELLE MONTEZ
Keep the change.

米歇尔·蒙特兹
保留零钱。

The ticket clerk responded by giving *Michelle Montez* one of the "sold out" tickets.
Bribes were typical for Russia these days, since everyone was now getting poor again
with the price of oil way down.

售票员给了米歇尔·蒙特兹一张 "已售完的" 票。如今，贿赂在俄罗斯很常见，
因为随着油价大幅下跌，每个人都又开始变穷了。

In Moscow people do not walk to private balconies without a proper ticket or they get
thrown out of the venue.

在莫斯科，人们没有正式的门票是不会走进私人包厢的，否则就会被赶出会场。

*Michelle Montez* knew this, so she had to be craftier tonight. She would find an empty balcony, take some pictures if there was a good shot then keep moving because it's harder to hit a moving target.

米歇尔·蒙特兹知道这一点，所以她今晚必须更狡猾一些。她会找到一个空的包厢，如果有好镜头的话就拍几张照片，然后继续移动，因为移动的目标更难击中。

Normally *Michelle Montez* would have been stopped, ticket checked and barred from the balcony entrance. But *Michelle Montez* was wearing highly fashionable French clothes that looked nothing like what Muscovites were wearing. The usher wrongfully assumed *Michelle Montez* was one of the aristocrats they were briefed that would be here tonight along with some high-ranking government official.

通常情况下，米歇尔·蒙特兹会被拦下，接受检票，并被禁止进入阳台入口。但米歇尔·蒙特兹穿着非常时髦的法式服装，与莫斯科人的穿着完全不同。引座员错误地认为米歇尔·蒙特兹是他们被告知今晚会和某位高级政府官员一起来的贵族之一。

The lights dimmed after the conductor walked on stage. There was some applause. Then the conductor took his position on the conductor's platform, he soon started giving some signals to the orchestra. Suddenly, the noise died down to an eerie quiet.

指挥上台后灯光暗了下来。掌声响起。然后指挥站上指挥台，开始向乐团发出信号。突然间，喧闹声渐渐平息，安静得令人毛骨悚然。

## MUSIC FOR THIS SEGMENT:

Tschaikowsky: 6. Sinfonie (»Pathétique«) · hr-Sinfonieorchester Lionel Bringuier

本部分音乐：

柴可夫斯基：第六交响曲 （》悲怆《） 法兰克福广播交响乐团 莱昂内尔·布林吉耶 （Lionel Bringuier）

Tchaikovsky's 6th Symphony began, with a somber almost funeral like procession.

柴可夫斯基的《第六交响曲》以阴沉的、近乎葬礼般的旋律拉开序幕。

Soon the conflict of emotion and exaltations gradually erupted as the orchestra gradually slid into that clearly Russian Tchaikovsky style unlike many symphonies that were built on a foundation of violins and strings.

很快，随着管弦乐队逐渐进入明显的俄罗斯柴可夫斯基风格，情绪和兴奋的冲突逐渐爆发，这与许多以小提琴和弦乐为基础的交响曲不同。

Tchaikovsky's 6th Symphony utilized a much wider range of instruments whose sounds flowed with this music.

柴可夫斯基的《第六交响曲》使用了更广泛的乐器，这些乐器的声音随着音乐流动。

The strings would make their impact, but when the brass section lit up the air, a major theme transcends time that wants to escape the confines of a symphony orchestra and bestow upon mankind sound elixirs of life.

弦乐会产生影响，但当铜管乐器组点燃空气时，一个超越时间的主旋律想要摆脱交响乐团的束缚，并赋予人类生命的声音灵丹妙药。

Tchaikovsky's music soon gave a temporal anomaly in the psyche of many in the audience.

柴可夫斯基的音乐很快就在许多观众的心理中产生了暂时的异常。

Alex, who grew more and more attached to Christina in each passing day suddenly felt a transcendence this music influenced.

阿历克斯对克里斯蒂娜的感情与日俱增，他突然感受到这种音乐带来的一种超越感。

Alex's bonding with Christina was exemplified by that rarified quality of compassion and understanding, intensely composed and evolved in such a very short time. Alex's whirlwind affair with Christina, that was nowhere near its climax now stood on the threshold of a dream, or was this reality?

亚历克斯与克里斯蒂娜之间的感情体现了同情和理解的珍贵品质，这种感情在如此短的时间内得到了强烈的构建和发展。亚历克斯与克里斯蒂娜之间的旋风式恋情还远未达到高潮，现在却处于梦境的边缘，或者这就是现实？

In Alex's senses his observation of Christina, smelling her perfume, looking at the glamor of her latest makeup and sweet hair sculpture added the ambience to the symphony that he might otherwise care less about. The quality of the sound was of course unquestioningly strong and gifted in the fantastic brilliance designed by the brilliant composer Tchaikovsky.

在亚历克斯看来，他对克里斯蒂娜的观察、闻她的香水味、看着她最新化上的迷人妆容和甜美的发型，为这首交响曲增添了氛围，而他可能并不关心这些。当然，这首交响曲的音质毫无疑问是强劲的，而且在才华横溢的作曲家柴可夫斯基设计的奇妙光彩中显得尤为突出。

About eleven minutes into the Symphony is a strong passage and a crescendo that conveyed the emotions of the composer is quite obvious. And right when the crescendo reached the peak, Alex felt a hand on his shoulder. He turned around and there was Vladimir Putin sitting next to Alina Kabaeva. Just like Christina, Alina Kabaeva was dressed up like a goddess and all smiles.

交响曲进行到大约十一分钟时，出现了一段强劲的乐段，而传达作曲家情感的渐强部分则十分明显。而就在渐强部分达到顶峰时，亚历克斯感到一只手搭在了他的肩膀上。他转过身，发现弗拉基米尔·普京正坐在阿琳娜·卡巴耶娃旁边。和克里斯蒂娜一样，阿琳娜·卡巴耶娃也打扮得像个女神，满脸笑容。

Alex smiled at Vladimir and Alina, both of whom conveyed the magic of affection as if there had been a recent magical trip to ethereal passages and celestial feasts.

阿历克斯对弗拉基米尔和阿丽娜微笑，两人都传达着爱情的魔力，仿佛最近刚刚进行了一次通往空灵通道和天堂盛宴的神奇之旅。

Vladimir Putin sat in a spot on the balcony that hid him and Alina from most of the audience. If a person in the front row seated were to look hard, they would see a person but due to the darkness could not make it out to Vladimir Putin who arrived in such a way as to avoid any public recognition and assure he and Alina's privacy.

弗拉基米尔·普京坐在阳台上的一个位置，大部分观众都看不到他和阿丽娜。如果坐在前排的人仔细看，他们会看到一个人，但由于天色昏暗，他们看不到弗拉基米尔·普京，因为他的到来避免被公众认出，并确保了他和阿丽娜的隐私。

Vladimir Putin's situation was 1000 times more intense and critical than Alex had been prior to his marriage to Christina when Alex was trying to protect himself and Christina from yellow journalism and public attacks by vicious scandal rags such as *Magazine Femmes Réelles Exigeantes*.

弗拉基米尔·普京的处境比亚历克斯与克里斯蒂娜结婚前紧张和危急1000倍，当时亚历克斯试图保护自己和克里斯蒂娜免受黄色新闻和《真实妇女》等恶意丑闻杂志的公开攻击。

How *Michelle Montez* managed to get into one of the most forward balcony seats would soon be the source of smoke-filled meetings in special rooms at Lubyanka Square in Meshchansky District of Moscow. Someone would soon get transferred to the border guards and reassigned to a border crossing at Chechnya for not properly indoctrinating the usher that night.

米歇尔·蒙特兹如何设法挤进最前面的包厢座位之一，很快就成为莫斯科梅尚斯基区卢比扬卡广场特别会议室烟雾缭绕会议的焦点。有人很快就被调任为边防警卫，并被重新分配到车臣边境口岸，原因是当晚没有正确指导引座员。

*Michelle Montez,* aside from knowing how to smell a story, acted like a well-trained blood hound on a hunt.

米歇尔·蒙特兹 (Michelle Montez) 除了知道如何嗅出故事的气息之外，她还表现得像一只正在狩猎的训练有素的猎犬。

*Michelle Montez's* extraordinarily keen sense of smell combined with a strong and tenacious tracking instincts, produced the results that made her so successful with

*Magazine Femmes Réelles Exigeantes*. The Alex and Christina Baxter marriage story would have been a career achievement had Alex Baxter not outfoxed her.

米歇尔·蒙特兹 (Michelle Montez) 嗅觉异常灵敏，再加上强大而顽强的追踪本能，让她的《Magazine Femmes Réelles Exigeantes》取得了巨大成功。如果亚历克斯·巴克斯特 (Alex Baxter) 没能智胜她，亚历克斯和克里斯蒂娜·巴克斯特 (Christina Baxter) 的婚姻故事将成为她职业生涯的一大成就。

Tonight was *Michelle Montez's* chance to get even with Alex Baxter. If rumors persisted and reports that Mrs. Baxter was seen at GUM today with Alina Kabaeva, she not only could get that story that Alex Baxter would shell out $5 million to prevent publishing but also cause some friction between him and Putin if he didn't pay up.

今晚是米歇尔·蒙特兹报复亚历克斯·巴克斯特的机会。如果谣言继续，并有报道称巴克斯特夫人今天与阿丽娜·卡巴耶娃一起出现在 GUM，她不仅可以得到亚历克斯·巴克斯特将支付 500 万美元阻止出版的故事，而且如果普京不付钱，他和普京之间也会产生一些摩擦。

Alex was so infatuated with Christina and in deep appreciation that Vladimir Putin would acknowledge him privately by placing his hand on his shoulder, which meant a lot to Alex.

亚历克斯对克里斯蒂娜如此迷恋和深深感激，以至于弗拉基米尔·普京会私下将手放在他的肩上来表示对他的认可，这对亚历克斯来说意义重大。

Vladimir Putin admired Alex Baxter. Building a half mile high *Dome City* as it now seemed to be probable design limitations, with five miles in diameter right over the top of historic Moscow was going to take a hell of a lot of nerve. It took the synergism of three big personalities: Putin, Baxter, and Rearden to entertain such an extraordinary undertaking.

弗拉基米尔·普京非常钦佩亚历克斯·巴克斯特。建造一座半英里高、直径五英里、位于历史名城莫斯科上方的圆顶城市（现在看来可能存在设计限制）需要极大的勇气。需要三位大人物的通力合作：普京、巴克斯特和里尔登，才能完成如此非凡的工程。

Alex understood the political reasons behind building the dome in Moscow. But for the sake of mankind, Alex felt it best to build Dome Cities in places like Siberia, Greenland, and Twenty-Nine Palms, where weather and soil conditions did not support plant and food growth.

阿历克斯明白在莫斯科建造穹顶背后的政治原因。但为了人类的利益，阿历克斯认为最好在西伯利亚、格陵兰和二十九棕榈村等气候和土壤条件不适合植物和粮食生长的地方建造穹顶城市。

Dome Cities in non-arable land would benefit mankind more by housing people where their food was not grown and saving the farmland from further reduction due to Urban sprawl.

在非耕地上建造圆顶城市将使人类受益更多，因为它可以为没有粮食种植地的人们提供住房，并防止由于城市扩张而导致的耕地进一步减少。

*Michelle Montez* got a few shots of the Big-4: Alex Baxter, Claude Reardon, James Walker and Howard Grady. It was too dark to make out who else was in the very private balcony that 95% of the audience could not see in.

米歇尔·蒙特兹（Michelle Montez）拍了几张四大明星的照片：亚历克斯·巴克斯特（Alex Baxter）、克劳德·里尔登（Claude Reardon）、詹姆斯·沃克（James Walker）和霍华德·格雷迪（Howard Grady）。天色太暗，95% 的观众都看不到非常私密的阳台上还有谁，根本看不清。

Timing and luck were again on *Michelle Montez's* side. Alina Kabaeva is a young woman. Young enough to be Putin's daughter. Hence, Alina Kabaeva sometimes overused her iPhone communicating and texting her friends. Vladimir didn't care if she didn't interfere with his agenda or delay him in any manner.

时间和运气再次站在米歇尔·蒙特兹这边。阿丽娜·卡巴耶娃是个年轻女子。年轻到可以做普京的女儿。因此，阿丽娜·卡巴耶娃有时会过度使用她的 iPhone 与朋友交流和发短信。弗拉基米尔不在乎她是否干扰他的日程安排或以任何方式拖延他。

Alina was semi-bored with this symphony having attended it dozens of times in her life. She was also answering a text suddenly and the brightness from her cell phone bathed Putin with just enough light where Michelle Montez could identify him!

阿丽娜一生中已经看过几十次这样的交响乐了，现在听着有点无聊。她突然回了一条短信，手机的亮度刚好照亮了普京，米歇尔·蒙特兹可以认出他！

Unfortunately, there wasn't enough lighting available to get a good photograph. Then enough time quickly passed and before the lights were turned on for intermission, Putin and Alina were gone.

不幸的是，光线不足，拍不出好照片。然后时间很快就过去了，在灯光亮起准备休息之前，普京和阿丽娜已经走了。

The Big-Four met in the Moscow Symphony lobby during intermission, each partner introduced their wives or girlfriends. Predictably Christina charmed the other women.

四大天王在中场休息时在莫斯科交响乐团大厅见面，每位搭档都介绍了自己的妻子或女朋友。不出所料，克里斯蒂娜迷住了其他女人。

***

*Michelle Montez* got into position in the lobby of the concert hall to try to capture some pictures, but there were just too many people, and it was far too crowded.

米歇尔·蒙特兹在音乐厅大厅就位，试图拍摄一些照片，但人太多了，太拥挤了。

*Michelle Montez* didn't think her pictures could be used, but the marvel of modern electronics got feedback from her photographic section of her office,

米歇尔·蒙特兹认为她的照片不能用，但现代电子奇迹从她办公室的摄影部门得到了反馈，

PHOTOGRAPHIC DEPARTMENT
(SUPERVISOR)

Picture not good enough to put in the magazine, but we can make out Vladimir Putin and Alina Kabaeva in the photograph which could be used to withstand any legal challenge for any story we wish to publish.

摄影部
（主管）

照片质量不够好，不能刊登在杂志上，但我们可以从照片中看出弗拉基米尔·普京和阿琳娜·卡巴耶娃，这张照片可以用来抵御我们想要发表的任何故事的法律挑战。

***

An usher soon came into the lobby and announced to everyone:

很快，一位引座员走进大厅，向大家宣布：

USHER

Everyone please, return to your seats as the 2$^{nd}$ half of the performances will begin shortly.

引座员
请各位回到座位，下半场演出即将开始。

As soon as Alex, Christina, and Garrison's were seated, the orchestra began.

亚历克斯、克里斯蒂娜和加里森刚就座，管弦乐队就开始演奏。

<u>MUSIC FOR THIS SEGMENT:</u>

<u>Mozart - Piano Concerto No.21, K.467 / Yeol Eum Son</u>

<u>本部分音乐：</u>

<u>莫扎特 第 21 号钢琴协奏曲</u>，K.467 / Yeol Eum Son M

During the intermission a grand piano was hauled onto the center of the stage next to the conductor's podium. A beautiful female Korean performer walked out onto the stage, there was applause, and the pianist bowed and smiled and took her seat at the piano.

中场休息时，一架大钢琴被搬到舞台中央指挥台旁，一位美丽的韩国女演奏家走上舞台，掌声雷动，钢琴演奏家鞠躬微笑，坐在钢琴前。

Soon the pianist delighted the audience with Mozart's Piano Concerto No 21. As it was getting near the end, Alex had another tap on the shoulder. This time it was Buster who spoke softly:

很快，钢琴家就用莫扎特的第 21 号钢琴协奏曲让观众欣喜若狂。当钢琴接近尾声时，亚历克斯的肩膀又被拍了一下。这一次是巴斯特轻声说道：

BUSTER
It's time to leave.

巴斯特
该走了。

*Michelle Montez* sitting across saw Alex and his family silently and quietly leave all taken out the side entrance hidden from public view. *Michelle Montez* knew Alex Baxter and his group would be worth following and immediately walked to the lobby and out the main entrance and proceeded to the corner to observe which direction they were heading.

坐在对面的米歇尔·蒙特兹看到亚历克斯和他的家人默默无声地从隐藏在公众视线之外的侧门离开。米歇尔·蒙特兹知道亚历克斯·巴克斯特和他的团队值得跟踪，她立即走到大厅，走出正门，走到拐角处观察他们往哪个方向走。

The convoy of Limo's pulled out of the adjacent driveway, made a right turn at the corner and drove right past the entrance to Tchaikovsky Concert Hall on Tverskaya St.

豪华轿车的车队驶出相邻的车道，在拐角处右转，直接驶过特维尔大街柴可夫斯基音乐厅的入口。

*Michelle Montez*, quick in her head and fast on her feet almost sprinted to the lead taxi outside the Tchaikovsky Concert Hall and quickly got in and announced:

米歇尔·蒙特兹头脑敏捷，行动迅速，几乎是冲刺着来到柴可夫斯基音乐厅外的领头出租车前，迅速上车并宣布：

*MICHELLE MONTEZ*
Follow that string of Limo's and I'll give you 15,000
Rubles if you don't lose them.

米歇尔·蒙特兹
跟着那一串豪华轿车走，如果你不把它们弄丢，
我就给你 15,000 卢布。

It didn't take long for the taxi to reach Bolshaya Nikitskaya 53 and Povarskaya Ulitsa 50, where the CDL restaurant is located.

没多久，出租车就到达了大尼基茨卡亚五十三号（Bolshaya Nikitskaya 53） 和波瓦尔斯卡娅乌利察五十五十号 （Povarskaya Ulitsa 50)，也就是CDL餐厅所在的地方。

Traffic was slightly snarled as security personnel were directing the Limo's in for unloading their distinguished guests which included the Big-4 and their wives and girlfriends.

交通稍微有点拥堵，因为安保人员正在指挥豪华轿车下车，让贵宾下车，其中包括四大巨头及其妻子和女友。

*MICHELLE MONTEZ*
Let me out here.

米歇尔·蒙特兹
让我出去一下。

The cabbie pulled over just behind the traffic snarl. *Michelle Montez* knew she could walk quicker than staying stuck in the taxi where she might miss the action.

出租车司机在交通堵塞后停了下来。米歇尔·蒙特兹知道她可以步行，而不是留在出租车里，因为那样她可能会错过精彩的表演。

Good thing *Michelle Montez* was wearing a hat and had sunglasses to hide herself enough to not spook Alex Baxter. *Michelle Montez* would get that damn picture sooner or later that would get another front cover on the magazine!

幸好米歇尔·蒙特兹戴着帽子和太阳镜，可以遮住自己，不至于吓到亚历克斯·巴克斯特。米歇尔·蒙特兹迟早会拍下那张照片，再拍一张，登上杂志的封面！

*Michelle Montez* was insanely brave. She caught up to the group entering the restaurant that seemed closed off to the public. She started her cell phone recording in video mode and got right behind Grady's girlfriend and followed her into the restaurant.

米歇尔·蒙特兹非常勇敢。她追上了进入餐厅的人群，餐厅似乎不对公众开放。她打开手机录像模式，紧跟在格雷迪女友身后，跟着她进入餐厅。

Just like the Lackadaisical usher back at Moscow Concert Hall, *Michelle Montez's* integration into the Big-4 crowd was so successful, she got inside and did a lot of filming before someone figured out, she didn't belong there and escorted her out.

就像莫斯科音乐厅那位懒散的引座员一样，米歇尔·蒙特兹 (Michelle Montez) 非常成功地融入了 Big-4 人群，她进去拍摄了很多视频，后来有人发现她不属于那里，并把她赶了出去。

It was good for *Michelle Montez* that Alex Baxter didn't recognize *her*, otherwise Putin would have arranged for her cell phone to disappear.

对米歇尔·蒙特兹来说，幸好亚历克斯·巴克斯特没有认出她，否则普京就会安排让她的手机消失。

*Michelle Montez* didn't have much time, possibly two or three minutes at the most, and was able to film the interior, The staircase in the Oak Hall, the fireplace, and the red walls and wood paneling gave it a surreal image.

米歇尔·蒙特兹 (Michelle Montez) 没有太多的时间，最多可能只有两三分钟，但她能够拍摄内部景观，橡木厅的楼梯、壁炉以及红色的墙壁和木镶板营造出一种超现实的形象。

What made the risky trip all worth it suddenly captured on film, Vladimir Putin with a very beautiful woman, welcoming and shaking hands with Alex Baxter and the rest of the Big-4 and their wives and girlfriends.

是什么让这次冒险之旅变得值得？影片突然捕捉到了这样一个场景：弗拉基米尔·普京和一位非常漂亮的女人一起欢迎亚历克斯·巴克斯特和四大成员以及他们的妻子和女友，并与他们握手。

*Michelle Montez* knew that in Moscow it did not pay to get greedy, cleared out of the restaurant and as she was leaving asked one of the perturbed bouncers:

米歇尔·蒙特兹 (Michelle Montez) 知道在莫斯科贪吃是没有好处的，于是她走出了餐厅，在离开时她问其中一位不安的保镖：

*MICHELLE MONTEZ*
Where can I find a restaurant nearby?

米歇尔·蒙特兹
我在哪里可以找到附近的餐馆？

*Michelle Montez* played the innocent role of a misguided tourist who didn't know Russian or understand the restaurant was closed for the evening for a private party.

米歇尔·蒙特兹 （Michelle Montez） 扮演的是一个误入歧途的游客，她不懂俄语，也不知道餐厅当晚因举办私人聚会而关闭。

RESTAURANT BOUNCER
Walk over to GUM, there are a couple of good restaurants there.

*Michelle Montez* left looking fully innocent and not suspected. She would be out of Russia long before *Magazine Femmes Réelles Exigeantes* got published this week, otherwise her departure might have been seriously delayed. *Michelle Montez* hightailed it back to the Baltschug Kempinski Hotel and showered, changed her clothes, got a bite to eat downstairs in the bar/restaurant and waited patiently for feedback from the Magazine on the video feed.

米歇尔·蒙特兹离开时看起来完全无辜，没有受到怀疑。她应该在《真实女性》杂志本周出版之前离开俄罗斯，否则她的离开可能会被严重推迟。她飞快地回到酒店，洗澡、换衣服，在楼下的酒吧/餐厅吃了点东西，耐心等待杂志对视频的反馈。

*Michelle Montez's* phone suddenly vibrated, and Michelle looked at the Text Message.

米歇尔·蒙特兹的手机突然震动了，米歇尔看了看短信。

PHOTOGRAPHIC DEPARTMENT
(SUPERVISOR)
(Text Message)
The video is fantastic. Charles Denning wants you to
come back to Paris tomorrow to work on the story.

摄影部
（主管）
（短信）
视频太棒了。查尔斯·丹宁希望你明天回到巴黎继
续创作这个故事。

***

## INT. DAY. MOSCOW, RUSSIA. SAFE HOUSE.

室内场景。俄罗斯莫斯科。安全屋。

The Chechnyan Grozny Demons gang had lived in safe houses in Moscow for months up until now.

车臣"格罗兹尼恶魔"团伙此前已在莫斯科的安全屋中居住了数月。

The Grozny Demons were plotting and a few of them would be sacrificed as they would soon stage the big event. They hoped it would shake the Putin administration and possibly help topple him from government to allow a more moderate leader come in and ease the heavy handedness that people in Grozny wished to escape.

格罗兹尼恶魔正在密谋，他们中的一些人将被牺牲，因为他们很快就会上演这一大戏。他们希望这能动摇普京政府，并可能帮助推翻普京政府，让一位更为温和的领导人上台，并减轻格罗兹尼人民希望摆脱的高压统治。

Ever since the end of the Soviet Union, two wars were fought. Following the First Chechen War, Chechnya gained *de facto* independence as the Chechen Republic of Ichkeria.

苏联解体后，爆发了两场战争。第一次车臣战争后，车臣获得事实上的独立，成立伊奇克里亚车臣共和国。

Russian federal control was restored during the Second Chechen War. Since then, there was systematic rebuilding of the Chechnyan Grozny Demons gang laying low to avoid being rounded up and shot. Fighting continued between the Russian Army and the Grozny Demons in the mountains and southern regions of the republic.

第二次车臣战争期间，俄罗斯联邦控制得以恢复。此后，车臣格罗兹尼恶魔团伙开始有计划地重建，并保持低调，以避免被围捕和枪杀。俄罗斯军队与格罗兹尼恶魔团伙在共和国的山区和南部地区继续战斗。

The Grozny Demon leader, Abukhadzhi did a final peptalk to his men before they headed to the SUBWAY STATION to make a shocking Terrorist attack that would shake the Kremlin so bad they would have to negotiate.

格罗兹尼恶魔头目阿布哈吉在他的手下前往地铁站进行一次令人震惊的恐怖袭击之前，对他们进行了最后的鼓舞人心的讲话，这次袭击将使克里姆林宫震惊不已，以至于他们不得不进行谈判。

ABUKHADZHI
Our transportation will be arriving shortly to take us to the subway station. Pray to Allah because now we go and do what we were sent here to do.

阿布哈吉
我们的交通工具很快就会到达，带我们去地铁站。向真主祈祷，因为现在我们要去做我们被派到这里来做的事情了。

DANILBEK
Most of us will be killed.

丹尼尔贝克
我们大多数人都会被杀死。

MAIRBEK
Danilbek, we've been over this quite a few times. The reason why we are going to hop on the subway train and kill the driver is so that he doesn't stop. We'll shoot up the train. Stop it two stops down the track, get off there leaving our guns on the train and walk off as if nothing happened with our transportation waiting for us. It's a bullet proof plan.

梅尔贝克
丹尼尔贝克，我们已经讨论过很多次了。我们之

所以要跳上地铁杀死司机，是为了不让他停下
来。我们会向火车开枪。在两站路程处停车，下
车后把枪留在火车上，然后像什么事都没发生一
样走开，我们的交通工具在等着我们。这是一个
万无一失的计划。

***

Alex with the "Big-4" and Vladimir Putin celebrated the progress towards Moscow Dome Inc. finally looking like it would soon become reality. Vladimir Putin and Claude Rearden entered a discussion of dome construction while others got involved in numerous topics.

亚历克斯与"四大"和弗拉基米尔·普京一起庆祝莫斯科圆顶大厦公司终于即将成为现实。弗拉基米尔·普京和克劳德·里尔登讨论了圆顶大厦的建设，而其他人则参与了各种话题。

**VLADIMIR PUTIN**
How will you manage to get the roof up half a mile?

弗拉基米尔·普京
你要怎样才能把屋顶抬高半英里呢？

**CLAUDE REARDEN**
At first it seems almost impossible until you start to figure out the construction plan. The structure is too tall to utilize the pillars like we did in Greenland and propose for Chita. So, we came up with a new design all together.

克劳德·里登
一开始，这似乎几乎是不可能的，直到你开始制定施工计划。这座建筑太高了，无法像我们在格陵兰岛和 克劳德·里登 所提议的那样利用柱子。所以，我们一起想出了一个新设计。

**VLADIMIR PUTIN**
And what is that?

弗拉基米尔·普京
那是什么？

**CLAUDE REARDEN**
We will put up Three pillars together that will support each other. That will produce the added lateral strength we need until the roof is covered and wind is no longer a factor.

克劳德·里尔登
我们将把三根相互支撑的柱子放在一起。这将产生我们所需的额外横向强度，直到屋顶被覆盖，风不再是一个因素。

VLADIMIR PUTIN
Wouldn't three pillars together be sort of an eye sore?

弗拉基米尔·普京
三根柱子放在一起会不会有点碍眼？

CLAUDE REARDEN
The three pillars can be corners of buildings which would give a different appearance and psychology. Because of the pillars, the corners of the building can be round or square. It all is depending on what the Architect designs for the building owner.

克劳德·里尔登
三根柱子可以作为建筑物的拐角，从而产生不同的外观和心理效果。由于这些柱子的存在，建筑物的拐角可以是圆形或方形。这一切都取决于建筑师为建筑物所有者设计的内容。

VLADIMIR PUTIN
Interesting idea.

弗拉基米尔·普京
有趣的想法。

CLAUDE REARDEN
Inside the area between the three pillars besides office space or high-rise housing, there could be elevators and other critical components.

克劳德·里尔登
三根柱子之间的区域除了办公空间或高层住宅外，还可能设有电梯和其他关键部件。

VLADIMIR PUTIN
What does that do for building height?

弗拉基米尔·普京
这对建筑高度有什么影响？

CLAUDE REARDEN
It allows buildings to be built all the way up to the roof potentially.

克劳德·里尔登
它可以让建筑物一直建到屋顶。

VLADIMIR PUTIN
Does that mean the public would then simply see tall buildings and not even realize a triple pillar is located inside the buildings?

弗拉基米尔·普京这是否意味着公众只会看到高楼大厦，甚至没有意识到建筑物内部有三柱？

CLAUDE REARDEN
That's correct.

克劳德·里尔登
没错。

VLADIMIR PUTIN
Will you put the roof on like you did in Greenland?

弗拉基米尔·普京
你会像在格陵兰那样盖上屋顶吗？

CLAUDE REARDEN
No, the dome will be too high.

克劳德·里尔登
不，圆顶太高了。

VLADIMIR PUTIN
Then how will you do it?

弗拉基米尔·普京
那么您将怎么做呢？

CLAUDE REARDEN
We will start building at the edge or circumference of the dome and spiral inwards and upwards and build an external road on the top of the dome as we go.

克劳德·里尔登
我们将从圆顶的边缘或圆周开始建造，然后向内

向上螺旋形建造，并在圆顶顶部修建一条外部道
路。

### VLADIMIR PUTIN

You will build a road that will lead to the top of the
dome?

### 弗拉基米尔·普京
你会修建一条通往穹顶的公路吗？

### CLAUDE REARDEN

Yes, absolutely. The road will be built on stantions like
a bridge off the dome surface with anti-skid surface
for better traction. Cranes and materials will come up
on that *Dome Top Road* as we built it and that area of
the dome.

### 克劳德·里尔登
是的，绝对如此。道路将建在类似于桥梁的支柱
上，这些支柱与穹顶表面相连，表面具有防滑功
能，以便更好地牵引。起重机和材料将在我们建
造穹顶道路和穹顶区域时运到那里。

### VLADIMIR PUTIN

Great idea but why is the road built on stations and not
on the direct surface of the dome?

### 弗拉基米尔·普京
这个想法很棒，但是为什么道路要建在车站上，
而不是直接建在圆顶的表面上呢？

### CLAUDE REARDEN

This design of the road built on stantions will keep
weight directly off any portion of the dome.

This spiraling corkscrew road will facilitate
construction and later benefit maintenance.

### 克劳德·里尔登
这种建在立柱上的道路设计将使穹顶的任何部分
都不受重量影响。

这种螺旋形道路将方便施工，并有利于后期维
护。

### VLADIMIR PUTIN

What are you concerned about that will require
maintenance?

弗拉基米尔·普京
您担心哪些需要维护？

### CLAUDE REARDEN

Remember we are creating something that's never been tried before, building a dome city that has a dome sticking up a half mile in the air. Massive amounts of material will need lifted. Therefore, a spiral road leading up to the top will facilitate hauling roof sections up.

克劳德·里尔登
请记住，我们正在创造一种前所未有的东西，建造一座圆顶城市，圆顶高出半英里。需要吊起大量材料。因此，通往顶部的螺旋形道路将方便将屋顶部分吊起。

### VLADIMIR PUTIN

You will not be able to turn the trucks around, it seems to me backing down would be a problem.

弗拉基米尔·普京
你无法让卡车掉头，在我看来，后退会是个问题。

### CLAUDE REARDEN

We have designed a double cab truck that bends in the middle and has steerage simultaneously at each end. With a cab on each end, on the way down, the driver simply shifts cabs because the steerage is all computer controlled by GPS. The trucks and cranes are self-driving.

克劳德·里尔登
我们设计了一款双驾驶室卡车，它在中间弯曲，两端同时有转向装置。两端各有一个驾驶室，在下行过程中，驾驶员只需换个驾驶室，因为转向装置全部由 GPS 电脑控制。卡车和起重机都是自动驾驶的。

### VLADIMIR PUTIN

If these are self-driving trucks and cranes, why do you need drivers?

弗拉基米尔·普京
如果这些是自动驾驶卡车和起重机，那为什么还需要司机呢？

CLAUDE REARDEN

The truck driver is really nothing more than a safety observer since computers will be controlling the trucks.

克劳德·里尔登

卡车司机实际上只不过是一个安全观察员，因为卡车将由计算机控制。

VLADIMIR PUTIN

What's the circumference of the dome?

弗拉基米尔·普京

圆顶的周长是多少？

CLAUDE REARDEN

Approximately 15.7 miles.

克劳德·里尔登

约 15.7 英里。

VLADIMIR PUTIN

It seems to me that it would take a lot of time to send as many truckloads of supplies as you will need.

弗拉基米尔·普京

我认为，运送你们需要的那么多卡车物资需要花费很长时间。

CLAUDE REARDEN

We will be able to send multiple double cab trucks at a time to avoid costly delays.

We will have passing lanes built on struts on the rooftop road every two miles.

Since the computer will track the progress of the trucks climbing up to the top, trucks that are returning to the bottom area for a reload of materials are lighter and easier to control and will go into the passing lanes and wait until the loaded trucks pass.

克劳德·里尔登

我们将能够一次派出多辆双排座卡车，以避免代价高昂的延误。

我们将每隔两英里在屋顶道路上修建一条超车道。

由于计算机将跟踪卡车爬上顶部的进度，因此返回底部区域重新装载材料的卡车重量更轻，更容易控制，并将进入超车道，等待满载的卡车通过。

## VLADIMIR PUTIN

So, let me get this straight. The roof will have a spiral road all the way to the top of it.

弗拉基米尔·普京

那么，让我把这件事说清楚。屋顶将有一条螺旋形的道路一直延伸到顶部。

## CLAUDE REARDEN

A service and construction road only. In the overall surface area, the road network will take up very little space.

克劳德·里尔登

仅一条服务和施工道路。在总体地表面积上，道路网络将占用很少的空间。

## VLADIMIR PUTIN

After construction is complete, do you plan on leaving double cab trucks to be used for dome maintenance and service?

弗拉基米尔·普京

建设完成后，你们打算留下双排座卡车用于穹顶维护和服务吗？

## CLAUDE REARDEN

Definitely. These special built trucks will be left at all domes constructed because they help eliminate turnaround areas.

There will be a need for service activities in case a solar panel or windmill fails, or damage is created by a severe storm.

Every few years we expect new models to come out integrating lessons learned and extended capabilities.

When new models are available, we will swap out the old trucks at no charge since we will have a substantial investment in the dome and want to maintain its condition.

克劳德·里尔登

当然。这些特殊制造的卡车将留在所有建造的穹顶上，因为它们有助于消除周转区域。

如果太阳能电池板或风车发生故障，或者严重风暴造成损坏，则需要进行维修活动。

每隔几年，我们都会期待新车型问世，融合经验教训和扩展功能。

当新车型上市时，我们将免费更换旧卡车，因为我们将在穹顶上投入大量资金，并希望保持其状况。

***

The dinner included anything on the menu. The Chefs were out to please and routinely brought out samples for everyone.

晚餐包括菜单上的所有菜品。厨师们竭尽全力取悦大家，并定期为每个人提供样品。

The CDL restaurant manager approached Alex and Vladimir Putin

西迪艾勒 (CDL) 餐厅经理联系了亚历克斯和弗拉基米尔·普京

### CDL RESTAURANT MANAGER
How is everything?

西迪艾勒 (CDL)餐厅经理
一切还好吗？

### ALEX
The food was fantastic, the service was superb, and the entertainment, (a soft jazz group), made it all an enjoyable evening.

亚历克斯
食物很棒，服务一流，还有娱乐节目（轻柔的爵士乐队），让这一切成为一个愉快的夜晚。

### VLADIMIR PUTIN
I thought so too and smiled at the manager in a very friendly manner.

弗拉基米尔·普京
我也这么想，并以非常友好的方式对经理微笑。

The waiters and waitresses were treated very respectful, and one could feel the friendliness, among friends truly was infectious.

服务员非常尊重你，你可以感受到朋友之间的友好，这种友好确实具有感染力。

### CLAUDE REARDON

Vladimir, when will you have an announcement to the public that the *Moscow Dome* is now beyond just a planning phase, and that construction will commence shortly?

克劳德·里尔登
弗拉基米尔, 您什么时候向公众宣布莫斯科穹顶体育场已完成规划阶段，并将很快开始动工？

### VLADIMIR PUTIN

We can't tell the public everything right away. They need to be conditioned because there will be some who do not want the *Crème De La Crème*, including Red Square under a dome.

弗拉基米尔·普京
我们无法立即向公众公布一切。他们需要接受训练，因为有些人可能不想要那些精华部分，包括穹顶下的红场。

### CLAUDE REARDON

Why is that?

克劳德·里尔登
为什么呢？

### VLADIMIR PUTIN

It will seem unnatural to them.

弗拉基米尔·普京
对他们来说，这似乎不自然。

### CLAUDE REARDON

I can understand that.

克劳德·里尔登
我能理解。

## VLADIMIR PUTIN

For now, we say, the study is in progress, and when your equipment arrives and we start condemning buildings and moving people out to make room for the triple pillars and other activities, then we'll make the announcement that the project has been given government approval and has started.

## 弗拉基米尔·普京

目前，我们说，研究正在进行中，当您的设备到达，我们开始拆除建筑物，将人员撤出，为三支柱和其他活动腾出空间时，我们就会宣布该项目已获得政府批准并已启动。

## CLAUDE REARDON

We'll need to start demolishing some buildings within three months.

## 克劳德·里尔登

我们需要在三个月内开始拆除一些建筑物。

## VLADIMIR PUTIN

That's when we'll announce.

## 弗拉基米尔·普京

到时候我们就会宣布。

## VOICEOVER

Claude was slightly nervous because three months is cutting it a little short to get the new Nuuk Dome Inc. General Manager fully up to speed.

Having the new General Manager in place and fully functional was a serious requirement since Alex Baxter, James Walker, and Howard Grady had unanimously stated *they would only go along with a Moscow Dome if Claude Reardon was on site for construction at least the first full year.*

To the casual observer, it took men of power and vision such as Vladimir Putin, Alex Baxter, and Claude Rearden joined at the hip to be able to pull off such a auspicious and challenging construction project.

## 画外音

克劳德有点紧张，因为三个月的时间对于让新任

努克穹顶公司总经理全面适应新形势来说有点太
短了。

让新任总经理到位并全面发挥作用是一项严肃的
要求，因为亚历克斯·巴克斯特、詹姆斯·沃克和霍
华德·格雷迪一致表示，只有克劳德·里尔登至少在
第一年全程参与施工，他们才会同意建造莫斯科穹
顶。

在旁观者看来，只有像弗拉基米尔·普京、亚历克
斯·巴克斯特和克劳德·里尔登这样有权力和远见的
人齐心协力，才能完成如此吉祥而富有挑战性的
建设项目。

During coffee, after dinner, Vladimir Putin suggested:

晚餐后，喝咖啡时，弗拉基米尔·普京建议：

### VLADIMIR PUTIN
Let's all get together and talk for a while, and the
women get together.

### 弗拉基米尔·普京
我们大家聚在一起聊一会儿，女士们也聚在一起。

For the women that was ok, but one could easily detect an element of jealousy because
Claude, James, and Howard did not have glamorous women that came close to
Christina Baxter and Alina Kabayeva.

对于女性来说这还算可以，但人们很容易就能察觉到其中的嫉妒，因为克劳
德、詹姆斯和霍华德身边并没有像克里斯蒂娜·巴克斯特和阿丽娜·卡巴耶娃那
样魅力十足的女性。

Nevertheless, the other women were mature, and their behavior was exemplary, and
that helped create a special bonding to the women who now had each other's contact
information. They had no option but to look out for each other.

尽管如此，其他女性都很成熟，她们的行为堪称典范，这有助于建立一种特殊
的联系，因为现在她们有了彼此的联系方式。她们别无选择，只能互相照顾。

### VLADIMIR PUTIN
Russia will pay for most of the Moscow Dome
Construction.

### 弗拉基米尔·普京
俄罗斯将承担莫斯科穹顶建筑的大部分建设费用。

Alex was surprised Vladimir Putin wanted Russia to pay for most of the Moscow Dome construction. But in the end, it was obvious why. Vladimir Putin, a great visionary and didn't want to give up all that air space to Alex Baxter.

亚历克斯很惊讶弗拉基米尔·普京竟然希望俄罗斯支付莫斯科穹顶的大部分建设费用。但最终，原因显而易见。弗拉基米尔·普京是一位伟大的梦想家，他不想把所有的领空都拱手让给亚历克斯·巴克斯特。

One reason why Alex was more than willing to finance the Nuuk Dome and Chita Dome was their air space would become extremely valuable as suddenly Dome city life meant good living could occur anywhere on the planet now.

阿历克斯之所以愿意资助努克穹顶和赤塔穹顶项目，是因为它们的领空将变得极其宝贵，因为穹顶城市生活突然意味着地球上的任何地方都可以过上美好的生活。

As the evening ended, a parade of Limo's formed out front of the 西迪艾勒 (CDL) Restaurant.

夜幕降临，一队豪华轿车在 西迪艾勒 (CDL)餐厅前列队行驶。

Word had leaked out with *Michelle Montez* report that Putin was secretly meeting Alex Baxter at the CDL restaurant, when people on the staff processing the pictures contacted special friends that such a meeting was occurring.

米歇尔·蒙特兹 (Michelle Montez) 的报道泄露了普京在 西迪艾勒 (CDL)餐厅秘密会见亚历克斯·巴克斯特 (Alex Baxter) 的消息，当时处理照片的工作人员联系了一些特别的朋友，得知了这一会面正在进行中。

The picture *Michelle Montez* took that had Putin, Baxter, his wife, and Alina together conveying warmth and affection on the front cover of Magazine Femmes Réelles Exigeantes in just a couple days.

米歇尔·蒙特兹拍摄的普京、他的妻子巴克斯特和阿丽娜在一起传递温暖和爱意的照片在短短几天内就登上了《现实女性》杂志的封面。

*Michelle Montez* might have thought she could blackmail Alex again and offer to shelve the story, which Alex would have gladly paid $5 million, but unfortunately Charles Denning had other ideas. His writers were hard at work generating a boilerplate for *Michelle Montez's* report when she got back to Paris the following day. *Michelle Montez* no longer had a vote.

米歇尔·蒙特兹可能以为她可以再次敲诈亚历克斯，并提出搁置报道，亚历克斯很乐意支付 500 万美元，但不幸的是，查尔斯·丹宁有其他想法。第二天，当米歇尔·蒙特兹回到巴黎时，他的作家们正在努力为她的报道写一份样板。米歇尔·蒙特兹不再有投票权。

*Michelle Montez* went back to the Baltschug Kempinski Hotel, had taken a bath, changed into more casual clothes, then decided she would go to the bar, then try to figure out where Alex Baxter was staying in this hotel. *Michelle Montez* might find something amusing to write about if she caught up with him coming and going.

米歇尔·蒙特兹回到巴尔舒格凯宾斯基酒店，洗了个澡，换上更休闲的衣服，然后决定去酒吧，然后试着弄清楚亚历克斯·巴克斯特住在这家酒店的哪里。如果米歇尔·蒙特兹看到他来来往往，也许她会找到一些有趣的东西来写。

Vladimir Putin's Limo was first in line and Moscow police officers redirected traffic off the street so that Vladimir Putin's car would have a somewhat empty road to traverse on his way back to his Dacha with Alina.

弗拉基米尔·普京的豪华轿车排在最前面，莫斯科警察疏导了街道上的交通，以便弗拉基米尔·普京的车在与阿丽娜返回别墅的路上有一条较为空旷的道路可走。

Security was tight and because of the leaks that sprang out of *Magazine Femmes Réelles Exigeantes*. A crowd had been forming that included locals and tourists who wanted to get a sight of Vladimir Putin, now one of the most powerful and successful leaders in modern times. Russia really had not had a powerful leader that compared since Leonid Brezhnev and most likely Stalin.

由于《真实女性》杂志的泄密，安保工作十分严格。当地人和游客聚集在一起，想要一睹弗拉基米尔·普京的风采，他现在是现代最有权力、最成功的领导人之一。自列昂尼德·勃列日涅夫和最有可能的斯大林以来，俄罗斯确实没有一位领导人能与他相比。

Alex and his family were shown to the next Limo, and the driver took them back to the Baltschug Kempinski Hotel.

亚历克斯和他的家人被带到下一辆豪华轿车，司机将他们送回巴尔舒格凯宾斯基酒店。

With the scarf and sunglasses on, sitting in an obscure area of the hotel bar/restaurant, *Michelle Montez* had a commanding view of the Baltschug Kempinski Hotel entrance.

米歇尔·蒙特兹 (Michelle Montez) 戴着围巾和太阳镜，坐在酒店酒吧/餐厅一个不起眼的地方，可以俯瞰巴尔舒格凯宾斯基酒店的入口。

*Michelle Montez's* planning paid off as Alex's group soon returned and *Michelle Montez* got a few more pictures taken covertly as she appeared as some woman in the bar simply Text Messaging someone.

米歇尔·蒙特兹的计划得到了回报，亚历克斯的团队很快就回来了，米歇尔·蒙特兹又偷偷拍了几张照片，当时她看起来像酒吧里的一个女人，只是在给别人发短信。

Alex, nor any of the others spotted *Michelle Montez*, nor were they even thinking about the woman they thought they had left far behind in Paris.

亚历克斯和其他人都没有看到米歇尔·蒙特兹，他们甚至没有想到这个他们认为已经远远留在巴黎的女人。

After *Michelle Montez* saw Alex Baxter's group walk past, she delayed getting up until she heard the elevator signal the doors were about to open. No others got on the elevator, so as it went up, it had only one stop.

米歇尔·蒙特兹看到亚历克斯·巴克斯特一行人走过后，她一直拖延着起床，直到听到电梯门即将打开的信号。电梯上行时没有其他人上车，所以电梯只有一个停靠点。

*Michelle Montez* now knew what floor Alex Baxter was on. She then pressed the elevator button and waited for it to return and then she got on and rode it up to the 7th floor where the more luxurious rooms existed.

米歇尔·蒙特兹现在知道了亚历克斯·巴克斯特在几楼。然后她按下电梯按钮，等电梯回来，然后她乘电梯到了七楼，那里有更豪华的房间。

The door to the elevator opened and all *Michelle Montez* had to do is look down what appeared to be approximately seven hotel doors, and she spotted four guys, two facing the other two by that seventh room door.

电梯门打开了，米歇尔·蒙特兹只需向下看大约七扇酒店门，她就发现了四个人，其中两个人在第七个房间门旁边面对着另外两个人。

*Michelle Montez* then immediately closed the door as if the elevator took her to the wrong floor, an honest mistake not to tip off the security detail. She went down to the 4th floor, which her room was on, and went down seven doors to see what room number the seventh room was located.

随后，米歇尔·蒙特兹立即关上了门，好像电梯把她带到了错误的楼层，这是一个无意之失，没有向保安人员透露情况。她下到 4 楼，也就是她的房间所在的楼层，然后下了七扇门，看看第七间房间在哪个房间号。

*Michelle Montez* decided based on her floor numbering system that Alex Baxter is staying in room 714. Now she knew where to ambush Alex Baxter!

米歇尔·蒙特兹根据楼层编号系统确定亚历克斯·巴克斯特住在 714 房间。现在她知道在哪里伏击亚历克斯·巴克斯特了！

But *Michelle Montez* would wait for the proper time and place and attempt to force him to answer some questions about: "What the purpose of meeting with Vladimir Putin all about? Is Alex Baxter going to build a Dome City in Russia too?

但米歇尔·蒙特兹会等待合适的时间和地点，试图迫使他回答一些问题： "与弗拉基米尔·普京会面的目的是什么？亚历克斯·巴克斯特也要在俄罗斯建造圆顶城市吗？"

Michelle Montez went back down to the Bar/Restaurant, had another glass of wine to celebrate her latest victory over Alex Baxter and possibly get the money out of him this time.

米歇尔·蒙特兹回到酒吧/餐厅，又喝了一杯酒来庆祝她最近战胜亚历克斯·巴克斯特，并且这次有可能从他那里赢到钱。

Alex had very politely said good night to his in-laws.

亚历克斯非常有礼貌地向他的岳父岳母道了晚安。

ALEX
Night mother and father.

亚历克斯
晚上的妈妈和爸爸。

Alex's behavior tended to create a sense of worth and respect for the Garrisons. Alex and Christina were immediately back in their hotel room, slightly tired and sleepy and decided to undress and try to get some sleep.

亚历克斯的行为往往会让加里森一家人产生一种价值感和尊重感。亚历克斯和克里斯蒂娜立即回到酒店房间，他们有点累，有点困，决定脱掉衣服，试着睡一会儿。

Alex Baxter's was looking out the window of his current view of Red Square and the Kremlin caused him to make a mental note:

亚历克斯·巴克斯特 (Alex Baxter) 正透过窗户望着红场和克里姆林宫，他心里记下了一件事：

ALEX (Thought)
*I need to get a room on the riverside next time I stay here.*

亚历克斯（想）
下次我住在这里的时候，需要订一间河边的房间。

Alex then closed the curtains then undressed.

It seemed kind of a strange sensation undressing in front of Christina, and she felt likewise, because they had never dressed or undressed in front of the opposite sex before in their lives.

But as a married couple, it simply became part of everyday life, which Alex didn't mind in the least bit. They did not hang their clothes up as they undressed quickly and in a manner that would manifest the horizontal tango later in the night when they felt like it. In the meantime, Christina's soft skin against Alex's chest felt very good.

***

*Michelle Montez* sent more pictures to *Magazine Femmes Réelles Exigeantes*. Charles Denning the editor felt there was some sort of confusion about expecting Michelle to be back in the office to make sure *Magazine Femmes Réelles Exigeantes* was ready to go to print in 48 hours. *Michelle Montez* had no intention of breaking contact and stalking Alex because she could smell that story.

***

The next morning, Alex suggested:

第二天早上，亚历克斯建议：

ALEX

Let's all walk over to GUM for breakfast, as there are several shops that cater to tourists that seemed to offer some very nice-looking Russian pastries.

亚历克斯

我们一起去古姆百货吃早餐吧，那里有几家专门为游客提供的商店，似乎提供一些看起来非常漂亮的俄罗斯糕点。

CHRISTINA

I'm all for that.

克里斯蒂娜

我完全同意。

MRS. GARRISON

So am I.

加里森夫人

我也是。

Mr. Garrison was content just to have a cup of coffee in the room, but Mrs. Garrison felt otherwise.

加里森先生只要在房间里喝杯咖啡就心满意足了，但加里森夫人却不这么认为。

MRS. GARRISON

William, you need to go with me, in case I need you to protect me.

加里森夫人

威廉，你得跟我一起去，以防我需要你保护我。

MR. GARRISON
I'm more than happy to do that, but when are we going
to let the kids have some time alone?

加里森先生
我非常乐意这么做，但是我们什么时候才能让孩
子们有时间独处呢？

MRS. GARRISON
They invited us honey.

加里森夫人
他们邀请我们了，亲爱的。

MR. GARRISON
That's probably because they feel sorry for us cooped
up in Moscow.

加里森先生
这可能是因为他们可怜我们被关在莫斯科。

MRS. GARRISON
No doubt, so let's just adapt, okay?

加里森夫人
毫无疑问，那我们就适应一下吧，好吗？

MR. GARRISON
There are things we should do together.

加里森先生
有些事我们应该一起做。

MRS. GARRISON
Such As?

加里森夫人
比如？

MR. GARRISON
Well for starters I'd like to go see the Moscow Subway,
it's one of the finest and best decorated in the world.

加里森先生
首先我想去看看莫斯科地铁，它是世界上最精
致、装饰最精美的地铁之一。

MRS. GARRISON
Ok let's think about that after breakfast.

加里森夫人
好的，我们吃完早餐再考虑这个问题。

In due time Alex led Christina and her parents over to the GUM stores and settled in on one of the pastry shops that had a pretty good variety.

不久之后，亚历克斯带着克里斯蒂娜和她的父母来到 GUM 商店，并在一家糕点品种丰富的糕点店里坐了下来。

ALEX
I hope you all have a sweet tooth.

亚历克斯
我希望你们都爱吃甜食。

MRS. GARRISON
Definitely.

加里森夫人
当然。

ALEX
What would you like to eat, mother and father?

亚历克斯
爸爸妈妈你们想吃什么？

MRS. GARRISON
Some of those pastries look good.

加里森夫人
有些糕点看上去不错。

Mrs. Garrison pointed to a pastry with what appeared to be powdered sugar on it.

加里森夫人指着一块上面似乎撒了糖粉的糕点。

MRS. GARRISON
What is this?

加里森夫人
这是什么？

### SALESCLERK
That's 'Hvorost'.

售货员
那是 "霍沃斯特"。

When Mr. Garrison bit into it he discovered the crunch, they produced similar sounds to breaking dry wood. Hvorost in Russian means dry wood. There are many variations, as with all other old recipes, including versions that are prepared with cheese or mashed potatoes.

当加里森先生咬下它时，他发现它发出的声音很脆，就像折断干木头一样。俄语中 霍沃斯特 (Hvorost) 的意思是干木头。和所有其他古老的食谱一样，它有很多变化，包括用奶酪或土豆泥制作的版本。

Mrs. Garrison ordered a Russian Strudel that had apple and blue berries in it. She shared some with Christina who ordered Rugalach, which is a rolled pastry, that is light and delicious, shared some with her mother as well.

加里森女士点了一份俄式卷饼，里面有苹果和蓝莓。她和克里斯蒂娜分享了一些，克里斯蒂娜点了 鲁格拉赫 (Rugalach)，这是一种卷饼，口感清爽可口，她也和她的母亲分享了一些。

Alex ordered Hungarian Nut Rolls. He shared some with Christina and Mrs. Garrison.

亚历克斯点了匈牙利坚果卷。他和克里斯蒂娜以及加里森夫人分享了一些。

The manager had seen a story in the newspaper about Alex Baxter including positive comments from his idol Vladimir Putin and wanted to be as hospitable as possible. When Alex and the group ordered coffee, he responded:

经理在报纸上看到了一篇关于阿历克斯·巴克斯特的报道，其中包括他的偶像弗拉基米尔·普京的正面评价，因此他想尽可能热情好客。当阿历克斯和其他人都点了咖啡时，他回应道：

### PASTRY SHOPS MANAGER
Let me make you a fresh pot of coffee, this one is getting stale.

糕点店经理
我给你泡一壶新鲜的咖啡吧，这壶已经不新鲜了。

### ALEX
Thank you, we appreciate that.

亚历克斯
谢谢，我们很感激。

After the manager started the automatic drip coffee maker using ground fresh roasted Columbian coffee beans, he brought out a sampler that had swirling sponge cakes, stuffed pastries, and other delightful creations.

经理启动了自动滴漏咖啡机，使用新鲜烘焙的哥伦比亚咖啡豆，然后拿出一个样品机，里面有旋转的海绵蛋糕、馅料糕点和其他美味的食物。

PASTRY SHOPS MANAGER

Here try these. This is a complementary serving to go with your coffee.

糕点店经理

来试试这些吧。这是与咖啡搭配的免费食品。

ALEX

Thank you, it looks good.

亚历克斯

谢谢，看起来不错。

The manager waited standing by Alex' table and watched the group sample his creations.

经理站在亚历克斯的桌子旁边，看着大家品尝他的作品。

PASTRY SHOPS MANAGER

What do you think sir?

糕点店经理

先生，您觉得怎么样？

ALEX

These are wonderful, you are very talented.

亚历克斯

这些太棒了，你非常有才华。

PASTRY SHOPS MANAGER

Thank you, I appreciate the feedback.

糕点店经理

谢谢，我很感激您的反馈。

ALEX

I will certainly inform people I know they should come here. You have great baked products.

亚历克斯
我一定会告诉我认识的人他们应该来这里。你们
的烘焙产品很棒。

PASTRY SHOPS MANAGER
I appreciate that sir.

糕点店经理
我很感激先生。

ALEX
Call me Alex.

亚历克斯
叫我亚历克斯吧。

PASTRY SHOPS MANAGER
All right Alex, I'm Richard Sorge.

糕点店经理
好的，亚历克斯，我是理查德·索尔格。

ALEX
Same name as the famous WW2 spy?

亚历克斯
与著名的二战间谍同名？

PASTRY SHOPS MANAGER
Yes sir, that's the same name as mine.

糕点店经理
是的，先生，这和我的名字一样。

ALEX
Incredible story. Did you see the Japanese movie they
made about Richard Sorge?

亚历克斯
令人难以置信的故事。你看过日本拍摄的有关理
查德·佐尔格的电影吗？

PASTRY SHOPS MANAGER
No, was it good?

糕点店经理
不，好吃吗？

ALEX
It was a very good movie.

亚历克斯
这是一部非常好的电影。

PASTRY SHOPS MANAGER
Richard Sorge helped save Moscow.

糕点店经理
理查德·佐尔格 (Richard Sorge) 帮助拯救了莫斯科。

ALEX
Yes, Richard Sorge informed Stalin the Japanese did not plan on attacking Russia so that Stalin could pull back 18 divisions from the Far East to help defend Moscow.

亚历克斯
是的，理查德·佐尔格告诉斯大林，日本人不打算进攻俄罗斯，这样斯大林就可以从东部撤回 18 个师来帮助保卫莫斯科。

PASTRY SHOPS MANAGER
You seem to know a lot about History?

糕点店经理
你似乎对历史很了解？

ALEX
I'm a history buff, just like my father-in-law, Mr. Garrison here.

亚历克斯
我是一个历史爱好者，就像我的岳父加里森先生一样。

PASTRY SHOPS MANAGER
It's a pleasure to meet you Alex and Mr. Garrison.

糕点店经理
很高兴认识你，亚历克斯和加里森先生。

ALEX
Thank you, Mr. Sorge.

亚历克斯
谢谢你，佐尔格先生。

### MR. GARRISON
I retired as a history teacher and today, I want to do some traveling on the Moscow Subway to see some of the fantastic artwork.

### 加里森先生
我已从历史老师的岗位上退休，今天，我想乘坐莫斯科地铁去看看那些精美的艺术品。

### PASTRY SHOPS MANAGER
Probably the only good thing about the horrible Russian Winter is we can ride in our beautiful subway trains to take some of the sting off the weather.

### 糕点店经理
也许俄罗斯可怕的冬天唯一的好处就是我们可以乘坐美丽的地铁列车来缓解寒冷。

### ALEX (Thought)
As soon as they start living in a domed city that may change.

### 亚历克斯（想道）
一旦他们开始住在圆顶城市里，情况可能会发生变化。

In a short while everyone had coffee and too much pastry. Mr. Garrison announced:

不一会儿，大家都喝完了咖啡，吃了一大堆糕点。加里森先生宣布：

### MR. GARRISON
I could probably use a walk now to walk off a few calories.

### 加里森先生
我现在可能需要散步来消耗一些卡路里。

Christina was hinting she and her mother wanted Mr. Garrison and Alex to give them some space so they could go do girls' things.

克里斯蒂娜暗示她和她的母亲希望加里森先生和亚历克斯给她们一些空间，这样她们就可以去做女孩的事情。

### CHRISTINA
Daddy, mother and I would like to go shopping in GUM, could you take Alex with you when you go for a walk?

克里斯蒂娜
爸爸、妈妈和我想去古姆商场购物，你们散步时<br>可以带上亚历克斯吗？

Mr. Garrison responded with an evil grin:

加里森先生露出邪恶的笑容说道：

MR. GARRISON<br>Sure, no problem if Alex can keep up.

加里森先生<br>当然，只要亚历克斯能跟上，就没问题。

Trever stayed with Mrs. Garrison and Christina, while the Russian FSB Agent Vasily Oryol and Buster followed along with Alex and Mr. Garrison.

特雷弗与加里森夫人和克里斯蒂娜待在一起，而俄罗斯联邦安全局特工瓦西里·奥廖尔和巴斯特则与亚历克斯和加里森先生一起跟随。

Alex and Mr. Garrison left the women, walked back towards the hotel then walked a bit along the waterfront of the Moskva River.

亚历克斯和加里森先生离开了女人，走回酒店，然后沿着莫斯科河的河岸走了一会儿。

After they walked a distance, Mr. Garrison turned around and asked the FSB Agent Vasily Oryol:

走了一段距离后，加里森先生转身问联邦安全局特工瓦西里·奥廖尔：

MR. GARRISON<br>How far is it to the nearest Moscow subway station?

加里森先生<br>距离最近的莫斯科地铁站有多远？

FSB AGENT VASILY ORYOL
We are two blocks away from the Okhotny Ryad which is on the Sokolnicheskaya Line in the Tverskoy District which is right by the Kremlin Manezhnaya Square.

联邦安全局 (FSB) 特工瓦西里·奥约尔
我们距离猎人商行只有两个街区，猎人商行位于特维尔区索科利尼切斯卡亚线，紧邻克里姆林宫驯马场广场。

Mr. Garrison turned to Alex.
加里森先生转向亚历克斯。

### MR. GARRISON
Alex I would like to go see a few Subway stations.
They are the most decorative in the world.

### 加里森先生
亚历克斯，我想去看看几个地铁站。它们是世界
上最具装饰性的。

### ALEX
Sure, Papa, if that's what you would like to do, I'm
happy to go with you.

### 亚历克斯
当然，爸爸，如果您愿意的话，我很乐意和您一
起去。

*Michelle Montez* got up out of her hotel bed and was ready to track Alex and discover more about him today.

米歇尔·蒙特兹从酒店床上起身，准备今天追踪亚历克斯并了解更多关于他的情况。

The first thing *Michelle Montez* wanted to know is whether Alex was still in his room. She dialed the room directly which the phone system allowed. The phone rang a dozen times, no answer.

米歇尔·蒙特兹想知道的第一件事就是亚历克斯是否还在房间里。她直接拨打了房间电话，电话系统允许拨打。电话响了十几次，没有人接听。

### *MICHELLE MONTEZ* (Thought)
*I missed my quarry dammit.*

### 米歇尔·蒙特兹(想法)
我错过了我的猎物，该死的。

*Michelle Montez* was upset with herself and started thinking maybe she should simply do what Charles Denning was demanding that she return to Paris immediately.

米歇尔·蒙特兹对自己很失望，开始想也许她应该按照查尔斯·丹宁的要求去做，让她立即返回巴黎。

*Michelle Montez* decided to go down to the lobby and get a coffee and a pastry at the Restaurant and Bar and take it back to her room and then decide her next move.

米歇尔·蒙特兹决定去大堂，在餐厅和酒吧买一杯咖啡和一份糕点，然后带回房间，再决定下一步的行动。

*Michelle Montez* knew she needed to get back to Paris, but thought she could stretch this adventure out for another half a day and, worst case, take the red eye home and be at the office first thing in the morning.

米歇尔·蒙特兹知道她需要回到巴黎，但她认为她可以把这次冒险再拖半天，最糟糕的情况是，坐夜班飞机回家，第二天一早到办公室。

During the day, in her spare time *Michelle Montez* would generate a story and email it to Charles Denning via her smart phone to help calm him down.

白天，米歇尔·蒙特兹利用闲暇时间写一个故事，并通过智能手机将其通过电子邮件发送给查尔斯·丹宁，以帮助他平静下来。

While *Michelle Montez* was eating the pastry and drinking coffee, she put on a pair of jeans that would make Kalvin Kline smile. Then she put on an undershirt and then a sweater that would help keep her warm but also decorated to an extent that men would have to acknowledge she had beautiful breast implants. Then of course she put on her comfortable almost knee-high boots.

米歇尔·蒙特兹一边吃着糕点一边喝着咖啡，她穿了一条牛仔裤，这会让卡尔文·克莱恩笑起来。然后她穿上一件内衣，然后穿上一件毛衣，这件毛衣不仅能保暖，而且装饰得当，让男人不得不承认她的隆胸很漂亮。当然，她还穿上了舒适的齐膝长靴。

*Michelle Montez* fabulous French perfume left no doubt that she could humble most men and get her way in most cases. Part of her success as a muckraker was the fact she disarmed her victims with her sexuality and poise just before she sunk her fangs into them.

米歇尔·蒙特兹 (Michelle Montez) 的法国香水令人难以置信地让大多数男人感到羞愧，并在大多数情况下得逞。她作为揭丑者的成功部分在于，在她用自己的性感和镇定解除受害者的武装之前，她就将尖牙刺入受害者的心中。

The makeup work *Michelle Montez* did for herself added substantial luster. She was an expert in applying makeup and anyone with slight bit of testosterone would acknowledge she was certifiable "eye candy."

米歇尔·蒙特兹的化妆工作为自己增添了不少光彩。她是化妆方面的专家，任何稍微有点雄性激素的人都会承认她是名副其实的 "养眼美女" 。

Sitting in her room looking up the road and sidewalk that paralleled the riverbank, *Michelle Montez* noticed a group of men walking, one of them was obviously an African American.

米歇尔·蒙特兹坐在房间里，抬头望着与河岸平行的道路和人行道，注意到一群男子正在行走，其中一个显然是非裔美国人。

**MICHELLE MONTEZ** (Thought)
*Could that be them?*

米歇尔·蒙特兹(思考)
那会是他们吗？

*Michelle Montez* quickly grabbed her eye piece which she used at the symphony and elsewhere and looked down to get a closer observation, and sure enough it was Alex Baxter!

米歇尔·蒙特兹迅速抓起她在交响乐和其他地方使用的目镜，低头仔细观察，果然是亚历克斯·巴克斯特！

*Michelle Montez's* heart was racing, and she almost tipped over her coffee as she got up so quickly and moved into action. Within one minute she was at the elevator on her way down and exited the hotel and swung to the right, hoping she did not lose sight of Alex Baxter.

米歇尔·蒙特兹心跳加速,她起身行动得如此之快，差点把咖啡都打翻了。不到一分钟，她就到了下楼的电梯旁，走出酒店，向右转，希望自己没有忘记亚历克斯·巴克斯特。

**MICHELLE MONTEZ** (Thought)
*They must be going on a morning walk.*

米歇尔·蒙特兹(心想)
他们肯定是去晨练了。

Several blocks up *Michelle Montez* saw the 4 men, just as they were turning the street corner on the way to the Subway Station. She had to hurry otherwise she risked losing them. Luck was on her side, a taxi was right by the hotel entrance, she walked over and hopped in.

几个街区之外，米歇尔·蒙特兹 (Michelle Montez) 看到了这四名男子，当时他们正转过街角前往地铁站。她必须快点，否则可能会失去他们。幸运的是，酒店门口就有一辆出租车，她走过去跳了上去。

**MICHELLE MONTEZ**
Drive on, I'll give you directions.

米歇尔·蒙特兹
继续开车，我会给你指路。

The cabbie pulled forward and as it approached Alex and the group and turned on, *Michelle Montez* announced:

出租车向前驶去，当它接近亚历克斯和其他人并转弯时，米歇尔·蒙特兹宣布：

*MICHELLE MONTEZ*
Make a right here.

米歇尔·蒙特兹
在这里右转。

Again, luck was with *Michelle Montez* as she saw the men ahead cross the street and were heading to the subway entrance a couple blocks away.

米歇尔·蒙特兹再次幸运地看到, 前面的男子穿过马路，正前往几个街区外的地铁入口。

Unknown to all of Alex's group, *Michelle Montez* following them is a professional tracker. *Michelle Montez* made sure she never lost physical contact, trailing Alex at a good distance to avoid counter detection.

亚历克斯团队的所有人都不知道，跟踪他们的米歇尔·蒙特兹是一名专业追踪者。米歇尔·蒙特兹确保自己不会失去身体上的联系，她一直跟在亚历克斯身后，保持着一段距离，以避免被反侦察到。

By the time the cab got to the Okhotny Ryad Subway Station, the men were already down at the departure platform.

当出租车抵达猎人商行地铁站时，两人已经在出发站台上了。

*Michelle Montez* looked up at the taxi meter and it said 291 Rubles.

米歇尔·蒙特兹抬头看了看出租车计价器，上面显示 291 卢布。

*MICHELLE MONTEZ*
Let me out here

米歇尔·蒙特兹
让我出去

*Michelle Montez* handed the cabbie 500 Rubles, got out and walked across the street, went to the Kiosk and bought a ticket, then was past the turnstile and on her way down the escalator.

米歇尔·蒙特兹递给出租车司机 500 卢布，下车穿过街道，去售票亭买了票，然后经过旋转栅门，走下自动扶梯。

The men did not get on the next train that went by as Mr. Garrison wanted to look things over and take a few pictures with his cell phone. The subway station was inspirational, and Alex took note of it for ideas concerning public transportation in his domes.

这些人没有上下一班经过的火车，因为加里森先生想看看周围，用手机拍几张照片。地铁站很有启发性，亚历克斯记下了它，为他的圆顶建筑中的公共交通提供了灵感。

### ALEX (Thought)

*For the Moscow Dome, no subways would need to be built since the vast subway complex already existed. All the Moscow Dome Construction Company had to do was avoid attempting to put a series of pillars over any subway line due to the 200-foot steel anchors.*

### 亚历克斯（思考）

对于莫斯科圆顶体育场而言，无需修建地铁，因为庞大的地铁综合体已经存在。莫斯科圆顶体育场建筑公司所要做的就是避免尝试在任何地铁线路上放置一系列支柱，因为有 200 英尺高的钢锚。

The Russian Federal Security Service (FSB) agent accompanying them today, Vasily Oryol knew some of the history and offered:

今天陪同他们的俄罗斯联邦安全局 (FSB) 特工瓦西里·奥廖尔 (Vasily Oryol) 了解一些历史，并说道：

### FSB AGENT VASILY ORYOL

The architects of this subway station were, Yuri Revkovsky, N. Borov, and G. Zamskoy, and was built in the early 1930's by Stalin.

### FSB 特工瓦西里·奥雷尔

该地铁站的建筑师是尤里·列夫科夫斯基 (Yuri Revkovsky)、N. 博罗夫 (N. Borov) 和 G. 扎姆斯科伊 (G. Zamskoy)，由斯大林于 20 世纪 30 年代初建造。

### MR. GARRISON

I wonder, where did that silvery marble come from?

### 加里森先生

我想知道，那块银色的弹珠是从哪里来的？

### FSB AGENT VASILY ORYOL

From what I understand it was imported from Italy for the finishing of the pylons.

### FSB 特工瓦西里·奥廖尔

据我了解，它是从意大利进口的，用于完成塔架的精加工。。

### MR. GARRISON

Did Russia import a lot of materials for the construction?

加里森先生
俄罗斯是否进口了大量建设材料？

FSB AGENT VASILY ORYOL
No, this is the only documented case where imported material was used in the Metro.

俄罗斯联邦安全局特工瓦西里·奥雷尔
不，这是唯一有记录的地铁使用进口材料的案例。

MR. GARRISON
The walls look impressive with that ceramic tile.

加里森先生
墙壁上贴着瓷砖，看上去很漂亮。

FSB AGENT VASILY ORYOL
Russia's best artwork is in subway tunnels.

俄罗斯联邦安全局特工瓦西里·奥雷尔
俄罗斯最好的艺术品就在地铁隧道里。

MR. GARRISON
Why then is such an extravagance shown here, when a lot of Moscow looks depressive?

加里森先生
那么，为什么莫斯科的很多地方都显得很压抑，而这里却展现出如此奢华的风采呢？

FSB AGENT VASILY ORYOL
With the 5th largest ridership in the world of subway users, the way to service the masses was to put the artwork in front of them which they could enjoy every day while commuting to and from work.

FSB 特工瓦西里·奥廖尔
作为全球地铁乘客量第五大的城市，服务大众的方式就是将艺术品放在他们面前，让他们每天上下班时都能欣赏到。

MR. GARRISON
I can see where that would help, especially in the middle of winter when everything is so dreary cold and dark during most of the commuter hours.

加里森先生
我知道这会有所帮助，尤其是在隆冬时节，大部分通勤时间，一切都阴冷而黑暗。

**FSB AGENT VASILY ORYOL**
Exactly.

FSB 特工瓦西里·奥廖尔
没错。

Soon they walked past a tourism information exhibit which stated:

不久他们走过一个旅游信息展览，上面写着：

**TOURISM INFORMATION EXHIBIT**
**INFORMATION PLACARD**
**MR. GARRISON READING OUTLOUD**
*The station was completed in just two weeks which included the installation of more than 3,000 square meters (32,000sqft) of marble, 20,000 square meters (220,000sq ft) of plaster, and thousands of square meters of tile as well as lighting and decorations.*

*In 2004, Okhotny Ryad underwent a major renovation which included replacing the lighting elements inside the spheres and repainting the plaster from light beige to white. A further renovation took place in 2007/2008 when the old ceramic tiles were replaced by bright marble, though a small, tiled section was retained.*

*An average of 42,110 passengers per day entered the station through its vestibules with an additional 241,000 passengers entering via Teatralnaya.*

旅游信息展览
信息牌
加里森先生朗读
车站仅用两周时间就完工，包括安装 3,000 多平方米（32,000 平方英尺）的大理石、20,000 平方米（220,000 平方英尺）的灰泥、数千平方米的瓷砖以及照明和装饰。

2004 年，Okhotny Ryad 进行了大规模整修，包括更换球体内的照明元件，并将灰泥从浅米色重新粉刷为白色。2007/2008 年进行了进一步整修，用明亮的大理石代替了旧的瓷砖，但保留了一小块瓷砖。

平均每天有 42,110 名乘客通过门厅进入车站，
另外还有 241,000 名乘客通过 地铁剧院线
（Teatralnaya 地铁线）进入车站。

Mr. Garrison, sensitive to Alex possible mood shifts asked:

加里森先生注意到亚历克斯的情绪变化，问道：

MR. GARRISON
Alex, I hope this isn't boring you.

加里森先生
亚历克斯，我希望这不会令你感到无聊。

ALEX
No father, this is good because it gives me ideas for Nuuk and Chita Domes.

亚历克斯
不，父亲，这很好，因为它给了我关于努克和奇塔圆顶的想法。

MR. GARRISON
That's good to know you picked up some ideas here. How would you build subways in Nuuk, it's mostly on solid rock?

加里森先生
很高兴知道你在这里学到了一些想法。你会如何在努克修建地铁，它大部分都是在坚硬的岩石上？

ALEX
According to Claude Rearden, it would be almost impossible to do much with the surface area under the dome because of the huge amount of rock we would have to blast through, which the public there would not tolerate because of all the shock waves the blasting would create.

亚历克斯
根据克劳德·里尔登的说法，对穹顶下的表面区域几乎不可能做太多事情，因为我们必须炸穿大量的岩石，而爆破会产生巨大的冲击波，公众将无法忍受。

MR. GARRISON
I would imagine so. How will you deal with it?

### ALEX

So, we are going to build a false floor for the entire dome area. Therefore, we can build underground parking and mass transit in huge volumes provided we plan for it initially, that's why we are pressing the Government of Greenland on the zoning rules and regulations.

### 亚历克斯

因此，我们将为整个穹顶区域建造一个假地板。因此，只要我们最初做好规划，我们就可以大规模建造地下停车场和公共交通，这就是我们敦促格陵兰遵守分区规则和法规的原因。

### MR. GARRISON

You said people would have parks and lawns, so how would they be created?

### 加里森先生

您说人们会拥有公园和草坪，那么它们将如何建造呢？

### ALEX

On the elevated flooring, in areas where we plan on putting in trees and lawns, except for Nuuk Hill area, we'll install large cement bathtubs with areas large enough to plant the lawns, trees, etc., and bring in about three to four feet depth of soil which would support trees, lawns, and whatever else is planted because wind and weather would not be a factor.

### 亚历克斯

在高架地板上，在我们计划种植树木和草坪的区域（努克山地区除外），我们将安装大型水泥浴缸，其面积足以种植草坪、树木等，并引入约三到四英尺深的土壤来支撑树木、草坪和其他种植的东西，因为风和天气不会成为影响因素。

### MR. GARRISON

Lawns and forests have natural drainage. How do you handle that in a park area bathtub in the dome?

### 加里森先生

草坪和森林有天然排水系统。在公园区域的圆顶浴缸中，您如何处理这个问题？

ALEX

The special bathtub areas will have a drainage system that takes the excess moisture to a reverse osmosis plant for recycling that will help remove salts and impurities, allowing the soil to remain with a neutral pH of 6.5 to 7.5.

亚历克斯

特殊浴缸区域将配备排水系统，将多余的水分送到反渗透装置进行回收，有助于去除盐分和杂质，使土壤保持 6.5 至 7.5 的中性 pH 值。

MR. GARRISON
Where will you get the soil?

加里森先生
你要从哪里得到土壤？

ALEX

We must remove a considerable amount of soil to get at the coal seams and limestone we need to mine to manufacture cement; we'll simply load that topsoil material on barges and ship it down to Nuuk to be used as the base materials for that type of development.

亚历克斯

我们必须清除大量的土壤，才能开采出制造水泥所需的煤层和石灰石；我们只需将表土材料装上驳船，运到努克，作为此类开发的基础材料。

MR. GARRISON
Is there that much material handy?

加里森先生
手头上有那么多材料吗？

ALEX

Yes, we must remove 200 feet of topsoil over the coal seams which are deposited materials left over from previous periods of time when Greenland was most likely a tropical paradise millions of years ago.

亚历克斯

是的，我们必须清除煤层上方 200 英尺的表土，这些表土是数百万年前格陵兰岛很可能是热带天堂时留下的沉积物。

**MR. GARRISON**

I would like to go see another half dozen stations, if you don't mind Alex, it should not take us too long, maybe an hour or so.

加里森先生

我想去看看另外六个车站，亚历克斯，如果你不介意的话，我们不会花太长时间，大概一个小时左右。

**ALEX**

No problem, Papa, this will be good for me too as I'm taking pictures and sending them to Claude Rearden with some suggestions for our dome construction in the future.

没问题，爸爸，这对我也有好处，因为我会拍照并将它们发送给克劳德·里尔登 (Claude Rearden)，并为我们未来的圆顶建造提供一些建议。

MUSIC FOR THE NEXT SEGMENT:

Alexander Fliarkovsky Symphony To Coeval - YouTube

下一段音乐：

亚历山大·弗利亚尔科夫斯基《同代交响曲》 – YouTube

In a short time, a train arrived, and the group got on. Nobody paid much attention to a woman who also got on the train several cars back.

不一会儿，一列火车到了，一行人上了车。没人注意几节车厢外也上了车的一位女士。

Mr. Garrison mentioned to the FSB Agent Vasily Oryol:

加里森先生向联邦安全局特工瓦西里·奥廖尔提到：

**MR. GARRISON**

I would like to go to the Mayakovskaya (Russian: Маяковская) station next.

加里森先生

接下来我想去马雅可夫斯基（俄语：Маяковская）站。

**FSB AGENT VASILY ORYOL**

Mr. Garrison, it's on the Zamoskvoretskaya Line, in

the Tverskoy District in central Moscow nearby, but we'll have to change trains at the next stop to get there.

联邦安全局特工瓦西里·奥约尔
加里森先生，它位于莫斯科市中心特维尔区附近
的扎莫斯科沃列茨克亚线，但我们必须在下一站
换乘火车才能到达那里。

The men got off the subway at the next stop and Vasily Oryol part of their FSB security attachment, led them to the change of tracks so they would not get lost and not waste a lot of his time. Since they had Buster also with them, they had no reason to fear or look around and did not spot the woman de-train and follow them to the next subway train that headed to Mayakovskaya.

两人在下一站下了地铁，俄罗斯联邦安全局安全人员瓦西里·奥廖尔　　(Vasily Oryol) 带领他们换乘轨道，这样他们就不会迷路，也不会浪费太多时间。由于巴斯特也和他们在一起，他们没有理由害怕或四处张望，也没有发现那名女子下了车，跟着他们上了下一班开往马雅科夫斯卡亚的地铁。

TOURISM INFORMATION EXHIBIT
INFORMATION PLACARD
MR. GARRISON READING OUTLOUD
The name as well as the Art Deco architecture design by Alexey Dushkin's is based on a Soviet future as envisioned by the poetry by the famous Russian Mayakovsky.

旅游信息展览
信息牌
加里森先生大声朗读
该建筑的名称以及由阿列克谢·杜什金设计的装饰
艺术建筑均基于俄罗斯著名诗人马雅可夫斯基的
诗歌所描绘的苏联未来。

The design exhibits a sense of Futurism. The subway station is a fine example of pre-World War II Stalinist Architecture completed in 1938 and one of the most beautiful Metro stations in the world. It has 34 ceiling mosaics depicting "24 Hours in the Land of the Soviets."

设计充满未来主义气息。该地铁站于 1938 年建成，是二战前斯大林主义建筑的典范，也是世界上最美丽的地铁站之一。它有34幅天花板马赛克，描绘了"苏联土地上的 24 小时"。

During World War II, it was used as a command post for Moscow's anti-aircraft regiment. And during the battle of Moscow, Stalin lived here for a while.

第二次世界大战期间，这里曾被用作莫斯科防空团的指挥所。莫斯科保卫战期间，斯大林也曾在这里居住过一段时间。

Mr. Garrison then turned towards Alex and Vasily Oryol and made an astute comment.

MR. GARRISON
The Art Deco columns and the ceiling arrangement create a very inspirational sense of awe to tourists who have never seen it before.

加里森先生
装饰艺术风格的柱子和天花板布置让从未见过它的游客产生一种非常鼓舞人心的敬畏之感。

ALEX
Father, I'm glad you suggested we visit here. This is fantastic inspiration and provides vast ideas. I will suggest to Claude Rearden to make Nuuk commuter terminals appear something like this.

亚历克斯
父亲，我很高兴您建议我们来这里参观。这是奇妙的灵感并提供了广阔的想法。我会建议克劳德·里尔登让努克通勤终点站看起来像这样。

MR. GARRISON
Alex, what are your plans for *Chita Dome*?

加里森先生
亚历克斯，你对奇塔圆顶有什么计划？

ALEX
We must do something different for the *Chita Dome*. We must give Muscovites reasons to visit Chita.

我们必须为赤塔穹顶做些不同的事情。我们必须给莫斯科人一个参观赤塔的理由。

Mr. Garrison turned to Vasily Oryol and offered:

加里森先生转向瓦西里·奥廖尔并说道：

MR. GARRISON
Mr. Oryol, you Russians should feel very proud of your subway stations, they are so beautiful and magnificently maintained.

加里森先生
奥廖尔先生，你们俄罗斯人应该为你们的地铁站感到自豪，它们非常漂亮，而且维护得非常好。

VASILY ORYOL
Thank you, Mr. Garrison. Yes, I'm proud of my heritage. Since we are on this subway line, may I suggest we go on to Belorusskaya Station?

瓦西里·奥约尔
谢谢，加里森先生。是的，我为我的血统感到自豪. 因为我们在这条地铁线路上，我可以建议我们继续前往白俄罗斯站吗？

MR. GARISON
Why certainly.

加里森先生
当然可以。

***

Deep in the mountains of Chechnya, the *Grozny Demons Criminal Terrorist Gang*, were also a proponent of forcing the Russians out of their country. Guerilla warfare was often discussed, designed and planned.

深藏车臣山区的 "格罗兹尼恶魔" 犯罪恐怖团伙也主张将俄罗斯人赶出他们的国家。他们经常讨论、设计和策划游击战。

Originally from the City of Grozny, most of the *Grozny Demon Gang Members* were on the losing side and fled to the mountains to avoid capture and either execution or forced hard labor in Siberia, often 10 years or longer.

格罗兹尼恶魔帮最初来自格罗兹尼市，大多数成员都是失败者，他们逃到山里，以避免被捕和被处决或在西伯利亚被迫做苦工，通常要服刑 10 年或更长时间。

Many of the Chechnyan prisoners taken to Siberia never returned home as most of them died from the harsh winters and exposure they were subjected to by their Russian masters.

许多被带到西伯利亚的车臣战俘再也没有返回家园，因为他们中的大多数因在俄罗斯主人的严冬和暴晒下死亡。

The current *Grozny Demon Terrorist Operation* had been under way for almost two months. The *Grozny Demons* had warned Russian government officials to lay off attacks on the rebels hiding in the mountains or they would retaliate in places the Russians would least expect.

目前的"格罗兹尼恶魔"恐怖行动已经进行了近两个月。"格罗兹尼恶魔"曾警告俄罗斯政府官员，停止对藏匿在山区的叛军发动袭击，否则他们会在俄罗斯人最意想不到的地方进行报复。

And since the Russian Metro stations were the psychological heart of the Russian City, the subway system as well as the *Bolshoi Ballet* were their top designated targets. Striking either target had technical problems.

由于俄罗斯地铁站是俄罗斯城市的心理中心，地铁系统和莫斯科大剧院芭蕾舞团是他们的首要目标。袭击任何一个目标都会遇到技术问题。

If the *Grozny Demons* struck the Bolshoi *Ballet Theater*, the likelihood that any of the attackers would get away was *considered* slim at best. Therefore, the decision was made to strike *Komsomolskaya-Metro-Subway Station*-in-Moscow with a bullet proof egress plan.

如果格罗兹尼恶魔袭击莫斯科大剧院，袭击者逃脱的可能性微乎其微。因此，他们决定袭击莫斯科共青团地铁站，并制定防弹逃生计划。

***

Alex and the group enjoyed Belorusskaya Station for a short while and were then back on the subway train and headed for Komsomolskaya-Metro station. They again changed trains at Okhotny Ryad and then headed up Northeast towards Komsomolskaya-Metro-station on the Sokolnicheskaya Line (red) where it intersected with the Koltsevaya Line at that station.

亚历克斯和团队在白俄罗斯站玩了一会儿，然后又坐上地铁前往共青团地铁站。他们再次在猎人商行换乘，然后向东北方向前往索科利尼切线（红色）上的共青团地铁站，在该站与科利采瓦亚线交汇。

Example of one of many beautiful Moscow subway stations

Once again, Alex and his group failed to detect their trailer who was now starting to get interested in why they were looking at subway stations.

再一次，亚历克斯和他的团队没有发现他们的拖车，拖车现在开始对他们为什么要查看地铁站感兴趣。

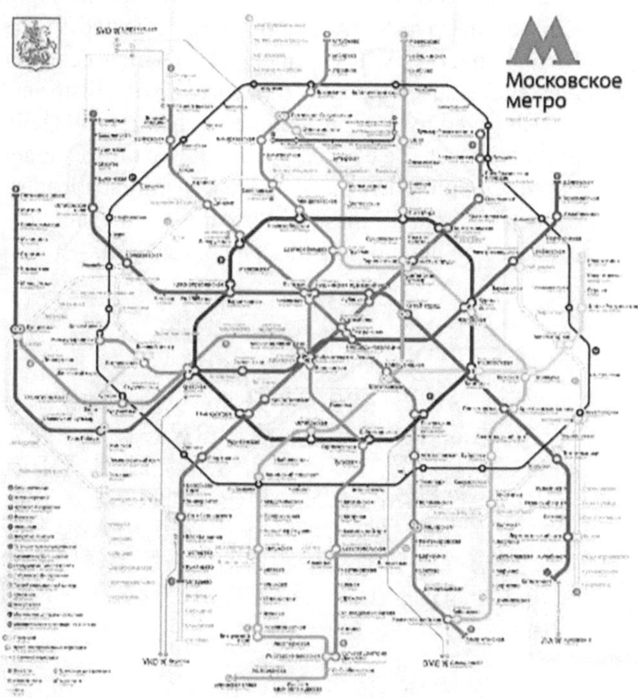


Since *Michelle Montez* had no idea this subway trip was all Mr. Garrison's idea, she assumed it was something Alex was doing and the first thought she had was Alex Baxter planned on building subway systems in the dome cities just like the way the Russians had built, with ample artwork.

由于米歇尔·蒙特兹不知道这次地铁之旅完全是加里森先生的主意，她以为这是亚历克斯在做的事情，而她首先想到的是亚历克斯·巴克斯特计划在圆顶城市建造地铁系统，就像俄罗斯人建造的那样，并配有大量的艺术品。

Michelle would never have gone to these subways on her own, and now was delighted she did, because she already thought of a story the magazine could do on the Moscow subway stations, most of which were unknown to the world. The artwork alone deserved some recognition. As a people mover, it was very efficient, and one of the major success stories of Moscow.

米歇尔永远不会独自去这些地铁，现在她很高兴自己去了，因为她已经想到了杂志可以写一篇关于莫斯科地铁站的故事，其中大多数地铁站都不为世人所知。单是这幅作品就值得一些认可。作为一种旅客运输工具，它非常高效，是莫斯科最成功的故事之一。

TOURISM INFORMATION EXHIBIT
INFORMATION PLACARD
MR. GARRISON READING OUTLOUD

The Komsomolskaya-Metro-station opened in 1952. Komsomolskaya-Metro-station was dedicated to the Victory over NAZI Germany. The chief designer Alexey Shchusev made it an illustration of a historical speech given by Joseph Stalin November 7, 1941. In Stalin's speech, he evoked the memories of Alexander Nevsky, Dmitry Donskoy and other military leaders of the past, and all these historical figures eventually appeared on the mosaics of Komsomolskaya.

旅游信息展览
信息牌
加里森先生朗读

共青团地铁站于 1952 年开通。共青团地铁站是为了纪念战胜纳粹德国而建。首席设计师阿列克谢·舒索夫将约瑟夫·斯大林 1941 年 11 月 7 日发表的历史性讲话的插图绘制在了地铁站上。在斯大林的讲话中，他唤起了人们对亚历山大·涅夫斯基、德米特里·顿斯科伊和其他过去军事领导人的回忆，所有这些历史人物最终都出现在了共青团的马赛克上。

***

The *Grozny Demon Gang* considered troublemakers to the Chechnya's who bestowed upon the countryside continuous Russian reprisals, wished they would knock it off, because they were not going to solve any problems and only cause more misery for the public. Hence the *Grozny Demons* were not well liked back in Chechnya.

格罗兹尼恶魔帮被车臣人视为麻烦制造者，他们不断对乡村进行俄罗斯的报复，希望他们停止这种行为，因为他们不会解决任何问题，只会给公众带来更多痛苦。因此，格罗兹尼恶魔帮在车臣并不受欢迎。

However, these *Grozny Demons* were willing to give up their lives and more. They were dedicated and martyrs, hoping they would one day trigger a general uprising and hopefully sever all future relations with the Russians.

然而，这些"格罗兹尼恶魔"愿意献出生命，甚至更多。他们是忠诚的烈士，希望有朝一日能引发一场全面起义，并希望断绝与俄罗斯的一切关系。

The *Grozny Demons* received a lot of financial support from Muslim countries and in particular Iran which demonstrated a really good ability to conceal their ties with terrorist groups. Even though Iran used Russia as a surrogate against the Americans, they knew they were playing a dangerous game financing the *Grozny Demons*.

格罗兹尼恶魔从穆斯林国家，尤其是伊朗获得了大量资金支持，伊朗表现出了隐瞒与恐怖组织关系的出色能力。尽管伊朗利用俄罗斯作为对抗美国的代理人，但他们知道，为格罗兹尼恶魔提供资金是一场危险的游戏。

But as Russia's appearance diminished in the Caucasus, so to it did Iran's influence increase. Most of the Iranian leadership and especially the *Clerics* looked forward to the restoration of the Persian Empire which would dovetail into the remaking of the Ottoman Empire. The Iranians viewed Iran as the future kings of the new Ottoman Empire, something the Turks would have to get used too.

但随着俄罗斯在高加索地区的影响力逐渐减弱，伊朗的影响力也随之增强。大多数伊朗领导人，尤其是教士，都期待波斯帝国的复兴，这将与奥斯曼帝国的重建相吻合。伊朗人将伊朗视为新奥斯曼帝国的未来之王，而土耳其人必须习惯这一点。

***

## INT. DAY. MOSCOW RUSSIA. BELORUSSKAYA SUBWAY STATION

国际日。俄罗斯莫斯科。白俄罗斯地铁站

Alex and his group departed the Komsomolskaya-Metro-station and in a matter of time arrived at the Belorusskaya Subway Station just before the Chechnya's Grozny Demons arrived to shoot it up.

阿历克斯和他的团队从共青团地铁站出发，没过多久就抵达了白俄罗斯地铁站，就在车臣的格罗兹尼恶魔到来并进行枪击之前。

What saved Alex and the group's lives was Mr. Garrison strolled further down the corridor to look and photograph some of the Belorusskaya Subway Station artwork and decoration.

拯救亚历克斯和团队生命的是加里森先生沿着走廊继续走下去，观看并拍摄白俄罗斯地铁站的一些艺术品和装饰。

Moscow Russi Belorusskaya Subway Station

The Chechnya's piled out of the Delivery Vans that dropped them off at the Belorusskaya Subway Station with the AK-47's partially hidden under their long coats, and they simply jumped over the turnstiles. When the Moscow security sentry tried to stop the group for avoiding paying for the subway ride, one of the terrorists simply shot him in the chest instantly killing him.

车臣人从送货车上走下来，将他们送到白俄罗斯地铁站，AK-47 步枪部分藏在长外套下，他们直接跳过了旋转栅门。当莫斯科安全哨兵试图阻止他们，因为他们逃避支付地铁票价时，一名恐怖分子直接向他的胸部开枪，当场毙命。

Buster did not bring any firearms from the plane because, the Russians can be very bad to someone bringing in firearms without a permit, and to obtain the permit was impossible unless you were part of the secret service protecting the President or something along those lines. However, this morning as they were preparing to escort Mr. Baxter and his family around Moscow, Vasily Oryol handed Buster a gun with a clip of 9 rounds for emergency purposes and announced:

巴斯特没有从飞机上带任何枪支，因为俄罗斯人对未经许可携带枪支的人非常严厉，除非你是保护总统的特勤局成员或类似人员，否则不可能获得许可证。然而，今天早上，当他们准备护送巴克斯特先生和他的家人游览莫斯科时，瓦西里·奥廖尔递给巴斯特一把装有 9 发子弹的枪，以备不时之需，并宣布：

**VASILY ORYOL**
Just be sure and give it back to me before you leave Russia.

瓦西里·奥约尔
你离开俄罗斯之前一定要把它还给我。

Square support columns come down from the ceiling about every 20 feet in the Belorusskaya Station. Alex's group had passed the 10th column heading away from the stairway when the *Chechnyan Grozny Demon Terrorists* came down and had planned to shoot their way aboard the train and waste anyone riding that day.

白俄罗斯站每隔二十英尺左右就有一根方形支柱从天花板垂下。当车臣格罗兹尼恶魔恐怖分子下来时，亚历克斯的团队已经通过了第　十分根支柱，准备从楼梯上下来，并计划开枪打死当天乘坐火车的所有人。

The *Grozny Demon Leader, Abukhadzhi* showing haste in judgement and feeling the effects of the opium, he took in preparation for this slaughter. *Abukhadzhi* knew he very well might be killed in a shootout with Moscow police, thus swallowed the large amounts of opium just before he got out of the Delivery Van and went into the subway station.

格罗兹尼恶魔头目阿布哈吉反应迟钝，他为这次屠杀做了充分准备，服用了鸦片。阿布哈吉知道自己很可能在与莫斯科警方的枪战中丧生，因此在下送货车、进入地铁站前吞下了大剂量的鸦片。

The combination of the drugs and the adrenalin rush from conducting this bizarre act now had the *Grozny Demon Leader, Abukhadzhi* higher than a kite. The Grozny Demon Terrorist named *Danilbek* moving right behind *Abukhadzhi* also buzzed up with opium looked towards Abukhadzhi as a mentor and would carry out any orders *Abukhadzhi* gave him. *Danilbek* demonstrated repeatedly, he was the useful idiot zealot that made these kinds of events hugely successful in striking terror into the hearts of Western Civilizations.

药物和肾上腺素的结合使格罗兹尼恶魔领袖阿布哈吉兴奋不已。格罗兹尼恶魔恐怖分子丹尼尔贝克紧随阿布哈吉身后，也吸食鸦片，他把阿布哈吉视为导师，并会执行阿布哈吉给他的任何命令。丹尼尔贝克反复证明，他是一个有用的白痴狂热分子，他使这类事件取得了巨大成功，在西方文明中引起了恐慌。

As soon as the *Grozny Demon Terrorists* got to the subway exit platform just down the stairway the *Grozny Demons* saw a dozen people standing waiting for the train that might pose a problem when the train was to arrive in precisely three minutes.

当格罗兹尼恶魔恐怖分子到达地铁出口站台时，他们刚走下楼梯就看到十几个人站在那里等火车，这可能会对火车造成麻烦，因为火车将在三分钟内准时到达。

*Abukhadzhi* gave the orders as he was now feeling the rush of the opium and his adrenalin flowing making him feel invincible.

阿布哈吉下达了命令，因为他此时正感受到鸦片的冲击和肾上腺素的涌动，让他感到自己无敌了。

## ABUKHADZHI
Shoot at these people, they will scatter and get out of
the way!

阿布哈吉
向这些人开枪，他们就会四散逃开！

The Terrorists had no idea there was a former Spetsnaz, Green Beret, and Navy Seal out on the platform, and two of them had guns and were great shots.

恐怖分子根本不知道站台上有前特种部队、绿色贝雷帽和海豹突击队队员，其中两人还带着枪，而且枪法高超。

The sudden firing and unmistakable sound of an AK-47 instantly sent Mr. Garrison to battle stations. Just like he reacted while on a SOG team, he led Alex to safety behind one of the support columns as bullets zipped past almost hitting them.

突然的枪声和 AK-47 的清晰声音让加里森先生立即进入战斗状态。就像他在 SOG 小队中做出的反应一样，他带着亚历克斯躲到一根支撑柱后面，子弹飞过，差点击中他们。

There were terrible screams, people were fleeing away from the shooters as fast as they could.

人们发出可怕的尖叫声，尽可能快地逃离枪手。

*Michelle Montez* was halfway between the shooters and Alex and his group. There were a dozen people between *Michelle Montez* and the shooters who were gunning them down just like they were shooting ducks in a barrel feeling enormous satisfaction in the killing they were doing.

米歇尔·蒙特兹站在枪手和亚历克斯等人中间。枪手和米歇尔·蒙特兹之间有十几个人，枪手们像瓮中之鳖一样向他们开枪，他们为自己所做的杀戮感到无比的满足。

Alex seeing the attractive woman who somehow looked familiar running towards him screaming jumped out and grabbed *Michelle Montez* and in the process the two tumbled to the floor with Alex somehow coming to stop on top of her, in direct view of the terrorists who would eventually get down there and waste them just as they were going to get on the train.

看到那个看起来有些眼熟的漂亮女人尖叫着向他跑来，亚历克斯跳了出来，抓住了米歇尔·蒙特兹，在这个过程中，两个人都摔倒在地，亚历克斯不知怎么地停在了她身上，就在恐怖分子的直接注视下，他们最终在他们准备上火车时冲到那里，杀死了他们。

Vasily Oryol called in support. Help was on the way, but it could be five minutes before they would arrive with enough fire power to make a difference. He had no choice but to defend those he was sent to protect.

瓦西里·奥廖尔呼叫支援。援军正在赶来，但可能要过五分钟他们才能带着足够的火力赶到，造成影响。他别无选择，只能保卫那些他被派去保护的人。

Seeing that Alex was in a very vulnerable position with the woman, Vasily Oryol did the only thing he could do to distract the terrorists.

看到阿历克斯在那名女子面前处于非常脆弱的境地，瓦西里·奥廖尔做了他唯一能做的事情来分散恐怖分子的注意力。

Vasily Oryol got down on one knee next to the support column and started shooting his Uzi sub machine gun, immediately cutting down a couple of the dozen terrorists each armed with AK-47's, hand grenades and a few other surprises.

瓦西里·奥廖尔在支撑柱旁单膝跪地，开始用乌兹冲锋枪射击，立刻击毙了十几名恐怖分子中的两三个，每人都手持 AK-47、手榴弹和其他一些突袭武器。

Buster also started shooting from the side of another support column further distracting the terrorists.

巴斯特还开始从另一根支援柱的侧面射击，进一步分散恐怖分子的注意力。

*Michelle Montez* was screaming and almost out of her mind. She thought she was going to die but knew the man had jumped out and grabbed her and pulled her to the ground. *Michelle Montez* had no idea how big a target she was and was only about two or three seconds away from receiving ten or more rounds into her backside. Alex had for the time being saved her life.

米歇尔·蒙特兹尖叫着，几乎失去了理智。她以为自己要死了，但知道那个男人已经跳出来抓住了她，把她拉到了地上。米歇尔·蒙特兹不知道自己有多大的目标，而且距离她臀部被击中十发或更多子弹只有两三秒钟的时间了。亚历克斯暂时救了她的命。

The terrorists ignored Alex and the woman for the time being they were now in a fire fight with someone who had guns.

恐怖分子暂时忽略了亚历克斯和那名女子，他们正与一名持枪者交火。

Suddenly the subway train arrived.

突然，地铁进站了。

Vasily Oryol knew if the train stopped there would be mass carnage and figured if he put a couple bullets thought the right side of the cab away from the subway train driver, he'd scare the crap out of the driver who would keep on driving to the next stop instead of stopping here where the terrorists could get aboard the train.

瓦西里·奥廖尔知道,如果火车停下来，将会造成大规模屠杀。他认为，如果他从车厢右侧远离地铁列车司机的地方射几颗子弹，就会把司机吓得魂飞胆丧，他就会继续开车前往下一站，而不是停在这里，因为恐怖分子可能会登上火车。

Just as Vasily Oryol figured that's all it took, and the train continued and sped up. The driver hit the floor of the train with the microphone in his hand screaming to his dispatcher the train was being shot at by terrorists at Belorusskaya Station.

正当瓦西里·奥廖尔认为一切就绪时，火车继续行驶并加速。司机趴在车厢地板上，手里拿着麦克风，向调度员大喊，恐怖分子在白俄罗斯站向火车开枪。

A terrorist named Ismael soon hit Vasily Oryol in the mid-section. The AK-47 round tore Vasily Oryol guts apart in a very painful and fatal wound.

一名名叫伊斯梅尔的恐怖分子很快击中了瓦西里·奥廖尔的腹部。AK-47 子弹将瓦西里·奥廖尔的内脏撕开，留下了非常痛苦和致命的伤口。

Vasily Oryol knew he was dying but also knew he could not waste bullets and had to make every shot count and would keep firing taking out terrorists as long as he could which he knew might only be another minute. Then he would throw his gun to the Americans when he felt he was about to pass out.

瓦西里·奥廖尔知道自己快要死了，但他也知道不能浪费子弹，必须让每一枪都发挥作用，他会继续射击，直到他能射出子弹为止，尽管他知道可能只剩一分钟了。然后，当他觉得自己快要昏过去时，他就会把枪扔给美国人。

Buster only had nine rounds. He also had to make every round count and carefully aimed and shot each time usually hitting his target but not necessarily killing them. By the time Vasily Oryol was feeling he was passing out, half of the terrorists were dead, and the other half were cowering behind the support columns and edging their way closer.

巴斯特只有九发子弹。他还必须充分利用每一发子弹，每次都仔细瞄准并射击，通常都能击中目标，但不一定能杀死他们。当瓦西里·奥廖尔感到自己快要昏过去时，一半的恐怖分子已经死了，另一半则躲在支撑柱后面，慢慢靠近。

The woman was screaming, but the man wasn't moving. The Terrorists assumed they had hit the man who was probably dead on top of the woman and continued to ignore him as Alex laid perfectly still and kept saying in a calm and low voice:

女人在尖叫，但男人一动不动。恐怖分子以为他们击中了那个男人，他可能已经死了，压在女人身上，于是继续无视他，而亚历克斯一动不动地躺着，继续用平静而低沉的声音说：

ALEX
Stop screaming or they may start shooting at us.

亚历克斯
别再尖叫了，否则他们可能会开始向我们开枪。

Just before he passed out, Vasily Oryol hit *Abukhadzhi* on the forehead just above the eyes. Vasily Oryol was finished but so was the leadership of the Grozny Demon Terrorist assault force.

就在他昏倒前，瓦西里·奥廖尔击中了阿布哈吉的额头，就在眼睛上方，瓦西里·奥廖尔完蛋了，但格罗兹尼恶魔恐怖分子突击部队的领导也完蛋了。

*Danilbek* knelt by his mentor Abukhadzhi quickly saying a prayer when Buster's shot hit him in the side of the head ending his jihad. The 74 virgins promised did not appear.

丹尼尔贝克跪在导师阿布哈吉身边，快速祈祷，这时巴斯特的子弹击中了他的头部，结束了他的圣战。承诺的 74 名处女并未出现。

*Grozny Demon Fighter Mairbek* an expert marksman hit Buster who now had a semi-fatal wound that was also very painful. Just as Vasily Oryol was passing out, he threw his Uzi to Buster yelling:

格罗兹尼恶魔战士梅尔贝克是一名神枪手，击中了巴斯特，巴斯特现在受到了半致命的伤害，同样非常痛苦。就在 瓦西里·奥廖尔巴斯特昏倒的时候，他把他的乌兹冲锋枪扔给了 巴斯特，大喊道：

**VASILY ORYOL**
Buster, take this my friend.

瓦西里·奥约尔
巴斯特，接住它，我的朋友。

Vasily Oryol's movement distracted Mairbek who wasted time and a bullet on a dying man which gave Buster though wounded and in intense pain just a second to hit Mairbek.

瓦西里·奥廖尔 (Vasily Oryol) 的行动分散了梅尔贝克 (Mairbek) 的注意力，他浪费了时间和一颗子弹，击中了这名垂死之人，而这让受伤且痛苦不堪的巴斯特 (Buster) 仅有一秒钟的时间来击中梅尔贝克。

Mr. Garrison, fully combat ready, adrenalin flowing just like on the SOG-teams doing penetrations into Cambodia during the Vietnam War, was standing behind the support column beside Alex, fearing the most for his son-in-law, yet realizing he too was a hero for saving that woman's life. He poked his head out and could see Buster was bleeding badly and knew he may be soon finished.

加里森先生做好了战斗准备，肾上腺素激增，就像越南战争期间潜入柬埔寨的特种部队一样，他站在亚历克斯旁边的支援柱后面，最担心的是他的女婿，但他也意识到自己也是救了那个女人的英雄。他探出头，看到巴斯特血流不止，知道自己可能很快就完蛋了。

Mr. Garrison had been a Medic in the Army. The three men Studies and Observation Group (SOG) teams (plus five Montagnard mercenaries) had one member who was a certified medic, and the idea was casualties were expected and having a medic along might save a few lives. Even though he was a medic, he also received the same training as the other SOG team members.

加里森先生曾在陆军担任过一名医务兵。三人 研究与观察组 (SOG) 小队（加上 五 名 蒙塔格纳德 雇佣兵）中有一名成员是经过认证的医务兵，他们的想法是，伤亡是意料之中的事情，有一名医务兵在身边也许能挽救一些生命。尽管他是一名医务兵，但他也接受了与其他 研究与观察组小队成员相同的训练。

One of the other members oversaw the communications equipment which was their lifeline in case the team needed to be extracted, which occurred on every single mission. Eventually Mr. Garrison became the team leader, but he also had duties and responsibilities as the team's medic.

另一名成员负责管理通讯设备，这是他们的生命线，以防团队需要撤离，每次执行任务时都会发生这种情况。最终，加里森先生成为了团队领导，但他也承担着团队医务员的职责。

Mr. Garrison saw Vasily throw the gun, but it landed a few feet on the other side of the support column. Buster's wounds were too severe for him to go after the Uzi. Mr. Garrison knew all their lives were now at risk, the terrorists still had a half dozen men and AK-47's.

加里森先生看到瓦西里扔出了枪，但枪落在了支撑柱另一侧几英尺的地方。巴斯特的伤势太重，他无法去追那把乌兹冲锋枪。加里森先生知道现在他们所有人的生命都处于危险之中，恐怖分子还有六个人和 AK-47。

No doubt the Russian police would soon be here thanks to Vasily having the foresight to shoot at the train which set off every alarm in town. Already police cars were pulling up to the station. But the terrorists were getting closer, and they probably knew they would all be dead soon, so their idea was to make one final gift to Allah by eliminating a few more of these infidels who screwed up their mission.

毫无疑问，俄罗斯警察很快就会赶到，因为瓦西里有先见之明，向触发全城警报的火车开枪。警车已经驶进车站。但恐怖分子越来越近，他们可能知道他们很快就会全部死掉，所以他们的想法是通过消灭更多搞砸了他们任务的异教徒，向真主献上最后的礼物。

Mr. Garrison waited until Buster weakly fired his next shot hitting another terrorist in the middle of the throat to dive for the Uzi. Having used an Uzi a few times during SOG missions, Mr. Garrison knew how to handle it just fine. Mr. Garrison's memories came back instantly and as soon as the Uzi was in his hand he pointed and shot, which forced the enemy to keep their heads down so that he could get back behind the column.

加里森先生等到巴斯特虚弱地开枪，击中另一名恐怖分子的喉咙中央后，才俯冲去拿乌兹冲锋枪。加里森先生在 研究与观察组 (SOG)任务中使用过几次乌兹冲锋枪，因此知道如何应对。加里森先生的记忆立刻浮现出来，他一拿到乌兹冲锋枪，就瞄准并射击，迫使敌人低下头，以便他能回到纵队后面。

Mr. Garrison's son-in-law Alex was brilliant, but extremely brave. The terrorists were not yet focused on him while there were 2 shooters, though Buster was not long for the world.

加里森先生的女婿亚历克斯非常聪明，但非常勇敢。虽然巴斯特很快就死了，但当枪手数量达到两名时，恐怖分子还没有把注意力集中在他身上。

Just as the police were starting to come down the stairway, the terrorists were now faced with shooting in two directions and they feared the police more and changed their orientation, but in one last desperate attempt the terrorists decided to storm Mr. Garrison's position, and they were extremely mad and agitated because whoever this was had just killed seven of them.

就在警察开始走下楼梯时，恐怖分子面临着来自两个方向的枪击，他们更加害怕警察，改变了方向，但在最后一次绝望的尝试中，恐怖分子决定袭击加里森先生的位置，他们非常愤怒和激动，因为不管这是谁，他刚刚杀死了他们七个人。

Buster who knew he was almost dying made one Navy Seal last stand, making each bullet count at the same time he was taking hits from the AK-47's. And as he fired his last round, now out of ammunition, he was also out of life, and with blood flowing now out of his mouth he was coughing up, fell forward face down dead. The two that were left of those charging were cut down by Mr. Garrison.

巴斯特知道自己快要死了，但他还是在海豹突击队中奋力拼搏，在被 AK-47 击中的同时，每发子弹都发挥了作用。当他射出最后一发子弹时，子弹已经用完了，他也失去了生命，他嘴里流着血，不停咳嗽，脸朝下倒地，死了。剩下的两名冲锋队员被加里森先生砍倒。

The Moscow police took care of the rest of the terrorists and shot one in the head just as he was getting ready to throw a hand grenade at them.

莫斯科警方制服了其余恐怖分子，并在一名恐怖分子准备向他们投掷手榴弹时击中其头部。

*Michelle Montez* didn't know if she should pee her pants, scream, or what to do was holding on to Alex for dear life. Then there was quiet.

米歇尔·蒙特兹不知道自己是该尿裤子，还是该尖叫，或者该怎么做，只为了保住性命而紧紧抱住亚历克斯。然后一片寂静。

ALEX
It's over, you are going to be safe now.

亚历克斯
一切都结束了，你现在安全了。

Up until this moment, *Michelle Montez* had not noticed all her senses. The voice sound reassured, and soft. *Michelle Montez* noticed the man's breath was sweet and his cologne was invigoratingly attractive. *Michelle Montez* owed the man her life and he indeed was a sweet-smelling prince.

直到此刻，米歇尔·蒙特兹才注意到她所有的感官。那声音听起来令人安心，柔和。米歇尔·蒙特兹注意到男人的呼吸很甜，他的古龙水令人精神振奋。米歇尔·蒙特兹欠这个男人一条命，他确实是一位香气扑鼻的王子。

*Michelle Montez* opened her eyes and seeing his face close to hers, she held on even tighter and kissed him as if there was no tomorrow.

米歇尔·蒙特兹睁开眼睛，看到他的脸靠近她，她抱得更紧了，亲吻他，仿佛没有明天似的。

With her endorphins flowing *Michelle Montez's* body stimulated beyond love making, she felt orgasmic. Alex calmly tried to dislodge himself and Michelle finally let go so he could get up and then with a sudden huge surprise *Michelle Montez* discovered:

米歇尔·蒙特兹体内的内啡肽在做爱之外受到刺激，她感到了性高潮。亚历克斯平静地试图摆脱自己，米歇尔终于放手，这样他就可以站起来，然后米歇尔·蒙特兹突然大吃一惊地发现：

*MICHELLE MONTEZ* (Thought)
*Oh my god, it is no other than Alex Baxter.*

An American woman who had been further down the train platform hiding behind one of the support columns came out right away when the police arrived, and the shooting stopped. She had her iPhone out and caught some of the action including Michelle Montez kissing Alex.

一名躲在火车站台下方支柱后面的美国女子在警察到达后立即走了出来，枪击停止了。她拿出 苹果手机拍下了一些动作，包括米歇尔·蒙特兹亲吻亚历克斯的画面。

Mr. Garrison sat the Uzi down on the floor and walked out toward Alex, hoping he was alive and witnessed the woman grabbing and kissing Alex.

加里森先生把乌兹冲锋枪放在地板上，向亚历克斯走去，希望他还活着，并亲眼目睹那个女人抓住并亲吻亚历克斯。

MR. GARRISON
Are you okay Alex?

加里森先生
你还好吗，亚历克斯？

The police approached everyone and asked what happened, Paramedics quickly arrived and notified the police that both Vasily and Buster were dead. Every single one of the Terrorists were dead, and because half of them were so arrogant they were going to shoot up the place, then walk out of there, had their identification on them. So further penetration and cracking of the Grozny Demon Gang was in the works. Russians in fact raided homes and were able to discover some of the mountain hideouts, which took down part of the apparatus.

警察走近每个人询问发生了什么事，医护人员迅速赶到并通知警方，瓦西里和巴斯特都已死亡。恐怖分子全部死亡，而且由于其中一半人太过傲慢，他们打算枪杀这个地方，然后离开，身上带着身份证明。因此，进一步渗透和破获格罗兹尼恶魔帮的计划正在进行中。事实上，俄罗斯人突袭了房屋，并发现了一些山区藏身处，并摧毁了部分装置。

The American lady approached *Michelle Montez* and did not know who she was.

这位美国女士走近米歇尔·蒙特兹, 但不知道她是谁。

### AMERICAN LADY
I was so touched watching you kiss the man, I took pictures.

### 美国女士
看到你亲吻那个男人，我很感动·我拍了照片。

### *MICHELLE MONTEZ*
May I have a copy for my memories.

### 米歇尔·蒙特兹
请给我一份作为纪念。

### AMERICAN LADY
After what you went through with bullets flying all around you, I would be delighted to give you copies.

### 美国女士
在您经历了子弹横飞的痛苦之后，我很乐意给您复印件。

Within minutes *Michelle Montez* texted Charles Denning and explained what just happened and sent the splendid picture of "the kiss.".

几分钟后，米歇尔·蒙特兹给查尔斯·丹宁发了短信，解释了刚才发生的事情，并发来了 "吻" 的精彩照片。

### CHARLES DENNING
That's an incredible story and picture of a kiss with

Alex Baxter. This will sell a lot of magazines. You need to come back to Paris immediately so we can put together a magazine article and be ready for the next publication.

查尔斯·丹宁

这是一个令人难以置信的故事，还有一张与亚历克斯·巴克斯特接吻的照片。这将会卖出很多杂志。你需要立即返回巴黎，这样我们就可以整理一篇杂志文章，为下一次出版做好准备。

*MICHELLE MONTEZ*

I cannot come back to Paris because the police wanted to question me about the terrorist attack.

米歇尔·蒙特兹

我无法返回巴黎，因为警方想就恐怖袭击事件对我进行讯问。

Alex still had not figured out nor did he care who the woman was, until the police started asking them names via translators for the most part.

亚历克斯仍然没有弄清楚也不关心这个女人是谁，直到警察开始主要通过翻译询问他们的名字。

FSB showed up shortly and took Vasily's body away and his guns. The Russian coroner's office took Buster's body and after Alex had some discussions with them, he was notified:

俄罗斯联邦安全局很快就赶到，带走了瓦西里的尸体和他的枪支。俄罗斯验尸官办公室带走了巴斯特的尸体，亚历克斯与他们讨论后，他得到了通知：

RUSSIAN CORONER

The American Embassy will have to ship the body back to the United States. Mr. Baxter, we will not permit you to ship Buster Fancher's body back to the United States. Your American State Department will be required to keep custody of the body until it leaves our country.

俄罗斯验尸官

美国大使馆必须将尸体运回美国。巴克斯特先生，我们不会允许你将巴斯特·范彻的尸体运回美国。美国国务院必须保管尸体，直到它离开我们的国家。

ALEX<br>Understand sir.

亚历克斯
明白先生。

Alex now heard the Russian Investigators talk to *Michelle Montez*.

亚历克斯现在听到俄罗斯调查人员与米歇尔·蒙特兹的谈话。

RUSSIAN INVESGTIBATOR
May I have your name miss?

俄罗斯调查员
请问您叫什么名字？小姐。

*MICHELLE MONTEZ*
My name is *Michelle Montez*.

米歇尔·蒙特兹
我的名字是米歇尔·蒙特兹。

Alex looked at Ms. Montez and felt astonished. The next publication of *Magazine Femmes Réelles Exigeantes* would feature that kiss as a centerfold piece. With Alex's picture with Putin on the front cover and that famous kiss in the centerfold, *Magazine Femmes Réelles Exigeantes* that week would be sold out in two days.

阿历克斯看着蒙特兹女士，感到很惊讶。《真实女性》杂志的下一期将以那次吻作为插页。阿历克斯和普京的合影出现在封面上，而那次著名的吻出现在插页上，那周的《真实女性》杂志将在两天内销售一空。

A member of the FSB approached Alex.

联邦安全局的一名成员走近了亚历克斯。

FSB AGENT
Mr. Baxter, we've arranged transportation back to your hotel. The Limo will be out front in a moment.

FSB 特工
巴克斯特先生，我们已经安排好返回酒店的交通。豪华轿车马上就到。

Under the circumstances Alex felt sorry for *Michelle Montez* who equally was probably still shook up and needed transportation.

在这种情况下，亚历克斯对米歇尔·蒙特兹感到难过，因为她可能同样仍处于震惊之中，需要交通工具。

ALEX
Could you also please arrange transportation for Ms.
Montez.

亚历克斯
您还可以为蒙特兹女士安排交通吗？

Alex nodded towards *Michelle Montez*.

亚历克斯朝米歇尔·蒙特兹点点头。

Even though her hair was slightly messed up, when she put her hat back on that she took care of that, and her Kalvin Klein inspirationally fit jeans quickly left an impression on the young FSB officer who quickly responded:

虽然她的头发有点乱，但当她戴上帽子时，头发就散了，她穿的　卡尔文·克莱恩(Kalvin Klein) 修身牛仔裤很快给这位年轻的 FSB 官员留下了深刻的印象，他很快就做出了回应：

FSB AGENT
Yes, I will personally see to it that she is taken back to
her hotel right away.

FSB 特工
是的，我会亲自确保她立即被送回酒店。

The FSB officer gave marching orders to one of his deputies regarding helping Ms. Montez, then turned to Alex.

联邦安全局官员向他的一名副手下达了帮助蒙特兹女士的命令，然后转向亚历克斯。

FSB officer
Mr. Baxter, I will escort you and Mr. Garrison to a
waiting Limo ready to take you back to your hotel.

联邦安全局官员
巴克斯特先生，我会护送您和加里森先生到一辆
等候的豪华轿车，准备送您回酒店。

ALEX
Thank you.

亚历克斯
谢谢。

Alex nodded to Mr. Garrison, who walked side by side with his son-in-law out to the Limo.

亚历克斯向加里森先生点点头，加里森先生和女婿并肩走向豪华轿车。

Inside the waiting Limo, Gennady Alexeyev was there to take them back to the hotel. A lot was not known yet, but Alex knew it was some sort of terrorist attack that failed.

在等候的豪华轿车里，根纳季·阿列克谢耶夫正准备送他们回酒店。很多事情还不得而知，但阿列克谢知道这是一场失败的恐怖袭击。

### GENNADY ALEXEYEV
Mr. Baxter, we are so sorry you just had this close call.

### 根纳季·阿列克谢耶夫
巴克斯特先生，我们很抱歉您遭遇了如此危险的遭遇。

### ALEX
Don't worry about it, today was not my destiny to die.

### 亚历克斯
别担心，今天不是我的死期。

### GENNADY ALEXEYEV
This was quite an extraordinary event, I promise you the Russian Government will quickly investigate it and bring those responsible to justice.

### 根纳季·阿列克谢耶夫
这是一起相当不寻常的事件，我向你们保证，俄罗斯政府将迅速展开调查，并将责任人绳之以法。

### ALEX
I have no doubt you will.

### 亚历克斯
我毫不怀疑你会的。

### GENNADY ALEXEYEV
I was just contacted by Vladimir Putin, and he wanted me to convey to you his warmest sympathy and also was glad to hear you were not wounded.

### 根纳季·阿列克谢耶夫
弗拉基米尔·普京刚刚联系了我，他希望我向您转达他最热烈的慰问，并且很高兴听到您没有受伤。

### ALEX
Nor was my father-in-law, thank goodness.

亚历克斯
谢天谢地，我的岳父也没有。

Mr. Garrison was equally alarmed.

加里森先生也同样感到震惊。

MR. GARRISON (Thought)
*Christina would take it very hard if something happened to Alex. She would also hold me responsible for taking Alex some place where he almost got killed. Life with Christina is going to be tough for a few days. And then there was Ethel who also will probably nit-pick me.*

加里森先生 （思考）
如果亚历克斯出了什么事，克里斯蒂娜会很难过。她还会认为我把亚历克斯带到了差点让他丧命的地方。和克里斯蒂娜一起生活几天会很艰难。还有埃塞尔，她可能也会对我吹毛求疵。

Alex would however be extremely appreciative of his father-in-law who saw Michelle Montez kiss him that he was being kissed not kissing the woman, even though *Magazine Femmes Réelles Exigeantes* said otherwise in a couple days.

然而，亚历克斯非常感激他的岳父，当他看到米歇尔蒙特兹亲吻他时，他说那是他在被吻，而不是在亲吻那个女人，尽管《真实女性》杂志在几天后发表了相反的看法。

***

Christina and her mother had been shopping and having a good time at GUM when the Russian FSB agent informed them:

克里斯蒂娜和她的母亲正在 GUM 商场购物，玩得很开心，这时俄罗斯联邦安全局特工告诉她们：

FSB AGENT
I'm sorry, you must return to your hotel at once.

FSB 特工
很抱歉，您必须立即返回酒店。

The FSB Agent gave that strange look to Trevor who was also quite interested in the change of events suddenly and the body language of the agent was not reassuring.

联邦安全局特工用奇怪的眼神看着特雷弗，特雷弗也对事态的突然变化很感兴趣，而且特工的肢体语言让人感到不放心。

CHRISTINA
We are not done shopping, why must we go?

克里斯蒂娜
我们还没买完呢，为什么一定要去呢？

FSB AGENT
Trevor, may I have a word with you privately?

FSB 特工
特雷弗，我可以和你私下谈谈吗？

The FSB agent took Trevor down the hallway away from where the two women could not hear. Then the FSB agent explained:

联邦安全局特工带着特雷弗沿着走廊走，远离两名女子听不到的地方。然后 FSB 特工解释道：

RUSSIAN FSB AGENT
Mr. Baxter and Mr. Garrison were at a subway station that was hit by terrorists. They are safe and are being taken back to the hotel, but under the consideration of the head of the FSB, it is determined that for Baxter's and Garrison's security, they want them back at the hotel until the police can discover the plot and who was all involved.

俄罗斯联邦安全局特工
巴克斯特先生和加里森先生所在的地铁站遭到恐怖分子袭击。他们目前安全无恙，正被带回酒店，但根据联邦安全局局长的考虑，他们决定为了巴克斯特和加里森的安全，让他们回到酒店，直到警方发现阴谋和所有涉案人员。

He also informed Trevor the bad news:

FSB AGENT
I'm also sorry to inform you that your colleague Mr. Buster Francher was killed in the attack.

FSB 特工
我还很遗憾地通知您，您的同事巴斯特·弗朗彻先生在袭击中丧生。

Those stunning words put Trevor into his security game plan state of mind.

这些令人震惊的话语让特雷弗进入了制定安全游戏计划的状态。

TREVOR (Thought)
*The two women needed extracted out of GUM right away in the event this was an attack on Alex and his family.*

特雷弗（思考）
如果这是对亚历克斯和他的家人的袭击，那么这两个女人需要立即撤出 GUM。

FSB AGENT
We have a Limo waiting at this exit and do not want them to walk to their hotel.

FSB 特工
我们有一辆豪华轿车在这个出口等候，我们不想让他们步行去酒店。

Trevor then approached Christina and her mother.

随后，特雷弗走近克里斯蒂娜和她的母亲。

TREVER
I believe the FSB is correct in their assessment we should go back to the hotel immediately.

特雷弗
我相信 FSB 的评估是正确的，我们应该立即返回酒店。

Fear suddenly struck Christina, and her only thoughts now were:

恐惧突然袭上克里斯蒂娜的心头，她唯一的想法就是：

CHRISTINA (Thought)
*Is my daddy and my husband, okay?*

克里斯蒂娜（想道）
我的爸爸和丈夫还好吗？

Since the ride was short and they only had a couple bags of shopping items, it was only five minutes before they were back in their hotel room.

由于路途较短，而且他们只带了几袋购物物品，所以只用了五分钟就回到了酒店房间。

Christina sat down on the king-size bed and her mother sat on a chair directly across from her in Christina's room for about 10 minutes, in total silence wondering what

Moscow had bestowed upon them. Soon there was noise at the door and Alex opened the hotel room door and walked in. Christina ran up and threw her arms around him and they hugged.

克里斯蒂娜坐在特大号床上，她的母亲坐在克里斯蒂娜房间对面的椅子上，大约 10 分钟，两人都沉默不语，想知道莫斯科给了他们什么。很快门口传来一阵响声，亚历克斯打开酒店房间的门走了进来。克里斯蒂娜跑上前去，张开双臂拥抱了他，两人拥抱在一起。

Mr. Garrison followed Alex into the room and knew he had to help soothe the women's fears since they both came out of it unscathed. However, if they knew how vulnerable Alex had been, and that it was a pure miracle he wasn't shot and killed, they might get really upset.

加里森先生跟着亚历克斯走进房间，他知道他必须帮助安抚这两个女人的恐惧，因为她们两个都毫发无损地走了出来。然而，如果她们知道亚历克斯是多么脆弱，而且他没有被枪杀简直是个奇迹，她们可能会非常难过。

MRS. GARRISON
What happened, William?

加里森夫人
发生什么事了，威廉？

MR. GARRISON

I took Alex sightseeing in a few Moscow subway stations to see the majestic construction and artwork and we just happened to get caught up in a terrorist attack that appears to have been planned for a subway train.

Had we not been there with Buster and Vasily, a lot of people on that train would have been killed.

加里森先生

我带亚历克斯参观了莫斯科的几个地铁站，欣赏了雄伟的建筑和艺术品，我们刚刚卷入了一场恐怖袭击，袭击似乎是针对地铁火车站策划的。

如果我们没有和巴斯特和瓦西里一起在那里，那列火车上的很多人就会被杀。

Alex knew that Christina and her mother had grown accustomed to Buster in a week or more traveling with them and felt he might as well tell them now before they learned from someone else.

亚历克斯知道克里斯蒂娜和她的母亲在与巴斯特一起旅行的一个多星期里已经习惯了巴斯特，他觉得最好现在就告诉他们，以免他们从别人那里得知。

ALEX
Buster and Vasily were killed saving our lives.

亚历克斯
巴斯特和瓦西里为了拯救我们的生命而被杀。

Mr. Garrison knew now would be a good time to leave the newlyweds alone suggested:

加里森先生知道现在是让新婚夫妇独处的最佳时机，他建议道：

MR. GARRISON
Honey why don't you and I go to our room and let
Alex and Christina have some time by themselves?

加里森先生
亲爱的，你和我为什么不回房间去，让亚历克斯
和克里斯蒂娜单独呆一会儿呢？

MRS. GARRISON
Okay dear.

Mrs. Garrison instinctively followed her husband's suggestion knowing she would get *"the rest of the story"* privately in their hotel room.

加里森夫人本能地听从了丈夫的建议，因为她知道她会在酒店房间里私下了解"故事的其余部分"。

Another FSB agent came to replace Vasily who would not be returning, and he told his partner the news about what happened to Vasily and Buster.

另一名联邦安全局特工来接替不会回来的瓦西里，并将发生在瓦西里和巴斯特身上的事情告诉了他的搭档。

Alex told Christina he just wanted to lay down and relax for a while. After he kicked his shoes off, he reclined on the bed with his clothes still on and then he held out his arms for Christina. She immediately moved beside him in his arms, and they held each other close.

阿历克斯告诉克里斯蒂娜，他只想躺下休息一会儿。他脱掉鞋子，穿着衣服躺在床上，然后向克里斯蒂娜伸出双臂。她立刻在他怀里移到他身边，两人紧紧地拥抱在一起。

Alex wept for a little while. He had known Buster from back when he was the security detail for one of his businesses. He had taken Buster fishing and bear hunting in Alaska a few times, not as an employee but as a good friend.

亚历克斯哭了一会儿。他认识巴斯特是在他一家公司的保安人员的时候。他曾带巴斯特去阿拉斯加钓鱼和猎熊几次，不是以雇员的身份，而是以好朋友的身份。

Christina knew it was best not to ask any questions, just to give her husband solace and understanding. And soon, both fell asleep in a natural reaction from a period of intense stress. They didn't wake up until 5:00 p.m.

克里斯蒂娜知道最好不要问任何问题，只要给丈夫安慰和理解就行了。很快，两人都睡着了，这是一段高度紧张时期的自然反应。他们直到下午 5 点才醒来。

Alex didn't feel jovial, but he was glad to be alive and decided to shift his personal psychology and felt the best way to do it was to get his family out of the hotel and go do something meaningful to obscure these bad memories for a while and suddenly asked:

亚历克斯并不觉得高兴，但他很高兴自己还活着，于是决定改变自己的个人心理，认为最好的办法就是带家人离开酒店，去做一些有意义的事情来暂时掩盖这些不好的记忆，然后突然问道

ALEX
Christina, have you ever seen a Bolshoi performance
of Swan Lake?

亚历克斯
克里斯蒂娜，你看过莫斯科大剧院的《天鹅湖》
演出吗？亚历克斯 克里斯蒂娜，你看过莫斯科大
剧院的《天鹅湖》演出吗？

CHRISTINA
No honey

克里斯蒂娜
没有蜂蜜

ALEX
Good, you get to see one tonight.

亚历克斯
很好，今晚你就能见到一个。

CHRISTINA
Sure, if that's what you would like to do.

克里斯蒂娜
当然，如果你愿意的话。

ALEX
We have about two hours to get ready, I'll have room
service bring us and your parents up a snack and we'll

then have dinner after the Ballet. Call your mother and
let her know what we are planning.

亚历克斯
我们有大约两个小时的准备时间，我会让客房服
务为我们和你的父母带来一些小吃，然后我们将
在芭蕾舞表演结束后吃晚饭。给你妈妈打电话，
告诉她我们的计划。

## CHRISTINA
Sounds good. I'll call my mother right now.

克里斯蒂娜
听起来不错。我现在就给我妈妈打电话。

Alex had a good snack including some of the Russians favorites including Caviar
served on toast. A shot of Vodka helped it down easily.

亚历克斯吃了一顿丰盛的小吃，包括一些俄罗斯人最喜欢的食物，比如烤面包
上的鱼子酱。一杯伏特加酒很快就把它喝下去了。

***

The sweet young makeup lady, who was not accustomed to all the big tips, was starting
to love Christina and her mother. And just as if nothing happened, Alex had the crew
ready to go right on time. Because of the Terrorist attack, Moscow was on pins and
needles and the Bolshoi almost considered canceling tonight's performance.

这位年轻可爱的化妆师不习惯大笔小费，但她开始喜欢克里斯蒂娜和她的母
亲。亚历克斯准时准备好了所有工作人员，就好像什么事都没发生一样。由于
恐怖袭击，莫斯科处于紧张不安的状态，莫斯科大剧院几乎考虑取消今晚的演
出。

When Alex contacted Gennady Alexeyev for assistance in obtaining tickets to a good
balcony seat, Gennady Alexeyev advised the Bolshoi management who wanted to
cancel tonight's performance:

当阿历克斯联系根纳季·阿列克谢耶夫，寻求帮助以获得一张好的阳台座位票
时，根纳季·阿列克谢耶夫告诉莫斯科大剧院管理层，他们想取消今晚的演
出：

## GENNADY ALEXEYEV
Vladimir Putin would be severely disappointed in them
if they canceled the performance for the distinguished
guest, Mr. Baxter.

根纳季·阿列克谢耶夫
如果他们取消了贵宾巴克斯特先生的演出，弗拉
基米尔·普京会对他们非常失望。

BOLSHOI MANAGER
We will not cancel tonight's performance, but we need
extra security.

大剧院经理
我们不会取消今晚的演出，但我们需要额外的安
保。

GENNADY ALEXEYEV
The government will bring in extra security for
tonight's performance. How many empty seats do you
expect to have?

根纳季·阿列克谢耶夫
政府将为今晚的演出增加安保人员。您预计会有
多少空座位？

BOLSHOI MANAGER
Maybe seventy-five.

大剧院经理
大概七十五岁吧。

GENNADY ALEXEYEV
We'll put agents in seventy-five seats.

根纳季· 阿列克谢耶夫
我们将在七十五个席位上安排特工。

BOLSHOI MANAGER
With that level of security, the management team has
no issues leaving the performance set for tonight's
scheduled time.

大剧院经理
有了这种级别的安全保障，管理团队可以毫无顾
忌地按照今晚的预定时间演出。

***

Alex's Limo pulled up in front of the Baltschug Kempinski Hotel and two minutes
later. Alex and his group walked out the front entrance of the hotel. *Michelle Montez*
again in the restaurant saw them leave, but she was catching a quick bite to eat then
heading for the airport.

两分钟后，亚历克斯的豪华轿车停在了巴尔舒格凯宾斯基酒店门前。亚历克斯和他的团队走出了酒店正门。米歇尔·蒙特兹再次在餐厅看到他们离开，但她正在吃点东西，然后前往机场。

*MICHELLE MONTEZ* (Thought)
*Tonight, Alex Baxter will have peace and quiet, but in a couple more days he will probably get angry over the magazine article.*

米歇尔·蒙特兹(想法)
今晚，亚历克斯·巴克斯特可以安安静静地过一晚，但过几天他可能会因为那篇杂志文章而生气。

The ride to the Bolshoi Theater was short. The building was of course immaculate and became more glamorous as they entered the building.

去莫斯科大剧院的车程很短。建筑当然是一尘不染的，越往里走越显得光彩夺目。

The Bolshoi Theatre Opera House in Moscow, Russia
俄罗斯莫斯科大剧院歌剧院

ALEX
The Russians are very under-rated on much of their arts and performances. This really is the best opera house in the world, nobody compares.

亚历克斯
俄罗斯人的许多艺术和表演都被严重低估。这确实是世界上最好的歌剧院，无人能比。

A beautiful white grand piano in the lobby was being played by an expert performing Chopin Nocturnes. Moreover, the pianist showcased the essence of the brilliance of the composition, and the performance did in fact create a surreal experience that heightened people's awareness and expectations of the ballet performance about to begin.

大堂里一架美丽的白色大钢琴，正由专家弹奏着肖邦的夜曲，钢琴家不仅将这首曲子的精髓展现得淋漓尽致，而且演奏也确实营造出一种超现实的体验，让人对即将开始的芭蕾舞表演更加期待。

Bolshoi Theater
莫斯科大剧院

The Bolshoi Theater has a lot of balcony seats. Some of which are orientated to prevent the general audience from witnessing who the occupants are. Some of them are long term leased to individuals such as Vladimir Putin. On nights he doesn't wish to attend, which is often, he would give out the seats for political favors, and they were the best seats in the house.

莫斯科大剧院有很多包厢座位。有些座位的朝向是为了让普通观众无法看到座位上的人。有些座位长期租给了弗拉基米尔·普京等人。在他不想出席的晚上

（这种情况经常发生），他会把座位送给别人以换取政治利益，而这些座位是剧院里最好的座位。

Anyone observing the geometries of the performance would know the performers were often giving signals to Putin's balcony even though choreographically appeared to be just reaching out into space.

任何观察过表演几何形状的人都会知道，尽管从舞蹈编排上看，表演者似乎只是向太空伸出援手，但表演者经常向普京的阳台发出信号。

In a short while Alex was sitting next to his princess Christina who looked stunning again. *The young Russian makeup artist had earned her tip ten times over.*

不一会儿，亚历克斯就坐在他的公主克里斯蒂娜旁边，她又一次看起来惊艳无比。这位年轻的俄罗斯化妆师赚到了十倍的小费。

Back at the Baltschug Kempinski Hotel prior to the performance, Mr. Garrison had informed his wife the entire details of the terrorist attack in the subway station.

演出前，回到巴尔舒格凯宾斯基酒店，加里森先生向妻子讲述了地铁站恐怖袭击的全部细节。

Mrs. Garrison now knew how brave her husband is then he informed her about the terrorist attack and Buster's death:

加里森夫人现在知道她的丈夫有多么勇敢，然后他告诉了她恐怖袭击和巴斯特的死亡：

### MR. GARRISON

I was quite shocked that of all the people *Michelle Montez* entered the picture and she has a picture of her kissing Alex on the lips because he saved her life.

### 加里森先生

我很震惊，在所有人中，米歇尔·蒙特兹出现在照片中，她有一张亲吻亚历克斯嘴唇的照片，因为他救了她的命。

### MRS. GARRISON

This will probably soon be shown in that filthy *Magazine Femmes Réelles Exigeantes*. I wonder how Christina will take it.

### 加里森夫人

这件事可能很快就会在那本肮脏的《真实女性》杂志上播出。我不知道克里斯蒂娜会怎么接受它。

MR. GARRISON

Anyone could tell Alex was not kissing *Michelle Montez* back.

加里森先生

任何人都看得出亚历克斯并没有回吻米歇尔·蒙特兹。

While Alex was sent out of the room to the Garrison's room so the women could be alone putting on their "war paint," Christina's mother explained to her how Mr. Garrison had informed her about the American taking the picture and gave it to Ms. Montez.

当亚历克斯被送出房间，前往加里森的房间，以便女人们可以独自涂上她们的"战争彩绘"时，克里斯蒂娜的母亲向她解释了加里森先生是如何将美国人拍照的情况告知她的，并将照片交给了蒙特兹女士。

MRS. GARRISON

Christina, expect a magazine picture in *Magazine Femmes Réelles Exigeantes* and DO NOT GET JEALOUS.

加里森夫人

克里斯蒂娜，期待杂志《Femmes Réelles Exigeantes》上的杂志照片，不要嫉妒。

CHRISTINA

I have no reason to be jealous. It was an extraordinary event, and my daddy was there as an eyewitness. Alex did a heroic act. The woman unconditionally reacted emotionally like most people would if their lives had just been saved from terrorists.

克里斯蒂娜

我没有理由嫉妒。这是一次非凡的事件，我爸爸当时在场，亲眼目睹了这一幕。亚历克斯做了一件英勇的事。那位女士毫无保留地表现出了情绪，就像大多数人在被恐怖分子救出后一样。

Christina was now well-armed and emotionally fortified for the next phase in the publicity war that *Michelle Montez* seemed to be hell bent on engaging.

克里斯蒂娜现在已经做好了充分的准备并在情感上做好了准备迎接米歇尔·蒙特兹似乎决心要参与的下一阶段宣传战。

<u>BACKGROUND MUSIC FOR THIS SEGMENT.</u>

<u>(4) Chopin: Complete Nocturnes (Luke Faulkner) - YouTube</u>

## <u>BACKGROUND MUSIC FOR THIS SEGMENT.</u>

<u>(4) Chopin: Complete Nocturnes (Luke Faulkner) - YouTube</u>

<u>本片段的背景音乐。</u>

<u>(4) 肖邦：完整夜曲 (卢克·福克纳) - YouTube</u>

The acoustics inside the Bolshoi Theatre Opera House were of course phenomenal. The Chopin Nocturnes, which had surreal piano sounds, instigated a mood in the audience causing them to expect a sensational two-hour ballet performance.

莫斯科大剧院歌剧院的音响效果当然是惊人的。肖邦的夜曲伴随着超现实的钢琴声，激发了观众的情绪，让他们期待一场长达两小时的芭蕾舞演出。

Gennady Alexeyev and his Russian movie star wife sat in the balcony box with Alex and his family.

根纳季·阿列克谢耶夫和他的俄罗斯影星妻子与阿列克谢耶夫及其家人一起坐在包厢里。

For good measure Gennady in what appeared to be an overstuffed suit, besides wearing body armor he also was packing an FN P90 made by FN Herstal in Belgium just in case there were any terrorists left, and Alex was the target.

为了保险起见，根纳迪穿着一件看上去塞得满满的西装，除了防弹衣外，他还携带了一把比利时 艾弗艾娜 赫斯塔尔 (FN Herstal) 制造的 FN P90，以防还有恐怖分子留下，而亚历克斯就是目标。

***

Just prior to the ballet, Vladimir Putin met with the head of the FSB, Alexander Vasilyevich Bortnikov to get an update about the terrorist attack.

芭蕾舞演出开始前，弗拉基米尔·普京会见了俄罗斯联邦安全局局长亚历山大·瓦西里耶维奇·博尔特尼科夫, 了解恐怖袭击的最新情况。

ALEXANDER VASILYEVICH BORTNIKOV
FSB has not fully determined the exact plan, though
it was likely the subway train was the real target, but
ballistics experts discovered two bullets in the subway
train cab were from Vasily Oryol's Uzi.

亚历山大·瓦西里耶维奇·博尔特尼科夫
联邦安全局尚未完全确定确切的计划，尽管地铁
列车可能是真正的目标，但弹道专家发现地铁列
车车厢内的两颗子弹来自瓦西里·奥廖尔的乌兹冲
锋枪。

**VLADIMIR PUTIN**
Why did he shoot at the train, was it an accident?

弗拉基米尔·普京
他为什么向火车开枪？这是意外吗？

**ALEXANDER VASILYEVICH BORTNIKOV**
FSB analysts have concluded Vasily Oryol's most likely determined the train was the terrorist target and didn't want it to stop at the station where people on the train would be slaughtered in large numbers.

亚历山大·瓦西里耶维奇·博尔特尼科夫
俄罗斯联邦安全局分析人员得出结论，瓦西里·奥廖尔很可能认定这列火车是恐怖分子的目标，因此不想让它停在这个车站，因为这样火车上的乘客就会遭到大规模屠杀。

**VLADIMIR PUTIN**
Why is it we have not found proof of that analysis?

弗拉基米尔·普京
为什么我们没有找到该分析的证据？

**ALEXANDER VASILYEVICH BORTNIKOV**
Since there were no living terrorist survivors to interrogate, until we find corroborating information, the conjecture the train was the target and not Alex Baxter remains the most likely scenario.

亚历山大·瓦西里耶维奇·博尔特尼科夫
由于没有活着的恐怖分子幸存者可供审问，在我们找到确凿的证据之前，最有可能的情况是火车是目标而不是亚历克斯·巴克斯特。

**VLADIMIR PUTIN**
What led the analysts to make this determination?

弗拉基米尔·普京
是什么促使分析师做出这一决定？

**ALEXANDER VASILYEVICH BORTNIKOV**
One other factor that pointed to the train as the target was the FSB agent Vasily Oryol who escorted Alex Baxter and Mr. Garrison to different subway stations on a random tourist visit, could not have been planned, nor give the terrorist a good location to whack them.

亚历山大·瓦西里耶维奇·博尔特尼科夫
另一个将火车作为袭击目标的因素是，联邦安全
局特工瓦西里·奥廖尔在一次随机的旅游中护送亚
历克斯·巴克斯特和加里森先生到不同的地铁站，
这不可能是事先计划好的，也不会给恐怖分子提
供一个袭击他们的好地方。

**VLADIMIR PUTIN**
Which means what?

弗拉基米尔·普京
这意味着什么？

**ALEXANDER VASILYEVICH BORTNIKOV**
I agree with the analysts, the only possible outcome of
the investigation appears to be that Alex Baxter, Mr.
Garrison, Baxter's security man a guy named Buster
Francher, and the FSB agent Vasily Oryol sent along
for security, accidently happened to be at the scene
when the terrorist crime was initiated.

亚历山大·瓦西里耶维奇·博尔特尼科夫
我同意分析师的观点，调查的唯一可能结果似乎
是亚历克斯·巴克斯特、加里森先生、巴克斯特的
保安人员巴斯特·弗兰彻以及被派去负责安全的联
邦安全局特工瓦西里·奥廖尔在恐怖犯罪发生时恰
好出现在现场。

**VLADIMIR PUTIN**
That makes sense.

弗拉基米尔·普京
这很有道理。

**ALEXANDER VASILYEVICH BORTNIKOV**
Vladimir, I would also like to point out that Agent
Vasily Oryol truly did prevent hundreds of people
murdered by terrorists when he valiantly gave his life
and prevented the train from stopping.

亚历山大·瓦西里耶维奇·博尔特尼科夫
弗拉基米尔, 我还想指出，特工瓦西里·奥廖尔英
勇献出生命, 阻止火车停下来，确实阻止了数百人
被恐怖分子杀害。

**VLADIMIR PUTIN**
Please write up an award for Agent Vasily Oryol and I
will immediately approve it. He's now a national hero
and deserves to be recognized.

弗拉基米尔·普京
请为瓦西里·奥廖尔特工写一份奖项，我会立即批
准。他现在是民族英雄，值得被认可。

**ALEXANDER VASILYEVICH BORTNIKOV**
Sir, it will be my distinct pleasure in doing so.

亚历山大·瓦西里耶维奇·博尔特尼科夫
先生，我非常荣幸能这样做。

***

MUSIC FOR THIS SEGMENT:

ROMEO AND JULIET at Bolshoi Theatre (05.12.2013) - Act I - YouTube

本片段的音乐：

莫斯科大剧院的《罗密欧与朱丽叶》（2013 年 12 月 5 日）- 第一幕 -
YouTube

It took something as surreal as the Bolshoi Ballet to take Buster's sad situation off
Alex's mind. The slender female ballet dancers were gorgeous. Their artwork was
unquestioningly outstanding.

只有莫斯科大剧院芭蕾舞团这样的超现实主义表演才能让阿历克斯忘记巴斯特
的悲惨处境。身材苗条的芭蕾舞演员非常漂亮。她们的作品无疑非常出色。

All Alex could think at the time was how this splendid performance and the fantastic
orchestra enamored his soul on such an auspicious occasion. It wasn't until he was
sitting here soul searching that he realized how pitifully vulnerable he was at the
subway station.

当时亚历克斯唯一能想到的就是，在这样一个吉祥的日子里，这场精彩的演出
和美妙的管弦乐队让他的灵魂陶醉其中。直到他坐在这里自我反省时，他才意
识到自己在地铁站是多么的脆弱。

Alex was also aware that Buster and his father-in-law as well as Vasily Oryol saved
his life when he foolishly tackled *Miss Montez* to keep her from being killed. He
wondered if that deed would somehow lesson the almost relentless attack *Michelle
Montez* and *Magazine Femmes Réelles Exigeantes* seemed to want to engage in. Day
after tomorrow he would get his answer.

亚历克斯还知道，当他愚蠢地扑向蒙特兹小姐，阻止她被杀时，巴斯特、他的岳父以及瓦西里·奥廖尔救了他的命。他想知道这一举动是否会在某种程度上减轻米歇尔·蒙特兹和《真实女性杂志》似乎想要进行的几乎无情的攻击。后天他会得到答案的。

But for now, Alex was safe and sitting by Christina, the woman he truly adored. And even though Alex didn't have parents of his own, since he grew up as a gypsy orphan child, Christina's parents substituted for the lack of his own parents.

但就目前而言，亚历克斯很安全，他坐在克里斯蒂娜身边，克里斯蒂娜是他真正爱慕的女人。尽管亚历克斯没有自己的父母，但由于他是作为吉普赛孤儿长大的，克里斯蒂娜的父母弥补了他失去父母的缺憾。

VOICEOVER
画外音

This terrorist incident did a lot of harm to the future *Moscow Dome* project. Alex would have to have discussions with Claude real soon, especially since this *Moscow Subway Terrorist Attack* hit the news cycle.

这次恐怖事件对未来的莫斯科圆顶体育场项目造成了很大损害。亚历克斯必须尽快与克劳德进行讨论，尤其是自从这次莫斯科地铁恐怖袭击事件成为新闻热点之后。

The impact on the *Moscow Dome* that would be built unlike anything that ever existed before, would be the mindset that it's vulnerable to Terrorism.

莫斯科穹顶的建造将产生与以往任何建筑都不同的影响，即人们认为它很容易受到恐怖主义的攻击。

Chita Russia is a much safer location. It would be much harder for Terrorists to get in the area as opposed to Moscow where they could simply drive in automobiles to launch future attacks, including Moscow Dome infrastructure.

俄罗斯赤塔是一个更安全的地方。与莫斯科相比，恐怖分子进入该地区要困难得多，在莫斯科，他们可以驾车发动未来的袭击，包括莫斯科穹顶体育场的基础设施。

Alex soon realized a security nightmare.

亚历克斯很快就意识到了一场安全噩梦。

During the intermission, Alex, Christina, and the Garrisons went out to the lobby, and once again the pianist adorned them with more Chopin Nocturnes as refreshments were being served.

中场休息时，亚历克斯、克里斯蒂娜和加里森一家走到大厅，钢琴家再次为他们演奏了肖邦的夜曲，同时供应了茶点。

## VOICEOVER
### 画外音

*If there was a silver lining in today's experiences, one thing showed clear and added some comfort was the fact Michelle Montez did not seem to be around. Alex realized he would have one decent night without worrying about newspaper headlines in the morning.*

如果今天的经历还有一线希望，那么有一件事很明显，也让人感到安慰，那就是米歇尔·蒙特兹似乎不在身边。亚历克斯意识到自己可以度过一个美好的夜晚，而不用担心早上报纸的头条新闻。

*Unfortunately, Alex could not escape the news cycle, the reports of the terrorist attack in the Moscow subway was already hitting the USA. Worse yet, Alex Baxter's name had been tossed around a few times, gleefully by the yellow journalists of some of the more prominent news agencies. Alex discovered such about when his cell phone vibrated and there was Claude's text message:*

不幸的是，亚历克斯无法逃脱新闻周期，莫斯科地铁恐怖袭击的报道已经席卷了美国。更糟糕的是，亚历克斯·巴克斯特的名字已经被一些知名新闻机构的黄皮肤记者津津乐道了好几次。亚历克斯发现这一点的时候，他的手机震动了一下，里面有克劳德的短信：

## CLAUDE REARDON
### (Text Message)
### Everything okay in Moscow?

克劳德·里尔登
（短信）
莫斯科一切都好吗？

### ALEX
(Text Message)
Yes, I'm alive and well, no problems.

亚历克斯
（短信）
是的，我还活着，活得很好，没有任何问题。

### CLAUDE REARDON
(Text Message)
Saw a news piece about you just now.

克劳德·里尔登
（短信）
刚才看到一条关于您的新闻。

### ALEX
(Text Message)
Yes, there was an incident.

亚历克斯
（短信）
是的，有一个事件。

### CLAUDE REARDON
(Text Message)
On your way home, how about stopping in for a little
discussion, I have some concerns.

克劳德·里尔登
（短信）
回家的路上，顺便过来聊聊怎么样，我有些担心。

### ALEX
(Text Message)
So, do I.

亚历克斯
（短信）
我也是。

### CLAUDE REARDON
(Text Message)
Good, we'll see you soon then.

克劳德·里尔登
（短信）
很好，那我们很快就能见到你了 。


ALEX
(Text Message)
Absolutely.


CLAUDE REARDON
(Text Message)
Good, we'll see you soon then.


The usher asked everyone to return to their seats right after Alex and Christina finished toasting her parents with a glass of Dom Perignon.

亚历克斯和克里斯蒂娜刚用一杯唐培里侬香槟王为她的父母干杯，引座员就要求大家回到座位。

During the performance, Christina whispered:

表演过程中，克里斯蒂娜小声说道：


CHRISTINA
Those ballet dancers' legs are so skinny.


克里斯蒂娜
那些芭蕾舞演员的腿真瘦啊 。


ALEX
That's because one performance is the same as walking
five miles on their toes, keeping them nice and thin.


亚历克斯
这是因为，一项表演就相当于踮着脚尖走了五英
里，让他们保持美丽和苗条。因为一次表演相当
于用脚尖走五英里，保持脚尖漂亮又苗条。


CHRISTINA
I hope I don't look too fat to you.


克里斯蒂娜
希望你看我没那么胖。


ALEX
No, you are built to perfection, I love the way you look.

亚历克斯
不，你生来就是完美的，我喜欢你的样子。

CHRISTINA
What about these women?

克里斯蒂娜
这些女人怎么样？

ALEX
Even though they are very pretty, they're too skinny for my taste.

亚历克斯
尽管它们很漂亮，但对我来说太瘦了。

***

After the Ballet, Alex and his family had dinner in an exclusive invitation only restaurant that Gennady Alexeyev took them.

芭蕾舞演出结束后，亚历克斯和他的家人在根纳季·阿列克谢耶夫邀请他们去的一家仅限受邀者参加的餐厅共进晚餐。

VOICE OVER
Alex could tell there was something strange with Gennady Alexeyev tonight. It really was nothing more than Putin was now terribly worried Alex might pull out of the *Moscow Dome* construction.

画外音
亚历克斯能感觉到今晚根纳季·阿列克谢耶夫有些不对劲。其实，这只不过是普京现在非常担心亚历克斯可能会退出莫斯科圆顶体育场的建设。

Without Alex's money and efforts, the *Moscow Dome* would never get off ground.

如果没有亚历克斯的金钱和努力，莫斯科巨蛋就不可能建成。

Putin had fully committed himself to build the first *Large City Dome* anywhere on the planet. Nuuk was nothing more than the size of a small city in the USA, nothing special.

普京已全身心投入建造地球上第一个大型城市穹顶。努克只不过是美国一个小城市的规模，没有什么特别之处。

Moscow on the other hand was one of the seven premier cities in the world. Putin understood just like Alex, the dome would change Moscow forever. Avoiding cold winters would vastly change Russians attitudes.

而莫斯科则是世界七大顶级城市之一。普京和亚历克斯一样明白，这座穹顶将永远改变莫斯科。避开寒冷的冬天将极大地改变俄罗斯人的态度。

Putin privately predicted once Muscovites grew accustomed to dome living, more domes would sprout up over Moscow which would end up with a Dozen Domes and never experience winter again.

***

Dinner came and went, and Alex was back in his hotel room planning for the morning. They would all leave and go to St. Petersburgh because Alex wanted to take his in-laws to the Hermitage

晚餐过后，亚历克斯回到酒店房间，计划第二天早上的行程。他们都会离开，前往圣彼得堡，因为亚历克斯想带他的岳父岳母去冬宫

***

The Hermitage, the former palace, is like no other on the planet. Its construction goes a long way to demonstrate the power and wealth the Czars had. The vast treasures and art works are on par with the Louver in Paris.

艾尔米塔什博物馆是一座前宫殿，世界上独一无二的存在。它的建造充分体现了沙皇的权力和财富。馆内珍宝和艺术品数量之多，堪比巴黎的卢浮宫。

As planned, Alex, the following day, was walking with Christina, Mr. Garrison with his wife and mother-in-law Ethel following behind, as they visited the Hermitage looking at all the artistic treasures.

按照计划，第二天，亚历克斯和克里斯蒂娜一起步行，加里森先生和他的妻子以及岳母埃塞尔跟在后面，一起参观了冬宫，观赏其中的各种艺术珍品。

https://hermitagemuseum.org/

CHRISTINA
(Reading from a museum placard)
Catherine the Great started the Hermitage when she had a building built next to the winter Palace to house her artwork collection. From then on it slowly expanded and grew until they were out of room and built the new Hermitage which was opened in 1852.

克里斯蒂娜
（读博物馆的标语）
叶卡捷琳娜大帝在冬宫旁边修建了一座建筑，用来收藏她的艺术品，从此便建立了冬宫。从那时起，冬宫便慢慢地扩大，直到没有空间，于是便修建了新的冬宫，并于 1852 年开放。

MRS. GARRISON
It could take us a couple days to see everything.

加里森夫人
我们可能要花几天时间才能看完所有东西。

MR. GARRISON
If we truly studied the artwork a few weeks or a month.

加里森先生
如果我们真的花几周或一个月的时间研究这件艺术品的话。

CHRISTINA
Alex, when do you plan on leaving Russia?

克里斯蒂娜
亚历克斯，你打算什么时候离开俄罗斯？

ALEX
Christina, if you want to spend more time in the Hermitage, perhaps an extra day.

亚历克斯
克里斯蒂娜，如果你想在冬宫待更多时间，也许可以多呆一天。

Then the *Magazine Femmes Réelles Exigeantes* article hit. Putin was not happy nor was Alex. In the hotel room that night, Alex proceeded to delicately discuss *Michelle Montez's* kiss with Christina.

然后《真实女性》杂志的文章就出现了。普京不高兴，亚历克斯也不高兴。当晚在酒店房间里，亚历克斯继续小心翼翼地谈论米歇尔·蒙特兹和克里斯蒂娜的吻。

ALEX
Christina, you know I did not kiss that woman.

亚历克斯
克里斯蒂娜，你知道我没有吻那个女人。

CHRISTINA
Yes Alex, I know. I had a long talk with my father. He was an eyewitness and no matter how the picture appears, I trust nobody in the world as much as my mother and father. His words are golden to me. So don't be concerned about the magazine article.

克里斯蒂娜
是的，亚历克斯，我知道。我和我父亲谈了很久。他是目击者，无论照片看起来如何，我最信任的还是我父母。他的话对我来说是金玉良言。所以不要担心杂志上的文章。

ALEX
I appreciate how you are handling this.

亚历克斯
我很欣赏你处理这件事的方式。

After another day at the Hermitage with private tours, they managed to see a lot of the great artwork.

在冬宫参加了另一天的私人游览后，他们欣赏到了许多伟大的艺术品。

CHRISTINA
We have nothing like this in America.

克里斯蒂娜
在美国，我们没有这样的事。

ALEX
Only small exhibits spread out all over the country.

亚历克斯
只有小型展品遍布全国各地。

CHRISTINA
Would you want to build a dome on St. Petersburgh?

克里斯蒂娜
你想在圣彼得堡建一个圆顶吗？

CHRISTINA
Would a Dome change all that?

ALEX
No, it doesn't need a dome, though perhaps a suburb might be ok, we need to preserve the City St. Petersburgh as one of the great cultural landmarks of history of the world.

亚历克斯
不，它不需要圆顶，尽管也许郊区也可以，但我们需要保护圣彼得堡市作为世界历史上最伟大的文化地标之一。

ALEX
Certainly.

亚历克斯
当然了。

<u>MUSIC FOR THE NEXT SEGMENT:</u>

<u>11 SHOSTAKOVICH Symph No 11 The Year 1905 in G min Op 103 Dir Valery Gergiev Mariinsky Orchestra</u>

下一乐段的音乐：

11 肖斯塔科维奇 第 11 号交响曲 1905 年，G 小调·作品 103 指挥：瓦列里·捷杰耶夫 马林斯基管弦乐团

That night Alex took his family to the Mariinsky Theatre and watched Valery Gergiev lead the orchestra performing Shostakovich Symphony Number 11 *The Year 1905* in G min Op 103.

当晚，亚历克斯带着家人去了马林斯基剧院，观看了瓦列里·捷杰耶夫指挥乐团演奏肖斯塔科维奇的第 11 号交响曲《1905 年》（G 小调·作品 103）。

Considering what Alex went through recently, this Shostakovich Symphony resonated well with him. Mr. Garrison could feel SOG missions in the music. There was an air of mystery behind it, but the composer certainly understood the emotions surrounding events in 1905 that gripped Russia.

考虑到亚历克斯最近经历的一切，这首交响曲引起了他的共鸣。加里森先生可以从音乐中感受到 SOG 的任务。这首交响曲背后有一种神秘的气息，但作曲家肯定理解 1905 年俄罗斯发生的事件所带来的情绪。

Note: *Shostakovich Symphony Eleven* serves as a profound reflection on the events of the Russian Revolution of 1905. Shostakovich's ability to weave together the emotional tapestry of a tumultuous allegros is evident in this composition. The music encapsulates tension, sorrow, and triumph expressed in this musical cacophonous presentation.

Russian Revolution of 1905 - Wikipedia

注：肖斯塔科维奇《第十一交响曲》是对 1905 年俄国革命事件的深刻反思。肖斯塔科维奇将动荡的快板的情感交织在一起的能力在这部作品中显而易见。音乐中充满了紧张、悲伤和胜利，在这种嘈杂的音乐表演中得到了表达。

1905 年俄国革命 - 维基百科

VOICEOVER
During the intermission, Alex noticed a lot of people staring at him in the lobby while getting refreshments.

画外音
中场休息时，亚历克斯注意到大厅里很多人在吃点心时都盯着他看。

Word travels fast and today's Terrorist Attack was in the Moscow and St. Petersburg NEWS.

消息传播得很快，今天的恐怖袭击事件已经登上了莫斯科和圣彼得堡的新闻。

The concert goers seemed almost in shock observing the Dome Guy Alex Baxter out in public after such a terrorist event.

在发生这样的恐怖事件后，当看到穹顶人亚历克斯·巴克斯特 (Alex Baxter) 出现在公众面前时，音乐会观众似乎都感到震惊。

People in the lobby getting refreshments and going to and from the restrooms displayed reactions to Alex Baxter tied in nicely to the music they just heard that was composed around similar events, especially the second movement:

大厅里享用茶点和往返于洗手间的人们对亚历克斯·巴克斯特的反应与他们刚刚听到的围绕类似事件创作的音乐完美契合，尤其是第二乐章：

Shostakovich's 9th of January symphony, second movement, a tumultuous Allegro referring to the events of *Bloody Sunday at the Winter Palace on 22 January 1905* encapsulated the emotions Alex felt and realized behind those stares were impressions he would never forget.

肖斯塔科维奇的《1 月 9 日》交响曲第二乐章是一段激烈的快板，它描述了 1905 年 1 月 22 日在冬宫发生的血腥星期天事件，概括了亚历克斯当时的感受，他意识到那些目光背后是他永远不会忘记的印象。

The evening's main event was over with the symphony just performed, and the following piano concerto was not so inspiring, so in the middle of it, Alex took his family out of the Mariinsky Theatre because he did not want to face the concert goers again at the end of the performance.

当晚的重头戏刚刚演奏完交响乐就结束了，接下来的钢琴协奏曲却不那么让人激动，所以中途，亚历克斯就带着家人离开了马林斯基剧院，因为他不想在演出结束后再面对音乐会的观众。

Few people saw Alex and his family slip out of the Mariinsky Theatre thanks to the location of their balcony seats.

由于亚历克斯和他的家人坐在阳台上，所以很少有人看到他们悄悄溜出马林斯基剧院。

It was a short Limo ride to the Radisson Royal Hotel in the center of St. Petersburg, at Nevsky and Vladimirsky Prospekts. Alex picked this hotel because it was just a few hundred meters from the Palace-lined embankments of the Fontanka River.

乘坐豪华轿车很快就到了位于圣彼得堡市中心涅瓦大街和弗拉基米尔大街的丽笙皇家酒店。亚历克斯之所以选择这家酒店，是因为它距离宫殿林立的丰坦卡河堤岸只有几百米。

The rest of the night was rather somber, and Alex was happy Christina gave him space and allowed him to get a good night's sleep and forget about all those tumultuous allegros and thoughts they caused.

The rest of the night was rather somber, and Alex was happy Christina gave him space and allowed him to get a good night's sleep and forget about all those tumultuous allegros and thoughts they caused.

***

MUSIC FOR THIS SEGMENT:

<u>Sergei Bortkiewicz (1877-1952) : Piano Concerto No. 1 (1912)</u>

本部分音乐：

谢尔盖·博特凯维奇 (1877-1952)：第一钢琴协奏曲 (1912)

The following day, Alex and the group flew back to Switzerland. Alex felt they would be safer at his Switzerland mansion and also give her parents a little rest before they flew back to America via Greenland to get another look at the dome.

第二天，亚历克斯和团队飞回瑞士。亚历克斯觉得留在瑞士的豪宅里会更安全，也让她的父母能稍事休息，然后他们经格陵兰飞回美国，再看一眼穹顶。

The staff in Switzerland was of course pleased that Master Baxter was once again visiting.

瑞士的工作人员当然很高兴巴克斯特大师再次来访。

Switzerland will now be a special place for Christina as well as Alex because, it was here that they crossed over the point of no return in their relationship.

现在，瑞士对克里斯蒂娜和亚历克斯来说都成为一个特别的地方，因为正是在这里，他们的关系跨过了不归路。

On that auspicious and magical night, Christina knew she had fallen in love. Alex had traveled the world over and looking but never finding the woman of his dreams. Then suddenly by accident Alex saw Christina Garrison in the elevator at 120 Wall Street.

在那个吉祥而神奇的夜晚，克里斯蒂娜知道她已经坠入爱河。亚历克斯走遍了全世界，寻找却从未找到他梦寐以求的女人。突然，亚历克斯在华尔街 120 号的电梯里偶然看到了克里斯蒂娜·加里森。

Accidents do have meaning. Just like when the Terrorist was about to lower his AK-47 and shoot Alex in the back which would have killed him, Vasily Oryol gave his life.

意外确实有意义。就像当恐怖分子准备放下 AK-47 并从背后射杀阿历克斯时，瓦西里·奥廖尔却献出了自己的生命。

Through Gennady Alexeyev, Alex learned the official time and date of a memorial service for Vasily Oryol. In bed that night before Alex made passionate love to Christina, he informed Christina:

通过根纳季·阿列克谢耶夫，阿列克谢得知了瓦西里·奥廖尔追悼会的正式时间和日期。当晚，在阿列克谢与克里斯蒂娜激情做爱之前，他告诉克里斯蒂娜：

ALEX
I'm going back to Moscow in the morning for a few hours to attend Vasily Oryol's memorial service.

亚历克斯
我早上将返回莫斯科几个小时，参加瓦西里·奥廖尔的追悼会。

CHRISTINA
Are we all going?

克里斯蒂娜
我们都去吗？

ALEX
No, I don't think it would be a good idea for your parents, they need to rest up a bit before they fly back to New York.

亚历克斯
不，我认为这对你的父母来说不是一个好主意，他们在飞回纽约之前需要休息一下。

CHRISTINA
What about me?

克里斯蒂娜
那我呢？

ALEX
I kind of prefer you not to go to Moscow.

亚历克斯
我有点希望你不要去莫斯科。

CHRISTINA
Why is that?

克里斯蒂娜
为什么呢？

ALEX
For your personal safety.

亚历克斯
为了您的人身安全。


CHRISTINA
Alex, if you are going to go back to Moscow, then I want to go.


克里斯蒂娜

亚历克斯，如果你要回莫斯科，那我也想去。


ALEX
I'll take you Christina, but I'd rather not, at least I know you are safe here.


亚历克斯
我会带你去的，克里斯蒂娜，但我宁愿不带，至少我知道你在这里是安全的。


CHRISTINA
Don't worry about my safety, if something were to happen to you, I would prefer to die with you.


克里斯蒂娜
你不用担心我的安全，如果你有事，我宁愿和你一起死。


ALEX
We'll have to hustle and get you some funeral clothes in the morning, I doubt you have anything with you in black.


亚历克斯
明天早上我们得赶紧给你弄些丧服，我怀疑你身上有没有黑色的衣服。


CHRISTINA
No, I do not.


克里斯蒂娜
不，我不知道。


ALEX
I'm going to ring Mary and have her come into the room so I can give her some Marching orders.


亚历克斯
我要给玛丽打电话，让她进屋来，这样我就可以给她下达一些行动命令。

Moments later, knock at the door.

过了一会儿，敲门。

ALEX
Please come in.

亚历克斯
请进来。

MARY
What can I get for you, Mr. Baxter?

玛丽
巴克斯特先生，我能为您做些什么？

ALEX
Mary, come in and shut the door for a minute, I do not want others to hear.

亚历克斯
玛丽，进来把门关上一分钟，我不想让别人听到。

MARY
Yes sir, what is it you want me to do Mr. Baxter?

玛丽
是的，先生，您想让我做什么，巴克斯特先生？

ALEX
Tomorrow I'm going to Moscow for a memorial service for a Russian official who lost his life saving mine.

亚历克斯
明天我要去莫斯科参加一位救我一命的俄罗斯官员的追悼会。

MARY
Alright.

玛丽
好的。

ALEX
Christina is going with me, but she doesn't have any

funeral clothes with her. In the morning, I want you to get ahold of the department store manager where we have shopped in the past and ask him to open around 7:00 so that Christina can get a couple garments to go to this memorial.

亚历克斯

克里斯蒂娜要和我一起去，但她没有带丧服。明天早上，我要你联系一下我们以前购物的百货商店经理，让他在 7 点左右开门，这样克里斯蒂娜就可以买几件衣服去参加追悼会了。

MARY

Understand Mr. Baxter.

玛丽

明白了，巴克斯特先生。

ALEX

I'm very sorry. We had no advance warning, and it's important for us. If you have any issues with the manager, tell him I will make it worthwhile to help.

亚历克斯

我很抱歉。我们没有提前收到通知，这对我们很重要。如果你对经理有任何问题，请告诉他，我会让他尽力提供帮助。

Knowing the story since it was in the news, Mary understood the importance it was for Mr. Baxter.

自从这件事见诸新闻后，玛丽就知道了它对巴克斯特先生的重要性。

MARY

I will be very happy to make all the arrangements, Mr. Baxter. Rest well, everything will be taken care of.

玛丽

我很乐意为您安排一切，巴克斯特先生。好好休息吧，一切都会安排妥当。

Mary and the staff knew all the key people around; she knew who she had to call for almost anything important, including the phone number to the department store manager himself.

玛丽和工作人员认识周围所有的关键人物；她知道几乎所有重要的事情都要给谁打电话，包括百货商店经理本人的电话号码。

MARY (Thought)
*No doubt the department store manager will want a little quid pro quo, which I'm more than happy to provide.*

玛丽（想道）
毫无疑问，百货公司的经理会想要一点交换条件，我非常乐意提供。

Mary went back to her private room, then she made the phone call to the department store manager.

玛丽回到自己的私人房间，然后给百货商店经理打了电话。

Alex and Christina collapsed in each other's arms as the passion flowed that night unlike many others. In a short period of time, they experienced a lot together. Making that sweet splendid euphoric transcendence towards a release of love and passion put their minds into a state that allowed slumber to come on strong. It seemed just like minutes before there was a knock on the door.

那天晚上，亚历克斯和克里斯蒂娜在激情四溢中倒在彼此的怀抱中，这与其他夜晚不同。在短短的时间内，他们一起经历了很多。在爱情和激情的释放中，他们甜蜜而又美妙，欣快而超脱，他们的思想进入了一种让他们沉睡的状态。似乎几分钟后，门就响了。

MARY
Mr. Baxter? It's time to wake up, we need to get Christina dressed so she can get to the department store.

玛丽
巴克斯特先生？该起床了，我们得帮克里斯蒂娜穿好衣服，这样她才能去百货商店。

ALEX
We are getting up.

亚历克斯
我们要起床了。

In fifteen minutes, Christina and Mary were off to the up scaled department store that had Swiss Quality garments, very pricey but for something like a funeral, essential.

十五分钟后，克里斯蒂娜和玛丽就去了高档百货商店，那里有瑞士品质的服装，价格很贵，但对于葬礼这样的场合来说，却是必需的。

Christina was the ideal woman. Not only did she pick out something that made her look like a person mourning, but also did not reduce her natural beauty in any manner.

克里斯蒂娜是一位理想的女性。她不仅挑选了一些让自己看起来像是在哀悼的人的衣服，而且丝毫没有削弱她自然的美。

Alex called ahead and made arrangements with Gennady Alexeyev, who deposited $1 million in a bank account for Vasily Oryol's widow. Alex would do a wire transfer to Gennady to fund it.

阿历克斯提前打电话与根纳迪·阿列克谢耶夫商量好，根纳迪·阿列克谢耶夫在瓦西里·奥廖尔遗孀的银行账户中存入了 100 万美元。阿历克斯将通过电汇向根纳迪汇款。

Vladimir Putin decided Vasily Oryol deserved some distinction and hence requested Patriarch Kirill to perform the Memorial. Patriarch Kirill's presence would elevate Vasily Oryol's status to someone very important to the Russian Public.

弗拉基米尔·普京认为瓦西里·奥廖尔应该得到一些荣誉，因此要求基里尔牧首主持追悼会。基里尔牧首的出席将使瓦西里·奥廖尔的地位提升到俄罗斯公众非常重要的地位。

Putin also took the extraordinary step to sit directly behind the Widow next to Alex and met him outside the Church and said what Patriarch Kirill had informed him:

普京还采取了非同寻常的举措，坐在寡妇亚历克斯旁边的正后方，并在教堂外面与他会面，并说出了基里尔牧首告诉他的话：

### VLADIMIR PUTIN
Alex, Patriarch Kirill informed me that it would be kind of you to say a few words after his eulogy about Vasily Oryol since you will one day be very famous in Russia for building the *Moscow Dome*.

### 弗拉基米尔·普京
亚历克斯，基里尔牧首告诉我，希望您在他悼念瓦西里·奥廖尔之后，能说几句话，因为您有一天会因建造莫斯科穹顶而享誉俄罗斯。

### ALEX
I will do what I can to help.

### 亚历克斯
我会尽我所能提供帮助。

### VLADIMIR PUTIN
Alex, your presence and comments will be very meaningful to Vasily Oryol's widow if you would say a few nice words about Vasily Oryol who singlehandedly saved a lot of lives.

弗拉基米尔·普京
亚历克斯，如果你能为瓦西里·奥廖尔说几句好
话，说说他独自一人拯救了无数生命，你的到来
和评论对瓦西里·奥廖尔的遗孀来说将意义非凡。

ALEX
I would be very pleased to do so if you want me to speak.

亚历克斯
如果您希望我发言，我将非常乐意这样做。

AMAZING New Russian Memorial Orthodox Christian Cathedral for Military

令人惊叹的全新俄罗斯东正教军事纪念大教堂

VLADIMIR PUTIN
I appreciate that. Shall we go in now?

弗拉基米尔·普京
我很感激。我们现在可以进去吗？

Alex nodded and followed Vladimir Putin into the church who was by himself. Christina followed a close distance behind Alex.

阿历克斯点点头，跟着独自一人的普京走进了教堂，克里斯蒂娜则紧随在阿历克斯身后。

## MUSIC FOR THE NEXT SEGMENT

### Mozart : Requiem in D K. 626 (Orchestre national de France / James Gaffigan)

下一段音乐

莫扎特：D 大调安魂曲 K. 626 （法国国家管弦乐团/詹姆斯·加菲根）

On Putin's own initiative, a small orchestra was there behind Patriarch Kirill, and a large Choir. They were performing Mozart's Requiem as everyone filed in. The new large Russian Orthodox Church Cathedral for Military had almost every seat taken. Those who came early were ushered in to good seats. Over half of the congregation was made up of former Spetsnaz buddies and KGB/FSB colleagues.

在普京的倡议下，基里尔大牧首身后有一个小型管弦乐队和一个大型合唱团。当所有人鱼贯入场时，他们正在演奏莫扎特的《安魂曲》。新建的大型俄罗斯东正教军事大教堂几乎座无虚席。早到的人被引导到好座位。超过一半的会众都是前特种部队伙伴和克格勃/联邦安全局同事。

These vast numbers of top Russian Intelligence Officials all knew Vasily Oryol had given his life so that others could live when he prevented the Grozny Demons Terrorists getting on the subway train.

这些俄罗斯高级情报官员都知道，当瓦西里·奥廖尔阻止格罗兹尼恶魔恐怖分子登上地铁时，他是为了他人的生命而牺牲了自己的生命。

Everyone attending the memorial, also knew Vasily Oryol saved the life of Alex Baxter a very rich and powerful man who had a lot of impact on the future of Russia.

参加纪念活动的每个人都知道，瓦西里·奥廖尔挽救了亚历克斯·巴克斯特的生命，后者是一个非常富有和强大的人, 对俄罗斯的未来产生了很大的影响。

Vasily Oryol did not let the FSB down. He demonstrated with his unselfish heroic actions the moral and ethical fiber expected from Agents that FSB leaders retained with the highest standards of conduct.

瓦西里·奥廖尔没有让联邦安全局失望。他用无私的英雄行为展现了联邦安全局领导人作为特工应有的道德和伦理素养，并保持了最高的行为标准。

Vasily Oryol did not let the FSB down. He demonstrated with his unselfish heroic actions the moral and ethical fiber expected from Agents that FSB leaders retained with the highest standards of conduct.

瓦西里·奥廖尔没有让联邦安全局失望。他用无私的英雄行为展现了联邦安全局领导人作为特工应有的道德和伦理素养，并保持了最高的行为标准。

In about five minutes after Alex arrived in the *Russian Memorial Orthodox Christian Cathedral for Military*, the Mozart performance ended after completing part III

(*Sequentia*). The rest would be played after the eulogy and Alex and Vladimir Putin's comments.

阿历克斯抵达俄罗斯东正教军人纪念教堂后约五分钟，莫扎特演奏结束，第三部分（Sequentia）结束。其余部分将在悼词、阿历克斯和普京致辞后演奏。

If it had not been for the fact this was a memorial, there would have been a standing ovation for the orchestra and choir and guest opera singer's performances. The guest singers were the best opera singers in Russia and performed around the world.

如果不是因为这是一场纪念活动，管弦乐队、合唱团和客座歌剧演员的表演一定会赢得全场起立鼓掌。客座歌手是俄罗斯最好的歌剧演员，曾在世界各地演出。

Patriarch Kirill gave a funeral eulogy that exemplified the courage and the dedication of this Great Russian man Vasily Oryol who not only saved those on the subway train platform, but with the firepower the Terrorist brought in perhaps the entire trainload of passengers during a busy part of the day.

基里尔大主教在葬礼上致悼词，彰显了俄罗斯伟人瓦西里·奥廖尔的勇气和奉献精神，他不仅拯救了地铁站台上的乘客，而且还利用恐怖分子带来的火力，在一天中的繁忙时段救下了大约整列火车的乘客。

After Patriarch Kirill finished the eulogy, he requested:

基里尔大牧首致悼词后请求：

**PATRIARCH KIRILL**
Vladimir Putin, please come forward

基里尔大主教
弗拉基米尔·普京，请上前。

Vladimir Putin rose out of his chair and walked up to the alter area with a podium, and stood there as he addressed Vasily Oryol's Widow and informed her:

弗拉基米尔·普京从椅子上站起来，走到有讲台的祭坛前，站在那里对瓦西里·奥廖尔的遗孀发表讲话，告诉她：

**VLADIMIR PUTIN**
Vasily Oryol is a hero of Russia and will always be
remembered as the man who saved a lot of lives that
day and will be fondly remembered by many.

Ladies and Gentlemen, we have someone special here
today who also would like to say a few words.

弗拉基米尔·普京
瓦西里·奥廖尔是俄罗斯的英雄，他将永远被人们
铭记，因为他在那天拯救了很多人的生命，许多
人都会深情地怀念他。

女士们，先生们，今天我们这里有一位特别的人
也想说几句话。

Vladimir Putin then gestured for Alex to come forward to the Podium, he then took a few steps backwards allowing Alex to say a few things.

随后，弗拉基米尔·普京示意亚历克斯走上讲台，然后他后退了几步，让亚历克斯讲了几句话。

ALEX
Mrs. Oryol, I'm truly sorry about what happened to your husband. I witnessed him giving his life for his country and many people that day.

亚历克斯
奥廖尔夫人，我对您丈夫的遭遇深表遗憾。那天我
亲眼目睹他为国家和许多人献出了生命。

I owe Vasily Oryol my life. I was laying very vulnerable on the platform after I attempted to get a woman running down the platform to safety because in a short while she would have been shot in the back and killed.

我欠瓦西里·奥廖尔一条命。我试图让一名妇女从站台跑到安全的地方，当时我正躺在站台上，非常脆弱，因为再过一会儿，她就会被从背后开枪打死。

Your husband Vasily Oryol saved her then he saved me by making a target of himself and firing at the Terrorists. I am deeply humbled and very sorry for his loss.

您的丈夫瓦西里·奥廖尔救了她，然后他把自己当成目标，向恐怖分子开枪，救了我。我对他的损失深感惭愧和遗憾。

Alex eyes were watered up and he struggled hard to not break down from the grief and sadness he felt for the fallen agent.

亚历克斯的眼睛湿润了，他努力抑制自己不因这位牺牲的特工而感到的悲痛和难过。

ALEX
I've been a newlywed for about a week, your husband saved me on my honeymoon.

亚历克斯
我刚结婚大约一个星期，你的丈夫在我的蜜月期
间救了我。

Alex choked up then, could only utter those special words, simple and brief but to the point:

阿历克斯当时就哽咽了，只能说出那句特别的话，简单而又一针见血：

ALEX
Thank you.

亚历克斯
谢谢。

Putin knowing human nature as good as any forecast in his mind the events that would unfold and followed Alex as he walked up to the widow and put his arms around her shoulders and hugged the crying woman.

普京深谙人性，在心里预测着接下来的事件，他跟着亚历克斯走到寡妇身边，搂住她的肩膀，拥抱了这位哭泣的女人。

ALEX
I'm very sorry.

亚历克斯
我很抱歉。

Christina who was very close behind stood up and walked around and beside Alex and then took her turn to bend over and hug the widow and say in Russian:

紧随其后的克里斯蒂娜站起来，绕到亚历克斯身边，然后弯腰拥抱了寡妇，用俄语说道：

Note: the actress speaks in Russian with English and/or Chinese subtitles on the movie screen.

KRISTINA
[КРИСТИНА]
{CHRISTINA}

Vash muzh spas zhizn' moyego muzha. YA nikogda ne smogu otplatit' vam za yego zhertvu.

[Ваш муж спас жизнь моего мужа. Я никогда не смогу отплатить вам за его жертву.]

{Your husband saved the life of my husband. I could never repay you for his sacrifice.}

克里斯蒂娜
你的丈夫救了我丈夫的命。我永远无法报答你的
牺牲。

Vladimir Putin then walked over and bent down and put his arms over the widow's shoulders and gave her a gentle hug and whispered a few words, that seemed to calm the woman.

随后，普京走过去，弯下腰，将双手放在寡妇的肩膀上，轻轻地拥抱了她，并低声说了几句话，似乎让这位女士平静了下来。

The Orchestra and choir started performing again the remainder of Mozart's "Requiem." Vasily Oryol's Widow was escorted to the casket, then out of the church in the leading Limo, followed by the rest of the congregation after Putin and Alex walked by and bowed giving great respect, then they two went out and got into Limo's and headed in opposite directions.

管弦乐队和合唱团又开始演奏莫扎特《安魂曲》的剩余部分。瓦西里·奥廖尔的遗孀被护送到灵柩旁，然后乘坐领头的豪华轿车离开教堂，普京和亚历克斯走过并鞠躬致意，其余教众也紧随其后，然后他们两人走出教堂，上了豪华轿车，朝相反的方向行驶。

Vladimir Putin was taken back to his Dacha while Alex and Christina were driven back to the airport where Brad and Gladys were patiently waiting for immediate take off. Oddly many in the church remained until Mozart's "Requiem" finished.

弗拉基米尔·普京被送回别墅，亚历克斯和克里斯蒂娜则被送回机场，布拉德和格拉迪斯在那里耐心等待飞机起飞。奇怪的是，教堂里的许多人一直待到莫扎特的《安魂曲》结束。

As Alex and Christina got out of the Zil Limo, Gennady Alexeyev got out as well wishing them off.

当阿历克斯和克里斯蒂娜从　齐尔豪华轿车下车时，根纳季·阿历克斯耶夫也下了车，为他们送行。

ALEX
I hope Vasily Oryol's Widow will be okay.

亚历克斯
我希望瓦西里·奥廖尔的遗孀一切安好。

GENNADY ALEXEYEV
Yes, and the money you gave Vasily Oryol's Widow
will improve her quality of life. An FSB agent salary
is not huge. Vasily Oryol's Widow disposable income
just went up by a factor of 20. In Russia a widow with

that kind of money will have no problems finding another mate quickly.

根纳季·阿列克谢耶夫
是的，你给瓦西里·奥廖尔遗孀的钱会改善她的生活质量。联邦安全局特工的薪水并不高。瓦西里·奥廖尔遗孀的可支配收入刚刚增加了 20 倍。在俄罗斯，有这种钱的寡妇很快就能找到另一个伴侣。

ALEX
I hope so.

亚历克斯
我希望如此。

GENNADY ALEXEYEV
Alex, thank you for coming to the memorial. It meant a lot to Vasily Oryol's Widow.

根纳季·阿列克谢耶夫
阿列克谢，谢谢你来参加追悼会。这对瓦西里·奥廖尔的遗孀来说意义重大。

ALEX
It's the least I could do for the man who saved my life. Because of where I was laying and playing dead, out of the corner of my eye I could see Vasily Oryol die. It truly rattled me.

亚历克斯
这是我能为救我生命的人做的最起码的事情。由于我躺在那里装死，眼角余光中我看到了瓦西里·奥廖尔的死状。这真的让我心烦意乱。

GENNADY ALEXEYEV
Alex, I would feel the same way too.

根纳季·阿列克谢耶夫
亚历克斯，我也有同样的感受。

ALEX
Thanks for all your help during this visit.

亚历克斯
感谢您在这次访问期间提供的所有帮助。

GENNADY ALEXEYEV
When Vladimir Putin makes the formal announcement
of the Dome Project, we would like you to attend.

根纳季·阿列克谢耶夫
当弗拉基米尔·普京正式宣布穹顶项目时，我们希
望您能出席。

ALEX
It will be my pleasure, but as you know, it's *Chita
Dome* I most look forward to building the most as
it's more ideally suited to take land that is not very
efficiently utilized to improve it immensely with the
dome.

亚历克斯
这将是我的荣幸，但如你所知，我最期待建造的
是赤塔圆顶，因为它更适合占用尚未得到充分利
用的土地来极大地改善圆顶。

GENNADY ALEXEYEV
It's kind of ironic Alex; the Russian Military agrees
with you. They would prefer to skip Moscow for now.

根纳季·阿列克谢耶夫
阿列克谢，这有点讽刺；俄罗斯军方同意你的观
点。他们现在更愿意跳过莫斯科。

ALEX
Very well. We'll be seeing you again soon.

亚历克斯
很好。我们很快会再见到你。

GENNADY ALEXEYEV
Stay well Alex.

根纳季·阿列克谢耶夫
保持健康，亚历克斯。

ALEX
You too Gennady.

亚历克斯
你也是根纳季。

Alex and Gennady shook hands then Alex climbed up on the GS650 following his wife.

亚历克斯 (Alex) 和 根纳季·阿列克谢耶夫 (Gennady Alexeyev) 握手后，亚历克斯跟随妻子爬上了 GS650。

In three hours and fifteen minutes, Alex's GS650 was landing in Switzerland, the sun was going down.

三小时十五分钟后，亚历克斯的 GS650 飞机降落在瑞士，太阳即将落山。

<u>INT. DAY. GENEVA SWITZERLAND. ALEX'S MANSION.</u>

The next day was somewhat subdued. Christina's parents were a little concerned when they woke up and discovered Alex and Christina had gone to Moscow a couple days before.

第二天的情况有些平静。克里斯蒂娜的父母醒来后发现亚历克斯和克里斯蒂娜几天前去了莫斯科，他们有点担心。

MRS. GARRISON
Why didn't they take us to Moscow with them?

加里森夫人
为什么他们不带我们一起去莫斯科？

MR. GARRISON
Alex wanted us to rest, for the long trip home.

加里森先生
亚历克斯希望我们好好休息，为回家的漫长旅程做准备。

MRS. GARRISON
We're fine.

加里森夫人
我们很好。

MR. GARRISON
It's an eight and half hour flight back to America
without head winds. 10 hours otherwise.

The Garrisons were sincerely happy to see Alex and Christina, knowing they were both healthy.

***

<u>MUSIC FOR THIS SEGMENT</u>

<u>A. Rawsthorne - Piano Concerto No. 2 (Tozer, Bamert) - YouTube</u>

本部分音乐

A. Rawsthorne - 钢琴协奏曲 2 号 (Tozer, Bamert) - YouTube

The following morning Alex and his family were in the air flying to Greenland. As the GS650 was approaching Greenland, Alex had Brad get permission to fly over the Dome Project.

第二天早上，亚历克斯和他的家人乘飞机飞往格陵兰岛。当 GS650 接近格陵兰岛时，亚历克斯让布拉德获得飞越穹顶项目的许可。

A lot of progress has occurred since they last looked. Twelve pillars now had roof sections installed, and six more pillars were going up. The Hill was showing a lot of trees now providing something Greenlanders around Nuuk had never seen. The plane landed and they were soon off to see the construction site in the Land Rover's.

自上次查看以来，已经取得了很大进展。十二根柱子现在已经安装了屋顶部分，另外 六 根柱子正在安装中。山上长满了树木，这是努克周围的格陵兰人从未见过的景象。飞机降落后，他们很快就开着路虎去参观施工现场。

Claude Rearden shook Alex's hand.

克劳德·里尔登与亚历克斯握手。

CLAUDE REARDEN
Glad you are still alive; the project would have folded without you.

克劳德·里尔登
很高兴你还活着；如果没有你，这个项目就会失败。

ALEX
Well, I'm certainly happy to be here.

亚历克斯
嗯，我当然很高兴来到这里。

CLAUDE REARDEN
The locals here at Nuuk are starting to realize the Dome is getting built.

克劳德·里尔登
努克的当地人开始意识到穹顶正在建造中。

ALEX
Just wait until we have 50 or 75 pillars up, and those roof sections, they will really know then.

亚历克斯
等到我们竖起 50 或 75 根柱子以及那些屋顶部分时，他们就会真正知道了。

CLAUDE REARDEN
I'm already getting comments about the hill and the
Trees we are planting.

克劳德·里尔登
我已经收到了关于这座山和我们正在种植的树木
的评论。

ALEX
Yes, their expensive, digging them up in Norway and
bringing them here.

亚历克斯
是的，它们很贵，在挪威挖出来然后带到这里。

CLAUDE REARDEN
Well, that is the quickest way to get a small forest
started.

克劳德·里尔登
嗯，这是开始种植小片森林最快的方法。

ALEX
I'm going to be sending you an artist conception of the
subway system we should build below the false floor.

亚历克斯
我将向您发送我们应该在假地板下方建造的地铁
系统的艺术构想。

CLAUDE REARDEN
I'll look forward to that.

Soon Alex and his new family were on the plane again, heading for New York. Five
and a half hours later, the GS650 touched down at JFK and Mr. Black was there to
greet them. Rodriguez was more than happy to take the family home to Queens.

很快，亚历克斯和他的新家人又登上了飞往纽约的飞机。五个半小时
后，GS650 飞机降落在肯尼迪机场，布莱克先生在那里迎接他们。罗德里格斯
非常高兴地把他们一家人送回皇后区。

Alex and Christina were at home in their modest Queens home. Christina didn't want to
give up working quite yet and after discussions with her boss, Alex convinced him that
more contributions would come in if he allowed Christina to work from the Minnesota
home part of the time. Alex bounced around a lot on the projects, but Christina's home
turned into his master residence since it was in the middle of everything plus next door
to her parents whom he also enjoyed visiting.

亚历克斯和克里斯蒂娜住在他们位于皇后区的简朴家中。克里斯蒂娜暂时不想
放弃工作，在与老板讨论后，亚历克斯说服他，如果他允许克里斯蒂娜部分时
间在明尼苏达州的家中工作，那么贡献会更多。亚历克斯在项目上四处奔波，

但克里斯蒂娜的家成了他的主居所，因为它位于一切的中心，而且毗邻克里斯蒂娜的父母，他也喜欢去探望他们。

As time passed, the construction on the Moscow dome started. In the face of terrorism, the project boldly went forward and in a dozen years, the Moscow Dome was eventually completed, about the time Vladimir decided his days in politics were over. He eventually married Alina, and they had several children together, and she continued to look like a beauty and remained a loyal friend to Christina. Alex's vision of building the *Chita Dome* proved the point he was going to make. It truly revolutionized polar living standards in cold regions like Siberia.

随着时间的推移，莫斯科穹顶的建设开始了。面对恐怖主义，该项目大胆推进，经过十几年，莫斯科穹顶终于完工，大约在那时，弗拉基米尔决定结束他的政治生涯。他最终娶了阿丽娜，他们有了几个孩子，她仍然长得很漂亮，仍然是克里斯蒂娜的忠实朋友。亚历克斯建造赤塔穹顶的愿景证明了他要表达的观点。它真正彻底改变了西伯利亚等寒冷地区的极地生活水平。

Nuuk eventually was completed and as Alex predicted, the locals wanted to move into the dome, and Alex Baxter ended up with a lot of property in Nuuk so that when the next adjacent dome was built, he owned a lot of real estate.

努克最终竣工，正如亚历克斯所预测的那样，当地人希望搬进圆顶建筑，而亚历克斯·巴克斯特最终在努克拥有大量财产，因此当下一个相邻的圆顶建筑建成时，他就拥有了大量房地产。

When Alex finally retired when his last dome was being built, no American City had agreed to build a dome. China was in negotiations for a couple Gobi Desert Dome Cities, but since they wanted to do the work and manage it themselves, t would take several more centuries before the rest of the planet hopped on board the Dome express. But eventually it happened as many of the inhabited earth cities would have DOMES. That's how it all started.

当亚历克斯终于退休时，他的最后一座圆顶正在建造中，没有一座美国城市同意建造圆顶。中国正在就建造几座戈壁沙漠圆顶城市进行谈判，但由于他们想自己动手和管理，因此地球的其他地方还需要几个世纪才能赶上圆顶快车。但最终还是发生了；因为许多有人居住的地球城市都拥有圆顶。这就是一切的开始。

Paul D. Escudero

保罗·道格拉斯·埃斯库德罗

April 9, 2025

2025年4月9日